MW00975359

Halls of Poison Ivy

B. B. Rose

Copyright © 2003 by B.B.Rose

Published by:
ngpress
4787 Riverview Road # 10
Atlanta, Georgia 30327

Publisher's Note: This book is a work of fiction. Names, characters, places and incidents are either a product of the author's imagination or are used fictitiously, and any resemblance to actual persons, living or dead, events, or locales are entirely coincidental. The use of real locales and similar situations are intended only to give the fiction a sense of reality and authenticity.

ISBN: 0-9724727-0-3

All rights reserved. No part of this book may be reproduced or transmitted in any form or by any means, electronic or mechanical, including photocopying, recording, or by any information storage and retrieval system, without written permission of the copyright owner and the above publisher, except where permitted by law.

First Edition

Printed in the United States of America

Higher Education has its secrets.
Some are deadly.

When Andy Dren, a graduate student at the historic Georgia Tech, is murdered in the president's office in the middle of the night, several people become nervous and a few turn vicious.

It is possible that the killing occurred because of international laundered "gifts" to the institution, it could relate to the president's affair with a beautiful coed or perhaps it is a case of mistaken identity.

Homicide Detective Wes Wesley finds tangled motives and a murderer with the help of a homeless man, with only a first name, who hangs around campus and several students who, by using their knowledge of technology, both help and confuse the investigation.

THIS BOOK IS DEDICATED TO

Detective Carl Lee Price,
Atlanta Homicide, my mentor and counsel while creating this story, who did not live to see the work completed.

and

Reverend William Hill,
my university advisor who always gave me the support and guidance that encouraged me to have a vision, which would create the direction for my life.

ACKNOWLEDGMENTS

A story is simply a collection of words if there is no human connection behind those words. Thanks to the help, advice, time, encouragement and criticism of the following people, this story and its characters took on their own reality. Members of the Atlanta Police Force for their advice and valuable lessons; Richard Belcher, WSB-TV in Atlanta, for his generosity to review the text and make suggestions for authenticity; the readers' time and thoughtfulness who gave freely of their advice; Patrick Helmer, for his overwhelming knowledge about computers, who organized the text; Richard John Livingstone Martin, my husband, who willingly gave me all the time I needed to finish the manuscript.

Prologue

A Murderer

A slim shadow seemed to creep up to the 100-year-old building always known as the Tech Tower. It avoided the street-lights that cast a soft, seductive light around the foundation that was almost hidden by thick bushes planted years ago as a reunion gift from the class of 1975. The walls were covered by trails of ivy, clipped frequently by the grounds staff so the vines would not overrun the entire structure. The shiny green overlay was in keeping with the old, pitted, red bricks and worn Georgia marble steps that delivered the message, "This is a traditional, conservative, reliable institution. We are proud to be Georgia Tech."

It was a stately building that reflected the classic image: The Halls of Ivy. Being in Atlanta and in every way a part of Southern history did not diminish Georgia Tech's desire to be listed among MIT, Cal Tech and other highly rated technical institutions. The Tech Tower was a symbol of generations that became politically honored alumni and commanders of industry. Alumni often returned to their alma mater and served as volunteer leaders for many more years than they studied to "get out of Tech." (Never do they say graduate!)

On this chilly, March night, the person who cast the slim shadow scanned the historic structure and its nearby parking area and saw the president's car, with its GT1 special license plate, was in its regular "#1" parking space. That was unusual. "Why would he spend time in his office in the middle of the night?"

On seeing the car, the dusky form tried harder to hide in the shadows that were spread like ink smudges on the lawn and parking spaces. Dark clothes blended into the late night blackness. The silhouette moved cautiously, watching in all directions. There was nothing stirring anywhere near the hill where the old building was located. The figure leaned back and looked up at the steep roof.

"Everyone here feels proud when they see the Tech Tower. To many, it's almost hallowed. I must be crazy to be hanging around in the middle of the night. What do I think I'm going to learn? Something I don't already know?"

Just as those thoughts passed through the hesitant individual's mind, a low light was noticed through the windows of the president's office. Reacting with surprise, the half-hidden form shrunk back into the darkness. The shadows cloaked the stealthy figure that crept forward to peer through the window.

"The son of a bitch is sitting at his computer."

Watching through the window, strong feelings began to take over. Anger. Fury. Rage. These emotions had been the reason to come to this place tonight.

"Why aren't you a man of integrity? For your own benefit, you're making this an intolerable place. You have no feelings for those who think this campus is special."

The thoughts tumbled and then their strength propelled legs toward the other car parked in the lot. There seemed to be no control of mind or body. The familiar deer rifle came to hand almost automatically. It was a shock, but the reason it was there was clear. Everything seemed to be moving in slow motion as if the air itself had thickened.

"Jonathan Lindholm, fate has brought us together in a quiet and secluded place. I need no other sign. It's time that you pay for your acts that are ruining good people and a good place."

Two shots shattered the quiet of the night. Then a short silence and the racing of a car's engine. The low light continued to burn in the office, but there was no sound beyond the hum of the president's computer.

• • •

THE ATLANTA JOURNAL-CONSTITUTION
Body Found in Georgia Tech's President's Office

Ms. Janeen Carson, assistant to three Georgia Institute of Technology presidents, found the body of a graduate student slumped over the president's computer early this morning. It appears that the man had been shot in the head from a location outside the building.

The murdered student has been identified as Oliver Andrew Dren, Jr., 30, a computer science graduate student. Mr. Dren, a native of Dalton, Georgia, had been at Georgia Tech for less than a year after having worked for Microsoft as a senior programmer and doing special computer projects for Olympic-related corporations.

Ms. Carson called campus security director, George Fancer, and then President Jonathan Agnew Lindholm III. Both arrived on the scene at the same time. Director Fancer called the Atlanta police immediately.

"I am personally saddened," said President Lindholm, "I have known Andy for almost a year, because he was working on some projects for the administration. He is, ahh, was tremendously bright and always hard-working."

When asked by Atlanta homicide detective, Wes T. Wesley, if he had a clue as to why Mr. Dren was in his office, the president said he had no idea.

The medical examiner said the cause of death appeared to be a bullet entering just in front of the left ear. The bullet, apparently shot from outside and through a window, also hit the corner of the back of the desk chair on which the victim was sitting. Campus police and Atlanta police have begun their investigation of the murder and are gathering additional information.

Detective Wesley found indications that the shooter may have stood in the bushes at the parking area to be able to see into the office. "If this is how the killing was done, we can eliminate the possibility of random shots gone wild." His suspicions were based on scuff marks on the ground and several newly broken branches in the bushes. It is difficult to determine if a car had been parked in the area, because the parking lot is so highly used.

Chief Fancer made an immediate visit to Mr. Dren's graduate residence apartment, which was shared with two other students. His roommates expressed amazement and horror. "How could this happen to someone like Andy? He was a quiet guy who had no interests beyond his computer and his studies," said Peter Kirk.

President Lindholm has been unavailable for further questioning at this time and has said, "Please contact the institution through our Vice President for Advancement, Charles Black."

Chapter 1

Danielle Jarvis Swain

"BreakIn!"

The television screen screamed the words. Anchorwoman Danielle Swain waited impatiently for the Channel 22's special format to complete its 15-second introduction. She knew exactly how it would appear in thousands of homes. She tapped her finger on the desktop—-seven, eight, nine —-.

"BreakIn!"

Big red letters on a flashing blue and white background. Designed to look like the piercing strobe lights so prevalent in any urban area. Blue and white. Blue and white. Blue and white. Lights that when concentrated on the screen created spots and stripes before the viewer's eyes. The visual irritant was coupled with a siren everyone relates to a police action. And why not? Most of the BreakIn! features brought to the public were related to crime.

Twelve, thirteen, fourteen—-

"BreakIn! WPTR-TV Channel 22. Just minutes ago, a body was found in the office of the president of Georgia Institute of Technology. There are no details at this time but both the Georgia Tech chief of police and the Atlanta homicide department have been notified. Stay tuned to Channel 22 for all breaking news happening about the apparent murder on the Georgia Tech campus."

Danielle relaxed when the hot lights went out. She took a moment to think back to the whirlwind half-hour she had just spent after arriving late for a manager's 8:00 AM meeting.

She had rushed into the station and immediately scanned the police radio, a constant source for the next BreakIn! report.

Even though WPTR-TV's scheduled news programs had constantly won national awards, its BreakIn! feature was what more people talked about at Atlanta cocktail parties, or over a beer at a favorite bar near the end of a day. Ever since CNN had made news a 24-hour entertainment, Channel 22 television had beefed up its already strong news focus. WPTR's top-rated investigative reporters and anchorpersons kept the ratings high from year to year. Their salaries rose in reflection of the channel's popularity.

The anchorwoman thought back to the evening before. She had learned of the manager's meeting as she was leaving the station about 7:30. Somehow she had missed the announcement on E-mail.

"Looks like Jimmy has a new idea. His last-minute meetings are always an adventure," Danielle said to the security guard as she opened the door leading to the parking lot. "See you early tomorrow, Tony."

"Right, Dani. I'll see all of you early. Guess it's my lucky day," Tony Jones smiled brightly. He liked Dani Swain, because although a 'star,' she was a sweet, kind and an open person.

Tony Jones watched Dani as she walked to her car. She was in no hurry. He imagined she was enjoying the fresh, light spring air. This was the time of year in Atlanta that everyone said was special. Even the camellias around the parking lot seemed to have been planted to quietly signal the short winter was past.

He thought about when Dani arrived five years ago. She was driving a beat up Honda that was covered with crusty, northern road dirt. Now she's driving a newer one, clean and shiny. She looked good in both cars. In Tony's opinion, she should do advertising for Honda, because she makes a Honda look as good as a BMW.

Tony never missed an attractive female. Danielle's finely drawn features reminded him of the African art he had seen several times at the High Museum on Peachtree Street. He saw her as a study of colors. Her skin looked like a handful of brand new, copper pennies, her eyes were a light hazel green, her short, curly hair as black as the inside of the Omni basketball arena when all the lights went out. Dani's choice of clothes was always vibrant shades of the rainbow. He didn't think he had ever seen this beautiful woman in black or white.

He didn't know a lot about her personal life. "How could I?" Tony asked himself. They were only in the same world here at Channel 22. "When she drives away from here, where does she go? Who was waiting for her?" He didn't know the answers, but he'd learned other facts about her and everything he learned, he liked. Yes, he felt she was a class act.

Tony Jones always read the WPTR's newsletter introducing new staff. He also listened as they passed by. Most people never notice security guards. He could add lots of details to the basic information that was circulated by Channel 22.

Danielle Jarvis Swain's arrival announcement said she was an army brat from Hilo, Hawaii and had worked her way east by having several jobs related to media. In high school, she was writing for the school newspaper when she was asked to host a radio show focused on both talk and music. When she agreed, it was suggested that she call the show: D.J.'s. She liked that. For several years she was known as D.J. rather than Dani before going to the University of California, Berkeley.

Tony had also learned about Dani from conversations with her standing by the door at the end of a day. She had told him that after graduation, she gravitated back into media by taking a job with a television station in northern California. Being a smaller market and with a bare-bones staff, she had the opportunity to learn many different jobs at the station and soon became an occasional backup for the regular newscasters. When the station was sold to a larger corporation, Dani was asked to move to one of the new owners' major locations in Cleveland, Ohio. Tony remembered her laughter when she told him, "I called my dad and whined, ' I don't know if I can survive in polar bear weather.' Then he reminded me that I used to whine in the same tone about wanting a sled. I stopped whining, vowed to buy a child's sled when I reached Cleveland and headed north."

When Tony heard that during her two years of cold winters, she became a local television 'star,' he wasn't surprised.

While he believed she had that special celebrity quality, she told him that she was constantly surprised that she'd be asked for autographs and receive fan mail. It was amusing, but she felt it was also a responsibility. She would never know, but she might be a role model for some kids who want to be in television. She believed she had to have an honorable reputation. Being the daughter of an army officer, honor and ethics were topics of discussion in her home from the time she was a small child.

Several years later, another call to her parents announced Dani's big chance to come to Atlanta when the Universal Television Corporation bought Channel 22, "I've been asked to be one of the anchors for WPTR-TV. It has the reputation for putting news first." She wondered if this focus was decided because they were actually a neighbor of Ted Turner's original CNN. Whatever the reason, Danielle Swain was ready to move to a bigger market and away from winter.

• • •

Tony remembered every detail he had learned about Danielle. He actually was thinking about her success the next morning when Dani arrived at the studio just seconds after 8:00. She smiled, called the Southern greeting - hey, and ran past him. She hated to walk into Jimmy London's meeting after he had begun to talk. The manager was never late. If he set the appointment time, you could count on him to be waiting for you. If you asked him to meet with you, he crossed your doorstep on the dot.

"I should have started earlier," Danielle said out loud as she headed to the conference room. As she heard her own voice, she also became aware of the voice on the police radio.

"What's that? Somebody shot on the Tech campus? A 50/48." She shuddered. She knew those numbers on a police report meant someone was dead.

Dani ignored that she was late and waited to hear the next message. Yes, Homicide was dispatching several detectives immediately. The campus police chief had called them. The hell with the manager's meeting. She had to interrupt Jimmy's monologue and get some reporters and equipment over to Tech. It was fortunate for WPTR that they were only a few blocks away. They may get there before any of the competition except CNN. It was located even closer; practically on the campus.

Dani rushed to the conference room, threw open the door and shouted, "There's been a shooting at Georgia Tech! The Atlanta police are already on their way."

Everyone looked astonished. For a moment there wasn't a sound. Then several people jumped up from their chairs around the glass-topped conference table and were through the door in a matter of seconds. Jimmy London didn't try to continue his meeting. They were in the news business and this was news.

"Monitor the police radio, pass it on to the mobile crew," London instructed. He knew that the filming crew and reporters on duty would already be in the mobile unit racing out of the parking area. They could move as fast as any firemen in town. "Dani, do a BreakIn! right away. Use the best pictures of Tech that you can get. Hurry. Something of the Tech Tower should be easy to grab. We want to be first with this story."

Danielle could feel the adrenaline racing through her body. A big story always did that to her. No matter how long she has been in the news business, she couldn't be blasé. This was what her whole life was dedicated to. She was already framing her opening sentences of the story. It'll be just like the day after the Olympic bombing. Even people who proclaimed not to watch TV became avid watchers for a few days. A shooting on the Tech campus won't capture the world like the Centennial Park tragedy, but it was going to be the major topic in the city and with students' parents and alumni everywhere.

• • •

When Georgia Tech had been the Olympic Village, it had almost become Dani's second home. She was the field anchorwoman for all of Channel 22's newscasts from the temporary home of the athletes. It had been a chance of a lifetime and she loved being a part of this special kind of history. So much news is about conflict and disasters, but the Village reporting was just plain fun. There were human-interest stories every day to intrigue the public and happenings that were of interest around the world.

Features were presented about dining tents the size of a huge parking lot where dozens of different ethnic cuisines were served daily. The public marveled at the need to store a million cans of Coca-Cola and the tens of thousands of condoms dispensed at the Olympic medical center. Athletes seemed to be as lusty as they were thirsty.

In addition to being assigned to the story of the decade in Atlanta, Danielle Swain enjoyed the opportunities to meet both international people and local residents in an electrifying environment. She had gotten to know several Tech faculty members who had volunteered to work for the Olympics. They would share a break at the athletes' coffee house, meet in the late evening around the pool or have a meal together in the huge, tented dining hall. She received as much information from these informal meetings as she did from some of the scheduled media briefings.

She had kept in touch with several of the international athletes through E-mail and had continued seeing the faculty members whom she now considered her close friends. She thought about Rex Shaw. They had met recently at Einstein's, a trendy Atlanta Midtown restaurant, and sat out on the patio in the warmth of the pale, early spring sun. Dani had insisted that they eat outdoors, because she was still reveling in being away from the northern climate. Rex had lived his entire life in Georgia. He had kidded her that it was too early to sit outside except with the assistance of the overhead patio heaters used by Atlanta restaurants. Dani had compromised and sat at the table Rex chose that was directly under the big umbrella-like heater.

• • •

After doing the BreakIn! broadcast, Dani decided to call Professor Shaw to inquire about what was being said on campus about the shooting. He had been a source for her to get campus background on several stories that she had done about the effects that technology has had on Wall Street and how Georgia Tech is the incubator for many new technically-based start up enterprises. She might get more good backup material for this story. She was always amused when someone called her backup footage

"*Dani's package*" rather than the standard *package*. She knew WPTR always wanted to "own the big story," to be first on the scene and last off, but her colleagues said "Dani's package" in such a way as if she owned the story instead.

The truth was that she sometimes did feel that way. She worked hard to get the most provocative and exciting story. She was adept at covering every part of a newscast from the live lead beginning to the live tag ending with the best package in between. To her, the anchor toss from anchorperson to reporter and back again was as thrilling as being a pitcher for the Atlanta Braves in a World Series.

Using her automatic dialer, she called Rex. He picked up the receiver on the second ring.

"Rex, it's Dani. We just got the police report about a suspected homicide at Tech. Someone was shot. What do you know?"

"Shot? I don't know anything. Haven't heard a word. Who was shot? Where?" Rex rambled.

"Right in the president's office, practically across from your office. "

"Isn't it crazy? We all feared something like this during the Olympics. Instead, it happens on just a normal class day."

"Right now I don't know anymore. I was hoping you had heard something, but it must be too soon. Will you ask around and see what you can find out? You have my private number. Call me anytime. This is going to be a big story. A homicide at our prestigious Georgia Tech is mega news. I'll be over soon to do some interviews."

"I'll see what I can learn, but no TV interviews for me, Dani. You know how I feel about those on-the-spot talks with people who are hanging around. Yuk! Never leaves the person watching the news with a positive impression of the citizens of Atlanta."

"I know how you feel, but the public loves it. Just like they want to call into those talk shows. Makes them feel that they're in the media. It's like a virus. The format has infected the whole country. —— But, back to the job. Call me when you have some news, and I'll let you know when I'm coming to campus. Right now, I need to go check out the police radio. See what the Good Guys are doing. Talk to you soon."

Chapter 2

Charles William Black

Gazing out the high Palladian window that overlooked his backyard garden, Charles William Black was in the shower reviewing his plans for the day. As the window began to steam over, the warm water relaxed his muscles after his early morning exercise routine on his own Nautilus. Charles smiled to himself. Out loud, he said to himself, "I have it made here as Vice President for Advancement at Georgia Tech. What a great decision to take this position. Working with the alumni and the foundation board members has been more than I ever hoped for. Why, I wouldn't even have my Nautilus, except for one of the board members!"

He was pleased with his job as well as his well-toned body. Although he had just celebrated his 43rd birthday, he looked years younger. The mirror, that he kept in the shower so he could shave while relaxing under the soothing spray, reflected the green eyes about which many people have said, "Reminds me of a cat." He felt that his resemblance to a cat went beyond his eyes. His whole style made him think of a sleek, fast cheetah in pursuit of a beautiful antelope.

Yes, he was pleased with his physical appearance, but he was even more proud of his ability to fit into any situation where he could convince everyone that he was in charge. He knew he was ruthless enough to intimidate his staff to do things his way. He had intelligence, flair and talent to realize what the board members and the president wanted. Very rarely did they get ahead of him because he worked at reading every sign and suggestion that could benefit him. It was that last quality that kept him in his comfortable position and guaranteed him a long tenure with many perks. Yes, this had become a perfect life for Charles Black, such a contrast to the life he had as the son of Margaret and Lewis Black.

• • •

He was reminded of the time his father had come through Atlanta about a year ago and called Charles to meet him at the airport. As he looked into the mirror, it was as if the reflection was a video of his father's visit.

"Charlie Boy! Here I am. You almost walked right by me."

Charles was amazed. Of course he had almost missed him. It was just 10 AM and his father was already sitting at the concourse bar with an empty beer glass in front of him.

"Come here, boy, and I'll buy you a beer. You can chew some damn gum so no one will know you were out drinking with your long lost dad. I can't wait to tell you about my latest deal. Your dad is never short on ideas."

Black shuddered remembering why he had not heard from his dad in five years. That was when one of Mr. Black's get-rich-quick deals had turned into a get-out-of-town-quick deal. Lewis Black had needed an even quicker loan which eventually turned out to be Charles's gift to his father. He could hear his cold words, "You never learn, Dad. Why don't you just get a job?"

"Shit, Charlie Boy, I can't be tied down. I'm a free spirit. Give me a fast buck and a hot woman, and I've got it all. You think I want some fancy, candy-assed job like you have? Sucking up to people who have so much money that they're willing to give it to a fucking college. Damn, just let me talk to them, and I'll get them to give to something really worthwhile: me!"

Charles hated his dad calling him Charlie Boy and despised his language. No one else ever called him anything except Charles. If they did, he would correct them. But he wouldn't correct his father. Their relationship had never been warm or humane, but now it was close to hostile. His dad knew that the name Charlie Boy bothered Charles, which is why he used it. The son wasn't going to give the father the satisfaction of mentioning it. He simply mumbled that he didn't want a beer and hoped that his father's plane was not delayed.

Charles had grown up despising his parents. His father deserved every venomous thought he could invent. His mother really didn't. She had simply done nothing. She had allowed his dad to be irresponsible, nasty, abusive, crude and slovenly. She never had the courage nor interest to improve the situation for herself, Charles, his five brothers or two sisters. His mother had been willing to go on having Lewis' children usually conceived after a roaring fight that would spread from husband and wife to most of the children. Charles would like to rewrite his whole childhood, but that wasn't the way life was. Best decision for him was to just write off his family and get on with his own successful life. He wanted to break away from the images that appeared to be held in his steamy mirror, but the scenes of the past seemed to be flowing as easily as his shower water.

• • •

"Charles! Charles!" Sally Black was screaming to be heard over the rush of water. "Charles, it's the president on the phone. He says it's an emergency and to get to the phone even if you're dripping."

Charles didn't like being interrupted during his morning routine. He got up early to have this time for himself. Sally learned this years ago and had made a point to stay out of his way until he made his entrance into the kitchen for breakfast. Today she broke their unspoken rule, because Jon Lindholm sounded, what was it, maybe desperate?

"It's not even 7:30. What could be bothering him so early? Probably wants more headlines with his name in them," he shouted back to Sally as he reached to turn off the water.

"I wouldn't joke right now, Charles. Your boss sounds like he has a big problem."

Charles grabbed a towel and dried some of the water from his body as he went to the telephone. Wrapping the towel around his waist, he sat on the edge of the bed and picked up the telephone.

"Good morning, Jon. What gets you up so early?"

"How about murder? Murder in my office," the president said trying to keep his voice calm.

"Murder? Who? What?"

"Ask your questions later. This may be big trouble for all of us. There are all kinds of problems that could arise," exclaimed Jon Lindholm. "Andy Dren was in my office in the middle of the night with my computer on and was shot through the head. So do you see that we might want to cover up some possible problems here?" The president was obviously on the verge of panic.

"Andy being in your office doesn't make any sense. But I can see why you're upset. I'll be there just as soon as I can. Have the police been called?"

"Of course the police have been called. They've arrived and are already starting their investigation. No one has any idea why Andy would be using my computer. I want to keep it that way. Who would shoot him and why? I hope I don't know the answers."

There was a pause. Both men were thinking about what had happened and how it could change their lives.

Jon Lindholm was as satisfied with his life as Charles was with his. They made a good team because both of them believed in being in control and had learned to make it work for themselves. Charles understood that when dealing with "his" president, it was Lindholm who was in control. That was fine with him. As long as he followed the Lindholm rules, he was safe in his high-salaried position. He could continue to flourish in a situation that not only carries perks and money but also prestige in certain circles of his venue.

Charles recognized the reasons why he and Lindholm were good teammates. He ran his department with fear and consequences and that was fine with the president. In fact that was the model that his boss had used for most of his professional and personal life. Jon Lindholm had no trouble with his staff as long as they needed their jobs and understood who was in charge.

The president's façade of being an attractive, congenial, fifty-something, happily-married, devoted father was the shell of a hard, driven, egotistic man who had spent years perfecting the appearance to make possible the filling of his very esoteric needs.

He enjoyed reading the features often written about him because he could say smugly to himself, "Good. No one has invaded the real Jon Lindholm."

Charles understood that Jon had no trouble with his family either, because he'd established his dominance even before he and his wife, Laurie, were married. Actually, Lindholm had once told him he felt that was the best time to get control, because then your lover was willing to agree to anything to get you to get married. His command in his home and in his office was the president's passport to big advantages. Black knew that Lindholm III would not want to lose any of his plush living just because of some computer nerd.

Charles also was having similar thoughts about himself, except he saw that he was in a much more fragile situation. If the president needed a fall guy in this predicament, with no hesitation, Charles Black would be the sacrifice. That was an obvious observation when you work for someone who is a mirror image of yourself. They may have a contrast in coloring, Lindholm having dark brown hair and eyes, but they were the same at the core of their personalities.

"Charles! Get down here now!" The shrillness of Jon Lindholm's voice brought Charles back to the immediate situation.

"I will be there within the hour."

Sally was still standing at the door waiting to hear what was happening. She felt some of the panic that both the president and her husband were feeling, but she didn't know why. She was quite good at reading Charles' moods and this morning she was reading big trouble. She stood quietly. She had learned over the years that it was better to wait if you really wanted to learn what was important.

She looked at Charles and stopped breathing.

• • •

Sally was what some referred to as "small and mighty." She wasn't sure that was true, but she was sure that she could direct the relationship between Charles and herself. Sometimes it took patience, but that willingness to wait had proven to be the way to get what she wanted. She was the one who made their personal decisions.

Four years ago she had seen the advertisement for this big advancement position at Georgia Tech. Charles had never been anything more than a free lance writer for educational and alumni publications, a college development director who lucked out getting credit for securing a $10,000,000 gift for that institution from a large corporation, and later an account rep for an inconsequential public relations firm in Peoria. His aspirations were to be a partner in that rinky-dink company, which had the distinct honor of being named The P R Company.

Sally had other ideas. She had been raised in a middle class home in Chicago with three older brothers. There never seemed to be enough money left from her father's salary, as a district manager of a soft drink company, to go beyond the basics. When it came to education, each one of the children was given two years of college, paid for by their dad. "I want to be fair," he said, "If you really think college is important, you'll find a way to finish."

And, each did. They found jobs and went to classes at night and weekends. Four years in a row, the family gathered and celebrated each graduation. There was always a party at their parents' home. Their dad and mom were proud that their children had gotten a good education, and they gave each of them a monogrammed, leather briefcase with a card that said: We're glad that you knew it was important. We're proud of you. Love, Mom and Dad.

The celebrations were all alike. It always was a festive time, but the four siblings looked forward to the time after the party when they got together and talked about their lives with their parents. Soon the guests had gone home and the family was talking about things they all felt were of value. They enjoyed the quiet time together and then went off in different directions.

The morning following Sally's celebration, her dad was found dead in his bed of a heart attack. Her mother said the last thing they talked about after the four children had gone was that her dad felt they had done a good job as parents and hoped their children would enjoy their future families as much as he enjoyed his.

• • •

Sally's thoughts stopped when her husband said, "There's been a murder at Georgia Tech. Janeen found a body in the president's office. Why did this have to happen now? Everything's been going so well."

Sally caught her breath and blurted out, "Oh, God, was it one of his girlfriends?"

"Sally! Don't ever say a thing like that again. Especially now when we've no idea what's going on. This has nothing to do with Jon's little 'adventures.' The person murdered was a male, graduate student who apparently broke into the president's office."

"Sorry. I spoke out of just plain shock. Of course, I'll be careful," Sally said feeling contrite and disloyal to a man who had been responsible for much of the good life they had. Charles' salary and perks had greatly increased since Dr. Forsythe, the former president, had died and Dr. Lindholm had arrived to be president.

His mind already miles away on the campus, Charles Black jumped up from the bed and started across the room. "Sally, why don't you pick a good suit and tie for me, appropriate for a long day?"

Sally enjoyed choosing Charles clothes. She liked to paraphrase that her man made the clothes rather than the clothes made her man. Sally looked at Charles' flat stomach and muscular legs. She knew how hard her husband worked at staying in shape and both of them were pleased with the results. She noted that his curly blond hair had faded slightly since she met him 15 years ago, but there was no obvious graying at his temples.

• • •

Black was good to his word. He walked into President Lindholm's foyer exactly 54 minutes after he said he would be there.

The door closed behind him and Charles reached up nervously and ran his fingers through his hair. He stopped suddenly as soon as he entered the foyer of the president's suite. He couldn't believe that this was the same place he had left only 14 hours earlier.

Just last evening, at the end of a long Georgia Tech Foundation committee meeting, this foyer was serene and staid. The president demanded the proper aura to be present for those who came to see him with information, with problems or to ask a favor.

The soft cream walls created the background to emphasize an interesting collection of student art. In the foyer was an outstanding example of the talent that had passed through the Georgia Institute of Technology in more than 100 years. The art was mostly paintings or drawings, but there were also sculptures and detailed models that dated back to the early 1920s. Simple, classic furniture had been chosen for those who must wait for their time with the president. The lines and muted colors of the pieces didn't draw one's attention from looking at the students' art.

"I'm surprised at this much artistic talent in an engineering and technical school," was a common remark.

This was exactly the kind of reaction Tech employees welcomed, because it gave them an opportunity to boast about the diverse student body at the Institute today and through the earlier years. Although these were the usual thoughts that Charles Black had when he entered the foyer, today his thoughts were on more pressing topics.

He was taking in all the frantic activity that seemed to be in every inch of the area. There was a yellow, plastic crime scene tape stretched across the doorway opening into where Janeen Carson, the president's assistant, usually sat directly outside Lindholm's office. Janeen, looking almost as cool and composed as any morning, was set up at what is normally the receptionist's desk and the receptionist was sitting at a folding table that was crowded with her telephone and other items that had been whisked off her desk to make way for Janeen. Two upholstered chairs that usually flank a matching sofa had been dragged to one corner where two policemen were in deep conversation with campus chief of police, George Fancer. It occurred to Charles that he should have been here long ago. After all, as the vice president of advancement, he's paid to be the front man. Why hadn't Janeen called him when she called the president? She had made him look bad.

Two men in dark suits and white shirts, carrying oversized imitation leather cases were stepping over the yellow ribbon. They said good bye to Janeen, thanked her for her assistance and for keeping everybody out of their way while they did their job. One of the men stopped at her desk and quietly added, "Thank you for your calmness and helping keep the others from freaking out."

Janeen gave him her everyday, warm, flashing smile and responded, "That's part of my job, Detective Wesley. We see crises here almost daily. That's the nature of a campus. You just let me know how I can help you, and I'll do my best to do it." She took one of her cards and handed it to the officer.

Wes glanced at the card but returned his eyes to Janeen. He liked what he saw —- Creamy complexion; gray eyes that often took on a different hue depending on the light; a full, honest smile framed by shoulder length chestnut-brown hair. Janeen had worked at acquiring a sense of style perfect for her slim body and glowing face. In all ways, Janeen added a simple dignity to the president's outer office. Her clothes were professional with a soft warmth that matched her personality.

Wes smiled and was turning toward the door when Janeen caught Charles' eye.

"Oh, Charles, Dr. Lindholm is waiting for you in the provost's office. That's his temporary location until the police complete their investigation of his office."

Chapter 3

Jonathan Agnew Lindholm III

When Charles entered the office and saw the president, he had the uncomfortable feeling that Lindholm was ready to pounce on him.

"I've told you many times that for a man with your responsibilities, you should live closer to the campus. Look at what has already happened here and you're not plugged in at all."

Lindholm's opening remarks definitely set the stage. Black knew that it was going do be difficult to lower the pressure that his boss was experiencing. Charles couldn't do it now, but he would find a way to transfer the blame to Janeen or one of his staff.

• • •

Jon Lindholm felt he was losing. He had not felt this stressed since coming to Georgia Tech two years ago. He was quickly reminded about his reason for pursuing this job. His muscles tightened. His head began to ache.

He had been doing quite well in his former position at Hewlett Packard in California plus teaching one course in strategic planning for higher education at Cal Tech. This had been a big "promotion" from earlier years when he taught Management of Research in the night school at San Jose State.

He remembered the day when he made the deal at Cal Tech. He jumped into his car, raced the motor and spun the wheels. Several coeds looked around and threw him high fives. Although he was practically middle age to them, for that moment they took him into their group, "Just you wait, young things. Soon you're going to know that Jon Lindholm has arrived on campus. I can afford to wine you, dine you and then bed you."

Jon saw no conflict between these intentions and his reputation as an expert in management that he was building as a conference keynoter. Using his vacation and sick time, he presented at every conference that he could work into his schedule and had become a sought-after speaker.

The professional persona Jon had created was in place and ready to work for him when Tech began looking for a president. The Board of Regents and the alumni who were on the search committee had decided this was the time to look for leadership with strong corporate background. When his vita showed corporate and academic expertise, he was considered to be the perfect candidate. It was unanimous that Dr. Jonathan Agnew Lindholm III would fill their needs for an administrator, fundraiser and team member.

His vita focused on that he was known from coast to coast as an authority on higher education administration and strategic planning. Oh, yes, it was easy to talk the theory everyone wanted to hear. It was easier to cash in on the hot issues and buzz words. Absolutely, he was an authority on marketing himself by talking about what was already being talked about and promoting himself as successful. His rhetoric was famous. He was often quoted. He hoped that no one in his conferences or those who listened to his statements ever investigated how he really ran his own shop. He found that fear and threats worked best for him.

Even with his complete belief in being in control, at Cal Tech, just three years ago, he lost it and with it his job and almost his wife and reputation. How could he have been so stupid? How could he have allowed himself to be out of control? One coed had forced a whole new life plan. It wasn't going to happen again. He would always protect himself with a person who is set up to take the hit.

"I may need that person sooner than I would have expected," Tech's president thought as he watched Charles walk toward him. "I may just want to pay more attention to Charles. He thinks he has it all here, but he has it only if I want him to have it."

• • •

As he crossed the room, Charles debated whether to sit down before being asked. The desire was strong, because his knees seemed to be quite a bit weaker than they were when he worked out this morning. The chair in front of the desk that matched nothing else in the room, looked inviting, but his instinct told him that he better play the dutiful servant.

"I'll tell you the important points that I want you to know and then you get on the job and find out everything you can to bring back to me. This may be the most critical assignment you've ever had, Charles. Don't fail me now."

Lindholm's opening words dripped like icy rain from the eaves of the Tech Tower roof. Charles could see all kinds of problems in trying to keep ahead of his boss and the police at the same time.

Leaving Charles standing beside the wooden chair that was painted with the Georgia Tech seal, the president filled in his vice president with the events up to that point and then lowered his voice.

"Since Andy was at the computer, we must assume that he had some suspicions about the work we asked him to do. I find it hard to believe that damn computer freak would have been taking such matters into his own hands or could he have been working with someone else? Might another person have directed him?" The president was spitting out questions and thoughts faster than Charles could consider answers or consequences.

"Charles, you must get as much information as possible from the police and the Tech security officers. They will assume doing that is just part of your job. At the same time, you must do some investigating on your own. See what you can find out about Andy, who were his close friends, who were his professors, etc. etc."

Black's head was reeling. His mind was a jumble of questions, partial responses, potential remarks and images of being thrown into a situation that would leave him completely vulnerable. The president sounded like he had several agendas and Charles wondered if he knew them all. There was no doubt that

Jon Lindholm was going to take care of himself with no concern for Charles Black.

• • •

Lindholm saw Black hesitating. In the chilly silence that filled the room, the president was unable to stop his mind from wandering back to California. He felt he'd learned a huge lesson at that time that would help guide the rest of his life, but now he was faced with a dilemma that really was not in his hands.

For years his salary at Hewlett Packard had provided a comfortable life for himself and his family. Laurie was kept busy with civic activities, their son, Jonathan IV, and her true passion, ballet. When he had met his wife, she was the cheerleading coach at San Jose State and part of her routine to stay trim was to study ballet. For more than 20 years she'd continued to learn and in the past 12 years, she'd been teaching children in urban, community centers.

Jon Lindholm welcomed her dedication to ballet and the children she taught. Sometimes it kept her occupied both day and night. That was perfect because Lindholm never had to wonder how he would keep busy. Not when he had so many young women in his classes who thought he was smart, handsome and intriguing. Actually, they had convinced him! He must be special to be able to attract lovely, intelligent students who were willing to play his game and not tell.

Yes, he had financial stability with HP, a respectable family, a part-time instructor's appointment at Cal Tech, and recognition through his speaking engagements; but his female students kept his life from being boring. Actually, some of them were boring (They were so much alike!), but pursuit and conquest were exciting. When he made his presentations on management and strategy, he often was tempted to use his successes with women as examples of how careful planning works. Wouldn't that get the attention of the listeners?

Fortunately for all concerned, he was as discreet as his many partners. He'd learned that he must strategically plan his sex life as much as he did his business life. He must also have a loyalty to both.

"Be true to your job and it will be true to you." he said often when he spoke to mid level managers.

His personal paraphrase was, "Be good to your lover and she will be good to you."

This thought always brought a smile to his face, and he could feel one starting now. Oh, yes, his idea of being good to his lover was not to have more than one during an academic year. This helped to prevent conflict. By the end of the academic calendar, he was already working at giving the young woman many reasons to find a way to end their relationship "without hurting him too much."

• • •

"Jon. Hey, Jon," Charles' voice brought Lindholm back to the present, "If you have nothing else to add, I'll go talk with the police."

"Yes, do that. And, bring back all the information you find. Do not miss anything that could be important to me."

As Charles turned quickly, he caught his foot on the leg of the chair, "That son of a bitch never did ask me to sit down," he thought as he left the room.

Preoccupied with his own discomfort, Charles almost walked into the president's son.

Chapter 4

Jonathan Agnew Lindholm IV

"Hi, Mr. Black. You and Dad must be going crazy. I guess you have been together planning how to deal with all the rumors as well as the facts. You know, like, be sure the image of Tech isn't messed up," Lindy said as he avoided being knocked down.

"What do you mean, Lindy? What kinds of rumors have you heard? How could your father and I be considering anything beyond how to help the police find the person who shot poor Andy? It's a terrible thing. Such a wonderful young man," Charles responded, wondering if there was a hidden meaning in the president's son's greeting.

"Oh, you know how the campus is. There are about as many theories as there are people. Remember, we are at a research institution. Everyone has an inquiring mind and is looking to come up with the answer before anyone else," and without even taking a breath, Lindy called across the room, "Hey, Dad, I've come to interview you for The Technique."

Lindy had been on the campus newspaper staff for almost a year and he hoped to be the editor next year when he would be a junior. He was careful not to take advantage of his familial ties and never mentioned that he was related to THAT Lindholm, but it was difficult to not be seen only as the president's son.

He wanted to make it on his own, but it sure was hard. Because of his interest in technology and talent for computer science, he had wanted to go to Georgia Tech most of his life. He never dreamed, when the time came, his dad would become the president! His parents always encouraged him to go to Cal Tech, his father's alma mater, but he'd never really wanted to go anywhere except the other Tech. He'd been wearing Tech sweat shirts and singing The Ramblin' Wreck from the time he was in grade school and had a teacher who gave Georgia Tech T shirts as prizes in the annual math competition.

It was a strange turn when he finally decided on Cal Tech and both of his parents were insistent that he come to this campus. Suddenly, his dad had left Hewlett Packard and was applying to become the president of Georgia Institute of Technology. Lindy had never heard his father ever mention wanting to leave the company, California, or his teaching position at Cal Tech. He certainly had never heard that he wanted to be a college president. When he asked about this new direction, his father said, "For years, I've been teaching thousands of people to run academic institutions and think it's about time I test my theories. So I might as well start at the top!"

At the same time, his mother was experiencing some "middle age" depression and was encouraging her husband to consider the job in Atlanta. She said she needed a fresh start in a different environment. Her attitude was also a surprise to Lindy, since his mother was a true California girl. She loved being close to the ocean and told stories of the 'olden days' when she spent every weekend at the beach and had surfer's bumps the size of lemons. Surely she would hate living in a city almost a day's drive from the ocean.

When it appeared that his parents were definitely going to move to Atlanta, Lindy began to have second thoughts about the school of his choice. He knew that it would be tough to attend college where your name was a carbon copy of the president's. He didn't want to constantly be compared to The Third. He looked at the options open to him and decided he would rather stay in California and go to Cal Tech. He had always thought it was a great second choice, if he didn't get into Tech. It wasn't a tremendous sacrifice, and it was better than having to adjust to being the Prez's Kid

He could not have been more surprised at his parents' reaction when he told them of his decision. He thought they'd be thrilled. Instead they were completely negative about him staying in the area and going to Cal Tech. During a heated conversation, his mother even suggested that he look at other colleges. He was confused. Why would he want to choose a place that he'd never considered when his two top choices were still open to him?

Lindy's reaction was that he was an adult and should make his own decision. He felt the same about his parents. They made the decision to go to Georgia Tech, which was fine with him. They should feel the same way about his choice. But when he said this, both of his parents pleaded with him, asking him to think about his changed intentions. To avoid a more unpleasant argument, the three Lindholms agreed to think about the conversation and discuss it at a later time.

A few hours later his dad came to his bedroom and asked if they could talk; just the two of them. The two men sat on Lindy's bed. Lindy waited for his dad to tell him what was on his mind.

"Lindy, there is more involved here than just where you go to college. I could not say this when your mother was with us, but you need to know that the three of us being together is critical to your mother's health."

"What's the problem, Dad? I have noticed that Mom has been very quiet and sad lately. I wouldn't do anything to hurt her. Tell me what's wrong?" Lindy asked, feeling the panic that a son feels when he thinks he may be losing his mother. "She's not going to die, is she?"

Lindholm carefully chose his words so that he could assure that his son would move away from Cal Tech, "No, Lindy, your mother isn't dying, but she's having some mental problems. The doctors say that the best thing for her at this time is to convince her that her family is safe and close to her. She has this obsession that something is going to happen to you or me. She's been struggling with this for the past few months and didn't want me to tell you. Now I think you need to know, if you're going to make a serious decision that could tip the delicate balance your mother is experiencing."

Jon Lindholm III listened to his own explanation. He felt that what he said sounded plausible. Not too serious but enough of a worry for his son that he wouldn't take a chance in hurting his mother. He would also know that he shouldn't talk to her about this, because it would embarrass her. Lindholm felt he had covered all the possible options that his son may argue why he should stay in California. There was no way either of Lindy's parents wanted him to be at Cal Tech where stories of why his dad had left his teaching position may begin to circulate.

Lindholm looked at his son and felt just a spasm of guilt. Here was a young man who could be a model for others in his age group. His face was nearing being handsome, still growing into its potential. He had deep brown eyes and sandy brown hair that he wore a bit long as was the style of all his friends. His smile had been enhanced by a well-known orthodontist who surely was able to drive a Mercedes because of the Lindholm case. Lindy's features were pleasing but what people noticed when they met him was that he radiated a sense of strong, ethical character.

"Your son makes me feel that the younger generation is way ahead of us," said Earl Prince, an alumnus of Tech and a long time member of the Georgia Tech Foundation board. "It's in his face as well as in his conversation, because he understands the importance of a strong value system. He belongs at Tech where integrity comes first. If we all don't live that way, we should leave or we fail the students and alumni."

Although he believed that Prince was radical on the topic of integrity, Lindholm loved to hear this. Yes, it meant that he had a fine son to carry on his name, but it also meant that the image he had created here at Tech was set. Old Earl would be mighty surprised if he knew about Tiffany Walton, Lindholm's current playmate.

• • •

"Dad, can I get some information from you about the murder and maybe a quote or two that I can feature in our lead story?"

The president looked intently at his son. He never would get used to the casual, no, "careless" was a better word, style of today's students. Lindy had on jeans that had at least four major holes in them and a knit shirt that must have been lying in a heap for days before he chose to wear it today. The boy took much better care of his body than he did his clothes. Lindy worked out daily at the Student Athletic Center and had a shape that was the envy of most men and a magnet to most women.

"Hey, Dad, it looks like I'm going to have trouble keeping your attention today. You seem to be in outer space. I probably shouldn't be bothering you, but we're working against a deadline, and Andy *was* found in your office."

Lindy spoke the words and then realized that this was not just another assignment. He'd known Andy Dren and now he was dead.

"I just can't believe this has happened. I knew Andy. We talked several times about the things we were doing and had worked next to each other in the computer lab. How could anyone be mad at him? He was a really nice guy."

Lindholm was jolted back to the present and caught the essence of what his son was saying: Lindy knew Dren and also knew about things he was doing.

Could that computer nerd have ever mentioned to Lindy the project that he was working on for his father? How much did they talk when they were in the lab or between classes or wherever?

"I didn't know that you knew Andy. I don't remember you ever mentioning his name."

"I guess that's possible, Dad. We weren't like, you know, real close friends. Actually, I don't think Andy had close friends. His whole interest was computers. Our conversations were only about computers. I don't even know where he lived or how he decided to come to Tech. I doubt if anyone else knew him much better."

Jon Lindholm felt relieved, but decided to have Charles look into this new information. This wasn't the time to overlook details.

"O.K., Lindy, let's get on with it. I must move along. Already my schedule has been ruined. Just getting Janeen calmed down was difficult."

"Ha! Are you kidding me? Janeen is the coolest person I know," said Lindy as he began to laugh. "I bet she had to help *you* calm down. You must've gone ballistic when you found someone had gotten your password, then been killed in your chair. Wow!"

"Why do you think Andy had my password?"

"Didn't he? The word out on campus is that he was into your computer and was reading your personal files. Hey, Dad, what does a straight guy like you keep in his personal files?" Lindy was enjoying this opportunity to make his dad nervous. Heaven knows, he'd done that to *him* enough times.

"How about a quote as to what you think Andy was looking for on your computer? I think the students and faculty would like to read about that."

"O.K., son, you've had your little joke. Now either you get to your assignment or you're leaving here empty handed. I've things to do," the president spit out the words in a way that Lindy knew he had gone as far as he should. He had learned long ago that his dad could have a very short fuse if the conversation wasn't on a subject of his choosing.

Lindy asked his questions. His father answered them succinctly. They were coming to the end of the interview, when Janeen Carson came to the door.

"Detective Wesley is on line one for you."

Chapter 5

Janeen Newman Carson

Many said, "Georgia Tech is really run by Janeen Carson."

This was an interesting observation, because actually she had outlasted three presidents, got to say hello and good bye to more than 25 deans, was chairman of the Tech United Way annual campaign three times, and was the unofficial leader of all the administrative assistants and secretaries on the campus. When someone needed a quick response to solving a problem, Janeen received a 'Please, help' call. If a faculty member could see the president only on Friday, Janeen found a way to work the appointment into the schedule. If the president forgot to get a birthday gift for his son or wife, Janeen was right there to rescue him. If the president wanted the afternoon to himself, Janeen found a way to detour people in a different direction.

A faculty member had often told the story that he once sent a new employee who was an alumna of the institution to the president's office to deliver a grant proposal. The young woman had not returned by the end of the day so he walked up to the Tech Tower. He entered the office and was greeted by his newest assistant, "Damn, Professor Martine, this day has been more educational than all my classes here at Tech. I haven't decided yet if Ms. Carson is an angel or a witch. She sure can create miracles. I bet she knows more than the president."

Janeen Ann Newman was just barely 18 years old when she answered a newspaper ad looking for a secretary in the Georgia Tech alumni office. She had graduated from a small high school in the North Georgia mountains and had come to Atlanta to attend secretarial school. Before she had completed one year, she saw the request for applicants for the alumni position. She asked an instructor if she could finish her courses at night so she could seek a job. Within a week, she had the job and was enrolled as a night student.

Still officially a teenager, Janeen was already a wise woman. She came from a closely-knit family —- an older sister, Lorene and a younger brother, Gene. Her mother, Nadine, was steady and stable and took seriously the responsibility of being a wife and raising three youngsters. If there was a choice between doing something for her family or herself, she found that her greatest pleasure was being with her husband, Eugene, and the kids.

Never once did Nadine Newman question her decision to marry when she was just out of high school. Eugene, Nadine's only sweetheart, was already a teller at the local bank and had what looked like a nice salary. The family grew at about the same speed as Janeen's dad's responsibilities and salary grew at the bank. He joined the employee stock plan when he was only 20 years old and never missed investing more whenever he was given the opportunity. Because of several bank mergers and his systematic bank stock purchases, when he retired at age 60, he was a millionaire. He never wanted to be a burden to his children, but he had not dreamed that he could give all of them a financial start when they were ready to be out on their own.

Within three years, Janeen had moved from the alumni office to being the president's secretary. On her fifth anniversary on campus, her mother took her to lunch, "I'm so proud of how well you have done at Tech. Not just because you've earned a wonderful salary but because you're respected and valued."

Janeen laughed, "Mom, you would be proud of me if I were a clerk just following directions. But what you really like is that I have the opportunity to use the good, common sense you and Dad taught us all. I've been able to learn from the different presidents I have worked for. So all of my life, I've had quality education."

To many at the college, she was the constant in the president's office: the person who would always be there. She often thought of herself as being just like her mother: She was loyal, hard working and satisfied with her lifelong choice.

Janeen grew with her job. She was pleased with what she had accomplished. When she was asked by her second president, Dr. Maynard Lionel Forsythe, "How would you like to get a degree? I can make it part of your benefits," she leaped at the chance. Within weeks, she again became a part-time student and six years later graduated with honors.

Janeen gained knowledge through her academic experience but gained wisdom from her professional life. She had done a lot more than 'survive' three presidents. She had supported each one, served them all, and gave gentle direction when each took his new position. She wanted all to succeed and make Tech an even better place than it had been before their arrival. This campus was her passion and her refuge.

• • •

As she turned from the doorway and returned to her desk, Janeen Carson was reminded of how different each of the presidents had been.

President Emanuel Joseph Pendleton had asked her to transfer from the alumni office to his office. He'd watched how well she did the routine work, but he saw the potential that she had to be the perfect contact person for him. She could handle stuffy faculty, doting parents, generous donors, nervous students, irate alumni and other staff with the same grace and warmth. Even when she was saying no or delivering an unwanted message, Janeen did it well. None of the presidents ever heard a complaint about how his phone was answered or how a person was greeted at the door. Pendleton often said that his secretary definitely did the things that made him look good.

Of course, Janeen would remark that Dr. Pendleton didn't need a fan club. He was a dear man who cared about his students, his employees and his institution. He was a widower with no children who poured out his affection to those around him.

Maynard Lionel Forsythe had become Tech's seventh president when Dr. Pendleton retired at 65, because he believed that the institution should have a younger man as its leader. Forsythe learned immediately that having a personality like Janeen's as his front office person was invaluable. It was when he knew how important she was to his operation that he suggested that she work on additional education. He wanted her to stay with him. First he offered her education and upon her graduation, he gave her a $5,000 raise.

"I'm glad that I told Dr. Forsythe that I would have stayed without a raise, but I was thrilled that he had improved the quality of my life," Janeen had thought many times.

Maynard Forsythe died of a heart attack after an alumni dinner meeting. He was found in his car parked at the curb in front of the President's home on the edge of the Tech campus. He had not quite reached the driveway that led to the impressive white- columned, Southern-style house when the Forsythe era ended.

Three months later, Jonathan Agnew Lindholm III had been chosen by a search committee and the Chancellor of the Georgia University System, Dr. David Nathaniel Deck.

Two weeks later, Janeen was welcoming 'her' third president. He was younger than Pendleton or Forsythe. The man was far more handsome; almost six feet tall with what appeared to be a perpetual tan. He was an engineer like Forsythe, so she was not surprised that he had a similar closed personality. Some days Dr. Lindholm barely spoke to her or anyone else. Those were the days when she worked her magic and convinced people that they may want to wait until another time to meet. It was her job to make the president look good and she was good at that.

She had dealt with the introverted President Forsythe for years and they had a productive, professional relationship. Lindholm was much more difficult. She accounted that to his lack of real academic administrative experience and almost secretive character. When he first arrived, she'd invited him to lunch to get acquainted and to find out what he expected from his assistant. In that conversation, she asked him about his teaching at Cal Tech, telling him that she had several friends who had been at Georgia Tech and now were on that west coast campus.

He said to her that he never spent much time talking about the past, "Life is only what's ahead of us," he told her shortly. "My job at Cal Tech was strictly that: a job. Nothing at all to talk about."

Janeen was embarrassed that she had even inquired. She was also shocked that he could feel teaching and being at a university was just a job. "What kind of a president will he make?" she thought while she made a mental note to ask her friend at Cal Tech if he had known Jonathan Lindholm, which she did several months later. His quick response was, "Cal Tech was glad to see him go."

She did the best work she could for Dr. Lindholm, as she had done for her other presidents, but from the very beginning, they were not a team. As she got to know him better, she knew he'd have her service and she'd work to always have the presidency be a position of respect, but for the first time in her career it was just a job.

Janeen remembered when she had said to her young husband, Roy, "I will never work in a situation where I feel it's just a job." But here she was doing just that and half a lifetime had passed since she made that statement. She was 16 years older, maybe wiser and Roy had been dead for 14 years.

It still hurt to think of her wonderful Roy. They had had such fun together, and they had so many plans for their future. They didn't know that there wasn't going to be a future for them. The young couple had only two years together before Roy was killed in a grinding car accident at the intersection of Peachtree and Piedmont Road.

• • •

Now, Janeen wondered, what will murder do to her life and to her campus refuge? Why would someone shoot Andy Dren? Would she ever forget that terrible scene that she found this morning? She squeezed her eyes as if to erase what she had seen. She knew she really couldn't forget what she saw, because she was the first one to observe the murder scene and would have to review her recollections later for the police as well as what she knew about Andy.

Chapter 6

Wes T. Wesley

Jon Lindholm picked up the receiver, "Detective, President Lindholm speaking. What can I do for you?"

Wes Wesley hesitated briefly as he contemplated that Jonathan Lindholm identified himself by his title rather than his name. "Being president must be very important to him. I better remember that," he thought before responding.

"Wes Wesley, Dr. Lindholm, from Atlanta Homicide. We met earlier today in your office." Wes was standing in the cheerless hallway just outside of the medical examiner's cramped cubicle. He had come here to talk to Dr. Glenna Rather about performing the Dren autopsy. Sometimes a lot was to be learned when the victim's life was virtually laid open for speculation. He had witnessed many of these procedures and usually it was simply doing the job. The body was another clue to be read. Only when the person lying on the cold, stainless steel table was one of his friends on the force did this aspect of the routine change his attitude and cut deeply into his own emotions. The detective had never been able to steel himself to a death when it was someone who had been in his life.

"Yes, of course. What a terrible thing to happen to one of our students. Have you learned anything yet? Do you know anything about what he might have been doing on the computer? We should get an update report out for the campus as soon as possible."

Wesley wasn't surprised at Lindholm's premature questions. The public always seemed to think that a real crime was solved in the same twenty minute period that it took to solve one on television. Wes often mused: Maybe we could eliminate all of the grunt work, if we had advertisers. Then we could hire more detectives and purchase state-of-the-art technology. Maybe we could even get caller ID on our phones. It's crazy that we still have to trace calls the old way when the criminals have caller ID and know exactly when we're calling them.

"No, sir, we're still putting together the facts. Actually, I'm calling you from the coroner's office before I start back to Homicide. They'll do the autopsy, so we'll have more information soon. In fact, the main reason I'm calling is because we want to move on this case as fast as possible. So while the docs and the other investigators do their jobs, we want to interview people on campus and talk to the victim's friends and family. I would like to start in the president's office. When may I see you to get your statement and answers to some questions?" Detective Wesley asked in his flat professional voice.

"Well, Detective, I told you all I know. I was home when Janeen Carson called. Of course, I came right over. As you probably know, the president's home is at the edge of campus."

"Yes, I know all of that, but we'll want to get some more information that might give us a clue as to why the student was in your office and who might have known he was there and who would want to kill him and why? Those are the kinds of answers that we need to put together our case background." He wondered how people feel the police can do their job without learning anything from those involved.

"You'll have to talk to Janeen Carson. She keeps my calendar. I just don't have time to do that. You will like dealing with Janeen. She has a real talent for accommodating everyone. If you'll stay on the line, I'll transfer you back. Maybe we can get together tomorrow. Of course, you understand what this murder has already done to schedules and the environment on the campus."

Before Wesley could say that waiting until tomorrow won't cut it, the president had switched him to hold and Janeen was picking up her extension.

"Detective Wesley, Dr. Lindholm said I should set up an appointment for the two of you. When would be a good time for you?"

"This afternoon would be perfect."

"Oh, I had the impression that you were interested in tomorrow."

"Ms. Carson, I surely wouldn't be doing my job or helping the campus very much if I was willing to put off my investigation for another twenty four hours. Do you think your president would consider it police negligence if there is another shooting tonight?" Wes Wesley asked with a decided edge in his voice.

"Detective, you're absolutely right. I must have misunderstood Dr. Lindholm. I am sorry if it appeared that either of us was thoughtless. Let me see what I can juggle to make time for you today," Janeen was already reading the day's appointments as she covered for her boss.

"Smart lady," Wesley thought. He knew she had not mistaken her instructions. "I wonder if she'll be in trouble for changing her boss's directive?"

"Could you come here about one o'clock? I think I can head off one of our faculty members in time to make that change."

"That'll be perfect, Ms. Carson. I appreciate the special effort you've made so we can move forward. It's important that other students not be in harm's way. I'll see you at one. By the way, as long as I'm there, after my appointment with the president, could I meet with you and go over anything else you might remember from this morning? I know this has been a terrible shock, but sometimes during a time of stress details surface later."

"I'll be available whenever you are. You'll find me in the president's suite. See you at one."

Detective Wesley replaced the receiver on the telephone and wondered about Janeen Carson. His short time with her earlier in the day had been relaxed and pleasant even though the topic of their conversation was strictly business. His business, unfortunately, is homicide. It had to have been a terrible time for her, but she had managed to keep her cool and make the ordeal for those around her as easy as possible.

Wesley cleared his head of his thoughts about Janeen Carson, and pressed the numbers on the wall phone's keypad. A rough, masculine voice boomed through the receiver, "Major Dilbert's office."

"Hey, Brassy, it's Wes Wesley."

"Before you say a fuckin' word, Wesley, I want you to know that the major will be at the door at one o'clock to personally welcome you to your annual qualification on the range," the man called Brassy said loud enough that Wes had to hold the receiver six inches away from his ear. Brassy had gotten his name because of his tough knuckles that he frequently tested in a variety of local bars, but Wes thought that the name should also be attached to him because of his very unpleasant voice. He had heard that was the attribute the major liked best about Brassy because it sent the message when you came to the office: you're facing a hard nose.

"Shit, Brassy, give me a damn break. I don't schedule murders in Atlanta on my fuckin' appointment calendar. I want to get this qualification behind me more than you or the major. Just hear my reason."

"Reason. Schmeason. Forget that! You've just come up with another *excuse*. You guys are all the same. You think administration is for the birds. Somehow you have gotten the idea that the Homicide squad is superior to the rest of us. Major Dilbert isn't going to accept another excuse from you."

Wes realized that Brassy was being his most charming. The man didn't have a clue as to how to relate to people beyond hostility. He wondered if this glorified secretary wasn't on the wrong side of his badge.

"Just listen, Brassy. Then pass on my message to Major Dilbert. She might even agree with me this time."

The detective explained about the murder at Tech, Brassy listened without cutting into his explanation. Wes closed his case, and waited for an explosion at the other end of the line.

"Now that's a new one. You usually give me some fairy tale about hoodlums and gang warfare and Atlanta's going to hell because Homicide is undermanned. This is more original. A shooting in our big deal, overrated In-sti-tute of Technology. We don't hear much big time trouble from there. Sounds like a great story, but who knows if the Major will buy it as an excuse to cancel for the third time? Just wait there. I'll be back," Brassy banged the telephone down on something and Wes could hear him charging away from his desk.

The detective waited at the wall phone. He switched his weight from leg to leg, he read numbers and an obscene note written on the wall beside the telephone, he took out his pen and drew a small gallows on the wall and wrote under it: mine

He was ready to repeat the same procedure when he heard rustling on the other end of the line and a voice, "Well, well, well. One of our golden boys has a 'scheduling problem.' Does this have a familiar ring, I ask? Have I heard this little story before?" Major Dagmar Dilbert said sweetly with just a touch of snake venom.

"Major, you know I wouldn't mess up your schedule if I had a choice. I would arrive early and stay late if I could control my own life," Wes tried to meet her sweet tones and eliminate the snake venom, although he might have rather presented her with the whole goddamn snake around her friggin' neck.

"Right, Detective, I understand your dedication to rules, regulations and the administration. I've always thought you'd lay down your badge and your life to help us keep this organization running smoothly. It's just that you simply have no time, right?" Dilbert's voice was still rather quiet, but Wes knew what was coming. He had surely been on its receiving end more times than he wished to remember. It was just about time for the major to sound like her flunky, Brassy.

"How do you jokers think I can keep us in compliance if all you do is postpone your annual qualifications? The chief is going to hear it again from me that Homicide *never* cooperates. You throw out the shit and expect us to pick up the pieces and cover up the missed dates. Enough is enough. You're scheduled for today. You should be here today," Major Dilbert was screaming and Wes was again holding the receiver half way down the hallway.

"Major, I would never do anything to make you look bad. You know I respect your position and would tell the chief that you do a tremendous job under the most difficult circumstances." Wes could hardly believe that he had sunk so low, but he had to postpone his time on the range this afternoon.

Major Dilbert had no desire to give in to Wes, but she didn't want to create a problem for her department. They were squeaky clean, which meant that she didn't get a hard time from above. That's the way she ran her shop.

"I'm a reasonable and humane person. I also understand that you could run into some political pressure on this case. I don't want to be attached to you not getting the perp. Here's the deal. You're off the schedule today, but your reprieve is only to the end of this week. You'll be on the range by the end of the day Friday or you're out of commission beginning Saturday." There was a moment of silence, "Wesley, I expect to hear nothing from the other end of this telephone except: Thank you, Major."

Wes swallowed, took a deep breath and said, "Thank you, Major."

"You're welcome, Detective. I look forward to seeing you in the next few days. By the way, I'd like to hear when the chief starts getting a hard time from those fat cat alumni, because I want to tell him what a team player I am by giving you this extra time."

"Yes, Major. I'll be in touch." Wes hung up the receiver, drew a small stick figure on the gallows and circled the word 'mine' before turning away from the wall.

Wes slowly returned to the autopsy room and smelled the acrid odors of death and chemicals before he heard the doctor talking into the recorder as she proceeded with her examination. Behind Dr. Rather's monologue, harsh echoes - cracking off hard, cold surfaces - clamored in his ears. How could it seem so noisy when only one voice was quietly reciting an autopsy litany? The actual surgical process didn't upset him, but he did feel sadness when the victim was young, healthy and promising. What had been Andrew Dren's mistake that he was lying here on this hard, clammy, sterile table with rows of sharp scalpels lying on a white towel on another table pulled close for the convenience of the doctor? Why had his right to life ended as a number in Atlanta's morgue? What can be learned in this frigid room about Andrew Dren that will explain his short life?

• • •

Glenna Rather began talking to Wes as soon as he entered the room, "Well, I don't think we're going to find a lot that doesn't fit your first opinion. He was killed by one shot in the head that entered about an inch in front of the left ear, traveled at a slight upward angle and exited the right side of the head about a half-inch behind and above his ear. No other obviously, noticeable marks on the body that would indicate that he may have struggled with another person. Of course, Wes, I may find more when I get into the details, but my gut reaction is that what you see is what you got."

"I'm planning to stay and watch for awhile, but you'll let me know the complete, official report as soon as possible after you're finished?"

Rather was not sure whether she was being asked a question or if Wesley had made a statement. Considering either case, she responded, "Right."

"This case is going to be high profile, and I expect the department will begin getting heat soon. With all the political pull that Georgia Tech alumni have, it won't be long until we have to justify every move. One of the alumni was a mayor of Atlanta back during the civil rights days so you can be sure that he'll be asked to get our asses moving," Wes explained to the medical examiner to which she responded, "Ummm."

The only sound in the room was Glenna's voice being recorded as she went through her routine. Wes knew there were sounds to her surgical procedures, but he'd long ago learned to tune them out. He related less to the visual image of a dead body than he did to the audio sensations. Sometimes when it was very quiet, he felt he could hear the sound of a scalpel opening a cadaver's chest from throat to navel. That was the time he'd reach over and switch on a radio or turn on the television. He was good at his work and knew that he had chosen the best career for himself, but there were negatives that would always remind him of the mortality of man in general and himself, in particular.

Wes checked his watch and saw that he should leave. As Dr. Rather predicted, nothing surprising surfaced. Tests may prove otherwise but his gut reaction said they wouldn't. "I'm going to head back to the office. I need to talk to Billy Joe and get back to the campus. Thanks, Glenna, for getting to this right away. The Chief is probably already getting calls to 'find the shooter.'"

• • •

Detective Billy Joe LaCrosse was not in his office when Wesley arrived. He knew he would turn up soon so Wes picked up his coffee cup, walked back to their dingy break room that for some unknown reason had fancy, silver, foil wallpaper on one wall that definitely did not become a decorator feature. It made the old Coke and snack machines look like worn-out prostitutes in the downstairs lounge of a second-rate whorehouse. He filled his cup and returned to his cramped quarters and tried to reach "Irish" Finn at the crime lab to ask whether he would be there later when Wes would bring out some of the evidence picked up at the crime scene. Irish's findings, along with Glenna Rather's, will give them the basic information needed to begin to create the track that will lead to the killer.

Wesley leaned back in his chair, clasped his hands behind his head, balanced on two chair legs for several minutes before hiking his long legs up on his desk. He often did things like that just to get a little exercise when he was stuck in the office. He kept a "cuff" weight in his desk drawer and sometimes did his 'desk workout' while talking on the telephone. At 42, he was still crazy about athletics and kept in shape by playing police league softball and basketball or working out at Haney's gym. He spent hours coaching the Little League baseball team that his son, Jason, had once played on. When he bothered to weigh himself, he was pleased that he was within 10 pounds of his college weight. His hair was still thick with just a touch of gray at the temples. Not bad for an old guy, he would brag to himself.

• • •

"Hey, Wes, have you got appointments with some of the folks in the president's office?" Detective LaCrosse asked as he came into the office. "We need to spend some time out on that campus and see what we can learn. I have a fuckin' funny feeling that there is somethin' here that ranks in the 'would you believe' category."

"I think I better sit up and pay attention. When LaCrosse gets a 'fuckin' funny feeling,' it usually means we have some work cut out for us. Now what has gotten your antenna up and circling?"

Billy Joe LaCrosse pulled up a straight, wooden chair and added his feet to the old, scarred desktop. Several decades of use and abuse had mellowed all the furniture into fodder for Goodwill Industries rejects. "I'm not sure yet, but this guy Black is just too intense for me. He's askin' questions like he needs to have detailed answers but doesn't have a clue how they might fit. Like maybe there's a hell of a hidden agenda that he wants to be sure we never find. Makes me feel that we need to find out what's happenin' at Georgia Tech besides a student's murder."

LaCrosse's attitude about keeping in shape was quite the opposite of Wesley's. When he put his feet up on the desk, it was simply to relax. He was a bigger man than his partner and had gained about 20 pounds in the 16 years he had been on the police force. He used to joke about a pound a year is a cost to being a policeman and enjoying the good life, but the past two years he had managed to increase weight at a faster pace. His bulky body fit well his large head which looked bigger since he still wore a full Afro. He liked lots of hair so the only reason he trimmed it at all was to comply with regulations.

Wes Wesley always took seriously Billy Joe's hunches."Tell me more. I want to know your observations before I see Lindholm this afternoon. I have a similar reaction to him as your feeling about Black. He has already suggested that I can wait until he's ready to talk to me but thanks to his secretary, I'll be seeing him today."

"I was with Tech's police chief, George Fancer, and we were

decidin' what he and his guys would do to help us," LaCrosse began to explain and then had another thought, "By the way, Wes, we don't want to ignore Tech's security guys. They can help us with a lot of the investigation. It'll be like havin' a whole new team that still has new energy and freshness. I don't think they're burned out with murder and mayhem like our guys. They probably spend most of their time savin' coeds from alcohol and testosterone attacks. Must be a tough way to make a livin'."

Wesley nodded his head in agreement and waited for Billy Joe to get back on track.

"So there we were exchangin' our thoughts on what would work best for the two police organizations and this pretty boy Black barges in and says that he's the contact for Georgia Tech, and he wanted to find out what I knew. I told him I'd be with him in a minute and turned back to Fancer. Black interrupted again and said he didn't have time to just wait around and turned to Fancer and said, 'Of course, you understand, George.'

"Fancer gave me a what-a pain-in-the-ass look and said he could get on with some information gatherin' and he'd see me later. It took him about two seconds to get the hell out of the room. I'd say that those two have tangled before. Maybe I'll make a point to find out what that might have been. Could be interestin'.

"So, I turned back to Black who had put on his best TV smile showing off every one of his ultra white teeth. They look almost as contrived as his cat-like-very-green eyes. Could they be colored contacts? Damn, Wes, in this day of appearance enhancement and virtual reality, how the hell are we ever gonna figure out who is the real person or what is the real scene? And in this case, it doesn't help to be on the campus of one of the best known high tech institutions in the country that is famous for creatin' its own reality. Maybe that's why they all seem to have an attitude. If they don't like the truth, they produce their own and then pass it off as the real thing.

"Did you ever see any of the damn computer stuff they did durin' the Olympics? It was way out. They'd take you through buildings that weren't even built yet and you felt you'd really been there. They made a diver go off the board, but when I saw it, I felt like it was me in the air and I was gettin' dizzy. I saw it once, and I was grabbin' for something to hold on to. It was weird."

Wes smiled and then started to laugh, "Billy Joe, are you telling me you think that some computer nerds on campus have created this murder? Surely you jest. I guaran-damn-tee you that we've a real body, and we better find a real murderer. No virtual shit. Now, how about getting back to your Charles Black encounter. You just can't tell anything without digressing all over hell's half acre."

"Hey, man, that's why everyone finds me so damn interestin'. I'm very colorful."

"Oh, yes, you're colorful, starting with that new purple Taurus you just bought." Wesley told him, "But let's face it. Your colorful digressions take you twice as long as anyone else to tell a story. So, LaCrosse, back to your observations on Black."

"Well, for one thing, the guy is a nervous wreck. He was lookin' cool, but he had trouble keepin' himself still. While we were talkin', he just moved around a lot and ran his hands through his hair all the time. Shit, its obvious that he drops a bundle on keepin' that blow dry look, but he sure messed it up today.

"He made it plain that he was the one that, get this, I was to report to. As if I was a member of his own damn staff. *He* wants to know everythin' we learn, and *he* would judge whether it had relevance to the damn case. I just have the feelin', Wes, that he's lookin' to hide somethin' and is afraid that we're gonna find it. He seemed to be waitin' for some revelation but he wasn't gettin' it from me at that time. Of course, I still didn't know anythin' anyway! But, then he asked if we'd taken anythin' that had been printed from the computer. That seemed to be what he was most interested in. He shit a brick when he learned that the president's computer was temporarily in custody of the Atlanta Police Department."

"Damn," broke in Detective Wesley, "I think maybe we have hit on something. Both Lindholm and Black have a bigger interest in why Dren was in the office than the fact that he was shot."

As if they had received a reminder call, both looked at their watches, "Let's go for lunch about 11:30 before we meet with Lindholm and Fancer. I don't want to be late for my friggin' appointment with Lindholm the Third." He had a feeling that the rest of the day was going to be spent listening to answers to his questions, and hopefully catching some comments that related to more than Oliver Andrew Dren's killing.

"OK with me. I've got some things to do now so I'll meet you outside," LaCrosse said as he left the office where he had been assigned when he was moved to Homicide and where he had become a victim of a fast moving criminal.

Everyone who was stationed in the Homicide Building thought it was a joke. Well, a joke if you didn't see it for what it really was: a close call. The space was an old office building that never had any renovations done to it from the day it became their quarters five years ago. The only time the office that Wes and Billy Joe shared with another detective was painted was when a perpetrator grabbed one of the detectives' guns and made a wild shot, hitting Billy Joe in the shoulder. Two walls were splattered with blood and fragments of his new Nike jacket. He started yelling about ruining his jacket before he paid any attention to his wounded arm.

The next day they requested fresh paint for the office, and the other members of the Homicide team began threatening to shoot their partners to get their offices painted.

The individual rooms were all crowded with desks, files and officers. The only chance for privacy was where they conducted interviews. That room was equally ugly with an unsteady table, battered from rough wear and cigarette burns; broken Venetian blinds hanging by one cord; folding metal chairs, with chipping paint and torn plastic seats; a bulletin board covered by rag-tag announcements; and walls of an unidentified color that obviously were not protected from damage caused by water and humidity. It was definitely the type of surroundings that encouraged criminals to speak up fast, because they felt even jail had to be better than this place.

As Billy Joe left the office, he called out an off-color remark to one of the detectives who had almost knocked him off his feet as they passed each other. The cop was paying more attention to the new secretary who was dressed in a tight, red skirt than to where he was headed. Wes sipped his cold coffee, looked at Janeen Carson's business card and thought about her offer: I'll be available whenever you are. He hoped she was serious. He'd wait and see if she sent another message that he liked.

Chapter 7

Oliver Andrew Dren, Jr.

Peter Kirk and Andy's other roommate, Frank Bostwick, were gathered in the living area of their campus apartment. The residence hall had been built just before the 1996 Olympics to be used as housing for athletes while Tech was the Olympic Village. Although new construction, already the rooms were beginning to show signs of wear. Moving athletes and students in and out of the housing frequently had put scuffs on the floors, scratches in the paint and chunks out of the doors, but the two roommates did not notice these things under normal times; and they certainly weren't noticing them today.

The two roommates had been on a roller coaster of emotions ever since learning of Andy's murder. Both were inexperienced with any deaths, neither ever imagined they would have roles in a real-life murder. They were surprised that they had cried and laughed earlier. To them, it felt what they had heard called hysterics. They had not been able to predict or master their actions. Why were they laughing with tears dropping onto their shirts? Why did they feel exhausted when they had done nothing physical? They didn't know the answers but they were both glad that they had finally reached a plateau that they were rational and calm.

"Maybe if we had paid more attention to Andy and his interests, like, you know, he would be alive. Or maybe we would have an idea who killed him," Peter Kirk said, remembering when he had first seen Andy Dren in the doorway to their apartment. Peter had extended his big, dark brown hand that could have covered both of Andy's. The two men didn't have to be concerned if they were going to get along, because within minutes they were talking about basketball. It always happened that way when people would mention Peter's height, 6 feet 6 inches.

Because he was already more than a head taller than anyone in his class, Peter had played basketball with a teen team at his neighborhood rec center from the time he was only 10 years old. For all his years from 10 to 21, it had been a serious pursuit. Now that he was in graduate school, he used it as R and R. It worked for him and it didn't cost a cent.

Frank Bostwick responded to Peter "There's no point in playing the 'what if' game. Andy was quiet about what he did and didn't share much of his life with us. I don't see how prying into his life would've been helpful."

"I didn't mean that I wanted to, you know, pry, Frank. I meant that we don't know enough to help the police find his, you know, murderer or that we have much to tell his family. You'd think living here together we should know something. I expect we will be, you know, investigated by someone. Like, you know, the campus or Atlanta police."

"Unless you know more than I do, we aren't going to be much help in this case, but I think we should do something in Andy's memory that he might like if he were still here." Frank considered himself to be the closest to Andy, but still he didn't know a lot about his life. They had more in common, because both had been working for several years before returning to college. Frank had the same youthful appearance that Andy had had, and often he was mistaken for an undergraduate. That didn't bother him until he was with a date who was a few years older than he, and a waiter made a big deal about carding him. Then he wished for gray hair or a few wrinkles.

Frank did know that the Drens lived in Dalton, a small manufacturing town in Northwest Georgia, and that Andy had a father, Oliver Andrew Dren, Sr., and a younger sister, Susan. He had met them when they had helped Andy move from his off-campus apartment to this one. His family seemed a lot like him. They were quiet and serious even as they helped him get all his boxes and bags from their two cars. They also had come to campus on Andy's birthday to take him to dinner at Pitty Pat's Porch, a popular tourist attraction near Georgia Tech. At the last minute, Mr. Dren had invited Frank to join them.

• • •

Frank felt that the Drens were nice people who were pleased that Andy had decided to go back to college and get his masters degree. His father, Oliver, Sr., mentioned several times, "You boys will be able to go anywhere and get the job of your choice with a degree from Tech. You know half of the successful men in Dalton went to Tech," he hesitated before adding with a chuckle, "The other half went to the University of Georgia!"

Frank and Peter often scoffed at the thought that successful men could come from UGA, which was the big, rival institution in the state. They believed that there was no comparison in the two campuses. Frank, his brown eyes sparkling with determination, responded strongly, "No one with any sense at all would go to Georgia."

All three of the Drens laughed and Andy confessed that his dad had gone there and graduated with honors.

"Oh, damn, I guess I should keep my mouth shut. Mr. Dren, I apologize. But, I suppose it's no surprise to you that Tech students think they are better than Georgia students."

"Don't worry, Frank. This argument has been going on since before both of us were born. I love UGA, but I appreciate that you guys are getting your education on North Avenue. We're glad that Andy is here where he can really get into his beloved computers. He's getting his degree and also having an opportunity to make some money helping the president."

"Hey, Andy, what *are* you doing for the president? Wish I could find a cushy job to help me finance my weekend activities," Frank said turning to his roommate.

"I'm just doing some programming and inputting for the administration. Dad always says it's for the president, but a lot of it is for the Georgia Tech Foundation and public relations. It's interesting and if it has to do with the computer, I think it's next to heaven."

Andrew Dren's eyes always seemed to take on a new sparkle when he talked about his passion for computers. His eyes, usually a medium shade of blue, would actually become the color of the spring sky. Then they were special and quite noticeable, but normally it was Andy's wide smile and deep dimples that got a person's attention. His face had a cherubic appearance, which he hated. He always felt that his round, childlike image was a disadvantage when talking about serious and important topics. One time he tried growing a mustache to look older, but even his mustache looked like something that a teenager would have: light and straggly.

• • •

The birthday dinner at Pitty Pat's Porch was a relief from campus cafeteria meals. You can be sure that the roast beef with horseradish sauce, Caesar salad, buttery rolls and chocolate mousse cake would never appear on the menu at Tech. The conversation was almost as different from everyday campus talk as the food. They talked about their own pursuits, politics, future plans and who Susan was dating. The Drens were at ease with one another, and they easily included Frank in their conversations.

When Frank thought about the pleasant time they had together just two months ago, he couldn't believe that Andy was gone. Why would anyone want to kill him? And, would that person kill someone else? Who? Why? What is going on? Whatever it was, he still wanted to do something in memory of their roommate and friend.

"Frank, when you say do something for Andy, do you mean like give money for a scholarship or put something on the campus like, you know, plant a tree?" Peter asked, having no idea what his roommate had in mind. Because he had dark, highly-arched eyebrows, he was always kidded about having a permanent look of puzzlement on his face, which fit his feelings now.

"Oh, those could be options, but I meant trying to remember what Andy had talked about that he would enjoy doing it if he were here," Frank answered, "A happening that is just for Andy. You know, like invent another G. Pitts Berdel."

Peter laughed at Frank's mention of the 65-year-old fictitious student who was 'conceived' by the class of '32 and has been enrolled at Tech every year since then. Fifty years later, a student claimed to have a photograph of old G. Pitts. When asked to produce it so it could be printed in a campus publication, he gave them the negative that was of a man rushing into the campus library whose face was a blur, because he'd been moving too fast for the film. After it appeared under the headline: G. Pitts Berdel Still Trying to Get Out of Tech, for weeks students and staff had a great time calling in Berdel sightings.

"Yep, that's the idea. But I wanted to do something original that would be remembered through the years just like Berdel," Frank said beginning to get excited about creating a memorial event for Andy Dren.

"Of course, this murder will be added to Tech's history, so we should make sure that in the future people don't forget who was the victim. Andy deserves to be, you know, remembered," remarked Peter Kirk realizing that he too was getting interested in this crazy idea of Frank's. "What're we gonna to do that won't get us expelled? Like, you know, the way they stole the T from the Tech Tower years ago." Students and alumni loved to talk about campus traditions that had become challenges of how not to get caught.

"What we do has to be specially invented for Andy. He was mostly serious and very pro Georgia Tech. Think of all the time he put in doing that computer work for the president. But he did hate the way the whole institution was being commercialized. He felt Tech was good enough to stand on its own. Why sell out to sponsors? Maybe he...." Frank began but was interrupted by Peter.

"Like, you know, he hated that electronic sign that some alumnus put up on campus to sell advertising. Sure, Tech puts coming events and big sports news on the board but, Andy said, it was 55 minutes of advertising to 5 minutes for Tech every hour. I think he actually timed it one day. Why the information wasn't even interesting enough to cause a traffic pile up. Maybe we could steal the sign like other students stole the T."

"Hey, Peter, I think you've hit on a good idea. I don't think we can steal it. After all, it's about as big as this apartment but we might think of something else to do with the sign. Shit, the best thing would be to blow it up, but I'm sure that would send us to jail."

"Well, we sure as hell can't move it. We'll never get them to take it away, not even in Andy's memory. Maybe we could cover it up with something. How about a disguise? Let's get the industrial design students to make it look like a big Varsity hot dog that somehow escaped across the highway."

Frank was referring to the famous, local, fast food drive-in that had been established by a Tech dropout over 40 years before. It was a joke around Atlanta that the founder did not make it at Tech, but he was smart enough to create a business that made him both a multimillionaire and known by millions of people. Some alumni had the Varsity cater their parties and said the big V chili-dog might be the best-traveled sandwich in the world!

"Hey, the other advertisers who pay to be on the sign would shit if the Varsity upstaged them. If they all got pissed, maybe they would like, you know, withdraw their support and then the sign would go away," Peter added.

"I like this idea, but I have something to add. Maybe we could block out the regular messages and put our own on the electronic board. Unfortunately, the person who could probably figure out how to do that was Andy since the messages are some-how linked into a computer. Who could help us do that?"

"If we're going to get a chilidog on there, we should ask the Varsity to help us," Peter threw in, half as a joke, "That's what the stupid sign is all about: getting money!"

"Yeah, right. We should do the same damn thing that we think Tech shouldn't do? No way."

"I think we've got our challenge. We should find a way to get a message up there, because it's the kind of project that Andy would like. It all fits together. Now all we've got to do is figure out how to do it and what we want to say. Let's see what we can find out about the sign without raising suspicion and then talk about it later."

"O K, but right now, I can only think about lunch. Don't you think we should satisfy my Grease Attack and go up to the

Varsity?" Frank suggested as he started toward the door already deciding whether he should have fried onion rings with three chilidogs.

"But it's not even 11:30!"

"Hey, we need to get to the Varsity and back to campus in time, so we can have lunch. I'm not going to miss a meal; even a bad meal!" Frank explained as he locked the door to the apartment that, until last night, had been Andy Dren's home.

Chapter 8

Tiffany JoAnne Walton

As the two roommates were heading to The Varsity to eat, a beautiful, young woman was talking on the telephone to Jonathan Lindholm. Her vivacious face had a shadow of deep concern that darkened her usually luminous features. She listened intently before responding to the president of her institution.

"Jon, I just can't believe that a murder has happened right in your office. Already my daddy has called and insisted I come home until the killer is found. I told him I would call him back just as soon as I knew more. I called you right away. Who do you think did this? Who did Andy Dren have as an enemy? Why in your office?" Tiffany blurted.

Lindholm was very upset with Tiffany for calling him at his office. She knew that he had made that one of the rules of their relationship. Good god, he didn't want anyone asking questions about Tiffany, a freshman coed. He was playing it carefully and that was part of his plan for keeping control. He admitted that this was an unusual situation and if anyone asked him about her call, he felt that excuse would work. After all, lots of parents are going to be pressuring their sons and daughters to come home at this time.

To cool down his anger with this girl, he decided to ask a simple question before trying to make her realize how risky her contact was, "How did your father know what happened?"

"Oh, it's all over Charlotte. Daddy said that the alumni director was talking to one of the alumni and told him that the campus was alive with rumors. That's true from what I have heard. Everyone has a theory. Everyone is trying to figure out why a student was in your office in the middle of the night. It's good it wasn't a female, Jonathan Lindholm, or you'd really be in trouble."

"You're using poor judgment today. First, you shouldn't have called here and second, this is not a time to make light of a tremendously serious situation. You wouldn't want someone to speculate why you called and perhaps get back to your father," the president's statement sounded like a threat to Tiffany.

"Well, well, you obviously have privileges that I'm not supposed to have," she retorted sulkily, "I believe that you call me whenever you're ready, and I'm left to think up some lie if someone happens to be at my condo. I assume you're as good at lying as I am, Jonathan."

• • •

Talking to Jon reminded Tiffany why she never had an interest in living on campus. When she was accepted at Tech, she knew she didn't want to live on campus or in any off-campus student-type neighborhood. She wanted a place where she would have her privacy and not have to spend all of her time with immature college students. She convinced her father that she could study better if she was not around students 24 hours a day. She explained that most students partied constantly or had loud music blaring. Her father agreed with her observation and decided that he would buy a condo for her if she would find a safe location.

Tiffany preferred privacy to safety and chose one of the new loft apartments in the area of the city called Five Points. It was right in the heart of the business district where residents were gone most of the time and when they were at home, they didn't pay attention to their neighbors. They were city dwellers and their lives were built around their professions and a few people who shared mutual vocations.

Tiffany admired her space as she reflected on the messages being sent to her by Jon. The condominium was spectacular with ceilings ranging from eight to sixteen feet high. The living area took up what was once two floors. Two sets of windows overlooked the triangular-shaped park that was named in honor of one the Woodruffs, a Coca Cola magnate. The park looked fantastic from her fifth floor balcony. Of course Tiffany didn't have to dwell on the homeless who spent most of their days on the park benches hoping for a little humanity and a handout. The fountain, tucked in one corner of the open area, could be heard on a very still night. Often Tiffany would close her eyes and pretend she was back in her beloved North Carolina mountains.

Mr. and Mrs. Walton had given Tiffany as a birthday gift the furnishings to complete the condo. "Comfortable Elegance" is what she called the style of furniture she had delivered to the freshly painted rooms. Her intention was to create an atmosphere in which her favorite companions would feel at ease and decide to stay awhile. To create the perfect background for her own pastel coloring, she had chosen soft peach and teal as a color scheme.

Tiffany had always liked her dramatic appearance and had used it often to her advantage. She highlighted her long, gentle blonde hair, usually worn loose and shining from a daily shampoo. Her aquamarine blue eyes appeared innocent yet encouraged others to take another look and enter her private sphere. Although her individual pallet was a misty pastel, her body was lush and brazen. She knew that the combination had made her the center of attention for years. When she chose her clothes, always as carefully as she had decorated her condominium, she heightened the message, "I'm a person you want in your life."

This is the young woman who caught the eye of President Jonathan Agnew Lindholm III on Tiffany's first day at Georgia Tech. As was the custom, Freshmen Convocation was held where the president and other Tech leaders delivered messages of welcome and hope while they asked for commitment to the Honor Code. It was a time of shyness and indecision for most of the new students, but not for Tiffany Walton. She could not remember when she might have been shy or indecisive. Her parents had taught their four children self-confidence and presented them with the skills to feel able to cope with many social situations. Her brothers assimilated this broad-based education, but Tiffany took it and put her own personal spin on it. She had decided she was going to make sure that others followed her suggestions and as the trail of admirers lengthened, her confidence grew. She wasn't the least bit intimidated when the president of this institution began to come on to her.

As was her style, Tiffany sat in the first row of the Roberts Theatre, named in memory of a beloved alumnus. She knew that she would be noticed more if she didn't join the huge, tight group that was jockeying for a place in the last few rows. She knew that she could walk straight down the aisle and find lots of empty seats, which she did. She was already in place when the speakers walked out on the stage and took their places ready to impress these new, young students.

Almost immediately, Tiffany was drawn to look directly at a man who sat in the middle of the group of five. He was a bit on the old side for her taste, but he surely was a handsome and impressive looking man. She looked him straight in the eyes and then picked up her program to see who he might be. Her eyes moved away from his, but she knew that his eyes remained on her. They would probably be riveted in the same direction when she looked back again.

Tiffany scanned the program. She couldn't guess by the speakers' names who he could be. A dean, a vice president, president of the student body (nope, not him!), an alumnus or the president of Georgia Tech. She then flipped to another page and found "A Message from the President" with a photograph of the man who was staring at her.

"E-gad," she thought, "The president of Georgia Tech is trying to get my attention. Is this going to be a great four years or what?"

She looked directly back at Jonathan Lindholm and just for fun winked and added a small smile. To her amazement, he nodded his head slightly before turning away to respond to a motion to start the meeting.

Lindholm rose from his chair, walked to the podium, scanned the audience with his serious eyes and looked at Tiffany one more time before he opened his presentation.

"The biggest and newest class of Georgia Tech, I salute

you. Today is the beginning of your challenge to prepare to be corporate, political and community leaders. You are our future, and that is why you have been chosen for the Georgia Institute of Technology. This is a special institution and each of you will add to its honor and its mystique.

"All of you have been recognized in your home towns and in your high schools. Many of you already have been active volunteers and successful participants in community service. A few of you have started and run your own businesses. I don't have to know each person's name to tell you that you are all above the average and will use your outstanding heritage as your foundation for an education that also is far above average. You've decided that you can face challenges and are ready for hard work and notable accomplishments. I'm proud of you as freshman and I'll be prouder of you when I hand you your diploma in four years.

"Yes, you begin your college experience by building on your individual history. We offer you a great institution and an excellent hundred-year academic record to help you fulfill your dreams........."

The words went on but Tiffany had tuned them out. Her imagination had taken over and she was pondering who was the real man behind the title president and the words that were so politically correct. All of her plans and dreams to come to Tech, where the male/female ratio was in her favor, had never included a scenario with the president. "I think my sights were too low," she thought, "I believe I'll broadened my possibilities."

Tiffany Walton left the Roberts Theatre with a scramble of thoughts in her head. She must be discreet and let time help to develop whatever had started during the Convocation. She would be here for four years. No rush when the prize could be tremendous. Being hasty could ruin the potential for making it to the winner's circle.

As she reached the plaza that was the entrance to the theatre, a group of other freshmen were gathering off to the side. One young man looked at her and called, "Want to join us at a party? We're going to go together."

"Sure. That's what being in college is all about, isn't it?"

"Damn right! By the way, my name is Lonnie. I'm from Waycross, Georgia."

"And, I'm Tiffany from Charlotte, North Carolina. Let's go party. In fact, let's go to lots of parties. I bet they're all over campus."

• • •

Jonathan Lindholm was not about to get into an argument with Tiffany on the telephone, in his office, on a day when there were police and other people paying close attention to everything that's happening.

"Let's talk about all of this later. I'll call you. This place is crawling with police and half of the campus wanting to know what's going on. You must understand the environment here. It's a zoo," Jon explained as quickly as he could and being careful not to use Tiffany's name.

"OK, I'll wait for you to call, but I don't like being pushed aside. You know where to find me or where to leave a message."

President Lindholm sat a moment, with the dial tone ringing in his ear, thinking about the good situation he had with this beautiful, young woman. She was inventive and enthusiastic in bed, she was willing to keep their relationship to herself, she had the perfect place for him to get in and out of unseen, she made no demands about going out to be entertained, and she said she loved him. He had learned that he had to be cautious that she did not feel like she took second place in his life. He had her convinced (and even sympathized with him) that his wife's health forced him to stay married. He didn't think Tiffany really wanted to get married, but she would like to have him free to do anything they wanted. What a ridiculous thought. As if, even if he were single, he would take her places as his date. The alumni, especially those who have such influence by being on the foundation board, would run him out of town. It was almost a joke to think of Tiffany Walton sitting next to him at some campus event.

But, that was not the issue today. He had gotten her to hang up and wait for him to call. She understood that he wasn't going to continue the conversation. Of course, he knew she also had chosen not to continue the telephone call. Whatever, she was out of the way for now.

When Tiffany replaced the receiver, she was already fuming at Jon's attitude. He wasn't the only one to be considered because of the shooting. She had to argue with her parents just to keep them in Charlotte. They wanted to come to Atlanta immediately, pack her up and escort her home. The best part of being in college is the freedom she had. She could see whomever she wanted and when she wanted and nobody even noticed. Her parents would want to commit their own murder if they knew that she was sleeping with the president of Tech. Another head would roll, not only the head of Jonathan Agnew Lindholm III. They would blame Jon, but they would be furious with her, too.

Well, she not only wasn't going home, she wasn't going to sit in her condo and wait for the exalted president to call. She picked up the receiver again, dialed a number by memory and waited for it to be answered.

Chapter 9

Lonnie Tedesco

"Hey, Lonnie, it's Tiffany. What're you doing? I was sitting here thinking about you and decided I would call. I'm so glad you're there."

"I'm glad you called too. In fact, I was wondering whether you were around or if maybe you had gone home like a bunch of the guys from my building did. You know, b-b-because of the, ah, because of the m-m-murder." Lonnie Tedesco had a tendency to stutter when he was excited. "It's been a scary d-d-day. Everyone has so many ideas of who could do this and if there will be another sh-sh-shooting."

"Relax, Lonnie. I don't think it's anything to worry about. After all, there's no relationship between Andy Dren and us. Whatever the reason for this murder, it had to be something that related to his own life. I didn't even know who he was, did you?" Tiffany asked in her soothing voice that she used when her friend, Lonnie, would get excited. It was almost comical when she was kissing him that his next words would be stuttered. She would hold him tighter and tell him that she was flattered that her kisses got him so excited.

"No, I d-d-didn't know him. When would a freshman get to meet a graduate student? He would probably think we're just kids. I heard that he already had a job and was at least 30 years old. His life was half over! I'm glad we aren't that old, Tiffany. Hey, why don't we get together? I don't have anything to do. One of my professors cancelled class because of what happened," Lonnie held his breath and hoped that Tiffany would say yes. He would like to go down to her condo and make love. She could make him relax and forget everything when they were in bed.

"Oh, Lonnie, I was thinking the same thoughts you were:

you know, like, let's just be alone. Wouldn't that be perfect?" Tiffany was putting on her most seductive act. She knew Lonnie would literally run from the campus to her building and up five flights of stairs to get into her bed.

It was lucky for Lonnie that he was - as her friends said - drop dead handsome. That was important to Tiffany. His dark hair and almost black eyes were an ideal contrast for Tiffany's pastel beauty. When they lay close as two sheets on the bed, they liked to look in the mirror that dominated her one bedroom wall to see the different shades of their bodies. They also talked about the contrast in their size. Tiffany was just a fraction of an inch over 5'4" and wore a size four dress. Lonnie was a foot taller than she and weighed 230 pounds. It was no wonder that he had been playing football since he was in middle school and hoped to go on to the pros when he got out of Tech. His family said that college was just a track to big time sports. They didn't believe college was necessary to be wealthy. None of them had a degree but his father and uncles all made lots of money

Lonnie was so attractive and so visible as a football player that he had many coeds chasing him on campus. He could have his choice of young women, but Tiffany had gotten his attention during the Freshman Convocation and captured his heart and his reason, even before he had unpacked all of his boxes and suitcases. She knew how to take advantage of his overactive testosterone. His Latin forefathers would be proud of his sexual performance. He had a reputation back home in Waycross for being a talented stud, but since Tiffany, he would return to South Georgia with a lot more tricks than when he left.

"Great, Tiffany, I'll be down right away. We c-c-can spend at least a couple of hours together."

"Hurry, Lonnie. We don't want to waste this found time. At least something good has come out of this awful day."

Tiffany decided to take time to call her father so he wouldn't do something stupid like turn up on her doorstep. She wanted him to stay in Charlotte and forget about trying to make her come home for awhile.

"Hey, Daddy. It's Tiffany. Everything's quiet here. I hope

you and Mommy aren't worrying about me."

"Of course we're worrying about you, honeychile. That's a terrible thing that has happened, and we don't want you in jeopardy," Howard Tiff Walton said hurriedly before Tiffany could break in. He knew his daughter's habit of trying to keep control of a conversation simply by doing all of the talking. "Your mother and I thought we would come down and look at the situation ourselves. I'm sure other parents have the same concerns that we do. What do you hear from other students?"

"Nobody's upset, Daddy. The student who was killed was practically unrelated to campus life. He was 30 years old, had been working for years and had come back for a graduate degree. Honestly, Daddy, graduate students have nothing to do with us. I talked to Lonnie, and he's going to come over so I can get some more information that he might have heard, but he didn't know the guy either. He said the guys in his building are hardly talking about the shooting and there are police all over the place." Tiffany never had trouble bending the truth when talking to her parents. Of course, she and Lonnie would certainly talk about the shooting, but it wasn't why he was coming to the condo. No way!

"Well, Lonnie is big enough to protect you, but I don't think having him around all the time is exactly what your mother and I had in mind. We really think you should come home until the police find this killer," her father pleaded gently so that he would not make her antagonistic. Tiffany was used to getting her own way having grown up in a family as the baby with five people willing to wait on her. Her brothers, from five to twelve years older than she, often acted the same as her doting parents.

"Daddy, I'll call you later just as soon as I know more. Oh, I hear someone at the door. Gotta run. Love ya, Sweet-dads," Tiffany made up a reason to end quickly and hung up. She really didn't have a good argument for her dad except that she didn't want to leave Atlanta now. It was exciting, and she'll get all kinds of inside news directly from Jon. She was sure that there was no danger to her. Besides, Lonnie was available when the president was too busy answering the questions of the detectives. She would not lack protection.

• • •

Lonnie Tedesco had proven to be the perfect boyfriend for Tiffany. He provided a handsome date whenever there were events on the campus. He also was so crazy about her that he didn't ask questions about what she did when they were not together. In fact, she often thought he made a point to not ask what she had done or whom she was with. Was he just sweet or did he prefer not knowing? Of course Lonnie was busy enough with his sports that he really didn't have a lot of time to be concerned how she spent her time. She was careful to learn his schedule so she would know when he'd be preoccupied.

As important as she was to his life, she knew that football was a close second. It had made him a celebrity in his hometown, and after making many touchdowns when he first came to Tech, he'd immediately become a hero to students and alumni alike. If their relationship lasted beyond college, she thought life would be even better as the girlfriend of a pro football player.

Tiffany went to her bedroom to be sure that it was ready for her visit from Lonnie. She stopped at her oversized mirror. Using the standards of today's Miss America, she was almost perfect, and on a campus where the ratio of men to women was about four to one, she was outstanding. Sometimes it was hard to believe that she also had an IQ of over 150. It was her talent in math that got her interested in and accepted at Tech. Her father had a dream from her first grade report card that included a comment: Natural ability in math. He wanted his daughter to get an engineering degree from Georgia Tech.

Howard Tiff Walton had managed to be successful with a degree from the University of Iowa, but living in the South, he was always competing against the hot shots from Tech. He wanted Tiffany to become a part of his construction business. It was going to be with special pride that he could say, 'This is my daughter, a Tech engineer and *my partner*.' He hoped that exuberant young men like Lonnie Tedesco didn't shatter his dream.

• • •

Tiffany carefully checked out her reflection. She knew she

was beautiful and felt that it was her special gift so that she could get what she wanted. She had used her face and body to get many things that she wanted and planned to continue to use what had been given to her. Yes, she was always conscious of the power she had because of her appearance. Surely, she wouldn't have gotten the eye of Tech's president if she looked like some of her class-mates in their army boots and baggy shirts separated by faded jeans from some second-hand shop.

Chapter 10

Jonathan Agnew Lindholm III

Wes and Billy Joe walked out of Thelma's Restaurant after a heavy Southern lunch of fried chicken, biscuits, gravy and boiled greens. Atlantans had been eating at Thelma's for decades. You could find tourists, professionals, the unemployed and often the city's hungry police waiting for a table at lunchtime. It was one place in the very diverse city that there was neither discrimination nor a need to be financially successful. Thelma's was one of the best bargains in Atlanta and was frequented regularly by local residents rather than being another formula-designed eatery for tourists and conventioneers. It was so popular, when the building the restaurant had called home for uncounted years was to be razed to make space for Olympic plans, a new place was found and hardly a day of cooking was skipped when it moved.

"I'm glad you're the one goin' to see El Presidente, because I think I'll go back to my office and go to sleep. I always feel that way when I've eaten at Thelma's," Billy Joe confessed.

"It might help if you just didn't eat so damn much. I'm always impressed when we go to Thelma's how much food you can put away. I know it takes a lot of food to maintain your 200-plus pounds of shifting muscle, but, son of a bitch, two complete lunches could be called excessive," Wes kidded his partner.

They had been working together more than five years and knew each other as professionals as well as being friends. Billy Joe had told Wes that he felt Wes understood him at times better than his wife, Cleo, because she often didn't want to listen to the perpetual problems of their day. Wes had countered with, "If I ever have another wife, I hope she's as patient with me as Cleo is with you and your long, drawn out stories and explanations. It's not that she isn't interested, Billy Joe. It's simply that she doesn't have enough time to hear four stories you have already told to get through one new one."

Standing in front of Thelma's, Wes watched Billy Joe stretch and yawn, "Maybe you should borrow a student's NoDoz, because I know you're really going out to Tech to meet with Fancer and some of the Tech police. You won't leave a good impression if you fall asleep on the chief's desk. Let's meet after our interviews and compare notes. We need to get something definite right away to pass on to the students. They and their parents must be going ape-shit. So I'll see you in the office later this afternoon." Wes headed off in the direction of his unmarked car. He had decided that even though he would like to borrow a flashy Atlanta police car to park in front of Lindholm's office, he would get a better reception from him if he were discreet.

• • •

Jon looked at his watch and noted that Detective Wesley would be arriving within 15 minutes. He was sure he would be on time. "Those types always are," he thought and then wondered exactly what he meant by 'those types.' He certainly didn't know this man.

The buzzing of the inner office line interrupted his concentration.

"Yes, Janeen. What is it? Don't tell me Detective Wesley has arrived early."

"No. You've a call from Rutledge Newborn," his assistant informed him.

Newborn was the newest member of the Georgia Tech Foundation board. Actually he had just been selected last evening at a meeting in the president's office. Could that have been only a few hours ago? With the terrible event of the morning, yesterday seemed like months ago. And, talking to Newborn was not going to improve the day.

• • •

Rutledge Newborn, an alumnus who had graduated 25 years ago, had never been considered for the board before Lindholm recommended him. Because he had a rather questionable business history, the older members challenged the president's recruitment.

One of the main reasons for calling the meeting of the nominating committee was to propose Rutledge as a trustee. The alumni members were not pleased to give up their time for a purpose that was negative in their eyes.

"I think Rutledge Newborn will be an asset," Jonathan had told the committee members as he sipped coffee prepared by Janeen before she left for home about 7:30. "He's enthusiastic about being on the board. He's from an old Atlanta family, so he has good Southern roots. Being in the top position of two software companies during the past five years has made him a wealthy man. Now he's retired so he can handle his investments. With our plans to do more fund raising, he's exactly what we need."

"Both of those companies went bankrupt during his watch. He was moving so fast that I guess the directors just didn't catch up with him. Let's face it, Jon, Newborn made his big money with two CEO exit packages," Earl Prince, chairman of the committee pointed out, "I think we can make a better addition than he, but, of course, we want you to feel that you can make recommendations as well as the trustees."

Lindholm liked Prince, a lawyer with one of the well-established Atlanta firms, and didn't want to argue with him, but he had to get Newborn on the board. He was happy that Earl added that they wanted him to suggest new members. He was going to take advantage of that generous statement. Rutledge had mentioned several times that he'd be honored to be one of those few alumni chosen to collect, invest and administer private monies for the benefit of their alma mater. He had been ignored. This closed group had its own ideas who should be in the inner circle. Being *in* not only carried prestige but could provide financial rewards as well.

Fortunately for Rutledge Newborn, returning to his home from a late evening meeting downtown, he'd decided to see if the president might be on campus to again broach the subject of membership on the board. He felt the discussion might be more productive if the two of them could talk about it in a relaxed, informal setting. After seeing a dim light on in the window of the president's office, he parked the car and walked into Lindholm's office. He was surprised to find Tiffany Walton there alone with Jonathan Lindholm.

"Oh, Jon, I'm so sorry to barge in on you. I saw the light and just assumed I'd find you doing a little extra, uh-um, work."

The president didn't miss the intent. He was sure that it looked exactly what it was: a clandestine meeting. He quickly responded, "Tiffany's one of our work-study students. She left her books in the office this afternoon but didn't discover the silly mistake until this evening. You can imagine how happy she was to find that the president works late. I always have something to do to run *your* alma mater, Rutledge. I told Tiffany I would wait because I knew it was important for her to retrieve her books."

He was sure it probably sounded lame but Newborn had been gracious—-or was it sly? He simply said that he'd stopped by to talk to Jon about a personal matter and would call him in the morning. There was something about his smile and the lingering stare that he gave Tiffany as he left the room that made the president shiver. It was at that moment that Jon decided he would invite Rutledge Newborn to be on the board.

The next morning, Lindholm made sure he called Rutledge before he received his promised call. "Rutledge, I'm sorry you couldn't stay last night. Ms. Walton left immediately, and you and I could've talked about what you had on your mind, and I could've told you about an idea of mine."

"Well, Jon, it just didn't seem to be the time for a lengthy conversation," Newborn hesitated for effect and then added, "Actually, I had not noticed how late it was until I got back to my car. None of us like to work way into the wee hours of the night."

"I frequently work in the evenings, Rutledge. I can get so much more done when there are no interruptions."

"Yes, there are 'projects' that go better without other people bothering us," Newborn agreed, "We should...."

Anxious to change the direction of the conversation, the president broke in, "Well, let me tell you what's on my mind. I want to recommend you for the Foundation board. I need to know if you're still interested before I mention your name."

Rutledge Newborn smiled and nodded his head like he was verifying his own thought. Why was he not surprised that Jon had finally decided to support his nomination to the board? He found the timing of this call positively condemning.

"Why, Jon, as they say, great minds etc. That was exactly what I wanted to talk about with you. I know I'll be an excellent member. You and I can be on the same team. We already understand each other so well. I accept your invitation. When will the next meeting be held? I want to put it on my calendar."

"It'll be the first Thursday of next month. I'll be sure that you get the notice when it's sent. Do you prefer fax or E-mail?"

"E-mail, Jon. It's appropriate communication for a high-tech institution like Georgia Tech. I'll look forward to receiving it. I'm so pleased that you had time to think about my interest in the Foundation. I must run now. There are several people waiting to see me," Rutledge added a quick good bye and returned the receiver to the telephone that was on his nightstand beside his bed. He leaned back on the double pillows and started to laugh. He was going to have a fine time on the board now that he had the president's complete attention and dedication. He had no idea how easy it could be to join the Tech power brokers. He wondered how each of them *earned* his honored place.

While Rutledge Newborn was enjoying his newly discovered clout, Jonathan was thinking about how difficult it was going to be to deal with him. It wasn't quite blackmail, but it surely has the signs of being something closely related.

• • •

Jon replayed in his mind all of the details and innuendoes of that recent conversation. Now he was going to be able to tell Newborn that he had actually passed the committee's vote. That ought to make the jackass happy. Earl Prince was right about his assessment of this alumnus. It had been hard for the president to argue his case when he really wanted to say: Damn, you're right! Who needs the bastard? But he did argue the case for Newborn and finally won. Only on the surface, had he won. He was going to have to kowtow to Newborn's demands and back him when he expresses his opinions. It wasn't going to be fun having him on the board.

The president picked up the phone and immediately told Newborn he was ' in.'

"That's great news, Jon. I look forward to meeting with the board and joining a team of truly outstanding men."

Rutledge Newborn couldn't have been more pleased if he'd won the Georgia lottery. This was an honor far beyond money. And, he thought, "This all happened because the president of Tech is sneaking a piece of ass with some little chippie...or several, who knows or cares at this point. What a wonderful decision of mine to stop in and see Lindholm on that particular night. I've always believed if you keep working at challenges, they can usually be won. I won big this time."

For a moment Newborn was so taken up with his own thoughts that he completely forgot about Lindholm being on the other end of the line. He raised his fist that was holding the telephone receiver and said out loud, "YES!"

"What did you say, Rutledge? This doesn't seem to be a very good connection," the president said wondering about the long pause followed by a distant word.

"I was going to say, Yes, I welcome the opportunity to serve my alma mater. Now that I have taken early retirement, I've an abundance of hours to give to Tech. But, as excited as I am with your news, Jon, I called to ask about this gawd-awful murder in your office. It surely was a stroke of luck that you weren't working late last night like you were a week ago," Rutledge almost laughed as he imagined the look on Lindholm's face when he referred to his late 'work.'

Jonathan had a quick thought, "The wrong person was shot. I would like to murder this son-of-a-bitch. He's going to really make me dance." His words were quite different, "You're so right. But, in answer to your question, I don't have a lot of information yet. I'm waiting for Detective Wesley from Atlanta Homicide to arrive. We have a one o'clock appointment."

Looking at his Rolex, Rutledge Newborn noted it was about

a minute before the hour. "I'll look for a call later to keep me informed. All board members should have the facts for when they're asked about this horrendous deed."

Already in a foul mood that was exacerbated by this pompous ass, Lindholm wanted to say, "Who would call you? Who would know you were a trustee? Who would imagine that you would *ever* be a trustee of the Tech Foundation?" Instead he said, "Of course, Rutledge, I'll call as soon as I have more details. In the meantime, you can enjoy your new honor by sharing the information with your lovely wife. Do tell Mitzi that I send my regards. I must run. Good bye."

Jon Lindholm didn't have time to have one more negative thought about a jerk who definitely had practiced for years to be one. Janeen was standing at the door of the office.

"Detective Wesley is here, Dr. Lindholm."

Chapter 11

Wes T. Wesley

"Well, Janeen, show him in. We shouldn't keep the detective waiting. He has an important job. And, all of us want to help him apprehend this monster as soon as possible," Jonathan said loudly enough so Wesley could hear. He wanted to be sure that he appeared to be cooperative. After all, he *was* cooperative, but he also was very busy and had other issues that needed his attention.

Janeen disappeared momentarily and returned with the Atlanta police detective dressed in a plain dark suit, light blue shirt with a red and blue regimental striped tie. No flash for this man. He would fit in any of the sections of the city from Buckhead, to Midtown, to downtown. Actually, he'd hardly be noticed in a group. The president supposed that was the point of his nondescript, average facade. Wesley created a different aura than the Tech police. They wore their uniforms as a deterrent for everyone on campus from doing actions that cause problems and to let students know that the police are omniscient. They wanted to be noticed. This detective wanted to be invisible. He may work at being invisible, but Jon was sure that his presence was felt strongly whenever he was on a case.

"Thank you for finding time to see me *today*, President Lindholm," Wes Wesley said as he extended his hand. The tone of his voice and the serious look on his face quickly set the stage for Lindholm who knew it would be difficult for him to control the meeting. Wesley was making it clear that this was his show.

"It's my pleasure to accommodate your schedule. Of course the reason we're meeting is not a pleasure. I'm so distraught about this unbelievable invasion of our campus and horrible killing of one of our outstanding students. Andy was truly a part of my office team." Jon carefully looked Wes in the eyes to deliver the message that he was open and willing to work closely to solve this mystery. He added, "Do sit down, Detective. May Janeen get you coffee or a Coke?"

"She already asked, President Lindholm, I don't need a drink at this time." His response implied what Lindholm had already ascertained: this is not a social call. Wes moved directly to what he wanted to accomplish at the meeting, "Do you mind if I tape our conversation? Although I may jot down some specific points, the tape is much more detailed."

Before Jon Lindholm had time to respond, Detective Wesley reached into his pocket and placed the small recorder on the desk between them, checked out the tape in the machine, and stacked several other tapes on a pile beside the recorder. He was ready.

"I have no objection to taping. I do it often myself. So many facts and figures to remember. And, in the academic environment, there are faculty and staff just waiting for me to forget something or quote the wrong numbers. E-mails start flying faster than rumors. So, let's begin. I'm sure we both have other people waiting for our time." Jon was not going to be intimidated by a glorified cop.

"OK," Wes said turning slightly toward the recorder to indicate that the tape had begun, "This is March 3, Detective Wes Wesley speaking with the president of Georgia Institute of Technology, Jonathan Lindholm, in his office. Now we're ready. Where were you on the night of March 2?"

Jon was shocked at the first question. Was this police officer intimating that he had something to do with Dren's death? He expected him to begin asking about Janeen's early morning call.

"Dr. Lindholm, did you hear the question?"

"Yes, of course, I heard the question. I was just surprised. Are you suggesting that I'm a suspect?"

"Not at all. I just want to know where you were when the victim was shot. I will..." The detective began but was interrupted by Lindholm.

"You want to know where I was. Well, I have to know exactly when the shooting occurred. How can you expect me to give you an intelligent answer, if I don't have all the information?"

"The autopsy report hasn't been completed yet, but you know that it'll show the killing was after 8:15 PM and before 7:00 AM," Wes said calmly and then returned to the thought he was expressing when he was interrupted, "I'll want to know where all of your office staff were last night. If anyone was here, he or she may have seen or heard something. That includes you, sir. Do you ever work late? Does any of your personnel put in evening work?" the detective threw out questions like a machine gun's rapid fire.

"Of course, I work late at times and sometimes no one else is here. And, I expect others do too. I really don't keep tabs on my staff. They are..."

"Those were easy questions to answer and you didn't have a problem responding so let's try again: Where were you last night?"

"Vice President Charles Black and I were here with four Georgia Tech Foundation trustees having a nominating committee meeting until a little after eight o'clock. I didn't look at the time, but my impression is that it was eight to eight fifteen. I went home and had a late dinner with my wife, Laurie. I noticed that we were in the kitchen cleaning up about nine. Laurie mentioned that she expected Lindy, our son, to stop in after he worked out. He had told her he would be there about nine."

"Who were the trustees in your meeting?"

"Earl Prince, chairman of the committee, Burl Mentor, Eddie Lee Johnson and Noble Adkins. I'm sure you'll recognize those names. They're all corporate and community leaders in Atlanta. You can get their addresses and telephone numbers from Janeen."

"I'll do that when I meet with her later. That'll make my job easier. As you might guess, much of our work is detailed research. We would probably make good librarians, if we could learn to be productive in a quiet environment," Wes added as a small joke to help the president relax.

"I'll keep that in mind the next time we have a vacancy, Detective." Lindholm actually chuckled, and Wes felt he had broken some of the tension.

"Now, you noticed it was nine o'clock. What did you do next?"

"I answered the phone. It was Lindy saying that he wasn't going to stop in. He was running late and had some studying to do. My son is a student here, but he doesn't live at home. Heaven knows, it's hard enough being the president's son. It would be harder if he lived here in the lap of luxury while the other students are in some of the older buildings or living four in an apartment.

"After our conversation, Laurie and I both decided to go to bed and read. Late evening is about the only time we get to have a little quiet time for just us. We probably turned out the lights close to eleven o'clock."

He ended his account and waited for Wesley to comment or ask the next question. Instead, he said nothing as if he was in deep thought. "I wonder what I said that he is contemplating?" Jonathan mused to himself, "I wonder if he's expecting me to say more? Should I add some details?"

Wes wrote a few words on his pad and asked, "Were you at home the rest of the night?"

"I just told you that. We went to sleep somewhere around eleven thirty. Both of us are good sleepers, so we didn't awaken until the alarm went off at 6:30. Janeen called from the office about 7:10 and I came here. Probably arrived by 7:20. I was already dressed and about to leave for the office when I received the call."

"Is it unusual for your secretary to come in that early?"

"Not at all. I surmise that Janeen arrives here most mornings about seven to seven thirty. She's usually here when I arrive. She's a widow, you know. Janeen lives alone near the campus, so it's no sacrifice for her to come to work early, She thinks this is her office, rather than mine. And, I can understand that. She's been here for about 20 years and has worked for three Tech presidents."

Wes didn't have to listen to every word when he had on his recorder, because he would review the tape and study the responses when he was alone, but he perked up and listened more intently when Janeen's name was mentioned. What great information. A widow who doesn't live with anyone. Hurrah! Knowing that is a wonderful way to start the meeting that he'll have with her soon.

"I find it interesting that Andrew Dren was shot in your office. How would he have gotten in if you locked up about 8:15?"

"Andy had a key to the office suite so he could do work or pick up his assignments before or after his classes and studying. It's interesting to me, too, that he was seated at my computer, because he had his own computer or could use the one on Janeen's desk. I guess we may never know what he was doing, right?" Even though Wes was the person officially asking the questions, it was difficult for Jon not to have a few of his own.

"Well, sir, I don't think any of us know that yet. Andy may have told someone, such as his roommates or family, that he was going to your office and why. Do you think there could be a relationship between where he was and what happened to him, Dr. Lindholm?"

"What are you suggesting, Detective?" Jon's voice tightened like his throat had closed up. He wondered why his mouth felt so dry? He reached for a cold cup of coffee that had been sitting on his desk and took a big swallow.

"I'm not suggesting anything. I'm just asking a question. We need to find a killer and to do that it's critical to know the motive for the crime. You say it would be unusual for him to be in your office and using your computer. The reason for those actions may have a bearing on the murder. By the way, what has been done to inform the campus and parents about what has happened? I'm sure that there are a lot of upset and scared people. That combination usually produces rumors and bizarre theories." Wes decided it was time to change the direction of his questioning.

Lindholm welcomed the new focus. He could relax and

show this policeman that he was on top of the situation.

"We made an E-mail announcement this morning and also asked the supervisors to tell their staff and faculty to announce it in each class. We also asked anyone who might know something or had seen anything that might relate to Andy to contact Chief Fancer. We told them that we'd have an update by mid afternoon. I chose that timing, because I knew you were coming at one and might have some news for us."

"We have no suspects now nor do we know enough about the victim to begin to put together a plausible theory. We've a lot to learn and appreciate the help your Tech police have offered us." Wes knew that it was good to throw in a thank you or two now and then.

The president gave the detective a weak smile and mumbled that they were there to help in any capacity. George Fancer had been with the Birmingham police force for many years and would be knowledgeable about the process that was needed to solve this murder.

Wes Wesley appeared to think of another subject, looked at Lindholm and asked, "How well did you know Andrew Dren? How long did he work here in your office?"

"Let me try to reconstruct the past year. I first heard about Andy during the Olympics. He was working for Microsoft but was freelancing on his own for some of the corporations that were loosely related to the games. He did a great job, and I heard about him because he'd told one of our trustees he was working for that he was going to be a student at Tech in August. Later he told me that he made enough money because of the Olympics that he'd be able to get his degree without working off campus. He started to work on special projects for the administration in October. He came highly recommended."

"And, Dr. Lindholm, what was the nature of those projects?" Detective Wesley asked in a very deliberate way.

The president knew that this question was coming and he'd been contemplating how he would respond so that it wouldn't encourage more questions on the topic, "We needed to catch up on data entry with both administrative and foundation material. Most people look at the Olympic experience as one big sports bar party. Well, it wasn't for us. Not only did it create monstrous amounts of extra work, it sidelined much of the normal flow of work.

"We had hundreds of people who simply took vacation during the Games and their responsibilities didn't get passed on, because there was no one there to receive the pass. We had many people who worked for the Olympics for most of the summer and consequently, nothing moved ahead toward our summer quarter that started the same week that the athletes moved out. It's rather like the notorious Lost Weekend, but it was the Lost Summer. We hired Andy in our area to play catch up. I'm sure *you* know about student work-study programs to give financial assistance."

Jon looked straight into Wes' eyes to see if he could read his reaction. He saw nothing that indicated that his response was an intended put-down. He waited for the detective to make a remark, but instead he picked up his pencil and wrote a few short words.

Glancing at his watch, Detective Wesley said, "I assume I can get a list of everyone who works in this office suite from Ms. Carson. One of my Homicide team will be talking to all of the members of your staff as soon as possible."

"I'll tell the chief to be available to your investigators until this nasty business is ended," Tech's president promised the detective.

"Then let's call it a day. I'll call you or come out to see you again if I need to follow up from this meeting. Thank you for making the time to see me. I hope changing the faculty member's appointment won't mess up his life too much."

"Many of them are prima donnas, but even they would understand that this situation takes precedence," Jon responded, rising from his chair to see Detective Wesley to the door.

Chapter 12

Jackson Burl Mentor

The two men walked out toward the foyer together chatting about education like they were old fricnds. The tension between them seemed to have disappeared as soon as Wes closed the interview. When they turned the corner to the secretary's area, a large man was standing at Janeen's temporary desk.

"Burl, what a surprise. We were just talking about you. Come over here and meet Detective Wes Wesley from Atlanta's Homicide Department," Jon said in a louder than usual voice, "Detective, this is Burl Mentor who's on the nominating and finance committees of the Foundation."

Burl stepped toward the two men, never taking his eyes off Jonathan. When all three were facing each other, he switched his attention to Wesley, extended his hand and said, "Detective Wesley, it's a pleasure to meet you. This is a dark day in the history of Georgia Tech. A dark day. What do you have to tell me about your investigation? I could carry your message back to the other trustees. They want this matter cleared up as soon as possible. It'll have a chilling effect on the campus until it is resolved. A chilling effect."

"How do you do, Mr. Mentor. Dr. Lindholm was telling me that you and a few others had been here last evening. I or one of my detectives will want to speak to you soon. We're still collecting information, but hope to have some leads after we speak to more people."

Jackson Burl Mentor appeared to be a few years older than Lindholm. His dark brown hair was streaked with gray and thinning at his forehead. He was looking at the detective with a steady gaze as he tried to determine if he was delivering a hidden meaning in his statement relating to last night's meeting. He was sure that Lindholm would be discreet, but a policeman could ferret out concealed facts by his clever questions and by reading body language, eye movement and tone of voice. He wanted to get Jonathan alone. He could learn exactly what he'd told this detective, but also he had some important business to conduct and didn't want the police in the middle of it.

"Here's my card to make it easy for you to reach me. I'll tell Earl, Noble and Eddie Lee that they'll be hearing from you. I'm confident they'll make time available for you just as I will. It was good to meet you and know that our competent Atlanta police are already on the job," Burl said as he moved toward the door of the private office area. He was putting an end to the conversation and hoping Wesley would take the hint.

"I'm meeting with Ms. Carson now," Wes Wesley told the two men as he turned and smiled at Janeen, "I don't want to keep her from her work waiting for me any longer than necessary. So, thank you again, Dr. Lindholm. Good to meet you, Mr. Mentor."

The president closed the door quietly behind him and Mentor. He felt that he had sighed as he heard the click of the lock. If he didn't, he surely felt that he should. He was pleased with how his interview went with Wesley. They seemed to end it on a friendly note. He didn't want to antagonize the police and have them looking into more than the murder of Andy Dren.

"Well, Jonathan, how did it go with the police detective?"

"Just fine, Burl. He asked who was here last evening, what time we all left, what else I did after our meeting, and if I had any idea who would have shot Andy. I had no trouble answering his questions. My question is: Why was Andy in my office at my computer in the middle of the night? That may be something that we don't want to speak about to Detective Wesley."

"Don't worry. We've been conducting our foundation business for years and have never had a problem. As you know, sometimes it has proved to be quite profitable. No reason why the police should be looking into what we're doing just because a student was murdered. He probably made someone mad and you know how it is these days. Drive by shootings, killings over s or a pair of Air Jordan shoes and neighbors who ildren on their own streets. Atlanta and our country filled with violence.

"But, I've more important business to discuss today. I've just received word that the Foundation will be getting another 'major gift' tomorrow. We need to compose our story as to where we got it before we hand it over to Charles Black. You know how important it is to have each of these windfalls *look like* a contribution to the capital campaign," Burl Mentor explained.

"Oh, yes, I do. This is too good a deal to mess up by not keeping up our strong front. How much is the 'gift'?"

• • •

Jon's mind was already wandering. He thought about when he first interviewed for the position of president of Georgia Tech and heard about the fund raising goals he had been astonished. He was told they were waiting to have the new president in place before announcing the campaign. They wanted it to be his venture. As president, he could accept all of the glory, they were there to help make him look good. Jon had no real experience in philanthropic endeavors and thought a goal of $750,000,000 was outrageous. He'd learned the amount from Burl who had been one of the trustees to interview him at that time. Mentor had taken him aside and said not to worry. It might appear to be a huge amount, but the Foundation trustees were supporting it, and they would guarantee success. The trustee then, as was his style, repeated the important words: guarantee success.

Jonathan heard what he said, but he went back to California wondering if he wanted to be responsible for the institution, the upcoming Olympic Village plans and for raising $750,000,000. It would be so much extra work and take a lot of extra time. He mentioned it to Laurie and she simply said, "That's part of the price you pay. If you're chosen for this position, we are going! And, we're going before Lindy gets suspicious about this change in our lives."

He knew that wasn't the time to argue with his wife because she was right. He couldn't stay where he was. He had no job. He possibly couldn't get a job in the area if people began to talk about why he lost his teaching appointment and his job at Hewlett Packard on the same day. So even without Laurie's ultimatum, he knew he had to do his best to get the president's position and be on the job immediately.

Lindholm had been president for exactly 18 hours when he found Jackson Burl Mentor standing at his office door, "We must talk. You and I need to reach an airtight agreement. An airtight agreement." His words and his voice were ominous. What could be so important that he had to meet with this man even before he'd sat in his presidential chair?

"Come in, Burl. What a terrific surprise. You'll be here to get my first day on the job launched with flair."

"We're going to get the day launched OK. Maybe with more flair than you ever imagined, Jonathan," Mentor announced as he came into the room, loudly closing the door behind him. He walked directly to the wing back chair that had been the favorite of President Forsythe. He sat down as if he owned both the chair and the office. He wanted to give Lindholm the feeling that maybe he also owned him.

The patronizing attitude of Burl Mentor was not lost on Jon. He recognized a message when it was being delivered. Now he wanted to know what this was all about.

"I'm pleased to see you, Burl, but we must remember that I have a day full of appointments set by Janeen so I can meet faculty, student and staff leaders. We must build a team here. That comes first."

"Wrong, Jonathan. Wrong! First is a damn meeting with me. You'll work at building the team of Mentor and Lindholm or you may not be in Atlanta very long. I hardly think you want to move back to California, do you? Do you?" The Foundation trustee almost hissed the last two words.

Jonathan's anger skyrocketed in a matter of seconds. He was the president and this loathsome man was only an alumnus who served as a volunteer. Yes, he sat on the board of the Georgia Tech Foundation, but he wasn't the decision-maker in this office.

Lindholm rose from his chair, "Relax, Burl. I don't know what is bothering you, but you can be civil. Of course, I want to be on your team. The Foundation is very important to Tech and therefore to me but, as of yesterday, I'm the president and it's my choice how I'll spend my day."

"Let's get a few things straight, *President*. That title doesn't mean shit to me. You're nothing, and you'll be less than nothing if you choose not to play my game. You're the president because I convinced the other trustees and the Chancellor that you were the man for us. You would be perfect. And, *sir*, I decided you would be perfect, because I knew why you left California in such a damn hurry. Now, unless on your very first day as President of Georgia Tech you want the media to learn about your sordid past, you'll sit down and listen to what you're going to do to continue being the fucking president of this great institution. This great institution." Burl had risen from his chair when he began to admonish Jon. Standing just over 6 feet and weighing 220 pounds, he was an imposing man who had maintained the strong, solid physique of a football player. Jon stepped back as if he were physically threatened and finally slumped back into his desk chair. His worst nightmare had become reality.

"What are you ranting about?" Jon bluffed, "What rumors have been spread about me?"

"How could you ever think that a past like yours wouldn't follow you? Fortunately, for us, we can take advantage of the mess you left behind. Personally, I think you should consider yourself damn lucky that I felt we could use you. You could have hung around Cal Tech and perhaps landed in prison." Burl was enjoying Jon Lindholm's discomfort. He knew the man looked like a respectable president but under that slick veneer was a man with no morals. He'll be the ideal front man for the Foundation and its plans for the future.

Mentor continued, "I don't think you want me to recite all the gory details, but let me say that Cynthia Maddox was in much better physical shape before she knew you than after. Than after. Do I make myself clear enough for us to get on with the business at hand?"

Jonathan Lindholm felt like his heart was going to pound its way through his chest. He couldn't breathe. His face flushed and the heat moved down his body until he wanted to scream. Cynthia Maddox. He did know. He wasn't bluffing. Burl Mentor would always hold Jonathan's life and sanity in his hands. He'd been sure that other than Laurie, no one in Atlanta would know why he wanted desperately to be the president of Georgia Tech. They had even gotten Lindy out of California before he heard rumors. Was it all for naught? Not if he would (What did Burl say?) play his game. Well, I guess I can make that decision. Now, I should find out what the game is.

"OK, Burl, let's get to what you want me to do. I'm sure it's for the good of your alma mater."

Burl chuckled and then was swept into a hearty, robust fit of laughter. "Yes, Jon, I sure can pick 'em. You're going to be perfect for us to expand our great, profit scheme inside the Georgia Tech Foundation. Your resume should have included: 'No morals. Just ego and instant gratification.' One would think you were part of the 'Me Generation.' I guess it isn't a generational thing. It's just a lust thing. Do whatever you want with your dick, because we're going to be making lots of money easier because of your appetite for young women. Yes, for young women."

Lindholm wanted to vomit. The way Burl Mentor said it, his life sounded sick. He wasn't really like what he was hearing. Mentor was such a crass degenerate that anything coming from his mouth was already soiled. It was Burl who was a sick man. He would watch out for the son of a bitch and would be careful to keep him satisfied by playing his little game, whatever it was.

"The Foundation for years has been playing penny ante money games. We've been able to bring in funds as gifts, get them into our non-designated account and make them work for the financial benefit of the trustees as well as for the institution. It not only is an honor to be a Tech trustee, it can be damn right profitable! We've multiplied our land holdings and been partners in some lucrative business ventures. What we've done to this point pales next to what you and I are going to do in a short period of time now that we have the campaign to use to bring in big 'gifts.' You'll be the front man who is *supposedly* going out and sweet-talking our alumni to contribute to the damn cause. It's so simple. So simple."

Burl Mentor was making his presentation with a sense of pride. He'd helped to develop the structure that provided a way to transfer real estate among trustees and the Foundation so all could make a profit, and it had been working for more than two decades. Development was the best business in Atlanta since railroads. But his newest strategy was going to be easier and result in large amounts of money. He was in the process of deciding how much he and the president would receive as a 'signing fee' for playing the game.

"Are you telling me that the trustees actually are profiting by being on the board?" the president asked in amazement.

"Don't make yourself look like such a damn fool, Lindholm. These are businessmen! They take care of their own. Deal in our own tight group. Write their own contracts. This kind of arrangement is everywhere, its legal and in many cases it's no secret. Ever pay any attention to the money maneuvers in Washington or on Wall Street? Well, we must be smarter than they are, because those bastards keep making the headlines, and we happily stay out of the media. Yes, out of the media. When Charles Black puts us in the news, it's for a 'gee whiz' story that says look at our terrific students. Those kids could learn a thing or two from us. Maybe I should teach a course in accounting practices or laundering money."

Burl was still talking when he started to laugh at his intended wit and then added, "OK, now that you've had your own education greatly expanded by me, and I don't have one of your damn PhDs, let's get down to what you're going to do to keep your job. To keep your job."

Mentor was enjoying the scenario. From the day that he learned about the kind of man Jonathan Agnew Lindholm III was, he'd looked forward to this meeting. He surmised, during Lindholm's series of interviews when vying for the job, that the man made a point of being in control. The joke was on him, because Burl was the man in control. He'll learn that the Southern way is not always sweet hospitality, fried chicken and magnolias.

"First, you're going to establish a center that will appear to have a legitimate reason to be associated with Hong Kong. It will actually exist and function. It can even serve some productive projects so it's not under suspicion, but its purpose is to create an excuse to accept Far East money. The Georgia Tech Foundation will be the conduit to get the funds into this country. We will......"

Lindholm spontaneously broke into Mentor's description, "But what will the money be going to? We don't want to be in the middle of a repeat of what has been happening to many politicians. We have to do what is ethical for Tech, Burl."

"Sure, Jonathan, I know how important ethics are to you. Well, if that's your attitude, I guess it's time for Tech to accept - with regret, of course - your resignation and look for someone who fits into our future better than you do. A one-day presidency may be a record. I'll have Charles start working on how he's going to pitch your reasons for leaving. Black is a fine example of someone who knows when to do as he is told. His compensation and perks are at least twice any of his counterparts, because we pay for loyalty and silence. Loyalty and silence."

"Now, Burl, don't jump to conclusions. I'm not backing out nor giving you any resistance. I just mentioned the path of the funds to be sure you'd thought of possible consequences. Just get back to what you want me to do. So far establishing a program that relates to Far East studies is a very wise move with all the attention on Hong Kong and Beijing."

"For chrissakes, Lindholm, this has nothing to do with altruism or that it's trendy to have Far East studies. This is about how to make money by doing a little slight of hand. The Tech Far East Center, or maybe we should call it Hong Hong Delight like the restaurant in the area, is just there for window dressing. In addition to getting the center on-line, you will devote what time is necessary to keep contacts in Hong Kong that we can continue to use. We need people who will *say* that they're the donors of the funds as they come to us. We have about 20 alumni living in Hong Kong, so you can begin with them. Get some of them to agree to appear to be the donors. You'll have to decide who has the same value system that you do and get them to join our camp for the good of our alma mater. Oh, yes, and you want them to know that they will receive a *commission* or *finder's fee* for being the "*donor*." That might help them decide whether your offer is interesting."

Jon liked the sound of his participation in Mentor's plan. Regular international travel and having time for his own pursuits while he would be out of the fish bowl of being the president of Tech had all kinds of possibilities. He thought this was going to be a downer, but things were already looking up.

"Burl, I'll be the front for you and these unknown monies. You can count on me...that is, umm,... if I can count on you," Jon watched for Mentor's reaction and was glad to see him shaking his head as if to say: We have a deal. He smiled back and then asked a very important question, "How much money are we talking about?"

"Over $500,000,000, Jonathan. Over $500,000,000. Minus *your* finder's fee, of course."

• • •

Lindholm's thoughts had been so overpowering that he had practically forgotten that Burl Mentor was still sitting in his office. He shook his head to air out the dark images and turned back to his antagonist.

Chapter 13

Laurie Rogers Lindholm

Laurie noticed as she pulled the car into the garage, that it was almost 1:15. She had planned to be back by one, because Lindy had left a message that he was coming over to the house to show her something important. She hoped he had not gotten tired of waiting or thought she wasn't interested, but during her last ballet class at Capitol Homes, one of the little girls slipped and scuffed her knee. Although it wasn't serious, the child was upset and began to cry. Laurie took time to comfort her, clean off the scrape and went out to her car to get a Band-Aid from her first aid kit. This took just enough time to make the rest of her morning schedule run late.

She opened the door to the house and knew that Lindy had waited. By the sounds of the loud music reverberating from every wall, it was guaranteed that there was a nineteen year old present.

"Lindy," Laurie called trying to be heard over the Grateful Dead, "Lindy, I'm sorry I'm late. Where are you?"

"I'm in the kitchen, Mom. I thought I'd see what you had to eat while I waited."

Laurie was always pleased when Lindy made himself at home. He really didn't consider the campus residence of the president as his home. As a student he had always lived in a dormitory or in one of the student housing apartments. Even during the summer, he had a full-time job with the Olympics and had the opportunity to share an off campus house with five other young people. He'd jumped at the chance for several reasons, but mostly because he didn't like being identified with the president's house. It made people treat him like an outsider.

Lindy Lindholm also felt that since his mother had been having some emotional problems, it would be easier on her if he was close by but not 'in residence' and driving her up-the-wall with his loud music and late hours. He made a point to stop in a couple times each week. He knew his mom liked to hear what he was doing, and he liked to get some good home cooked food while they talked. She was a cool lady. Not only as his mother but as the surrogate mom to all the little kids she taught dancing to in the inner city neighborhoods. He liked seeing his mother's enthusiasm when she was with her dancers. He always came home with a friend or two on the day that Laurie would have a class out to the house to go swimming in the pool and slurp up Smoothies and scarf down cookies. It was just like having a bunch of little brothers and sisters.

"Honey, I'm sorry to be late. Latisha Seton fell in class, and I had to play nurse before I left. I wouldn't want her to think I didn't care about her. Those kids need all the gentleness they can get. That's why I believe that the ballet classes are so well received. There's gentleness to that form of dance. Not like today's style. Which reminds me, could . . ."

".....you turn the music down?" Lindy completed his mother's question and went into the living room to adjust the CD player. "I had it turned up because you weren't here but planned to decrease the decibels when I heard you drive into the garage, but I didn't hear the car."

"I guess not. How could you hear anything, dear heart?"

Lindy saw that his mother looked youthful today. He had noticed many times that she had almost a girlish look when she returned from the ballet classes. Her face would be slightly flushed from working with the children so her blue eyes would be more noticeable and her skin had a sunny glow. Her dark blonde hair would be damp enough to encourage delicate curls to fall lightly across her forehead. And, the skintight leotard that she wore just for teaching would convince anyone that she was still in great shape. Looking at her today, he found it hard to believe that she had ever had any big mental problems other than those caused by stress. Since he wasn't supposed to know she was sick or question why, he didn't feel he could ask her about what his father had said, but he hoped that her illness was now gone. She had enough to handle as the wife of his dad and the Institute's First Lady.

"If you have time to visit, I was planning to make some fresh iced tea and take your favorite chocolate fudge cookies out of the freezer. It'll only take a few minutes."

"I always have time for your cookies. And I hope you have time to look at something I wrote. I brought you a copy," the young Jonathan Lindholm said reaching into his backpack that was heavy with papers and books.

• • •

Laurie ran water into her old teakettle that once sat on her mother's range when Laurie was in college. She liked having material ties with her family even though they were all gone. Her father had died soon after he retired from his dental practice. He was so active and happy when he was working but seemed to lose that zest when he took down the Dr. Benjamin Ephraim Rogers, General Dentistry sign that had been out in front of his office for 35 years. He never got around to clearing his office space of equipment or records. Just closed the door like it was simply the end of the day but didn't open it for patients ever again.

Her mother suggested several times that they could do a little work on it each day, but he wasn't interested. Two years later he duplicated the retirement process. He went to his bedroom one afternoon for an early nap, closed the door but never opened it again. Laurie's mother found him there several hours after he had died of a massive heart attack. Unfortunately it was too much for her delicate mother to survive. Three hours before her father's funeral service, her mother also had a heart attack. His service was postponed and the two of them were buried side by side after a combined service that seemed to be proof that their marriage was not to end with death.

Laurie had thought that was how all marriages were. Her parents were the best role models that a daughter could have. But, you must have two people who believe the same philosophy.

Good marriages are not made in heaven nor by only one person. Laurie chose the wrong person for her values and dreams. Jon Lindholm wasn't satisfied with one woman nor willing to work at being a family. He had his own needs. Laurie and Lindy were just a small part of those needs. Other than having an explosive temper, he was a good husband in his own home: helpful, considerate, entertaining. The problem, Laurie figured out after several years, was that he was somebody else when he was not at home. Since he liked that other Jon, he spent a lot of time outside their home. It was usually called work, but once she discovered that late work really was another four letter word, she entered into a contract with herself.

Lindy was going to grow up in a two-parent home with the advantages that come with a father who makes a good living and a mother who is at home. She wouldn't sacrifice his security for her pride. Outwardly, Laurie, Jon, and Lindy Lindholm were models for a television series in the 60s. The facade had almost shattered three years ago in California, but Lindy had been protected and here they were living a new life in Georgia. Here they were drinking iced tea and talking about another sad life, or death, of a murdered student.

• • •

"This is my article on Andy Dren's murder. The Technique published a special edition because of the murder. Even though it was expensive, we ran Xerox copies so we could get it out ASAP. Because the editor felt I was the only one who could get to Dad, I was the reporter assigned to the lead story. I did get to him, so I was able to include quotes from him and from Janeen. Copies were hand delivered to every building on campus. I don't think it has decreased the rumors or the fright, but at least we gave them the facts up to press time. Now I'll be quiet and eat cookies so you have a chance to read it."

Graduate Student Shot at President Lindholm's Desk
By Lindy Lindholm

O. Andrew Dren, a graduate student in the College of Computing, was shot to death last night as he worked at the desk of the president of Georgia Tech. The body was discovered by the administrative assistant to the president, Janeen Carson.

"Andy had been a work-study student in this office since October. He was a brilliant young man. He taught everyone in the office new methods to be more efficient and was always available to help solve computer problems. He understood the technology as well as the programs and was empathetic to the users' frustrations. Andy was also a friend to all of us. I cannot imagine what kind of person would want to harm him," Ms. Carson said as she stood by her temporary desk in the foyer area of the president's suite.

President Lindholm's formal office area is surrounded by yellow crime scene tapes. Police technicians are examining all of the area in and around where the body of Andrew Dren was found. Homicide detectives are methodically questioning dozens of people as they put together their case. The body has been moved to the morgue, but blood is visible on the walls, furniture, and computer marking where the crime was committed. A broken window suggests the killer was outside the building, perhaps standing in the parking area, when the victim was shot.

"This is a dark day in the history of Georgia Tech," President Lindholm said, "We have lost one of our outstanding students whose education was important enough for him to leave a successful career with Microsoft to return to school to earn an advanced degree. Andy Dren had been one of my students on staff for almost six months. He did most of his assignments after classes, so it wasn't unusual for him to be working at night. If someone disliked Andy, I don't know who it could be.

"Andy lost his life doing a job for Tech, so I assume a personal responsibility for this dastardly deed. Therefore, I personally pledge a $5,000 reward to anyone who can identify the murderer or give the police information that will lead to the arrest of the murderer. You may contact Detective Wesley of Atlanta Homicide or get the information to our office. We must all work together to find this monster."

Andrew Dren was the son of Oliver A. Dren, Sr., Dalton, and the late Gloria Pinellis Dren. Andy was a graduate of Dalton High School and Purdue University. He had been a senior programmer at Microsoft before he entered Georgia Tech to pursue a graduate degree. His sister, Susan, a senior at Dalton High School, also survives Mr. Dren.

Dren lived on campus and shared an apartment with two roommates. Frank Bostwick, a graduate student in the Ivan Allen College, spoke for them, "We were devastated when we heard about Andy being murdered. We felt that such things can't happen at Tech. This was a safe campus. I guess we'll never feel that way again. If it can happen to a nice guy like Andy, it can happen to any of us. They better soon find the b*****. We want the killer caught, and we want everyone to remember Andy. He deserves his place in our history."

Additional security officers have been assigned to the campus and everyone is cautioned to not be out after dark or alone. Detective Wes T. Wesley and his partner Detective Billy Joe LaCrosse of the Atlanta Homicide Department head up the investigation. If you know something that will help the police, contact Detective Wesley or Chief Fancer on campus.

To assure that everyone knows what progress is being made to solve this murder, we will publish as often as necessary. Contact The Technique office if you have comments or questions relating to this emergency.

• • •

Laurie read the article, feeling pride that her son was on the campus news staff. She was happy that his choice to come to Tech had worked for him. She had understood his reluctance to enroll at Tech once his father had been chosen as president. It surprised her that he had capitulated as easily as he did but she was also relieved. If he had insisted on going to Cal Tech, there would've been a terrible battle. She no longer cared about protecting Jon, but she didn't want to have to tell Lindy the truth about his dad.

She was embarrassed and furious because Jon had made such a fool of her and a mockery of their marriage. Sometimes she wished that he hadn't gotten away with his crime. Now that they were in Atlanta, Jon acted as if nothing had ever happened. He seemed to be three people: the Jon who was a partner in family activities when he was in his home, the controlling president that she heard others whisper about, and the glamorous, congenial public image that was seen at community events and alumni gatherings. Who was the real Jonathan Lindholm? Were any of these personas the real person? She didn't care who was the real Jon, because she hated them all. They were all contrived and phony. He was whomever he needed to be to get his own way.

Knowing this, she had stayed with her husband for a variety of reasons, including her commitment to the family unit for the benefit of Lindy. As long as she lived as Mrs. Jonathan A. Lindholm III, she would honor their marriage contract and be a model wife. She played her role so well that even Jon thought she had forgiven him. What sustained her when she allowed her mind to drift back to ignoble memories was anticipating the day when she could reveal them all and therefore force the great Lindholm III to become yet another person as he tried to explain to his diverse audiences what he really was.

She looked back down at the article and felt like she was seeing a vision. As she looked at the name Andrew Dren, she thought she heard the words: You are having your revenge.

"Hey, Mom, whadda you think?" Lindy brought her back to the reason for his visit.

"I think you've done a fine job with a tragic subject. It's so sad that this could happen on campus. Everyone must be scared. I know I am. Which reminds me of something that happened last night. It was like a premonition or some kind of message from beyond."

"Mom, this doesn't sound like you who is always so practical. Maybe it was an out-of-body-experience.... Now, dear little lady, tell me about this strange episode," Lindy said in a joking way pretending to stroke a beard that he felt a shrink would wear,

"Just relax on my couch and tell me your story."

Laurie smiled warmly at her son, "Your dad and I went to bed soon after we had a late dinner. We read awhile and turned out the light about 11 o'clock. I was asleep in a few minutes but was awakened 15 minutes later. It seemed like something awakened me, but I couldn't identify anything. I just had a feeling of foreboding that not only woke me but kept me awake.

"I tried to settle down again for maybe a half an hour, but I was wide awake. I finally got up in the dark and went down to the terrace room and read. I fell asleep there and was suddenly awakened again with that same feeling like something bad had happened. This was about two hours after I had gone downstairs. I wondered again if some noise had wakened me, but I couldn't remember hearing anything. At that point, I went back to bed and slept until Janeen's early call. Lindy, I *knew* that it was going to be bad news. Even though I've been busy all day, I keep thinking that maybe I had a premonition about Andy Dren's murder but also wonder if it could be something else. All of this makes me nervous. Maybe you should come home until they find and arrest the murderer."

"Now, Mom, that isn't necessary. You just had a bad dream that you didn't remember after you woke up. It happens all the time. I'm sure it didn't relate to the shooting. I'm OK, as you can see. Besides, what makes you think it's safer here than in my apartment? Remember that Andy was killed right in Dad's office so it looks like being in the president's domain doesn't guarantee safety."

"That's a chilling thought. Maybe I'll move into your apartment until this is cleared up," Laurie joked. She didn't feel at all light-hearted, but she didn't want to sound like an alarmist. Surely there was no relationship between the shooting, it happening in the president's office and her sleepless night.

"Hey, you're welcome anytime. The guys would love a home cooked meal or two. You might find our housekeeping a bit on the raunchy side, but the roaches thank us for a great place to live."

"Oh, yuk, Lindy. Even joking about your apartment condition is an awful thought," Laurie made a face that definitely reflected her opinion of roaches as roommates.

"I'm meeting some friends in 15 minutes at the Student Center, so gotta get going. Keep that copy and show it to Dad tonight. Tell him that his favorite reporter will be in touch," Lindy told his mother as he slung his backpack across his shoulder and headed for the door.

Laurie followed him to the door. Lindy turned around and gave her a hug and a peck on her forehead before leaving the kitchen. He raised both arms and waved his hands as a closing to his visit and quickly jogged down the driveway.

Laurie watched tenderly as her son disappeared down the sloping driveway that led to 10th Street once the northern most point of the campus. Now there were several new graduate residences and some ugly flat-roofed Tech apartments across the street. It could be thought of as a college neighborhood, but the truth was that no one considered the president's house, set in acres of beautifully landscaped yard complete with two swimming pools, as being a part of the otherwise modest surroundings.

Laurie missed being a friendly neighbor who knew the folks who lived in the vicinity. Unfortunately, she was held apart, because she was the president's wife. She was happy for her son that he had his own circle of friends and wasn't constantly reminded that he was the president's son. She wondered how Lindy's friends and the other students were reacting to the turmoil on campus today. It must be the only topic of conversation.

Chapter 14

Tiffany Jarvis Walton

Two of those students seemed to not have a thought in their heads beyond themselves. Tiffany and Lonnie were lying in her bed on a rumpled pile of peach colored sheets, a darker shade of apricot blanket and their own clothes. The pale peach drapes had been drawn allowing a muted light to enter the room. Sometimes at night Tiffany would light candles before they made love, but during the daytime, closing the drapes created almost the same soft atmosphere.

"Damn, Tiffany, making love to you is more strenuous than going to football practice. The coach at least has a heart and let's us take a break now and then. But you're like that Energizer Bunny: You go on and on and on. Look at your clock. We have been here for two hours. I must weigh ten pounds less than when I arrived," Lonnie was almost out of breath, and he pretended to be just minutes from expiring, "You're going to have to deliver my body to Coach Sam."

"Right, Lonnie. I can see it now. 'Here he is, Coach. He thought he was really macho, but I proved him wrong,'" Tiffany improvised as she laughed and gave Lonnie a playful punch on the back which was the only place she could reach in her current position. "You said today you're going to break our record of coming four times in a row, but you didn't do it. I'm just going to find someone with more staying power, my boy."

"Don't even kid about t-t-that, Tiff. If you want five, you'll get five. There's no hurry. I'll be ready to go again by the time you untangle us from these sheets. In fact, I think I'll roll you up like a mummy so you can't escape while we're working on my dork. Of course you're going to be the only mummy whose hands are free to do their j-j-job," Lonnie was already off Tiffany and beginning to roll her up in the sheets as she wiggled and thumped on his back. She opened her mouth and bit hard on his shoulder, which made him loosen his hold on her. As she laughed, she scooted from his embrace. He reached quickly for her body just as she slipped off the bed with him on top of her. They were both laughing and playfully hitting each other.

Lonnie could feel himself getting excited and hard. Tiffany had a magical quality about her sex play. She could read what turned him on and knew how to get him to be bigger and better. It was going to be a real treat to take her right here on the floor.

"Lonnie," Tiffany gasped, "Let me up. Let's get back in bed. This is crazy."

"It sure is, baby. I like crazy when it comes to sex. You have shown me some new tricks, but I'm about to show you what it's like being raped."

"Lonnie, come on. Let me up. Get back in bed. You don't have to go for five. I was just kidding. Making love isn't ripping one off on the floor!"

"Tiff, we're both going to do something we've never done before and so far I'm loving it. Now fight me and it'll be that much better. You're so b-b-beautiful and you're going to be mine today in a very special way," Lonnie was panting as he forced Tiffany's legs apart and placed his hands on her shoulders holding her against the carpet. She was still trying to get away and looked longingly at the bed. In all their months of making love, Tiffany had never resisted and sometimes took the lead. Today, he decided, was going to be different. It was going to be his show.

"Come on, Lonnie. You've never done anything that I didn't also want to do. You've always been sweet. Right now you're scaring me," Tiffany squeezed out the words as Lonnie squeezed her whole body deeper into the carpet.

Lonnie made no response, saving all of his energy for keeping Tiffany down and in the right position. He was amazed that he was ready again. This was really going to be a day to remember. He might go back to his room and paint a huge red 5 on his wall.

"Lonnie, stop right now," she cried as she struck out wildly, "You can't do this. I'm not ready. You're going to hurt me."

Neither her voice nor her words slowed him down even one stroke. It was almost like he wasn't there. He felt detached and simply an observer. He raised his hips and plunged into her with almost the same force he would use making a tackle on the field. There was a slight resistance and then he was fully buried beyond the soft hair and delicate lips. He called out her name and then yelled, "Five!"

Tiffany's resistance dissolved into a few gasps and an outpouring of tears. How could Lonnie be like this after an afternoon of making love? Did he even hear her pleas? She felt that he was enjoying her dismay and distress.

It was only a matter of minutes until Lonnie rolled over on his back and sighed. They slowly turned their faces toward each other. "Tiffany, why is your face all wet? I must be a sloppy kisser."

Tiffany was careful to not tease him again. She supposed that she insulted his macho ego. "I guess I was a bit emotional but everything's OK now."

"I feel like I'm in a dream. I guess you do that to me. After t-t-today, number five may be a very special number. I b-b-bet you'll never forget me now."

"I can't believe that you were so rough and domineering. I believe you just got carried away with your own power. You better keep this latest talent hidden. Or you might get arrested, and you wouldn't like being in jail without me," Tiffany warned him.

"No, I wouldn't. I like my life as it is. You aren't g-g-going to squeal on me, are you?" he said in a joking manner, but he knew that the words he spoke were really the way he felt.

"You don't have to worry about me, Lonnie, if you get your butt up, dressed and out of here in 10 minutes. I have some notes to review before leaving for my 3 o'clock class, so let's get moving," Tiffany said as she sat up wondering what her back looked like. She knew how it felt but hoped that there weren't carpet burns from her shoulders to her hips. She looked down at the carpet and thought that it looked the same as always. How could it be?

"Yep, Tiffany. I'm on my way. No more excitement for me. I'm just meeting the academic advisor at 3:30. So I need to move almost as fast as you do," Lonnie was up and headed toward the bathroom for the guest bedroom. He learned that Tiffany didn't like to have someone use her bathroom and Lonnie preferred to be alone when he was cleaning up after his times in Tiffany's bed.

Lonnie took a quick, cold shower, picked up his clothes that were scattered around the bedroom, threw on those clothes and was ready to go before Tiffany finished her shower. Lonnie stood at the door and raised his voice to be heard, "Tiffany, I'm going. You better hurry or you'll m-m-miss your class. I'll call you later. Don't forget about this day. It's going to change our lives. Bye."

Tiffany caught some of the words over the water and hoped one date rape wasn't going to change her life. She would have to talk to Lonnie about that later.

Tiffany hated to rush and decided that everyone was so upset at Tech today that she wasn't concerned about being late to her class. She would enjoy her shower before getting dressed. She needed the warm water to ease some of her bruised and scraped spots. What a surprise Lonnie was today. He wasn't just the sexy pussycat that she had thought. She'll have to be more careful of what challenges she tosses out to him.

As she stepped out of the shower, wound a towel around her head and reached for another towel to dry her body; the telephone began to ring. She wrapped the second towel across her breasts and let it drape below her hips.

"Hello."

"It's Jon. I hoped I'd catch you at home. How did I get so lucky?"

"I had some studying to do before I went to my 3 o'clock class, and I absolutely lost track of time." Well, that part was true! "I guess I'm going to be late now."

"Some professors have canceled their classes because so many students have gone off campus. Maybe you'll get there and find yours canceled. You'd probably like that, right?" Jon asked, knowing that Tiffany's main interest at Georgia Tech was not class work.

"If that happens, I'll go over to the Student Center and see who's around."

"Be careful around the campus until the murderer is identified. Chief Fancer has asked that no one wander on campus alone. I don't want anything to happen to you."

"I won't do anything that'll put myself in jeopardy, Jon. I'll make sure I hang out with a gang or a couple of my friends."

"Well, I was hoping you would spend some of the time safely at home. I may be able to stop down sometime later. But I'll call and let you know," Jonathan explained.

"That would be great, Jon, but I won't be here all the time. Give me a call or leave a message. I'll probably be back here by mid-evening. I want to find out what's happening on campus as well as be with you. I may learn something that you don't know. You'd be surprised how much goes on that a president never knows."

Lindholm was both disappointed and angry that Tiffany was going along in her own way rather than waiting for him. Maybe she was still miffed from their conversation this morning. He wished that she was more pliable, but she had her own little life as a student. Right now, he wasn't going to let her know that she was annoying him. When he was ready to end their relationship, then he would show her how much they can annoy each other.

"OK. If I get the chance, I'll call later. I want to see for myself that you are all right. This is a very stressful time. The telephone has been ringing constantly, detectives still in my office and now the media has trucks and equipment parked all over the hill. I couldn't get my car out if I had to. So take care until I see you, which I hope will be this evening," Jon saw three lights flashing on his telephone and knew he had to get back to the job.

"Love ya', Jon. Talk to you later," Tiffany was also ready to end the conversation, because she really did have to at least do a walk-on for her class.

Chapter 15

Janeen Newman Carson

Before Dr. Lindholm and Detective Wesley emerged from the office, Janeen had greeted Burl Mentor, cleaned up her desk and wondered what the policeman was asking and what they were discussing. She was sure that Dr. Lindholm didn't know anything about the shooting. He had heard about it for the first time when she called him this morning. He must've wondered what might have happened, or not happened, if he had been here later last evening. Would he have seen someone or even had been the victim? Probably Andy wouldn't even have come into the office if the president had been there.

Both Janeen and Burl turned when the door of Lindholm's office opened, and he and Wesley came out into the foyer area talking enthusiastically as if they were simply enjoying a break from their usual responsibilities. Janeen thought: It must be strange to have a job that just relates to death. ' Oh, Mr. Wesley, what do you do?' 'I count bodies.' Seems a lot different to her than, 'I write letters and manage an office.'

Dr. Lindholm greeted the Foundation trustee, introduced him to the detective and was quick to notice that Mentor was anxious to talk to him. The two men left Wesley at Janeen's desk and went into Jon's temporary office.

"Detective Wesley, if it's agreeable to you, I've asked Dr. Jungstone if we could meet in his office. If we stay here, we'll be constantly interrupted. Everyone who comes to see the president feels that my time is their time."

"It's best to have privacy when we talk about what you know regarding the murder."

Janeen Carson took the lead and walked toward the outer

door, took a turn to the left and opened a door at the top of the carpeted stairs that went to the office area on the lower level. Because the old, ivy-covered, brick building was built on a hill, the space below the president's suite also had a ground level entry. Wes was surprised that it was almost as bright and pleasant as above. He noticed four open doors that seemed to say, we're here to do business, come on in. He must be sure to get the names of these staff members who might've been here the night before.

"Here we are. Dr. Jungstone said he would be out of the building until later this afternoon, so we'll stake our claim," Janeen said as they walked into one of the offices which was a lot like what he remembered his professors' offices were at the University of Virginia. There were orderly piles of papers everywhere and four bookcases filled to overflowing with heavy tomes for reference or kept as remembrances of an earlier, personal education. He glanced at the computer which had on the monitor a letter that began: Dear Mr. and Mrs. Holly, I appreciated your call today, and was pleased to be able to tell you that we and the Atlanta police have everything under control....... Wes didn't know where Dr. Jungstone got his information, but he hoped that he was correct.

"Detective Wesley, sit here in this comfortable chair. I'll sit in the desk chair. If you want to take notes, you can pull it closer to the desk." Janeen was doing her assistant to the president job, trying to make the 'guest' feel at ease. She wasn't sure that was the proper protocol when the 'guest' was investigating a murder, but she did want this man to feel relaxed and understand that they were all trying to help him do his job.

Wes reached back and closed the door before he settled in the chair. He asked Janeen if she was agreeable to having their discussion on tape. She responded that it was fine with her so he took the small machine from his pocket and placed it on the desk. He pondered what fun it would be to replay their conversation and hear her voice that he had decided was quite enchanting. It was the perfect complement to her overall gracefulness. He was astonished that he was so captivated by Janeen Carson when he had only met her today. He had his share of dates and women who would like to share his home and his bed. He liked some of them a lot, but none had the same immediate attraction that this lovely woman had. He wanted to ask her about herself and tell her about his life but instead he started the interview as he always did.

"This is March 3, Detective Wes Wesley speaking with Janeen Carson, the executive assistant to the president of Georgia Tech, in the office of Dr. Jungstone. Now we're ready," he adjusted the location of the recorder to better catch Janeen's voice and added, "Where were you on the night of March 2?"

"I was here in the office until about 7:30, because Dr. Lindholm had a trustee nominating committee meeting. I usually stay around until they get started so I can get coffee and to be sure no one needs anything else for the meeting. When I left, I stopped at the grocery store on my way home and got there before 8:30. I live only about a mile from campus but had to go out of my way to go to the store. I made something to eat and had my dinner in front of the television watching the news. Other than returning a couple telephone calls, that's all I did before I got ready for bed. Sounds dull, doesn't it?"

"Actually," Wes laughed, "It sounds wonderful. My news often comes from the police radio. Not quite CNN," he paused and then added, "Is it normal to have after hour meetings in the office?"

"Well, it's not an everyday occurrence, but it isn't unusual. Some are planned and others just happen when they happen. You know what I mean?"

"Sure, I understand. Now what about staff working in the evening? How about the president? Does he work after regular office hours?" Wes asked the questions in series, because they all related and could be answered together.

"Oh, yes, all of us work at night from time to time, Dr. Lindholm probably more than any of us. He's the model for today's workaholic. Type A, no maybe a double A. I'm sure Mrs. Lindholm wishes that he didn't have to work so much," Janeen added even though he had not asked for her opinion on anything. She thought: Just the facts. Like in the old Dragnet television series: Just the facts, ma'am.

"That reminds me, would you give me the names, telephone numbers and addresses of the trustees and the staff in this building? On the trustee list, please mark who was here. We'll be talking to many of the staff and the trustees as we proceed with our investigation."

"Of course. When we go back upstairs, I'll make copies for you. However I can help you find Andy's killer, you just ask. Don't worry about my other work, I can always find time to do things that are important. Georgia Tech is practically my home. I've worked in the president's office for about 20 years," Janeen said wistfully and then quickly added, "I guess I'm getting off the track. Sorry. What other questions do you have?"

"OK. Tell me something about Andy and his relationship to the office? Is it unusual for him to be here at night?"

"No, Andy would come in early or late, depending on his studies. It *was* unusual for him to be in Dr. Lindholm's office. That was really strange. He could pick up his assignments or use my computer and never even get close to the other office. I haven't been able to figure out why he was there."

Janeen had thought about that a lot today. She wondered if Andy had learned something from the computer files that intrigued or bothered him. She knew more about some of the deals happening from this office than Jonathan Lindholm would suspect, and she knew that he often conducted some of that business by E-mail. This could be interesting information, but there was no reason for Andy to know this, and that was the only reason she could think of for Andy to be in the president's computer file. Obviously, he had figured out the password, because when she found the body, she noted that he had been looking at a document that was addressed to Hong Kong. She didn't touch anything, but later when she was talking to George Fancer, who was standing near the president's desk, she noticed that the screen was filled with the new curriculum schedule.

"Janeen, what're you thinking about? Have you remembered something important?"

"Nothing particularly important, Detective. I was remembering that the document on the computer had been changed from when I arrived to later when George Fancer and I were talking. I imagine that Dr. Lindholm had been looking for something to respond to a faculty member or one of the administrators."

"What was on the screen when you saw it in the morning?" Wes leaned toward her. She saw his jaw tighten.

"It was a memo to one of the alumni in Hong Kong. We have people all over the world, but since Dr. Lindholm has been here, he's gotten to know most of the alumni there. I think it's because he likes to travel to the Far East," she said and then added, "Of course, that's my opinion. No one has ever said that."

"Sounds like a great way to do the job. I guess it's something like me getting to know all the sleazeballs who are 'alumni' of the Atlanta jail," Wes threw out as he laughed.

"Not quite the same, Detective, but you get the picture, I'm sure. It's a part of the president's job to build strong, productive relationships with our alumni. Especially now during a big capital campaign."

"How big, Janeen?"

"The goal is $750,000,000. We already have pledges for half of that. The reason that the Hong Kong alumni are so important is that almost half of the $370 million raised has been from them. It's no secret that there is lots of money being made there."

"Right. Just ask the politicians in Washington. They've been tapping that well for years. It's surprising that you have that many alumni in Hong Kong. Half of $370 million is a big chunk of change. I guess I don't know a lot about the people who come to Tech. Like Andy Dren. What do you know about him as a student, his friends, family, and even a girlfriend or two?"

"Actually, we don't have a lot of alumni in Hong Kong. Maybe 20 or so, but they must be big time wealthy. They've begun to support the institution tremendously in the past year. It's a big surprise to me. I get the impression that Hong Kong is the pot of gold at the end of the rainbow. At least Georgia Tech's rainbow," Janeen commented before talking about Andy, "You may have already heard the same information about Andy that I know. Just tell me if I'm repeating what you already have."

She did repeat some of the facts that Wes already had but she got into more detail than he'd already heard today. Obviously, Janeen Carson was accustomed to being observant and a good listener.

"Andy was recommended by Earl Prince who's on the nominating committee that met here last night. Mr. Prince had met him through the work he did during the Olympics and was very impressed with him, his work and his character. Andy was close to his family. I'd met both his father and his sister around Christmas when they came to go shopping with Andy. There's no doubt in my mind, Detective, that Andy came from a fine family. They are devastated. They called earlier and said they would come here later this afternoon. They want to see the president.

"As far as friends are concerned, from my observation, Andy spent more time working than he did making friends or partying but he was close to his roommates. Andy didn't talk about any girl in particular and I never got the impression that he did much dating. I think most of his money was going toward his education and daily living expenses. He was really smart when it came to numbers and budgets. One time he and I were looking over the documents that he was going to input, he just glanced at the figures and immediately said, ' These are wrong. Someone didn't check the math,' and he was absolutely right. We redid the entries and found that they were off by a few thousand dollars."

Janeen Carson wiped her hand across her eyes before adding in a tight voice, "I really liked him. I can't understand how anyone would, uh, kill him."

Wes felt that Janeen was going to lose her carefully-held-in control, so he changed the subject away from Andy, "When you get me the information about the staff and Foundation members, would you add the names and telephone numbers for Andy's roommates?"

"Of course. I'll help you anyway I can."

"Would you review your arrival this morning? Just start at the beginning and take your time. Mention anything that comes into your mind. Let me decide what's important."

"I got here a little after seven and parked on the road just below this building. There were a couple of cars already parked but mostly the area was empty."

"Did you recognize any of the cars, and did you notice whether they were there when you left the night before?"

"Yes, the one car was Dr. Jungstone's. That's whose office we're in. I didn't see him, of course, because I went directly to my own office. The other one I must not have paid much attention to, because I'm not even sure what make it was. I parked next to Nils Jungstone's car, which is why I noticed it. I wouldn't have known whether they were there when I left, because when I'm going to be at the office after dark, I move my car up to the parking area in front of the building."

"That would be the parking area where it appears the shot came from, right?" Wes didn't wait for a response, "Did you notice any cars there when you left?"

"Oh, yes. Most of the places were taken. I'm not sure what cars all the trustees drive; but I recognized Earl Prince's. It's a Mercedes. Burl Mentor's is a Jaguar, and Dr. Lindholm's, a Lincoln. Oh, yes, Dr. Lindholm's sports car was there too. He had some work done on it, and it was returned yesterday afternoon. I assume that Mr. Johnson's and Mr. Adkins' cars were in the same area, because it's the closest to the building but I don't recollect seeing them. Since he always walks to meetings here, Charles Black's car would have been parked in the Billy Williams Building. There may have been someone else parked there, but I really don't remember."

"OK. That's good. If the president had two cars in the evening, which one was still there in the morning?"

"What a good question. I'm so used to his cars that I completely forgot about his Lincoln being in his # 1 parking spot. So he went home in his convertible, " Janeen added, feeling that she had somehow failed her test.

"Janeen, this is exactly why I asked you to go over the whole story with me. Our memories sometimes need some help when we're asked to remember all the details, because that's not our normal way of getting through a day. Now, you parked the car and..."

"I walked up the hill and came to my office. Before you ask, Detective Wesley, yes, I had to unlock the door. It was locked just like any other morning that I arrived first."

Wes laughed and said brightly, "Hey, you're getting ahead of me. Now don't put me out of a job."

Janeen joined in his laughter and noted how easy it was to talk to this man. He had a certain charm that she had never associated with her impression of a rough, tough police detective. Maybe she'd been seeing too many movies lately. She wondered what there was about Wes Wesley's life that he seemed so out of character and wished she had more time to have him answer her questions instead of being the one providing the answers.

There was a moment or two of silence. Both were searching. Back, back. Then Janeen continued, "I hung up my coat, went to my desk, put away my purse and switched on my computer. That's the way I begin every day... unless I don't wear a coat. I went right into Dr. Lindholm's office to pick up cups, throw away napkins, get rid of any mess that was still there from last night. He wouldn't like to come in and not have everything in good shape. I noticed that his computer and monitor were on. He normally turns off the monitor but not the computer. Although I didn't remember them being on during the meeting, I assumed I was wrong and that he had been in a hurry and forgot his regular procedure.

"If you're wondering why I had time to think about all of these trivial things, it was because the desk chair was turned with its back to the door. I had to come much farther into the room before I saw, I saw, uh... Andy's body. He was slumped over the computer, a hand still on the keyboard, like he had just gotten tired and fallen asleep," Janeen stopped and struggled to keep from crying. She would never forget that moment or that scene.

"Detective, at that point, I didn't even know who it was. My first thought was that it was the president. I think I screamed.

I'm not really sure. My next thought was that maybe he, still thinking it was Dr. Lindholm, was alive. I don't know how I did it, but I went over to the body and put my hand on the wrist, hoping to find a pulse. Even though.... oh, it was awful," Janeen squeezed her eyes closed and covered her face with her hands."It was awful. Awful. There was blood and other stuff everywhere. There was a very dark spot near his ear. At that moment is when I saw it was Andy. I turned and ran out of the office, called Chief Fancer and then Dr. Lindholm. All of that, I realized later, took only a few minutes, but I felt like I'd been looking at all of that gore for hours. How do you do this everyday? How can you ever forget what you see?"

"Ms. Carson, you've done just fine. I know how difficult this is when you know the victim. That's the difference in my position and yours. I usually don't know the people who've been killed. I guarantee you that when it's someone I know, like another police officer I have worked with, I'm as emotional as you are. Let's go get those lists and I'm out of here."

"I've been so upset. I just haven't been thinking. It just occurred to me, Detective Wesley, that I should have called 911."

"Maybe you should take off the rest of this afternoon. Get away from this office," Wes said, wanting to take her hand, put his arms around her and comfort her in some way. She was so vulnerable and yet she had a strength that must have come from other sadness in her life. She is young to be a widow. Obviously had faced another untimely death. He decided then that he was going to try to get to know this woman better.

Chapter 16

Charles William Black

Since he left the president's office, Charles had been running around like the wild cheetah. The image was not chasing a sleek antelope but rather chasing his own tail in frustration.

The frustration had begun when he had left Jon and his son, Lindy and his first stop had been at Janeen's desk. As he waited for her to answer a call, he had random thoughts about the president and his executive assistant. He knew that she was wired into the best network on the campus. Her 20 years of service, building relationships, and collecting information probably qualified her to be president. Jon Lindholm would be lost if she didn't provide background and documentation on people with whom he dealt.

"Janeen, are you doing alright? I've been so concerned about you ever since I learned that you were the first one here this morning. If it would help to talk to someone, just let me know. I'll drop whatever I'm doing … maybe we could have coffee together later," Charles smiled his brilliant for-the-camera smile. He knew how much women liked to receive the impression that they had a support system all ready to help solve their problems.

Janeen looked at his fake smile and thought what a colossal phony he was. Did he really think that she couldn't see through his act?"Thank you, Charles. It's thoughtful of you to offer, but I'm doing fine. I'm devastated about what happened to Andy, but other than that, I can handle the day. I'll have to talk later to Detective Wesley and that will be enough talking for me."

Charles was disappointed but not surprised at Janeen's

response. Of course he wouldn't share the information either if he had it. He'd get what he needed from someone else. He didn't know whom yet, but there are people out on campus who know what he wants to know.

"Well, you just give me a call, if you change your mind. I'm available," Charles said seriously as if her welfare was truly a concern to him. He turned and left the building, heading for George Fancer's office. The Chief was his second best chance to get some information in a hurry.

Black parked his car close to the Georgia Tech police station in a No Parking zone, locked the doors, and strode briskly into the building. He looked for George Fancer and saw him talking with a man in a navy blue sports jacket that looked like it had seen too many seasons of wear. Attached with a heavy-duty clip to his yellow and blue tie was a shiny gold shield of the Atlanta police. Black would rather speak to him than the campus chief. Fancer was available to him anytime.

"Hi, George, I see you're right on the job," he said walking directly toward the two men. He turned toward the sports jacket, offered his hand and said, "I'm Charles Black, Vice President of Advancement. I've just come from speaking with President Lindholm. He wants all information to come through me."

"Hey, Mr. Black, I'm Detective Billy Joe LaCrosse, Homicide. Good to meetcha. If you'll just wait over there a few minutes, I'll be right with you. The chief and me were just about done with our conversation."

"I really don't have time to wait. George, you understand my problem. If I could talk to Detective LaCrosse now, then he could finish up with you after I'm on my way."

Fancer looked at LaCrosse. His shrug spoke: Let's humor the son of a bitch and get rid of him ASAP."No problem, Detective. I'll begin getting some of the things you wanted. We can talk again before you leave."

The chief smiled at Billy Joe, neglected to deliver the same courtesy to Charles and walked away. Black had always made him feel he was there simply to serve him. He sometimes wondered if Charles Black treated him with disdain because he knew Fancer had a file on him.

• • •

He was reminded of the time that Black had left an alumni meeting after a few too many drinks (white wine, he was sure, for this pretty boy!), got into his car and backed into a student's car. He threw the transmission into drive and was headed for the parking lot exit when two students jumped out of the car he had slammed and took chase. Black was moving fast enough that the students could not stop him, but they did get his license number.

The students went back to their car and drove to the Tech police station and made a report. Fancer had checked out the damage and whistled, "Wow. How fast was he going? He must have really gunned it when he was in reverse."

After checking the license registration, George decided the best way to handle it was to drive out to his home, talk to him face to face. He knew it would not be a pleasant meeting. He was right. Not only was Black belligerent, he first lied about the incident and then told him that he knew the trustees would cover the expense. That was exactly how the situation was settled and kept quiet.

• • •

As the chief walked away, Billy Joe said, "We can talk right here. I don't think we have to put anyone out of his office. I saw you earlier when you came into the president's office. If I had known your role then, I would've made a point to talk to you."

"That's OK, Detective. I wouldn't have had time then anyway. The president was waiting for me. But, now, why don't you tell me what you've learned?" He would finish this interview and get on to other people.

"Detective Wesley's the detective in charge. He's already talked with the medical examiner as well as the coroner who is takin' a particular interest in this case because it's a student at Tech. APD and the Tech police are interviewin' a variety of people to begin to put together the facts that could identify the killer."

"Well, don't expect much from Fancer and his gang.

They're like boys playing cops and robbers."

Billy Joe wasn't sure whether Black was trying to ingratiate himself to him or if he simply wanted to take a swipe at Fancer.

"Mr. Black, I've only heard positive reports about your police. We're glad to have them on our team," LaCrosse said stiffly in defense of Fancer and his staff. He was surprised that a vice president would purposely create a negative image of members of the campus staff.

"That's wonderful to hear, LaCrosse. I hope you're not disappointed. If you have nothin' else to tell me, I'll get on to the next people I must see this mornin'," Hereafter, he would deal directly with Detective Wesley. This man obviously was the second string.

"We'll be seein' more of each other, I'm sure. I think it's important that you know much of what we know so you can keep the media happy."

"Detective, I believe I should know *everything* you learn. Not just, as you say, much of what you know."

"We don't spill our guts, sir, because our job's to find a murderer, not feed egos or satisfy the public. This's become friggin' impossible in our current open-information environment, but we do what we know is right even if it ticks off other people."

"Very reluctantly, I'll accept that philosophy, but don't forget that I'm to be your primary contact here on campus. What information you can share should be shared with me." Charles sounded like he was reading a proclamation.

"Fair enough. Stay tuned for the next announcement. See ya' around," Billy Joe responded as he backed up. He intended to find George Fancer to continue their earlier conversation.

Chapter 17

Oliver Andrew Dren

Frank Bostwick opened the door to the apartment, acutely aware of the silence inside. It was the same place that he'd lived for six months, but it felt different today. He wished that Peter had already returned from class. He didn't want to be in Andy's space alone.

He felt hot tears in his eyes and looked up at the ceiling to prevent them from trailing down his cheeks. That usually worked when he wanted to be macho. Not show his emotion. He raised his arm and wiped away the glistening tracks with the sleeve of his jacket. "Until now, I really *did* think I was going to live forever. I never was close to anyone before who died. Murder just happened to bad people. But, Andy was a good guy. He should still be here sitting at his computer doing his thing. Why? Why?"

Frank went into the bathroom and splashed water on his face. He looked into the mirror and was surprised that he looked exactly the same as he did yesterday. Now he knew what it was like to feel real grief, helplessness. He wanted to find the killer. Then he wanted him to be executed. Why did he say *he*? Why not *she*?

Frank looked into the mirror again. Cold eyes stared back at him. He was astonished that he had thought about an unknown person dying in the electric chair. He abhorred capital punishment. Now he'd like to be on the jury. He'd vote to fry the bastard.

Then, his thoughts also flicked to another subject —- the Andrew Dren 'memorial.'

Frank turned and stared at the computer on one of Tech's regulation desks. It had been installed in time for the Olympic athletes to use. He noticed the pile of disks, a half filled cup that had the Microsoft logo on it, an old desk lamp, and a small, furry, gray, toy mouse. It wore a necklace that said Take me home. I need a pad. Andy and his life were everywhere in this apartment. Frank wondered if there was a clue to his murder here. Could he help find the killer?

He felt frustrated because he had no answers, but he could still create the memorial that he hoped would become part of the Institute's history. He'd do it because it would make him feel close to the Andy who had shared the apartment; not the Andy who no longer existed. In fact, as he looked at Andy's desk, he decided that he might get an idea of what to do from some of the computer games they had all played together.

Frank slid into Andy's chair. Dren had his own work to do to get his degree, but he spent hours at a time inputting information for the administration and writing new software when it would improve what was already available. He had most of his disks separated in piles and in different colored boxes by topic: administration, Tech classes by number, personal documents, games, etc. Frank had never paid much attention to the system because he was usually busy enough trying to keep his own programs and schedule under control.

He lightly touched the green, blue, yellow and red boxes and thought about how Andy had reached for them in exactly the same way. The difference was that Andy knew what was in each one. He hardly needed to look at them when he was ready to change from one disk to another. Today Frank didn't even know what he was seeking. He looked at the boxes again and said out loud, "Here's the history of Oliver Andrew Dren. His experiences, his work, his talents, and maybe his dreams. Dreams that'll never become reality. On these disks, he's still alive. The disks are here for a purpose."

He and Andy had exchanged each other's computer passwords, so if one of them wasn't there and needed some information, he could get it by calling back to the apartment. It had been a good plan, because both of them had had to ask for help several times. Once Frank had told Andy that looking up something for him was like having old textbooks in high school. He learned concepts and understood programs that he never had figured out for himself. As he reached for the first disk, he wondered what he'd learn without Andy being available for direction.

Frank arranged the boxes in the order that he wanted to peruse the material: games, personal documents, administration and classes. He went through more than 15 games, before he began to get bored. He wasn't getting any ideas to use for the memorial. They were fun and Andy had been an expert opponent for the computer, but today they seemed shallow, without merit.

The personal documents file was a mega-mix of subjects. Andy must have saved every thought he ever had. Did he review and use the information in his daily routine, or was it his daily journal to be savored years after it was written? The first disk Frank chose reminded him of his own sister. She kept a diary, named 'Zelda.'

Here was Andy's disk titled 'Worth Remembering.' Things that just seemed to catch his attention. Quotes of friends and even some from quotable professors. Frank found a statement that he obviously had made to Andy. He didn't even remember the context of their conversation. "Everyone talks about 'dissing' (disrespecting) others. Why don't they talk about 'ressing' (respecting) others?"

He went through many other notations, quotes and reminders for a few birthdays. Frank was surprised again to find another of his own statements. This one he had made after returning from a week of leadership training. He remembered this one, because he had been so 'high' from the experience that had taken place at the Rock Eagle State Park over the winter break. It said: Frank said that he was surprised how honest all the students were during the retreat. He used as an example a statement that was made by a student introducing a skit about how to improve leadership at all levels on campus, "I would describe Tech in three words- Apathy, Arrogance and Indifference. The apathy of the students, the arrogance of the faculty and the indifference of the administration." Andy had added: (Note) I wish

I could discuss this observation with Dr. Lindholm. He should know that the students feel the indifference and arrogance that begin AT THE TOP! Maybe I'll do this sometime when no one else is there. Frank wondered if that conversation ever took place.

He was ready to look at another disk when the telephone rang. He turned around in his chair and straddled the back as he picked up the receiver and said, "Yoh."

"Frank, this is Oliver Dren. Susan and I would like to come over after we leave the president's office. Are you going to be there?" Andy's father's voice sounded dry and lifeless. Frank could feel the hot tears again behind his eyelids. He didn't know what to say. What were the proper words for a father who had just lost his son?

"Mr. Dren, I'll be here whenever you want to come. I'll do whatever you want me to do. I can't think of the right things to say that you'll know how awful I feel."

"Let's not talk about it now, Frank. We should be there by 4:30. We'll see you then. Thank you for being Andy's and our friend," Oliver Dren said quickly and hung up like he couldn't say another word.

Chapter 18

Jackson Burl Mentor

Burl went directly from meeting with Lindholm to his own office, where he knew some of the foundation trustees would be waiting for him. They had all been in touch by telephone earlier, voted for Mentor to meet with the president and then they would gather to discuss their own personal concerns about the murder before reporting back to the entire board. Their main objective wasn't finding the murderer, that was the job of the police, but to be sure the Foundation and Georgia Tech were not harmed in any way.

Burl parked his Jaguar in his reserved spot closest to the side door of his office building in the Midtown Technology Park that had been developed on an old railroad and foundry site. Because of its proximity to the center of the city, it was prime property. In the late 1800s and early 1900s, Atlanta had been a hub for the railroad industry. It was an ideal center for transporting steel, produce and people to a variety of Southern cities. The automobile frenzy hadn't yet taken over the city creating a whole new Atlanta that followed the ever-expanding highway system.

Mentor and several other Foundation trustees had been the first investors in the development of MidTech Park, as the business/technology complex was now called. The property, bordering the campus on the North, had been the topic of many discussions of how its land value was escalating and adding future wealth for each of them. None of the trustees had built expensive buildings. They knew the profit would be made in reselling the property, not in these Atlanta *disposable* structures. Because of the clout that they had in the city as Georgia Tech Foundation board members, they'd made millions of dollars for the inner circle players.

Mentor noticed Eddie Lee Johnson's Mercedes parked next to Noble Adkins' Cadillac. Farther down the parking lot, parked diagonally over the white divider stripe to protect it from another car door chipping the paint, was Austin Cruise's new Lexus. It annoyed Burl that Cruise always took up two spaces and he often thought someday he'd park close enough for his car door to reach the Lexus. Today was not the day. There were important actions to be discussed.

The three men were sitting at Mentor's large, highly polished, cherry conference table that could seat 16 comfortably. The table had two matching credenzas that were along one wall. It faced a window wall that provided a spectacular view of the skylines of midtown and downtown Atlanta. At night it was especially alluring because of the special lighting that was installed to bring attention to the fancy tops on the newer buildings. It seemed to have become a competition with Atlanta building owners to have the highest and the most unusual pinnacle. However the trend began, it was there to the benefit of those who were located in MidTech.

"Good afternoon, gentlemen," Jackson Burl Mentor greeted his colleagues as he entered the room. He noticed each one had either a glass or cup in front of him, "I see you have been well cared for by Bettianne."

"Yes, Burl. You're the perfect host, even when you're not here. Some day I may try to steal away your wonderful secretary," said Eddie Lee Johnson, continuing a long standing jousting with his friend. He would no sooner steal Burl's secretary than he would try to take his wife. Some things a real friend just did not do. There were rules they followed about hands off employees, family or mistresses that didn't hold fast for business deals. They all knew when it came to making money, rules were bent, ignored or changed on the spot. They laughed that it was best to do business with your back to the wall.

"Bettianne did the job, but we really have been more interested in hearing what you know about the unfortunate event on campus. We're ready to give you center stage." You could always count on Austin Cruise to keep them on track. He liked to do his business and get on his way.

"Well, I don't know a lot more than before I went. Lindholm seems to be in the dark and is a very nervous man. He can see that he's expendable if this incident reflects poorly on *our* school. A president is easy to find, and he knows it. He knows it.

"The police are everywhere. The Homicide detective in charge is Wes Wesley. He..." Burl was interrupted by a laugh from Eddie Lee.

"Wes Wesley? Like the street? Who would name their boy after a street?"

"It might sound strange, but that's the man's name. And, he appears to be intelligent and experienced. He's not what I thought an Atlanta policeman would be like up close and personal, as they say on TV. As they say on TV. One could say he had a certain Southern polish, but we don't want to underestimate this detective's expertise. Of course, we've no reason at this time to think that the murder will in any way slop over onto our reputation or concerns," Burl continued after they all had their little laugh.

"That may be so, Burl, but we must be prepared to face that possibility. That's why we're here now. If we're going to be questioned, or even suspected of complicity, we must make our stories match," Austin Cruise said gravely.

"You're absolutely right," Eddie Lee agreed, "We should be ready."

"Of course, we'll be ready, but I really don't think that the police will get into the Foundation's operations," Noble Adkins added.

Noble was the most senior of the Georgia Tech Foundation trustees in both age and tenure. He'd be retiring as an active member this year as he turned 70. He'd been asked to be a trustee when he was just 40 years old after he'd become an instant mega-millionaire when oil was discovered on his Texas ranch.

"I agree, Noble. What we're doing now is just playing it safe. The biggest question for us to ruminate is: What did this

Andy Dren know that he was at the president's computer? Yes, at the president's computer," Mentor threw out as their major assignment.

Although the thought had crossed the minds of the four men, having it thrown out for discussion had a sobering effect on the group. None of them had paid any attention to the student who was helping get carefully selected Foundation financial records up to date and fitting into the context of the capital campaign. As an example, the Hong Kong monies were being brought into the not-for-profit structure as alumni gifts. They made the campaign look tremendously successful but they were more like a business deal. All of the staff and volunteers were so proud of their efforts to meet the record-breaking goal of the endeavor. It was good that they didn't know that Tech kept only a percentage of the funds to act as the conduit to get the dollars into the United States for Chinese ventures.

"Maybe we should find out more about this Dren person from Earl Prince. He's the one who recommended him to Lindholm," said Eddie Lee Johnson.

"That might be helpful, but I think we want to be sure we have our cover story well-rehearsed before any of us are questioned by the police. We don't want to be surprised and we don't want to contradict each other," Noble pointed out the obvious.

"We just stay with the same explanation that we've used with everyone else. Why would the campaign come up? How can it relate to this unfortunate shooting?" Austin Cruise asked the group.

"I believe you're thinking in the right direction, Austin, but we must be prepared for the worst," Mentor replied. "If this student discovered something or made a wild guess, he may have been looking for confirmation of his suspicions. Or maybe he may have told someone. And, then, why was he shot? Could Lindholm have done it to protect himself? He does have a lot to lose. A lot to lose."

"Burl! Surely you're joking. Jon couldn't have shot that young man. I find it hard to believe that such a thought would even enter your head," Eddie Lee exclaimed.

"Well, it happened in *his* office. The boy was at *his* computer. Jon knew more about him than any of us. He can be the big loser if our Foundation financial gyrations become known. Who would've known that Dren was there? Lots of possibilities to say the least. To say the least," Mentor said looking at each of the men as he made his points.

"It's true that there might be some reasons for suspicion, but it doesn't fit Jon's character. No, the murderer doesn't relate to the president or us. That's my opinion," Eddie Lee countered.

"You're probably right, Eddie Lee, that Jon didn't do it, but the reason is not because he has great character. Definitely not that," Burl retorted. Sometimes he was tempted to tell his friends about Lindholm's past, but this wasn't one of those times. They needed to get their act together and this information would start a whole new conversation.

"There are times, Burl, when I think you're not pleased with our president," Austin Cruise said.

"Oh, no, Austin, I think we have the right president for us. We have the right president. You know how well he's taken to the Hong Kong deal. But, I don't think that indicates that he has great character," Burl Mentor responded, "Now, let's get on with our problem of how we cover ourselves with the police, if it's necessary."

"OK. We're already using the capital campaign as our cover to help bring easy dollars to Tech. We have the names of the 'donors' and Jon has created a track record that looks like he's met all of them, gotten to know them and encouraged them to become 'major givers' to their alma mater. We know he has initiated some special programs on the campus to make it look like the Hong Kong alumni have a reason to be giving. That seems good to me," Austin carefully laid out the steps that were already in place.

"Austin, you need to tell us more about how the money is being used by Tech. How the cover works. Even faculty or other alumni might question what happens to millions of dollars," Noble suggested.

Both Burl and Austin looked at each other as if to say: his

memory isn't as good as it used to be. They had talked at length about the token use of a small percentage of these funds from time to time. Now they were going to do it again. But, that's why they were meeting: to be sure all of them were in sync. They just hoped that Noble wouldn't forget the drill if the detective in charge interviewed him. They could plan better if they knew why Andrew Dren was in the president's office.

Although Noble Adkins had addressed his words to Austin, it was Burl Mentor who responded, "Remember, Noble, we had Jon set up those projects that he named Presidential Programs. We wanted a name as broad as possible so we can slip almost anything into it without questions from faculty or alumni. Currently, all the programs in the series relate to Asian studies. That can also be construed to mean China studies. In fact the one I like is the one Jon titled The Middle Kingdom. Since that is what China has called itself for centuries, he's able to throw in any topic that relates to the Chinese. The Hong Kong "donors" love it. They get to launder their money for their own enterprises, back the US politics that suits them and still see courses at Tech that are targeted for their Asian scholars. It's worked like a charm." Burl explained quite slowly and louder than normal as if Noble had a learning disability.

"You don't have to talk to me like I'm deaf or retarded, Burl. I don't spend as much time devising these plans as you do. It's not a crime to ask to be reminded of a part of this whole intricate arrangement," Noble said indignantly.

"I'm sorry if I sounded like that, Noble. You're quite right to ask about something that you may not understand. We must protect this windfall for Tech. We surely don't want to damage our Hong Kong money machine. Yes, our wonderful Hong Kong money machine," Mentor said directly to Noble, ending his apology with a friendly smile while the other men held their breath, hoping that this altercation wasn't going to set off sparks that could ignite a large fire.

It seemed that Burl often could be short with Noble, because he felt the older man was over the hill. He also felt that Noble had just fallen into his position with the Foundation because of his father's lucky ranch purchase. In Burl's opinion, Adkins wasn't very sophisticated about business and certainly wasn't up to the complexities that it took to operate in the international financial world. Unfortunately, it was too late to drop him from their plans. He'd been a trustee many years before the others in the room and was part of the original dealings that started with buying, selling and trading real estate.

"Well, gentlemen," Austin began as he stood up and took a few steps away from the table, "Is there anything else we need to review at this time? I have an important meeting in half an hour and will just about make it on time. My feelings are still that we have nothing to worry about. This murder could have been a grudge between two students or just the usual, Atlanta drive-by shooting. Let's face it. The city has grown around and beyond Georgia Tech. Some questionable areas now border the campus. We may love the place, but it's not a problem-free Disney World. It's sad that a student was killed, but it's not a surprise."

"Thank ya'll for coming," Burl said in his best Southern host style, "We'll keep in touch as we learn more. If anything seems strange, I'm available to talk or meet. I expect y'all feel the same."

"We'll, do it, Burl, absolutely." Eddie Lee added as he pushed his chair back and stood next to Austin. "Unless there are other comments or questions, I'll follow Austin's lead and be on my way, too." Without further discussion, it was understood that the meeting was adjourned.

Chapter 19

Danielle Jarvis Swain

"This is Danielle Swain on the campus of Georgia Institute of Technology. I'm standing in front of the Tech Tower, the symbol of the tradition and academic achievement of this fine institution. Just six months ago it became part of Olympic history when Tech was the home for athletes from more than 190 countries. Today it's become the scene of the murder of one of its students.

"Oliver Andrew Dren, Jr., a graduate student in the College of Computing, was found early this morning shot to death in the president's office. Ms. Janeen Carson, executive secretary to Dr. Jonathan Lindholm, discovered the tragedy and immediately called Chief George Fancer, Tech's head of security, and President Lindholm. Atlanta Homicide squad was notified by Chief Fancer.........." Danielle was taping her opening statement for the evening news.

Dani knew this was going to be a hot story in Atlanta. Depending on motive, perpetrator and personality of the deceased; this could be a story that was picked up by many other news services.

When she was gathering background for the story, she considered how the public is always interested in events that seem personal to them. Many feel that way about education, because they can say: that could have happened to me or my child or my friend when we were going to college. Also she didn't lose the fact that this could be picked up by other news teams, because it will intrigue everyone who felt related to the Olympics. The public and media were waiting for something like this to happen in the Village during the Games. Now it happens a few months later.

Dani finished the taping and decided to walk across the campus to get the reaction of the students and faculty about the shooting. She asked one of the camera crew to go with her.

Dani left the administrative area of Tech known as The Hill and walked toward the library. Traditional, red brick buildings that had been used constantly since the opening of the institution more than 115 years ago surrounded her. Dani loved the atmosphere of academia. The thick ivy covering the buildings. The ground slashed in several directions by irregular paths. The people all about were the only signs here that reminded her that this really was the beginning of another millenium.

As the campus opened up to less green space and more modern buildings, she passed several groups of students who were obviously rushing to make their next class or to go back to their dorms. She approached a young man and woman who were sitting on a bench along the walkway enjoying the early, wan, spring sunshine. She recalled the lateness of spring's arrival in Cleveland and said a little thank you to her special guardian angel that sent her South.

"Hi. I'm Danielle Swain with Channel 22. This is Loretta Regan, one of our camera crew. Do you have time for a short interview, which we may use on the news?"

"I guess you want to ask us about the murder," the young woman on the bench responded quickly.

"Yes. How do you feel about this happening here on your campus."

"It's unbelievable. Totally incredible. Who's going to be next? Everyone I've talked to today is afraid it's just the first shooting." The young man nodded his head in agreement. He then added, "I'm in the College of Computing, too. I probably saw Andy in the laboratories."

"Oh, did you know him?" Dani asked, her interest piqued.

"No, but I *could have* seen him during any day. I think I remember him."

It always intrigued Dani that whoever she interviewed about an incident could make a personal connection—-even when there was none.

"What's the attitude on campus since the announcement of the murder?" Dani asked the young woman.

"Mostly disbelief and some distrust. It's hard to even imagine that there's this horrible person possibly right here. Some students have moved off campus or have actually gone home."

"Thank you for talking to me. All I need now are your names and for you to sign these releases that we can use your statements on Channel 22." Dani took out two forms for their signatures.

Dani and Loretta were walking away from the bench where the students remained seated, talking excitedly to each other. Most people were more than willing to appear on television.

Danielle Swain was an intense observer whether she was on an assignment or if she was simply living her own life. She knew she had a real nose for news. She felt that she probably was never off the job because she couldn't turn off her inquiring mind, couldn't stop sniffing. She knew she had chosen the perfect career for herself.

"Loretta, let's try to talk to that young man who seems to be holding court over there in front of the fountain. This was a site that we used a lot during the Olympics. In fact the fountain was built right before Tech became the Village," Dani added as they approached the plaza area. Several students were taking advantage of the soft, balmy, spring day. There were a few with books open, but it was easy to see that most of the young men and women didn't have studying on their minds.

Dani and Loretta joined the group of students that surrounded the young man. Some were asking questions. He was responding with ease. He'd be good on camera. Might he be running for a campus office?

"Lindy, what does your dad say about why Andy was in his office? Did he break in to steal something?" a boy called out.

Before Lindy could answer, another student called out, "Is it true that the police say that Andy vandalized the office before he was shot?"

"Slow down. I'll tell you what little I know, but I don't want to add to the rumors. That won't help anyone. First, there was nothing missing. Theft does not appear to be a motive. Second, there was no vandalizing of the office. I've been there.

It's a tragic shooting and nothing else. Maybe the shooter thought he was somebody else. The office window is broken so at this point it's assumed that the murderer was outside. But this is not a fact yet, just a theory! Andy was in the office probably doing some work. He had a part-time job doing programming and computer inputting for the president and the vice president. He didn't break in. He worked a lot with the president's secretary and had his own key. Everyone there knew Andy." Dani was surprised by Lindy's maturity.

"Loretta, let's get this on film. We can edit later. This kid's good. He must be the son of Tech's president," Dani whispered. Her nose had picked up the scent of news.

"I'm way ahead of you, Dani. We're already rolling."

"Lindy, where was he shot?"

"Some information just has to wait until the police are ready to tell us. We don't want to mess up their investigation. My dad's going to meet with the detective in charge today and then maybe they'll be willing to make a statement for the paper. As we keep all of you informed, we want to report only the facts. Rumors can not only be scary, but they can create more problems. The Technique staff has promised to print updates whenever we have them. That'll be a lot more reliable than just asking questions when right now none of us knows much."

Lindy looked at his watch and added, "I need to be going so watch for the Technique later today."

"Hi, I'm Danielle Swain from Channel 22. Could I speak with you for a few minutes before you leave? I have some questions and Loretta will get some footage for the program package. Without her work, we might as well be on the radio."

"I don't know much more than I just told the guys. What more do you want to ask?" Lindy responded.

"It appears that you have some good information. I got the idea that you've already talked to people who are close to this crime."

Lindy laughed before he said anything, "Today I've become

very popular because I interviewed the president and quoted him in our first story about the murder. Lots of the guys think I know more than anyone else. Well, I don't know about that, but I'm trying to pass on information as we learn it. If that helps you, Ms. Swain, I'm willing to tell you what I know."

"That's great. I guess we could start with who you are, in addition to being on the paper's staff, and what's happening here?"

"I'm sorry. It was such a surprise to see you in the group, I didn't even think about introducing myself. I'm Lindy Lindholm, a sophomore here in the College of Computing."

"Lindholm? Like the president?" Dani said, making her question appear to be one of complete surprise.

"He's the Third, I'm the Fourth. He's at the top of the institution. I'm at the bottom. We're definitely related, but we have our own lives. Often pointed in different directions," Lindy responded.

"That's the way we all should be. I can tell you, Lindy, when I was growing up, it was hard for me to just be me. My dad was the commanding officer of the base and everyone knew his daughter and every move I made. It's not always fun to be recognized. I understand your predicament." Dani told Lindy hoping that he would feel a kinship and comfortable with her. She knew that Loretta would cut this out for the news presentation.

"Wow! I guess it would be hard to be the commanding officer's kid. Maybe even worse than the prez's kid, because everyone's life depended on your dad. In my case, because lots of the students don't even know who Tech's president is, I'm not always the center of attention. And, my dad has only been the president for about a year and a half. Up until that time, he wasn't any different than other kids' father. He worked during the day and taught a class at night. He was never home."

"You sure are the center of attention today, Lindy. When we arrived, it looked like everyone wanted to hear from you."

"It's just that they know that I've talked with my dad and have actually been in the building where Andy was shot. They all want the inside story that I don't have. Even if I did, I think the police would be pissed off if I was out telling things they might want to keep quiet at this point. I knew Andy, and I want you to know, Ms. Swain, that this is a real tragedy. He was a good person, liked by everyone."

"I'm sorry that this has happened to a friend of yours. Did you know Andy Dren because he knew your dad?"

"No, we were both in the same college and often would use the laboratory at the same time. Andy was so smart. He could do anything that related to a computer. He was smarter than some of the professors, because he had real life experience as well as education and training. He was always willing to help the other students when they were having a hard time. I wonder what he was doing using my dad's computer, but I bet he was doing it better than my dad could do it himself," Lindy said feeling proud that he had known Andrew Dren.

"You mentioned a special edition of The Technique about the murder. Could I get a copy of it? I would like to use it for my newscast later today."

"Sure. I've a copy right here. It's no big deal. I'm sure you will think it's amateurish. You're the famous professional."

"I don't think it's going to be amateurish at all. I've a feeling that you know what you're doing and that you do it well. In fact, if you want to visit the studio sometime and see how we put our news together, just call me," Dani said as she handed Lindy her card. She wasn't sure that any engineer from Tech would be interested in Channel 22, but she was quite sure that Lindy Lindholm would be.

"Wow! I'd love to do that, Ms. Swain. That would be cool."

"OK. We make a deal. You're welcome to come spend time with us and you stop calling me Ms. Swain. My friends call me Dani. You make me feel like I'm old enough to be your mother

"It's a deal, Dani. I'll call you. And, it won't be long. I really want to see Channel 22 up close and personal....as some of the news people say."

Lindy couldn't believe this stroke of luck. He often heard people say: timing is everything. After today, he'll believe it. He now had a friend in the real news business. He thought maybe he could write a Technique feature on Dani Swain later and also get her to come and talk to the staff. He felt sure she would say yes to both. He couldn't wait till he told the guys and then tune into her program tonight. Maybe he should call his parents, too.

"Let's keep in touch," Dani said. Lindy smiled and waved as he turned away to go back to the newspaper office.

Chapter 20

Oliver Andrew Dren, Jr.

After Frank Bostwick hung up from his brief telephone call with Oliver Dren, he returned to his project to find a phrase or topic to use for his memorial for the younger Dren. He knew he'd never review all the files that were Andy's, but surely he'd find something usable soon.

He continued to peruse the 'personal documents' file because he felt that's where the special words would appear. He hoped he was right, or he may still be looking weeks from now. Andy seemed to have kept everything.

He read some documents that related to follow-up from Dren's Olympic work, noted a few names titled: Possible contacts for jobs after I get degree, reviewed a remembrance from his Microsoft days and found a calendar of days he would be 'available to work for Black and Lindholm.' Frank stopped there and saw that March 3 was on that list. Whatever he was going to do that day would never be known to anyone.

Frank glanced at the clock and was surprised to find that he'd been at the computer for more than an hour and he was still looking in the 'personal documents' file. He said to himself, "Andy, you were a real pack rat when it came to your computer files."

He clicked on to another screen and stopped to scan it. No title, but just a few letters and a question mark: HKIIICC? That was followed by short notes with more letters and some numbers. At first glance, it could be Greek or hieroglyphics, but he knew it was Andy's code that told him a lot in a very small space.

"No quotes here to use for our memorial, but I wonder what this all means? It's like figuring out what the messages are on vanity license plates," Frank said like he was addressing the computer, "Andy always said that his computer was his best friend. It seemed that they talked to each other."

He continued to surf through all of the files, reading quickly and not in detail. He was looking for some fun or provocative phrase. He knew that they would only get a short time on the electronic sign before someone questioned what it was. Then all hell would break loose, and hopefully they could just sit back and watch everyone try to figure out how this happened. If all went as planned, this'll get enough attention that it'll give the idea to others. Maybe start another Tech tradition.

He slowed down and looked at the screen with more interest. He had passed through the letter/number code and now the words seemed to be random thoughts:

Investigate computer pass through, who benefits, who knows, how was it done in Washington?

Frank stared at all of the cryptic messages and felt bewildered. There was no doubt in his mind that there was something here that was important, but what was it? Was there a message here for him? Would Andy want him to follow up on what he had begun? Shit, he didn't understand any of this. Maybe he would just make up his own tribute and give up on the computer.

Did Andy enter these words just for himself or did he file them in case something happened to him? Why would he have thought something might happen to him? This was just too strange. Is a clue to his death right here to be read? It's really scary to think that his roommate might have been murdered because of something he'd discovered through his computer. On one hand, the reference to computer pass through hints at such a possibility. On the other, his shooting may not have related to what was here on the screen.

Frank was so deep into his own thoughts and questions that he jumped when he heard a knock on the door. He looked at the screen, clicked back to another section and then turned off the monitor before he got up to see who was trying to get his attention. As he stepped toward the door, he wondered why he felt compelled to 'hide' the information he was reading.

"Hi, Frank. We're a bit late. I hope we didn't keep you from going to dinner." Oliver and Susan Dren came through the door that Frank had opened wide.

"Not at all, Mr. Dren. I told you that I'm here to do whatever I can for you. I didn't mind waiting at all."

"We just came from seeing the president and we stayed longer than we expected. He was quite cordial, but seems to be as perplexed as we are about why this has happened to Andy," Mr. Dren said after the door was closed, "It appears that the Atlanta police have a real mystery on their hands. It must have been some random shooting. All the times I've heard about Atlanta's drive-by shootings or about someone being at the wrong place at the wrong time, I never imagined that we could be involved. I believed good people just were somehow immune to such barbaric situations. I surely was naive."

Frank realized that Oliver Dren wasn't talking to him. He was talking to himself; trying to sort out the tragedy that had struck his family. Frank looked from Dren to Susan and noticed that her reddened eyes were filled with tears. She was so young to be losing her only brother. Frank knew that Susan and Andy had been close and that she often had called him to ask his advice or tell him about her day. Andy seemed to be her mentor and role model as well as her big brother.

"We can get Andy to take him back to Dalton tomorrow. We're planning the funeral for the day after tomorrow from the Baptist church. Frank, will you be a pallbearer and take care of asking others to join you? I think Andy would have liked for them to be students and faculty whom he knew and admired."

Frank nodded. Mr. Dren continued.

"The service will be at 10:30 AM, the internment following and then we want everyone to come to have lunch at our home. As sad as this is for Susan and me, we believe we should celebrate Andy's wonderful life. Having him in our lives for 30 years was a gift," Mr. Dren said quietly, but with much pride in his voice.

"I'm honored, Mr. Dren. Thank you for asking me to do

this. Of course, I'll begin with our other roommate, Peter. I'll talk to Andy's favorite professors, and we'll be ready. What else can I do to make it easier for you and Susan?"

"It doesn't have to be done now, but if you would help pack up Andy's things that are here in the apartment, I'd be grateful. Perhaps you and your roommate would give his clothes to one of the missions or even directly to some of the homeless. Is that asking too much with your class schedule and other activities?" Oliver Dren knew that the job he requested wasn't going to be easy for anyone who cared about his son, but right now it was unthinkable for him to touch those items that had been a part of his son's life.

"No, I can do that. It's no problem. It's a great idea to give Andy's things to the homeless. Do you know that we have homeless who're on this campus everyday? Andy knew some by name and would sit down and have a Coke with them now and then or give them a couple dollars."

"Yes, Andy had mentioned that he was interested in the people who had very little but liked to think of themselves as part of the campus. I hope the ones who he knew can use his clothing. That would please Susan and me." Mr. Dren obviously had not made his suggestion by chance. He knew of his son's compassion.

"Andy had all of us saving aluminum cans that he gave to a homeless guy named Walter. He and Walter often had long discussions about computers. A few months ago, I came home and Andy was showing Walter the basics of using a computer. He later said that Walter was quite smart and maybe would learn enough to someday get a better job than the one he had," Frank told Andy's family.

"I hope that can happen. It'd be a nice legacy for Andy if this Walter person was inspired by Andy's interest and vote of confidence."

"Daddy, we need to pick out some clothes for Andy to wear," Susan said very quietly trying not to cry again."If we're able to have the casket open, we want him to look handsome." She looked so forlorn and lost. Frank noticed her pretty, pale face was blotched from sobbing. Her dark blonde hair appeared to have lost its luster as did her hazel green eyes. The freshness that had always seemed to emanate from her sweet face was wilted and still.

"You're right, honey. Do you want to pick the outfit or do you want me to do it?" Mr. Dren asked almost as softly as Susan.

"I'd like to do it. Andy and I used to joke about what he wore and what looked good. You know how he wasn't all that concerned about his clothes."

"Oh, yes. I've heard that argument between the two of you often. He thought you wanted him to appear in GQ magazine and you thought he dressed more appropriately for Rolling Stone. If Frank will show you where to look, I'm sure you'll choose exactly the right things."

Frank walked to Andy's room with Susan following silently. He then returned to where Oliver Dren seemed to be deep in thought. Frank wasn't sure if he should say something or just wait until Andy's dad was ready to speak. He chose to wait. He knew that Oliver Dren had much to think about right now.

Breaking the silence, Dren asked, "Frank, do you have any kind of information for the police? Do you have any idea who might've done this or why?"

"I've tried to remember anything that could be helpful, Mr. Dren. I just don't have a clue. Andy had no enemies and never spoke unkindly about anyone. I haven't been asked yet to talk to the police, but when I am, I don't think I'll be helpful."

"Well, don't worry, Frank, but if an idea comes to you, be sure that you call Detective Wesley. He's the person in charge and will welcome whatever you might know. A murderer must not be left out there to hurt others."

They could hear Susan opening drawers and moving around in the bedroom. She soon appeared at the door with an armload of clothes, "I made a compromise, Daddy. I sorta went half way with what Andy usually wore and what I'd like to see him wear. We want his friends to remember him looking special."

Frank was tempted to tell them about his plan to create an Andy memorial but decided against it. He knew what he was planning to do was probably breaking the law, so he better not involve anyone else. Besides, he didn't want Mr. Dren to talk him out of it, which he'd certainly try to do.

"Thank you, Frank. I'll be talking to you tomorrow about the pallbearers, and then I'll see you the next day. Please, come to our home about 9:30 and we'll all go to the church together."

"We'll be there," Frank said. Then turning to Susan, he added, "That'll give Susan time to check out our clothes."

With a hint of a smile, Susan retorted, "You know I'm not going to do that, Frank, even though you do dress just about the same as my brother."

The Drens left immediately. Frank felt exhausted and sad. If he could feel so wasted, he couldn't imagine how badly Andy's family felt. He knew it was better to keep busy during a stressful time, so he was glad that Oliver Dren had left him with an assignment. It would fill a lot of time, and he wouldn't have to think about how much he was going to miss Andy.

Chapter 21

Janeen Newman Carson

It had been one of the longest days of Janeen's life. She'd gone through the motions of the work and the usual routine that had to be done, had met with Detective Wesley, had answered at least 'a million' questions about Andy's murder and finally, about 7 o'clock was ready to go home. She reached for her coat on the rack and was surprised to find another one under hers. She caught her breath when she realized that it was Andy's jacket. She hadn't noticed it when she put her own coat there in the morning, but then she had been rushing to clean up the president's office before he arrived.

Thinking this might be important to the investigation, Janeen glanced at the clock and noted that it was long after normal work hours, probably too late to call Detective Wesley at the Homicide office. After what had happened last night, she didn't want to leave the jacket in her office. For some reason, she felt it should be protected. She went back to her temporary desk and looked at the detective's card that was still tucked into the corner of the desktop protector. He'd written in his home number in case she needed it. She would take the jacket home with her and call him from there.

Janeen Carson locked the office and went to get her car with Andy's jacket carefully folded in the crook of her arm. Feeling the soft material reminded her how fast life can change. Andy was gone but the lives of many others like Susan and Oliver Dren are altered forever. Janeen knew what it was like to lose a loved one quickly and have to go on in an empty, darker life. She wanted to do something to help the Drens through this painful time. Unfortunately, grief cannot be shared, but an offer of friendship can be comforting.

After parking her car in the garage of her Midtown home, she entered the house through the foyer and den that were on the first level of the three-story townhouse. The den was her favorite room, because it was very personal as well as cozy. The informal, stone fireplace was usually the focal point for guests who visited, but her focal point was the wall that was filled with photographs of her family and friends. The earliest pictures were of her four grandparents with their children, her parents. There were many photographs of the Newmans at various ages and then a few of Janeen's life with Roy. All of the collection was valuable to her, but the limited number of pictures she had of Roy were truly precious. Tonight she barely glanced at the wall that gave her such deep pleasure. While thinking of the events of the day, she placed Andy's jacket on the sofa beside her briefcase.

As soon as Janeen threw her coat on a chair and kicked off her shoes, she sat down at the telephone and called Oliver Dren. She had brought his card home with her, because she knew she wanted to extend her hand in sympathy. She wasn't surprised to have her call received by an answering machine. Of course they would be out with other family or friends as they made their plans for the next few, difficult days.

"Mr. Dren, this is Janeen Carson from Georgia Tech. I'm calling for two reasons. One to ask if there is anything I can do for you or Susan, and two to tell you that the staff in the office will be at the services. Together we'll bring food for the luncheon you're planning. We all wanted to do this because Andy was important to us, and it's a small way to let you know that we share your loss. Count on us to be there and to help you with the lunch."

She pushed the off button on her phone and pressed the keys again. She wanted to tell Laurie Lindholm that they were going to take food for the Dren's luncheon. She knew Laurie would want to join them. The telephone rang four times and she was prepared to hear another message when Laurie said quite breathlessly, "Hello, this is Laurie Lindholm."

"Mrs. Lindholm, this is Janeen. How're you doing tonight?"

"Oh, Janeen, I'm fine. I was just coming in from the yard when you called. That's why I sound like I've been running....because I have been. The days I don't teach the little ones, I try to get out and do some slow jogging. Jon isn't here, but I'll tell him to call when he gets home. I guess he's at another of his thousands of meetings."

Janeen thought about Laurie's assumption that her husband was at a meeting. Very interesting, she thought, because she didn't have a meeting on his calendar. Janeen usually knew where he was, and tonight Jon Lindholm was not at a meeting. She wondered how long Laurie could be blind to her husband's affair. He's such a fool. He had a lovely wife and a terrific son and he was stupid enough to fool around with a coed.

"I wasn't calling for Dr. Lindholm. I was calling to tell you that the people in the office had decided to take food up to Dalton to help Oliver and Susan Dren host a luncheon after the funeral, I..." Janeen was interrupted by Laurie.

"Please, let me join you. I've more time than many of you do, so I can make some potato salad and dessert to add to what you all are taking. Is there anything else you want me to do? Whatever we do, Janeen, is only a tiny help when you think of what they're experiencing. It's so sad."

"Yes, I've been thinking of them all day and wanting to be a comfort. You're right that the food is a small gesture, but it's something that we can do. Thank you for helping,"

"I feel so close to this horrendous incident, because I almost had a premonition about the murder," Laurie explained and then told Janeen how she had been awakened and not been able to go back to sleep.

"That's really weird. If only you could've told someone. But then what would you have told them?"

"I did finally go back to sleep while I was reading in the terrace room. But you're right when you say it leaves you with a weird feeling. I didn't go back to bed until almost when you called in the morning."

"Well, don't let it bother you, Mrs. Lindholm. Your feelings were just a tremor in the night. I'll talk to you before we leave for Dalton. Thanks again for making the potato salad and dessert," Janeen said.

"Thank *you* for thinking of me. See you soon."

Getting ready to make a third call, Janeen placed a card on the table beside Oliver Dren's card and looked at it for a few moments. She wondered why she hesitated about dialing this number. It was no different than doing what she just did, but she felt rather shy. Somehow this seemed very important to her own life.

She broke into her questioning thoughts and tapped out another number. She listened to the ringing with anticipation and was jolted when she heard, "Wes Wesley."

"Detective Wesley, this is Janeen Carson from Georgia Tech. I hope I'm not bothering you, but you said I should call if I had additional thoughts or questions. I assumed that you'd no longer be at your office."

"You got that right. If you saw my office, you would know why I spend as little time in it as possible. It's the dregs. Don't worry about calling. You're not bothering me at all. It's good to hear from you," Wes said, meaning every word. It sure was good to have her calling, even if it was business.

"This may not be important, but I felt I should tell you what I found as I left the office." She hesitated and took a deep breath as she noticed that her heart was pounding.

"Yes?"

"When I took my coat from the rack to go home, I found Andy's jacket under it. I was so surprised."

"Wasn't it there this morning, Janeen?"

"I don't really know. I was rushing at that point to clean up Dr. Lindholm's office from last night's trustee meeting. I would assume that it was, and I didn't notice it."

"You're probably right. What did you do with the jacket?" Wesley asked.

"I brought it home. Maybe that was a strange thing to do, but I didn't want to leave it in the office. Was that a stupid thing for me to do?"

"Not at all. It may help us find some answers, but even if

it doesn't, it's best to have it in a safe place. Should I assume your home is safe?" Wes asked in a lighter tone than his previous questions.

How lucky he was that this lovely woman takes her responsibilities seriously. Without that attitude she wouldn't have taken the jacket home nor called him about it right away. Maybe this was the sign he was hoping for: that she wanted an opportunity to talk to him outside of Tech. He was going to take a chance, "How about if I come to your place and pick it up now? That would spare you from having me arrive early in the morning on my way to work."

Janeen found that she was again holding her breath. She realized that she had hoped that he would suggest coming for the jacket. It still surprised her how attracted she was to Wes Wesley and that she wanted to see him again.

"That would be great. I live in the Midtown area on Juniper Street."

"Terrific. I live in Home Park. You're only a few blocks from where I am. As they say, it's a small world. How much smaller could the circle be than Juniper, Home Park and Tech?"

"Come over whenever you can. I've just gotten home and have no plans besides catching up on the news on CNN."

"You might want to check out some of the other channels, Janeen, because you're a star of the evening news 'entertainment.' You and a kid with the same name as your president."

"You're kidding me. It never occurred to me that I would actually be mentioned on television. I don't know if I even want to be. Yuk! Most people appear to be so dumb when they're the subjects of the news. Danielle Swain asked me a few questions, but I thought it would just be background. I'm not sure this is good news, Detective Wesley," Janeen said in mock horror, then she added, "What did you say about a kid with the president's name?"

"On Dani Swain's news show. She featured a student who was identified as Lindholm IV. Very impressive. Hey, I taped the show and if you have a VCR, I'll bring it with me."

"I do, so bring it. We'll make a trade. You get the jacket, and

I get to see what Atlanta's popular anchor person said about my rotten day."

"It's a deal, young lady. Tell me your address and I'm on my way."

Janeen hung up the phone and sat for a minute. She had practically thrown herself at this man, and he had responded with the same urgency. It felt good. There was a real chemistry between them. Her thoughts sobered for a moment when she thought about why they had met. She would always feel badly about Andy, but maybe Detective Wesley being assigned to the case was going to be the good out of the bad. Her mother always said that was how life was planned.

Janeen took a sweeping glance at the den and decided that it looked fine for a special guest. The VCR and TV were built into the cherry bookcases that lined both sides of the fireplace. The red poppy, print sofa with many loose, plump pillows faced both the fireplace and the television screen. The coffee table that she had made from an antique trunk sat on a creamy-white, area rug. She loved the bright reds and dark greens of the sofa contrasting with the light, wood floor and plain rug.

Yes, the room looked fine but taking a quick inventory of herself in the mirror over her desk, she jumped up and made a beeline for the stairs to go up to her bedroom to change clothes. She didn't want to look 'business formal' as all the ads would call her suit and a simple blouse.

Chapter 22

Wes T. Wesley

"Yes!" Wes exclaimed as he raised a fist and pulled his arm down toward his side. This was a motion that he had learned from his son, Jason. Wes had always thought it was too trendy to use, but tonight it felt just right. If Jason were here, he would definitely laugh at him and say, "I thought you were too cool to be 'in', Pop." Wesley was lucky to have a relaxed and comfortable relationship with his only son who was now a 19-year-old university student majoring in criminology. Jason seemed to have an honest interest in the field. He didn't make the choice simply to please his father. Wes used to take him to the office when he was a young teenager, and Jason was relaxed with the squad from the first day. As his doting dad, he was pleased that his partner and associates always treated Jason like one of the team.

His son loved to tell the stories about when he was asked to give his opinion of how young men of his age would perceive certain events or react to particular incidents. The best story being when his response helped Homicide find the perpetrator they were seeking. He had said to Billy Joe LaCrosse, "I know three witnesses have ID'd this guy, but I don't think your teenage suspect would ever wear the Florsheim shoes that match with those foot prints. No way! It's Nike or Adidas. Your suspect has got to be older." That day they were more than father and son, they were colleagues.

While enjoying the thoughts about his son, he rewound the tape and took it out of his VCR. He placed it beside his car keys and took the steps two at a time to run his razor over his day's growth of beard. He always avoided after shave lotion but decided that tonight was the time to break a few of his stodgy habits, "Getting bold in your old age, Wesley?" he asked the face that peered back at him from the bathroom mirror. He took a second look and wished there were more to do to improve his face (like trade it with Harrison Ford, maybe?) but being cleanly-shaven will just have to suffice.

"I'm only going out to do my job, for god's sake," he said defensively to his image."You're acting like Jason when he finally got a date with the Homecoming Queen."

After taking another few seconds to run a brush through his hair, he was out the door with the video. He bolted to his car, did a U-turn and headed toward Juniper Street.

Janeen had told him to park in front of her garage because finding a space on the street at this time of evening was impossible. The neighborhood was spilling over with cars and drivers cruising slowly looking for room to leave their automobiles for the night. It was good that Janeen Carson had a garage, because she shouldn't be walking alone on the city streets after dark. His buddies who patrolled the streets of Atlanta did an excellent job, but they couldn't be everywhere nor recognize every weirdo in a neighborhood.

Wes rang the doorbell, stood in the pool of brightness from the porch light and tossed the video from hand-to-hand as he waited for Janeen to open the door. He looked like some nervous kid whose voice would crack when he finally had to say, "Hey."

The door opened and Janeen said with a broad smile, "Hey, Detective Wesley." He did love her voice.

"Hey," he squeaked and then quickly cleared his throat, "Sorry about that. I've had a touch of laryngitis. Never know when it's going to hit."

"It's that time of year, Detective. Lots of colds and flu. Come on in, before you catch a worse cold," Janeen said standing back so he could come into the foyer; leaving the crisp, clear March night behind.

As he passed her, she thought how different he looked out of his proper, dark suit and standard dress shirt. Tonight his very casual style of jeans and an opened necked, plaid sports shirt seemed more suitable to this handsome and energetic man. When he appeared to practically bound into the house, she was reminded of a big, overgrown puppy. She wasn't sure of his age, but everything about him tonight was much more youthful than when he was on the job earlier today.

"I see you brought the tape. The television is in the den so make a right turn and we'll be where we want to be."

He scanned the room and its aura gave him a deeper insight of this interesting woman. Warm, vivacious and dependable were the first words that came to his mind. When he did investigations, he always felt that seeing where a suspect or victim lived gave him a better understanding of with whom he was dealing. This evening wasn't truly an official investigation, but his instincts were on high. He saw and felt in this room a Janeen Carson who was intelligent, sweet and caring.

"This is quite a photo album," Wes said walking to the wall filled with the history of her family.

Janeen found it amusing that the first thing he noticed about the room was her family, "Yes, even though I don't have my family living in town, I feel close to them by keeping them here in my favorite room. I could bore you with stories that go with each picture, but I won't do that the minute you walk into the house. But look out, if you stay too long, you'll have to submit to: Once upon a time in the Newman/Carson family."

"OK. I hope that's a promise. I bet you tell a good story." Wes was feeling that this might be just the first of more visits in this home. He again felt that the message was there that Janeen wanted to know him better. That fit right into his own plans that she not get away. He met hundreds of women every year, professionally and personally. Many were attractive, some intelligent, a few were successful and next to none demonstrated a caring nature for others. In Janeen Carson, he was sure he'd found all of those qualities he'd been seeking for many years.

• • •

Wes was surprised that he suddenly was thinking of his life more than 20 years ago. He knew that his judgment of others was keener today than it had been when he met the woman whom he later asked to be his wife. He had recently graduated from the University of Virginia and had been recruited by the FBI. His first assignment was St. Louis. He was excited and couldn't wait to become a team member of the highly respected government agency. The only negative he faced was that he had to leave the beautiful Linda Sue Allcott in Charlottesville. She had another year to graduate with a degree in Fine Arts. Linda Sue was already preparing for her senior art exhibit focusing on her extraordinary talent as a painter. After being invited to exhibit her paintings in a local gallery when she was only 15 years old, she began selling her work which she signed LinSua. Wes had seen her oils and watercolors in many homes and businesses in the Charlottesville area, and each time, he felt an intense pride that she was his fiancee.

When Wes first met Linda Sue and they became a steady twosome, he was convinced that he'd won the prize of his life. Even when he moved to St. Louis, and they only saw each other once a month, life was still fantastic. They spent whole weekends in his small apartment when she flew west or in her studio when he flew east. He thought her graduation would never happen. How could one year be so long?

The graduation week was full and exciting. Wes drove to Charlottesville to be there when Linda Sue received her diploma and a special art award given by an aging alumnus who was dedicated to being a patron of the arts and young artists. Two days later Wes and Linda Sue were married in a small, charming church dating back to before the Civil War. They left for a short honeymoon in the Smokey Mountains before driving to St. Louis. Wes was sure that the honeymoon would last forever, but he'd overestimated by about 100 years.

Linda Sue painted, Wes investigated, they played together, and made love in their apartment, out in the woods, beside a misty lake, in motels when taking short trips away from St. Louis, and even on the roof of the FBI office building. Love and life were sweet. The first year of their marriage went so fast they were both surprised it was their first anniversary that was celebrated with another weekend of non-stop lovemaking.

Six weeks later, their marriage ended. Linda Sue bought a pregnancy test kit at the drug store that read: positive.

"A baby!" she screamed, "That's not in my plan. I've more important things to do."

"Calm down, honey. It's a shock to both of us, but think how lucky we are. We've made a copy of us, and he or she'll be surrounded by love. We've so much to share. Even though we haven't talked a lot about a family, surely we're going to have a child sometime. We're just going to have it sooner than we thought."

"I didn't talk about it because I've no interest in cluttering up our lives with a baby. How can I paint with crying and some little snotty-nosed kid running around?" Linda Sue cried shrilly, "I like our life just the way it is. I don't want any changes. We've often talked about our perfect life. We never added that it would be better with a child. I just won't have it!"

"No, Linda Sue, don't say that. Don't even think about it. This is ours. We're already its parents, and we owe this baby the same love that created it."

"I'm sorry, Wes, I'm an artist, not a mother. I like being your wife because I still can pursue my passion that is art. You're into your work too. We fit. We work together, but I'm not going to be a babysitter and a nanny. No way!" Linda Sue's words had a ring of finality.

"We don't have to decide now, honey. We're still in a state of shock. Let's talk about it later. We need time to get used to this new idea." Wes heard himself pleading. There must be a way that everyone can win, including this new, delicate life.

"Right, Wes, we'll talk about it later. But there's not much more to say. Just because I couldn't tolerate taking the pill and somehow a condom didn't work, I'm not being enslaved for the next twenty years. This is when I establish my name as an artist. No one gives a shit if I'm a mother," Linda Sue spit out the words like she hated him as well as the baby. His life was shattered; lying in shreds in the bathroom wastebasket with the ripped pieces of the pregnancy test kit.

The encounter ended abruptly with Linda Sue's words filling the room with their venom. Their little, cozy apartment would never feel the same. It had lost its glow of young, easy love; a daily serving of fun and spontaneity that didn't include family responsibilities. Where had their precious love gone that had carried them happily through this first year of marriage? He'd scoffed at the people who told him the first year was the hardest. It was one year and six weeks that were hard. Nothing could be harder than seeing all your dreams dissolve in less than ten minutes because of "The Home Test.... the quick way to plan the future." 'Sorry, marketers, your product is...."The Home Test....the quick way to ruin the future."' Wes thought sadly.

When he replayed the day, he was convinced that it was just like a poorly-rated television movie: fight, cool off, go to bed, reach out for the comfort of love making, and .....be rejected!

"Wes, leave me alone. This is not the time. It may never be the time after I tell you that I'm going to have an abortion as soon as I can. I'm not waiting to talk again, and I'm not changing my mind. I will not ruin the rest of my life," Linda Sue's voice was suspended in the darkness of the room. It didn't appear to be connected to his wife whom he had loved so intensely. Its coldness, along with the stiffness of her body lying beside him, delivered a message that there was no hope for them. He was nauseated when he realized that it meant there was no life for their child. At that moment, he gave up on Linda Sue and Wes, but was not ready to give up on the baby.

"OK, Linda Sue, I get your message. I hate that we can't both rejoice in this event, but there has to be a compromise. You must give me something for losing you. You must still have a shred of memory of our love and life together. Have you cared so little about me that you can just end our lives together as well as our baby?"

"Our life together doesn't need to end. I can have my tubes tied when I have the abortion. We can replicate this fantastic year 30 or 40 or 50 more times. We don't need a baby. We have each other," Linda Sue's voice sounded more relaxed as she explained her vision of the rest of their lives.

"No, Linda Sue. We would have a terrible life with this

hanging over our heads. It wouldn't work. It might even change the empathy and passion that is so beautiful in your paintings. You may no longer be able to transfer your joy and love of life onto the canvases and paper. If we kill this child, we might just be killing your talent." Wes knew his wife well enough to attack her passion.

The thick blackness of the room seemed to press in on them as they lay unmoving, not touching. Wes listened intently but couldn't hear his wife's breathing over the pounding of his heart. Minutes seemed to drag, making only a few feel like an hour. He wondered how she could be so still and quiet. He closed his eyes and waited. He closed his eyes and prayed for his unborn child.

There was an intake of breath, another long pause and then Linda Sue asked softly, "What's the deal? I know you have something to offer."

"Yes, I have a deal. We stay together long enough for you to have the baby and then you go your way and we go ours. We'll make no demands on you for the rest of your life. In addition, I'll give you $10,000 to help you get resettled or to stay on here. The baby and I will leave town."

"We don't have $10,000, Wes. You can't make that offer."

"I can borrow it," he said simply. He thought it was a small amount to buy a life.

"Well, I don't like the idea of having to go through all of the discomfort and pain, but it would solve our dilemma. I think you have a good point that we don't want to weaken my artistic talent. That would be a sin."

Wes thought about her use of the pronoun *we* and almost laughed. His offer had nothing to do with her career. Linda Sue just lost his devotion and support of her career. Eight months and $10,000, and she was only a bittersweet interlude in his life. He would move ahead with his son or daughter. He replayed her words and said to the darkened room, "It would be a sin to kill our child."

• • •

"Sit here, Detective," Janeen motioned toward the sofa,"It's the best place to watch the tape. Tell me, do I want to see it at all? My short talk with that anchor woman really wasn't much to keep for posterity."

"It's fine. You're right that your cameo appearance is limited, but the entire report is quite interesting. You can tell me how you like being on the six o'clock news when it's over."

"My dad was famous for telling us that it was not desirable to make the news and he didn't want to see any Newmans there. He told us even as youngsters: the people who make headlines usually were there because of problems or they were dead. He would be appalled at the news of the 90s when everyone wants to get on TV or radio to tell their darkest and most disgusting secrets," Janeen mused.

"Your dad was right. All dads should tell their kids that. I know I have said practically the same thing to my son, Jason."

"Oh, how old is your son?"

"He's 19 and a sophomore at the University of Virginia, my alma mater," Wes said and added quickly, "I'm a single parent. Have been since the day Jason was born. My wife wasn't overjoyed with motherhood."

Janeen passed through several emotions as Wes told her these important facts about his life: first, disappointment because he was probably married; second, relief that he wasn't; third, disbelief that a mother could leave her newborn son; and fourth, respect that Wes had raised his son on his own.

"Sounds like a story there, too, but it can wait until you hear my family tales. We can inflict each other with: Our lives by Janeen and Detective Wesley."

"Wes. My name is Wes Wesley. Easy to say even if you stutter," Wes corrected.

"That's fine with me. Wes is so much shorter to say than Detective and a whole lot easier to spell," Janeen told him, liking the idea that all vestiges of formality were being set aside.

"OK. Time to be quiet and tune in on Janeen Carson, Channel 22's special guest."

Chapter 23

Danielle Jarvis Swain

Janeen took the video from Wes, turned her back to him as she set up the VCR, and inserted the black container. Although she appeared to be concentrating on her action, she was thinking about what a great evening it had been so far. She definitely had her stereotype of what a policeman would be, but Wes Wesley didn't fit that mold. She found him gentle and understanding of people. Somehow the meanness of the lives he encountered daily didn't seem to have hardened him. She felt the tough veneer he wore was a protection from the misery he faced constantly rather than a barrier to keep all emotions and people out.

Wes broke into her thoughts, "Are you ready? I can't wait to see you as twins: one here and one there."

"Many folks would feel two Janeens were too many, so let's not even suggest that possibility." She crossed over to the sofa, sat down and tucked her feet under her.

'She reminds me of a kitten. I sure would like to hear her purr in my ear,' Wes was having his own thoughts that had nothing to do with the news video. His daydreaming was broken by a familiar voice:

"This is Danielle Swain on the campus of Georgia Tech. I'm standing in front of the Tech Tower, the symbol of the tradition and academic achievement of this fine institution. Just six months ago it became part of Olympic history when Tech was the home for athletes from more than 190 countries. Today it's become the scene of the murder of one of its students.

"Oliver Andrew Dren, Jr., a graduate student in the College of Computing, was found early this morning shot to death in the president's office. Ms. Janeen Carson, executive assostant to Dr. Jonathan Lindholm III, discovered the tragedy and immediately called Chief George Fancer, Tech's head of security, and President Lindholm. Atlanta Homicide was notified by Chief Fancer. At this time a suspect has not been identified.

"Ms. Carson had known Mr. Dren and was shocked that he was killed. She's here with me on the steps outside of the office where she found the body."

"Andy worked in the office with us and was truly one of our Georgia Tech family. He was a wonderful young man who couldn't possibly have an enemy. It's a real mystery that we all hope Detective Wesley and his associates will solve quickly." Janeen was standing just outside the main door with Danielle Swain holding the microphone just below her chin. Although Janeen had never liked her image on videos, she decided it wasn't extremely important, since she was on camera for only a few seconds before Danielle cut to the plaza area and was standing with Lindy in front of the campus fountain where a large group of students was assembled.

"Lindy Lindholm is the son of the president of Georgia Tech and on the campus newspaper staff. He has been responding to questions about the murder."

Another voice shouted in the background, "Lindy, is it true that the police say that Andy vandalized the office before he was shot?"

"Slow down. I'll tell you what little I know, but I don't want to add to the rumors. That won't help anyone. First, there was nothing missing or even disturbed. Theft doesn't appear to be a motive. Second, there was no vandalizing of the office. I've been there, and it was a tragic shooting and nothing else. The office window is broken so at this point it's assumed that the murderer was outside. Andy was in the office probably doing some work. He had a part-time job doing programming and computer inputting for the president and the vice president. He didn't break in. He worked a lot with the president's secretary and had his own key. Everyone there knew Andy."

"Lindy, where was he shot? What news will you report in

your next Technique?" "Some information just has to wait until the police are ready to tell us. My dad's going to meet with the detective in charge today and then maybe they'll be willing to make statements for The Technique."

Almost in a whisper like a fairway announcer at a golf tournament, Dani explained, "We are in front of the same fountain where Channel 22 did dozens of live Olympic Village interviews. Today we have another drama unfolding as his peers question a prominent student.

"You certainly are the center of attention today, Lindy. When we arrived, it looked like everyone wanted to hear from you."

"It's just that they know that I have talked with my dad and have actually been in the building where Andy was shot. They all want the inside story, which I don't have. Even if I did, I think the police would be (bleep) if I went out telling things they might want to keep quiet at this point."

Dani turned directly to the camera and said, "The mystery deepens here on campus. Everyone agrees that Andrew Dren was a model student and well-liked young man. As we follow this tragic story, we echo Lindy Lindholm's remarks about the police investigation: this is the time to wait for them to find a brutal killer who will allow this campus to return to its normally relaxed environment.

"This has been a special news report with Danielle Swain at Georgia Tech in Atlanta."

The screen went blank and the audio sounded like a noisy machine shop. Neither Wes nor Janeen said a word for a few moments, both into their own thoughts.

"You may not have been the star, but you surely will be mentioned for an academy award for best supporting actress."

"Right. I don't think my dad will be too upset about my appearance. I'll have to call my family and tell them. They are absolutely the doting parents and love to talk about their kids. Could I make a copy from your video?"

"Of course. I would give you this one except I'll keep it in the file as part of the case."

"You must have lots of tapes that relate to your cases. Maybe you're the star on some of them."

"Actually, I've been on the news before with Dani Swain. She's quite the girl. Did you like her when she interviewed you?" Wes asked Janeen as she turned back from setting the VCR on copy.

"Yes, actually, I did but then I had already known her from last summer during the games. She changed my opinion that TV anchors just might be rather stuck on themselves. She was real popular in the Olympic Village. She was genuinely interested in the athletes and their stories; and they responded to her as a person, not a personality." Janeen explained as she again curled up on the sofa.

"As pretty as she is, I bet some of those athletes would really enjoy being interviewed and spending some time with her to develop their stories. Fortunately she's a lot more than a pretty face."

"You sound like maybe you know her better than just seeing her on the six o'clock news."

"I've met her several times at City Hall events. She has been dating one of the mayor's special aides. He's a down to earth guy, so it doesn't surprise me that she's the same."

"I just don't see her as a down to earth *guy*. I wonder about your eyesight," Janeen joked with Wes.

"Just an expression. I have no problem picking out good-looking women. I didn't miss you when I arrived at Tech this morning," Wes hesitated and added very quietly, "Janeen, you're a beautiful TV personality, and I'm so glad that you found Andy's jacket."

Janeen was flustered. She felt like maybe he was picking up her own thoughts about him. Hoping that she wasn't quite so transparent, Janeen sat up straighter, placed her feet on the floor and changed the subject, "Hey, I don't know about you, Wes, but I didn't have any time to get supper, and I'm hungry. Would you like a sandwich? From the fridge, I can manage a hamburger, hot dog or grilled cheese. Take your pick, and I'll head for the hot kitchen and demonstrate my gourmet chef talents."

"Great offer, pretty lady. Do you also feed the neighborhood homeless as well as the lonely? I bet you're as kind to stray animals as you are to stray people." Wes trailed her out of the den and up the stairs toward the kitchen.

"Let's see, should I consider you lonely and stray or just lonely or just stray?" she threw over her shoulder as she gave Wes one of her sparkling smiles. Suddenly, Janeen stopped and turned toward Wes. It was such a surprising move that he almost knocked her down. He grabbed each of her arms and steadied her, "Whoops, you should give hand signals. I might have to give you a ticket for endangering others on the stairs."

"I'm sorry. Obviously my mind was still moving but my body was not. I couldn't believe that you would imply that you are lonely. You seem to have everything under control, and I'm sure you don't lack friends or dates. I bet you have women standing in line to get to know you better."

"You're right. I'm with lots of people, on and off the job. You're wrong that that solves being lonely. Being lonely is solved by spending time with the right person or people. My life had been quite full when Jason was still home. We're best friends. Until six years ago, I also had my father around. We three had lived together since Jason was a baby. We needed help, and we gave it to each other. It was a good arrangement, because we all liked each other, laughed a lot and shared the activities of three generations. Believe me, that can be quite a challenge at times: a little boy who goes to the seniors' meeting because his grandfather doesn't like to go alone, a grandfather who's sitting with all the young parents at the school Thanksgiving play, or the father in between who tries to go along with the interests of both of them. It's been a full, rich life.

"But, the life I have had should have been shared with a woman who cared about what I cared about and she would have people and a life that I could care about. Our society calls this a good marriage or at least a good, lasting companionship." Wes reached up to touch Janeen's face and pressed his hand against her cheek, "I'm sorry, pretty lady. That was much too heavy a speech for the first hour of our relationship, and much too long to be made as we teeter on the stairs. If the sandwich is still an option, I'll take a hamburger."

Janeen actually felt a lump in her throat. Why were tears boiling behind her eyelids? She wanted to put her arms around this sweet man and hold him until his loneliness was gone. How could she feel like a lover and a mother all at one time? Her emotions were so askew that she was weak. She *wanted* to put her arms around....no, she *did* reach out and pull him closer, his head at her shoulder because she was higher on the stairway. Wes did not resist. He moved slightly toward her as if they had been the best of friends for years. Neither spoke nor moved again once their bodies touched. She felt him breathe, he heard her heart beat. There wasn't another sound for either of them. They both wondered how they got through yesterday without knowing each other.

"How do you like your hamburger? Well done, medium or rare?" Her words were muffled in his hair. Her thoughts seemed muffled, too, but she did remember that they were headed for the kitchen.

"Rare. Just warmed through. After that it should be used to patch the roof."

"Me, too. Let's get to the kitchen before you give me another ticket for causing a traffic jam." Janeen winked at him before she continued to the kitchen.

Chapter 24

Janeen Newman Carson

Wes stood in the doorway and observed Janeen and the kitchen that she had created. It was small, but in every corner, on every wall he could see her signature. The room was a perfect reflection of the woman who lived here. It had the same cheerful, cozy aura that was in her den. The walls were covered with a lemon yellow checkered wallpaper with saucy, gathered valances, over two big windows, made from a companion material of daisies casually strewn over the same yellow and white checks. Above the range and sink were yellow, handmade tiles with imprints of real daisies in every other square. Sparkling white cabinets and floor gave the impression that every inch of this small room was as fresh as the daisy's reputation.

He perused the room, tucking it away in his memory, but he seriously studied the woman who made the surroundings come alive. Janeen was at the range with a built-in grill, heating it to the proper temperature so the hamburgers could be seared quickly. She had cut several tomatoes and arranged them on leafy, green lettuce. She appeared as comfortable and at home in the kitchen as she did in the president's office. She moved with such grace from range to sink to refrigerator. As she turned to him and smiled, her slim body looked elegant from every angle.

"How about a beer with your hamburger?" Janeen asked.

"If you have no imported champagne, beer is next best."

"I forgot to pick up the champagne in my haste to get home to call you," she laughed, "I forgot that you like the beverage of a royal table with the food of an ordinary backyard barbeque."

"Nothing is ordinary when you're around, Janeen, but do remember the bubbly the next time."

"The next time? Whatever gave you the idea that you would be invited back? You've made me miss the CNN news. You've completely upset my routine. I may never get to doing my laundry."

He took several steps and stood in front of her and, since they were no longer on the stairs, she looked up at him, "Don't worry, honey. Remember CNN news is on 24 hours a day and repeats the same stories about every hour. In the meantime, I'll try to keep you from missing the television or washing clothes," Wes leaned toward her and kissed her lightly on the lips."Maybe we can make some news of our own," he whispered and kissed her again, a little longer and a little harder.

Janeen returned both kisses and then put her arms lightly around his waist. He felt so good. He looked so good. His words sounded so good. Was he as good as he seemed? She realized that at the moment she liked everything about him.

"That's it, Detective, or you'll have to go patch the roof with your hamburger. You're definitely diverting my attention from cooking."

"It's a hard decision to make, but I'll unhand you temporarily so you can cook our perfectly-rare hamburgers," Wes said as he stepped back, crossed his arms over his chest and continued to watch Janeen's every move.

They sat at the small, made-for-two table with their knees almost touching as they pulled their chairs close enough to eat. The sandwiches were juicy from both the hamburgers and tomatoes, the beer frosty. They agreed that the meal couldn't be better if they were at the Ritz Carlton. Each secretly added that enjoying the meal together made the simple fare taste better. Following what they sarcastically called the main course, Janeen took homemade chocolate chip cookies from the freezer and announced that these were to make up for no champagne.

"I never turn down homemade cookies, but the sandwich and beer have already made me forget special, imported, exotic, expensive, choice, French champagne. Not to worry. As they would say in my hometown: you dun good," Wes told her as he leaned back in his chair satisfied and happy.

"You must tell me where that hometown is that doesn't teach grammar but encourages champagne tastes."

"I was born just outside of Atlanta but grew up in the city in the same house I now live in."

"Well, that fits. The citizens of the Atlanta area don't want to pay taxes for an excellent school system, but they don't object to the price or taxes on wines. Yikes, don't get me started on the public schools. I really get nasty."

"I'm right with you there. Jason went to private school after fourth grade. Maybe he would have done OK in the Atlanta system, but I wasn't willing to experiment with my son's future."

Janeen again noticed a softening of the look in Wes' eyes when he mentioned Jason. He was definitely a proud father. She decided that he was probably a good father who had always been close to his son. Someday she would like to ask more about his life as a single parent. She had often wondered how she would have been as a mother if she and Roy had had a child.

"Earth to Janeen. Where are you? The cookies must have sent you into orbit," Wes said as he reached across the table and tapped her on the hand.

"Oh, I'm sorry. Just thinking about what a wonderful evening this has been. I've never enjoyed a meal here in my kitchen this much. I'm glad you were willing to take a chance on my cooking," Janeen told Wes as he took her hand in his, raised it to his lips and gave her fingers a quiet kiss.

"It wasn't a risk, pretty lady. You give the impression you do everything well, so I knew this would be the best hamburger I ever ate. Janeen, you are simply a very special woman."

Never letting go of her hand, Wes pushed his chair back and stood up in one fluid motion. He took a step to put himself beside Janeen and guided her to stand next to him. With no other movement or sign, he kissed her on the lips and waited a moment to read her reaction. She turned toward him and kissed him back. Her body leaned into his and she found she fit perfectly in the curve of his body. Tenderness and excitement warmed her. She was confused that she could feel like she had known this man forever and yet tingled with the electricity of a new relationship.

They kissed again and held each other in silence. Nothing else was needed. It wasn't the time for words; they didn't need them. They knew their bodies and emotions were in harmony. The world was momentarily severed from them. He touched her shiny, brown hair, traced his fingers along her nose, across her lips and down her throat. Everywhere he touched he found a woman, silky and smooth.

Janeen copied the same trail along Wes' hair, face and throat. She found a gold chain just above where the hair on his chest curled against his skin. She leaned forward and kissed him, taking the initiative for the first time. She felt comfortable being close to him but was uneasy that she could have that feeling with a man she hadn't known for 24 hours.

"Wes, the world is moving too fast for me. We've had a day that may be both awful and wonderful at the same time. Since this morning, I've not been acting or reacting like me. I need some time to recover from all of the shocks. And, believe me, you're a shock in some ways as strong as finding Andy in the office. As the students would say, I need my space."

Wes took a small step back. The tiny space seemed to create room for each of them to take a deep breath.

"You're probably right, but I really want to talk you out of being sensible. I want to get so far into your head that you can't think one straight thought. That's what I want, but I'm still conscious enough to know that you're calling the plays," he stopped and added, "You remind me of when I'm coaching Little League and I tell them: slow down, it's only one play. Tonight you're the coach and I'm going to save this play for later in the season. I just want you to plan to be at all the games this year because you're my star pitcher."

"I guess I have been pitching but it's time to call the evening on account of confusion. Do they ever do that?"

Wes laughed, "No, but I can think of a lot of times when that call would have been perfect. Now, send me back to my home dugout with one jacket under my arm. It was better than a ticket to the game. It got me into your house and you into my heart."

Chapter 25

Oliver Andrew Dren, Jr.

Frank Bostwick and Peter Kirk had watched Danielle Swain's report of the murder while they consumed two large pizzas from Papa John's. It was just an hour after each had eaten a greasy, fried chicken dinner in the Student Center cafeteria, topped off with double dip ice cream cones, but both of them seemed to be starving.

Frank tossed the empty boxes into the huge, black trash bag that they kept in the kitchen and said, "Maybe we should've offered to be on the news. We know Andy better than Lindy."

"I doubt if he offered. I got the impression, you know, that the anchorwoman just saw him on campus and started to talk. That's the way they do it. Anyone hanging around, you know, becomes part of a program," Peter Kirk explained, "At least he sounded like he was smarter than some of the red-necks who are usually interviewed. Those TV reporters can find the weirdest people when they want local opinion."

"It was interesting, but we gotta talk about a bunch of other things that relate to Andy. First, do we have all of the pallbearers?"

"I think so. It was really easy. Kinda like everyone wanted to do something but didn't know what." Peter reached for a paper that had a list of names on it. "There're the two of us. Then I asked Professor Mah, the Chinese guy in Computing who Andy considered his best instructor, and Professor Martin, who teaches the Ethics of Technology, because Andy was really into that subject, and you asked Khalid Siddiqi and Marc Balam, two other students who Andy talked about a lot. Wow, I just realized that we're going to look like a meeting of the United

Nations. Those are the kind of friends that Andy had. We didn't plan it that way, but there you go."

"OK. Now, second topic: do we know how we're going to get our message on the electronic sign? This is where we need someone like Khalid or Professor Mah, but unfortunately we can't tell anyone," Frank said, emphasizing with a shake of his head that Peter not talk about their plan. It might be fun to let people know how clever they were, but it would probably get them thrown out of school. They must be like the inventors of the fictitious student G. Pitts Berdel and stay anonymous for at least 50 years before they announce their creation at their big Gold Reunion.

"I think we got, you know, lucky on this. It pays to listen to some of the nerds around here. When we got talking about this, I remembered that one of the guys in my Thursday computing class had talked about having an easy job that gave him enough money to buy special software that he wanted. The job is to input the messages on the electronic signboard! He talked about himself like he's a published author, or something, because his work is in lights. He actually goes out and rides by to see what's flashing. What a dork. I didn't see him today, but I'll look for him tomorrow either in class or in the lab. He's always around. I don't know his name, so I can't call him."

"That's great, but how do we get him to put on the sign what we want?"

"That's going to be easy, you know. I'm going to get him talking about his cream puff job and act like he's the same as, you know, a rock star or something. Then I'm going to get all excited about what he's telling me and ask if I can watch when he, you know, sends a message. I'll either learn how to get into the right address, and we can do it, or I'll suggest he fool around with some crazy message that I'll, you know, 'make up' on the spot."

"Good thinking. It might work if this stupid shit is as impressed with himself as you say. It's amazing how many geeks there are around, but if this works maybe we should do a tribute to nerds on the fuckin' board, too," Frank suggested, only half as a joke.

"Let's not get carried away. If we can do this once and not get caught, I think we should consider ourselves lucky." It wasn't Peter's plan to end up begging to be allowed to stay at Tech."The best honor we can pay to Andy is for us to be as smart and innovative as he was. He wouldn't be proud of two dummy roommates who would be residing in the Atlanta jail. So, I'll work on getting to this guy. Now our biggest challenge: THE message."

"Yeah, I know, and I've been working on it. I just can't come up with something that's really clever. We owe it to Andy to have it worth doing," Frank sounded dejected, like he thought he was a failure."I've been looking at some of Andy's computer notes but even they haven't inspired me to greatness."

"That would be a real trick, Bozo. You can't become a genius overnight. It's good there are two of us, so we can pool our mental resources. Of course, some of our better friends would say that even then, we don't have a full brain."

Peter, Frank and Andy had always liked kidding each other. They were all intelligent and dependable but better than that, they knew how to have fun. The two remaining roommates wondered how different their lives were going to be now that Andy was gone. Their synergy had been broken. Even though money was a consideration, they hoped that they couldn't find another student right away to move into Andy's room. It just wouldn't feel right.

"OK. Let's hear some ideas. Now that you've found this dippy dork to input our memorial, we need to be ready." Frank was trying to encourage some original thoughts. He dragged himself out of the chair that he'd been slumping in, moved over to his computer and entered the word: MEMORIAL. "I'll add what we say, so we'll have all our suggestions."

Just like when a professor asked for answers or ideas, both minds went blank. They struggled to come up with even one idea. Maybe they were trying to be too clever. Maybe they each thought his idea would be laughed at. Whatever, someone had to get them going.

"How about: In memory of Andy Dren, a computer whiz?"

"Andy Dren, inspiration of all hackers."

"Andy Dren, connoisseur of computer information."

"Connoisseur? Are you crazy? Who can even spell it? We go to Tech, schmuck. We aren't expected to spell. If it doesn't have an equation, we're lost," Peter cried out in horror.

"That brings up an interesting thought. Andy had a code in his file that was kinda interesting. Maybe we could do something with it. The cool thing of that is that it would keep everybody guessing and talking. Maybe we could get The Technique to ask for ideas of what it means, or something."

"Well, what is it? Let's see if it has possibilities."

Frank hesitated just a moment to be sure that he had it right and said, "HKIIICC."

Peter repeated it to himself and commented, "What the hell could that mean? Maybe it's a cowboy holler. You know, Eye-yi-yi in the middle of four letters that're a mystery."

"That's interesting. I saw it as seven letters that absolutely don't spell anything or can't be pronounced."

"Of course, Frank, you're not known for your over-active imagination. That's why you're a good engineer. Stay in the box! That's your mantra." Peter laughed. "How about: HK meaning hacker and CC could stand for College of Computing? So if we put those together, we have Hacker eye-yi-yi College of Computing. My mother always says eye-yi-yi when she's amazed at something so maybe this Hacker (Andy) is amazed at the College of Computing. Since he'd so much experience at Microsoft, he might have felt that the College really wasn't as good as it could be."

"Man, *you* sure do have an imagination, but it's the best we have so far. Even if it means something else, we can have it mean this for our purposes."

"How about if the III is for three? We often use those numerals when outlining or listing items on our menus," Peter sent them in a new direction."Hey, I got it. It's referring to Three Hackers in the College of Computing. You know: The Hackers Three. Maybe he worked with two other students on a project and they referred to themselves as The Hackers Three."

"I like that! I wish Andy were here to tell us if we're even close. I think we should use the HKIIICC as the focus of our message." Frank felt relieved that they had come up with something that will be enough of a mystery to make it a topic of conversation on campus. It may get enough attention that the tale will be repeated just like the G. Pitts Berdel stories.

Peter nodded his head and smiled. He was pleased that they saw a provocative missive. They didn't want to get the credit for this crazy idea, but they did want to hear the students, and maybe even faculty, talk about their creation.

"OK. We'll say: In memory of Andy Dren: a computer expert who knew more than HKIIICC," Frank read as the memorial message appeared on the monitor. "We've done it. Now, Peter, you need to work on your geek."

"I'm ready. It's not, you know, going to be hard. He's going to, you know, love being the center of attention. Remember, the nerd probably thinks he should get a literary award for his sign messages like: Duke vs. Tech, January 22 or Spring Break begins March 4. Trust me, this guy is out of it," Peter was quiet for a moment and then cried out, "Hey. I just had another thought."

"Shit, look out. When the guy gets rolling, he gets dangerous."

"No, this is about us. If you think of the III as a number, *we* -Andy, you and me-we're The Hackers Three invented by Andy. So maybe this message was about us from him. Maybe he wanted us to find this. Maybe he's left us a disguised message that we haven't figured out yet. Could he have thought that he was in danger?"

"Damn, Peter, when you get going, you're a menace, but who knows at this point. We can hope our sign tribute will give the police a clue as to who shot Andy. I hope it does. The bastard must be caught."

Chapter 26

Tiffany Jarvis Walton

Jonathan Lindholm left his office feeling completely exhausted at the end of the day that had started with Janeen's shocking telephone call. He thought that would be the low point of the day, but he was wrong. The day continued to deteriorate with Burl's visit, the detective's interview and Tiffany's telephone call. Those were all unpleasant, but what was eating away at his confidence and adding to his misery was the growing sense that his whole life was closing in on him. Many times during the day, he was overcome with the same intuition of disaster that he had experienced during his darkest days in California. He tried to cheer himself by thinking that he'd gotten through that and had actually improved his life. He certainly lived better now, had a lot more money, was highly respected by many people (Burl Mentor didn't count.), still had a great playmate and, although she'd drawn definitive lines for their lives together, still had a wife who acted like the perfect partner for the president of Georgia Tech.

He told himself to forget all the negative vibes that were hovering around his head, buzzing in his ears. He had no reason to be concerned. Andy's shooting had nothing to do with him, and it had no more importance to his circumstances than other ripples that now and then disturbed the smooth surface of the campus. Shit happened, as the students said.

Jon reached his little sports car, and felt his mood lighten as he slid into the seat that was designed to make the driver feel powerful and in charge. This car did as much for his ego as any other possession he had. He loved driving the Mercedes SL 230 and having people turn their heads and take a second look when it went past them. Damn, he wasn't going to let the day spoil his evening. He was making a big deal out of one of life's blips on its radar screen.

Lindholm parked his car in a guest space in the basement of the building where Tiffany lived. When he parked there, he always backed in so that his GT 1 license plate wasn't staring blatantly into the sight line of all the other people who parked in the garage. Usually he'd park in outside parking lots so if he was seen he wouldn't be identified with this building, but tonight he was in a hurry. He knew that he only had a short time before Laurie would raise her antenna and be waiting for him with fire in her eyes. If he wanted to keep her under control, he had to be careful and clever. No problem, he thought, I'm good at both, only lost once in over 20 years.

He rang Tiffany's number and was actually excited when he heard the buzzer in return. She was there. By the quick response, he was sure she'd been waiting for him and was as anxious to see him as he was to see her.

No one was in the elevator lobby nor in the elevator. He breathed a sigh of relief. He'd never run into anyone he knew, but he couldn't be sure that others didn't recognize him. After all, his picture was often on television or in the newspapers. This public life did indeed make it harder to lead a clandestine life here than in California. Maybe that was part of the excitement of seeing Tiffany, because there were times when beyond recreational sex, she was a bit of a bore. Jon was able to tolerate the boredom for the sex. That frisky woman was the best piece of ass that he'd ever had, he thought as a rush of heat raced through his body.

"Hey, there, I thought you were never going to get here, baby. Has my big man had a busy day?" Tiffany was waiting in her open doorway looking sexy in a tight, red crop top that stopped just inches below her full breasts and inches above her tiny skirt. Jon would bet that she had on no bra....and probably no panties.

"It's been shit from beginning to right now. Seeing you, Tiffany, is the first good thing that's happened in over 24 hours,"

Jon confessed as he followed her into the condo and closed the door quietly behind him.

He slipped his hand under her arm and caressed one of her breasts. He had been correct, no bra. He was thrilled that she didn't need one, because he loved the tautness of young bodies. With a little pressure from his fingers, he turned her around to be facing him. She moved into the circle of his arms and pressed her body tightly against him. The angle was very subtle, but he didn't miss that she gently extended her pelvis and rubbed against him in a sensual and deliberate motion. She looked him square in the eyes as if to dare him to miss any of her message before slowly closing her eyes as she kissed him with her lips and tongue. She'd already taken control.

Jonathan felt limp everywhere except between his legs. He still was surprised that this half-grown woman could make his body act like a teenager's. Damn, did he have no power to time his own actions? His mind screamed 'No' as he pushed her backwards while never taking his lips from hers. Their bodies moved in perfect unison like they were ballroom dancers who were so in tune that music was unnecessary. He had a painful thought that if they didn't hurry, he was going to come right in his shorts. What a waste. Let's get going.

He found no resistance from Tiffany as he began taking off her clothes in the hallway and on through the living room. By the time they fell across the bed in her darkened bedroom, she had on only a gold chain that held a delicate GT. Not a word had been spoken from their initial greetings. It swiftly crossed his mind whether they could be together during the entire visit with no words at all beyond her 'Hey, there' and his final 'Good-bye.' They surely didn't need words to fuck.

Because he knew she preferred it, he tried to get into some foreplay, but he knew that it would be dangerous if he wanted to complete the act inside of her rather than on the sheets beside her. He rolled Tiffany over on her back and moved on top of her shimmering body. As intent as he was on penetration, a wild question popped into his head, 'What had she put on her body that gave it the aura of clouds and stars?' The thought was fleeting, because the tip of his penis had touched the dampness waiting his probing. Jon thrust only once, and he felt that they had crossed from ordinary to unique, encouraging each other to soar. He pumped against her, feeling their perspiration mingle, and their breathing become one. It was perfect except that it was over in a flash. He wanted more but rolled over and was content to just relax.

"Baby, what happened? You're usually a leisurely lover. Tonight you were just like Speedy Gonzalez," Tiffany asked in a mocking tone.

"Tonight, Tiffany, just thinking about you had me almost past the point of no return. Maybe it was your voice. Maybe that shirt you had on for about a minute or maybe it was your body. You shine like you have been polished with stardust," Jon carefully pronounced his words between the panting from their brief lovemaking.

"It's my little surprise for you. When I saw this 'sex enhancer' advertised, I knew it would please you. I didn't know it was going to almost ruin our evening. You're so impressionable, Jon, and I love it." She was proud that the Moonmist Body Spray had the desired effect. She didn't have a lot of time, because Lonnie was coming over at 8 o'clock.

Jon liked that Tiffany always kept some faint light in the bedroom. Because they would reflect in the mirror, she'd placed five candles on the dresser. It was enough light for him to scan her luminous skin. The flickering candles seemed to animate the outline of her body with thousands of miniature fireflies. Jon had never seen such artistry in a woman's figure before. She was so beautiful, and she was his for this year. Maybe he'd change his pattern and extend their relationship into the next academic year. At the moment it seemed like a magnificent idea, but he knew that he was being influenced by her mastery of creating powerful, sensual vibes.

"You're always full of surprises, Tiffany, but this might be the best one ever. You have no idea how breathtaking you are shining here in the dark like you were just delivered by a cloud lit by a stream of moonbeams."

"You're wrong, Jon, I know how I look. I wanted to have this effect on you. It was to be my gift to you and a reminder for you that I'm in your life, waiting for you even during your busy and crazy days. I want you to sit at your desk, or be in a meeting, or be talking to faculty but be thinking of me as I look right now. Won't that be fun, Jon? They'll think you're paying attention to their words, but you'll probably be trying to keep your erection down," Tiffany's words rolled softly off her tongue and across his body leaving tiny chills.

"Baby, you're a sadist. How will I ever concentrate on my job again? I'll see tiny sparkles everywhere, because they'll be permanently engraved in my mind. As you look tonight, you should be preserved as a work of art," Jon was still feeling breathless from both the exertion and the images she created for him. He wanted to become lost again in her body. Instead he struggled to clear his head and start the process of leaving.

Jon Lindholm stretched, rolled to his side and sat up on the side of the bed. It helped to feel closer to sanity in a sitting position with his back to his young lover.

"You drove me to such a frenzy, baby, that I didn't get a chance to go to the bathroom before you had me in bed. Don't go away while I make a quick trip so I can really relax." Jon was headed out of the bedroom before he had completed the sentence.

Tiffany jumped out of the bed and looked at the clock that was on her nightstand. It was already 7:10. She blew out the candles to reset the stage for the final curtain, their good night scene. She needed to get Jon on his way before Lonnie arrived. She knew that would be easier if she had her clothes on, so she scurried around the room finding what had so recently been flung aside. She was just buttoning her very tight skirt when she heard water running. Her timing was perfect.

A moment of bright light, pointing toward the middle of the room, stretched across the plush carpet and quickly disappeared as Jon came back, sat on the edge of the bed and reached for Tiffany. He was surprised that she wasn't where he left her.

"Tiffany? Has that shimmering apparition dissolved into

thin air?"

"Back to reality. Never want to get too much of a good thing, Jon. You might become bored with what's now a fantastic relationship," Tiffany said brightly while she headed toward the living room.

"Ummm, it is that, baby. But I don't think I'll get bored with a sex magician like you. You keep me guessing all the time," Jon sneaked a look at the clock, hoping Tiffany wouldn't notice, and added in a voice that he hoped sounded unhappy, "Today's been a bitch, and I still have work to do to get caught up. I've just enough time to catch a cup of coffee with you and then it's back to the office."

"If you weren't so terrific, Jonathan, I'd get angry that you don't have more time for me tonight. Fortunately for you, I do understand the terrible pressure that's all around you, and I don't want to add to it, Sweetheart."

"Go put the water on and I'll get dressed. I'll be there by the time you're ready to spoon out the instant coffee," Jon said, looking at his clothing on a rumpled heap beside the bed. He was sure that they hadn't been there long enough to be wrinkled. He often worried, when he left Tiffany's condo and went home, that he looked like they came directly out of a laundry basket. So far Laurie had never mentioned that he looked like he had slept in his clothes, which sometimes he had.

Jon was knotting his tie as he joined Tiffany in the kitchen. The room was the only one in the condo that didn't reflect her personality, or maybe it did. She wasn't a cook and believed that fast food became a gourmet meal when you put it on a real plate! The kitchen was exactly how the contractor left it after his final owner's inspection: completely equipped but bland.

"I love the aroma of freshly ground coffee brewing in a time-seasoned pot," Jon joked as he buried his face in Tiffany's shining hair.

"Then you should be hanging around with my mother instead of me, Sweetheart. I need a map just to find the microwave to heat the water."

"I'm sure your mother is quite something if she produced

you, but I guess I'll skip the gourmet coffee and take gourmet sex instead."

"Good choice. I don't need a map to find your most interesting body parts. Now, tell me what happened today so you can get back to your boring li'l ole office. Oh, are you able to be in your office?"

"Not really. I've been operating in the provost's office, and he's downstairs in another one. It's been like musical chairs. Everyone has been temporarily displaced," he took a breath and continued to tell just enough so he could easily be on his way. "That makes everything more difficult to do, but the harder part of the day has been having the police around always asking a million questions. They make us all feel like we are suspects!"

"They should be nice to you. You're being inconvenienced and upset just because the shooting was in your office. It wasn't your fault that some silly student broke into your office and got killed. You're a victim too, Jon," Tiffany said in amazement, "Police have no compassion. Everything you read these days confirms that victims are just a forgotten group. They're treated worse than the guilty who have all the civil rights people working for them."

"Don't get carried away, baby. I know your viewpoint that almost everyone is a victim of something, and that our parents probably started the whole process. I don't like being questioned about where I was at the time of the shooting and how did I feel about Andy, but the detectives are just doing their job. The objective is to find the murderer and, unfortunately, so far they haven't a clue. They've no time for related victims."

Jonathan hoped that he didn't sound like he was delivering a lecture, but it annoyed him that the young people today never wanted to accept responsibilities for their actions. Oh, no, they were *all* victims. But, surely not this little sex machine, he thought. Before she met him, she probably left a whole pile of victims behind her. Jon felt that Tiffany would always be ahead of her peers and needed someone with his experience to reign her in. He knew with her schoolwork, campus activities and their time together, she had no time to produce new victims. He could consider himself as a protector of the young men who were not caught in her aura.

"I guess in this case, if you can be generous, I can too. But, I do hate the idea that those police would even suspect that you could be involved. I think I could actually feel such serious guilt if I was with the person who did this. And, Jonathan-love, the only guilt I feel from you at the moment is that you believe you must get back to Georgia Tech business. So drink up your coffee, and be off," Tiffany said cheerily as she noted on the oven clock that it was already 7:35.

"You're the best, baby. You can read my moods and react in the most positive ways. You have many talents. I'm so glad we were able to see each other tonight but you're right, I must get moving."

Tiffany knew that she could gently push him out the door in about ten minutes. They liked to prolong their good byes, leaving a powerful incentive to see each other soon again. If they stayed on her time schedule, he would be gone in time for her to jump into the shower and get rid of this messy Moonmist before Lonnie arrived.

Chapter 27

Lonnie Tedesco

Lonnie was rushing to be at Tiffany's by eight. He knew that she didn't like to wait, but also he was anxious to be with her. Their time together earlier in the day had given him an immediate rush and a daylong high. He had no idea that their lovemaking could take an entirely new turn. He hadn't planned on his aggressive attack, but he wasn't sorry that he had done it. He felt truly macho today.

Lonnie drove down Peachtree Street as fast as traffic would allow and screeched his tires when he stopped at the last red light before the driveway into her parking garage. He was impatient and tapped his fingers on the steering wheel, commanding the light to change. Because of being held up at the intersection, he also had to wait a few seconds as another car exited the same driveway. He was attracted to the sleek, sports car, thought it looked familiar and took a second glance at in his rearview mirror.

"Son of a bitch! That license plate is GT 1. That's the p-p-president's car. I wouldn't have expected to see him off campus when the whole institute is going fucking nuts. He's supposed to be the leader. He should stick to his job." Lonnie said out loud to himself.

Lonnie Tedesco parked the car and went to the phone to call Tiffany. He waited through six rings, hung up, looked at his watch and thought, "I'm only five minutes early. I would've thought she would be right there to answer my call. I guess she's just too busy. Maybe cleaning up the condo," he thought cynically.

He waited and watched the second hand go around the

face of his watch three times. Each minute seemed to be forever. He was sure that once he was with Tiffany the same amount of time would fly by. At the end of three minutes, Lonnie picked up the phone and dialed again. It rang twice.

"Hey, this is Tiffany. Is this Lonnie?"

"You bet your sweet, beautiful ass it's Lonnie. Buzz the door, and I'll be there before you can reach your door to tell me how glad you are to see me."

"OK, Speedy. I'll race you to the elevator door on my floor. You know I can beat you, but it'll be fun for me to be the winner and get a prize."

"I'm only speedy until I get to your condo. Then we want to exercise my s-s-staying power. I'm on my way," Lonnie said as he could feel himself getting excited as he anticipated the evening with her.

Tiffany was waiting for him in the hallway in the shortest skirt and tightest top he had ever seen. Her hair was wet and her face glowing from her shower. He often wondered why she didn't pose for Playboy magazine. She had more outstanding equipment than any woman he'd ever seen and she didn't mind showing it.

"As predicted, I won. Of course it really wasn't fair, because I only had a few feet to go and you had to come up in the elevator, but you still owe me a prize."

She led the way and Lonnie gave her a playful caress on her denim clad behind. The material barely covered her rounded butt and couldn't possibly be flexible enough for her to sit down.

They closed the door and Lonnie reached out and pinned Tiffany to the wall as he asked, "And, what s-s-should that prize be?"

"A chance to make up for your rude behavior today."

"Hey, I was just doing what my old man has told me that a real man does. It's c-c-called staking my claim."

"Well, your dad isn't my idea of a role model. But let's not talk about him. Loosen up your grip. Who wants to hang around my hallway?"

Tiffany wiggled artistically to suggest that Lonnie let her

loose, so they could go into the living room. Instead he responded by pressing his body tightly toward her, pushed both her hands above her head, flat against the wall, and kissed her hard. He was already excited as he felt his jeans tight against his cock. Physically he was in control of her and liked thinking about his earlier actions and how good he felt making Tiffany submit. He hadn't forced any girl to do it since his first time when he was only 14 years old, and believed then if he stopped, he was admitting that he wasn't macho. To preserve his own ego, he raped his little sister's best friend and told her if she said anything he would do it again. She never came to their house again and he easily convinced himself that it was just part of growing up.

When he thought about Tiffany struggling on the floor of her bedroom several hours ago, he had no remorse. It wasn't as if they had never had sex before. It was his choice to be dominant. As he often thought when he was the star of a football game, "I'm strong. I'm smart. I'm omnipotent. I can beat them all. I'm a winner.' He would call the plays...on the field and with this woman.

While Lonnie held her in the vice of his own strength, Tiffany felt a moment of panic. She knew she couldn't physically overcome him. That had been proven this afternoon. Lonnie's strength and determination would simply create pain for her, but she believed that she could beat him with her ingenuity. She'd been developing that as long as he'd been developing his body. She relaxed under the pressure of his entire body, returned his kiss and then looked at him with eyes half closed and said softly, "Lonnie, you're really strong. I bet there isn't a football player who can do more than you can. When I watch you play, I'm so proud. I actually get tears in my eyes. I jump up and down and scream for you to make the touchdowns, and that no one will hurt your gorgeous body. That would really break my heart: if something were to happen to you. You're always on my mind and in my soul." Then Tiffany sighed and closed her eyes as if in passion or prayer.

Tiffany very slowly moved her body and felt the first softening of Lonnie's muscles. His hands loosened around her wrists and the blood began to flow again out to her fingertips. She placed her one arm across Lonnie's shoulder and stroked the back of his head. He too sighed with a sound of contentment. She put her other arm behind his neck and cradled him like they were slow dancing. She moved her feet in time with a little tune she began to hum. Lonnie encircled her waist with his arms and moved to the same beat that she had started. Hoarsely he whispered, "I l-l-love you, Tiffany. I l-l-love you."

She knew the crisis was passed and that she could simply take him by the hand and walk into the light of the living room. They'd make love tonight, but it would be on her terms. He wasn't scary anymore.

"Hey, Sweetheart, how about a beer or a Coke? We can have a drink and some munchies and snuggle up while we catch our breath. Sometimes we just can't think straight when we get together, Lonnie."

"You got that right. You drive me crazy. A beer sounds like something we both need and of course munchies to go with the beer. Then get back here in a hurry, because I like that snuggling part the best."

Tiffany went to the kitchen, where she had just put away the cup from Jon's coffee, got two beers, a glass and several bags of chips and pretzels. As she was returning to the sofa, Lonnie said loudly, "Hey, I saw the president's car leaving the garage when I drove in. I s-s-saw him here once before."

"Bill Clinton?" Tiffany asked being careful that her voice sounded completely natural.

Lonnie looked at her like she was playing some game and said slowly, "Nooo, Tiffany, the president of Georgia Tech. You know, the old guy, Lindholm."

"Really? Wonder why he would come here? Must know someone in the building," Tiffany said glad that she could pay attention to juggling the beer, the glass and the snack bags.

"He must have a very close friend here to get him off campus hours after a shooting. I guess he doesn't feel that it's related to him. It was only a st-st-student. When I saw the GT 1 car, I thought maybe you would know, that maybe you'd s-s-seen him here too."

"No. Never have. Here's your beer. I know you don't like a glass so just take the can. Now move over and make room for me. I want to know if you've heard anymore about that shooting?" Tiffany changed the subject easily.

Lonnie took a long draw from the can while he examined Tiffany's face. She didn't seem the least bit interested in the president or his visit to the building. He assumed she would show some reaction. Instead she moved over and situated herself against him in the crook of his arm, tilted her head back and waited for his response.

"No, lots of talk but no one seems to know anything. I heard that the other Lindholm was on the news talking about the guy who was shot. Everyone says that the Atlanta police couldn't find a criminal if he wore an arrow and a sign that said: 'Here Is a Criminal.' They also say that the Tech police are even dumber. I heard the killing relates to drugs, the guy was trying to steal a computer, it was a drive by shooting, and that he had t-t-trashed the office because the president insulted him one day he was there. Must be every p-p-possible theory out on campus," Lonnie said as he took a huge handful of chips.

"I heard that he had broken into the president's office so all of those things could be true. I would think that the police could figure that out without much help."

"We'll see but I think the rumors are true: Atlanta police are just wasted. Anyway, who wants to talk about this, I'd rather fool around. Why don't you help me take off your teeny, tiny blouse and let me have a good look at your not so teeny, tiny boobs?" Lonnie drew Tiffany's top up over her head. She raised her arms and he buried his face in her cleavage in one continuous movement like his head was on a string attached to her hands. His tongue moved rapidly from between her breasts, across the soft, rounded flesh until it found a hard nipple. That was what he was looking for. He wanted to feel her erection like she could feel his. He pushed her skirt up out of the way and explored between her legs as he continued to suck on her nipple.

"We can do it here, Sweetheart, but we'd be more comfortable in my bed, "Tiffany whispered.

"Let's not waste a minute moving. Besides, here with the lights on, I can see your body move and the look at your face. I feel like when we do it with the lights on that we're doing something completely honest and open. Nothing to hide. What more could we want than to be honest with each other?" Lonnie felt his mouth begin to get dry in anticipation and excitement.

"Lonnie, you're so special. I'll watch you, too. I love you and your great body," Tiffany said very softly as Lonnie slipped out of his jeans and pulled her down to the floor on top of him."Take your time, love. We have hours and hours and hours..."

Chapter 28

Oliver Andrew Dren, Jr.

It was still dark when Frank awakened and wondered momentarily why he felt depressed. Of course. This was the day of Andy's funeral. A time when a conclusion is formally and ceremonially drawn on his short life. Frank and Peter had watched the weather channel before going to bed, and the forecast was for a sunny, balmy March day. The kind of day that Georgia was known for and bragged about. They were glad that the weather wasn't going to lower their already gloomy mood. With much reluctance, he dragged himself out of bed and alerted his roommate that it was time to get his butt on the road. He had promised to have the pallbearers at the Dren's home early.

The plan was for all of the pallbearers to meet in the Student Center parking lot and then drive together to Dalton in two cars. The professors had offered to drive. To casual observers, the group may have looked like they were going on a corporate field trip, but the serious expressions on the six faces would have created doubt for that theory. To many on campus, there would've been no question where these men were going, because the Technique had announced the funeral plans in a late edition the night before. It also had carried short statements from Detective Wesley and President Lindholm.

Under Lindy Lindholm's byline, Wesley was quoted as the lead into the promised follow-up article:"We've met with the president, Chief George Fancer and others on campus to compile information to use in our investigation of the shooting of Andrew Dren. The state crime lab is examining evidence from the crime scene. There are no serious suspects at this time. We're working closely with the Georgia Tech police and support the precautions they're taking to protect everyone on the campus."

The statement from the president followed toward the end of the report just above the time and place of the funeral."It's been a difficult day for the Tech family. We mourn the loss of one of our outstanding students. I implore you to come forward if you have information. I'm confident (because it's the right thing to do) you'll do this in any case, but in addition to my personal $5,000 reward I announced earlier, Microsoft has added $20,000 for information leading to the apprehension of the killer. Andy Dren was employed by Microsoft before enrolling in the College of Computing to earn his masters degree. Their regional manager, Robert Wolfson, said that Mr. Dren was a valued employee, and they had looked forward to his return to the company upon his graduation."

• • •

"I brought several copies of the directions to the Dren's home in case we get separated, and I picked up extras of the two special editions of the Technique for anyone who didn't see them yesterday," Frank told the other five men."It should take us about an hour and a half to get to Dalton and Mr. Dren may have special instructions for us. I've no idea what pallbearers should do. I've never even been to a funeral."

Within minutes the two cars drove out of the parking lot and headed for I 75, a professor and two students in each vehicle.

Spread throughout the campus were similar clusters of people preparing to drive north to attend the funeral. Those who knew Andy went with a sadness in their hearts. Some were going only to see who else had felt it was important to be there and others were going out of curiosity feeling more like they were going on an adventure. Many of those, getting dressed like they were having job interviews, probably were going simply because classes had been suspended for the day, which gave a particular importance to attending the funeral. In each group, they talked about three subjects: whether the murderer was still on campus, if he (or she) would be gutsy enough to attend the service, and the $25,000 reward.

Tiffany Walton had made plans to go to Dalton with three other coeds who were in her calculus class. One of them was in the College of Computing and said that the murder was the only topic of conversation she had heard since it happened. The three girls felt that they should be there so the family would see that Andy had lots of friends. Tiffany had another reason for going. She knew Jon would be there, and it would send him ballistic to see her hanging around. He was always concerned that people would notice. Sometimes she hoped that they would, like the night that old alum caught them in Jon's office. She thought it was really funny how Jon had pretended that he was just being a good guy for one of the students. Yeah, right! Surely the old guy wasn't that dense. He might've been old, but if he went to Tech, he wasn't stupid.

Janeen was organizing the cars and food that would be going to Dalton. At the same time, she was orienting two secretaries from the College of Architecture who would cover the office for the day. She was glad that she was being kept busy with a myriad of small chores so she didn't have to think about why this day was not routine. Even getting dressed this morning had taken on a different meaning. She had chosen a tailored navy blue suit with a cream silk blouse with tiny rose and blue dots, because the outfit was somber, but not dull. She looked around the office at everyone who was assembled, ready to leave, and noticed they all had made the same decision. The proper dress for funerals had softened over the past decade. She was glad they weren't all wearing black.

• • •

Oliver and Susan Dren both were awake before dawn but didn't hurry to start the day. Finally they heard the noises of the other one as they showered and dressed. Father and daughter met in the kitchen where Susan was making coffee and pouring juice from a container.

"Morning, Daddy," she said as he kissed her on the cheek and gave her a quick hug."The coffee is almost ready. Do you want anything else?"

"No, honey, anything would taste like straw this morning, but I think a cup of coffee is just perfect."

He sat down at the kitchen table, unfolded the newspaper

and turned to the obituaries. He knew what he was going to find there, but he had to see it in print on a page that he wished was reserved for old folks. Each act since the call about 'an accident' at Tech he felt was a farewell to his son: learning he was shot, identifying the body, ordering the hearse to pick up Andy and bring him back to Dalton, seeing the headlines in their local paper, reading the obituaries and finally, today, going to the funeral. Today was the final goodbye, but he was determined that it be a tribute to Andy in his many roles: as a good son, close friend, admired employee, serious student, and fine young man.

"Daddy, you're letting your coffee get cold. I can pop it into the microwave and heat it up again."

He took a sip and shook his head, "No, ma'am, it's just the way I like it. In fact, Susan, you make a great cup of coffee. Lots of people can't do that."

They heard cars in the driveway and Oliver looked at his watch: 9:35. Frank was right on time. He looked out the window and said to Susan, "Do you think we should make more coffee to go with the muffins that we got last night? The students are probably going to be hungry."

"I used mother's big, party pot, Daddy. I think we'll be fine for now. We'll need more when we come back for lunch but then we'll have others to help." Oliver Dren stopped and took an appraising look at his daughter. She'd grown up a lot since her mother died and today she was simply taking over as a reliable hostess. Life would be hard without Andy, but he wouldn't be lonely because Susan was there.

• • •

"Damn, Wes, this looks like as many people as there were at the funeral after the Olympic Centennial Park bombing. I thought it was going to be easy to check out the people attending this one. Small town. Small group. Shit, we'll be lucky if we even see them all," Billy Joe said. They had parked their unmarked car on the street.

"At least we get three shots at them: here, at the house and from the van. When I called Mr. Dren about being at the funeral. He invited the two of us to lunch with everyone else," Wes told his partner.

"We blend right in. In these dull threads, do you think they will mistake us for professors?"

"I hope so. For sure you would've been noticed if you'd worn your normal screamin' tie, pink shirt, shades, and we arrived in your purple Taurus. Today we'll not even be noticed—- for awhile. By the way, do you see our police van? It's so plain looking that I haven't noticed it in the crowd."

"Yep. It's over to the right, the vehicle where they're unloadin' some flowers. Damn! Luis Carrero should've been an actor. He loves the role playin'. There he is, Wes, in basic black with a white flower in his buttonhole, lookin' exactly like an undertaker's assistant. If I know Luis, he made a run on a cemetery in Atlanta to pick up the flowers for his props." LaCrosse saw the Atlanta police technician point and say something. Then two young men helping him disappeared into the church, each lugging two huge floral displays.

"It's amazing that the chief agreed to sending the mobile laboratory. He probably has worked out every mile they must drive so the guys can't add to the cost of the trip by detouring for a break or lunch. If the old man gets any cheaper with the way he runs our department, we'll all have to volunteer our time."

"Yeah, Wes, he's a piss ant, for sure, but he's our piss ant. The bastard's probably ours for life since no one else would take him."

"I think at this point, we separate and go listen and watch all of these nice people with hopes of finding the clue to just one rotten person. That's all we need. So let's see what we can learn."

LaCrosse nodded and walked away like he'd never spoken to Wes in his life. There was no reason to think anyone would be looking for them or know them, but they still simply would prefer to fade into the background. They would look for people they already knew had a relationship to the victim, watch for anyone who seemed, perhaps, out of place or somehow suspicious, and listen carefully for conversations that might include clues.

As Billy Joe walked in one direction and he walked in another, Wes took a quick glance at his watch. Fifteen minutes until the service would begin. At the rate people were arriving, he was sure there'd be some mourners left on the outside of the church.

The first person he saw who he knew by name was Lindy Lindholm. He noticed that the young man was surveying the crowd in the same manner as he."He has the typical media stance. Looking for anything that can make a good story, while I look for the person who will give him the ultimate story," Wes thought as he skirted around the group where he saw Lindy enthusiastically greet Dani Swain. He really didn't want to be drawn into an interview nor even be recognized.

He watched as a black Mercedes pulled up to the front of the church, three doors opened and Jonathan Lindholm, an attractive, middle aged woman and an older, tall, gray haired man got out. The driver's side door didn't open so Wes assumed they had a driver who would park the car. Several people, including Charles Black, greeted the president as he shook hands and said a few words to them. Wes was reminded of a politician who needed votes and was on the circuit the day before the election. He didn't recognize the taller man, but remembered that Janeen had said a trustee named Earl Prince had a Mercedes

He was watching the car pull out of the driveway when he caught sight of Janeen walking with four other women. She looked so pretty this morning. As fresh as the day itself or maybe as fresh as those daisies in her kitchen. She walked directly to the woman who was with the president. She smiled as she saw Janeen. The two women seemed to have important things to talk about and walked a short distance ahead of the two men.

Wesley often thought of the persons who became part of each case as actors in a play. While he continued to study the crowd he had an image in his mind of a page in a playbook that was titled: Cast of Characters as they enter the scenes. Jonathan Lindholm, president of the institution; Mrs. Lindholm, wife of the president; Lindy Lindholm, president's son; Janeen Carson, executive assistant to the president; etc. etc. Act one had closed and this was act two, scene one: a church in Dalton.

As if responding to a sign, the crowd began to move into

the church. Wes saw Billy Joe following the flow behind a cluster of young men who looked like they should all play football. Seeing those big, healthy bodies reminded Wes of how inappropriate a funeral was when the deceased was a young person. It just shouldn't be that way.

Wes kept his eye on Billy Joe as he went into the church and situated himself at the opposite side of the sanctuary. He also managed to note where Janeen was sitting, directly back of the rows reserved for the family. She was with the same four women she was with when he first spied her. He decided that the Georgia Tech administrative entourage was all in the same area. Student types seemed to be congregated together farther back like they would be in a classroom. Wes concluded that the rest of the assemblage was Dalton friends, neighbors and relatives.

As he looked around for any kind of a sign that could help their case, he categorized the three groups. He was still interested in the president's group because of where the shooting had occurred, and that there was an undercurrent of something that they wanted to keep secret. He was interested in the students because he knew that firearms were easily available on the campus. He had much less interest in the local crowd. Of course the murderer could be in that group, but he doubted it. He was beginning with the premise that the person they were looking for was definitely related to Atlanta and maybe to the campus. As a last consideration, Wes admitted that the trip to Dalton could be a wild-ass idea that produced nothing. There was no guarantee that the murderer would be bold enough to come here today.

Wesley caught an unusual motion out of the corner of his eye and turned slightly to see what it was. He saw Billy Joe raising his hand slightly as if he were greeting someone across the room. Billy Joe nodded his head toward the right of where he was standing and then immediately looked away and took a few steps forward like he was looking for a seat.

Wes scanned the congregation in the direction of his partner's motion. At first he saw only the sea of students and wondered who had gotten Billy Joe's attention. Then he zeroed in on two men who did not look at all like students: too old, shaggier hair and clothes that didn't quite fit right. He watched for a few minutes and was intrigued that although they looked like they would be more at home at the Atlanta Union Mission, a center for homeless men, they seemed to know many of the students and were quite comfortable in their surroundings. They were certainly his biggest surprise.

As Wes was concentrating on the two men, his eye caught a beautiful young woman. Just as he switched his gaze to her, he noticed that President Lindholm had turned slightly in his seat also, as if scanning the crowd, but his attention was fixed on the same pretty face. Because of her youth and where she was sitting, the detective decided that she was a coed. He could see the full face of the woman and was amazed at the expression she returned to the president. She very slowly licked her lips, lowered her eyes demurely, gave him a Mona Lisa smile, and then mouthed a short but obvious message: I love you. Wes was so shocked that he almost missed the president's hasty nod as he turned away and looked straight ahead.

"Son of a bitch! Did I really see what I thought I saw? A chippy and the damn president sending cutesy signals?" Wes thought as he checked out who the girl was with. He also glanced at the president's wife to see if anyone else had intercepted the I love you. No one seemed to notice. Wes could almost believe that he imagined it except, *he didn't*. He was so engrossed in his newest finding that he almost missed the beginning of the ceremony. "Andy's family has asked me to thank ya'll for sharin' this day with them. They want it to be a celebration of the 30 years that Andrew Oliver Dren, Jr. was with us and added to our lives. Each person who knew him is richer because of his fine character and moral integrity. Collectively we have lost a piece of our future and the world will be less because of Andy's untimely death. He and the other students who gather here today have been our hope and our salvation. We of the older generation trust that today can act as inspiration for them to go on and do the kind of good works that Andy would have done if he were still alive. Let us all raise our voices together by turnin' to page 87 and singin'."

Chapter 29

Wes T. Wesley

The two homicide detectives situated themselves in strategic locations as the congregation filed out of the church. A few people stopped to talk to Oliver, some were sobbing out of control and couldn't say a word so they turned away quickly and were gone. The students' reactions were mixed. Several seemed to have never experienced a funeral before so they hung back wondering what was expected of them. The football players spoke a few words to the Drens and then walked toward their cars. Billy Joe overheard one say, "He must've been one hell-uv-a guy. I wish I'd known him better." Another responded, "He couldn't have been as good as the preacher said, if he broke into the president's office." The first voice explained as the six athletes went on down the driveway, "He didn't do that. He worked in the president's office.""Oh, yeah? I didn't know that."

Wes looked at the doorway just in time to see the pretty coed come outside surrounded by her friends. She glowed in the morning sunlight and looked lovelier than she did in the church. The detective automatically looked for the president and found that he, the gray haired man and Charles Black were together deep in conversation. Mrs. Lindholm and Janeen were directly behind, walking silently.

As Wes expected, the young woman's head swiveled as if she had heard a familiar voice. She looked directly at the president, daring him to speak to her. Instead he looked away and said something to his companions. Wes glanced at the president's wife as she looked at the young woman with serious interest. The coed didn't seem to notice that she had gotten Mrs. Lindholm's attention rather than her husband's and continued to look at the back of Jon's head.

Janeen reached out to Laurie Lindholm, leaned closer to her and said a few words. Laurie's eyes left the student, looked at Janeen as she responded to her question.

Wes and Billy Joe joined together, went to their inconspicuous Ford and waited until most of the cars had lined up in the procession that was going to the cemetery. They didn't want to be near the head of the line nor at the end. They wanted to be unnoticed. As they waited for an opportunity to cut into the line, a car stopped and the driver motioned for them to go ahead.

"You go first. I don't mind following you......anywhere," said a sexy female voice that made Wes look at the driver rather than positioning the car into the line. He was amazed that the face he was looking at was the beautiful woman he'd seen in the church. He hesitated a moment and heard the other girls in the car were giggling and one said, "Tiffany! You're just wicked."

"Thanks, gorgeous. Your gentility is as preeminent as your face," Wes said using a line that he knew would be remembered when he spoke to her later.

"Where did you learn to speak like that? I love it," Tiffany said just before the Ford settled into the space in front of her T-bird. As Wes returned his attention to the road, he heard another peal of laughter from the girls.

"That's fuckin' jail bait, Wes. She's a knockout, but she's probably not as old as Jason," Billy Joe chastised his partner.

"Maybe I'll just take her home as a gift for Jason. She'd be quite a daughter-in- law, don't you think? Besides I know who she is, and I was just about ready to tell you."

"What do you mean, you know who she is? She, obviously, doesn't know who you are, punk."

"Not yet but she will. That's Lindholm's playmate."

"You're full of shit. That girl's a fuckin' student. A baby girl student. As arrogant as that bastard is, he's not stupid," Detective LaCrosse exclaimed.

Wes proceeded to tell Billy Joe what he'd observed in the church and at the doorway. He added how Janeen had diverted Mrs. Lindholm's attention, so he believed that she knew what was going on.

"You're usually right about these kind of vibes, but I can't imagine that the son of a bitch could be stupid enough to fool around with a fuckin' coed."

"Would you like to turn those words around, Billy Joe? How about: the son of a bitch could be stupid enough to be fuckin' around with a foolish coed."

"Damn, Wes, there are more side bar stories to this murder than we need. It sure is gettin' interestin'. Which reminds me, you know when I tried to get your attention in the church. Did you see those two guys that looked like they were homeless?"

"Yeah, I saw them. I can't guess why they were there. What do you know?"

"I got closer to the pew where they were sittin'. Not close enough to really get all of the conversation but I got a feelin' for the relationship of the group. Six students seemed to all be together, and I'm damn sure that the two men had come with them.

"The two older guys definitely are well-acquainted with the students. One's name is Walter. It's fuckin' strange, but I could see that he's very upset. There was a time durin' the service that this Walter dude wiped tears away. One of the girls reached over and patted his arm several times. That's all I know now. I'm hopin' they'll be at the lunch and I can learn more, because no one else, other than ole Billy Joe, seemed to even give Walter and his buddy a second glance."

Everyone walked toward the gravesite and quietly waited. The minister again took charge. His words were brief before the casket was lowered into the ground. Susan and Oliver Dren stepped forward holding hands and carrying the toy gray mouse from Andy's computer and a single sunflower. They dropped them on top of the coffin and turned back to join the other mourners.

Wesley found himself having to wipe away a tear that had somehow already reached the middle of his cheek. He'd seen many funerals and grieving families and hadn't felt the depth of emotion that he felt at this time. He was surprised at his tear, but not surprised that he was thinking of the tragedy of a father's loss and of the goodness of his own son, Jason. He wished he'd known Andy Dren.

Chapter 30

Tiffany JoAnne Walton

The house was already filled with people when the two detectives arrived. Most were unknown to them, but both were beginning to recognize more of Wes' growing cast of characters. As a case crystallized the individuals involved took shape, materialized out of shadows. One-dimensional individuals became three-dimensional human beings.

Wes and Billy Joe looked for familiar faces. They would have a short time to move about anonymously. After that, someone, knowing why they're there, will tell a friend or another person will overhear a comment and their unobtrusive observing will become a topic of conversation.

Wes scanned the crowd and located the president, his wife and the trustee surveying the tremendous array of food. It ranged from baked ham and yams, to poached salmon with cheese grits, to beef stroganoff over noodles, to spicy carrot cake and a Southern tradition, banana pudding. Wes watched the Lindholms as they filled their plates, standing next to each other but not talking. From the body language, he was convinced that their silence was not a comfortable condition of two people who had been married for more than 20 years. Wes' gaze drifted beyond the table, looking for Little Miss Muffet. He was sure she was close at hand.

Tiffany and her three giggly friends were at the opposite end of the table. She looked cool and completely in control of herself.

Even though Wes was careful to never allow his eyes to rest long on one person, he found himself looking directly at Tiffany as she turned and their eyes locked. She gave him a tiny smile as she left the buffet table and walked straight in his direction.

"Hey there again. Could we be following each other?" Tiffany asked as she reached his side.

"The last time I noticed, I was the one in front—-because you were so kind to make room for my car in the procession."

"Exactly! So I must be following you. By the way, I'm Tiffany Walton."

The detective hesitated knowing she expected him to tell her who he was. He could feel her anticipation as he said, "Hello, Tiffany Walton. What brings you to this sad occasion?"

"Andy was a student at Georgia Tech and so am I. My friends and I wanted Mr. Dren to know the students sympathize with him and his daughter. It's such an awful thing. Are you related to the Drens?"

"No, not related if you mean like family. My name is ..." Wes began, but was interrupted by Janeen.

"Wes. I didn't know you were going to be here. Hey, Tiffany, I'm surprised to see you here too. Did you know Andy?"

"No, Ms. Carson. I was just telling 'Wes' that many of us are here to give support to the Drens."

"That's very nice, Tiffany. I'm sure the Drens appreciate the effort. It's very thoughtful," Janeen told the young woman just as she saw Laurie Lindholm walking toward them.

"Wes, here comes Mrs. Lindholm. Have you met her?" Janeen asked Wes but had her eyes on Tiffany.

"Janeen, do you want to join us for lunch? We won't be staying long. Jon and Earl must both be back to Atlanta for meetings this afternoon."

"That would be fine, Mrs. Lindholm. By the way, have you met Wes Wesley? He's the detective in charge of the murder investigation."

"No, but I've heard Jon and my son Lindy speak of you, Detective Wesley. We all hope you'll find this terrible person soon," Laurie turned to Tiffany, "I'm sorry. I didn't mean to ignore you, my dear. I don't believe we've met. I'm Laurie Lindholm."

"I'm Tiffany Walton. I'm a student at Georgia Tech, but you wouldn't know me, I'm sure," Tiffany said in her sweetest, Southern style.

"No, I just don't know all of the students and that's my loss, Tiffany," Laurie said almost beating Tiffany with her sweet-voiced response.

"Yes, I've heard that you haven't been well, Mrs. Lindholm. I hope you're doing better."

Laurie was shocked. The comment confirmed her earlier suspicion that there was a relationship between this coed and Jon. She'd learned in California that he'd been using that excuse with his 'girlfriends' to explain why he was tied to his marriage."I feel fine, thank you. But enough about me, Tiffany, since you're a student at Tech, perhaps you know my son, Lindy."

"Everybody knows Lindy because he's on the Technique staff. I believe he's even interviewed Detective Wesley," she said coyly, "I really must go or I may lose my riders back to Atlanta. It was my pleasure meeting you both and seeing you, Ms. Carson," Tiffany quickly turned, walked past Jon without even nodding and rejoined her three friends. What Wes, Janeen or Laurie didn't see was the sly wink that Tiffany gave the president as she passed.

"What an attractive young woman," Laurie said as Tiffany crossed the patio, "Do you know her, Janeen? "

"Yes, like hundreds of Tech students, I've met her a few times. I can't always put names and faces together. I'm glad that she introduced herself. I might've made a gross error," Janeen responded, making an effort to not meet Wes' questioning stare.

"No one expects you to remember all the students on campus. I know Jon certainly doesn't remember most of them. Of course he works harder at remembering the names of alumni—especially donors," Laurie said, sounding like it was a private joke, "Well, Janeen, do join us if you want. It was good to meet you, Detective Wesley. I wish I'd known you the night Andy was shot. Maybe then I could have helped."

Up until Laurie's surprise statement, Wes was being courteous but hadn't considered Mrs. Lindholm as being involved with the case. Now, he looked her eye to eye with a perplexed expression on his handsome face, "What a provocative statement, Mrs. Lindholm. Can you be more explicit? Or is this not the time nor the place?"

"No, this is fine. I've already told Janeen about my strange experience. It's just that I suddenly awakened the night of the murder with an oppressive feeling — like a premonition. I couldn't get back to sleep, so I went down to the terrace room and read until I was finally just plain, worn out. I went back to bed about dawn.

"I'd told Janeen, if I'd known what was happening that night, maybe I could've warned somebody or something. I, well, I feel I received a 'message' of sorts."

Laurie seemed to falter, almost stutter, "Oh, Detective, you must think I'm a crazy lady. I suppose it was just a bad dream."

"Perhaps, Mrs. Lindholm, but there are definitely such responses as intuition or anticipation of good or evil events. I wonder what Dr. Lindholm had to say relating to your premonition after learning about the murder."

"Actually, I never have mentioned it to him. He doesn't believe even a little bit in that kind of thing. He probably never knew I was gone for most of the night. You can't hear any sounds from the terrace room up in the bedroom. They're two floors apart and the house is quite large."

"Didn't he say anything when you left or returned to the bedroom? Wouldn't he wonder if you were having a problem?"

Laurie laughed in a throaty, sensuous way and her eyes sparkled, "You obviously are not married, Detective Wesley. If spouses awoke each time the other one got up or back down for a variety of reasons, sleeplessness would be a worldwide problem. No, I didn't even notice if Jon was in his bed during my nocturnal wanderings, and I would bet he didn't notice that my bed was empty for hours. Oh, there's Lindy with the pretty anchor lady, Danielle Swain. Will you excuse me while I go say hello to my son?"

Laurie was off in another direction, waving to get her son's attention. She never saw Tiffany Walton join her husband, say a few words and wait expectantly for a response. To the untrained eye it might appear she was inquiring about the quality of the buffet, to Wes it appeared she had challenged him and he had lost.

"Mrs. Lindholm is an interesting woman," Wes said more to himself than to Janeen and then added, "You like her, don't you?"

"Yes, I do. She's a kind, thoughtful person. Laurie's the perfect president's wife."

Wes detected a true admiration in Janeen's voice. He wanted to learn more about the Lindholm's relationship, but it could wait.

"Hey, wonderful woman," he almost whispered, "I've got to do my job, but I'll call you tonight."

"I'll be there, Wes. I imagine I'll be exhausted by the end of this day but I'll look forward to talking to you later. Now, please, go solve this murder. You're our only hope."

Already Wes had learned a lot but whether it related to the killing of Andy Dren, he wasn't sure. His discoveries did open up some intriguing avenues to pursue. It now appeared that Jon Lindholm's response that he and his wife went to sleep and woke up the next morning was too simplistic and didn't match with her description of the night. And, then there were the Tiffany-Jon encounters and Janeen's less than positive reaction to Tiffany. Add the out-of-place homeless guys and one could call this a successful fact finding mission.

The detective headed for the door opening from the patio to the family room adjacent to the kitchen. He'd just stepped into the noisy room when he was stopped by a hand on his arm.

"You weren't going to tell me that you're with homicide, were you, Detective Wesley?" asked Tiffany Walton as she moved closer than necessary to him.

"Oh, I might've. We just hadn't gotten that far yet, Tiffany," Wes said as he sidestepped away from her advance.

"Well, can we get that far now?"

"Too late. You already know. Instead, why don't you tell me why you really came here today?"

Tiffany read this as a serious question and decided to be

completely honest, "I came to see and be seen. It's that simple."

"Well, happy hunting, Tiffany," Wes said as he began to move through the clusters of friends and relatives; perhaps even through clusters of other shallow individuals who wanted 'to see and be seen.'

"Happy hunting to you too, Wes," Tiffany called, drawing out his name to sound like the wind blowing gently through tall grass.

Chapter 31

Billy Joe LaCrosse

Wes drove. Billy Joe slumped in the passenger seat munching on cookies that Susan Dren had given to him in a small bag as they left the luncheon. His eyes were half-closed so that Wes would have assumed he had dropped off to sleep if he hadn't been constantly eating the delicious morsels made by some of the finest cooks in Dalton.

"Damn, Wes. That was one of the best assignments I've had in ages. Two hours of non-stop eatin'. It's good my eyes and ears keep workin' even when my mouth is movin'. I always thought black folks cooked better than white folks, but I may have to reassess my own opinion."

"If you can slow down your attack on the Dalton cookies, I'd like to hear what you learned."

"Right, pardner. That's interestin' too. Let's start with Walter, the one homeless guy. The other one, by the way, is Sander. If they have last names, they didn't feel I needed to know. Walter was damn close to Andy. He says, ' He was my bro at Georgia Tech.' I think that says a lot for the deceased: He had friends from the trustees to the homeless."

Billy Joe popped another small cake into his mouth, chewing for a few seconds, before continuing, "Walter has a part-time job loadin' and unloadin' cartons at Green's Beer and Wine on Ponce. Says he makes about $60 a week. He's been collectin' cans on campus for years. He can make another $50 from that. It's shitty but here's a guy who probably works as many hours as we do but at the end of a week he's got about $110. No wonder he's homeless.

"Walter said that he first got to know Andy when Andy

talked to him one day when he was pushin' his grocery cart filled with cans. Andy asked him if he'd like him to save cans from his residence hall. Walter said he figured he was bein' set up somehow, so he just said he'd think about it and kept movin' along. Andy walked a short distance beside him and said fine, not makin' a big deal of it. I guess he understood how Walter could mistrust a student who looked to him like he had everythin'. For several weeks, their paths crossed by chance, Andy would greet him, say somethin' to get a response from Walter and then just say so long and go wherever he was goin'. Finally one day, Andy asked again if he wanted him to collect cans in his hall. Walter asked, 'What's the drill, man? What do you want from me?' Andy responded, 'Nothing. Cans don't cost me anything, and no one on campus wants 'em.'

"The next day, Andy met Walter at the door of the buildin' and gave him five garbage bags full of cans. Walter exclaimed, "Shit, man. Do you drink 24 hours a day?' Andy laughed and said, 'Of course not. I've been collectin' these since the first day I talked to you. I hoped one day you would trust me.' "

"Walter told me that he was impressed that a white man was concerned that he would trust *him*. Usually it's the other way around. That was enough for Walter. Andy was his friend for life. He didn't know that the friendship would be so short. Then, Wes, Walter said somethin' almost poetic:"The sands are numbered that make up our life."

"That's a quote from Shakespeare's Henry IV. Walter must've paid attention in school. I paid attention to my dad. He thought Shakespeare was the best."

"Maybe he learned it after school, because he said Andy loaned him lots of books and, get this, he was teachin' him to use a computer."

Wes always felt there were several Billy Joe LaCrosses. There was the rough-talking, hard-nosed detective who could see through a person's lies immediately. He believed everyone was guilty of something and had trouble accepting the popular philosophy: I'm a victim, therefore I'm excused from responsible behavior. There was the fun-loving friend who would go out for a couple of beers at Manuel's Tavern and talk for hours about worldwide news and personalities. There was the sensitive family man who was at Little League games and dance recitals sitting proudly next to Cleo, his wife of fourteen years.

Wes sometimes saw where the three Billy Joes would come together in harmony and support his current challenge. Wes felt that was happening in this case. Billy Joe saw how the facts emphasized the good while the bad was still elusive. Why is a young man who appears to have earned the respect and love of so many lie dead in a Dalton cemetery? Whose actions and relationships were in direct opposition to the positive image of Andy Dren? Wes felt they were probably stumbling along a murky course to the answers, but there were several trails to be discovered and investigated before the killer was found.

As Wes thought about Billy Joe and Andy, he took his eyes from the road, looked at his partner and asked, "Do you have a guess about who we should be concentrating on?"

"Nope, only some questions that have no answers yet but seem to go beyond the murder. The undercurrents that surround the president's office are damn strong."

"Gotcha. I agree. We both need to review some of our interviews for hidden messages. I think we should put less attention on the person, Andy, and look more into what he was doing, what unexpected information he might've had,"

"Exactly, Wes. In fact, my next lunchtime eavesdroppin' fits right into that train of thought. I was zeroin' in on that fucker Charles Black, when I realized his wife was with him - a little lady who could be easy to overlook. I stayed to his back and he never realized I was there and she didn't even notice me. She was tellin' him that he better relax and stop apologizin' to everyone. He hissed back, 'Get off my back, Sally. Who'm I apologizin' to?' She struck right back with, 'The president, the trustees, Janeen. Is that enough?'

" Black said quickly, ' OK. OK, Sally. Just forget it. This isn't the place to get into this discussion. You don't know who's around. For god's sake, the murderer could be right in this room!' Before Black spotted me, I was outa there."

"Shit, Billy Joe, I think we've had enough hints that something weird is going on at Tech. Let's look at our notes and tapes when we get back to Atlanta. It'll also be interesting to see what our techno-brats picked up from their van."

"You're right, Wes, we've got a pile of crap to wade through before this incident is erased off our open cases board."

Chapter 32

Jonathan Agnew Lindholm III

Billy Joe and Wes were still on the highway when Jon and Laurie Lindholm, Earl Prince and Janeen Carson got back to the campus. They dropped Laurie at the president's house and went directly to the office because Burl Mentor, Noble Adkins, Eddie Lee Johnson and Austin Cruise were waiting to hear about the funeral and to talk about receiving the latest mega-gift from Hong Kong. Earl stopped on 'The Hill' just long enough to say good-bye and walk with Janeen from the car to the door.

"It was so nice to see you, Janeen. By the way, my dear, you're looking radiant today. I'm so glad that you decided to ride back with us. I'm sure Laurie felt the same. It must get quite boring for her to be stuck with our business conversations all the time. I did think that she was unusually quiet on our ride from Dalton. Don't you agree?" Earl opened the door to the foyer of the Tech Tower.

"I believe the funeral was difficult for her as it might be for any mother who has a son. I've no children, and it was hard for me. I remember so many nice things about Andy." Janeen was feeling teary again.

"I know, I know. I liked him from the first time I met him and that was why I suggested that he talk to Jonathan about helping here in the office," Earl said in a tone of reverence and then added in a much more gruff tone, "The police must find this killer. He must not go unpunished."

"OK, you two. We have to get back to work. Earl, you always seem to have a myriad of things to discuss with Janeen. I guess it's because you've known each other for so many years," Lindholm said sounding peevish.

"You're right, Jonathan, we've been working together for this great institution since Janeen was just a child. She probably knows more about its secrets than any other living soul," Earl Prince said cheerily as he gave Janeen an exaggerated wink. "And, now I bid ya'll farewell. I'm on my way."

The president and his assistant turned and went into the building. He was surprised that the trustees weren't waiting for him, since it was a few minutes past their meeting time.

"Dr. Lindholm, the trustees are waiting for you in your conference room. They said they'd have some privacy there and could begin their meeting," the temporary secretary announced as soon as she saw them enter.

"Oh, start the meeting? I guess I better go right in. I don't want to hold them up."

"Believe me, Dr. Lindholm. Your absence wasn't slowing them down one little bit. They had their heads together before I ever walked away from delivering their sodas."

John didn't like the idea that Burl and his fellow trustees didn't feel it was necessary to wait for him or that they were already covering topics that he may wish to hear.

He walked to the conference room and found the door closed tightly. He definitely wasn't going to knock. It was *his* conference room.

"Good afternoon, gentlemen. I'm so pleased to see that you were all able to be here. This is going to be an important meeting," the president announced as he opened the door wide, walked to the table and sat down. He noted that Burl had chosen to sit at the head of the table as if this was his meeting. "We just returned from Dalton. There must have been 200 students at the funeral. A sad occasion but done with graciousness. The only jarring point was the attendance of two of the detectives from Atlanta."

"That's interesting. Interesting. I wonder what they hoped to learn and what they did learn?" Burl asked.

"I've no clue, Burl. I just wish they'd get the job done and exit the campus. They just seem to be snooping everywhere."

"What do you mean, Jon?" queried Noble Adkins.

"It's just that everyone wants to talk to them, and we've no way of knowing what theories they're putting forth. Even my son and Janeen have been captivated by them."

"Exactly what've they asked or been told that may be of concern to us, Jon?" Burl asked quickly.

"Actually, Burl, I don't have definite statements, but I do have a feeling of foreboding that lingers around my head like the proverbial black cloud," Lindholm responded, locking Burl Mentor's eyes with his own."I guess it still disturbs me that we've no earthly idea why Dren was in my office."

"It should bother you only if the kid knew something about how our money is coming in. You've never given me the impression that he did. Might I be mistaken? Might I be mistaken?" Burl asked still not looking away from Jon's eyes.

Sometimes Burl's habit of repeating himself annoyed Jon and today was one of those times. It was as if he were suggesting that he was not honest with the trustees. He knew the risks he took to do that and was careful to not give them that sense (even when he had to protect himself by bending the truth).

"Burl, I've no proof to believe that Andy knew more than he should, but I'll feel better when this is closed and becomes ancient history."

"Well, Jon, do you have anything to report that happened at the funeral?" Austin asked.

"No. As I said, it was well done. Most of the town turned out for the service and almost as many for the luncheon that followed. I was surprised to see several of our campus homeless there dressed quite nattily for the day."

"Campus homeless? What do you mean?" Eddie Lee exclaimed with surprise.

"Oh, we've several homeless men who use Tech as the place to gather their aluminum cans. It's perfect for them since our students empty multi-thousands of cans every day. The students know the men by name, and it wouldn't surprise me if on very cold nights they might be found in one of the rooms or apartments."

"Doesn't sound like a particularly good idea to allow them

here, but that's your business. I'd have them chased off by our campus police," Burl said in a way that he seemed to have just tasted something that was spoiled."Let's change the subject. It's a joke to mention the homeless and a gift of $30 million in the same breath."

"Son of a bitch, Burl. Is that the size of this newest gift? They grow larger and larger. Let's hope that these Chinese guys want to go on laundering their money forever!" Austin croaked. "It's outstanding that we can get this money so easily."

"You must remember that Tech gets to keep only a percentage of the 'gift' and sometimes the opportunity to earn a little interest before it gets passed on to the political party of choice of the Chinese or into their questionable businesses," Burl stated."Now, Jonathan, where're you going to put some of this money so that it looks reasonable for the Chinese to give it to the Foundation?"

"I'm ready for this, gentlemen. We're going to add a Far Eastern Studies Center in the College of Architecture that will include the art and technology of 5000 years of Chinese architecture. We'll build a small wing on the current building so that we've an actual location that we can point to if anyone questions the legitimacy of the program. It'll include an exhibit area, a classroom and small library. The addition will cost about $2,000,000 and a program endowment of $4,000,000 will be established and invested with the other Foundation funds. It's a sweet deal."

"That sounds perfect, Jon." Eddie Lee said nodding his head in agreement, "I think it's a stroke of genius to make the Hong Kong gift results very visible. The Chinese alums who have helped by being the "donors" should be impressed to see that Tech has done this with some of their 'gifts.' Looks to me like everyone wins."

"Don't you ever wonder where the big hunk of the money goes when it leaves Tech? Some of the stories you read and see in the news make me wonder if funding big Chinese ventures is really for the good of the USA," Austin mused, as much to himself as to the others.

"Forget it, Austin. You always see some problem. It's good to get foreign money circulating in this country. Even if all the businesses aren't Chinese restaurants or another silk flower factory, it's none of our concern what they do with their own money." Noble said sourly. He didn't want to be reminded about the use of the money beyond Georgia Tech. This wasn't a matter of some shady ethics. It was just business as usual. It just happened to be *big* business as usual.

"I think Noble's right, Austin. Of course if you want to resign from this committee, you're certainly welcome to do that. Welcome to do that. Whatever will make you more comfortable. After all, we've all been friends for years as we worked deals through the Foundation that have benefited our alma mater and sometimes ourselves." Burl told his fellow trustee.

"No. No, Burl. I wasn't suggesting changing anything. I was just saying that I think what the Chinese do must be very interesting," Austin backed out smoothly.

"Well, gentlemen, have we covered all of our business? I see that we've almost missed the dinner hour with our families. It's been quite a day for the institution, and of course for us," Jon interjected. He hoped that Tiffany was back from Dalton. He might just stop at her condo before he headed home. He could call Laurie and tell her the meeting was lasting longer than expected.

"Good suggestion, Jon. With the traffic from downtown, it'll take us longer than usual to get back to Buckhead. I know there's already a martini waiting for me so I'm zeroed in on that," Eddie Lee said as he got up and pushed his chair carefully back into place at the table.

Jon Lindholm said good-bye to them at the door and went into his office. The rest of the suite was quiet because most of the staff had gone. He looked at his watch and saw that it was just about 6:15. Laurie should be in the kitchen making a light supper. They had both had more than their usual lunch at the Dren's luncheon.

Using the automatic dialer, he called his home and waited as the rings echoed through the phone.

"Hello."

"Hi. I'm going to be a little late. Our meeting is not quite finished."

"Is that right? How convenient, Jon," Laurie spat at him.

"Now, Laurie, what's your problem? You've a certain edge in your voice that's extremely unpleasant."

"Let me say very shortly and very simply that if your late meeting relates to a certain young woman who answers to the name of Tiffany, you better adjourn your meeting and get your overactive testosterone home within a few minutes. I'm in no mood to be kept waiting."

Jonathan Lindholm was stunned. What had she heard? What did she know? Laurie hadn't acted strangely earlier in the day, or yesterday or last week. He'd begun to think she'd forgiven him for the situation in California. Something must've happened today in Dalton. Could that little vixen, Tiffany, have said something to Laurie? He hadn't expected her to be there, or he wouldn't have asked Laurie to go along. Well, actually, he didn't ask her. She told him that she was going and that she'd helped to put together the luncheon food. Something Janeen and she had arranged. Maybe Janeen said something that seemed suspicious to Laurie. No, what would she say? Janeen hardly knew Tiffany. Whatever happened he'd just have to go home and handle Laurie. He'd always done this successfully in the past.

"Jon, you're so quiet that I'm assuming you're already starting out the door. Good idea, loverboy. See you soon, or maybe I'll go see one of your precious trustees who is supposed to be waiting for you back in your conference room." Laurie had never raised her voice and had ended the call by hanging up the receiver gently. She wasn't an explosive person, but her family always knew when she'd reached her limit of patience.

The president hung up the phone and closed his briefcase, but didn't pick it up immediately. If he went directly home, Laurie would know that he had not had a meeting. He had to take a little time for it to appear to have been an honest call, but he couldn't be too long or in her present mood, his wife might just call a trustee. He'd wait about fifteen minutes and then go home.

Chapter 33

Oliver Andrew Dren, Jr.

Frank and Peter had returned to their apartment by 6:00. They were glad to be back on campus, the funcral behind them.

Peter Kirk had talked again to Russell Biers, the student who programmed the electronic sign, and had invited him to visit them that night in the apartment. Frank was anxious to meet this computer whiz because he had decided not to even drop a hint of what they wanted unless he was convinced Russell Biers could keep a secret and act dumb if he was questioned.

Peter had suggested to Russell that he come to meet his roommate about 7 o'clock, so the two young men had only a short time to put their enormous 'doggie' bags in the refrigerator and change their clothes. If they'd met their guest in their somber suits and white shirts, he surely would've thought they were strange.

"What if he doesn't show? Or what if he won't cooperate?" Frank asked, "Then we have to find another way, and we've no idea how to do that."

"He'll come, Frank. He was, you know, really glad that I'd invited him. This isn't the most popular guy on campus. I've never seen him anywhere with anyone, you know. He spends most of his time hugging his computer."

"We just have to impress him that joining us will be good for him. Not forever, though. We don't want to have him hanging around the rest of our lives just because he knows how to put messages on a technically-oriented blackboard."

"Don't worry about that. Let's just get the memorial done. That's all we want today," Peter said in a serious way.

"You're right, Peter. I just....." Frank was interrupted by a knock at the door.

"He-e-ere's Russell! Right on time. Ready to join our secret club. Maybe we should have him think he's being allowed into a new fraternity or something. This can be his initiation," Frank got up from the sofa to open the door."Hey, I'm Frank. You must be Russell. Peter has mentioned you several times. He says that you have been a big help to him in class and Peter needs all the help he can get."

Russell Biers looked questioningly at Peter, assuming he might be embarrassed that his roommate was insulting him. He liked Peter and didn't want to be a part of 'dissing' him,"Oh, Peter's one of the leaders in our computer class. He never needs help."

"I keep trying to set an example for Frank, but he isn't smart enough to get it."

Russell stood in the middle of the room with his narrow shoulders slumped and head slightly bowed. He was watching them with eyes wide and blue behind round, wire rimmed glasses. He appeared to be shy or dull, but they knew he wasn't dull, since Peter had compared his computer skills to Andy's.

Frank felt that their visitor was very uncomfortable. Maybe Peter was right that Russell didn't have any friends. It was up to them to help him feel at ease. No matter if he was going to help them or not, as fellow classmates, they should be friendly.

"Russell, sit down. How about a Coke or a beer? We just got in and haven't had time yet to get ourselves something to drink or eat. We've a bunch of food that wasn't eaten at Andy's family's lunch. Let's get some of that stuff out and dig in. Trust me, man, this isn't the usual Tech food. This's great," Frank said as he opened the refrigerator and took out one of the packages and waited to hear whether Russell wanted Coke or beer.

"A beer would be fine," Russell answered. Frank handed him a can, got the same for himself, placed it on the counter and unwrapped some of the delicacies Susan had given them.

"Peter, what do you want?" Frank asked idly as he tossed a can through the opening to the living room, "I don't have to wait for an answer from him. He loves his beer. Now, let's tell

Russell what we're thinking about. You'll be the only person who'll know what we're planning, so we're asking that you join the two of us in keeping this a secret. It's really important." Frank felt immediately that Russell was a sincere and reliable person. He decided that they weren't going to have to take a vote on this kid.

Russell sat on the straight chair that was at the computer desk, putting his can on the desk and wiping his wet hand on his jeans, "OK. I'm good at keeping secrets, but I don't know anybody at Tech well enough to tell anyway."

Frank took the lead and laid out the whole story in the order that it had happened. He described the kind of a person that Andy was, how the idea had evolved and how they thought their plan could start a whole new tradition at Tech. He almost sounded like he was telling an age-old legend when he went into the history of G. Pitts Berdel.

"It was a big time when at their 50th alumni reunion, the men proudly announced that they were the creators of G. Pitts. We can repeat a similar announcement in another 50 years."

Peter was as captivated by Frank's speech as Russell was. He convinced his roommate again for the second time. He felt that it was more important than ever to do this memorial for Andy Dren.

"I guess what you want from me is to tell you how to get a message on the sign, right?" Russell asked when Frank ended his presentation.

Peter didn't expect this all to be so open and direct. He'd been surprised that Frank had been completely truthful with their guest. He'd thought that they'd have to sneak up on Biers and somehow trick him into doing what they wanted.

"Right on, Russell. We want you to be part of our exclusive team to make this happen. Then we want you and us to forget about it. We think that some other computer experts will follow suit and figure out how to put other messages up on the sign. We start this now and we celebrate it at our 50th reunion," Frank explained so that Russell would feel that he was special and a maker of history.

"I don't know. I've never done anything like this. Actually I've never taken any big risks in my life. It just isn't my style. Peter knows that even when I know the answer in class, I don't speak up. I'm the type that no one ever sees," Russell confessed.

"Don't feel you have to decide this minute," Peter interjected, "Remember we've had a couple days to think about this. We were both close to Andy so that might be different for you."

"Oh, I knew Andy," Russell Biers enjoyed the surprised expressions on the faces surrounding him, "I was in Dalton too."

"You knew him? Tell us about it," Peter sputtered.

"It's not surprising that two computer nerds would get to know each other. Professor Mah suggested that I talk to Andy way back in the fall, because I was interested in the technology of the Olympics. He was just like you said he was, Frank. He always talked to me like an associate. No matter what I asked, he never made me feel like I was some stupid jerk. He was always honest with me. Like you've been. That's important. Too many people have no respect for others anymore. Andy respected everyone. I'd like to do something for him. I'm just not sure that this is OK. Do you think there's any way that this could hurt some innocent person? I wouldn't want to do that," Russell said thoughtfully. As the other students looked at him, they felt that Russell Biers was sitting straighter, his head was held higher and there was a new brightness in his eyes.

"We've thought of that too, but haven't been able to project any problem. We've chosen one of Andy's own computer file codes as part of our memorial message so it won't relate to other people anyway," Frank told the young man.

"What do you want the message to be?"

"Move over, man. We have it right here on the, you know, computer. Let me bring it up for you," Peter said, quickly reaching for the mouse. He was really feeling good that he'd found Russell and brought him into their group.

Russell stood beside the chair as Peter sat down and brought the monitor to life in what seemed to be one motion. It was only a matter of moments until all three young men were looking at the 'In memory of Andy Dren: a computer expert who knew more than HKIIICC' message. Peter and Frank waited in silence and wondered what Russell's reaction would be at this point.

"What does it mean?"

"We're not absolutely positive but we think that HK refers to computer hackers and the CC are the letters used for the College of Computing. We aren't sure about the III, because they could be a number, like in Roman numerals, or just three letters. Russell, maybe you have an idea since you worked with Andy," Frank suggested.

"Do you guys believe in messages that might be kinda supernatural?" Russell asked as he watched the two roommates look at him in amazement.

"Supernatural? What're you thinking? We just picked out a code of Andy's. It's, you know, nothing special," Peter said breaking the silence.

"Hey, Peter, don't toss aside a thought from one of the original thinkers here on campus. I want to hear what Russell has in his mind," Frank added quickly.

"Well, when I saw HKIIICC it just looked strange. Then when Peter said what you had already figured out, suddenly the meaning of the III came to me. It felt like a message from Andy. Of course you may think I'm crazy, but I see the III being pronounced like the plural of one or 'ones' which said just a little differently becomes 'once.' So the message becomes: A hacker once in the College of Computing. Since you can add *of* in the College of Computing, why not add *in* after once: A hacker once *in* the College of Computing?"

"Wow! Then it would mean Andy, now that he's dead. Russell, are you suggesting that maybe he knew he was going to die and that we might be doing this memorial?" Frank asked incredulously.

"No. I wouldn't go that far. I'm just saying that sometimes a sign seems to fit a certain situation. You often hear people talk about intuition or dreams that seem to project a future event. That's kinda how I feel about this. Can you say why you chose these few letters from hundreds of thousands of letters on the computer?"

"Nope. We just looked at stuff and said: let's use this," Peter told him.

"That's part of why this may be a real message. That's what you're saying, right, Russell?" Frank asked cautiously.

"Yeah, that's what I'm saying. You don't have to go for it. It's just what I saw when it flashed up on the screen."

"Well, I like it," Frank said nodding his head as if to add emphasis to his statement, "It sure is as good as what we came up with and makes it even more important to use it as our memorial. I don't think it's just by chance that Peter found you. I think maybe that was supposed to be, too."

Russell was thrilled. After all of his time at Tech that he didn't have a friend or was ever a part of any student gang, tonight after only about half an hour, he was actually a member of this group. They weren't looking through him like most people do. No, they were looking right at him. They were giving him the same respect that Andy had given him. This was the best time he'd ever had in college, and he felt that Andy had been the one to make it happen.

Chapter 34

Danielle Jarvis Swain

Having cut it very close for the 6:00 news show, Dani and Loretta pulled into the parking area of Channel 22 about 5:20. Immediately behind her was another car that parked beside hers. Lindy Lindholm jumped out. His hair seemed to have been created in the popular blow dry casual style, but the fact was that he liked to drive with his windows down and sunroof open. He quickly ran his fingers through it and was satisfied that he was presentable. He was one of those handsome young men who really didn't seem to notice his appearance. Dani felt that he looked quite mature still dressed in his dark suit, white shirt and a blue tie with tiny peach pits woven in one diagonal row just below the loosened knot.

Dani had once been told the story of the peach pit ties. She smiled when she noticed Lindy's and thought about the Georgia Institute of Technology faculty member who had designed the tie as a joke for the opening of classes about ten years ago. For the first one he'd bought a plain blue tie and painted the design in place so it would appear just under the knot. At the very bottom edge, he had painted the name that he'd chosen for his "work of art": It's the Pits by G. Pitts Berdel. The students loved it and asked that he create more for them. That was the beginning of a whole line of "It's the Pits" products.

Dani thought about the day and the tag line "It's the Pits" and decided that it was certainly appropriate for Andy's funeral. She was sure that Lindy saw the irony of his choice. She was also pleased that she'd seen him at the luncheon, and he'd agreed to do a live interview on the program this evening.

Loretta went into the studio to set up the footage she'd use taken in Dalton. An abbreviated version had been used earlier on a mid afternoon "BreakIn!" Channel 22 news people had decided that every newscast today would feature the funeral.

Dani smiled at Lindy as he walked toward her, "Thanks for inviting me to come here for tonight's show."

"Just remember, Lindy, you're theoretically paying your way for the grand tour. You're going to be on the show live for a couple of minutes. There's been lots of interest in this murder in Atlanta and beyond. One paper in South Carolina has named it the Halls of Ivy Murder. But, this killing is more like poison ivy. Something we don't want. It's amazing how this story has been picked up. I want to be right there when they identify the killer." Dani and Lindy approached the back door. Tony Jones was waiting, looking official in his dark gray uniform.

"Hi, Tony. I want you to meet our star for tonight: Lindy Lindholm. He's one of the reporters for the Georgia Tech Technique, their campus newspaper."

"Hi, Mr. Lindholm. Any friend of Ms. Swain's a friend of mine. Welcome to Channel 22."

"Hi, Tony. Glad to be here."

"We must hurry, Lindy. We only have a little time to be ready for the camera. See you later, Tony." Dani opened the door and was swiftly moving toward the newsroom with Lindy following closely.

"Why don't you have a seat over there. I need to check on some things before we go on camera. I'll interview you right after the tape from today. We'll leave one of the Dalton scenes in the background until we're finished. That's all there is to it." Dani pointed toward a comfortable chair that was at the side of the room.

Lindy sat where he was directed and watched several people busy at work. He liked the feeling of being on the "inside." Since meeting Dani, he actually looked forward to seeing the news program because of her professional manner and pretty face. Tonight her bronze-toned skin was a pleasant contrast to her pale lemon-colored business suit and matching blouse. He was sure that Dani chose her clothes to accentuate her wonderful complexion and to support her image of a successful television star.

He took out a Palm Pilot from his coat pocket and made a few notes that he planned to use later when he wrote a feature on the anchorwoman, Danielle Jarvis Swain. He'd do it for the Technique but hoped that he could place a version of it in other publications. He couldn't think of any local newspaper or magazine editor who wouldn't be interested in an in-depth story about the young woman who electronically entered many homes at least five days per week. That's probably more often than they see their own family members! Maybe he'd write the article as if she was in everybody's family. Maybe.... maybe he better just pay attention to what he was supposed to do tonight. It wasn't as if he was used to being on television.

Dani returned and told him they were about to begin. He should be ready to join her when she finished the story about the funeral and they ran 30 seconds of Loretta's video. She'd introduce him, ask a question, and give him enough time to respond. Then the camera would cut off them and she'd return to her desk to finish the news. They were ready to begin. The lights that focused on the news desk were switched on and she slipped into her seat.

"Hundreds of Georgia's future leaders gathered today in Dalton, Georgia. They were not assembled to discuss leadership nor the next millennium. They were there to pay solemn tribute to Oliver Andrew Dren, Jr., known to all as Andy, a Georgia Tech student who was found murdered Wednesday morning in the office of Tech's president, Jonathan Agnew Lindholm III.

"More than 200 students traveled to Dalton this morning to say good bye to their friend and classmate. Mr. Dren was a graduate student in the College of Computing who had enrolled at Tech last year after working for Microsoft. He had worked on several special projects for corporations during the Olympic Games. His extraordinary talents and skills were recognized later by Dr. Lindholm who hired him to do computer programming for the institution. He continued to be both a student and a part-time employee until his tragic death.

"We have with us tonight a reporter from the campus newspaper. He's Jonathan Lindholm IV, who, in addition to being a sophomore and a reporter for the campus newspaper, is the son of the president of Georgia Tech. Lindy has written several special editions about the murder, reactions on campus, and the investigation that's being conducted by the Atlanta Homicide Squad under the direction of Detective Wes T. Wesley." Dani opened the news broadcast in a tone that portrayed both the seriousness of the topic and her own sympathy for the loss of an intelligent, healthy, young, graduate student at an institution that had been important to Atlanta for more than a century.

"Lindy, I've been reading what you've published about Andy Dren's murder but tonight would you share your own personal feelings about this tragedy?"

"The Dren's, Andy's father and sister, Susan, and Andy's friends have experienced a heartbreaking loss. Every family that's heard about this shooting will empathize with them. But, in addition, Georgia Tech has lost to violence one of its exceptional students. Now that a senseless killing has occurred in its most famous building, the campus will never be quite the same.

"If I may, Ms. Swain, I'd like to make an appeal to anyone who might have information that could lead to the apprehension of this killer: Contact Detective Wesley or Chief Fancer at Georgia Tech with any facts that seem that they could have a bearing on this case. The only way to begin to turn around the cultural movement toward indifference is to stand up and be counted. If necessary, whoever might hold the knowledge that could identify this murderer can do it anonymously. Just do it and do it now. You may save other lives on the campus or here in Atlanta," Lindy ended his appeal and looked at Dani waiting for her to take back the lead.

She looked directly at the camera and said, "Lindy Lindholm has put a personal and community responsibility to this killing. He's right that this goes much deeper than one death. Violence has become a way of life in the United States, and we can use the murder of Andy Dren to be our call to action. If it's easier to call Channel 22, our lines are available to you. We're committed to helping solve this murder."

Dani ended just in time for the first commercial break. She turned to Lindy, shook his hand and gave him a big smile."We'll talk later. I must get back to my desk."

Lindy stepped off the set but stayed as close as he could to Dani as she smoothly segued into the next story. Once he had time to realize that he'd spoken to hundreds of thousands of people, the thought actually scared him. He'd spoken spontaneously. He was amazed at how quickly he'd made his decision to ask for help. It hadn't even been in his mind while he sat waiting for his time to join Dani in front of the camera.

Being lost in his own thoughts, he was surprised that the sign off had already happened and Dani was gathering some papers and walking in his direction. He felt he should say something about his unusual actions.

"Gee, Dani, I think I should apologize or something. I just got carried away."

"No reason to feel that way, Lindy. You did great. I don't believe you were nervous at all. It's just like you've been doing this all your life."

"Well, when I thought about it while you were doing the rest of the show, I got plenty nervous. Not about being on TV, but because of what I said. I guess I should have asked you before what you wanted me to say," Lindy said sounding more the boy that he still was than the man he looked to be.

"Not at all. That's the fun of doing interviews live. It's a risk every time, but it's what the audience loves. They're sitting there hoping something unique will happen. One thing I guarantee is that your words will create some response toward the police department."

"What do you mean?"

"Someone will take your words as a challenge to give the police a hard time that they don't already have the killer in custody. They'll call the chief of police or maybe even the mayor, but they'll call. Of course we want them to call with solid information so let's hope that happens too. That's how our news programs can help."

"I'd like to feel I helped. That would be awesome."

"We'll just have to wait and see. I'll be sure to tell you how many calls we get here and if anyone mentions your appearance. Now, are you ready for your tour of the rest of our facility?"

The two new friends left the studio and Dani was already describing equipment and showing him the heart and soul of Channel 22. Lindy was following along taking in the words and the atmosphere. He'll never again watch television with the same 'take-it-for-granted' attitude. He'll be able to *see* what's happening behind, beside and around the picture on the screen.

Chapter 35

Jonathan Agnew Lindholm III

Jon walked slowly to his car. If anyone saw him, they would've said hello and never noticed that he was agitated. He was annoyed at Laurie for speaking to him like he was someone far beneath her. Even though he had his idiosyncrasies, he was smarter than she and had a far better education. He felt that Georgia Tech had made its best choice when he was asked to become president.

Many people had written in press releases and said in introductions before he was to speak: 'Dr. Lindholm looks and sounds like a president.' Jon was careful to maintain those attributes. He was careful to always be well dressed, keep a modest tan and never let more than ten days go between haircuts. Before coming to Atlanta, he had special public speaking training and always practiced at keeping his voice modulated with no discernible accent. He made an effort to have the alumni and his community colleagues think that he cared about them, was impressed with what they were saying and interested in what they did.

Laurie took no particular interest in any of these things. She looked attractive, as the wife of the president should, but not because she spent time perfecting a style. She wasn't seriously attracted to clothes as a statement of her personality. She was college educated, but her dedication was not to academic pursuits. It was to dancing and keeping fit so she could continue teaching her young students. Laurie never went out of her way to impress others nor try to be a member of their group. Jon had wished many times that his wife would work harder at being the wife of the president, but she was often too busy with kids in the urban neighborhoods or with what Lindy was doing at the time.

He thought about his wife as he drove away from his #1 parking space and decided that tonight she was going to be a real pain in the ass, but he'd keep control of the confrontation. His main objective was that she didn't go off and talk to a trustee as she'd threatened. Whatever her problem, she could only have a suspicion. If she had proof, all hell would have broken loose by now. He had quelled her suspicions before by being smooth and sounding sincere. He'd do it again.

It took Lindholm a few minutes to cross the campus and park his car in the garage that led to the kitchen. He opened the door, expecting to find Laurie standing in the room waiting for him. She was not. He could hear her voice and wondered if someone else was there. He closed the door and saw his wife in the hallway talking on the telephone.

"...It won't be easy. Oh, Jon has just come home. I'll talk to you later." Laurie reached around the doorway and replaced the receiver, with its extra long cord, on the wall console. She loved to wander around when she was having a telephone conversation. For years, she'd said it helped her to think better.

"Who was that?" Jonathan Lindholm asked trying to start the evening off on a light and natural tone.

"Oh, ah, it was Janeen," Laurie responded curtly without looking at her husband.

Jon felt that her answer was forced. "Was she not telling him the truth," he wondered, "What was she saying when he walked in? Something like: It won't be easy? Was she talking about her conversation about to happen with him?"

"What were you two talking about?"

"Just about the day." Laurie's response was chilly.

Since his wife was being difficult, he decided there was no reason to pursue that conversation, "Why don't we go out and get a bite to eat?"

"I'm not going to be put off or cheaply bought off from saying what I have on my mind, Jon. So just forget it."

"I guess we might as well get it done, Laurie. It seems you are determined to spoil the rest of what has already been a trying day."

"Don't attempt to make me feel that I'm the problem. You've been the problem for years and obviously continue to be one," Laurie said quickly. She hated confrontation, but there were times when she couldn't back away from it."Jon. I'm not going to *nicely* see you through another disastrous affair with some student. The last one cost you your job, forced us to give up our home, ruined our relationship, and almost cost the girl's life. That is enough for one lifetime."

"Laurie, we've been through this a thousand times. We have our understanding, and we have our new life here in Atlanta. We've gotten through our past troubles well. You've been my partner in helping to make our lives whole again. Let's just put it to rest," Jon Lindholm said feeling quite proud that he commended Laurie for her actions. That will certainly please her.

"Absolutely, Jon. We'll set aside all of the past misery. That's what we agreed to. I've nothing to add to that fiasco. I'm talking about the present. I brought it up only as a preamble to tell you that you have broken your side of the agreement and therefore I am not bound by mine. I haven't yet made up my mind if I'm going to talk directly to Tiffany Walton or if I'd rather tell your precious trustees about your little sweetie," Laurie's voice was hard, her eyes icy as they met Jon's.

He was shocked again. He still couldn't believe that his wife knew about Tiffany. Damn that girl. She must have said something at the luncheon. Well, he'd just fake it and get through this as he has other crises.

"Calm down, Laurie, your hysteria is addling your mind. I'm not so dumb as to jeopardize our whole existence, including our income, for a student younger than our son."

"You are that dumb, Jon. You're killing just about everything you've touched: your career, your family relationships, your reputation, and the family of a stupid, immature, oversexed coed. Tiffany herself will hardly lose a day worrying over whatever became of the old guy who used to be president of Georgia Tech. Her parents will never forget, that I guarantee."

"Laurie, your imagination is simply working overtime. You meet a student at a funeral of another student and you just get carried away with emotions and wild ideas. What could've been said to send you into this frenzy? Or do you really have some mental problems that should be addressed immediately?" Jon responded thinking as fast as he could to turn Laurie around to feeling guilty about her outlandish accusations.

"Oh, yes. My mental problems. I heard about them quite enough! Poor Lindy has been so concerned about me thanks to you poisoning his mind. You're a piss-poor father, Jon. Just like you're a piss-poor husband. I bet you're a piss-poor lover too. Maybe I should compare notes with Ms. Walton."

"Take it easy. I don't know what you're talking about. Who's been talking about mental problems until just now? I'm just trying to figure out why you're making all these crazy statements. I wouldn't want you to make a fool of yourself by going downtown and talking to Tiffany Walton," Jon said keeping up his act of indignation.

Laurie noticed that Jon had placed Tiffany 'downtown.' That must mean that she didn't live on campus. Why would he know that about her? He rarely pays any attention to students, he certainly doesn't ask where they live —- unless he wants to go there. She decided to take a wild guess, "Yes, she said she didn't want to live on campus, because she had many interests and friends who weren't related to being a student at Tech. She added that she felt so much safer downtown than she does right now on campus."

"Oh, yes, she said the same to me this afternoon at the luncheon." Jon invented, glad that Laurie had provided him an opening for him to cover his stupid 'downtown' remark.

Laurie continued, "Then your little friend said the strangest thing. She said, 'I hope since you haven't been well, Mrs. Lindholm, that this murder hasn't been too much for you.' I told her I was quite well and that this murder is still upsetting. What have you been telling this girl, Jon?"

"I have barely spoken to her, Laurie. We had a short conversation at the buffet table today. I have no clue as to why she would say that to you. Who can predict students? They all live in their own little worlds. Now that we have this settled and behind us, let's seriously think about something to eat. It's getting late."

Laurie looked at her husband in amazement. She couldn't believe that he felt that he'd never have to keep the promises made at the wedding altar or at a time when he emotionally made a commitment to live as a model family man in exchange for a public picture-perfect wife. One commitment was made more than twenty years ago, the other only two years ago. She knew now that he was never going to change his pattern, and it's time to do something drastic about their lives. She'd tried to wait until Lindy was on his own, but he was almost there. He'll understand.

"Jon, this is not the end of the topic. It's just the end of our marriage. I'm going to take steps to solve the problems you have caused. I'll let you know what my direction will be just as soon as I make that decision." Laurie nodded her head signifying that she was closing her announcement.

"Forget it, Laurie. Damn it, this isn't the time to talk foolishness. Already on the negative side, we have the murder investigation staring us in the face and on the positive side, we have a huge amount of money coming through the Hong Kong alumni. We can personally profit greatly by this. Having this "commission" is going to free us of the California obligation. When the next Chinese gift comes, I'll give my cut to you and you can buy a whole new wardrobe, get a new car or take an exotic trip. That should please you and help you forget your outrageous ideas." Making a quick decision to tantalize her with the potential of big money, Jon told her about the most recent windfall coming their way.

"Do you really think that I can be bought for some clothes or a car? You have really lost touch with basic morality, Jon. I know you've been using your commission from the Hong Kong money to pay off Cynthia and her tremendous medical bills, but I'm not another Cynthia. I'm overjoyed that your efforts in soliciting the Chinese alumni have eliminated a huge financial burden, but it doesn't make you a better man in my eyes. You did a job and Georgia Tech rewarded you. That's all there is to it,"

Laurie told him sadly. She felt that she had just altered the course of the rest of her life. She was finally giving up on Jon and her sham of a marriage.

"Laurie, you're exaggerating an innocent remark made by an insignificant student. She could've heard anything that she just assumed it meant you were not well. Maybe she knows Lindy and he said you had a headache or something."

"The conversation is over. There's nothing else to be said. I don't want to have to say another word or hear any from you," Laurie said almost in a whisper of desperation. She looked at her watch and added, "I'm going out for awhile. I might just take a ride or a very long walk."

"You're going out? Where would you go at this time of the evening?"

"I'm quite capable of going out after dark, or are you suggesting that I have no friends who I could go see?"

"That's not what I meant, but it's true that you haven't tried to make any close friends here. Surely, you aren't going down to the projects where you know all the children as well as you know your own son," Jon responded sarcastically.

Not wanting to continue the argument or to become the target of Jon's sharp tongue that always took over when he was backed into a corner, Laurie picked up her purse and started for the door.

"I'll be back. Right now I need to put some distance between you and me."

Jon reached out and roughly grabbed her arm, "Stay here, Laurie! Don't put yourself in a situation where you might react in a stupid manner. Remember, we both will see this evening in the fresh light of morning. Tomorrow we can forget that we were angry."

Hardly feeling the sharp pain in her arm, Laurie shrugged off his hand and said quietly, "Sorry, Jon. This sounds like a line from a soap opera, but there is no tomorrow for us. I'm going out. Don't try and stop me." She closed the door without a sound.

Jon couldn't believe that his wife had actually walked out on him practically in the middle of their conversation. He took a step toward the closed door prepared to make her return but decided that there was nothing to be gained. Let her drive around town wondering where to go or stopping in a restaurant or movie to fill in some time. She would realize that she'd put herself in a ridiculous situation. When she comes back, she'll say she lost it and was sorry. Laurie was in no position to walk away from him and this comfortable life. He'd give her another chance, but he wanted her to ask for it.

Laurie backed the car out of the garage and drove down the curving driveway. To have a destination, she decided to go to Barnes and Noble Bookstore where she could get a cup of coffee and browse through the shelves. She stopped where the driveway intersected Tenth Street and checked for traffic. It was quite light which may be why she noticed that there was a car stopped at the curb just below a No Parking sign. As she made her right turn toward Peachtree Street, she saw a person sitting in the car.

"Someone must be waiting for one of the students to come out of Stein Hall across the street. Life does go on, even when your own seems to be ending," she thought. She glanced into the rear view mirror and her eyes were staring back. She then said out loud to that person in the mirror, "This is not a shock, dummy. You just chose to hope about a lost cause."

Chapter 36

Tiffany JoAnne Walton

Jon opened the door to the garage and stood in the doorway watching Laurie. He wanted her to see him as she drove away, but she never looked back. He was disappointed. He was sure if she saw him that she would get smart and change her direction. He knew if she gave the whole unpalatable scene a second look that she'd realize that she had nothing to gain by this preposterous behavior. As upset as she was, he still didn't believe that she'd go to a trustee as she threatened.

Feeling that she would return shortly, maybe drive around for fifteen or twenty minutes to make him uncomfortable, Jon opened the refrigerator and took out some baked ham, mustard and rye bread and made a thick sandwich. Before sitting down at the kitchen table, he opened the refrigerator again, took out a beer and twisted off the top. He really was hungry. He hadn't been talking about going out for dinner simply to change the subject.

Lindholm pulled the morning Atlanta Constitution off the counter and placed it in front of his sandwich on the table. He began to browse the business news, looking for names of successful alumni. It was amazing how many of the Tech graduates headed up corporations that were constantly making headlines. He saw no names that were familiar on the front page and opened to the second page. By that time he had already lost interest in the news. His mind was back on the unsettling argument with Laurie. Why did he even agree that she could go to Dalton with him? He could have made up a good reason if he had tried. Better yet, maybe he should've stayed away. Then Laurie would've been in Atlanta and so would he. Tiffany was so brazen with him that he could imagine that she was the same with his wife.

Tiffany. Was she going to turn out to be a problem? She'd been the perfect lover until now. Available, willing and private. Why would she change today? Was there a reason why the funeral of Andy Dren would send her off in a tizzy? He didn't even realize that she knew him. How well did she know him? What an interesting thought. Was there a relationship between Tiffany and Andy? He was shocked that he felt jealous.

Jonathan Lindholm looked at his watch. Laurie had been gone for almost half an hour. Could he risk a telephone call to Tiffany? Why not? If he used his cell phone and stood at the bedroom window, he could see the entire driveway. If he saw the Mercedes, he would cut off the conversation and be ready to play the injured husband when Laurie came into the house.

He got the phone out of his briefcase and took the stairs two at a time. As he walked into the master bedroom, he was already pressing the numbers. It rang three times and was picked up, "Hi, there."

"Tiffany, it's Jon. How're you doing after this very emotional day?"

"Oh, Jon, it's amazing that you called now. Actually I was just sitting here decompressing and thinking about the events in Dalton. There were so many surprises," Tiffany said leading him on to ask: what surprises.

Instead he said, "The biggest surprise was seeing you there. I didn't know that you knew Andy."

"I didn't know him... actually. A group of us went to represent the student body. He *was* one of us, Jon. Isn't that why you and your wife were there?" Tiffany asked sounding like she was a hissing snake.

"That's one reason, but also because he worked in my office. Oh, what surprises did you encounter?"

"Maybe the most interesting one was meeting an Atlanta homicide detective right there at the church."

"It's an important case. After all, Georgia Tech is always big news in Atlanta and this murder did occur in my office."

"Oh, yes, that would make it important. Certainly everybody is talking about this murder right there in the Tech Tower."

Not wanting to rehash the details again and beginning to worry that Laurie may return, Jon decided to divert the conversation in another direction, "Tiffany, all of this is intriguing, but I called to find out if you were OK after the strain of the day. I wish I could be there right now."

"Of course, Sweetheart. I wish you were here too. That would be perfect but having you at the end of the telephone is second best." Jon wondered if Tiffany had to practice to make a word like perfect sound like the purring of a tiny kitten.

"It might be second best, baby, but it's a far second best. Nothing can come close to being with you."

"Oh, Jon, it's just dreadful that we can't be together. I bet we could make each other forget some of this tragedy if we were."

Jon's mouth had gone dry as he thought about Tiffany and felt that tonight he was a prisoner in his own home. This was not the time to be unaccounted for. He was hardly paying attention to the driveway and had forgotten Laurie's tirade. Tiffany could get him off track with just a few words.

"Damn, Tiffany, you're right. You can make me forget lots of things. You're some woman."

"That's true, Sweetheart," Tiffany laughed and then added, "By the way, Jon, your wife says she's in perfect health. Aren't you thrilled that she's finally recovered from her long illness?"

The president was jolted again by Tiffany's words. How could she be so cruel? He was overcome with sensual images just by the sound of her soft voice and she was throwing biting reality at him. He didn't respond. He wasn't sure that he could.

"Well, Jon, I hear a beep on the phone. Someone else is trying to reach me. Gotta go. I wouldn't want to miss a call. See ya'." Tiffany hung up as she continued to laugh.

Tiffany transferred to the other call and said, "Hi, there."

"Hey, sweet lips, what's so funny? You sound like you're in a good mood."

"Right, Lonnie. I'm in a good mood. I'm so glad you called. I've been wondering about you ever since I saw you today in Dalton. Wasn't it awesome how many students were there?"

"Yeah. I wouldn't have gone except that two of my roommates knew Andy. I didn't know him at all. I never heard you mention him. How did you know him?" he asked cautiously.

"I didn't. I did the same as you. Went with a couple of friends who did know him. My friends are really going to miss him, because he was their unofficial tutor in computing."

"Yeah, that's what some of the guys I was with said too. Everyone thought he was so smart. Too bad he wasn't smart enough to stay out of the president's office," Lonnie said, "Great lunch. Wow!"

"Lonnie, how can you talk about food at the same time we're talking about the horrible death of an almost friend?"

"Hey, I can't be upset about every person who gets in the way of a bullet. In Atlanta, I'd have to be crying every day. You and football come way ahead of anything else for me."

"OK. Since you can't go playing football tonight, why don't you come over now and we'll have some quiet time together?"

"I'd love it, babe, but not tonight. I've got a couple things that I must give my attention. If I were there, my attention would be only on one thing. Can you guess what that is?"

"Sex. So come on over, Lonnie," Tiffany whispered.

"Don't tempt me, Tiff. I'd rather be with you than anything else, but it can't be tonight. In fact, I need to get back to my job for the evening. How about if we get together tomorrow? I have no afternoon classes."

"OK, Lonnie. Go do your little job, and I'll go take my nice, warm shower. Tomorrow you can take a shower with me but that's hours and hours away," Tiffany was still trying to entice him into a visit tonight.

"Absolutely! I'll meet you in the shower. Don't use up all the hot water and soap tonight. I'll come plenty dirty and you can clean me up. See you tomorrow just after lunch," Lonnie signed off with his usual 'bye' and Tiffany repeated the one word and hung up.

She snuggled down into her soft pillows and thought that she was a lucky woman. She had two interesting and sexy men dangling at the ends of her fingers. What a tremendous way to go to college.

Chapter 37

Wes T. Wesley

He stood in the middle of his kitchen waiting for Janeen's voice. The telephone had rung four times. He knew the next sound would be only the answering machine. He wanted, just like the old Coca-Cola ads, the 'real thing' to respond. He looked at his watch and saw that it was almost 7 o'clock."Come on, pretty lady, come on. Pick up that telephone. I want to come over and see you."

"This is Janeen. I'm not able to answer the phone right now but your call is important........ Hello," her real voice cut in and for another few seconds it was the Janeen Carson duet. Wes waited patiently and very happily. She was there!

"Hey, there. I was beginning to slip into a depression. I thought you weren't at home," Wes said as soon as the message clicked off.

"Oh, Wes, I just walked in. As usual, I got a late start from the office. Just like you, most of my day was spent away from my desk. I had a pile of things to do, but I decided to let them wait until tomorrow. I wanted to be here not there."

"Me, too. I want to be there not here. May I come over? I'll bring a pizza so you don't have to make your own supper. Mr. Domino loves to cook for you. He told me that when I called and told them to get ready, because I was going to come in soon and get their best pizza for my best friend."

"Mr. Domino has always been a good buddy. He probably knows my address without even looking, but with or without a pizza, come over. I'm here and wish you were here too."

"I'm almost on my way. I'll change from my double-drab suit and be there within a half an hour. See ya'." Wes hung up the receiver and bolted up the stairs, tugging off his tie and unbuttoning his shirt as he went. He was in high gear and loved the rush of energy that flowed through his body. He knew one cool lady had captured his attention. He felt like he'd been invited to the biggest party in Atlanta, and he was the guest of honor.

Janeen held the dead telephone in her hand for a second as a huge smile spread across her face. She wondered how she could be a winner because of a tragedy. She thought about the moment that she first saw Wes when he arrived at the office to begin the investigation of Andy's murder. She'd thought that he wasn't what she had imagined a homicide detective would look like. He had regular, interesting features, not tough and burly. His eyes weren't hardened from ugly things he saw daily. He looked like someone she wanted to know better. She looked forward to adding to her knowledge of this fantastic man who had walked straight into her life.

She was still thinking about Wes when the doorbell rang. He'd gotten there within the time stated. She opened the door and said, "Oh, great. It's the pizza man. You better get it into the kitchen quickly so we can eat it while it's still bubbling."

"Clear the way, woman. I know exactly where your kitchen is. The other pizza men have told me that you give generous tips. I have this moonlighting job for the tips, you know," Wes said lightly as he climbed the stairs to the second level of the townhouse.

"Those stories you heard about tipping must have been for deliveries on payday. Sorry, you're not here on a payday."

Wes put the big, square red and white box on the table and turned to see Janeen walk into the room behind him. Her eyes sparkled and her lips were soft and smiling. She was as pretty as she was at the luncheon, but there was an added glow tonight that Wes hoped was because he was there. He wanted to be a special person in Janeen's life. He reached out and brought her gently against his chest; her head touching his shoulder. She smelled of spring and wild flowers. He raised her chin and placed a sensual kiss on her full, pink lips.

"No tip is necessary, Ms. Carson. Just be glad I'm here,"

Wes whispered without taking his lips from hers.

"I'm glad you're here, and I can save my money all at the same time," Janeen paused and then said, "Your kissing is the perfect way to end a long day or start a short evening, but let's get that pizza box open. It's been a long time since lunch."

Janeen wiggled out of Wes's embrace and opened the cabinet to get some dishes, "How about a beer? I put the mugs in the freezer so they're frosty. That's one way I like beer: icy cold with hot pizza."

"The perfect meal. For years that was always my dad's and my Friday night dinner. Jason thought it was like camping out, because we'd eat right out of the box. Of course he constantly asked why he didn't get a bottle of beer, too."

"Well then, I think we should eat directly out of the box too. It may not be Friday but it sounds like a good idea to me. You sit over there while I get the beer. Just pretend I'm your Dad."

"Yeah, right. Go take a look in the mirror. No way can I pretend you're my dad. He was a neat old guy, but I'll let him rest in peace and keep you just the way you are."

Janeen could feel herself being captivated by the Atlanta detective. She continued to be surprised by him. He was thoughtful, fun and actually charming. She expected that he was quite different when he's with other police officers or criminals, but so far she'd seen only a Wes who would be at home in almost any social situation. She'd think about that more when the murderer was found. She wondered if under more normal circumstances, their relationship would continue to grow.

Janeen cut the pizza while Wes poured two beers. She sat down across from him. Both were eating and drinking before another word was said. They had a lot to discuss but the food came first.

Finally, "How, did things go today, Wes? Do you think you learned anything of value?"

"We didn't make the perpetrator, if that's what you're asking. Actually we created more questions." Wes's seriousness changed the mood in the room.

"Might I help with those questions? Remember I've been

around Tech half of my life."

"Actually, you probably *can* help me with some confusions that arose today. You might think some of my observations are strange, but at this point, Billy Joe and I are still collecting all possible information. We haven't figured out yet the exact direction that we'll take."

"OK. Shoot. Oh, no, I probably shouldn't say that to a man who regularly carries a gun. Just go ahead and ask."

"What do you know about the homeless on campus? Do you know the two older men, Walter and Sander, who were with the students today?"

"Yes, I know them both. I would bet almost everyone on campus knows who they are. They've never been a problem and I'd be surprised if they were involved in the shooting. I'm sure that they were at the funeral because Andy was a friend of Walter's. You may think it was a strange friendship but not if you had known Andy. He took a personal interest in Walter, hoping that he could help change his situation. Andy would talk about inviting Walter to have dinner or lending him books. Andy had everyone saving cans for Walter to collect."

"OK. Let's try another subject. What kind of people are Charles Black and his wife? He always seems to be covering up something."

Janeen hesitated a moment before answering. Wes wondered if she was simply finishing some of the pizza or thinking about the question."How honest should I be with my opinions, Wes? I shouldn't be influencing your assessments, should I?"

"How else do you think we learn about people except from other people? We certainly don't have time to become close enough to our cast of characters to do this all from our personal observations."

"I guess that's a good point. I simply don't trust Charles and feel like I shouldn't say that. He's willing to float in any direction if it's going to benefit him. He says what he thinks people want to hear. As far as Sally Black is concerned, I suspect that she knows he's a lightweight so she gives him direction or covers for his self-serving personality from time to time. If he's involved with Andy's murder, it would be only because it would help Charles."

"He's given Billy Joe the impression that he could be hiding something that might relate to Tech. Of course it could also relate to Dren, but it may not," Wes told Janeen before leading to his next question, "Lindholm gives off the same vibes. He seems nervous about what Andy was doing at his computer. I think he'd rather I give him that answer than who did the shooting. So, Janeen, what might Andy have known that both Dr. President and Mr. Vice President wouldn't like to get out?"

She was completely still. She didn't want to be interrogated. She just wanted to have a light, enjoyable evening with one of her favorite people. Could she change the discussion? She decided to be honest, "Wes, I don't want to talk about the office or my boss. I've always been careful to not carry the institute into my personal life. Many times friends are intrigued about what happens at a place that's so visible in Atlanta, but I'm not prone to entertain them with stories."

Now it was time for Wes to be quiet. He emptied his beer mug. He had several thoughts ready to verbalize but was taking stock as to what this murder investigation could do to the warmth that had happened so naturally and beautifully between them. He didn't want to ruin what he hoped to be a serious connection, but his first responsibility is to find the killer of Andrew Dren.

"OK, Janeen, you have a point. This isn't the time nor the place to pursue these questions. This is our time and this is your home. I won't force the issue now even though I think you may have some critical information. But, I do have some other questions and I'll be asking them. But it'll be on Atlanta police time and turf. I want you to know that they aren't going to get any easier, because I want to know about the relationship between the president and a sexy coed, named Tiffany."

Janeen was shocked. She couldn't believe that Wes' short encounter with Tiffany Walton at the luncheon could cause him to guess correctly about the affair. She'd never mentioned what she knew to anyone and no one had ever said a word to her. She didn't want to talk to Wes Wesley about this, now or later!

Although she wasn't cold, she shivered.. She was looking at her hands in her lap as if she were inspecting something of great importance. Janeen didn't want to respond. She wished she had never offered to answer Wes' questions. The mood of the evening had changed. At the moment, they weren't even friends. They'd been torn apart by just a few words. What could she say to rebuild the warmth of the evening?

"Wes, I appreciate your decision. I don't want to spoil our short time together. How about if we have a cup of coffee and some more of those chocolate chip cookies you like? Maybe we can forget about your job for now," Janeen got up and reached for the coffee maker that sat on the counter. She turned her back to Wes, ran water into the pot, put ground coffee into the filter and then got cookies out of the freezer. She was afraid to look at him, because she might see a change in his eyes. He might not have that little smile on his face that he had when they sat across from each other eating pizza.

Wes looked at Janeen's back and noticed that she seemed to look like she had lost the buoyancy that had been so obvious when he'd arrived. He got up from his chair and stepped behind her. He put his arms around her slender waist, laid his cheek against her hair and whispered, "I like you too much to make you mad at me. Please don't turn your back on me, Janeen. Be my girl no matter what we're talking about."

Janeen turned in the circle of his arms and looked into his eyes. They didn't look any different. They were still soft and warm. She felt better and reached up and gave him a light kiss, "I like you, too. And it feels much nicer to face you than to turn away. Thank you for reminding me of the joy of being with you."

Wes held her closer and tighter. He moved his hand to stroke her hair and let his fingers move slowly across her cheek to the corner of her mouth, "No more questions or answers from here. This beautiful mouth is now for serious kissing."

Janeen leaned into his body and kissed him again. He felt they'd passed a test, although he wasn't sure what the thesis had been. He didn't think he cared. He was happy that they were back to being friends.

The coffee made dripping sounds and there were the usual dim noises from a busy city just outside the kitchen window. Janeen and Wes heard nothing except their own breathing, together. They both sighed as if to say: we're OK, we haven't lost the magic. Both jumped when they heard the doorbell ring.

Chapter 38

Laurie Rogers Lindholm

Janeen looked at the clock on the range top and was surprised that it was already 9 o'clock, "Who would be coming here at this time of the evening?"

"This is a mystery that can be solved very easily by just going to the door. I'll wait here in case you don't want your visitor to know you're consorting with the police."

"OK, Detective. Be ready to dive out the back window if I whistle. It's only one story down to the ground, so it shouldn't be a problem for a Super Cop."

Wes listened to Janeen as she bounced down the stairs. When he heard no sound for just a moment, he assumed she was looking through the peephole in her door. Then he heard the door open and Janeen greet someone who she obviously knew well. Then he heard a voice that sounded familiar but that he couldn't identify immediately.

"Janeen, I hope this isn't too late for me to stop in. I was at Barnes and Noble and thought I'd see if you were here."

"It's not too late at all. Come in, Laurie. It's always good to see you. I must say that it's also a surprise."

Laurie stepped into the foyer and closed the door behind her. She looked attractive in her trim gray slacks and bulky, wine-colored sweater, but Janeen thought the president's wife looked tense.

"Come on up to the kitchen. The coffee is still dripping so it couldn't be fresher, and I've taken some cookies out of the freezer. You can join us for a mid-evening snack."

"Us? Oh, Janeen, I didn't mean to interrupt you if you have company. I'll go on my way, "Laurie stopped and turned toward the door.

"Absolutely not. You just come right up to the kitchen. You've met my guest, and he'll be glad to see you. You met him this afternoon at the Dren's luncheon."

Hearing the conversation from the upper floor, Wes wasn't so sure that Laurie Lindholm would be glad to see him. Most people who have met a homicide detective while doing his job quite often would prefer not seeing him again. He decided against diving out the window and tried to look relaxed with the hope the president's wife would feel the same.

"Wes, it's Laurie Lindholm. You met her today at the lunch."

"Of course. It's good to see you."

"I feel that I should apologize for breaking in on you two. I don't often just stop in to see people in the evening. I should've called from the car, but it didn't occur to me," Laurie said quickly, "Janeen, I really should leave."

Janeen looked at Wes over Laurie's shoulder with a questioning glance. She wanted to try to make her feel welcome and she wanted Wes to help do this.

"I'm so glad that you stopped in, Mrs. Lindholm. I was going to have to eat a whole bag of cookies so that Janeen would know that she's a great cook. Just between you and me, I'm so full of pizza that I was about to make my hostess very unhappy. Now she may not notice that I'm not eating my share. We were ready to pour coffee, so I'll add one more cup." Wes opened a cupboard to get the third cup.

"Well, I can stay long enough for a cup of coffee. It would be nice to visit for a few minutes. I hope Detective Wesley will call me Laurie. That seems much friendlier if we're going to share cookies."

Wes poured coffee. Janeen placed a tray on the counter and added the cookies that she had put on a plate, "Laurie, would you get the milk out of the fridge? Wes, if you'll put the coffee and the sugar on the tray, we can go down to the den and be much more comfortable."

"Whoops! It only took a minute for you to begin giving

orders. You probably had one of those mothers like I did who said: it goes much faster with more hands. Hey, Laurie, do you use that line on Lindy?" Wes asked jokingly.

Laurie smiled and looked a bit more relaxed than when she entered the kitchen,

"You bet I do. We mothers all think that we can make it work. Of course who can argue with the truth?"

"Surely, not I. OK, ladies, I'll carry the tray. You go first and be sure there's a place to put the tray. If it's like my house, there will be papers and magazines everywhere."

"Not in Janeen's house. Her home and office are always neat, Detective," Laurie said as she went down the stairs first.

Janeen looked over her shoulder at Wes and he gave her an exaggerated wink. She felt he was saying: She's OK now. Being nervous about walking in on us has passed.

They talked about the funeral, the luncheon and that Wes was still at a loss to identify a murderer. Wes asked Laurie again about her uncomfortable premonition the night of the killing. She said she was sure it was a premonition about something but maybe not Andy's death.

"What do you mean, Laurie?" Janeen asked.

Laurie looked at Janeen and said without hesitation, "Janeen, I'm going to divorce Jon. I'm sure he's having an affair with that student, Tiffany. And I'm not going to go through another fiasco. I guess that's why I stopped here tonight. I needed to talk to someone, and you're as close to me as anyone in Atlanta. I'm sorry, Detective, I didn't mean to barge in on your evening."

Before Wes could say a word, Janeen took Laurie's hand and said sympathetically, "Laurie, you must be wrong. Tiffany's hardly more than a child. Don't even worry about her. Dr. Lindholm has better things to do than be interested in a student."

"Oh, he might have better things to do, but I know he's finding time for Tiffany. I know the signs, Janeen. I've been through this before. Jon is not trustworthy. He likes young women and being around a university is a great place to find them."

Janeen had a hard time taking up for Jonathan Lindholm to make Laurie feel better. She, too, was sure that he was seeing Tiffany, but she didn't want to confirm his wife's suspicions. It wasn't her place to attack her boss. She was in an awkward position, but her heart went out to Laurie. Whatever she suspected or knew, must be hurting.

As if Laurie Lindholm had forgotten that Wes was there, she continued to talk directly to Janeen, "These young women aren't truly innocent, Janeen. They know that Jon is married and has a grown son. They must like the attention. Jon has been lucky up until a few years ago when he chose Cynthia Maddux. That has cost us a lot of heartache and money. Of course, he's been able to use his commissions on the Hong Kong money to pay her off. I don't know what we would've done without that. Her medical bills and what she asked for was over a million dollars."

Janeen was shocked. When her friend at Cal Tech said they were glad Lindholm was gone, she thought they just didn't like him or he was a poor professor. That she could understand. Later she heard more details, but Laurie was saying that this cost the Lindholm's a million dollars. Could it be blackmail?

"A million dollars!" Janeen gasped.

"Yes. It was a very nasty situation. I thought we'd never recover financially. We obviously haven't recovered any other way since the pattern seems to be repeating itself, and I'm in the same dilemma as two years ago. What do the kids always say: Shit happens? My question is, how often?"

Wes was listening with acute interest. He considered Mrs. Lindholm as simply a person related to a principal of his case, but she may be adding important information to weigh with other evidence. Lindholm apparently wasn't what the media portrayed him to be. He had a dark side. He was making some kind of 'commission' for something that added up to a million dollars. Wes may have just learned what he and Billy Joe have been feeling about secrecy surrounding the president's office.

"A million dollars is quite a substantial commission. If I remember the numbers, Janeen, the Hong Kong 'gifts' were in the range of $ 185,000,000. I wonder if it's technically a gift if there's a commission?" Wes asked looking directly at Janeen, "Is that what happens with all gifts to the institution?"

"Oh, no. Absolutely not. Most of the contributions given to Georgia Tech are true gifts. Many of our alumni sacrifice to support their alma mater. This Hong Kong situation is entirely different. It was more like a business proposition and Dr. Lindholm was the salesman. It was a deal made by Dr. Lindholm and Burl Mentor. I believe Mr. Mentor put the strategy together. And then the Chinese alumni had to be 'sold' on the idea to give huge amounts of money for the capital campaign. The people from Hong Kong insisted on some conditions that they wanted, so Burl Mentor added a Tech condition that there would be a commission to cover the extra time and effort that was needed from us to get the funds. Dr. Lindholm has spent a tremendous amount of time abroad and here working out all the necessary aspects of the deals," Janeen explained to Wes knowing that Laurie already knew much of the arrangement, "Of course, Andy was a big help to them, because he kept the accounting records. Because the dollars keep coming, they'll need someone else to do the work. Right now, it's like a guaranteed income."

"Very interesting. I had no idea that this is how contributions to my alma mater could be handled," Wes said innocently, waiting to hear if Janeen might have more explanations; especially more that might relate to Andy Dren.

"Lots of people give restricted gifts for specific purposes and programs, then projects must be designed. This money is the same. I've been waiting for an announcement about how they were going to use the Hong Kong gifts, and that's now been decided. In fact I typed the proposal for Dr. Lindholm to present to Burl Mentor and the others on that committee just the day before the murder."

"Are you at liberty to tell us what they're going to do with the gifts?" Wes asked cautiously.

"I don't think it's a secret except that we wouldn't want to ruin the surprise when the announcement is made within a few weeks." Janeen said to both Wes and Laurie.

"I'm not asking to publicize it, and I'm sure Laurie isn't going to insist on an interview with her son, right?"

"Well, now, Lindy might like to scoop his dad with a story, so you better be careful what you tell me," Laurie said laughing as if she were really enjoying the evening, "And, don't forget that his newest friend is Danielle Swain."

"Beware, Janeen, you have a spy in your house. If you need help, I'll handcuff her so she can't get away."

"You two are just giving me a hard time because I sound like I don't trust you. I do, but I also work for the president, and I don't think I should be the one responsible for announcements out of the president's office," Janeen said seriously, feeling strongly her responsibility to Georgia Tech and Jonathan Lindholm.

"We're kidding you, Janeen, but we also agree with you. It's not our job to be out front for Tech. I hope we aren't going to tell anyone about any of our conversation tonight. I want to be the one who announces my decision, too," Laurie said quickly, "Jon is already furious that I've said that he has deceived me once too often. Why would I add more fuel to his hot temper?"

"You're right. I'm sorry that I acted like a jerk. Sometimes I respond in the typical Tech style of no one trusting anyone. I hate that and here I'm behaving the same way. Maybe I've been on campus too long," Janeen said feeling guilty that she had offended both the people who meant a lot to her.

"Don't worry. I'm sure Wes and I both understand your dedication. You have a fantastic history at Tech. You probably know as much as any president who ever held the position. You should be the model for other employees; including Jon."

"Thank you for making me feel less like some old "sleaze." You're going to love what has been proposed for the money from China. It's only proposed, but I'm sure that it's going to be approved by Burl's committee. They plan to add a wing on the new architecture building that will be The Center for Far Eastern Studies. It'll include the art and technology of 5000 years of Chinese architecture. The building and an endowment to help run the program will cost about $6,000,000. Isn't that great?"

"It sounds like a wonderful plan. I assume it'll be good for recruiting and to catch the interest of our growing Chinese population in Atlanta," Wes said in response to her question but wondering what was to become of the other $179,000,000. He decided that this wasn't the time to ask that question. Maybe he wasn't the person to ask that question, because this new information pointed to more strange happenings on the campus that might or might not relate to the homicide investigation. It was interesting that Andy was somehow involved through his computer work and that he was killed at the president's computer.

"It's amazing what an effect the Hong Kong money will have on Georgia Tech, Jon's life and maybe even Burl Mentor. I guess no matter how angry I am, I can't say that Jon has never done anything right, can I?" Laurie asked without really expecting an answer.

"What do you mean: maybe even Burl Mentor?" Wes queried.

"I understand that both Jon and Burl received some of the commission. I wonder if all the trustees have such a great opportunity to do business, and make profitable contacts?" Laurie asked simply.

Wes always thought it was because alumni wanted to give back to their alma mater for giving them a good education. He guessed that was still part of it, but now there seem to be other motives. Someday he would like to learn about what drives the people who appear to already have everything. But what he needed to learn soon was who else was on the Georgia Tech board might relate to his murder investigation. Maybe it is not just Mentor and Lindholm. Not bad 'pay' for a volunteer or administrator. It was beginning to sound like the financial gyrations of the Olympics. He couldn't help to again wonder about the other trustees of the foundation. The list that Janeen had given him must have had twenty or twenty-five names on it. He and Billy Joe had not yet talked with them, but now he had another compelling reason to interview these respected, successful alumni.

"I can attest that the trustees work hard for Tech. I've seen it for years. I've never known any of them to blatantly profit by being on the foundation board. Of course, they are available to do business with the institution. And, it *is* the job of the president to help raise money. But this particular arrangement is so different than anything I've ever seen that I'm convinced that I just don't understand it all," Janeen said this for both Wes and Laurie. She knew what Burl and Jon were doing wasn't how it would be done if either Dr. Forsythe or Dr. Pendleton was still president, but she wasn't going to discuss that with two people who aren't as committed to the campus as she was. She liked them both a lot, but they wouldn't understand how much can be done for the students with this money from Hong Kong.

"Probably none of us completely understand what motivates those men to spend so much time away from their businesses and families so there is no reason to try and guess. I'm sure, Janeen, that you know them better than anyone. You've been on campus as long as some of them. I bet they pat you on your head and say you're their girl," Wes felt the need to lighten the conversation. He didn't want to have to recover from two crises in as many hours.

"You got that right! Sometimes I feel that they see me as one of their kids. They can be so sweet. The best of the bunch is Earl Prince. He's named perfectly. He is a prince of a man. When I wanted a lawyer to close this house and draw up a will, I went to Earl. He was so easy to talk to. The others are good men too, but Earl is tops in my book."

"Someday may I check out that book? I want to learn how to get listed."

"It takes a little time, Detective Wesley. But you have a chance to make it one of these days," Janeen tossed a smart remark back at him along with one of her dazzling smiles.

"I don't think I should hear all of this personal banter. I was going to stay for one cup of coffee and that must have been at least three cups ago. Thank you both for sharing your evening with me. I really didn't want to be alone," Laurie said as she rose from the sofa.

Janeen reached over and gave Laurie a quick hug, "You're

welcome here anytime, Laurie. If you're going to be going through some hard times after this evening, consider me your friend and my home your home. You don't have to be alone when I'm only a mile away."

Laurie's eyes sparkled with shy tears but she managed a weak smile as she returned Janeen's hug and turned to leave. She was already at the door when Wes said, "I'll walk you out to your car. How could I ever explain if something happened to you with an Atlanta policeman just a few feet away? You never know who might be hanging around the streets."

He took Laurie's arm and they both waved to Janeen like they were taking off on an extended trip. They laughed together as they talked and walked past a few cars.

"This one's mine. Thank you for walking along." Laurie pushed the electronic remote control key.

"What a super car, Laurie. It must be a hit on campus," Wes exclaimed when they got closer to the Mercedes.

"It certainly is a hit with Jon, and I doubt there are many of these driven by students. Although, there are lots of cute, little, sports cars at Tech."

Even though the street was empty and quiet right now, Laurie was glad that the detective had suggested walking her to her car. Suddenly she was reminded of the car that was parked at the end of the driveway when she left their house several hours ago. She almost mentioned it but decided it wasn't really important.

Janeen had cleaned up the cups and empty cookie plate while Wes was outside with Laurie. She was returning to the den when she heard him ring the doorbell and she felt the same excitement that she felt when he had arrived earlier in the evening.

Chapter 39

Jonathan Agnew Lindholm III

Laurie drove away from Janeen's house seeing Wes in the rear view mirror as he watched her approach the traffic light and stop. She'd been so surprised, almost embarrassed, to find him there; but after a few minutes she felt quite relaxed. She wondered if Janeen had known him before this investigation. Actually there would be no reason for Laurie to have known that. Janeen never talked about dates or steady men friends so Laurie had assumed she didn't have a close relationship with any male. "Now, wasn't I silly?" she thought.

She approached the campus and slowed down, getting set to make the sharp left hand turn into the driveway. Just as she put on her turn signal, she noticed the same car parked by the curb. There was no one in it this time, but she was surprised that Chief Fancer or one of his police hadn't gotten the owner to move it away from this area. She guessed that probably the driver had a breakdown and a tow truck had not yet arrived. She didn't like being reminded that those problems can be serious when a woman is out driving alone at night. She smiled and thought, "Of course it's different when you have your own policeman hanging around like Janeen does."

Laurie parked the car in the garage and pressed the button to put the door down behind her. She always felt better when the light came on to eliminate the dark corners and shadows, "I better get used to doing things on my own, because that's what I'll be doing from now on. I'll go see Earl Prince tomorrow."

She walked toward the door to the kitchen and was surprised that there was a computer carton right in front of the door. She was going to have to move it to get into the house.

She wondered why Jon would leave it there and hoped that it was empty. She just wasn't in the mood to have to wrestle with a heavy box.

Laurie leaned over to move it when the door opened suddenly, and Lindholm was standing in the doorway with a dark kitchen behind him.

"Oh! You startled, me but as long as you're here, would you move this carton out of the way?" Laurie said tightly without looking at her husband.

"Sure, but why is it right in front of the door? Who would just drop it there?" Jon asked as he stepped into the garage to pick up the box.

"I assumed you did since it wasn't there when I left."

Jon felt a shiver go up the back of his neck. If it wasn't there a few hours ago, someone has been in the garage. He hadn't heard anyone. He didn't see a car come up the driveway. He asked Laurie, "Did you leave the door open?"

"I must have. I don't really remember, but it was open when I came back. I drove right in and then closed the door." Laurie wondered if there could be a person still in the garage. She turned her head, looking at Jon for the first time and rolled her eyes as if to ask him the same question.

Lindholm reached for the main switch and the garage was flooded with twice as much light. The two of them could see the full garage. There were no places to hide. Fortunately the institution's physical plant staff kept the area clear of clutter.

"No one's here now but this box was put in this spot by someone. Why would you even have a big computer box sitting around anyway?" Jon asked his wife.

"I never saw it before. If it's not yours, it's not ours. You're the person who's into computers," Laurie said with a bite in her voice. She really didn't want to stand here having a normal, everyday conversation with the man she was going to shut out of her life because of his repeated infidelities. She didn't care why the damn box was sitting in the garage. She wanted to go to bed and get on with tomorrow.

Jon again felt the shiver rippling up his neck. When Laurie

said 'into computers,' his eyes dropped to the box that had printed on it in big blue letters WARNING!! COMPUTER, Handle with Care. His mind locked in on where Andy Dren had been found. Was this simply a strange coincidence? Or was this only an extremely strange week? What else can happen? Maybe if he'd been paying more attention during the evening, he would've heard a noise in the garage. The truth was that after talking to Tiffany, he was completely preoccupied with his own private thoughts.

"Didn't you hear anything, Jon? I would think if someone made this delivery, that you would have known. Surely they would've seen lights on in the house and knocked on the door."

"Actually, I dozed off. I was awakened by the sound of the garage door closing. I looked at my watch and couldn't believe how late it was."

Laurie ignored his accusative tone and words about the time and said coolly, "Well, move the box, please. I'm going to bed."

"Going to bed? I think we have some talking to do. I've been waiting so we could clear up any misunderstandings that were there when you flew out of here in a huff," Jon said trying to get control of the conversation and his wife.

"Then you waited in vain, because I've nothing to discuss. Our talking about your affairs is finished, completed, concluded, ended and final. Do you get the message? How else can I say it, Jon? You may have rotten judgment and no morals, but you aren't stupid when it comes to the English language."

Jon Lindholm was amazed. Even in their darkest time in California, Laurie had not taken this attitude. She always spoke with a tone that said: I think we can make this work. How dare she now put his career and the opportunity to make big money in jeopardy by implying that she's going to make all of this public?

"Laurie, I think it's time for *you* to not act *stupid*. If you don't calm down and get hold of yourself, you're going to regret your rash behavior. You aren't going to walk away from our life here with any of the comforts you have now. I guarantee you that!"

She knew they had reached the point where Jon Lindholm would no longer be able to keep his temper cool. She knew if she said one more argumentative word that he would raise his well-modulated voice hoping to intimidate her. 'Not tonight. He won't intimidate me tonight,' she thought.

"Comforts, Jon?" Laurie said almost too low to be heard, "Do you think it's comfortable to wonder every time you're late whether you're chasing some little coed? Do you think it's comfortable worrying whether you have contracted a venereal disease or AIDS, compliments of your latest fling? Do you think it's comfortable having to agonize over how we would survive another financial burden like Cynthia Maddux? I'll take my chances with physical comforts to give up all the discomfort you cause daily."

Jon listened as she spat back the words *you* and *comfortable* over and over again. He could feel his temperature rising and probably his blood pressure along with it. He couldn't remember when he 'd been this mad at his wife. She was usually so calm and, and, yes, predictable. Tonight was different. She had walked out and had been gone for hours. Where had she been? Who had she been with?

Jon stood squarely in front of the kitchen door and said loudly, "I've heard enough, Laurie. My goddamn wife is not going to impugn my reputation. Everyone here knows me as a model president and family man. We've been working toward getting over a very unfortunate mistake that was cast upon us in California. I've done a lot to make this work. I have fucking won! I won't allow you or anyone else to destroy the new life that's available to me here. You'll agree with me one way or another. Now, how much do you want? Money seems to be the solution that works best with women."

Laurie Lindholm was stunned. Jon obviously saw himself as a victim. How typical of our culture. No one ever takes responsibility in today's society. Find a way to blame the circumstances or your heritage or anything but yourself and then ask, 'How much will it cost me to keep this beautiful self image?' Over twenty years ago, she realized she had married a man's body with a child's mind. He stood before her today unchanged.

"Sorry, Jon. My silence will not be bought. If you'd be honest, you'd realize that you've had that for years for nothing. You had it because it was the right thing to do, because I still believed you were worth salvaging. Well, you aren't. You're simply trash that shouldn't be salvaged nor saved. Now will you please let me pass? I'm exhausted and want to go to bed." Laurie's words were spoken coolly and with precision. She felt that somehow she had prepared for this moment of strength. She certainly had had enough dress rehearsals leading to this ugly scene.

Suddenly Jon raised his hand and slapped her across the face with one hand and grabbed her arm roughly with the other. It was that double motion that saved Laurie from falling. She was astounded that he'd crossed the line between yelling and physical action. She expected him to be verbally abusive, but she hadn't believed she had to fear being injured.

Her tiny scream was delayed because of the swiftness of his movements. When she heard her plaintive voice, she was furious but an inner sense warned her to be cautious. Suddenly she felt in danger.

"OK, Jon. Let's both cool down. I think we need some time between now and when we have more conversation about this. We need to each be alone with our thoughts, so let's call it a night."

Jon sighed. He'd done it again. He'd forced Laurie to look at what she had to lose and had come around. It had been harder this time but he still had the control. He would agree to some *contemplation time* and then have a quiet and productive conversation in a day or two. He'd plan a Hong Kong trip soon and put some space between himself and Laurie and let Tiffany know that he wasn't going to be around for awhile. It might be a good break for them all. He certainly needed a rest from these two demanding women. One overtaxed his body and the other dug into his mind.

"Yes, Laurie, I think you have a good idea. I'm sorry that I was forced to bring you back to your senses. It's just that I was afraid you would do something to ruin your life."

"You go up, Jon. I'm going to make a hot cup of tea and then I'll follow you. I think I should unwind a bit. That will make it easier to sleep," Laurie told her husband calmly. She didn't want to rile him again. She would prepare for her future tomorrow, but not tonight. She looked forward to talking to Earl Prince.

Jonathan Lindholm felt good. He would have no trouble sleeping. His biggest worry now was where had that computer box come from and what message did it send.

Chapter 40

Oliver Andrew Dren, Jr.

It was the Friday morning rush hour in Atlanta. A record number of commuters were heading out of the suburbs to fight for their own turf on the packed, bumper to bumper I 75 and I 85 as each converged into the 'Connector' just north of the Georgia Tech campus. The question had been asked for years: Why did the highway designers direct most cars to exactly the same spot at the same hour of the day as they carried their riders to conduct the business of the city? Today, Andy's three friends were thrilled with the highway engineers' plan.

Russell Biers had not specifically chosen a Friday to put the memorial on the electronic sign that prominently faced all the traffic coming from the North, but he knew this was the best morning in the week for visibility. He wondered how many people would see it before he would have to pull the plug. At least hundreds of thousands, maybe more. Sometime he'll go back and look at the stats on viewership that were done for marketing to prospective advertisers. He was sure his "partners" would like to know that number. But, not this morning. Today they all had agreed to have Russell be on his own, the way people were used to seeing him.

The two roommates were sitting in Frank's car in a campus parking area close enough to the sign that they could take some fast photographs before the words disappeared. Then they planned to disappear! They didn't want to be anywhere near the sign when Russell got the call to get the memorial off the board. That's when security might send an officer to see if anyone was around.

Frank and Peter had each brought cameras and would snap

enough frames to guarantee having pictures of the entire series. Peter was also the driver poised to leave immediately when the documentation was on both slides and negatives. Russell said he would complete the message on three consecutive boards. The first: In memory of Andy Dren. The second: A computer expert who knew more than... The third: HKIIICC. The third was done in much larger letters and would certainly have drivers asking: HKIIICC? What's that? The missive would repeat once before the regular ads would be shown and then repeat twice again before the next advertising time. This would be the pattern until someone realized that the message wasn't intended to sing the praises of the basketball team or some other superfluous declaration. If traffic on the Connector was slow enough this morning, Russell figured that a driver could see the whole signal before passing on toward the south.

Russell had set up the message from one of the computers available to all the students who were taking computer courses. That's practically every one of the 14,000 plus students. He hoped that his precaution would create enough doubt that he could beg ignorance of the unauthorized words being viewed by a huge number of Atlanta area residents. If necessary, he'd accept the responsibility of the deed, but he hoped that he didn't have to do that. Why didn't they just blame it on old G. Pitts Berdel? He'd been doing tricks on campus for over fifty years, and everyone still loves that whimsical mirage.

The first appearance of the memorial was set for 7:30 AM. Russell Biers would see the first three boards and then would head for his breakfast at the Student Center as he ran to his 8:00 class. He hoped he'd be in class before he got an emergency call on his pager. Russell had worn the pager for six months and had only received one call about the sign. He always thought it was overkill and felt he looked like the street corner drug dealers downtown.

By 7:31, Russell was on his way to breakfast. When he first saw the letters in lights, he'd experienced an excitement that he'd never felt before about anything. Part of it was because he'd wanted to do this for Andy and part was being an accomplice to what he hoped would remain a mystery. He decided that this must be what it's like to be a criminal. Russell wondered if the person who killed Andy had the same moment of exhilaration as he did this morning. Maybe that's how criminals were created: ordinary people looking for a thrill.

He was so deep in thought that he reached the cafeteria without noticing any of the campus that he'd hurried through. He was careful to walk at a pace that wouldn't draw attention to him. He stood in line waiting for some of the usual early morning fare. He wasn't hungry, but he wanted to be able to say he was here if asked about his schedule. He looked again at his watch: 7:45. He must leave for class in ten minutes. He didn't want to be noticed coming in late. So far all was going according to the plan. He wondered about Peter and Frank but knew he had to wait until much later to hear their story.

Peter and Frank started snapping their photos at 7:30 and had used most of the film by the end of the second round of the memorial words. They had sat impatiently for two long minutes while the advertisers got to tell the commuters to buy their product. The roommates were nervous. Peter began to sweat while noticing Frank's head, which reminded him of a flashing blue light turning and turning on top of a police car, as he watched for anyone coming in their direction.

Shit! Why did he have to think of the police? Was it a damn omen? They had to get out of this location but wanted to take pictures the next time the message came up. At last they had two exposed rolls and were driving slowly toward Tenth Street. Peter would drop Frank at the residence hall so he could go back to bed, and he would park the car on a street near the campus as if he couldn't find a better place. It happened all the time. Parking was one of the continual problems on the campus. When students said: It's the Pits, they were often talking about the lack of parking.

The young man walked away from the car with the film in the pockets of his jacket. The cameras were in a backpack in the trunk of the car. He looked like all the other students starting a day of classes but he felt like an international conspirator. He kept telling himself to be cool. Peter remembered when he had called Frank G. Pitts Berdel's protégé and Frank had laughed. Thinking about that seemed to break the tension and he turned his thoughts to the basketball game on Saturday evening.

The day had begun and everyone was in his place. Three young men hoped that they had created a tradition and it wouldn't get them expelled.

Chapter 41

Jonathan Agnew Lindholm III

The telephone rang. Again. Again. Jon opened one eye and saw that it was barely gray outside. What now? What else could go wrong? Expecting the worst, he reached for the annoying, harsh-sounding instrument, "Hello. Jon Lindholm here."

"Hey, Dad, you don't have to be formal with me - especially at seven thirty in the morning. I knew I could call early because your alarm has been set for 6:30 or earlier for years," Lindy said cheerfully.

Jon glanced at the clock accusingly. He was reminded of all that happened the night before followed by the revelation that he really didn't remember setting the alarm."Damn," he thought, "I don't seem to be in control of many things this week. At least Laurie's back in the right frame of mind." As he looked over at her still quietly sleeping, he thought nothing seemed to be bothering her this morning. She hadn't even stirred when the telephone rang.

"What gets you started so early, Lindy? You're not famous for seeing the sun come up."

"You got that right, Dad, but today's different. Today I may be famous for appearing on television again. I was on Dani Swain's live show last night. I wondered if you and Mom saw me," Lindy's voice actually crackled with excitement.

"No, son, we missed it. If we had known, we would've been glued to the screen. This is getting to be a habit for you. Don't let all of this attention go to your head."

"Don't worry, Dad. I feel just the opposite. I feel lucky that Dani is willing to share her prime time with me," Lindy said still thrilled with his new friendship.

"She didn't tell me what to say, or anything. She says I could be successful in media if I changed my mind about being a computer nerd."

"I'm sure she didn't call you a nerd, Lindy. Surely, she knows who you are," Jon replied rather stuffily while he looked over at Laurie's bed and saw that she was now wide awake and listening intently to his conversation.

"Oh, yeah, she did, but the cool thing is that she doesn't give a shit. Actually, Dad, she said exactly that about me being a nerd. In case you don't realize it, most of the rest of the Western world calls the students at Tech nerds. We accept it as truth. You should too. If Mom's awake, may I tell her too about Dani's show? I know you must be rushing off to the office."

Jon was relieved that Lindy wanted to talk with his mother, because he did have to get moving since he'd already overslept. He was going to have to move fast to be there for his dean's meeting at 8:30. Also he was transferring back into his own office today so he hoped that Janeen was there now getting it all arranged. This had been a very inconvenient and upsetting week.

"Your mother is right here staring at me wondering why you're calling so early. I'll let you have the honor of telling her yourself."

Jon handed the receiver quickly to Laurie and headed for the bathroom. He could hear her chattering away, excited about Lindy's news. The two of them had always had a close relationship. They understood what was important to each other. People who met his son often mentioned to Jon that he seemed to be a caring and sensitive person. Laurie and Lindy were so much alike in many ways, but his son's interest in others was the most noticeable.

• • •

At the same time Jon was showering, getting dressed and drinking a cup of coffee; Burl Mentor was in his car driving South on I 75 to attend an eight o'clock meeting downtown. He was frustrated that traffic was so slow this morning and made a mental note to do his best to avoid future Friday meetings. His car was crawling along like a sloth. As he proceeded on the

Connector, he glanced up at the campus electronic sign wondering if the announcement of the basketball game would be there. He was surprised to see a jumble of letters: HKIIICC. The messages go fast, Burl thought, but this must be flawed input. It made no sense. Then new words flashed: In memory of Andy Dren.

Burl looked ahead and saw that the vehicles in front of him had moved almost two car lengths. He immediately pressed the gas pedal to catch up just as another car cut in front of the Jaguar, "Son-of-a-bitch! That car practically hit me," he exclaimed. When he blew his horn, the other driver turned in his seat and shook his fist at Mentor. "Crazy bastard. I'm not cutting him off. Who does....... Hey, that's Charles Black. What kind of a driver is he anyway? He's driving like some ignorant sixteen year old."

Black's car zipped past Burl Mentor's and into the exit lane for North Avenue. He didn't slow down until he caught up with the last car waiting to head toward the congested surface street. He jammed on his brakes as he lowered the window. Charles looked back at the Jaguar and yelled, "Stupid, you thought you could cut me off. Well, it didn't work." He wished that he could see the driver's face but the morning sun was reflecting too brightly. He rolled up the window satisfied that he'd made his point.

Burl Mentor realized that Black had yelled something but was unable to hear any of the words, "As soon as I get a chance, I'll call Jon. He should know how ridiculously his vice president acts, and I'll tell him what a nice idea it is to have the memorial sign for Andy; probably something the students will like," Burl thought.

Mentor exited at Martin Luther King Boulevard and parked near the Capitol. He glanced at his watch and decided to try to reach Lindholm before the meeting. He sat in the car and waited for someone to answer.

"President's office, Janeen Carson speaking."

"Good morning, Janeen. Is Jon there? I'm in the car and don't have much time."

"He's right here having his first cup of coffee, Mr. Mentor.

He really looks like he needs one this morning. It's been a hard week."

Jon motioned that he would take the call in his newly regained office and closed the door behind himself. He sighed quietly, slumped into the overstuffed chair that he used for relaxing between appointments, and picked up the phone

"Good morning, Burl. What gives you such an early start?"

"It's not early, Jon. It's not early. I'm already downtown for a meeting. I'm calling you about several things that happened on my way down the Connector."

Jon rubbed his eyes. He felt like he had no sleep. He wasn't ready to hear about Burl's complaints

"This won't take long, but both topics are important. First, you need to talk to Charles Black about his behavior. He's no credit to Georgia Tech. The alumni expect employees, and that's all any of you are, to act with proper decorum. Your vice president does not do that. He practically ran me off the road this morning and then yelled at me as if I had been the instigator. He acted more like a student than an administrator."

"This doesn't come as a surprise, Burl. Charles has had several incidents when he's been driving. I've spoken to him and so has Chief Fancer. It just appears that the man cannot control his temper. Sorry that you were the subject of his anger. Fortunately, you're OK. I'll speak to him first chance I get." Lindholm wasn't going to take the blame for Charles. What he did out on the roads was his responsibility, but he expected him to act as a professional when he was doing his job, and relating to the Tech alumni.

"I will count on that. Absolutely count on it. The second incident this morning was more pleasant. I wanted to commend you on the memorial message for Andrew Dren that's on the electronic sign. I think the students will like it."

Jon had no idea what Mentor was talking about, but if he liked it, he was willing to take credit for it."Yes, I thought we should do something unique." He decided that was bland enough to cover his ignorance. He'd have Janeen to check on it.

"Well, that's it. One positive report and one negative report.

One of each to start the day, Jon. One of each," Burl Mentor chuckled and then went on, "I almost forgot. You also want to check on the programming of the board because there's one messed up message. It's just a bunch of letters. They don't mean anything."

"Do you remember what they were? If I know, then I can tell them exactly what to look for."

"Yes, it's only a few letters so it's easy to remember. They are HKIIICC. Isn't that crazy?"

Jon felt a chill start at his head and whip through his whole body. Even his feet shivered. HKIIICC. He knew who used those letters and why. How could they be on the electronic sign? What was happening?

"Jon, I must run. I'll talk to you later. Maybe I'll stop in after my meeting. Have a good day. Yes, a good day," Burl signed off with one of his repeated comments.

Charles Black. A memorial message for Andy Dren. HKI-IICC. That was more than Jon Lindholm wanted to address this morning. He felt that the room was closing in on him. He did-n't want to get out of the chair. Too many incidents seem to relate to Dren. Maybe it wasn't such a good idea to move back into a murder scene. There seemed to be a chill in the air. Actually now that he thought about it, it was almost creepy. Why had he been in such a hurry?

Like it or not, Jon couldn't hide from the rest of the day. He still had the deans arriving in less than half an hour. He had to see what was happening on the sign. He'd check it for him-self and be back before 8:30. He dragged himself out of the chair and picked up his car keys from his desk.

Janeen looked surprised when her boss strode past her desk."I'll be back soon. I forgot something at home. If the deans get here before I return, tell them I'm on my way." He broke his rhythm and looked directly at her, "And, do something about the temperature in my office. It feels like the air-conditioning is on!"

Janeen didn't even have time to acknowledge Lindholm's directive. He was gone through the door and out of sight. She glanced at her watch and noted that it was almost ten after eight. She knew there was no problem about the president's return in time for the meeting. It was only five minutes to his house. She'd check on the continental breakfast and then see about the heat. Perhaps the thermostat needed a boost. She hadn't noticed that it was cool, but she had lots of other things on her mind from yesterday: some bothersome and some just wonderful.

Jon Lindholm jumped into his car and was across campus in a matter of minutes. He noted that it might be the first time he didn't get caught behind one of the campus mini-buses known as The Pits when it was picking up students at a Pit-Stop. If it hadn't been that he was stopped by a red light, he probably would have arrived at the parking lot where the sign was located at least 60 seconds faster. He knew every second was critical to accomplish his objective to be back for the meeting on time.

He made a u-turn and faced his car toward the south where he had the best view of the sign. He looked up and saw: Cheering is thirsty work, drink Coca-Cola. He had always liked that phrase, born during the Olympics. Seeing the normal, familiar advertisement, he could feel some of the tenseness leaving his body. The next light message was the traditional red and white Coca-Cola logo. He was beginning to feel like he'd made an unnecessary trip.

Coca-Cola disappeared and he saw all white letters flash: In memory of Andy Dren. They blinked off and were followed by: A computer expert who knew more than... Just a second behind those words, large capital letters flashed brightly: HKIIICC."Oh, shit!" Lindholm groaned. His eyes stayed on the sign and exactly the same message was repeated before the ad for Amoco became the focus-message. It all couldn't have taken more than 30 seconds but it seemed he'd been staring at the sign forever. He turned and glanced at the thousands of cars that were poking along on the Connector, some at almost a complete standstill. How many people have already seen this?

At that point, Jon's attention went back to the electronic board, and he saw that the same memorial notice was repeating. He was sure that it was just seconds since the first two flashed off.

It didn't take him long to realize that the missive was programmed to run between the regular ads. That meant that it was probably shown three or four times every few minutes. How long had it been running? He was getting warm. Beads of perspiration glistened on his forehead. He felt no one could know the reference of the cryptic message, but he assumed that somebody must have information about its origin and the Hong Kong funds. Who did this? Was the computer box placement last night a sign that someone was on to their scheme and that person was still alive?

Lindholm looked at his watch and was astonished that it was almost 8:30. He'd been sitting here for almost fifteen minutes. He must be, as Lindy would say, really losing it. He felt that he'd truly lost those minutes. He could remember seeing the message on the sign and then his thoughts were a jumble. He needed some time to himself, but he had to go play president for the deans.

• • •

Janeen was just coming out of Dr. Lindholm's office where she had raised the temperature degrees four points when the telephone began to ring. It was just 8:20, but most people on campus knew that she was already on the job.

"President's office, Janeen Carson speaking."

"Janeen, its Laurie. You've gotten your usually early start. I thought after our long conversation last evening, you might get started later this morning."

"That's a great idea. I should've thought of it *before* I switched on my alarm last night. I was here just a little before Dr. Lindholm but very little. Of course, now he's on his way back home because he forgot something. In fact, he ought to be walking into the house this minute."

"How interesting, but I was calling you, not him. I was calling to thank you and Wes for being so patient and kind last evening. I do believe I just babbled on and probably spoiled your time together."

"No and no," Janeen told Laurie, "You didn't babble on and you didn't spoil our time together. Actually, Wes liked you a lot. Said he was glad to get to see you again.

And, Laurie, you don't have to be concerned that we'll ever repeat what you said about Dr. Lindholm. My boss will never learn any of this from me. That's a promise."

"Not to worry. He'll be learning it all from Earl Prince and me. I plan to make an appointment with him as soon as he'll see me. I'll obviously be shocking Earl, but he and the other trustees will have to get used to the idea that Jon Lindholm isn't what he has led them to believe."

Janeen was still amazed that Laurie was planning to divorce her husband. She thought about how this would affect the institution. She wondered if all of the sordid details could be kept confidential. It was strange, but she believed that Laurie no longer cared to keep Jon's questionable behavior private; maybe just the opposite. Janeen was reminded of the day she talked to another friend at Berkeley who knew the whole story about the car chase when Jon ran Cynthia Maddox off the road, causing serious arm injuries. She spent a month in the hospital and had a series of operations. Even with the excellent medical care, she would always have a disabled arm. Although it was shocking, she didn't believe that it was simply juicy gossip. Jon's personality, quick temper and interest in Tiffany Walton pointed to the fact that it could happen.

"Whatever you decide to do, Laurie, remember I'm your friend. I'm sure Wes would say the same if he were here."

"You're right. That's about what he said last evening when he walked me to the car. It was so thoughtful of him to do that. I was reminded of his caution of being out late alone when I got back to the house and found a car parked by our driveway. Gave me a moment to wonder about people lurking around until I decided that it was probably a student who had car trouble or was waiting for someone from Stein Hall. I must run. I see it's almost 8:30. Thanks again for having a warm house and understanding nature. I realize you're in a difficult position being Jon's assistant, so don't feel you owe me anything. You can't choose sides. As far as he's concerned, he need never know that I visited you last evening."

"Let's not worry about that right now. You do what you have to do and know that my warm house is there for you anytime. I must run too. The deans have just arrived and Dr. Lindholm should be back in a moment. Bye-bye."

It wasn't until Janeen hung up the telephone that she realized the president obviously never went to his house. Laurie would've said something if he walked in while they were talking. He probably got detoured by someone on campus when they recognized his car, but she wished he'd get here soon before the deans began to get restless. As fast as she made her wish, the foyer door opened and Lindholm barged into the room. He had the same air of agitation surrounding him as he had when he left.

"Janeen, get Charles Black immediately. Tell him I want to see him ASAP in my office. I'll get to him as soon as I get rid of the deans. There's too much going on to vegetate in an inane meeting while each dean tries to prove to me and his colleagues that he's the most important," he blustered as he stood over Janeen. He added, "Cancel whatever appointments you must so that I can meet with Black. We may have some tasks for you to do after our meeting. Be sure you are available."

Janeen Carson didn't respond. She knew this was a time to just follow instructions.

"What's going on?" Janeen asked herself as she reached for the telephone to find the vice president, "What's Charles done to make the president so mad?"

Chapter 42

Wes T. Wesley

Wes entered the Atlanta homicide headquarters with a cardboard container of coffee and a small bag of Krispy Kreme donuts. He'd stopped at the shop on Ponce de Leon so often, the counter clerks called him by his first name. Another breakfast. Only on his days off did he think about what might be healthy. He headed toward his cramped, ugly office but was stopped by a huge banner stretched over the door: Qualification Day... or else????? The words were followed by a drawing of a skull and crossbones.

"I see Billy Joe has gotten here early. I can't imagine that he thought I'd forget. It's Friday. It's D-Day. The or else is: Death. Committed by Major Dagmar Dilbert. So it must be Triple D Day," Wes said to his colleagues. He knew they were waiting for his reaction. He'd just be cool.

"No! No! Not that! Death by Dilbert is too fuckin' brutal," one of the detectives called from his equally dingy office.

Wes ducked under the sign, put his coffee and donuts on the pile of papers covering his desk and turned to take down the banner. There was always a joker in every group, but homicide had more than its share. Wes had decided long ago, it was their way to decrease stress. Working with death daily just wasn't like selling bubbly, brown water, Atlanta's most well known product, Coca-Cola. The two 'industries' had one thing in common: neither would run out of 'customers.'

Wes knew he and Billy Joe had to reach some decisions this morning. Besides the Georgia Tech case, Wes had been assigned a murder of another young man. In between these two difficult cases, as he had been visually reminded, he must be on the range to qualify this afternoon. Quickly, the detective began to gather all of the material he had on the Dren case: his interview notes and tapes, medical examiner's report, Luis Carrero's tapes and photos, crime lab reports and the many questions and thoughts that were in his mind, but not yet on paper. All the homicide detectives agreed getting it written was the toughest part of any case. There were always too many things going on to enter data on the antiquated computers. It would help to have faster computers or a really good transcriber to process all the details while detectives actually did detective work instead of typing. Won't happen! No point to going through that routine again.

Billy Joe appeared at the door carrying his own huge coffee cup. It was decorated to look like a mug of beer."Let's meet in the interrogation room. We've too much crap to lay out to work here." Billy Joe stopped to take a long swallow from his mug.

"How long do we have before you must make your command performance for The Dilbert? I've about two hours before I have to be down at the medical examiner's to talk to Glenna about that little girl who was found dead back of the Pussy Kat Klub."

Billy Joe began to turn toward the interrogation room. He stopped a moment in the doorway and shook his head."I still have trouble believin' that kids not much older than my own are already hookers. This one is about eleven years old and she's dead. Her own father was her pimp. We live in a goddam sick world. "

Wes nodded his head. He followed his partner with a handful of paper and his breakfast. They were so used to their grim surroundings that the repulsive environment of the room wasn't even noticed. The blinds hanging at a forty-five degree angle; the paint peeling off the walls making a trail of what looked like giant hunks of dandruff on the cruddy carpet. All they saw was an empty tabletop that could accommodate their collection. Fortunately, today the table wasn't even sticky from either blood or vomit often left behind by perpetrators. They closed the door and went to work.

They knew exactly where the killer had stood, they knew

that the person was probably of average height, and they had the make on the bullets: two 150 grain Winchester silver tip bullets. Quite possibly, they had theorized, a hunting rifle. But on Tuesday, it was used to kill a man instead of an animal. The rifle was handled by an unknown person. Two shots were fired from the parking lot. One broke the window and lodged in the wall. One clipped the corner of the chair back before hitting Dren in the head. He died instantly.

"I think Andy turned toward the window when he heard the glass break. I'm guessing that up to that moment, the shooter could not completely see him. If someone is working on that computer, the chair back is mostly turned away from the window," Wes concluded.

"You're askin' me to consider that the shootin' of Andy Dren could have been a mistake, right? That can really fuck up our investigation at this point."

"Well, Billy Joe, I want to add some new information I learned last night that may confuse our investigation more."

"Sounds like you're fixin' to drop a bomb. Maybe I should know where the hell you were last night."

"As strange at it may seem, I was visiting with the wife of the president of Georgia Tech."

"Who? Where did you see the president's wife?"

"I saw her at Janeen Carson's house." He waited as he saw the look on Billy Joe's face change from bewilderment to growing anger.

"You were at the house of one of our fuckin' main people in a case and you don't even mention it? As I've heard you say many times: Surely you jest," Detective LaCrosse was just winding up for one of his dramatic scenes. Wesley could see it starting and began to smile. When he decided it would demonstrate his mood, his partner had a real flair for theatrics.

"I thought we were buddies. Son of a bitch, I thought we shared our lives. You're our kid's godfather. You spend most holidays at our house. Shit, Wes, I just might revoke your godfather license. You can start lookin' for another place to get your home-cooked meals. And, believe me, Cleo will agree with me. She understands that friends aren't just friends when they're hungry or it's damn convenient. I don't know why you haven't told me that you were seein' Janeen Carson." Billy Joe ended his speech and sat pouting.

Wes was laughing out loud by the time Billy Joe was half way through his diatribe. He looked him in the eyes and said simply, "I just told you," He waited a few seconds before he continued, "I've only known her since Tuesday. It's not like you and I've been sitting around this week just shooting the breeze. Last night was only 12 hours ago. I've told you, already. So I've told you."

Billy Joe watched Wes laugh again. He could feel his mood spreading across the table. He tried to keep a stern expression on his face but found it difficult. He wasn't really mad at his friend. He was just damn surprised. Wes usually mentioned when he was meeting someone after work, but since he was playing this differently, maybe this lady was special.

"OK. What do you want to tell me?"

Wes explained about Laurie Lindholm coming to Janeen's and the surprising information she shared with them. That some of the personal side of it was a complete surprise to Janeen, but that she already suspected there was more to the Hong Kong money than appeared on the surface. When Wes mentioned the commission amount, Billy Joe exclaimed, "A million fuckin' dollars? Son of a bitch! How much money has to be involved to produce a commission that large?"

"In the ball park of $185,000,000. There could be a possibility that additional commissions are going to another foundation trustee. The questions are: Did Andy know any of this, and if so, did he learn that there was something strange happening or is this all a coincidence?"

Billy Joe had a lot to contemplate. He picked up his pen and doodled on his note pad. He wrote the numbers that Wes had mentioned, arrows to several stick figures and on the top of the page, he wrote HK with a larger arrow toward all the other marks.

"It just feels wrong, Wes, that the president and vice president don't want us sniffin' around in their business."

"I'm not sure how this all fits together, but I want to talk to our own FBI in residence. I knew sooner or later there would be an advantage to having him housed here in our offices. Up to now it's just been more bodies in the same crummy, cramped space. I want to learn from him about the ins and outs of moving huge amounts of money around the world. Why does my mind keep coming back to the suspicious fundraising mess in Washington that has a direct link to China? Why wouldn't Tech be hyping the shit out of such huge gifts? Everyone else does it." Wes had been thinking about this ever since he heard the numbers related to Tech's capital campaign."As I said, this all adds new facets to our investigation. We need a motive for this killing."

The two detectives continued to organize their notes. With all the information they had on Andy, they couldn't see a motive for killing him. Billy Joe rose from his chair, stretched and commented, "If Andy was the target, who wanted him dead and why? If Andy wasn't the target, then who? The most obvious answer is Jonathan Lindholm. That's who usually sat in that chair at that computer. And, maybe the Hong Kong news provides a clue to a motive. The problem is, it could be a motive that fit either Lindholm or Dren."

"What if the killer wanted to waste Lindholm? If that were the case, our efforts to find a killer related to Dren are getting us nowhere and we're losing precious time looking for a killer who fits an entirely different set of criteria. Do the trustees relate somehow? Let's try a new approach and start a list that....." Wes was interrupted by the door opening and Luis Carrero saying, "There's a telephone call for Wes. Some guy who says he'll talk to only the detective in charge of the death of Andy Dren."

"Son of a bitch! Maybe we're going to have our luck change!" Wes jumped from his chair.

"I'll take it in my office, Billy Joe. You listen in on one of the other telephones. In case he won't say who he is, you can be tracing the call. It sure would be good to have Caller ID but the powers-that-be wouldn't want to make it easier to speed up the process called justice."

Chapter 43

Walter

Wes had taken many of these calls that usually led nowhere. He wished he had a dollar for each time he responded with great hope only to find a kook at the other end of the line. He sat down at his cluttered desk, “Detective Wesley.”

“Yeah. Are you the po-lice in charge of Andy Dren’s shootin’?”

“Yes, sir, I am. And who’re you?”

“I’m Walter. I saw you at the funeral. I want to talk to you.”

Wes was shocked. He gave Billy Joe a wave. His partner gave him a high five sign back.

“Yes, I remember you, sir. You were with a group of students from Tech. It was a sad day for you and the others. You must’ve been a good friend of Andy’s,” Wes said carefully, not wanting to scare off the man. Many homeless persons have a strong aversion to being connected in any way with the police.

“Yes, I was. When can I see you, Mr. Detective?”

Walter was obviously a man of few words but Wes wanted to hear those words. “I can meet you now. I can pick you up, if that would be helpful.”

“OK, man. Pick me up in front of the Union Mission. What will you be drivin’?”

“A gray Taurus. I’ll know you when I see you, sir, so I’m sure we can find each other. It’ll take me about ten minutes.”

“I’ll be waitin’.” The phone clicked. Dead. Wes looked again at LaCrosse.

“Not enough time to trace the call, but it doesn’t seem like you’ll need it. I believe he really wants to talk to you. Just to be cautious, I’ll ride along. He may not want to get in a po-lice car with a honky," Billy Joe kidded Wes.

"Yeah? He'd probably feel safer with me than some huge, overgrown bro, but sure, ride along. How much time do you have before you need to be downtown about your infant hooker?"

"I gotta 'bout thirty minutes. We'll be back in plenty of time. Let's get movin'," Billy Joe was already standing in the foyer.

The two homicide detectives drove west on North Avenue and took a left turn toward downtown. The Union Mission sat on the edge of new housing that was developed during the Olympics on former government housing project land. The Union Mission was not considered a good neighbor to the middle class residents now enjoying living near downtown. They would have preferred something more upscale.

"It sure looks different. Wonder where all the folks are who once lived on these same streets?" Billy Joe mused.

"A well-kept secret. Next thing is that the mayor's office is going to be asked to gentrify the Union Mission. Maybe add some flower boxes, a paladium window and a hot tub," Wes added sarcastically.

"There he is, Wes. Let's just pull over in back of the pickup truck. Looks like someone is haulin' his workers for the day."

Billy Joe opened the door and got out. He reached back and opened the back door and stepped toward it as he extended his hand to Walter, "It's good to see you again. You get in the front and I'll bring up the rear."

Walter shook Detective LaCrosse's hand without a word and got into the passenger seat beside Wes. He reached out and shook his hand, saying quickly, "Thanks for pickin' me up."

"No problem. Our offices are only a few blocks away."

Wes noted that Walter wasn't dressed as formally as he was at the funeral. He had on jeans, a plaid flannel shirt and a light windbreaker. His crinkled hair was neatly cut and he was cleanly shaven. He wondered how Walter had become one of the thousands of homeless in the city. Since he knew he worked regularly, he assumed he just didn't make enough money to get a start.

"Do you mind if we stop at Pizza Hut and pick up some lunch?" He explained to Walter, "Detective LaCrosse and I're eating on the run today and this would guarantee that we get some food before dinner time."

Billy Joe assumed there was some truth in Wes' statement, but he knew that Wes was making it easy for them to provide a meal for Walter. They'd done this many times. They both saw so much misery in the city that they tried to do their part, even though it might be a small gesture.

With stopping for the pizza, they got back to Homicide just in time for Billy Joe to grab his share of the food and transfer into another unmarked car. Wes and Walter carried their boxes into the building and headed for Wes' office. The detective pushed up a chair from another desk and dumped the bag of drinks beside the boxes of pizza. He motioned for Walter to sit. He did the same.

"Walter, do you want to talk while we eat or would you prefer to eat first?"

"I'll talk and eat. You have a busy day."

"Don't worry about my time. Getting your call was the highlight of the morning. All we hear is that Andy was a great guy. Yet, someone shot him. It doesn't make sense."

Wes pushed the pizza box aside, placed his tape recorder in its place."By the way, do you mind if I tape our conversation?" The homeless man shook his head.

"Well, Detective, we all gotta work harder. We owe it to Andy to find this bastard. He was all that people say he was. He didn't have an enemy anywhere. If puttin' my sorry voice on tape is gonna help you solve this, you go right ahead."

Walter looked almost as forlorn as he did at the funeral. It wouldn't have surprised Wes to see him teary-eyed again.

"If I could be a po-liceman, I'd work until I dropped to catch and kill Andy's murderer. Then you could come and get me. I wouldn't care because I had wasted the son-of a-bitch," Walter said, sounding like he meant every word, "Don't hate many people, Detective, but I hate this fuckin' coward!"

"Walter, be calm. Don't think about doing anything that

could mess up your life too. Andy wouldn't have wanted that. We can all work together and then hand over the perp to the authorities. They can fry his sorry ass and you can be cheering, if you want. But you want to have the last word. Getting yourself executed isn't having the last word," Wes was moved by Walter's sentiments but he was serious when he cautioned him to be temperate.

"I know you're right, Detective, but I don't want this excuse for a human bein' to get away. I've been thinkin' about what I'm gonna tell you and hope it means somethin'. So, this mornin', I was doin' my can rounds and thinkin' about how Andy would save thousands of them for me every week. Those students sure can put away the soda pop and beer. Anyway, I'd been checkin' out the trashcans behind some dormitories. That's about where the Tech sparkle-board is. I ...."

"The what? A sparkle-board?"

"Oh, shit, it's not really a sparkle-board. That's what I call that dumb electronic sign that makes advertisin' money for the college. So I looked at the sign, and it knocked my socks off. It was like a message to heaven," Walter hesitated to give Wes an opportunity to react again.

"You mean a message *from* heaven?"

"Nope. I mean what I mean: *to* heaven. Hey, don't you know about the sign? I thought you'd already know about it. Hell, you're the po-lice."

Wes laughed. There were two main misconceptions out in the world: one was that "po-lice" knew everything and the other that "po-lice" knew nothing. He was pleased that Walter believed the former.

"Man, I don't know shit when it goes beyond homicide. I assume this sign hasn't killed anyone, right. So, tell me what you know that I don't know."

"Sure, man, I'll tell ya'. There on the sparkle-board is a message about Andy."

"About Andy? Is this the information that you wanted us to know? Who put up the message?"

"It's part of it. But not the main part, man. I'm stopped in my tracks. It's like I'm hypnotized or whatever. The sign sparkles: In memory of Andy Dren...A computer expert who knew more than...HKIIICC. Then it does it again. Then some ads, and up comes Andy again. It's the coolest sparkle-message I ever seen. I'll always remember it. That's why I say: a message to heaven. I know that Andy knows that Tech cared enough about him to do that sign. That's why I say, Mr. Detective, Andy had no enemies. Even the president came to see the sign. I watched him drive up and park almost in front of it and just stare.

Wes again broke into Walter's story, "The president? He came to look at the sign?"

"Yeah, man. You know that Andy worked for him, right?" Wes nodded his head and Walter continued, "He never saw me, and I didn't try to get his attention, but as I watched him sit there in his little convertible, I had a vision."

"A vision, Walter? That must have been one helluva powerful message."

"Oh, you know, man, like, I remembered somethin'. I could mentally see somethin' that I guess I had forgotten until I saw that little fucker of a car. I remembered the night of Andy's murder. I was sleepin' on campus. Sometimes I do that. I don't have a regular place that I stay. Just curl up some place when I'm ready to sleep. That night I was back against the hill that's in front of the old buildin' where Andy was killed. The hill protects me against wind and I had my big overcoat and a couple plastic bags. Snug as a bug, as they say. I was long gone when I heard a car racin' its motor and zoomin' down the road from the hill. That son-uva-bitch was tearin' ass. It was almost gone when I sat up and..."

"What kind of car was it?"

"It's really weird, man. I don't know jack about cars, so I can't answer that, but it was seein' the president's car this mornin' that made me even think about it again. The car that was haulin' ass on Tuesday night was a small sports car. Kinda, all round and sleek. Looked like a dark color, but then my eyes weren't really wide open. I know it was small, shaped like a goddam sneaker. I'm gonna look for those kinda of cars around the campus and the neighborhood. I'll get Sander to help. No one'll notice us writin' down licence plate numbers. Most people look right through us. We're just bums in their eyes. Well, one of them, if he's still around, is gonna wish I wasn't around at all. I'm gonna help you grab that motherfucker," Walter was quite emotional at this point. Wes wanted to try to get more recollections from him, "Why do you say 'he'? Did you see a man?"

"Nope. I can't imagine a woman doin' this. How many women can handle a gun well enough to hit Andy right in the head?"

"Better be careful, Walter. If the National Organization of Women hears that remark, they'll probably sue you for sexism. Gotta be PC these days," Wes joked.

"I don't know much about this PC shit, but it's still my opinion that men like guns more than women. Well, Mr. Detective, that's what I had on my mind. If it can help, I'll be glad. If it can't, I know I tried. That's sorta what Andy always told me: nothin' ventured, nothin' gained. That's what he said when he asked me if I wanted to learn to use a computer. He was right. I was gettin' damn good. He thought I'd be able to get a job by summer. I guess that won't happen now."

Wes looked at the clock on Billy Joe's desk and saw that it was almost 12:15. If he was going to get out to the range by one, he's going to have to wrap this up. He didn't want to rush Walter, but he wanted to keep his job.

"Walter, I can't tell you how glad I am that you told me all of this. I don't know how it's going to fit in, but please make me a promise to keep in contact. You know how to reach me, but I don't know how to reach you. I have to rely on you, man. You can watch out for anything that might add to our information," Wes told the homeless man, talking to him as if they were business colleagues.

Walter sensed the respect that Wes was paying him and it felt the same as when Andy would talk to him. He knew how important it was to earn respect and to give respect. He felt this mutual exchange with this Atlanta po-lice."You won't lose me, Mr. Detective. I'm gonna be lookin' for that car and gettin' the word back to you. You just got yourself a dep-u-ty. A regular Columbo; that's me."

"I've got to run, Walter. My next appointment can't wait if I want to stay on the job."

"Let's jam it. You can drop me off at Green's Boozer's Bonanza. It's just around the corner. I'm workin' there this afternoon."

"I never heard it called that before, but it fits," Wes laughed again. He had enjoyed his interview with Walter,"Let's go. I can get you there and then hope I do the same for myself." He wanted to get his qualification behind him and go downtown about the guy who had been killed last night. The body was found at the Dome with two basketball tickets under his body and no money in his pockets. Could've been a fight over scalpers' rights; which of course there were none, since it was illegal to scalp tickets. If he could do all of that and get a little luck, he'd be back on the Dren case by evening.

Chapter 44

Jonathan Agnew Lindholm III

"Gentlemen, I appreciate your being here. Several problems have come up that I need to address immediately, so I'm going to ask you to make this as short a meeting as possible. Nothing's on the agenda as far as I'm concerned except what you consider an emergency. So who has a dilemma that must be faced right now?" Jon took no time in setting the rules and letting his deans know his mood.

Each dean felt he'd wasted his time crossing the campus for no reason. Surely their time was as valuable as the president's was, but they didn't have the option to beg out of one of his meetings. Lindholm was considered a control freak, and they'd each learned the hard way that you never make an independent decision if it related to the president's agenda.

"I understand the tremendous pressures that are being placed on this office, Jon," said Dexter Dudley, the dean of the Engineering College, "But we need some information about the murder and its investigation. We've all had calls, letters, E-mails, and visits from alumni, parents and the media. We have scores of students who have left campus at the insistance of their families. It's three days now and you've not seen fit to bring us together and tell us what's happening. We must have facts, and we should decide here and now exactly what is our party line!"

Dr. Dudley was usually the spokesman for the deans. He'd been at Georgia Tech since he was a student; thirty years now. His tenure through several presidents, his tight relationships with influential alumni and his own ego had made him an adversary to Jon from his first day on campus. Dudley was secure in his position and knew, to most of the faculty, he was really the leader of the institute. Since he didn't aspire to have any other position, he conducted himself with complete autonomy. He liked the place he had carved out for himself at his alma mater. The president could deal with the foundation, Dudley would continue to lead the faculty.

The president wanted to tell Dexter Dudley to go see Charles Black and not to bother him, but he knew that nothing would be gained by drawing a battle line with this man today. The most expedient way to end this meeting was to give him an answer. He would cast some of the blame on Black, but he'd graciously respond to what is a legitimate request.

"Dexter, you are 100% correct. I'm surprised that you haven't heard from Charles Black. I understood that he'd be contacting all of you, but I'll bring you up to date," Jon's voice dripped with sincerity. How could anyone question his intent? "It's still a mytsery, but the Atlanta Police have been on the case constantly. They're finding it a real challenge. There are so few clues. Because Andrew Dren did not appear to have problems, like drugs, drinking, history of confrontations etc., there are no obvious suspects. Of course, we may never know why he was in my office."

Dexter Dudley nodded his head and said sarcastically, "Well, Jon, maybe it's important that he was at your desk or maybe someone assumed it was you in your office."

The deans all laughed weakly to show that they knew this was a joke, but they were enjoying the reaction from their president.

"That's not funny, Dexter. This is a very serious situation and not something to joke about. I don't think there is a doubt that Dren was the target. This is probably as good a time as any to decide on our party line," Lindholm said shortly. He did not want this line of guessing to proceed.

They discussed their plan, agreed on a reasonable story and adjourned within half an hour. Jon returned directly to his office and found both Charles Black and Janeen Carson waiting for him. He wouldn't get any smart remarks from these two. They did not have tenure.

"I'm pleased to see that Janeen found you so promptly,

Charles. We have a lot to talk about. It seems my list of topics related to you keeps growing at a fearful pace," Jon's greeting was terse. Charles didn't know why yet, but he knew that he was in trouble again.

"Janeen, I've a few things to talk with Charles alone. I'll buzz you when I want you to join us. Be sure that you're at your desk."

The president and the vice president disappeared into the office and closed the door. Janeen definitely wasn't a fan of Charles Black's, but she felt a wave of sympathy when she saw the door close.

"It seems you've been a busy boy related to some things and a complete laggard on others. There are times, Charles, when I question your judgment, and this week is one of those times."

Charles waited. He could feel his temperature rise with the anticipation of what would come next. He had no idea what he might have done, but he hoped he could pass on the problem to others.

"First, you have not been keeping the deans informed about the murder case. They're bothered constantly with calls and you obviously have not spoken to them with enough information to field those questions. I do believe that your responsibilities include external relations. Am I correct?

"You should have been conferring with Chief Fancer and Detective Wesley regularly, then keeping in touch with all key people on campus. Surely, you list the deans as key people, Charles. They may be egomaniacs, but they still are our academic leaders."

"Yes, Jon, I know all of that. The fact is that I had given the responsibility of passing on the information to campus people to Sharon. With all of the things happening on campus this week, I believed it was more efficient to spread about the duties. I can't imagine why she's not been doing this, but I'll speak with her immediately," Black felt he had covered that oversight well.

"I want a complete report at the end of each day on every activity and task related to the murder. It should include all details, and who's doing the work. Is that clear?" Jon expected no response and continued on, "In addition, you again have demonstrated your personal lack of control. You chose Burl Mentor this morning to cut off on the highway and then yell at him like he was at fault. I guess I'm lucky that you didn't chase him down the road."

Damn. Out of the thousands of drivers, how could Mentor be the one in his way? He could pretend it wasn't him, but he decided he wouldn't chance that. The trustee obviously saw him. "I did try to sneak in a very small spot to get off at North Avenue. It was a solid line of cars, Jon, and if I didn't push a little, I would have been headed right downtown. I guess I should've been more patient."

"If it wasn't that this is your usual pattern, I could accept that explanation. Sorry, Charles, you give an apology to Burl and you get a warning from me: You control your temper or you start looking for another job. You're becoming dangerous, and we have enough of that around here right now."

Jon found it interesting that the personality traits he would not tolerate in others were the ones he often was reminded that he possessed. How many times had Laurie told him to keep his temper under control? He knew she often exaggerated, but he wasn't exaggerating the seriousness of his threat to his vice president. The man just didn't have the professionalism that he should for this important position. Just because Lindholm had inherited Black from another president didn't mean he had to keep him.

Wanting no further discussion on this subject, Jon reached for the intercom buzzer and summoned Janeen. It was time to address his last topic.

Janeen appeared at the door, Jon motioned for her to have a seat and began talking before she was settled, "I received a call from a trustee this morning about our thoughtful Andy Dren memorial message on the electronic sign. I assume you both know about this."

Janeen said she had had several people call about it in the last few minutes. Charles hesitated because he couldn't tell if the president wanted a yes or a no. If Jon would respond to Janeen, maybe he would know which way to answer.

"So, people are noticing. What were the comments, Janeen?"

"Each thought it was a nice gesture but mentioned that the one board was messed up. I was going to call about it when you buzzed me."

"Yes, the concept shows that we care about our students."

"We should always do that. Sometimes Tech is perceived to be without passion. A memorial message for Andy will help support another attitude," Black said quickly, feeling that he knew which way the president was leaning.

"Did you authorize the message, Charles?"

Again the vice president was unsure how to respond. He wanted the credit for it but didn't know any details to report.

"Some students wanted to do it and it seemed like a good idea," Charles Black tried to wiggle out a positive statement.

"Did they tell you what the message would be?"

"Not exactly. Just that they wanted to have a memorial message. It didn't seem to raise any problems at the time. Is something wrong?"

"I want to know how this confusion of letters got mixed up in the message. It makes it look like we are not technically proficient. It's everyone's responsibility to be sure the public sees us as a leader in technology education. I'd assume that you, Charles, agree since you're in charge of our public relations. As a dual responsibility, I'm assigning the two of you to investigate the origin of the message, discover the reason for the screw up of the message, make the correction of the message and then program the termination of the message by the end of the morning. It might be thoughtful, but I don't think we need to be reminding the public that we could have a murderer roaming around our campus.

"Now get on with it and, Janeen, report back to me by noon what you two have accomplished. Charles, you have several things to report back to me, this is only one of them," Jon completed his instructions and felt he had covered his own agenda without raising suspicion. He wanted HKIIICC off that board and he wanted to know who put it there.

Chapter 45

Danielle Jarvis Swain

"Hey, Dani, have you seen the Georgia Tech electronic sign?" Tony Jones greeted Dani as she got out of her car at Channel 22. He noticed that she looked like a fresh Spring day in her apple green pants suit with a pink, white and green floral print blouse. Her appearance made Tony think about the beautiful azaleas that would soon be blooming throughout Atlanta. The prettiest season in the city was just a few weeks away, and he felt that Dani had chosen to usher the glorious days in a bit early.

"The sign? No, I don't come that way, Tony. What about the sign?"

"It has a memorial message on it for that murdered student. Isn't that nice? You might want to have Loretta take pictures. It could make a good human interest follow up story."

"Tony you're getting to be a regular news hound. If you think it's a good idea, I bet it is. I'm going to take your advice and go find Loretta. If she has some down time, she can make a quick run across the Connector. Thanks for the tip."

To put the memorial on the sign that touted most campus events was typically Tech. She wondered if it was the idea of some students or the administration. She'd like to talk to the creator, so maybe she needs to ask some questions. She decided to call Charles Black as soon as she found Loretta. She also had to call Wes Wesley and see if they had any new information. She wanted to be right there when he was ready to say, "We have identified the murderer." Her day was going to be busy. It appeared that the public was captivated by stories of violence and misery.

• • •

"Charles Black, here. Hi, Dani. How can I help you this morning?"

"I'm wondering about the story behind the memorial sign. Everybody is talking about it."

"Yes, here on campus too. It seemed a nice idea. I'm glad that it's gotten positive attention. That should please our advertisers. We're always trying to find messages that get lots of notice."

Dani was surprised that Black's attitude seemed to set aside the reason for the memorial and comment on the commercialism of the sign. She didn't think that he had the warmth to be the creator of the sentiments. His tone confirmed her guess.

"Who can I talk to about the origin of the sign, Charles? I'd like to get some background in case I decide to use it as a followup story of the murder of Andy Dren."

"Just talk to me. The president has told me to handle this. What would you like to know, Dani? I don't have much time, but I can always find a few minutes for you."

"Whose idea was it to have the memorial?"

"Actually, I suggested it and then my staff worked out the details," Black responded confident that there was no way that Dani would find otherwise. He hoped that she might mention it on her prime time show.

"That's great, Charles. Then you can tell me, and the people who have called us about it, exactly what HKIIICC means? Is it a campus code for something? Or something that was special to Andy?"

The vice president hesitated. He wasn't sure how to reply."Well, that part is just a blooper. We're going to eliminate it momentarily. I can see why it has so many people intrigued. Just like you, Dani, they must think it's a secret message. How about telling me later how many calls you get about the message. I can include it in my market research for this month."

Dani wanted to end the conversation quickly. Charles Black's attitude was really bothering her. She was sure that the students at Tech weren't interested in the marketing value of the tragic death of one of their classmates. Black was a real loser.

Dani hung up. Her good feelings about the memorial had been tainted. She decided to account it to the ego-driven personality of Charles Black. He never was one of her favorite people, but she did have to deal through him so she'd just forget his attitude.

She tried to reach Wes, and was told that he was on a job and wouldn't be available most of the morning. They'd give him her message. She asked for Billy Joe and received the same response. She concluded that there were too many homicide cases in Atlanta for the number of detectives. Maybe that would make a good investigative story sometime, she mused.

Her hand was still on the receiver when the telephone rang, and she found her favorite contact on the campus on the other end."Dani, it's Lindy. Thanks again for having me on your program last evening. Lots of students saw it. I feel like a celebrity."

Dani laughed, "You are a celebrity, Lindy. I hope you're enjoying it."

"It beats being called the Prez's Kid, for sure. It's nice to be just me. The reason I called was to be sure you've seen the memorial message for Andy."

"Actually, I haven't seen it, but I asked Loretta to go get it on film, and I've had several conversations about it. What do you know about it?"

"Only rumors but I can tell you about them. No one's sure how it got there, but the opinion is that some students did it."

"Some students? I heard that it was Charles Black's idea."

"I don't think so. I talked to Janeen Carson just minutes ago and when I asked her about it, she said that my dad and she were surprised about it and Charles just seemed confused. She added that she was happy that it was done. She really liked Andy. Do you want to hear the really funny part of the stories going around campus?" Lindy asked excitedly, already having forgotten that Dani heard that Charles Black was the creator of the memorial.

"Absolutely. You're usually full of good information."

"I know that you know about old G. Pitts Berdel our Tech

student for more than sixty years. The guys around campus are saying that old Berdel did it! Isn't that cool? Our most famous Tech legend has moved into the era of technology. Nobody cares who really did it. They just like talking about G. Pitts doing his thing at Georgia Tech."

Dani liked the story. It was fun and this was a time for some fun on campus. The kids needed a little relief from the stress of this week. She joined Lindy in feeling that she didn't care who did it."How about the odd message: HKIIICC, Lindy? What do you hear about that?"

"You've gotta remember that this institution is made up by a huge collection of theorists. The theories are going ballistic. Most guys believe that the HK means hacker, you know, like computer hacker. Some see the III as three letters, others see them as numbers but many think that it loosely represents Andy's age: 30. Most of us agree that CC stands for the College of Computing. That's where everyone is at this point. The one definite is that everybody is talking about the sign and Andy. That's way cool."

Dani wasn't going to tell Lindy that Black said it was a mistake. The young man, and obviously many other students, had strong feelings about the message. She thought it better for them to have their fun.

"I've got to get to the Technique office. We've taken some photographs and we're going to feature the sign in our next special edition. Keep in touch, Dani. I'll do the same."

Dani said good-bye and smiled to herself. The Lindholm's had raised a fine son.

Chapter 46

Wes T. Wesley

Wes got back to the Homicide office just before 8:00 after grabbing a Chik-Filet on the run. He kept thinking about a thick, rare steak, a steamy baked potato and a big dish of chocolate ice cream. The chicken sandwich just didn't push those thoughts out of his head. He decided he'd ask Janeen to go to Bones tomorrow where he knew he'd get one of the best steaks in town. That would be a great way to end his day off this week. He was supposed to have had Friday off, too, but with the qualifying and the two homicide cases, his weekend just became a *weak-end* instead of the week's end.

Wes looked in his message box and saw a pile of pink slips. He frowned. He didn't need anything more to do. He was meeting one of the FBI agents in 15 minutes. Dickerson 'Dixie' Packard; a thirty-something man whose description would include words such as average, medium, ordinary, perhaps even beige; had been with the FBI in Atlanta for almost three years. He and two other agents were now assigned to the Homicide building. This worked out well for both the Atlanta detectives and the Feebee agents when they were collaborating on a case, otherwise it simply made the quarters more crowded and chaotic. Was there never to be an end to the chief's red pencil and penny pinching? The man was a good policeman and a likable person but was absolutely shit-zoid when it came to running his department for less than he was allocated.

Wes shuffled through the messages as he walked into his office."There's a pattern here," he said to himself, "I bet I can guess why there are three calls marked 'Urgent' from the chief, two from the mayor's office with a note 'call anytime' and one from a man who identified himself as a Georgia Tech alumnus. Yep, Tech big shot alumni are on the rampage."

The pressure was on. Wes wasn't surprised. He'd call the Chief Alan Princeton first. Surely there was no one in the mayor's office at this time of night.

"Hey, Barnes, it's Wesley returning the Chief's call."

"You mean calls, that's plural. Three to be exact. He had decided that you'd taken early retirement or left town to look for another job," Officer Roscoe Barnes said sarcastically. "This is your lucky day, because he's standing in the doorway headed for home. I know he'll take a minute or two to talk to you."

Wes waited. He could imagine Barnes holding out the receiver, Chief Princeton coming back to the desk and......"Where the hell have you been, Detective? Every time I called, someone had a different excuse."

"I hope they were reasons, sir, not excuses. I've been working on the Tech case and the shooting at the Omni with my time at the range mashed in between. I just got back to the office. I called you even before the mayor's office."

"Oh, shit. The mayor's office. I've been receiving those calls too, which of course is why I've been chasing your butt, Wes," Alan Princeton said in a voice that sounded like they both should be sympathetic to one another's problems."I need to have a response for the calls I'm getting about the Tech murder."

"Yes, Chief. I understand. Unfortunately, I don't have any spectacular news. It's a strange one," Wes proceeded to elaborate about all the information that says no one would kill Dren, the absence of material clues and that a witness had seen a car racing away from the crime scene. He tacked on some details and then bluntly added about the suspicious behavior of Lindholm and Black. When he mentioned the amount of dollars, Princeton whistled.

"I had no idea that alumni gave at those levels. Damn! We sure are in the wrong business. Do you think there's a relationship between the dollars and the shooting?"

"I'm back here at the office now, Chief, to meet with Agent Packard. I want to get his thoughts on this, since he's the expert on international funds coming into our country."

"That's good. He's the man. It'll be excellent to have his counsel before you return your call to the mayor's office. Why not wait until the morning? Then you can respond that the FBI and we are collaborating. The mayor'll like that. Doesn't hurt for us to look like we're covering every possibility. Sounds good, Detective. Maybe you can get some more from your witness. We're OK as long as there isn't another shooting. Does Fancer still have on his extra security?"

Wes confirmed that there were twice as many officers on the campus now as normal. Some were their own Atlanta officers doing some moonlighting. He was thrilled to hear that the Chief didn't expect him to return the calls to the mayor's office now. He wanted to talk to Dickerson and go home. He might have enough time to return the call from the Tech alumnus before the FBI agent arrived.

Wes pushed the disconnect button and immediately dialed the number, according to the note, that belonged to Rutledge Newborn.

"Rutledge Newborn speaking."

"Mr. Newborn, this is Detective Wesley, Atlanta Homicide. I'm returning your call."

"Yes, Detective, I wanted to discuss the murder at Georgia Tech. You can imagine how upset all of the alumni are, and they look at us, the Foundation trustees, for information and leadership. It's imperative that we know exactly what you've discovered."

Wes wondered if all of the men related to this Foundation have taken lessons on sounding like they had a corner on intelligence, power and position. There was the same tone in Newborn's voice as is in Lindholm's and Black's. They're probably nice guys, but they could be better received if they didn't talk down to those they believed to be the common man.

"I'm happy to tell you how the investigation is progressing, sir, but we're still gathering the evidence and interviewing people," Wes told him and then repeated most of what he had just told Chief Princeton.

"I'd hoped that you would be closer to an arrest, Detective. It's unacceptable to keep the alumni under such stress."

"I appreciate your concern, Mr. Newborn, but we're much more concerned about the strain that the students are under. Being on campus with rumors and fears is much more difficult than living elsewhere. We're working day and night to find the killer. If you'll pass that information on to your alumni friends, it would be greatly appreciated." Wes managed to keep the respectful tone in his voice.

Rutledge Newborn hesitated before responding. He listened closely to Wesley's voice and felt confident that the Homicide detective understood the importance of this call. He sighed and said quietly, seriously, "I acknowledge your efforts. I'm sure you know your job, but what you do not know is our job as trustees of our alma mater. Detective, we're in the middle of a significant fundraising campaign, and we must keep the institute's image above reproach. We can't allow a single event to discourage our alumni from giving. Actually we're expecting a mega-gift this week. Surely you wouldn't want to feel responsible for our donor changing his mind."

"I don't fully understand, sir, how a tragic shooting of one of Tech's outstanding students would affect alumni giving, but you're correct that I'm not enlightened about your responsibilities. Our focus is on finding the criminal and preventing another murder. I'm in the office tonight to meet with one of my colleagues to discuss and review information that hopefully will help solve the case." Wes was beginning to feel weary. This alumnus didn't appear to have a concern for the victim or his family. The concern was alumni giving. No, he didn't understand the trustee's mindset.

Wes turned away from the phone and saw Dickerson Packard enter the building, "Mr. Newborn, my colleague has arrived. Thank you for calling today and don't hesitate to contact me again if you have questions."

"Yes, Detective, I'll do that. I'll be watching the news for a conclusion to this embarrassing situation. Good night."

"Wes, you look like you need a good night's sleep. Too

many women chasing you these days?" Agent Packard asked as he pulled up a battered chair, turned it around and straddled the rickety back.

"Not the problem, Dixie. I've just had a bastard of a week. This Tech murder is a real bitch and now the chief, the mayor and the alumni are standing right behind my every step. I was on the phone with one of the more pompous alumni who is afraid this killing will affect alumni giving. Let's talk about humanity here."

Dixie Packard shook his head slowly as he empathized with Wes." Money comes before all other considerations these days. Since the institution is state supported, I don't see how some alumni dollars can be all that important."

"It might get your attention that we're talking about hundreds of *millions* of dollars; probably from Hong Kong, my friend. That's why I wanted to talk to you tonight. I need your expertise and opinion."

"Son of a bitch! I guess you better tell me the story. This sounds like my kind of crap."

Wes related their progress and findings on the investigation beginning on Tuesday and brought Dickerson Packard right up to the telephone calls tonight. He mentioned that Rutledge Newborn said that another huge gift was due this week. That might be a clue that Dixie needed to move quickly.

"I can't give you hard evidence about electronic transfer of funds, Dixie, but these large amounts surely aren't being carried in suitcases. The president's executive assistant says that Tech has already received $185 million from Hong Kong, but is about to announce plans for a big Asian program that will cost only $6 million. Now we have an alumnus who calls about the shooting and happens to say they are expecting another mega-gift this week. I'd like to know if it, too, is from Hong Kong and if it could relate to the motive for Dren's murder. I think it's possible that the victim knew something he shouldn't and that's what's making the bastards nervous. What was Andy doing at Lindholm's computer? Why, when he was found, did the screen show a Hong Kong file but when we arrived, it was some nonsense about curriculum?" Wes ran his doubts, questions and speculations along in one continuous line, almost without a breath as if there were no punctuation marks.

"It could be a problem. We're looking at more and more international influence in the US of A. Some feel that elections at every level are being decided because of foreign money. Georgia Tech could be being used as a way to launder funds to get them into the system here. The money could come in here and go out of here in several transfer operations. We can get a subpoena for the records. If there's no funny business going on, we'll get cooperation from both the foundation and the bank or banks involved. After all, they do want to find a killer who's probably loose on campus."

"Yes, let's do it," Wes exclaimed. "Having these answers will give us a better indication of where we should be looking for our killer. I've got a second hunch. It could be that the wrong man was shot. I've a theory that the victim was supposed to be the president."

"The president?" Dixie exclaimed in dismay, "That's a switch. If that were the fact, your investigation would take a different direction in a New York minute. Let me work on the subpoena and get back to you tomorrow. Unless you've more bombs to drop, I'm going home before there's an APB out on me."

"Nope, no more bombs. You now know about what I know regarding this case. Thanks for giving up your evening, Dixie. I owe you,"

"...again! You owe me again. It's amazing how many times the FBI has to bail out you little, pissant city cops. You'd think we were assigned here to be your guardian angels."

Wes laughed as the two friends walked toward the door. They liked working together. Each knew that his particular expertise was an asset to the other. Wes had many more years experience in police work, specifically homicide; but Dixie had broader experience and access to funds that sometimes helped to unearth information needed to close a case. Even though the addition of the Feebees overtaxed the facility, Wes thought it was great to have them on the team.

Chapter 47

Dickerson Packard

Since it was Saturday, Wes had slept in late. It was already after ten o'clock, and he'd been lying in his bed, dozing off and on, enjoying the inactivity of both his mind and his body. After six days straight of following leads of several cases, putting together reports of the progress, and trying to keep one step ahead of Major Dagmar Dilbert; he had no desire to get beyond the kitchen for his special Saturday breakfast of freshly squeezed orange juice, pecan pancakes and country-made sausage. Thinking about his opinion of morning banquet fare, he was almost enticed to crawl out of the bed. Maybe another twenty minutes and his body would catch up with his appetite.

He wondered what Janeen was doing right now and knew that his inactive body could be sent into orbit if he could reach over and find her warm and willing body beside him. He tried to picture how she would look after a night of sharing his bed and making love. She would have the covers pulled up to her bare shoulder that was the preview of her beautiful, unclothed body that was lying just inches away from his. He would reach over and stroke her back, down her arm and lightly cup her warm, soft breast in his hand. She'd move under his touch and slide those couple of inches so their bodies would join as naturally as if they'd been born together. She'd turn toward him exaggerating every motion so that they could enjoy the full ecstasy of their eager bodies. He'd kiss her with a passion that he imagined she would return. He wouldn't wait for more clues that they were both ready and accepting. He would simply continue the love-making. He would reach down and feel the wetness....

Wes jumped when the telephone began to ring. He squeezed his eyes closed to retain the erotic image that had brought him fully awake. He cursed the loss of a perfectly good erection. Whoever was calling him at this time of day was risking making the weekly homicide report. He wondered about the caller being Jason, but knew his son liked his Saturday sack time even more than Wes did.

"Wesley." No time to waste words.

"It's Dixie. I've been working for you since last night. Now you owe me BIG time. I will fax my list of what you can get for me soon, but now I want you to know that you've picked up something on that Tech funding. I don't have all the details, but it's been worth inquiring about."

Wes sat on the edge of the bed, his mind fully functioning on a different level by Dickerson Packard's third sentence. He could've dozed through all of his prattle about what he was owed, but the funding information was eye opening.

"What have you found, Dixie. Shit, it's only ten o'clock in the morning. What've you been doing?" the detective asked excitedly. He was wide awake.

"Here's what I know: When I left you last evening and drove home, I kept drifting back to the statement that you made that you thought there might've been an interesting funds transfer this week. I decided if something big was possible now, right after the murder, I better get a handle on it. If it relates to your investigation, being corporately courteous and waiting for business hours on Monday just wouldn't hack it. I called the U.S. Attorney, Gil Bronson, and talked turkey to him. He agreed to give me the subpoenas that I needed, then conferenced in Judge Forrest Owens and repeated to him what I needed and why it couldn't wait until Monday. We've worked on several cases together and I have downed a pint or two with him at that Mexican joint out on Chattahoochee, so we understand each other.

"Gil was able to use his influence to get the three subpoenas early today, and I was in touch with the three major banks to tell them what we're investigating. Each of the officials asked if it related to the student's murder, and I pleaded the fifth. They can make their own guesses without my help but their own questions did put certain urgency to my request. That made it easier to get them to do some work on a Saturday," Agent Packard had covered hours of effort and accomplishment in just a few sentences. He not only was reliable, but he was succinct.

"And?"

"Small question. Large answer. Wachovia Bank received a wire transfer of $13 mil from the Bank of China in Hong Kong on Friday that was for the Georgia Tech Foundation. When they checked the file today at my request, there was a transfer of the entire amount to the First National Bank in Washington, D.C. It moved so fast that it's like it wasn't even there. Also on Friday, Sun Trust received a wire transfer of $10 mil from the Bank of China in Hong Kong for the Georgia Tech Foundation. When they checked today, there appeared to be $2,400,000 remaining and a transfer of $7,600,000 to Summit Bank here in Atlanta. And lastly, Bank of America received $7,000,000 yesterday and this morning there was $600,000 still in the account with a transfer for the difference to a Canadian Bank in the Cayman Islands. Since those are the three main Atlanta banks handling The Foundation's funds, those are the banks that I asked to be subpoenaed. $30 million deposited on Friday; $3 million remaining on Saturday. I asked if this was a repeat pattern and each bank found several similar transfers in and missing amounts the next days. Before this week, total received for all three banks was $185,000,000 and remaining the next days $18,500,000. A neat 10% for a day for what? Quietly moving money into the United States?"

"I know that number $185,000,000, Dixie. Tech calls those funds campaign "gifts" from Hong Kong alumni. It made up half of the money they have toward their campaign goal. Adding this $30,000,000, the total is $215,000,000. Quite a campaign!"

"It surely is, Wes. It could be true, but where's the bulk of it a day later? One banker said that he'd been given the impression that Tech transferred it to one of the other banks that handle their business, but it didn't show up in the records of the other two main banks here. I don't know how this can relate to your murder, but it still needs to be investigated," The FBI agent told his colleague.

"I'm not sure either, but the student was at the president's computer and the student also helped to enter campaign data into the system. Maybe he figured out what was going on. That could be dangerous. You feds frown on questionable funds floating around the US of A, don't you?"

"Well, you know what a big mess is being investigated related to political funds. In fact, I wonder if this could be a part of that? I've a feeling that we might not be able to trace exactly where these monies have gone, but as I dig deeper, I'm going to seriously consider illegal political contributions as a final destination. Hard to believe that Tech personnel and alumni are involved in this, but right now it looks damn suspicious. Wes, have you looked at Andrew Dren's computer file? That may give us both some clues and answers to our questions."

"No, I haven't done it yet but that's in my plan next. Why don't you go with me? I don't think we'll have any problem getting access. Andy's roommates have been quite vocal about wanting to help find the killer. By the way, I have one of our computer nerds going over the president's computer but so far he has been bored out of his head."

"Can you set up checking Dren's computer for tomorrow? I can probably meet you on campus any time. If not, it should be done anyway."

"Dixie, I can't thank you enough that you moved on this so fast and are willing to team up on this. We might be following two different crimes but we might be on the same track."

"We might get two for the price of one if we work it right."

"I'll call Fancer and get this set up. With this new information, we might be looking for the wrong motive and therefore missing the killer. I hope you can have the rest of today for your family. I don't want your wife and kids hunting me down."

"Unfortunately, Wes, they're used to this. The same as Jason. I've heard how he used to spend lots of time in the office with you. Maybe I should soon break in my son to being my partner," Dickerson Packard mused, "See you tomorrow. Hey, I hear you're bird-dogging an interesting woman."

"Billy Joe could be competition for the gossip talk shows. I'll call you, Dixie."

Chapter 48

Walter

Saturday was the first day since the murder that most persons who were involved could say that their routines and lives were beginning to get back to normal. Every crisis has a life of its own. It comes suddenly from nowhere and disappears almost as fast. The memory will alter some lives, but in most cases it will simply be another event in a long series which is called life.

Campus people noted that tonight was a basketball game between Duke and Georgia Tech. Many of the students who traveled to Dalton for the funeral would be in the stands tonight; their attention on basketball players and scores. They'll hardly give a thought to Andy Dren and the memorial message that had a life of three hours.

That missive would live through the front-page feature in the Technique but otherwise it was gone with the push of the delete button on a computer keypad. Russell Biers felt he'd destroyed a modern day masterpiece when he followed Charles Black's direction to remove the memorial ASAP after being chastised for not having kept control of the sign. He also was told to find the culprit but Russell knew that he was not going to follow those instructions.

The students had loved it while it lasted, but it was gone as were all other activities that had happened during the week. Now it was the weekend and a time to party and roar with the crowd.

The students' memories were much shorter than Walter's. He'd looked forward to the game because of the opportunity it gave him to check on lots of cars at one time and one place. He could get maybe a hundred license plate numbers for Detective Wesley. He didn't care if Tech beat Duke or visa versa. It was just some kids playing around with a ball. It wasn't much different in his opinion than all the guys he grew up with who threw hoops in empty lots on almost every inner city block in Atlanta.

Walter came prepared with a pen and a bunch of torn up little pieces of paper that were in the deep, buttoned pockets of his army fatigue pants. It might be the first time in his life, when he crossed campus, he was not pushing a grocery cart piled high with crushed, aluminum cans. Tonight wasn't about making some money. Tonight was about finding a killer. Tonight was about the value of friendship.

As Walter approached the intersection at Tenth and Fowler Street, he saw Sander waiting for him. Just like he'd predicted, his buddy was as enthusiastic as he'd been to help with the homicide investigation. Sander was armed with papers and pen too. Their plan was to cover the parking lots and the streets adjacent to the Robbie Cremins Basketball Coliseum. They figured they had about two hours to do their work. Some of the older alumni or students trying to beat the traffic will begin to trickle out of the building about then.

Walter was amazed at how few cars basically had the same size and shape of the one he'd seen in the middle of the night. He decided to note color too even though he wasn't sure of that detail. It just might be important; like if he was asked to reconstruct his sighting in the dark. Maybe a light- or bright-colored car just wouldn't look the same as what he remembered — or then maybe it would.

He was completely absorbed in his task and enjoying having a more meaningful reason to be on campus than he usually had. He liked the feeling of being a part of something that can make a difference. It had been a long time since he'd felt like he was a person with value. Walter was concentrating on that thought and jotting down another license number when he was startled by a rough voice close by, "Hey, punk, whatta ya doing near my car?"

When he turned to face the person, Walter shoved his pen and the paper into his pocket. As he had learned from being on the streets, he put his hands out to his sides to indicate that he wasn't armed. He didn't want any hotheaded student or tottering alumnus to get the wrong impression and call the po-lice.

"Nothin'. I'm just walkin' down this street decidin' where

I'm gonna to stay tonight."

"That's not what it looks like to me, you motherfucker. I think you were planning to jack my car. Get over here, where I can see if you're carrying something."

Walter didn't want any problems, so he accepted the insults without a word. He could see that his accuser looked young and strong. Probably a student rather than an alumnus. He would back off and be on his way. He got this license number anyway, could ask Detective Wesley who it belonged to, and make a point to stay out of his way—-forever.

"Don't get excited. I don't want your car. I couldn't afford to put gas in. Besides, I don't have a license to drive. You got me all wrong, mister."

"That's your story, jerk off. You probably never told the truth in your life. Who do you think you are that you can hang around this campus? You homeless shits should be run out of town permanently, not just during the Olympics time," the young man said in a voice that was building in volume.

"I'll just get outta your way and go along where I was goin'. Sorry that my bein' here right now has upset you, but I can be outta sight in a minute," Walter apologized thinking that this student would like him to act subservient. He proceeded to walk away from the car. He'd given the young man the indication that he wasn't a threat and that he was leaving to accommodate him. That was why it was such a surprise that he was hit on the side of the neck by a hard fist. He grunted and turned toward his attacker, raising his arm to defend himself from another blow.

"Don't raise your fucking arm against me, slimeball. You're not gonna get away with attacking me," the student said through clenched teeth. He came at Walter and hit him twice with the power of a professional boxer. As Walter fell to the ground between the small sports car and a pickup truck, he saw the man pick up something from the curb, raise it above his head and..... he saw nothing else.

The student kicked several times at Walter's chest as he stepped over him and unlocked the door of his red Miata. He got into the car, slammed the door and put his key into the ignition.

Just before he started the engine he heard someone running and two voices cry out,"Hey, stop! Stop! Police."

"Oh, fuck. Now I'll have to explain how this piece of shit was trying to steal my car. I don't want to waste any time now, since I told Tiffany I would meet her after she had dinner with her folks. These cops should be quicker, and they'd have caught this guy instead of me."

Lonnie continued to pull out of his parking place but jammed on the brakes when he saw a man appear directly in front of his headlights. He rolled down his window and waited just like he'd done many times waiting to be given a traffic ticket.

The "uniforms" approached the car from the street. One hanging back to cover the lead officer. They had their guns drawn and ready but didn't feel they would really need them. It appeared from a distance that there were two men fighting, but they saw only one. Both officers had asked the other, "Carjacking?" as they called out, but it looked like they were wrong.

"What's the hurry, son?" asked Joe Garcia, an off-duty Atlanta police officer. "You must've heard us say: Stop."

"Stop? No, I didn't hear you. I was getting into my car and guess the noise from opening the door was louder than your voice." Lonnie Tedesco did not want to antagonize the policeman.

"I thought I saw another person with you. Have a fight with your date and she left you in the lurch?" Officer Garcia asked leaning over to get an interior view of Lonnie's car.

Before Lonnie could decide how to respond, he and the officers heard groaning from behind the car. Joe Garcia stayed in place with his pistol aimed toward the driver while his partner, Marla Eichmann, moved swiftly toward the sounds. Lonnie looked Joe directly in the eye and said quickly, "That's some homeless guy who was trying to steal my car. I hit him to get him to leave, and he fell. It's good you came along, because you can arrest him right now. I'll file charges."

"Hey, Joe, this guy is in bad shape. His head is a mess. I'm going to radio for the medics," Marla cried out from somewhere behind the car.

Joe had an uneasy feeling that this young man was not being truthful. All the part-time officers had been told about the Tech campus homeless and their can businesses. They weren't forced to stay off the property, because no one felt they were a problem. Since Joe and Marla were moonlighting at Tech this week, they'd seen some 'aluminum entrepreneurs,' and found them to be accepted by students and staff.

"May I see your license? Then, please, get out of your car, son. I'd like to take a look at what you're carrying," Joe asked politely thinking maybe instead of walking into a carjacking, they had walked into a drug deal. That seemed to make more sense.

"Don't act like I'm the criminal. I'm the victim. Can't you guys get anything right? This is so damn obvious that even a rookie could see that I was going to lose my car," Lonnie said less carefully as his temper rose but he reached for his wallet to get his license and handed it to the officer

"Lonnie Tedesco, I see that your address isn't in Atlanta. What're you doing here?" Joe asked quietly.

"I'm a student at Tech. Why else would I be on this campus? I was coming from the basketball game and found this guy trying to break into my car. It happens all the time around campus."

"Breaking in. How was he doing this?"

"Well, he was hitting the side window and grabbing at the door handle. It was lucky I locked the door. Sometimes I forget."

"The window seems to still work, and I don't see any marks on the door. I think your car fared quite well. Now, Lonnie, will you get out of the car so we can look around? You can give me the keys so we can check your trunk," Officer Garcia was using his most professional voice hoping he wouldn't get any resistance. Sometimes these very casual encounters can turn nasty.

"You don't have any right to search my car? I haven't done anything. It was that guy behind the car that was c-c-committing a c-c-crime," Lonnie told Garcia. He made no move to get out of the car. He was getting excited which always caused the stuttering to begin.

"We're not talking about the other guy. It's apparent that he's not saying anything. You must've really worked him over, Lonnie. Now get out of the car," Joe Garcia moved fast as he spoke in a soothing, mellow tone. He reached into the car and removed the keys from the ignition."Get out of the car, or I'll have to help you out."

Eichmann, Garcia and Tedesco heard the siren of the ambulance and saw the flashing light. Eichmann said, "That might be the fastest response on record. We may have to give these guys a commendation."

The vehicle pulled up beside them and the door opened, "I bet you thought we weren't coming, right?"

"If you're looking to break your own record, Melvin, I do believe you've done it. We're impressed. Now take a look at the man," Marla said, never leaving her place between the car and the truck.

"We cannot tell a lie. We were on the other side of the coliseum in the parking lot. Tech always has an emergency crew stationed outside the building during basketball games. We were in your back pocket, and you just didn't know it. Move over and let us get to work," the medic said pushing the officer gently out of his way.

"Now that Melvin the Medic has taken over, let's look at what surprises you may have for us, Lonnie. Anything you would like to tell us before we search the car?" Garcia asked in an almost friendly tone.

"Yeah. I have a p-p-permit for the gun in the glove compartment. My folks insisted if I was going to be in Atlanta, that I should be able to p-p-protect myself. Don't go getting excited over nothing. I have a hot chick waiting so can we make a deal and all go on our way?" Lonnie wanted to get away from the very piercing eyes of Officer Garcia. He knew from his own family that Latin types can explode at anytime for any reason. If this guy goes ballistic about the gun, he's liable to drag him in.

"No deals now. Let's see if we even need a deal, Lonnie. Right now we're just looking around. Stay calm, son."

Marla reached into the glove compartment and found the small handgun that Lonnie had mentioned. She found a packet of condoms, breath mints, the owner's manual and a scrunched up baseball hat. The officer checked the back seat and found a few schoolbooks, a pair of running shoes and an empty beer bottle.

"The car at first glance is real clean, Joe. Except for the gun, the stuff looks like what most students would have. Let's take a look at the trunk."

"Nothing there except some stuff for fun and games," Lonnie said quickly. He really didn't want the officers to search his trunk. "No need to waste your t-t-time."

"Thank you for being so thoughtful, but we've lots of time. We'll do a fast drive-through and decide if we agree with you," Garcia said as Eichmann took the keys and moved toward the back of the car where Walter had been lying.

Lonnie became more nervous as the trunk was opened. He'd just thrown some stuff in there that he was taking to Tiffany's, and he didn't want to discuss it with these two cops.

Marla used her flashlight in addition to the trunk light and noted that the trunk was quite clean, but several of the items stored there were rather unusual: a pair of handcuffs, rope, a black silk scarf, a box of ammunition, and five footballs. She ticked off each article loud enough for Joe to hear and waited for his reaction.

"Handcuffs and rope? Now what kind of fun and games were you planning?" Joe asked Lonnie with true interest.

"Oh, you know, I was on my way to see my girl. We like to do some kinky sex just to try something different. The macho thing t-t-turns her on." Lonnie wondered if he should have lied and said they belonged to his brother.

"Must be quite a girl. You better be careful and not let your rough stuff get either of you in trouble," Joe felt like an old uncle giving advice to some little kid and yet he knew that he was probably not more than a few years older than Lonnie Tedesco.

"Hey, Marla, come here before we take off for the hospital, "Melvin called from the open door of the ambulance.

Officer Eichmann slammed the trunk and walked the short distance toward Melvin's voice. She listened to what he was saying, nodded several times. On an impulse, she reached out and took Walter's hand. She placed her head close to the face that was now covered with temporary bandages and whispered a few words of encouragement. Melvin began to close up the doors and Marla backed away. She hoped the homeless man would be OK. He already had a lousy of life.

She walked away from Joe and Lonnie, far enough so she could talk in privacy. She called a number, waited until the beeping ended and punched in a number.

Chapter 49

Lonnie Tedesco

Wes had picked up Janeen about seven o'clock. He thought she looked especially pretty tonight in a soft, white woolen dress topped by a matching white and pale gray plaid jacket with chunky gold buttons. Her face positively glowed. Her smile warm. To him, Janeen looked like a very happy woman and hoped that he was the reason for her radiance.

They drove to 'Bones' for the steak that Wes had been fantasizing about for two days. He didn't have to look at the menu to decide on his meal and tried to be a good host by not insisting that the waiter bring the meat before they had even been seated at their table. He wanted this to be a special evening. To do that he knew he'd have to follow a more civilized pace.

"Janeen, would you like a drink before dinner? Wine or a cocktail?"

"Actually, I'd prefer to have wine with dinner. You'll probably think I'm really gauche, but I'm starving. That's not very ladylike, but I never had lunch today."

"Wait a minute, Madame Janeen. How long have you been in the mind reading business? It's a scary situation to think you know what I have in my head. Are you carrying your crystal ball or Tarot cards in your purse?"

"None of the above, sir. I'm just a hungry woman who is lucky enough to find herself in a great restaurant with another eager eater. We should ask the waiter if we can go directly to the kitchen to help them get our steaks on the fire."

Wesley motioned for the waiter and told him that they were ready to order. He thought they could linger over coffee and dessert rather than a cocktail. It'll be a better evening on a full stomach of lots of choice beef and all the trimmings.

While they waited for their food and through the meal, Wes and Janeen began talking about the past week, but they soon had moved to much broader topics as they began to get to know each other. Wes talked about Jason, his years as a detective and told a couple funny stories about living alone. Janeen related more details about her family, her long tenure at Tech and her volunteer work in Juvenile Court. They had so much to learn, and they were enjoying each new discovery.

Janeen was looking at the dessert menu when she saw Wes reach under his coat and look at his beeper.

"Damn. Who'd call me on a Saturday evening? I'm sorry, honey, but I need to find out who's trying to reach me. Take your time on that dessert decision, and I'll be back to add my order for a huge dish of chocolate ice cream." Wes got up, gave Janeen a quick kiss on her cheek and was out of sight in a few seconds.

Using the desk phone, he punched in the number left for him and waited for one ring. It was answered immediately, "Officer Eichmann."

"Detective Wes Wesley returning your page, officer. What can I do for you?" he asked tentatively, because he did not know this policewoman.

"Detective Wesley, I'm on special assignment at Georgia Tech. My partner and I were patrolling near the Cremins Coliseum and came upon what looked like a possible carjacking. We found a student about to drive away and another man on the ground unconscious. The reason I called you is that as the injured man was being put into the ambulance to be taken to Grady Hospital he regained consciousness and whispered your name several times. I thought it was strange since all the officers on this special duty have been told to call you if we saw anything unusual. This man doesn't look like an officer, detective. He looks more like a homeless person," Marla explained, speaking quietly and turned away from where Joe was still waiting with Lonnie.

"What's the man's name, Officer?"

"At this point I don't know. The only things we found on

him were lots of little pieces of papers with what looks like license numbers and colors written on them."

Knowing the man could only be Walter, Wes said, "You're right. He's not an officer. He calls himself my deputy, and he's very important to me and to the Tech murder case. Be sure he has the best care, Officer. Who's the student and what is this about a carjacking?"

"The student's name is Lonnie Tedesco. He's accused your 'deputy' of trying to steal his car and that's why Tedesco hit him. This Lonnie guy is real pissed at us for detaining him, because he was headed for a hot date with his handcuffs, blindfold and rope. Officer Garcia and I aren't at all convinced about the carjacking story," Marla Eichmann explained and added gravely, "Detective, this man has been badly beaten."

"Don't let this Lonnie Tedesco go. I want to talk to him. Why don't you take him downtown, and I'll meet you there in about thirty minutes? I'm not far away. Keep him away from a telephone, and we'll read him his rights when I get there. Also, at this point, don't make any mention that I'm from Homicide. As a courtesy, call Chief Fancer and tell him what you're doing with one of his students. If he chooses to join us, ask him not to say anything until I get there. Thank you for calling, Officer Eichmann."

Wes returned to the table, asked the waiter for the check and sat on the edge of his chair. He leaned toward Janeen and said in a hushed tone, "You're going to have to skip the dessert, but I'll make a deal with you. If you'll leave with me now without kicking and screaming, I'll take you to a dessert place just as soon as I can arrange it. I owe you a big dish of calories. Right now, Janeen, I must go to down to the jail. Someone has beaten up Walter."

"Oh, no. Why would anyone do that?

"Dunno. I need to get downtown. I'll drop you off on my way." He was deep in thought when he realized that she'd asked him a question. He turned his head slightly to let her know that he was tuned in.

"Oops, I thought I'd lost you there for a minute, Detective.

I was asking whether you'd call me when you're ready to leave the jail? I'll be waiting to hear what you've learned."

"It might be late, pretty lady. I'll go to the hospital after I'm finished at the jail."

"That's OK. Really it is. I won't sleep until I know you and Walter are both managing. Don't worry about the time. I'll be waiting for your call."

• • •

Wes and Janeen walked to her door."Yes, ma'am. Whatever you want, light of my life, you may have. I'll call you no matter when I get to a telephone. Now, Cinderella, your prince is about to turn into a frog and your carriage into a police car," Wes kissed Janeen lightly on the lips. She slowly returned his kiss. Wes felt he had been given a beautiful gift but had no time to show his appreciation. He quickly sprinted back to his car, went to his office to trade cars and headed to downtown Atlanta.

Wesley arrived at the Atlanta jail in a little more than the predicted thirty minutes. He was excited with anticipation. He knew from his many years of experience as a detective that most cases were solved through a combination of hard work and a lucky break.

Chapter 50

Wes T. Wesley

Wes approached the building that he had visited many times in the years he was on the regular Atlanta police force. He stopped at the electronic reader that was placed at the left side of the short driveway. He rolled down the window, took out a small leather case from his pocket that held his badge and ID card, held it up so it could be read, and then watched the huge, solid, heavy, garage door open in front of the car.

He parked his car and went through the first locked door into the foyer area. If Lonnie had been with him, he'd have been patted down for weapons at this door and again at the next one that opened from the foyer. He wondered how Lonnie felt being treated like a criminal instead of a student. So many people when they get this far begin to panic and make an attempt to get away. Of course there's no place for them to go once the garage door is lowered behind a car. It's a forlorn sound when a person hears the heavy clank of the locks.

"I'm looking for Officer Eichmann. I'm Detective Wesley, Atlanta Homicide," Wes said quietly to the young, black policeman he didn't recognize sitting at a desk close to the door.

"She's in the first room on the left, Detective. She said to give you this copy of items found in the suspect's car. You're to go right in."

Wes opened the door and saw four people in the room - two uniforms, George Fancer and a young man who obviously was the student, Lonnie Tedesco.

"Hey, Chief. Sorry that you had to end up back on the job on a Saturday evening. Officer Eichmann, thank you for calling me. Good to see you, Officer Garcia." Wes had always been good at remembering names.

"Thanks for joining us. The officers brought in Lonnie - he's a freshman at Tech - about half an hour ago. We wouldn't have called you except that the man who was beaten mentioned your name," George Fancer explained.

"He was stealing my car. He should be sitting here, not me."

"Well, Lonnie, maybe he'd be if he could sit up. From what I'm told, he's in bad shape. I want to hear about what happened, but first, let's do it just like they do it on TV," Wes said as he took a small card out of his wallet, "You have the right to remain silent. Anything you say can be used against you in a court of law. You have the right to talk to a lawyer and have him present with you while you are being questioned. If you....."

"Don't you think this is overkill for me protecting myself and my car?"

"Actually, no, Lonnie. We want you to have all the rights that are due you. Why would I not want to give you every courtesy that you, as a citizen, deserve?" Wes was using his very best 'good cop' manner.

"I think it's a waste of time. I haven't done anything that any other guy on campus wouldn't have done, but if you want to Mirandaize me, go at it," Lonnie said looking smug when he used the formal name for the warning.

"That's good. We'll all feel better to be able to do our job as we're instructed. If you can't afford to hire a lawyer, one will be appointed to represent you before any questioning if you wish," Wes hesitated looking like he had to take a breath and swallow. He knew from long years of experience that often the perpetrator broke in at this time.

"I don't need to have a lawyer appointed. I don't need a lawyer at all. I haven't done anything except handle my own business."

"That's what we're here to talk about. We want to hear your story. Now if you'll let me get through reading the rest of the, as you obviously know, Miranda warning... You can decide at any time to exercise these rights and not answer any questions or make any statements. Two questions, for you, Lonnie. 1. Do you understand each of these rights I have explained to you?"

"Of course, I understand. I was smart enough to get into Georgia Tech, wasn't I?"

"That's a point. 2. Having these rights in mind, do you wish to talk to us now?"

"Yeah, I wanna talk to you. I wanna bring charges against that bum," Lonnie made it clear by his tone of voice and his body language that he was really ticked off.

Wes pulled up a chair, placed it directly in front of Lonnie, sat down facing him and leaned forward, "Well, let's hear from you what happened this evening."

"I was at the basketball game. Tech and Duke. I left early because I had a date with my girl. She's not crazy about the game, so I told her I'd be late. At this rate, I'm gonna be damn late. I left the coliseum and walked to my car. Before I even got to it, I saw someone trying to get into my car," Lonnie began.

Wes hitched his chair a few inches closer and asked, "How could you tell in the dark that this person was trying to get into the car?"

"It wasn't all that dark because there's a street light close by. We're told that Chief Fancer added a lot of lights for the Olympic Village," he smiled at Fancer before continuing, "That guy was sorta scratching around the window and door. Maybe he had a tool of some kind. I'm not sure about that. I yelled at him, and he ignored me. Just continued to break into my car. I was afraid that he was going to slit the top or break a window. When I got closer, he turned around and got ready to hit me. I saw something in his hand. I don't know what it was. I was scared shitless. He seemed like he was determined to take my car even if he had to get rid of me first. It's good I'm younger and faster, because I got in the first punch instead of him. He fell down, and I got in the car. That's when these officers came out of nowhere yelling at me. At me! They should've been protecting me," Lonnie stopped his story. He thought it sounded good. If he worked this right, he'd be on his way to Tiffany's in a few minutes.

"How many times did you hit him, Lonnie. I'm not sure of

that," Wes said never taking his eyes from Lonnie's.

"Just once. He turned out to be a cream puff. Went down like a rock."

Officer Eichmann interrupted, "Do you want to tell more about hitting the man, Lonnie? His head was bleeding. His eye was already swollen and his nose no longer dead center."

"Well, I didn't do it. That must have happened when he fell. Maybe he hit the truck on the way down and then hit the street. That could mess him up, but I didn't do it. I want to know how I file a charge against him. I'm lucky to still have a car." Lonnie said trying to work up sympathy for his predicament.

"Chief Fancer can look into your story about the car later, Lonnie. Are you sure you didn't hit him more than once? It would be understandable that being afraid you might have hit him twice and momentarily forgot. After all, Lonnie, at that point you were afraid for yourself and your car." Lonnie saw some empathy for his side for the first time. His story must have sounded good to this guy. He was practically giving him the words to say.

"Well, I don't think I hit him more than once, but I was *scared*. Why, I didn't even hear these officers when they first called me. It's almost like I was out of it. Don't remember much. I wonder if maybe that guy did hit me, and I just don't remember that. So maybe I don't remember that we both got a couple punches in," Lonnie Tedesco felt he was on a roll.

"Those things happen fast. It's hard to predict what we're going to do or recollect our actions in detail. Officer Eichmann seems to feel that the injuries are more than a single punch. One thing you don't want to happen to you, Lonnie, is to get caught in a lie. That would look real bad on your part. But a normal reaction to fear is understandable." Wes moved a little closer to the student as he spoke in a sympathetic manner.

Lonnie thought for maybe a minute and then responded slowly, "Well, sir, I'm just not sure. That's the truth. I wouldn't lie; really I wouldn't. I think I hit him once and he went down, but as afraid as I was, I might just not remember. You might be right. Is it possible that it will come back to me later?"

"Oh, yes, Lonnie. That often happens. Stress causes all kinds of strange responses. You think about all of this. I'm sure we'll be talking again,"

"Lonnie," Officer Garcia said causing all heads to turn in his direction, "I'm still wondering why you feel you must carry a gun to a basketball game."

"I didn't take it to the game," Lonnie said feeling nervous again, "I always keep a gun in my car. Because I drive all over Atlanta, my folks, you know, said that I should be able to protect myself. They gave it to me as a gift when I came to Tech. Remember I told you that I have a permit for it, officer."

"I'm sorry that your parents feel that way, Lonnie," Chief Fancer broke in, "I think I need to talk to them about security and the chances of getting into serious trouble when a gun is too available. But no matter what your parents say, you know that guns are not to be on this campus. Yours will not be returned to you until you're ready to take it back to your parents."

"OK, Chief. That's all right with me. If you think it's a problem, I don't wanna cause any shit for you. You keep it. I know where it is and can get it next time I go home. I'll give your message to my dad. He may call you."

"That's fine, Lonnie. I'm sure your dad knows how to reach me."

"OK, Lonnie, we'll be charging you with aggravated assault and you have a choice of staying here tonight or getting someone to put up bond for you. I'm going to suggest the bond be $100,000 so you need a bondsman or a friend with some big dollars and willing to believe in you." Wes' explanation was short, but it was enough to infuriate Lonnie Tedesco.

"Whatta ya mean bond? Whatta ya mean $100,000? How c-c-can you be acting like I done something wrong? Whatta ya trying to p-p-prove?"

"That's the law, Lonnie. It appears that you assaulted another person with something more than your hands and the law looks at that quite seriously. You say he was trying to steal your car but there is no proof to back up your statement. The officers who were there within seconds, saw no indication of an attempted theft but did find indication and proof of a damaging assault. The question is simply: do you want to spend tonight with your girlfriend or in jail? The choice is yours. Bond or no bond." Wes rose from his seat giving Lonnie breathing room for the first time since he'd entered the room, "If you need to think about it, you can sit in one of the cells, and we can get on with our own Saturday evening plans."

Lonnie blanched at the word *cells*. The idea of actually being locked up in a jail was frightening. With all of the crazy things he'd done in his hometown, he'd never been locked up. His dad was always there to talk the police out of doing anything this drastic. If they were in Waycross, these punk officers wouldn't be riding their high horses. His dad had lots of connections. He probably had connections here in Atlanta too, but Lonnie didn't want to call his dad for help. He'd tell his son he was a stupid jerk. Lonnie didn't want to hear that tonight.

"Sir, isn't there any other way to handle this? If I promise to pay for the medical expenses for the guy? If I promise not to have any guns on campus? What can I do? I don't want to have a record," Lonnie said humbly.

"It's too late, Lonnie. You should've asked the man why he was near your car and listened to his answer. You shouldn't have beat him to the point that Officers Eichmann and Garcia had to call the paramedics. You had multiple choices earlier this evening, but you've only one now: bail or jail." Wes may have sounded sympathetic, but he wasn't. He'd seen too many of these young Turks who truly believed that they could walk away from their own mistakes and poor judgment.

Lonnie lowered his head. He'd lost his cocky assurance. He felt defeated. He could think of only several outcomes and all were upsetting. When he again raised his head, he looked Wes directly in the eyes and said in a breaking voice with tears welling up in his own eyes, "This is gonna r-r-ruin my life. My dad is gonna kill me, he'll say I'm not smart enough to be his s-s-son. Probably I'll lose my football scholarship at Tech. My girl's family will tell her not to see me. Can't you see why you s-s-shouldn't do this to me?"

"I understand how you feel, Lonnie. But that's not how life or the law is decided. You now have another decision to make and only you can make it. You can take some time to think about it, but the four of us are leaving." Wes started toward the door and the other law enforcement officers fell in behind him.

"No, don't leave me here by myself. Let me c-c-call my uncle and get him to bring the money. He can do that. He lives a lot closer than my dad. He'll c-c-come."

Lonnie felt like a child again. He didn't even realize that he'd made a transition from a confident, cocky college student and football star to a whimpering little boy afraid of his father. He thought of Lorenzo Tedesco, his father, and how everything about the man screamed macho. He had a highway paving company that he ran like he was really the Godfather. Yeah, just like the movie that Lonnie had seen six times. When Renzo, that's what everyone called him, wasn't running his business, he was playing cards and drinking with his friends. Sometimes he'd let Lonnie hang around, but usually he was told that this was macho shit and he didn't qualify. Then all the friends would laugh. Lonnie knew from when he was little that they were laughing at him not with him.

"OK, son, make your call," George Fancer broke in. This was not a new experience for him. He'd spent many Saturday evenings here and knew the routine, "I'll wait here until you call your uncle so the other officers can get back to their responsibilities."

Lonnie felt relieved that he wasn't being locked up in a cell. He felt maybe after he had time to think about all of this that he could handle it better. There was too much at stake to let something like a scuffle with a homeless guy mess up his plans.

"Lonnie, take some time to think about what has happened tonight. If you have information to add, you'll have a chance to include it at your hearing," Wesley commented as he approached the door.

"Yes, sir, I'll think about everything. Maybe after I relax awhile, I'll be able to remember m-m-more. I'm sure that when I do, you'll see what a misunderstanding this has been."

Lonnie felt new energy as he stood up next to Chief Fancer. These police thought they were so smart, but if he stuck to his story, they'll be on his side. Even if the cruddy, homeless piece of shit said differently, he was sure the judge would believe a student from Georgia Tech.

"Oh, Lonnie, if your uncle brings your bond, don't disappear from campus. You wouldn't want it to look like you were trying to bug out on us. That wouldn't do you any good at all. You understand what I mean?" Wes warned.

"Yes, sir, I understand. I'm not going any place. I've so many tests and projects to do that I barely have time to do anything else. I'll call Chief Fancer tomorrow, like, if I think of more details," Lonnie was still talking as Wes went out the door. He paused only for a moment and added, "Tiffany, will never believe this excuse for being late."

Wes stopped, and took a step back toward the room, "Chief, could I talk to you before I leave? Then you can give Lonnie a hand in reaching his uncle."

"Sure. I'll be right back, Lonnie."

The two policemen stepped away from the door so their words wouldn't be overheard.

"Damn, Wesley, I almost choked when you suggested $100,000 bond. I know you want to teach the kid a lesson, but this is going to make it tough for him to get out of here tonight."

"Chief, I don't want him out of here. There are too many questions raised because of his attitude. I want him to stay put, and I want you to meet me at the campus when I get back from the hospital."

Fancer looked into Wes' eyes and saw a graveness that he'd not seen before. He realized that the detective had something important on his mind."I'm getting a message from you but I'm not sure yet what it is."

"I think there could be a relationship between Lonnie Tedesco and Andy Dren. I want to look at Lonnie's dorm room tonight before he gets to any of his relatives. It looks like he prefers talking to his uncle than to his dad. That might mean that he has something to hide."

"Shit, Wes, surely this football player isn't a murderer," Chief Fancer said in amazement.

"Don't know yet, but there are a couple things that move my opinion in that direction. 1. A car similar to Lonnie's was seen leaving the crime scene. 2. The ammunition found in the trunk of Lonnie's car is similar to what killed Andy Dren. Lastly, just added a minute ago, Lonnie has a relationship with a girl named Tiffany and so does the president." Wes waited for a reaction from Fancer.

"Son of a bitch. Where did you get that information? How do you know about Tiffany and the president? We don't talk about that at Tech."

"Confidential information right now, but reliable, I guarantee you. But even without that newest fact, the other two reasons are enough to look seriously at Tedesco. So, will you go with me to take a quick look at his room? If I find what I think I will, in the morning I'll get a search warrant. I just don't want something to disappear before we even see it. That's why I want him in jail tonight. Hopefully, his uncle won't turn up right away carrying a big wallet full of money."

"OK, Wes. We'll take a quick look/see. I'll go back, see if Lonnie gets his uncle, and if he's going to get out of bed to come to his rescue with the family jewels. Then I'll meet you at Grisham Dormitory on Fowler Street. That's our freshman residence. How about if we get there in an hour? That would be before Lonnie can ask this uncle to go check out his room. If there's something there, we'll know it soon."

"It's a deal. And, Chief, thanks for your cooperation. I've a hunch that this is important to the campus. See you in an hour." Wes shook George's hand and headed for the door.

Chapter 51

Walter

Wes parked in the area saved for police cars near the emergency entrance of Grady Hospital. He locked the car, waved to the security guard, and was out of sight in less than a minute. As he approached the desk, he said who he was and asked where Walter had been taken. The nurse coolly informed him that she needed a better description of the patient so Wes slowed down and took the time to tell her Walter had been injured on the Tech campus, what kind of injuries he had and that he had been brought by the paramedics.

She checked her ledger, running her finger up from the bottom, stopping about four names from the top, "I think this is the one. He came in about two hours ago. That was about 45 patients ago. We're having a slow night! No last name is recorded, but the first name is Walter. They took him directly to the OR. Since it's quiet right now, let me make a call and see if I can get more current information, Detective."

Wes relaxed and leaned on the counter, half listening to the nurse talking to someone who was supposed to know the answers. He noticed that her name tag declared that she was Ellen Warren and thought that was a good, solid name for a woman who chose a career that needed strength and stability. He decided that Ellen Warren was as efficient as she was attractive and managed to look fresh and alert even though it was now almost midnight.

"The word is that your man is in recovery as we speak. You can go up, but you won't be talking to him for awhile. I'm sure you have been here enough times that you don't need directions. Stop back later if you need more information or maybe a cup of coffee so you can stay bright eyed and bushy tailed," Ellen Warren said, sounding friendly and like she might be looking for some diversion from more than forty emergencies.

"I'll let you know, Ellen. Unfortunately, I have another police officer waiting for me as soon as I leave here. But, believe me, I appreciate your offer." Wes smiled warmly and took off down the hallway.

He started looking for doctors on the loose before he'd reached the OR area. He wanted to get information as quickly as possible. He wanted to know that Walter was going to be all right. He didn't deserve to be in this situation simply because he wanted to help find Andy's murderer. Wes felt that he'd have to somehow take over where Andy was forced to drop off. Maybe Jason could help Walter learn more about computers. His son may not be the whiz that Andy Dren was, but Jason had been using his own computer since he was seven.

"Doctor," Wes called out as he approached a woman in a long white coat, "I'm Detective Wes Wesley, Atlanta Homicide. I'm looking for information on one of your patients in recovery."

"That's strange," she replied, "If the patient is in recovery, then it isn't a homicide, is it? We pride ourselves that we send them to recovery to recover."

"Yes, I'm sure you do. The man I'm inquiring about is a witness in a homicide case. He's also a friend. For both reasons, I'm interested in his condition. His name is Walter, and he was beaten, mostly the face and head."

"I didn't know that we were seeing a VIP, Detective. He looks more like the usual homeless guy who might be sent to us after a brawl at one of the centers," she said rather skeptically.

"You're right about him, but so am I," Wes responded testily. He felt that the woman was showing no respect for Walter, "He's a VIP to me. He may be the key to finding the Georgia Tech murderer, so if you know his condition, I ask that you tell me now."

The woman seemed to take a new interest in the conversation, which is what Wes had planned. She said, "I've heard about that shooting. There are so many alumni around this city that they seem to be taking a personal affront because a student was killed on *their* campus. Anyway, Detective, your Walter is doing fair. We won't know the extent of the damage until he's completely awake, and we can observe his movements and functions. His skull was cracked but not badly. Lots of blood loss from the head injury, facial cuts and broken nose. No wounds below the neck so the body mending system can concentrate in one area. He'll probably be fully awake by morning. You can go see him, if you wish, but I must ask you not to try to question him until he's stronger. Let him rest without being agitated."

"OK, Doc, I'd like to look in on him, but I won't say a word. I'm not here to make him sicker," Wes understood the woman's attitude but she still annoyed him.

The two of them walked silently side by side. There was no reason for small talk, and Wes didn't like this person well enough to try to make conversation.

They entered the recovery area with the doctor leading the way. She stopped at a bed. Wes came up beside her, looked at the person lying as still as if the bed linens covered only a lumpy mattress. Protruding from the sheet was a large, round mound of white bandages and multiple tubes and wires. It all looked so painful. Tomorrow Walter would feel the pain and learn that it would be awhile before he could go back to picking up cans and loading cases of soft and hard drinks. Wes would have to find a place for him to recuperate. They wouldn't keep him here one hour longer than he had to be.

"I think you've seen it all, Detective. You'll probably agree with me now that being here isn't going to help either of you. Why not go home and come back in the morning?" the doctor asked in a whisper.

"If he asks, please, tell him I was here, and I'll be back early." Wes put his hand over Walter's and squeezed very gently. He wanted him to know that he wasn't alone. He thought he felt a small response from the cool hand that lay quietly under his.

Chapter 52

Wes T. Wesley

Wes checked his watch as he drove onto the Tech campus: 12:15 AM. Saturday evening had passed and little of it had been what he planned when he picked up Janeen and started for Bones. He still hadn't had the chocolate ice cream that he'd been craving for several days. The steak dinner was superb, the wine mellow, and having about an hour with his most favorite person had been fantastic. Unfortunately, that's where the superlatives ended. And now, here he was looking for a parking space so he could go snooping around some college freshman's room. Wes wondered: what's wrong with this picture?

He saw a Georgia Tech police car and noticed Chief Fancer standing on the sidewalk in front of Grisham Dormitory. He parked the car and quickly walked back to meet his colleague.

"How did you find Walter?" the chief asked. Wes told him."I'm glad he doesn't seem any worse than that. I'll check again in the morning so I have the answers for anyone who might be inquiring, like maybe Lonnie's uncle."

"What happened with Old Uncle Godfather? I have the feeling that the Tedesco gang might consider that culture a fine model," Wes mused.

"Well, the old boy wasn't home. Lonnie got an answering machine. He was really upset, but when I asked him if he wanted to call his dad, he was adamant that he'd wait and try his uncle again. I waited about 20 minutes, he dialed again and still no response. The Atlanta officers were going to put him in a cell by himself for the night. I don't want something to happen that'll drive the alumni and parents crazy. I'm sure that Lonnie will be fine for a couple hours. Now, I checked out the room while I waited for you, and his roommate isn't there. That's about the way it is on a Saturday night. They're sleeping with someone or they've gone away. If you took Saturday census, you'd think that Tech was about half its size. So we've a clear field at the moment."

"I guess we're just lucky. So let's do it and go home."

George Fancer unlocked the outer door and led Wes up the stairway to the second floor. A long hallway with about 15 doors on each side intersected the small landing. The walls had marks and knicks in the paint, the carpet was worn in the middle but still quite attractive at the sides. Most doors had paper signs with names of these modern-age cliff dwellers and some doors had posters or flyers announcing something thought to be important. There was a musty smell that reminded Wes of an old locker room. "I wonder why we keep pining for the good old days? I wouldn't want to live like this anymore, would you, Chief?"

"No way! Not only is it unappealing now but during the days and evenings, it's noisy as hell. I'd much rather go home to my cozy three and two. OK, Wes, here we are. I hope your hunch is way out in left field this time."

Fancer unlocked the door and opened it like he expected a fire-snorting dragon to be waiting for them on the other side. Less dramatically, they found an ordinary, messy, crammed-full-of-junk room of two freshmen with about the same amount of things hanging on the walls as strewn on the floor.

"Yep, in comparison, my little house in Virginia-Highlands looks better and better. Shit, Wes, it may be hard to find anything in here. It's like a Where's Waldo Puzzle."

Both men scanned the area, but it was Wes who noted that the one desk was pulled away from the wall. A strange arrangement when the room was so small that every square inch of floor space was precious.

"Let's take a look back here, George," Wes suggested as he leaned to the back of the desk, "Uh, oh. I don't think you want to see this. Maybe you ought to go home now before you ruin your whole friggin' night...and maybe tomorrow too."

The chief stood beside the detective and leaned in the same

direction. Behind the desk was a small arsenal. There were at least four rifles and three boxes of ammunition. Wes wasn't surprised. The clues had seemed strong.

"Well, one of these rifles is a Remington 30/06 and one of the boxes of ammo is 150 grain Winchester silver tips. They could be a match for us. I think we've a better direction to our case. I want to get the damn search warrant tomorrow and get back here early. It's not going to be a pretty day for you, Chief." Wes knew that his associate was going to get heat for the firearms on campus and who knew what else some of the alumni and others will blame the chief for. They might say that the murder wouldn't have occurred if this nest had been cleaned out.

"What have we found? A militia trainee? A Mafia understudy? Two students who like to go hunting and whose families can afford a rifle for each day in the woods? I don't like to think about it, but there are probably other rooms that are similar. These kids would tell you that they have their rights!" Chief Fancer said gloomily. He always hoped that the rules and the explanations given periodically would have an effect, but seeing what's here in this room, he would have to admit that he and his officers are failing.

"Don't take on the guilt of the world, George. You know you can have only limited influence. Values begin in the home and there are many homes where having firearms available for everyone is the norm. At this point, all we've found is a cache of rifles. Someone could've come in and stolen one or more. Someone could've known they were here and taken advantage of easy access. We don't have the shooter yet. My hunch is strong, but I've been wrong before. We need to get our search warrant and then take these out to the crime lab," Wes didn't want George Fancer to take on the emotional responsibility of this crime, but he felt certain that in many ways the chief thought of all the students as his extended family.

"You're right, Wes. How soon can you get the search warrant? If you want me, I'll be here when you're ready to do this officially."

"I hope to get to the municipal judge at the crack of dawn.

This needs to be done ASAP. I'll beep you as soon as I have the paper in hand. Under the circumstances, she's going to be cooperative, so it'll be just a phone call," Wes outlined his plan, "Now it's almost 1:00 AM. Let's call it a day. Son of a bitch, just think of all the overtime we made tonight. We'll soon be rich and able to retire to the peaceful shores of Florida where hopefully they don't even need a police department."

"What are you smokin', Wes? No crime is a dream. That's way beyond the American dream and overtime is just a word. Just like I hear people talk about an eight hour day. Bull shit! Haven't seen one of those very often. But I do like your idea of going home. Let's do it."

The chief of Tech security locked up, walked Wes to his car, said good night, and went back to his own vehicle. Off in the distance he could hear loud music. These kids loved their parties. That seemed to be a constant no matter what the night of the week. It didn't sound like the party animals were concerned about a murderer on campus. But then, at their age, they felt they were invincible.

Wes sat in his car for a few minutes thinking about the events of the evening. He still didn't have a motive but he felt confident that he had a direct line to the murderer. If it wasn't young Lonnie, it was going to be someone Lonnie knew. While replaying the last few hours, he reached for the telephone and dialed Janeen's number. It was 1:00, but she had been insistent that he should call *anytime.* Well, this was certainly anytime.

"Wes, is that you?" she didn't even take time to say hello.

"It is. I'm headed for a mini market to get chocolate ice cream, and if you were serious, I'm on my way to your front door. My little mice are all worn out from dragging me all over town, but they say they can make one more trip. Then they want some ice cream and a long nap," Wes had picked up at the same place where he had left their make-believe conversation hours ago.

"You, your steeds and your ice cream are all welcome. Just like Motel 6, I will leave the light on for you. But in addition, I'll be at the door waiting."

"Ohhhh, I like that. I'm heading in your direction now. See ya' soon."

• • •

He found the light was on and Janeen was sitting on the stoop wearing a pair of jeans and a Georgia Tech sweatshirt. He thought she had looked beautiful in her soft wool suit, but right now she looked absolutely gorgeous. Obviously, in Janeen's case, the woman made the clothes rather than the reverse. He was thrilled that she was there on the porch to say, "Good morning, Wes."

"And, good morning to you, Janeen. Has anyone walked by while you were waiting and told you how lovely you look sitting there in the glow of the porch light?" Wes bent low and kissed her on the lips.

"No one mentioned how I looked but two cars stopped and the drivers made me an offer," Janeen laughed, "I told them that they better move on or the police will show up without even a call. Haven't seen them since. I'm ready for my dessert and to hear what you've been doing since my prince turned into a police-frog.

He gave her his hand and gently turned her toward the door. They both went up the stairs and settled in the kitchen. Janeen opened the cupboard to get dishes, but Wes stopped her by putting his arms around her waist and holding her close, "Ice cream will be wonderful, but you're even better. Do you have any idea how much I wanted to be here ever since I drove away? Janeen, you've put me under your spell. I'm willing to stay there, if you don't use your power to change me into that frog again. He's too short for you."

"I thought it was ice cream that was on your mind? It was a good idea, but I like the second option better: just being with you. I promise to not create a frog, unless you choose ice cream first," Janeen said huskily as she moved her body closer and in rhythm with his.

Keeping his one arm around her, Wes opened the freezer door and placed the box of ice cream inside. When he closed the door, he lifted her face to his and kissed her like a lover who had just returned from a long absence. Hours had seemed like days for him, and he believed that Janeen felt the same.

"There's something about this kitchen and us, pretty lady. The combination seems to create the most beautiful, erotic images. Would you consider letting me into your bed tonight? I want you to know how much you mean to me," Wes asked looking at Janeen with an understanding that this was to be a special experience for both of them.

"Tonight, honey, my bed is our bed. If you hadn't asked, I might have insisted that you share my most private space. We can talk later and break out the ice cream, but that's later...much later."

Wes Wesley could not believe his good fortune. In less than a week, he was sure that he'd found the woman who could fill the dreams and needs that he'd been contemplating since the day he walked away with baby Jason in his arms. He was sure that it had been worth the wait. Until this week, he had always scoffed at 'love at first sight' and called it silly. When he pulled the Tech murder case, he had no idea that this assignment was going to change his life. It was an exciting surprise to find a pleasant outcome grow from a normally devastating action.

Wes kissed Janeen again, then he raised her two hands to his mouth and kissed her slim, delicate fingers. She then lowered them to his waist and below. It was no longer a secret that he was ready to make love. He bent slightly and laid his face on the soft material that covered her breasts; discovering that she had on no bra. He reached under the sweatshirt and caressed the warm, smooth skin of her back and tummy. Slowly he raised his hands, taking each breast in a hand, feeling the tiny erections that indicated that she too was ready to open her body to his. In unison, they vaguely heard the other make a soft sound; not a word, hardly more than a deep breath but a message that each understood. They walked out of the kitchen to the stairway and climbed to a part of the house he'd never seen. He wasn't sure he was really seeing it now, but he knew it was where he wanted to be.

As they stood beside the bed, quiet but not shy, Wes pulled Janeen's shirt over her head and watched as her breasts bounced from the movement. She was so lovely. Her body was tight as if she exercised regularly. He realized that he didn't know those details about her. He had so much to learn. Fortunately, he had the rest of his life to be a student of the woman he hoped wanted to spend that much time with him. She smiled while she unbuttoned her jeans, her eyes moved from his face down across his body as if saying we don't need your clothes either. As she stepped out of her jeans, Wes already had created a pile starting with his tie, shirt and tee shirt. He was moving faster than she, but then he knew how close he was to losing all control. He didn't want that to happen while he was still standing at the side of the bed.

"I feel like a damn adolescent, baby, but we need to try out your bed now before I ruin the whole night. Love me, Janeen. Love me now," there was an urgency in his voice that she was glad that she shared.

"I love you, Wes Wesley. Don't wait. We've maybe years of time to perfect our loving, but tonight let's just be together. I don't want to wait for anything," Janeen looked up at him from the bed and liked everything she saw. There was nothing on her mind except that they were one as she thrust her body against his.

Chapter 53

Wes T. Wesley

Wes sat on the edge of Janeen's bed trying to get oriented. He'd been beeped, but he wasn't yet focused onto the number calling him. He was exhausted. The night had been fantastic, but face it, he thought, you aren't as young as you thought you were several hours ago. At four AM they had gotten up, made coffee and talked for almost two hours before returning to bed. By squinting one eye he saw by the bedside clock that another two hours had passed. Eight o'clock on a Sunday morning and someone was beeping him. He opened both eyes and recognized the number as Dixie Packard's.

"The man never sleeps," he said to himself. He pulled his wrinkled pants from the pile of clothes on the floor and put them on as he stood up. Seeing that Janeen was still asleep, he headed for the telephone in the kitchen.

"Dixie, Wes here. What can I do for you at this early hour?"

"You got it all backward, buddy. It's what I'm doing for you. I've been on the telephone and have subpoenas for the three banks where the Tech Foundation's banks sent the money. They all know that I want to speak to them this morning and have told me that they'll have staff available. Here at Summit Bank, I'm to meet their person at ten o'clock. The other two, I'm going to call at eleven and twelve. I figured you'd want to know and maybe even join me"

"Ummm, let me get my brain operating. I was still asleep when you beeped. A lot has happened since yesterday. Everything about the Tech case is moving like a bat out of Hell. I was at both the jail and Grady last night before being back on the campus at midnight," Wes told the FBI agent the details of the evening from jail to campus.

"I'd like to go with you, but I need to get that search warrant and get back to Tedesco's room before he has someone move the rifles. I'll take them out to the lab. This could be a big break for us and for Georgia Tech. If I'm free by ten or so, I'll meet you at the Summit Bank, but you don't need me. This international money business is your baby. I just pointed you in the direction."

"That's true, but I believe that the Tech Foundation has some real sneaky shit going on, and we're going to have to talk to the trustees. There is a way you can help me, Wes. If after I interview the bank guys, I want to talk to those alumni, will you get me the names and how to contact them?"

"I can do better than that, Dixie. If you want to see them, I'll have them called and make appointments for you in one location, so you don't have to run all over town. I can take care of that just as soon as you make your 'go or no go' decision." Wes knew that Janeen could handle that better than anyone.

"Well, son of a bitch, Mr. Casanova. You sound like you have a direct line to someone on the Tech staff. I knew those rumors were true. You *are* bird-dogging the President's secretary. Hot damn, nothing like having an inside track."

"No comment, you creep. Just because Billy Joe likes to create his own virtual reality doesn't mean you have to hang on his every word." Wes was feeling a bit guilty as he pretended the rumors were false, but he didn't kiss and tell. He also wanted to savor the private time and relationship that he had with Janeen. Anything that felt this good deserved to be kept between the two people who were responsible.

"OK, OK. I'll just enjoy my porno fantasies. Back to the business of the day. If I don't see you before I leave the bank, you'll know that I'll be in the office using the phone and the fax machine. Go break in a few doors and tell me about it later," Dixie Packard hesitated and then added, "By the way, my friend, I have caller ID on my phone. See ya'." Wes sat for a few seconds listening to a dial tone.

So much for privacy! His life was almost an open line thanks to technology, but in the homicide office, they still had to trace a call manually. "What is wrong with *this* picture?" he thought.

He picked up the receiver again and made a call to his colleague Municipal Judge Olivia Stone Martin. He was lucky that the judge hadn't yet taken off with her family for church. Wes quickly told his story and made his request for a 'no knock' search warrant. He emphasized that the reason was murder, added Georgia criminal code:16-5-1, and that he suspected that the firearm and type of ammunition used at Tech would be found in the student's room. When he was asked why these were his deducements, he responded easily that the information came from a confidential witness who saw the student's car fleeing the scene of the crime. When the student was arrested for another offense, similar ammunition was in the trunk of his car.

"Sounds like you have this pretty well tied up, Wes. You know all of us will be grateful when you close this case. It's amazing how many people in local government are acquainted or beholden to a Tech alumnus. The telephone lines have been blazing," Judge Martin said in her very quiet, sweet voice.

"That's the truth, Judge. Those guys have been calling right up to the mayor. I expect that the chief will soon be answering an urgent call from the governor if what I want to do this morning doesn't work."

"I'll get the warrant for you, Detective. You can pick it up within an hour. Then I'm going to go to church and pray that your clues and your skills are on the right track. Let me know later if the Lord is still on your side. With all the outside interest in this case, I'm sure you appreciate all the help you can get."

His next call was to Billy Joe to ask whether he wanted to be in on the search. His partner said he wouldn't miss this part for anything that often happens on Sunday morning like church, a big breakfast or some serious sex. He could get to all of them later, but closing this case may only come now. He offered to pick up the search warrant and meet Wes at Grisham Dorm about 9:30.

Wes had just said good-bye when he felt someone soft and fragrant press against his back and encircle his neck with slim, shapely arms.

"You feel mighty good this morning, Detective Wesley. Too bad you had to creep out of bed and get back to work."

"I wouldn't have planned it this way, but I got beeped by the FBI and thought I better respond." Wes turned around and put his arms around her waist and drew her as close as physically possible. He noticed that Janeen had on a pale coral, silk, wrap-around robe. He ran his hands over the smooth material feeling her sensuous body under the sheer silk."My dear Ms. Carson, I'm truly intrigued to know what you have on under your pretty robe."

"It's my designer outfit, sir. Probably designed by my parents and God. I believe it was your gift last night, sweetheart."

Wes had already forgotten the calls that had been keeping him so preoccupied. His body stirred against the smoothness of her robe. He gently pulled at the sash that was holding the material in place. The two edges fell away to either side. Wes looked down at Janeen's body and was overwhelmed by both passion and lust. She was beautiful in a fresh, wholesome style. She was correct when she joked about being designed by a hand that was greater than those highly touted creators of clothing. He slipped his hands across the shimmering silk and touched her warm skin. He'd often read about the magic of skin on skin, but this was the first time he'd ever felt the full power of that experience. His hands tingled, his mind floated and his penis was hard. He thought last night was the pinnacle, but he felt more emotional now than he had then.

"I'm going to take you back to bed, baby. You've cast your spell again. You're the only one to ease my painfully, delicious hex." Wes was so high, so ready to make love, that he felt that he didn't even care if they made it back to Janeen's bed.

"It's my spell, Wes, and I give the directions. If you can't make it to the bedroom in twenty seconds, you'll be banished to the kitchen to make breakfast." Janeen giggled in her appealing way and broke away from Wes' grasp. She was to the stairs and already taking them two by two before Wes reached the hallway. He caught up with her at the door of the bedroom and said as he dove toward the bed, "Fourteen, fifteen, sixteen...."

Janeen landed right beside him in a montage of coral silk and pale blue sheets, "....Seventeen, eighteen, ninetee...."

Wes had just missed the edge of the bed, slid to the floor and raised himself to the bed. He was laughing so hard that he just barely heard Janeen's counting. He lay his body alongside hers, feeling her presence from his head to his toes and relaxed a moment and said, "Twenty. Now you must pay for diverting me from my job, and I'll receive all of your unearthly powers. I can't cast a spell, but I can be your lover. That's all I want anyway, Janeen,"

• • •

Janeen now lay quietly looking at Wes who was struggling to stay awake. This lovemaking is a tremendous way to start the day, but Wes thought it would be better if he didn't have to get up immediately and head out to Georgia Tech. If he didn't move now, he was going to be late to meet Billy Joe and...."Shit, I forgot to call Chief Fancer!" Wes cried as he sat upright and reached for the telephone. He had promised to call the Tech's head security man and tell him when to meet him at the dorm. He looked at the receiver in his hand but didn't mash the numbers.

"Could it be that you don't know his number?" Janeen asked.

"You're right. "

Janeen rolled over and pressed one of the keys to the side of the dial pad."There you are. I have that number programmed for quick use. Get to work, Super Detective, and I'm going to take a shower. See ya'."

George answered on the first ring. He told Wes that he'd been waiting for his call. In fact he'd been sitting at his desk for almost an hour reading the paper. He added that he guessed Wes had overslept.

A fleeting stab of guilt crossed his mind, but it was gone before he explained that he and Billy Joe would be there in less than twenty minutes. They'd have the warrant with them.

Wes replaced the receiver and bounded for the bathroom. The shower was already steaming up the mirror and Janeen was stepping into the hot spray.

"Hey, do you know what all the environmentalists say?" Wes asked as he followed her.

"No. What do they say, pushy?"

"They say: Save water; shower with a friend!"

"Those environmentalists are just horny. But I guess if I can share my bed with you, I can extend the courtesy to my shower. But this is serious cleanup time. No fooling around!"

"Absolutely, Ms. Carson. I'm not one to waste water. Besides I've got to be at Tech in 18 minutes so move your pretty derriere so I can get wet." Wes gave her a bump with his hip.

He was out of the shower almost as fast as he had gotten in. Janeen was relaxing under the water and humming some simple little tune. It was all too appealing, but he made an effort to think only about the job he was headed to do. He wanted to get this killer and give the campus back to lighthearted kids, dedicated faculty and a handful of homeless men. None of them should have to be afraid to be at the institution. It should be a sanctuary for those who thought of it as their home.

Wes called out goodbye and left his clean and beautiful lover still dripping wet in the shower. "Don't even think about it," he directed himself, "Just get on your way."

• • •

George and Billy Joe were sitting in the Tech police car and got out as soon as they saw him pull up behind them. Billy Joe handed him the warrant.

"Let's go," Wes said.

They entered the building and went directly to the same door that they had opened last night. Chief Fancer took out his master keys and nodded toward the door, "Fortunately, we don't have to kick it in. You've no idea how much fucking grief I would have to take if you damaged campus property," he said in a whisper.

The door was open and all three men in the room before they saw that one of the beds was occupied.

"Police. Just stay where you are and you'll be OK," Wes said loudly. He figured the young man was both sound asleep and nursing a hangover.

"P-p-p-police? Why? What? This is my room, isn't it?" the groggy young man stuttered.

"Well, actually we don't know if this is your room. Who are you and what room is yours?" Billy Joe asked.

"I'm Alan Buckner. My room is 214 in Grisham. It looks like my room. Where is my roommate?" The voice was getting stronger as the student got awake.

"Who's your roommate?" Wes asked.

"Lonnie Tedesco. You know, he plays football. I guess he spent the night at his girl's place. It's a lot better than this room. That's for sure," Alan Buckner said as he swung his feet to the floor, wondering if he should stand up or stay where he was. He also wondered whether he'd done something last night that he was being arrested for. He couldn't remember a lot about being at a fraternity party last night, but he thought he'd had a good time.

"You can stay where you are, son. We're here to search your room and maybe take a few things with us," Wes told Alan. He saw the young man's face take on a look of surprise and then fear.

"What did I do last night?" he croaked and then cleared his throat and shook his head as if to clear his muddled mind.

"We don't know what you did? Don't you know?" Billy Joe asked, almost laughing. This surely reminded him of his days when he was in school. Saturday night was a time to howl.

"No, sir. I was at a fraternity party and had a couple beers, well, maybe a few more than that. I just left there and came right back here. I wasn't drivin' or anything."

"Then you probably don't have a problem unless the Chief wants to talk to you about underage drinking. He might want to do that later but right now, Alan, you stay right there and we'll look at what you and your roommate keep in this room," Wes said as he headed for the desk.

"Ohhhh, no. I told, Lonnie, a dozen times. More than a dozen. I told him that he shouldn't have guns in the room. He's so macho. He said his family had guns everywhere and this was the same as being in his own home. He never shot them here, sir.

Honest, he never shot them or even pretended. He liked to have them for, well, you know, kinda like being a big deal," the freshman was wide-awake now. He was sure that the police were here because they had a small arsenal stashed in their room. He just knew he was going to get blamed for this as well as Lonnie. His parents were going to kill him!

Alan Buckner sat looking both dejected and disheveled. His curly, brown hair was standing wildly out from behind each ear, and he could feel the color draining from his face. He was scared that he was in big trouble. Shit, he had to face all of this by himself. The stuff was Lonnie's, but he wasn't even here. This was worse than the hazing that he had seen at the fraternity party last night. Oh, yeah, now he was beginning to remember what he did last night. It was nothing. Just drank too much beer.

The two men continued to look everywhere: in drawers, behind furniture, under the beds, in boxes, in bags ("We sure have a lot of stuff," Alan thought). They didn't seem to be in any hurry. They'd already been there for about 30 minutes. They were checking every inch of the room. They were also creating a pile of things in the middle of the room. Yep, it's the guns they're most interested in. They had all four of the rifles in the pile, several boxes of ammunition and on the floor beside all of that was the appointment calendar book that Lonnie carried everywhere with him after he took the Psych 1010 class. He said that the instructor hammered the idea that students had to be organized to be successful.

"Sir, I can't wait any longer. I've gotta pee."

"Chief, why don't you walk Alan down to the john." Wes then added sympathetically, "I'm amazed you could wait this long. You must have the best kidneys in town, Buckner."

By the time they got back, Billy Joe and Wes had gathered up the items they were taking with them. Next stop was the crime lab.

"Now, Alan. Let's talk. I think it would be best for you to not be blabbing to all your friends and relatives that we were here. Right now we're not going to take you downtown. You know, like to jail? We aren't going to do that, but if you're getting in our way by talking about our little visit, we might just come back with something other than a search warrant. You understand what I'm saying, Alan?" Wes had a slight smile on his face, but he definitely delivered his message with a menacing tone.

"Yes, sir, I understand. I'm gonna go back to sleep and then do some studying. I'm not seeing or talking to anybody. Trust me, sir. I'm not talking. You aren't going to call my parents, are you?"

"No reason to call your parents, Alan, unless you create some problems for us."

"No, sir! I'm not talking and you're not talking. Sorta like a partnership."

"Absolutely, Alan. We're partners just like Detective LaCrosse, Chief Fancer and I are. So even if you get some visitors today, you aren't talking."

The kid was still shaking his head in agreement when the three men left the floor and returned to their cars. Alan was going to be a great partner. He didn't want his folks getting a call that started out, "This is the police and your son....."

Chapter 54

Lonnie Tedesco

Wes and Billy Joe met back at the homicide office and left one of their cars before heading to the crime lab. The evidence that had been picked up earlier at the crime scene was already there, and the two detectives were feeling confident that they had a match with one of the rifles from the Tedesco/Buckner room. If anybody could give them that kind of information it was Timothy Brian O'Rourke "Irish" Finn, head of the crime lab for more than twenty years. All of the homicide squad feared the day that Finn would announce his retirement, because he'd gotten his outstanding reputation honestly: he'd earned it. He was considered the number one expert in the entire Southeast. Many thought that his rating for excellence in the field went far beyond that geographic area. Of course as you got closer to New York City, there was *always* a fabled, special authority who came from 'The City's' police force. New York police really believed all the TV shows that portrayed them as supermen. They never talked about the times when they brought some particularly sticky evidence all the way down to the Irish Good Ole Boy.

Wes parked the car and he and Billy Joe each carried two rifles, which they had carefully bagged, and two boxes of ammunition. He hung the plastic bag that held Lonnie's planner-calendar over his wrist and followed his partner into the building. The foyer was empty which was a reminder that most people were still in bed or at church on this Sunday morning, "Workin' on Sunday sucks!" Billy Joe announced to the empty room, "I'm glad one of my regular days off is the same one that my wife and kids have off."

They opened the inside door and could feel the change in

tempo. Several people were talking and another one was on the telephone. The crime lab was always active. The staff was professional but friendly in weird little ways. They liked to deliver first-class work, but they wanted to enjoy the time while they did it. Some theorized that was the only way to stay sane when the job at hand normally related to mayhem and murder. It wasn't unusual for them to find black humor in their tasks and often played jokes on each other as well as the police whom they served.

"Is Irish around?" asked Wes.

"Yeah. He's testing the water before making his coffee. He reads all of the reports on Atlanta's pollution and is convinced that he's going to be murdered by the Water Department," the sergeant said as he pointed his thumb over his shoulder toward a desk down in the corner farthest from the door.

"Hey, Irish. We brought you some shit that's going to get you on every newscast and weekly news magazine in the US of A," Wes called out.

"Who needs it, my boy? I'm as famous as I ever want to be. I prefer the peace and quiet of anonymity. Let me fade away like Jack the Ripper into the London fog."

"Too late, Irish. You're already a legend. Today you're going to become the savior of the next generation of corporate leaders." Wes and Billy Joe walked toward Irish. They could see that they had gotten his interest.

"You've surely chosen the proper day of the week for me to become a savior. Now, what is it you're carrying so lovingly? Do I see a collection of superior gangsta' rifles? Have you been stopping cars speeding north from the Keys? Let's take a look."

Wes and Billy Joe deposited the rifles and the boxes on the nearest desk and stood back while Finn looked at their precious loot. He nodded his head several times, and then said, "Someone has purchased, or stolen, only the best. You guys have brought me some fine weapons. You must be hanging around with the rich Buckhead crowd again."

Wes explained where they'd gotten the items and how they believed that one of the rifles was related to the Georgia Tech murder. He added that they had the suspect in custody, but that he might get out on bond this morning. They wanted to get these guns here to the lab before someone "lost" them. Irish told them he'd do the tests now. After all, it was in his job description to keep all of the homicide squad happy and looking good.

The three men went into the laboratory and proceeded to advance toward the solving of the crime or eliminating a false lead. The guns would be tested by Irish Finn and while that was happening Wes and Billy Joe were also carefully looking through Lonnie's planner. They made a special effort not to disturb fingerprints, so that it could be dusted later.

"What does it say for the night of the murder, Wes?" Billy Joe inquired.

"Actually nothing. There're a couple classes marked during the day. 12 o'clock says: lunch-Tiffany-didn't come! This is interesting. On the last line, after all the numbers for the hours, there is a small red dot, but nothing written beside it. I almost missed it. The next day, written across 12 and 1 PM is a big 5!!!!! and later at 8 PM is *III*. The boy feels he has a need for codes."

"Looks that way. I never trust anyone who won't just spell it out. You know, Wes, like tryin' to hide a girl in your life from your best friend," Billy Joe took the opportunity to let Wes know that he hadn't forgotten his dishonesty.

"OK. OK. Let's stay on the subject. I feel like I've seen that *III* before. It's just in the shadow of my mind. Can't quite get it into the light."

"Yeah, I've seen it too. Let me think about it for a minute. I always try to remember exactly how the fucker looks. Not just in print but how I saw it first. This I see in.... YES!....in lights. Wes, it's part of the memorial message to Andy Dren!"

"Damn, that's right. We're on to something. We aren't going to lose this one, Billy Joe. This is too fuckin' important," Wes was as excited as his partner. This murder had become very personal to him, because he wanted there to be nothing threatening in Janeen's life at Tech. He also wanted to be able to say to Mr. Dren that the killer had been found and charged. He believed, as a father, that it was critical to know what and why a tragedy has taken your son.

Wes continued, “I think we have our murderer, but we must be positive of our case. We don’t want him to slide out from under us. You know, like another OJ. We also want to get the friggin’ alumni off our backs. Wait till they hear that the shooter was one of their precious football players. Should be a great story for Dani and Lindy Lindholm.”

“We’re almost home, for sure, except what’s the motive? Does it really relate to the Hong Kong money that Dixie is chasin’?” Detective LaCrosse asked.

“I’m not sure yet how the Hong Kong bucks play in the scenario, but I’ve a theory on the motive. Try this: Lonnie and the president are both screwing Tiffany. Lonnie finds out. Hey, hey. I just got another piece of the puzzle. In Lonnie’s planner, the III stands for Lindholm III. How do you react to that?”

“I think you’re right on. What’s next?”

“Lonnie goes to the president’s office to confront him. Maybe he wants to scare him or even beat him up or whatever. He sees a person in the poor light and thinks it’s Lindholm and decides to waste him. Never meant to kill Andy and probably didn’t even know his mistake until the next day. Surprise, Mr. Georgia Tech football star, you have just given your main squeeze to the president while you go to prison or worse.”

“It does make sense, but it also makes me want to puke. If the theory is correct, a perfectly good, young, promisin’ human bein’ is gone and his family permanently damaged because some hothead punk wanted exclusive rights to pussy. Stupid! And speakin’ of stupid, what kind of a man is the president who is jammin’ one of the freshmen coeds practically in front of his own son? And we still don’t know how the elusive funds relate. Georgia Tech has always been respected and revered, except by their big rival - Georgia. From the outside, Tech looks like a model, academic institution. It must keep Charles Black busy keepin’ positive news out in the public. Yeah, how does his role relate? He must be bein’ paid well to keep the lid on all of this kind of crap.” Detective LaCrosse was on a roll. He didn’t like the direction it was taking, but his thoughts all fit.

There were many parts of the case that still needed details

and discussion. The two detectives looked forward to talking later with Dixie Packard about his investigation. They now suspected that Andy had learned something through his work for the president. Could the president have paid Tedesco to off Dren and not even know he was dealing with another lover of Tiffany Walton? Surely that's too bizarre.

"Wes, we need to get a warrant for Andy's computer files as soon as possible. They would have to be mighty, damn simple for me to understand them, but I'm sure I can get some hunches from them. That's what we need now, so we aren't gettin' lost in all the muck. I'm beginnin' to feel like we're shaggin' around the swamp land, and it happens to be located in the middle of Atlanta instead of South Georgia."

"Billy Joe, we should split up when we leave here and see how much we can get done today. As soon as I know the results from Irish's tests, I'm going down to talk to our football hero. Why don't you get the search warrant for Andy's room and go do some surfing? Judge Martin should be easy to find after church. Later we can both catch up at the office when we meet Dixie. Shit, what a day," Wes was exhilarated but was also beginning to feel the effects of very little sleep and the emotional high that he gets when a case is coming to a dramatic conclusion.

In less than an hour, the two detectives left the building with a renewed spring in their steps. The one rifle had proven to be the murder weapon. They were both ready to take on their next tasks.

Wes drove to the jail by way of the Pizza Hut. He ate two pieces in the car, finishing the last bite as he pulled up to the ID monitor."Seems like I just did this. Sometimes I feel I should have my own room here to save time. Of course the sheriff doesn't have enough room for just ' his guests'," he thought as he waited to be recognized.

Lonnie was brought into the interview room where Detective Wesley was waiting. He seemed to have lost some of his youth and vigor in the few hours that he had been incarcerated. His dark beard was already casting a shadow on his olive complexion. He still wore the clothes he had on the night before, but now they were wrinkled from sleeping in them.

"This isn't right, Detective. Just because my uncle's unavailable, I shouldn't have to stay in this c-c-crummy place," Lonnie decided that he would start on the offensive. That's the way he liked to start a game. He liked to always be a few steps ahead.

"I'm sorry about your misfortune, Lonnie. Did you try your dad?" Wes asked quietly wanting to see the young man's reaction. He knew that Lonnie had a problem with his relationship with Lorenzo Tedesco.

"No. He's going to freak out. I k-k-know him. He'll do better if my uncle, that's my dad's older brother, can t-t-talk to him before me."

"Well, then, Lonnie, you'll just be cooling it with us until your uncle comes back from his world cruise or wherever. You and I are going to go over to my office and talk for awhile."

"I don't know where that is, but it's got to be better than it is here," Lonnie said feeling better that he wasn't going right back to the cramped cell.

"Don't be too sure of that, Lonnie. We're part of the city's low budget plan."

Wes indicated that he had to put handcuffs on Lonnie, "Those are the rules when transporting a prisoner. You're still theoretically a prisoner." Wes explained in the quiet voice he used to build confidence that there was nothing to fear from him. He was just doing his job.

Lonnie didn't like the idea that he was going to be restrained, but he could understand the detective's predicament. Rules were rules. He knew that from playing football. You just did as you're told if you wanted to play the game.

It was good to see the sky and the city. Everything looked just as it did yesterday. People doing their own thing, walking and riding from here to there. How come it felt so different to Lonnie Tedesco? Nothing was the same as yesterday. That homeless prick surely did change his weekend plans. He wanted to call Tiffany and tell her why he wasn't there last night but he had to save his call to reach his uncle. Maybe this Wesley guy will let him call from his office.

"Could I call my girl when we get to your office, DetectiveWesley? She probably has w-w-worried all night long." Lonnie's voice was almost humble.

"I wish I could let you do that, Lonnie. But we were just talking about rules. You know how rules are. They have no heart. Just a head. Sorta the opposite of your dick that makes you want to make that call, right?"

"Shit, you got that right. I was going to have one hell-uv-a time last night. I got me a girl who never gets tired of s-s-sex. She's hot. I don't want her to think that I've been with some other girl. I'd have to waste a lot of time trying to get her to reverse her wild imagination."

"You'll just have to wait. When you finally reach your uncle, maybe he'll call this hot woman." An image of Tiffany at the funeral flashed through his mind. Yes, he could imagine that she was a sex machine. But then he thought: The president had the same impression. I wonder who else was on her personal roster?

They arrived at the homicide building. Lonnie saw the sign and his mouth went dry and he felt a cold, icy feeling blanket his body."H-H-Homicide? Why're we h-h-here?"

"This's where my office is located. We investigate aggravated assault as well as homicides." Wes' explanation was delivered in his coolest, matter of fact voice.

"Oh," Lonnie heard the words but they weren't comforting at all. Why is this policeman in the homicide building? No one had ever mentioned that Detective Wes Wesley was with homicide. What had they said? It was that he's involved because the homeless guy had asked for him. What does this all mean? "Stay cool, Lonnie," he thought.

Wes motioned for Lonnie to take a seat in the small interrogation room. Wes had already pushed a chair into the corner while he kept his hand on the only other chair in the room, leaving the boy no choice.

Lonnie sat with his spine so straight that it didn't come close to the back of the chair. He was tight as the laces on one of the footballs that he threw so well. He wanted to look relaxed and unconcerned, but the truth was he was scared shitless and he showed it. His eyes darted about the room until he forced himself to look Wes in the eyes and hold his stare. He wasn't going to be intimidated. He could surely hold his own with a dumb flatfoot. If he kept his control, he knew that this little pissant policeman would be wasting his time trying to catch him in something. He'd been thinking about this minute all night long, and he was ready.

"OK, Lonnie, let's go over last night again. Just tell me the story about finding the man at your car."

Wes appeared to be so detached that Lonnie was sure that he was asking this question simply to fill in time. Shit, he already knew the story, "We already did that, sir. You must remember. It's only been a few hours."

"I remember what you said, Lonnie, but if you'll think back on our conversation, you'll recollect that I suggested when you had a chance to reflect on the evening, you might begin to remember other details. You were very angry last evening, Lonnie. Hot heads usually aren't level heads. Let's go through it again," the detective's voice was pitched so that Lonnie had to listen closely to hear all the words.

Lonnie nodded his head to indicate that he understood and reviewed what he said last night. He didn't make any notable changes, because he felt his story was believable. There was no one to contradict him except a homeless bastard who had already tried to commit a crime: steal Lonnie's car. He felt warm and swiped his hand across his forehead several times to wipe away any perspiration that had appeared under his dark hair that fell casually to his eyebrows. He ran his fingers through his bangs, so that they wouldn't be adding to the heat that he was generating.

Wes watched the young man as he fidgeted with his hair. He noticed that Lonnie had also moved in his chair and his jacket was now pushed tightly against the chair back. Wes moved his own chair closer to the young man. A piece of paper would barely fit between the four knees that almost touched. Wes could feel the tension growing in Lonnie Tedesco's body.

"That's probably enough about the encounter last night.

By the way, how many guns do you own, Lonnie?

Lonnie was jolted by the abrupt change of topic. He thought, "The police know about the gun in my car, but what does this jerkoff know about any of my other guns? He's probably fishing. Trying to get me to say something that'll get me in trouble."

"You already took the gun out of my c-c-car. Chief Fancer has it. They've searched me enough since I got here, that I couldn't be hiding a t-t-toothpick."

"That's true, son. How about other guns? Do you have any that you keep some place other than your car?" Wes watched Lonnie as he brushed his hair away from his eyebrows again. He could see perspiration glistening on the handsome face.

Lonnie Tedesco was undecided what to do. Should he admit he has more guns in his room and have Fancer get him expelled from Tech? Should he lie and then get Alan to move them out before anyone sees them? That's a funny thought, since his roommate has been trying to get him to remove the rifles for months. A not so funny thought was that Lonnie wished that he'd paid attention to Alan. He didn't want to have those guns taken by the police. He again thought of his dad. Lonnie was feeling desperate. There's no way that his father wouldn't find out about what he'd done. His dad would hear about ten words, look at his son and say," How could my son be so damn dumb?"

"Well, I've a deer rifle that I use during h-h-hunting season. I'm not sure if it's at home, or in my dorm room, or if someone has b-b-borrowed it." There - that covered all kinds of possibilities! He could say other students borrow his rifles, and he can't be sure where they are. So he did say, "I hardly ever use 'em but lots of other guys do."

"I've a deer rifle too. I like to hunt. How about you, Lonnie?" Wes asked, again changing the pace of the interview.

"Yeah, I like it. I don't get to do much because of football season."

"Do you go with your family or your roommate? I like to go with my partner, Billy Joe. He's a dead eye. Never misses. Even on the range, he makes the rest of us look like beginners,"

Wes was shaking his head like he couldn't believe how good Detective LaCrosse was.

"I go sometimes with my family but usually with my friends. That's more fun. I'm a good shot, man. I usually bag my limit when I go deer hunting. Even squirrels and rabbits aren't safe when I'm in the woods. That's why my d-d-dad got me some expensive rifles. He said I deserved to have the best *when* I was the best," Lonnie was proud of his skill and never had a problem bragging about himself.

"Them? I thought it was one deer rifle."

"Oh, yeah. I've one that I usually u-u-use. You know, a favorite. That's what I meant, but sometimes I've my dad's rifle or my b-b-brother's. We grew up with lots of guns around."

"Guess it's easy to have lots of guns when your family has lots of money."

Lonnie was beginning to relax again and actually enjoy the conversation with the policeman. He decided that Wesley wasn't so bad. He didn't seem at all like the jerks on the TV shows who were always yelling and knocking people around."Yeah. My dad has always made a lot of money, and he likes to spend it because he wants people to know that he's got it. He wanted me to go to some big fancy school so he could say: My son's at Harvard or Stanford, but I always wanted to go to Tech. Even though it's a public institution, my dad agreed because it still has prestige. Damn, everyone knows the song The Ramblin' Wreck. Did you know that President Nixon once sang it at a meeting with the Russians?"

"No shit? That's news to me," Wes watched as Lonnie took on a whole different attitude. He was starting to appear that he was there having a friendly chat."Lonnie, you were carrying ammunition of the same kind that killed the student, Andrew Dren. Is there a connection?"

Lonnie felt the iciness flow throughout his body. Then he experienced a flash so hot that he was sure somehow his clothes had caught on fire. He wanted to jump out of the chair and run. It took all of his self-control to sit still and say, "W-W-Wow, that's interesting. I guess there are lots of those kinds of b-b-bullets around."

"Chief Fancer doesn't think so. He thinks that there aren't a lot of guns on campus, Lonnie."

Lonnie Tedesco laughed a tight, forced sound and exclaimed, "He just doesn't know, Detective. There's lots of s-s-shit in the dorm rooms. And where there aren't any g-g-guns, the other students have access to what is there. I bet t-t-ten guys have borrowed my rifle since the fall."

"I'm amazed that you're so relaxed about your possessions. Especially like a rifle. That's a very personal item. Too many people don't return borrowed things anymore. What does your dad say about you loaning your rifle?" Wes knew when he mentioned Lorenzo Tedesco, Lonnie didn't keep his cool. He wanted his father to see him as perfect.

"Fuck, I wouldn't tell my d-d-dad. He'd shit a b-b-brick. We grew up in a f-f-family being told to not even share with our b-b-brothers. I never gave them anything, not even a c-c-cruddy pair of jeans or anything. I kept all my stuff to m-m- myself. My dad would have gotten both of us for breaking his r-r-rule."

"I don't see how you would feel differently now. A father has a lot of influence on his kids."

"You got that right! Almost all that I d-d-do or don't do is because my dad beat it into my head. D-D-Do this. D-D-Don't do that. Most of the time me and my brothers were too s-s-scared to do anything but follow his shitty rules. He said he was teaching us to k-k-keep what we had, but me and my b-b-brothers think he's just plain mean."

Lonnie was temporarily lost in his remembrances of the past so Wes moved even closer where his knees would weave a V pattern between Lonnie's."I bet he gave you a hard time if you ever lost a girl to some other guy."

"Ha! Worse than a hard t-t-time. He would make fun of us. Tell us we weren't macho or that our th-thing was too small or that we were lousy lovers. He ought to know. He's out s-s-screwing every woman over eighteen in our town," Lonnie's voice was becoming shrill. He was experiencing again all the humiliation he'd felt over the years, since he brought home his first date and tricked her into his bedroom. Since Lonnie was only fourteen at the time, his dad thought that was cute, but when Lonnie could never get the girl to come back again, his dad made fun of his sexual skills.

"I bet he gave you a hard time about Tiffany and all the boys a looker like that could get," Wes said as he leaned closer to Lonnie's face.

"Oh, yeah. I think my d-d-dad wants to nail her himself, but no one's going to g-g-get her away from me."

"What about the president of Tech, Lonnie? Can he get her?" Wes waited for Lonnie's explosive or calculated response.

"That p-p-prick! He's ancient and he's an idiot. He, he.... why did you bring him up? I hate that b-b-bastard!"

"Do you hate him enough to kill him, Lonnie?"

"Yes," Lonnie's voice broke and his eyes glistened with tears, "Tiffany is mine. She loves m-m-me. She just fools around with him because he's a b-b-big shit," Lonnie bent over and began to sob."I love her so much, I'd do anything to keep her."

"Would you kill to keep her?"

Lonnie continued to sob and then began to mumble. He repeated over and over again, "I thought it was the p-p-president, I thought it was the p-p-president. I never hurt a good guy before. I thought it was the p-p-president."

Wes reached out and took Lonnie's chin in his hand. He raised the boy's face and looked at the tears that were covering his face. He pushed his head back so that their eyes met. When he was sure Lonnie Tedesco was seeing him, he asked, "You shot Andy Dren, didn't you? Tell the truth, and I'll ask that they go easy on you. You were trying to right a wrong. You were trying to teach the president that he shouldn't be messing with your girl."

"Yes. I thought it was the president. I never even knew Andy. The president should be dead. He's a dirty motherfucker. He ..." Lonnie was lost in sobs again. Wes felt a wisp of compassion for this young man who had ruined his own life over a fleeting affair with a girl. His feeling was short lived when he also thought about the lives that had been destroyed because of uncontrolled anger and easy accessibility to a gun. Always a lethal combination.

"Lonnie, this isn't all your fault. You've been made a victim by your father, the president and your girl. Of course all of that'll come out in court and surely the judge will consider these factors. We need to make this look like you've been completely open and forthcoming. Let's get this all down on paper so I can tell the lawyer who'll protect you and your rights how cooperative and helpful you've been. You've stood up like a man. I'm proud of you, Lonnie. What you have done today proves that you're strong and, yes, macho." Wes was as gentle as if he were dealing with a small child. In some ways he was. Also he was encouraging Lonnie to put his confession on paper. Then the chips will fall where they fall.

Chapter 55

Billy Joe LaCrosse

Wes worked with Lonnie and a secretary to get the confession on paper and signed. Then he returned the young man to the jail. Lonnie still had his one call to make, but Wes wasn't concerned, because he had the facts. Now no matter what lawyer the Tedesco family hired, he'd have his work cut out for him. The kid was pathetic, but he was also a cold-blooded murderer.

After leaving the jail and starting back to his office, the detective dialed Danielle Swain's number to tell her the events of the past 18 hours. She was always fair to homicide and all week she'd been working closely with young Lindy Lindholm. They both might have the jump on the other news media, although he wondered how the son of the president would react to what's going to be said about his father. It would be only a matter of minutes until the news was going to be all through Atlanta like Sherman's army. Since television news had become a mode of entertainment, there was no such thing as a secret.

"Dani, Wes Wesley here. I got a big one for you and your protégé, the campus reporter. We have a confession in the Tech shooting."

"Fantastic. Tell me more, Wes, but first thanks for calling. I appreciate the thought. I really do!"

Being careful not to mention Lonnie's name, Wes reiterated some of what happened the night before and on through the morning. No solid details. Just enough to give her a short lead time before all the other media got the information. Dani was a good listener and only interrupted once when she needed to clarify a detail. She cut the conversation short, so she could activate their BreakIn! feature for Channel 22 before the other stations began their announcements. She would be the first. But only for a short time.

"May I call you back in a little while and talk about this more? Right now I'm gone. Thanks again." The line went dead.

Wes could imagine her running to be the star of the biggest local story in Atlanta since a series of bombings started during the Olympics. This story was going to hit the city hard. A big name associated with a prestigious institution was going to be splattered far beyond the Atlanta Journal and Constitution and other local media.

Billy Joe was seated in his office when Wes returned. It was obvious that he'd been there awhile. The remains of a fast food lunch and an empty coffee cup supported the notion that he'd taken over the room quite some time ago. A heavy aroma of onions and deep-fried potatoes hung in the air.

Wes grabbed the only chair available. Its seat was ripped and the back rattled each time it was moved. Before his butt touched the aging fabric, Billy Joe was giving his report on the search of Andy Dren's computer.

"Don't get comfortable. Son-of-a-bitch, Wes, I've so much to tell you, but let me do that in the car. We're travelin'. Now that you have your boy safely locked up, it's time to look at the other shit goin' on at Tech. Between me and Dixie, we've stumbled into a whole fuckin' snake pit," Billy Joe had not given Wes a moment to settle in before he hit him with the essence of what he and Dixie had discovered and was pushing him back toward the outside door."We're gonna make a surprise visit on pretty Charlie Black. I'll bring you up to shit in the car."

The two detectives took Wes' car from the parking spot where he'd left it only minutes before and headed north on the connector to I75.

Billy Joe continued his debriefing, "I was a big surprise to Andy's roommates. They thought they were gonna sleep off their Saturday night, but it didn't work that way. Both of his roommates were there. After the one named Frank got awake, he was a friggin'gem. Man, that guy can do anything on the computer. We ought to hire him to run our system. That is if we had a system.

Anyway, back to Frank. I bet Frank could find us some perps that we've been chasin' for months. He thinks like a detective but, you know, like, related to the computer. We know other police forces are doin' a lot of their work through technology, but not Atlanta. Our number of solved cases could go way up with serious technical support..."

"Hey, Billy Joe, back to Frank."

"Yeah, right. I gave the guys the search warrant and told them that I was there to search Dren's computer as well as the apartment. Frank spoke up immediately and said that he'd decided that there could be a clue on Andy's system, and that he'd been surfin' through some of his files. He'd be happy to help me, but he'd also stay out of my way if I wanted to do it myself. Is that a joke? I never did tell him that our computer literacy is about minus 10. If my kids didn't teach me stuff, I'd never learn it here..."

"Back to Frank."

"Yeah. Yeah. So Frank and I sat in front of the computer talkin' about what might be a clue, what might lead us in the right direction. It was neat how this kid immediately put himself on our team. He was close to Andy and wants the murderer fried, but he also got into *our* thought patterns in walkin' through a case. That kid had already found the financial files that Dren worked on for the president and the foundation.

"Sure enough those numbers that we've already run into were there, plus some earlier transfers from Hong Kong. I said I found it fuckin' amazin' that alumni could give away $185,000,000. Frank said that it appeared to be from several sources, because the banks sendin' the funds from Hong Kong differed. He also told me that international bankin' business was big in Hong Kong so havin' many banks wasn't strange, but it's a point to think about.

"Frank could track the Hong Kong gifts into the foundation account but then we saw that we could also track them out. It always occurred within two days; never longer and usually it happened the next day. After those moves, there was a cool 10% left in the account. Everything else was gone. It had gone to several banks located in Atlanta and Washington. That's where Dixie picked up the trail." Billy Joe stopped talking and paid some attention to passing several trucks and lighting a cigarette.

"As you know, Dixie had appointments with staff from three banks today. He found the pattern similar to the foundation accounts: in for a short time and out. The difference was that *nothin'* was left in these accounts. If Georgia Tech's percentage is a commission of some kind, these second conduits didn't get a cut. The funds then being transferred from the second banks went to other banks in Washington. One was an institution that's been the 'home' for the Democratic Party for more than four years. Do you think that might be a coincidence? Dixie doesn't think so."

"Are you deducing that Tech has been a laundering institution for Chinese funds that have been directed into our government?"

"All the signs are there. Hard to believe when you consider who is involved, but Dixie is ready to talk to the finance committee of the foundation. He wanted to know if your offer is still on the table to have Janeen Carson set up those appointments. I told him that to hear you talk, you barely know the woman, but that I'd ask you." Billy Joe smiled as he gave Wes a hard time.

"Let's save that conversation for later. Where's Dixie? I thought he'd be at the office."

"Dixie left about fifteen minutes ago for the president's house to talk to him. He didn't want Lindholm to hear about you pickin' up Lonnie before he'd a chance to question him nor to have an opportunity to contact anyone else. He figured you would be back in time for us to go out and interview the vice president while he's still with the president," Billy Joe responded and then asked, "Why don't you call Ms. Carson now to set up the appointments? Honest, Wes baby, I won't listen if you want to talk dirty."

Wes chose not to be baited by his partner."I'll call the president's assistant right now."

"Great. I'll hum soft, romantic songs in the background. Just pretend, loverboy, that you're all by yourself. As soon as you finish your call, I'll tell you more about the findin's of Frank and Billy Joe, the new homicide team. The kid is all right."

Janeen answered on the second ring, listened carefully to Wes' request, and told him she would do it immediately. He added that he'd like her to set up the appointments in the president's conference room at one-hour intervals starting at 5 o'clock today. She told him that anyone she couldn't reach now she would try again in an hour. The conversation was completed in a matter of minutes.

"She didn't sound all breathless and excited to hear from you, but she was quick to do what you asked without even a why? Or what? You have great power, partner."

"That's true. I've got it. Now, you smart ass, how about continuing your report."

"OK. I'd like to be able to take credit for the next part but the truth is that Frank and Andy really did it."

"Andy? That's interesting. Do you mean that he actually spelled out some of this on his computer?"

"In detail. Andy kept a journal: a diary of his life and, more importantly, his thoughts. What I read this mornin' would never make Playboy Magazine, but it'll probably make a sizzlin' news story. He began to suspect that there was somethin' fishy about the funds from Hong Kong about a month ago. Because the transfers didn't happen regularly, he decided to wait and watch what would happen with the next deposit or so. He'd tried to find the 'gift' money to balance out what he was doin' and couldn't trace the bulk of it after the first day. What was left was always the same percentage. He believed that it appeared to be a commission. Then one day, he watched the news on TV and there was a report that the Democratic Party Fund Raising Committee was being questioned about a gift of the same amount of money that he'd seen come in and go out of the Tech Foundation just months before. He thought that was too much of a coincidence but wanted to know who was involved before he talked to the FBI. That was when he decided to check out the president's computer files. He even made a comment like: I know I'm breakin' the law to get this information, but this can affect our whole country. That was the last entry. I think we know the rest of the story.

"Except that we don't yet know who's involved. We've a fairly large cast of characters startin' with the president himself, the pretty-boy Charles, the possible not-so-trusted trustees, and maybe someone we haven't even thought about yet. Talk about unlikely perps. Georgia Tech has always been the shinin' star here in Atlanta. There's soon to be a large group of disillusioned people readin' about how a few have dishonored their institution. Then they're gonna start callin' the chief and the mayor and probably up to the governor screamin' their heads off for us to keep this all out of the media. Well, it's not gonna work. When you've a story that includes money, power and sex, it's a winner. The public loves to know the down and dirty shit.

"One thing I learned from Frank is so damn cool. It's a hell-uv-a closin' line on this whole case. Wes, this is in strictest confidence. Just us, baby. Frank and his roommates are the guys who did the memorial sign for Andy. They got another computer nerd to break into the usual message and do the HKIII-CC missive in lights. When I asked why that particular message, Frank said because they found that code in the computer files and thought it was 'boss.' That was the file name Andy used to relate to the president and the records on the Chinese funds. We're damn sure that it means Hong Kong, Lindholm III, Capital Campaign. Once we got that, we had all the information I've told you and easy access to lots more. Lindholm must've gone ballistic when he saw the memorial, because he would've assumed someone besides Dren knew about the friggin' deal."

"Knowing all of this, Dixie must be having a damn picnic interrogating that son-uva-bitch, Lindholm," Wes added.

"I doubt whether he's havin' any better time than we're gonna have in a few minutes with his bastard of a VP. Accordin' to the directions I got from George Fancer, we should just about be there. Look for Tall Timbers Drive. That's our next turn."

Chapter 56

Danielle Jarvis Swain

Dani had just signed off the BreakIn! feature having told the viewing audience that a murder suspect in the tech shooting had been arrested. She emphasized that this news was conveyed to her just minutes ago. At this point it was believed Oliver Andrew Dren was killed by mistake. Dani suggested that the viewers stay tuned for more breaking news that she'll bring to them as it happens.

She rushed off the set and ran to the telephone. She wanted to get to Lindy Lindholm either before he heard this news or soon after. She hadn't used the confidential information about the triangle between the president, a student and a freshman woman. She wanted more confirmation on this to save Channel 22 from the risk of a lawsuit if it was misinformation. Lindy was going to be in a difficult situation by being both a reporter and Lindholm's son, but Dani wanted to be there to be his friend and help him during a bad time. Dani could hardly believe that this twist could be true, but then she'd seen many real events that were stranger than those written as entertainment.

Lindy had given Dani his cell phone number which she used. He answered after the first ring, "Hi."

"Lindy, it's Dani Swain. How are you doing? I just got off the air and thought I would call to find out if you had seen BreakIn!" No point in being coy. She asked the most straight-forward question that came to her.

"No, Dani, I've been working out. I'm standing in the locker room now getting ready to get cleaned up and go hit the books. How come you're working on Sunday?" Lindy asked as he walked toward the showers. He was looking forward to a leisurely, hot shower.

"I had some news that was just on our BreakIn! show. Why don't you come over here before you go study, and we'll talk about what's happened in the murder case?" Dani didn't feel comfortable telling him what she knew over the telephone.

"Gee, Dani, that would be great. Sounds like something big has happened. Maybe I can use it for another special edition of the paper. I can't wait to hear your news. I'll be there in twenty minutes. I can survive just as well with a short shower as a long one. Thanks for calling. Tell Tony to let me in. He's so good at his job that I never have been able to talk myself past him. See ya'."

Dani was sure that someone would tell Lindy about her news before he got off the campus. Maybe that would be easier for her. Then she wouldn't have to be the one to drop a bomb on him that might change his life completely. When he got there, she would let him know that he could count on her but now she had some more calls to make. She hoped that she could reach Wes, but if not she would go directly to the chief. She was going to continue to scoop her media colleagues. This story was very important to her.

She picked up the receiver to make another call to the Tech campus. She hoped to find Rex to get a statement from him to use as faculty reaction to the news. He'd be perfect for that type of filler, because he was typical of faculty that usually paid no attention to anything outside of the classroom

The anchorwoman immediately dialed Rex's number, "Hey, Shaw's residence."

Dani recognized the sweet Southern drawl of Rex's wife. "Missy, this is Danielle Swain. Is Rex there?"

"He sho' is, Dani. He will be soooo happy to hear from you."

Dani greeted Rex and was about to ask him if he heard the news, but Rex was already into the same topic, "Dani! I can't believe you're calling. We just saw your news flash. We're so pleased that the murderer has been caught. We can relax again."

Dani rolled her eyes and thought, if Wes was correct, the next news wasn't going to be as pleasant. She then said to Rex,

"Would you make a statement that I can use on the follow up of the confession? It'll be for the faculty's initial reaction. "

"Who cares what I think? No one would even know my name. But my reaction is that students and faculty will be celebrating this news. The president might even make a special award to the police."

"Rex, the perpetrator says he meant to kill someone else. What do you have to say about that?"

"The situation is crazy, but I hope that somehow this tragedy can be a serious lesson for our students. Each life is of value and should be protected and cherished; not deleted like yesterday's E-mail, " Rex Shaw was quite sober with his calmer, more reflective thoughts.

"I like that Rex. If it's OK with you, I'll include your quote in my next news show. I think it's important for the public to know that this has been a time of sorrow and contemplation on campus. You show that there is concern for the students who're entrusted to your tutoring for at least four years."

Rex Shaw agreed that Dani could quote him if she felt it had a positive purpose. He felt that at this time, Tech needed to look as strong as possible. After all, every rival school is going to be taking potshots at them. Dani thanked her friend and moved to her next call.

She tried the detective's beeper but didn't receive an answer. He was probably with someone so would get back to her later. That wasn't good enough. She wouldn't just wait idly. Already she'd sent Loretta and her assistant to the homicide office to get some footage and told her if nothing was happening to take a quick trip over to the jail and check it out before returning to homicide. She was going to meet them later.

Danielle Swain called Chief Princeton and was told by his assistant that the chief was out. She explained carefully who she was and why she was calling before adding that she'd like a statement from him before she went on the air. She thought it important that the chief speak for the department in this very visible case.

The voice on the other end of the line asked her to wait a

minute. He thought he heard that Chief Princeton had stopped in on his way to a brunch. Dani was put on hold for what seemed like ten minutes but by her watch was closer to two.

"Ms. Swain, how good of you to call. I was on my way to the Marriott and stopped here for a minute. How may I help you?"

"I'm calling to get a statement from you on the arrest in the Andrew Dren murder case. I've already done a short BreakIn! feature but am preparing my longer follow up spot."

Obviously, she could guess why he was in the office. "You're right on the job, Ms. Swain. I hope you'll mention the excellent work done by our outstanding homicide squad. We've been getting all kinds of flak from the alumni of Georgia Tech that we haven't been fast enough. One of these days we should have these big time businessmen ride with detectives to see how many hours are put in on their case load," Chief Princeton mused and then added," But that isn't why you called. You want a statement."

"Right, sir, I want to send my camera person over to your office, and I'll meet you both there in about 30 minutes. She's already out on this job taking background shots at homicide and at the jail."

"I'll be here and looking forward to seeing you. This is a big case for us both. Is there anything else I can do for you?"

"Not really. Of course I'd like to ask you to give me an exclusive but understand your position on that."

"I'll tell you what I will do," the chief laughed, "I'll go spend that half hour in the men's room. Hardly anyone bothers me there except in an emergency. We'll see if that protects your exclusivity. Then one of these days, you and I should talk again about how you, too, can project our image in the media. See you in 28 minutes."

Dani was thrilled with the banter from the chief. Of course he wasn't going to sit in the men's room, but he at least delivered the message that he understood the importance of her getting the first story. She would enjoy a discussion with him about their mutual interests. She'd follow up on that before he forgot his generous offer.

Danielle Swain made several other calls including one to Loretta to tell her to meet her at the chief's office before they go to homicide. She hoped to cover all possibilities before her next newscast.

She was trying to reach Wes again when she saw Lindy approaching the door. He did indeed look like he'd just stepped out of the shower. She was reminded of the old saying 'squeaky clean.' His hair was still glistening with water and his face flushed and vibrant. She thought that if she had a younger brother, Lindy would be the perfect model. It was no wonder that she wanted to protect his innocence.

"Hey, Dani. I bet you never knew a person could move so fast. Of course it helped to be a Sunday. There's no traffic between here and Tech," Lindy greeted the television news anchor as he entered the room.

"Totally awesome. Maybe your speed relates to all of that technology that's hovering over the campus. You know, you can propel yourself like E-mail, virtual reality or fax and be in two places at almost the same time." Dani smiled and looked the young man in the eye. She really didn't want to address the reason for his appearance.

Dani motioned for him to sit in the chair that was beside the desk, "Lindy, I heard from Detective Wesley that they have a confession for Andy Dren's murder."

"Wow! I was beginning to think they were getting nowhere. I guess we'll never completely understand all that goes on in the work of the homicide squad. Do you know who it is?"

"No, but I believe the Chief will announce that later today. The amazing information is, according to Wes, it was a mistake," she hesitated and then said pointedly, "The perpetrator says that he meant to shoot your father. I didn't want you to hear it on the news."

Lindy Lindholm was stunned. His reaction was a moment of complete disorientation. He didn't respond for several long seconds. The silence felt as painful as hearing Dani's words. His mind went from a blank to a collage of thoughts; none that were pleasant.

"My dad? Did Detective Wesley say why he was supposed to be the target?"

"He mentioned a theory, Lindy. Of course it may not be true. The suspect might've been making up a story to turn some of the blame from himself. He could be looking for some sympathy or setting himself up to look like a victim." Dani waited silently. She felt he needed time to get used to this new idea.

Lindy felt cold and detached. He felt that what he was about to learn was going to have a profound effect on his life and that of his family. Lindy hadn't forgotten what he'd learned quite by accident about why the Lindholm family had moved to Atlanta. His parents had no suspicion that, before they left California, he'd heard the story of his dad and a coed from a complete stranger. Could this be another situation like that?

"Dani, why was my dad the target?"

"Lindy, this is so hard for me. I don't want you to be hurt, but I thought it was better for us to talk about it before you heard it from others. In only a few days you and I have become not only colleagues but almost family."

"Dani, I appreciate your concern and I appreciate how you've allowed me to be a part of this story. You've made me the star in many ways. You didn't have to do that. I'll make this easier for *you* by asking: Does this relate to a female student?"

Danielle Swain was amazed. She thought she was going to help Lindy through the shock of this information. Instead he was helping her."Yes, Lindy, the murderer says that he wanted to kill your dad because he was taking his girl away from him."

"It could be true. In fact, I'm afraid it's just history repeating itself. Unfortunately, my dad lives in an unreal world. Before this minute, I've never admitted out loud that my father has a real problem. My mother doesn't even know that I know this. She's such a nice woman, that it's hard for me to empathize or understand my dad's actions," Lindy swallowed, sighed and looked directly at his friend, "Dani, thank you for being honest with me. Thank you for taking the time now to tell me, even though your time is precious at this point of the story. You're both my friend and role model. I guess I'd like to be like you when I grow up. I've been playing at being a real reporter, but my role now is being a son. My mom's going to need me, and I'm going home. Maybe we can talk later so I'll have a story for the Technique. Would you help me write it so it's true but won't completely make the Lindholm family look like fools?"

Dani could feel tears in her eyes. She'd been right in her judgment of this young man. He had depth and honor. He didn't ask for more details, nor was he offering any of his own. He was concerned about his mother and was going to be there for her.

The public isn't kind to visible personalities who have fallen from their pedestal. Jonathan Agnew Lindholm III, as president of the prestigious Georgia Institute of Technology, had been awarded a celebrity status in Atlanta that automatically gave him his own pedestal. It had nothing to do with earning it. It was a gift. The place of fame had been given easily, but now the same people who had bestowed it would take it away. Fame can quickly change to infamous when the receiver doesn't respect the responsibility that accompanies recognition.

"Lindy, you go do your job, and I'll do mine. Then let's put our heads together and write your special edition so you're ready for the students tomorrow. Call me anytime you need to talk, and I'll call you after the six o'clock news."

"That sounds like a good plan for a bad day. I'll be at the president's house, not my dorm room. I need to tell my mom what I know, but she already knows a lot of this. I can tell you, Dani, one of the first things she will say will be: That poor young man. He's dead because of Jon's weakness."

Chapter 57

Jonathan Agnew Lindholm III

Dickerson Packard drove up the curving driveway and parked his car in front of the stately, white mansion known simply as The President's House. Living in this grand style had always been a visible perk to serving as the CEO of Tech. The grounds were carefully attended and the building professionally maintained. Dixie wondered if any of the Hong Kong funds were used to keep the president and his family living so eloquently.

He stood before the double doors and waited for someone to respond to him. He often bet with himself whether a house was empty or not, because he believed that he could feel when the dwelling was occupied. He was right about eight times out of ten. Today he felt a presence behind the classic-style doors and waited patiently to be greeted.

The door opened and an attractive woman was standing in the doorway with her hand on the inside knob. She was dressed in navy blue slacks and a blue and burgundy, paisley print, tailored shirt. He assumed it was Mrs. Lindholm but didn't address her by name.

"Is Dr. Lindholm at home? It's important that I talk with him."

"He doesn't usually see people on Sunday unless he's made an appointment."

Dixie handed her his card, "FBI. Agent Dickerson Packard. And, no, I don't have an appointment. Please tell him I'm here."

Laurie was shocked. Lots of people came to see the president, but an FBI agent was not just a casual visitor. Jon may not want to see this young man, but that's his choice, not hers, "Come in, Agent Packard. You may wait in the living room. I'll tell Jon you're here."

Laurie motioned toward the wide archway that faced the outside door. A large room tastefully decorated in cheerful yellows and greens was flooded with sunlight from a full wall of windows. Dixie could see that this was a room for entertaining friends and staff of the institution. He decided quickly that he wouldn't like to live a fishbowl existence. He walked across the thick Oriental rug, looked out the windows and saw a wide verandah that overlooked a pool."Well, maybe I could get used to living in a fishbowl. This is damn nice!"

"Mr. Packard, I'm President Lindholm. Should I have known you were coming? It's quite unusual to have people just stop in on a Sunday," Jon said stuffily. Dixie felt that Lindholm had been practicing that demeanor for years. It probably intimidated most people but that wasn't Agent Packard's reaction.

"No, Dr. Lindholm. You wouldn't have known that I was coming. In fact, I didn't know I was going to be here until a few hours ago. You may want to sit down, because we have some talking to do."

"I beg your pardon. I believe this is my home. Whether I sit or stand is my choice, Agent Packard."

"Have it any way you prefer. I was only thinking of your comfort, because we may be here awhile. We'll be discussing how the Georgia Tech Foundation handles its gifts from outside sources. To get started: Who's responsible for accounting for these monies?" Dixie wanted to shake the arrogance and cockiness of this man, so that his responses would be spontaneous rather than calculated.

Lindholm's eyes widened. A feeling of emptiness clutched him like he had just lost his most valued possession. He didn't know yet why this man was pursuing this topic, but he could guess. He was going to have to be careful and not give away any information than wasn't absolutely necessary, "I don't see how this is the business of the FBI. Why would you care about our private gifts? Every college and university in the United States is conducting a funds campaign. Are you visiting every president?"

"Not yet, but maybe we should. If we do, Dr. Lindholm, I'll

be sure to give you credit for the idea. I'm confident that your colleagues will want to thank you for your thoughtful suggestion. Please, answer my question. We've a lot of ground to cover."

Jon had seen many scenes in movies and television where there was a good cop and a bad cop to set a stage for questioning. He felt he'd inherited only the bad cop and wanted to ask this self-confident man where his better partner was. He tried to give the impression that he wasn't threatened; only annoyed. To keep his dominant position, he chose to remain standing, being about eye-to-eye with the FBI agent.

"In response to your question, we have a vice president responsible for foundation relations. I'm sure that you understand the structure of a not-for-profit organization, so you also would know that the volunteers who serve as trustees really do not report to the vice president. I guess you could say that they work together."

"Yes, I do understand that well, but I don't believe that answers my question. Do the volunteers keep the books, record the funds that come into the foundation? Do they create the books that are needed to determine the financial standing of the foundation?"

"Of course they don't do the actual daily accounting. We have staff members who do that. Mr. Packard, a lot of gifts are given to Tech. Keeping the records is a job that keeps several people busy full-time. Vice President Black supervises the entire staff."

"And who supervises Black?"

Jon didn't like that question. To answer it truthfully, he placed himself with the full responsibility of accounting for the funds. He wanted to leave it with Charles Black and his staff, "Charles Black is a very responsible employee and handles his department in a professional manner."

"I would assume that's true or you wouldn't keep him, but who gives him his marching orders? Surely he isn't autonomous and acting without your knowledge."

Jon made the decision to sit down. He felt a bit off balance. It was his house, and he would sit when he felt like it. He settled in the closest chair as he said, "He reports to me."

Dixie chose a chair that was close to the president and sat stiffly on the front edge of the seat, leaning toward Lindholm. The posture he selected matched perfectly with his severe gray suit, white shirt, navy blue tie, and short military-style haircut. He'd often heard that the only government employee visit feared more than one from the FBI was one from IRS. Even he thought the IRS could be a scary encounter!

Dixie asked a series of innocuous questions as he gathered information and momentum. He was creating the path that would take them to the reason for this Sunday visit.

"Why do alumni and others give to the campaign?"

"Of course they give to support their alma mater, or to show confidence in the education that's being offered, or to help build buildings and create programs. Those are some examples. The generosity of many helps to make this an outstanding institution instead of being average." Because he was citing his usual case for support, Lindholm felt more comfortable. This should be easy enough for this pain-in-the-ass to understand.

Dixie said slowly, "Very impressive. With those thoughts in mind, would you explain why funds from these generous and concerned donors would then be withdrawn from the foundation accounts within a day?"

The FBI agent's stare bore into the president's eyes and seemed to reach deeply into his mind. Jon felt flustered. This man had some information that only a handful of people had. Who had he already questioned? What details did the agent have, and had someone set him up by passing Packard onto him. He didn't like the feeling that he might be targeted to take the fall. What else could go wrong this week? Did all of this relate directly back to Andy and his murder? He felt that he had as many questions as this uninvited guest, but he couldn't ask them. The interrogation was one sided.

"We invest our money with many banking institutions. Part of our annual income is the return on investments. Our trustee committee responsible for investing capital is practiced and knowledgeable in the field." Jon had regained his pompous facade.

Again Dixie said slowly, "Very interesting. The institutions you chose for this 'investing' also withdrew the funds within hours of their transfer. They have no records of instructions to 'invest.' Why do you think this was done, Dr. Lindholm?"

"I would imagine that they decided to invest the monies with an institution that could return more revenue. That would be the smart financial move, don't you agree?" Jon felt his confidence waning again, but he was sure that the agent wasn't versed enough in financial advising to know whether this was a normal procedure.

Drawing his words out like he'd been born in the deepest South, Packard said, "Just doesn't fit. The funds were not 'invested' with the second bank. Does that information bother you?"

"As a matter of fact it does. It looks like someone has not assumed the proper funds stewardship responsibility. I appreciate that you have brought this to my attention. I'll speak to Charles Black and the finance committee tomorrow. I cannot fathom that they've been this lax with our donors' gifts." Jon hoped that he sounded indignant and uninvolved with this part of the money handling."The foundation is independent of the institution. That's the purpose of establishing it: to be in charge of private contributions." He was pleased that he'd covered the responsibility being the trustees and Charles Black. Packard may think he hasn't been diligent, but at least he won't believe that the president was doing something shady.

It was time to make Lindholm wake up again. Dixie saw that he was getting comfortably back into his role of being the head of a prestigious institution."Perhaps you can explain why the only donations that followed this pattern were mega-gifts from Hong Kong?"

There it was. He'd finally gotten to where he was headed from the minute he walked into the house. Jon didn't know how the FBI knew all of this information, but he was smart enough to know that he had to consider that this conversation was serious enough to change his life. Nothing about his carefully calculated life had been the same since Janeen's call on Tuesday morning. Could all of this been started on this collision course before Andy was killed? Did Andy himself talk with the FBI before he was shot? What should he say? What was left to say? He made a decision, "This discussion is ended, Agent Packard. I'll have my lawyer with me if you choose to continue your interrogation." Jon rose and walked out of the room.

Chapter 58

Charles William Black

Wes drove slowly along the quiet suburban street. Houses all appeared to be the same, but the owners took great pride in pointing out that their homes were different from the others: one had a double doorway, another a huge chandelier that was visible through an oversized window in the foyer, another had faux stone trim instead of brick. All had fancy, customized mailboxes at the curb with numbers on both sides. Wes was looking for 7624 and pulled into the driveway that was beside the correct box.

"We've arrived in Suburbia USA. Seems like we've driven far enough to be in the outskirts of Chicago. I'd hate to drive from here everyday just to end up at the homicide building. I'd probably have to give up and join the county police force instead," Wes said before opening the door and waiting for Billy Joe to join him at the gracefully curving walkway leading to the postage stamp-sized front porch.

"You'd last about a week in this fuckin' atmosphere. It's like livin' under a Christmas tree in the miniature train yard. This sub-division is planned for impressin' rather than livin.' Wes, you'd be dyin' from boredom and quiet in a damn minute," Billy Joe observed.

"You're probably right. I love being in the city. It's real. It's in my soul. I guess I have city blood, and these folks have suburb blood."

Billy Joe rang the doorbell and stood silently beside his partner. He too believed that it was best to live in the city, but he sometimes wondered if being away from the faster life in the urban environment would be better for raising his kids. This thought was interrupted when the door opened, and Sally Black greeted them.

"Hello. May I help you? Do you need directions?"

"No. We're in the right place. Is Charles Black at home?" Billy Joe asked.

"Yes, my husband is here. I'm Sally Black. I don't believe I know who you are?"

"I'm Billy Joe LaCrosse and this is Wes Wesley. Atlanta Homicide."

"Oh, you must be here about the murder at Tech. Come in. I'll call Charles. He's watching television. If there's a sports program on, Charles is there," Sally explained as she walked the detectives into the living room and then disappeared through the dining room. They could hear the din from the television and Sally's voice mentioning their names before hearing a masculine voice reply, "I hope they've found the killer. Then we can go back to a normal life."

Wes looked at Billy Joe and said, "I don't think so, Black. I believe we're going to add to the chaos."

Charles Black entered from the direction where Sally had disappeared. He was wearing running shorts, a Coca-Cola T shirt and no shoes. He looked much softer here in his own home than he did in his usual campus uniform of a double breasted suit, stiff white shirt and conservative tie.

"Detective Wesley. Detective LaCrosse. What a surprise. I hope you're coming with good news."

"We came to talk about some of our findings. We do think we have a direct line to the murderer of Andy Dren, but we need to get some background and details to make our case solid," Wes told him as much as he wished to at the time.

"You bet. I'm here to help you anyway I can. This's been a terrible week at Tech. I feared we'd never know who did this terrible thing. Could Sally get you some coffee or a Coke?" he motioned to his shirt, smiled and added, "We're a Coke family. The corporation is one of Tech's major donors, and we're loyal to our givers. Loyalty is part of being in the institutional development business."

"We'll pass. We're pleased to hear that you're enthusiastic about filling in some information. Often people don't want to talk to the police." Wes said in a friendly and relaxed tone of voice.

"Not me, detective. I want to do what will get this case closed. It has everybody nervous."

"Would you tell us how the Georgia Tech Foundation accepts gifts and who's responsible for keeping the records of the transactions?"

Charles felt the breath leaving his lungs like he'd been punched in the chest. Actually maybe he had been. He was hit with the words rather than by a fist. He'd talked himself out of the idea that there was a connection between Andy's death and the work the student was doing for the foundation. Now the detective had brought up the thought again. There must be a connection. If he didn't suspect a tie, Wesley wouldn't have mentioned it. He knew that he had to give plausible responses, but no one said that he had to tell the truth.

"That is a surprising question. I thought you'd want to know about what I knew about Andy's friends and habits. His personal life must have a bearing on his murder. We know very little about most of our students. In a sense, many of them are just casual visitors within the 'halls of ivy' for a few years"

"That's a very poetic way of looking at time spent in college. It may have been how it was for Andy but still the question shouldn't be a surprise. Andy Dren was working with the foundation. That fact is part of the case of why he was in the president's office. Why would you be surprised?" Billy Joe asked.

"You're absolutely right. I should've expected that train of thought. Andy did work for months with the president and the foundation finance committee. But Andy didn't accept gifts. He just recorded them."

"Yes, I believe we understand that, but who did accept and account for them?"

"Well, now there are several answers to the question. 1. Development officers usually accept gifts and if not them then one of our accounting staff." As Charles Black proceeded, Wes felt that he was being lectured like he'd signed up for a course in Fundraising 101. He had to be patient. He wanted to learn how Black would handle this query and those to follow."2. Sometimes the volunteer asking for the gift accepts it. 3. The accounting of all gift falls under my department, but of course there's the foundation's finance committee, made up of alumni volunteers, which is also responsible, because the members are the stewards and the investors of the funds. 4. Even faculty can be responsible. You can see that it's difficult to just give you a simple, short answer."

"To point you in the exact direction that interests us, let's get more specific so we can get to our main concern: What son of a bitch is responsible for the mega gifts that have been coming from Hong Kong?" Wes said in a precise, clipped style that he used when he wanted to convey the feeling that this wasn't just fooling around time but instead: let's get serious.

Charles didn't want to hear the words: Hong Kong. Although he had a story ready for just this moment, he didn't feel any confidence that he could divert the track or speed of the course that Wesley and LaCrosse had set for this meeting.

"Hong Kong gifts? Why they in particular? We have hundreds of other donations that Andy worked on. The contributions from Hong Kong were just representative of a few persons."

"That's *why* we're interested, Black. They were from a few people but made up about half of your friggin' campaign." Wes knew that Black was aware of where they were going. The stupid bastard was trying to play a game while he created his next lines.

Indeed Charles Black was trying to stay ahead of the detectives, but he could sense himself dropping behind. It gave him an instant feeling of defeat. He wasn't going to get stuck for everyone's involvement. After all, he only got a part of the benefits. Right now, his commission hardly seemed worth facing the APD detectives. He was truly amazed that these two bozos obviously knew what was going on. Who knew this and was willing to talk to the police? Could Jon have set them on him?

"Hey, Black, you seem to have forgotten the question. Let's try it again: Who's responsible for the Hong Kong funds given to the Tech Foundation?" Wes allowed the tone of exasperation to be reflected in his voice.

"Yes, yes. I know the question, but as I said, it's not a yes or no response. The president is responsible for getting the gift and ultimately deciding how it is spent. In the case of the Hong Kong gifts, they'll go into a magnificent Asian studies building...." Wes interrupted Charles.

"Asian studies building. Sounds impressive. How much does something like that cost?"

"It is impressive! It's going to make the donors very happy. The building and program will cost about $6,000,000."

"Interesting amount," Wes nodded his head and drew out the two words slowly hoping Charle Black would begin to grasp how Wes was going to nail him. He preferred those persons he questioned to be nervous and feel threatened. To move the process along, Wes continued, "Does that means Tech isn't using the remainder of $179,000,000?"

In his mind, Black heard the words: "That's it, Charles." He felt it was time to get himself out of this link, "The president and the trustees make those decisions. I only follow their directions and do what's expected to keep them all happy. The vice president is simply a hired hand. I'm not a decision-maker. You could ask Jon Lindholm or Burl Mentor, chairman of the finance committee. They're the ones in charge."

"As vice president, I got the idea that you headed up the department. Actually I got the impression from you that you held a rather important position on campus," Billy Joe injected.

"Oh, no. I'm just one rung higher than any of the development staff. If you were looking for someone who has daily hands-on resposibilty of the accounting for the gifts, you should talk to them. Yes, indeed, they are much closer to all of the gifts."

"It sounds to me like maybe you aren't in this loop at all," Wes told Charles.

Charles Black laughed a small, brittle sound that made Wes think of the gurgle that was referred to as a death rattle. He'd heard enough of those in his career that he wouldn't mistake it for something completely viable."You got that right. I'm a possession of the State, much like a desk or one of the buildings on campus. I guess it's the same with you guys but your owner is the city."

"You have a point there, Black. Now, even though you are *not* responsible for these funds, just for the record, tell us where the other $179,000,000 is that have been transferred to Georgia Tech Foundation from Hong Kong in the last few months? A straight answer will be just fine without all the options and footnotes," Wes' tone indicated that he was losing patience.

"I don't know," was Charles' tight response, "It's none of my business. The president has been quite emphatic that the Hong Kong money was his. He told me just to forget it and don't include it in any budget. Detective, there's no reason to question me. The responsibility is his; I guess his and Burl's. They were the masterminds of how their efforts would profit Tech and their own wallets. But, may I ask how this relates to the murder?"

"It may not relate at all. We'll decide later after we meet with the FBI."

"The FBI? Detective Wesley, if the FBI is involved, you must tell them that I only follow instructions. I don't want my career ruined because the president is a sleaze. Between his money manipulation and his fooling around with a coed, this jerk is a real slimeball. If you need someone to testify, you just call me. I know a lot....of course, I don't mean about the Hong Kong operation. But I know this isn't an honorable man. This story needs to be told…I mean, about him," Charles Black was talking faster and faster. He wanted to be sure that his ass was covered. He would divert their interest. He wasn't going to be caught in the middle when Lindholm was taking care of himself.

"Well, it sounds like the prez isn't gonna to be able to count on you. Your loyalty seems to end with the donors. Then, he may even be plannin' to dump some of this mess in your lap. Won't the bastard be surprised to know you already fingered him?" Billy Joe asked.

"He'd be the first to sell me, or even his wife, if he thought it would help him. I just got there before he did. I don't owe him anything. There's no loyalty on this campus. No one gives it and no one expects it. Sometimes I think of the whole campus as being poisoned. We might look like the fabled 'Halls of Ivy,'' but that's just an outsider's view.

"The trustees will continue to take care of me when they know the whole Lindholm story," Charles sounded almost proud that he could snitch on his boss and then added, "I'll make a great witness for you. I fit the part. Everyone says that I look like a person who can be trusted. That's a real advantage in court."

Chapter 59

Wes T. Wesley

Janeen laid her head on Wes' chest, feeling her hair touching against his chin. She moved her body closer to his as he held her gently. He felt her warmth through the delicate material of her silk shirt. The one thin layer of fabric between his hand and her bare back and breasts added to his sensual anticipation. If left up to him, he could erase the events of the day and concentrate fully on making love, but Janeen had too many questions that needed to be answered first. He contemplated matching his immediate agenda with hers. Certainly he could satisfy both.

"Waiting for you into the wee hours of the night is becoming a habit. I can't believe that it's already 1 o'clock and you've just closed your workday. You must be exhausted. How about some coffee or something? I can make you a sandwich."

"No way, Janeen. I don't want you to do anything that will move your gorgeous body even one inch from me. Just be here, not in the kitchen or any other place. We're going to relax here on the sofa, and I'll bring you up to date while I show you how much I love you," Wes was easing the two of them onto the soft cushions. He stretched out, tipped off his shoes and settled comfortably along the full length of the sofa. Janeen followed his lead and gave him a long, warm kiss before saying another word. His tongue explored her eager mouth and for a few minutes she, too, forgot about being interested in the eventful day.

"I don't believe that I think as clearly when you're so close," she whispered, "but I can still vaguely remember that you've had a busy day. So tell me what's happening."

"I'd rather just lie here and kiss you and touch you and look at you and smell you and taste you and then...."

"Put that on hold for a little while," Janeen broke in, "But not too long. There's not much left of the night."

Wes reviewed the day, starting with the morning and Lonnie's confession. Janeen asked a few questions as he proceeded but his recounting was quite complete. He'd been making and writing statements about cases for years so this was routine. He instinctively knew what details to include and what could be skipped over that didn't have great impact on outcome. He watched Janeen's face as he spoke and could see what surprised her and what she already knew or sensed. She was very observant in her job and her life and some of his words were definitely not revelations.

Wes stopped the flow of words and kissed her again. He was excited that her response had the same enthusiasm that he felt. He opened his eyes and studied her lovely face for a few moments. Her eyes were sharply delivering a message of sexual expectations.

As Wes quietly reviewed the day, he reached for the buttons of her shirt and unfastened them. He lowered his head until it rested between her breasts and Janeen could feel each word he spoke, "So when we left Charles Black's, Billy Joe and I went to the campus where you and Dixie were waiting with the trustees. They're an amazing group, and that statement includes the president and the vice president. From the outside, we all see great men who give so much to their institution and for each new generation of students. They collectively look like heroes but I guess there are always one or two in every group just looking out for number one."

Janeen had a response formed in her head, but as Wes trailed his tongue across her breasts and down the warm crevice between them, she thought only of Wes and being together. She heard a small sigh, which she realized was her own, brought her mind back to the conversation and said, "Wes, don't judge all alumni and staff by only a few men. I've been at Tech for more than twenty years and have seen true dedication and deep commitment. I saw a president actually give his life for Georgia Tech. Right now the campus just needs a different leader."

Janeen didn't want Wes to see only the negative facade that was now so visible. Her words were almost detached from the sexual sensations she felt as Wes touched her body with his hands, lips and tongue.

"The interviews with the finance committee were a revelation. Some had absolutely no inkling that anything was amiss. A few didn't seem to think it was all that bad when Tech got so much from the transfers. Then there were the ones who suspected that something was strange about the sudden windfall from Hong Kong and now want to do whatever needs to be done to undo the wrongs. Burl Mentor added that maybe he should have shared the California scandal with the board after he learned about it, but felt everyone deserves a second chance. Oh, yes, Mr. Mentor is such a fair person. Right? So fair that he didn't give his so-called commission to Tech. He just added it to his fortune."

Janeen had to strain to catch all of Wes' words as he spoke but continued to criss cross her body with his mouth. Sometimes she was sure she 'felt' the words rather than heard them. She wondered how he could appear to have such a clear mind when she could barely pay attention.

"Anyway, they all were very careful about what they said until Dixie started bearing in on them suggesting that the Hong Kong money might be directly tied to the motive for Andy's murder. That's when the perspiration popped, handkerchiefs appeared to blot foreheads and the steady eye contact that had been so benign began to waver. These guys aren't used to being in the hot seat. Although I bet they've been on the opposite end of similar scenarios a few times. We'll see how their stories hold up the next time we question them. Dixie says he thinks we've just scraped the surface with some fund manipulation and might find earlier deals. He's talked to a lot of other people so far and a real strong picture is developing."

Wes caressed her hip and then stroked the inside of her legs. He was very conscious of the contrast of materials from the smooth silk of Janeen's shirt and the rougher wool of her slacks. His hand stopped and rested on the button above the zipper of her tailored pants.

Almost unknowingly, he moved his fingers in a gentle massaging motion. Before adding to his narrative, he unbuttoned the waistband, lowered the zipper and slid Janeen's slacks down over her hips and legs. He felt his own arousal when he touched the smoothness of her body and saw the glow of her skin in the low light of the room.

"I knew the Hong Kong gifts were different than anything I'd ever seen, but I didn't suspect it was money laundering. That's something that I read about in the newspaper. I never imagined that I'd actually know people who were mixed up in it. Damn, I'm really dumb. This was all going on just a few feet from me, and I still saw it as a stroke of luck for Tech. I've been trusting people for so long that it's simply automatic."

"Don't change. You're a better person to believe in others. As you probably have learned, I'm just the opposite. I've seen every possible way that one person can do in another one. It's not a nice life out there, Janeen. Enjoy that you can still see the good in your friends and acquaintances. I think that's a wonderful gift. Cynicism sucks!" Janeen wasn't sure whether Wes was really talking to her or perhaps to himself. He'd seen so much of the ugly side of human beings. She wished that she could somehow help him see a better side to people.

"Someday when our minds are clearer, we can talk more about that. But right now, I have to concentrate on removing your clothes, because, Detective, you seem to have been able to give a full report and undress me at the same time."

"I'm just good, Sweetheart. It's a combination of duty and desire. Have no doubts, I'm making love to you. The words don't matter. It's how you hear them. If I place my lips against your ear and whisper what happened today, I hope you're hearing: Wes loves you and is almost as close as he can be... Almost."

"OK, Super Detective, let's see if your report changes pace if you're giving it buck naked!" Janeen laughed as she helped Wes take off his shirt.

"No problem, baby. My mind is clear as the Georgia clay on a rainy week. So you just listen as you struggle to get my pants off," Wes said with a bravado he didn't feel. He was indeed having a problem reviewing a day that no longer seemed critical. So he solved another case. Was that any big deal? "As you know, I left Tech and went to the hospital to see Walter. He's still shaky and floats in and out because of the crap they are pumping into him, but he knew who I was. We had a short conversation that took a long time. I was there at least an hour, but I believe he was brighter when I left than when I arrived."

Wes' words were muffled against Janeen's tummy. He'd been true to his word that he could keep his thoughts on track. The question was: for how long? He stopped speaking and sucked a spot just below her navel."I'm taking a break to put my mark on you. Like it or not you will now have an identifiable love-bruise so be cautious where you wear your bikini."

"Just keep talking, Detective, while I match you mark for mark. Your job is to tell your story and mine is to pick a special place for Janeen's Seal of Approval."

Wes looked up at Janeen and slid his body along hers until he was looking directly into her eyes, "You really know how to test a guy. You're making this very difficult. But I can do it, if you can."

As Wes again began to tell about Walter, he rested his hand on Janeen's head and twined her silky hair around his fingers, "I'm going to see that Walter wins for his loss of a friend and for taking a beating from the person who caused that loss. It's because of his information and actions that we have Lonnie's confession. The reward money will go to him. He's going to get off the streets with a bang," Wes caught his breath and said in a hoarse whisper, "Speaking of a bang..."

"Just tell your story, Wes. Don't be concerned about what else is happening."

"Yeah, right. Surely you jest. Ummm. OK. I don't have much more to say. Actually, I don't know if I *can* say much more. Back to Walter. I got Walter to agree that when he leaves the hospital, he'll stay with me a couple weeks until he's steady on his feet. Then he wants to take some more computer lessons and get a substantial job. He says that was what Andy had discussed with him, and he's not going to disappoint him. He can't change what's already happened, but he can change his own future. He was interested in not only what would happen to Lonnie Tedesco but how this would affect the president and Georgia Tech."

Wes was amazed that Janeen interrupted him, "That will first be a decision of the chancellor. He's going to be getting a big surprise or two."

"We're full of surprises tonight. Some of them relate to words, but it's getting too hard to concentrate, baby. It's time to just focus on non-verbal communication. Lovemaking involves the whole body and mind. Let's not miss any of the feelings, because we're still talking."

"OK, honey, my mind is closed to words, but the rest of me is open to you."

Epilogue

"BreakIn!"

The television screen screamed the words. For seven seconds all screens tuned into Channel 22 boldly announced the special feature. Regular watchers knew that something important had happened. They knew that one of the news anchors would appear immediately. Many stopped what they were doing and waited.

The camera zoomed in on Danielle Swain's lovely, radiant face. The Tech Tower majestically was projected in the background.

"Just weeks after Georgia Institute of Technology weathered the murder of one of its brightest students, Chancellor David Nathaniel Deck has accepted the resignations of President Jonathan Agnew Lindholm III and Vice President for Advancement Charles William Black. When asked for details, the spokesperson for the chancellor's office responded, 'No comment.'"

The image behind Dani changed to two middle age men in front of a desk and floor to ceiling bookshelves. They were shaking hands, smiling broadly as if they already knew the secret that Dani was about to announce.

"Deck has appointed R. Kurt Landman, CEO of Miami-based International Finance Group, Limited and past chairman of the Georgia Tech Advisory Board, as interim president.

"This is the time to reach beyond the campus for solid leadership. Mr. Landman is known for his excellent management skills, outstanding ability to relate to his personnel and effective skills to handle a company in crisis. His own actions earned national attention when his corporate headquarters were destroyed during Hurricane Andrew in 1994 but the corporation was back in full-scale operation within several days. Because of this experience, in 1995, Landman was invited to head up the United Nations Committee on International Crisis Aid."

When reached in his office and asked for a comment, Mr. Landman remarked, "I willingly accept the challenge of this interim position. Georgia Tech is a fine institution and will always stand above the people who manage its daily operations. We must never confuse the importance of the Institute with the individuals who are charged with its administration. Tech has already served and flourished for over 100 years. It will continue to do so for the next 100."

Again the screen became frantic with the big red "BreakIn!" logo, flashing lights and police siren. The news was over. The "BreakIn!" signature was already practicing for its next appearance.

Watch for The Bad Old Boys Club by B. B. Rose

A serial killer is loose in Atlanta. Surprisingly the victims are all prominent men who are used to running the city and being in the headlines. Their final headlines they will never see.

First published by Charles Skilton in 1952

This edition published 1992 by:
HAWK BOOKS LTD
Suite 309
Canalot Studios
222 Kensal Road
London W10 5BN

Copyright © 1992 Una Hamilton-Wright

ISBN 0 948248 63 7

All rights reserved. No part of this publication may be reproduced, stored in a retrieval system, or transmitted in any form or by any means, electronic, mechanical, photocopying, recording or otherwise without prior written permission of the copyright holder.

Printed in England by Redwood Press Ltd.

"WATCH HIM, TIGER!" THE KEEPER POINTED TO THE FAT JUNIOR ON THE BRANCH

Page 21

BILLY BUNTE
AND THE BL
MAURITIUS

By

FRANK RICHARDS

Illustrated by

R. J. MACDONALD

CONTENTS

CONTENTS

CHAPTER I

FOLLOW YOUR LEADER

"Buck up, Bunter!"

"Beast!"

"Put it on, old fat man!"

"Shan't!"

"Look here, you fat ass——"

"Yah!"

It sounded as if Billy Bunter was peeved.

And, in fact, he was!

Bunter was tired. And when William George Bunter was tired, peevishness was wont to supervene.

Six Greyfriars juniors were tramping along the tow-path by the Sark. The sun was sinking. The Sark ran like a stream of gold under the sunset. Shadows were lengthening in the woods along the river.

There was none too much time for Harry Wharton and Co. to reach Greyfriars, if they were to arrive at the school in time for calling-over. Nobody wanted to be late for roll, and face Mr. Quelch's gimlet-eye in his study afterwards. Five fellows were prepared to put their best foot foremost. One was not.

Billy Bunter generally modelled his pace upon that of the tortoise. Now he seemed to have modelled it upon that of a very old, very frail, and very tired tortoise.

Bunter had already walked half a mile. Half a mile, after a picnic up the river, was enough for Bunter. It was yet another mile to Greyfriars by the tow-path. In that mile there were one thousand seven hundred and sixty more yards than Bunter could contemplate with equanimity. It was no wonder that the fat Owl of the Remove was peeved.

Now even his tortoise-like progress had come to a stop. At a point where a leafy footpath led up through the woods from the river, he halted : and the urgings of the Famous Five passed him by like the idle wind which he regarded not.

"We shall be late for roll, if we hang about, Bunter," said Frank Nugent, mildly.

"Beast!"

"What the thump did you come for if you're too jolly lazy to walk home?" snorted Johnny Bull.

"If that's what you call civil, Bull, after asking a fellow to a picnic——"

"Nobody asked you, sir, she said!" sang Bob Cherry.

"Oh, really, Cherry——"

"There's too much of the picnic inside Bunter, for him to put on speed," said Bob, thoughtfully. "What about up-ending him, and rolling him home like a barrel?"

"Beast!"

"Look here, Bunter, step out," exclaimed Harry Wharton, impatiently. "Do you want lines from Quelch, you fat chump?"

Billy Bunter did not step out. He remained where he was, and jerked a fat thumb up the woodland footpath. That shady path wound through Popper Court Woods : forbidden territory to all inhabitants of the county of Kent outside Sir Hilton Popper's estate.

"Lots of time, if we take that short cut," said Bunter. "It cuts off more than half the distance."

"Out of bounds!" said Nugent.

"Never been out of bounds in your life, I suppose," jeered Bunter.

"We don't want a row with old Popper!" growled Johnny Bull.

"Blow old Popper!" yapped Bunter.

"Well, I suppose we might chance it," remarked Bob Cherry, glancing into the deep, dusky wood that bordered the tow-path.

Snort, from Johnny Bull!

"Oh, let's!" he said, "Let's trespass in old Popper's woods, and have him come yowling up to the school about it, and go up to the Head and explain that we did it because Bunter was too jolly lazy to walk a mile. Never mind if we get six all round from the Head. What does that matter ? "

This was sarcasm !

" The short-cutfulness is not the proper caper, my esteemed chums," said Hurree Jamset Ram Singh, with a shake of his dusky head. " The estimable and ridiculous Popper would be terrifically infuriated."

" Nobody's about," said Bunter.

" Might run into one of old Popper's keepers," said Bob.

" Who's afraid of old Popper and his keepers ? " sniffed Bunter. " I jolly well ain't, if you fellows are."

" You cheeky fat ass——! "

" Yah ! "

" Look here, come on," hooted Johnny Bull, " we're not going trespassing——"

" 'Tain't trespassing," said Bunter. " It's a right-of-way, only old Popper makes out that it ain't."

" It's out of bounds, anyway."

" Who cares ? "

" The carefulness would be terrific, my esteemed idiotic Bunter, if there was a report to our ludicrous head-master."

" Rot ! " said Bunter, " I say, you fellows, what you want is a spot of pluck."

" What ? " roared the Famous Five, with one voice.

" Pluck ! " said Bunter. " I'm ready to chance it. I ain't afraid of a keeper. I'd knock him down as soon as look at him. There's nobody about—I mean, I don't care a bean whether there's anybody about or not. Have a little pluck, and chance it. You'll be frightened of your own shadows, next."

Five separate and distinct glares were concentrated on the fat face of William George Bunter. The Famous Five of the Greyfriars Remove had, in fact, more than a little pluck : while that quality, in William George Bunter, could only have been discerned with the aid of a very powerful microscope. But Billy Bunter feared no foe, when no foe was in the offing. At that moment Bunter was thinking chiefly of an ache in his little fat legs, due to the extensive weight they had to carry. And there certainly seemed to be nobody about, in the silent and solitary wood. So—for the moment—Bunter was full of valour.

"You fat, frowsy, cheeky porpoise——!" said Bob Cherry.

"Yah!"

"If you saw a keeper a mile off, you'd bolt like a rabbit!" roared Johnny Bull.

"Yah!"

"We're not going out of bounds," said Harry Wharton. "Step out, Bunter."

"I'm going to take the short cut," said Bunter, obstinately. "If you fellows funk it——"

"Who funks it?" howled Johnny.

"You jolly well do!" retorted Bunter. "Look here, screw up your courage to the sticking-plaster, as Shakespeare says——"

"Oh, my hat!"

"Ha, ha, ha!"

"Blessed if I see anything to cackle at. Screw up your courage to the sticking-plaster——"

"Do you happen to mean the sticking-point?" asked Nugent.

"No, I don't! You can't teach me Shakespeare, Nugent. Look here, you fellows, screw up your courage to the sticking-plaster, and come on! I'm going."

"Look here, you fat ass——"

"Yah!"

"Stick to the tow-path——"

"Rats!"

"You blithering, burbling barrel——"

"You can call a fellow names," said Bunter, disdainfully, "but I'm going by the short cut, and you're too jolly funky. So yah!"

And Bunter settled the disputed point, by turning off

the bank, and rolling into the footpath through Popper Court Woods. Harry Wharton and Co. stared after him, as he rolled, and then looked at one another. Their looks were expressive. To be called funks by the fat and fatuous Owl was exasperating : to hang back where Bunter ventured to lead, was quite intolerable. Bob Cherry stepped into the footpath after the fat Owl.

"Come on !" he said.

"Rot !" growled Johnny Bull. "It means going up to the Head if we're spotted. Let's get on, and leave that fat ass to it."

"That's sense," agreed Harry Wharton. "But——"

"But——!" murmured Nugent.

"The butfulness is terrific," remarked Hurree Jamset Ram Singh.

"Can't let that fat frowster crow !" said Bob.

"Let him crow, and be blowed to him !" growled Johnny.

But Bob was already marching on, and Wharton, Nugent, and Hurree Singh followed. Johnny, with his usual solid common-sense, was undoubtedly right : but it was said of old that wisdom cries out in the streets and no man regards it. Four members of the Co. at least, were not going to be outdone by Billy Bunter : and Johnny, finding himself in a minority of one, grunted and followed on. The river was left behind, and six fellows threaded their way through the leafy wood : five of them with wary eyes open for keepers.

CHAPTER II

ONLY A FALSE ALARM

"HALLO, hallo, hallo!"

It was not Bob Cherry's usual cheery roar. It was a whisper.

Even the exuberant Bob realised the need for caution, in the heart of the deep wood surrounding Popper Court. The thick trees and bushes and drooping boughs that bordered the footpath might hide anyone within a yard or two. And it was a sound of rustling close at hand that caused Bob to halt, with that hurried whisper.

"Hold on!" breathed Harry Wharton.

"Oh, crikey!" mumbled Billy Bunter.

"Keep quiet, you fat ass."

"Oh, really, Wharton——"

"Shut up, you blithering owl!" hissed Johnny Bull.

"Beast!"

Bunter, however, shut up. So far, the fat Owl had rolled on, regardless of keepers, thinking only of getting in at Greyfriars in the shortest possible time, and bestowing his weary fat limbs in an armchair. But the sound of footsteps close at hand made quite a difference.

The fat Owl blinked at the wall of green beside the path, with his little round eyes popping behind his big round spectacles.

It dawned upon Bunter's fat brain that a burly keeper was not a trifle light as air, to be lightly disregarded. Billy Bunter's valour, in fact, lasted just so long as no danger was nigh. When danger accrued, it evaporated quite suddenly.

The juniors came to a halt, listening. Someone was close at hand in the wood, a little ahead of them. It could hardly be anyone but one of Sir Hilton Popper's keepers, so far as they could see.

Five fellows felt like kicking themselves. Still more they felt like kicking Bunter. They had let the fat Owl lead them into a spot of wholly unnecessary trouble, and, too late, they wished that they hadn't. But it was no time for kicking Bunter. Silence was essential.

No doubt it was true that there was a right-of-way through Popper Court Woods. Everyone believed so, excepting Sir Hilton Popper. But that did not alter the fact that Dr. Locke had placed the wood out of school bounds, to avoid friction with a local land-owner who was also a governor of the school. If the juniors were discovered there, it meant a report to their head-master, with a painful interview to follow. Nobody wanted that : least of all, Bunter, now that he came to think of it !

The rustling came nearer, as the juniors stood listening. If the unseen man in the wood was heading for the path, he would emerge into it a little distance ahead of them, and in a matter of moments. But there was a good chance that he might pass on without seeing them, in the dusky shade of the thick branches overhead : if they made no sound to draw attention. Five fellows stood as still as mice.

But one fellow did not.

" I say, you fellows——! " breathed Bunter.

" Quiet ! "

" But I say, let's bolt——"

" He will hear us, idiot ! Quiet ! "

" Beast ! "

Billy Bunter's eyes, and spectacles, fixed on a spot a little distance up the path, where low boughs swayed and rustled, and a glimpse of a form could be seen through the thickets. The man was emerging.

That glimpse was enough for Bunter.

The fat junior backed into the wood on the other side of the path, and plunged away among the trees.

A loud crackling and rustling accompanied his flight, echoing through the wood. Any keeper within a hundred yards could hardly have failed to take warning that trespassers were about.

"Oh! That funky fat ass——!" breathed Bob Cherry. "The game's up now."

"The upfulness is terrific."

"Oh!" exclaimed Harry Wharton, "it's not a keeper!"

The man ahead emerged into the footpath, as Billy Bunter crashed away into the wood on the other side. He turned quickly to stare in the direction of the juniors, with a startled stare.

That he was not a keeper was evident at a glance. He was a small, slim man dressed in dark clothes, with a spotted tie, a bowler hat a little on one side of a bullet head, a pasty-complexioned face adorned by a variety of pimples, and a cigarette, unlighted, hanging in one corner of a loose mouth. Nobody, in fact, could have looked more unlike a gamekeeper: which was a tremendous relief to the Greyfriars juniors. Apparently the man was simply some member of the public who was making his way through the wood—which did not matter in the least to Harry Wharton and Co.

But it was only for a moment, or little more, that they saw him. He gave them a startled stare, like an alarmed rabbit, and then backed quickly into the thickets from which he had emerged.

In a moment more, he was out of sight: and the sound of rustling dying away told that he was departing, in haste.

Bob Cherry chuckled.

"Only a false alarm!" he said. "That johnny was more startled than we were—he's trespassing too!"

The juniors laughed. Evidently the pimply man had been startled, indeed alarmed, at being seen, and they could only conclude that he was some trespasser as uneasy about keepers as themselves.

"For this relief, much thanks—Shakespeare!" said Frank Nugent. "But where's that fat idiot Bunter?"

"Oh, the ass!" said Harry.

"The benighted bandersnatch," said Bob. "He's gone!"

Bunter was gone—there was no doubt about that. In the belief that a keeper was at hand, the fat Owl had gone plunging frantically through the wood to escape, quite forgetting that he was tired. Somewhere in the deep wood, already at a distance from the footpath, was the terrified fat Owl, still on the run.

" The frabjous fathead ! " growled Johnny Bull. " That's the chap who was going to knock down a keeper as soon as look at him ! "

" Oh, the fat chump ! "

" The howling ass ! "

The juniors stood staring at the wall of greenery. There was nothing to keep them from going on their way, and getting out of those dangerous precincts—and delays were dangerous. But they were reluctant to go on without Bunter, exasperating as the fat Owl was.

" Shall I give him a shout ? " asked Bob.

" Oh, do," said Johnny Bull, sarcastically. " We want every keeper at Popper Court to gather round. Go it ! "

" The shoutfulness is not the proper caper," said Hurree Jamset Ram Singh. " Silence is the cracked pitcher that goes longest to a bird in the bush, as the English proverb remarks."

" Well, we can't go after him, and hunt him through the woods," said Bob, " and he jolly well won't come back, as he thinks that that pimply merchant was a keeper. So what ? "

" Push on," said Harry, at last, " Bunter will wriggle out somewhere, I suppose, sooner or later. Bother him, anyway."

" Bother him, bless him, and blow him, and then some ! " said Bob. " Come on—the sooner we're out of this, the better. The next johnny who shows up mayn't be a harmless trespasser. Put it on."

The Famous Five tramped on, putting on speed. Billy Bunter had to be left to his own devices. Ten minutes later they were glad to emerge into a lane, leaving the forbidden precincts of Popper Court Woods behind them. They walked on to Greyfriars—minus Bunter.

At the school gates they stopped, and looked back along the road. But there was no sign of a fat figure to be seen.

"That fat chump must have got out of the wood by this time," said Nugent.

"Must have," said Bob. "Even Bunter couldn't lose himself in Popper Court Woods. He'll come rolling home in time for call-over."

"Unless a keeper's got him," said Johnny Bull. "It would be like Bunter to run right into one."

"The likefulness would be terrific."

"Oh, he's all right," said Bob. "Bet you he'll come rolling into hall before Quelchy calls the names."

But in that the cheery Bob was mistaken. When Gosling clanged the gates shut, Billy Bunter was still outside them: and when Mr. Quelch called the roll in hall, the fattest member of his form failed to answer "adsum" to his name.

CHAPTER III

TREE'D

" OH, lor' ! " gasped Billy Bunter.

He came to a sudden halt.

The fat junior had run, stumbling and scrambling through tangled thickets, till his fat little legs could run no longer. Then he had dropped into a walk, peering round him through his big spectacles, like an alarmed and wary owl.

What had happened to the other fellows, Bunter did not know : and, sad to relate, did not care. He did not, in fact, give them a single thought. His presence of mind had, he had no doubt, saved him from the keeper : and all he had to do now, was to find his way out of the wood, and get clear. That was only a matter of time—if he did not run into a keeper !

Which, unfortunately, was exactly what Bunter did !

Coming round the massive trunk of a big oak tree, he came suddenly in sight of a burly figure in gaiters—not ten feet away from him. The stranger on the footpath hadn't been a keeper : but this man, undoubtedly, was one : and Bunter gasped and halted at the sight of him.

The man stood with his head a little bent, listening : no doubt having heard Bunter stumbling among the bushes. He saw Bunter at the same moment that Bunter saw him, and made a movement towards the fat junior of Greyfriars.

" Oh, crikey ! "

Bunter backed hastily round the oak he had just circumnavigated.

" Here ! Stop ! You ! " called out the keeper gruffly.

" Beast ! " groaned Bunter.

The man was tramping after him, round the big oak. Bunter would have fled, but there was not a run left in his little fat legs. In sheer desperation, he clutched at the gnarled trunk of the ancient oak, and climbed.

Billy Bunter was not much of a climber. It was not really easy to lift his avoirdupois. But the dread of a clutching hand behind spurred him on. How he got into the branches of that oak he hardly knew. But he did get into them, clambering frantically: and he was ten feet from the ground when the man in gaiters came tramping round the oak.

He lay extended on a stout branch, holding on with both fat hands, breathless and palpitating, with the perspiration trickling down his fat face. From the branch he blinked down through his spectacles at the top of a cap.

The man did not look up. He seemed puzzled, for the moment, by the sudden disappearance of the fat schoolboy, but did not immediately guess that he had taken to tree-climbing.

He stood almost directly under Bunter, staring round him, angry and frowning.

"Here, where are you?" he called out. "Where are you hiding, you young limb? I've got you all right."

Bunter hardly breathed.

He hoped that the keeper might proceed to search for him in the wood, which would give him a chance of dropping from the tree, and cutting off in the opposite direction. But the man remained where he was, staring round, and listening. He could hear no sound from the thickets, to indicate that a fat schoolboy was scuttling away. Finally, he looked up: and gave quite a start, at the sight of a fat face and a large pair of spectacles just over his head.

"Oh!" he ejaculated. "There you are!"

"Oh! No!" gasped Bunter. "I ain't here! I—I mean——"

"Come down out of that tree."

"Beast!"

"What?" ejaculated the man in gaiters.

" Beast ! "

Billy Bunter certainly had no intention of coming down. The keeper was quite near enough—he did not want him any nearer.

The man stood staring up. Bunter squatted on the branch, blinking down. There was a pause. The keeper looked at his watch. That was a hopeful sign, to Bunter. It looked as if the man had other business on hand, and was not disposed to hang about. If only he went, it was all right for Bunter. If once he got away, he could hardly be reported at Greyfriars, as the man did not know who he was.

" Look 'ere, you come down, you young scamp," said the keeper, at last. " I know you belong to the school."

" Oh ! Yes ! Highcliffe," said Bunter, astutely. He did not mind if Sir Hilton Popper carried a complaint to Highcliffe.

" 'Ighcliffe ? " snorted the keeper. " You got a Greyfriars cap."

" Beast ! "

" What's your name ? " demanded the keeper.

" Smith," answered Bunter.

The man eyed him suspiciously. Certainly, there was no reason why the fat schoolboy should not have borne the ancient and honourable name of Smith. But the man seemed to doubt.

" Gammon ! " he grunted.

" Beast ! "

" Look 'ere, I've got no time to waste on you," exclaimed the keeper, impatiently. " Come down out of that tree."

" Shan't."

" I'll take you to the master, and he'll find out what your name is soon enough," growled the keeper.

" I've told you what my name is," yapped Bunter, " and if you don't believe that my name's Jones——"

" Jones ! " ejaculated the keeper.

" I—I mean Smith," amended Bunter, hastily, " and if

you don't believe that my name's Jones—I mean, Smith—you can ask any fellow at Greyfriars—I mean Highcliffe——"

"Are you coming down ?" roared the keeper.

"No, I ain't."

The man glared up at him. He did not seem to fancy tree-climbing in pursuit of the fat schoolboy: but there was no other way of getting at Bunter. He glanced at his watch again, and Bunter's hopes rose. If only he went——!

"I tell you I got no time to waste 'ere," snapped the keeper. "I got to see the master, and I was going up to the 'ouse when I heard you rooting about. You come down out of that tree, and done with it."

If Billy Bunter had needed encouraging to stick where he was, that would have done it. He squatted tight.

The man gave him a glare, and seemed undecided. Finally he put his fingers to his lips, and emitted a shrill whistle.

"Oh, crikey!" gasped Bunter, in dismay.

He had no doubt that that whistle was a signal to another keeper. But the sound of a distant bark answered the whistle. It was not another keeper. It was a dog that came scampering through the bushes.

"Beast!" groaned Bunter.

"'Ere, Tiger," called out the keeper, and the dog came scampering up. He was a Yorkshire terrier, very lively, and full of beans. Bunter noted, without pleasure, that he had a fine set of teeth.

"Now, then, young feller-me-lad, you coming down ?" demanded the keeper. "If you don't, I'm leaving the dorg to watch you, and keep you safe till I come back."

"Oh, crumbs."

"Now, then, yes or no!" snapped the keeper.

"Beast!"

"You coming down ?"

"No!" yelled Bunter.

"That does it! Watch him, Tiger!" The keeper pointed to the fat junior on the branch, and Tiger barked, snapped his teeth, and pranced. "Watch him! You up there, if you come down while Tiger's watching, I'm sorry for your trousis!"

With that, the keeper tramped away, and disappeared into the wood, in the direction of Popper Court.

Tiger remained. He frisked about cheerily under the oak, evidently full of spirits, every now and then giving Bunter a look. The fat junior gazed down at him. If he had not been disposed to descend while the keeper was there, he was still less disposed to do so, with Tiger watching him. It would have been very unpleasant to be marched into the majestic presence of Sir Hilton Popper, with a report at Greyfriars to follow: but it would have been ever so much more unpleasant to drop within reach of the terrier's teeth.

Billy Bunter's last state, in fact, was worse than his first: as he realised when the keeper was gone. The long minutes passed, and the shadows deepened and deepened in the wood. Bunter realised that it was past the time for calling-over at Greyfriars. From the bottom of his fat heart, he repented him that he had insisted upon taking that short cut through Popper Court Woods. A short cut is sometimes the longest way round: but really this seemed to be the longest way round ever.

The hapless fat junior began to wish that the keeper would return. But the keeper did not return. Tiger, tired of frisking around, sat down, and kept a steady eye fixed on Bunter above. Gradually, as the shadows deepened into dark, Tiger became invisible, except for his eyes, steadily watching.

"Oh, lor'!" groaned Bunter.

He had missed lock-ups at Greyfriars—he had missed calling-over—now it was time for prep, and he was missing prep. He began to wonder, with dismay, whether he was going to miss dormitory too. If only that beastly dog would go——

But there seemed no hope of that. Darkness lay on the wood, black as a hat, but whenever the tree'd junior looked down, he discerned two greenish eyes glimmering in the dark, watching. And the hapless fat Owl could only groan, and wonder how it was going to end.

CHAPTER IV

TROUBLE FOR FIVE

" THAT fat ass ! "

" That fat chump ! "

" That podgy piffler ! "

" That bloated burbler ! "

" That terrific fathead ! "

Harry Wharton and Co. made those remarks, in the Remove passage, outside the doorway of No. 7 study. They were perturbed and exasperated. There was a small spot of anxiety, and a large spot of exasperation. It was after prep, and Bunter had not come in.

Bunter was well-known in the Greyfriars Remove to be every imaginable kind of an ass. But why even Bunter, ass as he was, should have stayed out of gates till such an hour, was quite a mystery. It was absurd to suppose that something might have happened to him. But if nothing had happened to him, why didn't he come in ?

He had cut roll, but it was not uncommon for fellows to be late for roll, and to be duly rewarded with lines. Now the Famous Five discovered that he had cut prep, which was a much more serious matter. They had gone up to their studies to prep, with little or no doubt that Bunter would roll in while they were thus engaged. But when, after prep, Wharton and Nugent came up the passage from No. 1 Study, Bob Cherry and Hurree Jamset Ram Singh came down the passage from No. 13, and Johnny Bull from No. 14, and they all looked into No. 7 to see whether Bunter was there, they found him not at home. Peter Todd and Tom Dutton, his study-mates, were there : but the fattest and most fatuous member of the Remove was conspicuous only by his absence.

To questions, Peter Todd could only reply that he hadn't

seen anything of Bunter. Bunter had cut prep. He hadn't come in. Hence the uncomplimentary remarks the Famous Five were making on the subject of the Owl of the Remove.

"The howling ass!" said Bob Cherry. "Could even Bunter lose himself in Popper Court Woods?"

"Might after dark——" said Nugent.

"But why should he stay there till dark?"

"Goodness knows."

"Might have been copped by a keeper," said Johnny Bull. "But he would be back before this, if that was it. Old Popper wouldn't keep him there."

"Bother him!"

"Blow him!"

"This means a row with Quelch," growled Johnny Bull. "If that fat ass doesn't blow in before dorm, we shall have to tell Quelch where we left him."

"Oh, the ass!"

"Oh, the chump!"

"We'll jolly well boot him, when he does blow in."

"The bootfulness will be terrific."

"But—I—I suppose nothing can have happened to him?" said Harry Wharton.

"What could?"

"Blessed if I know. He's ass enough for anything. It will mean a row if we have to tell Quelch that we came back through Popper Court Woods," said the Captain of the Remove. "Lines all round—after getting through all right!"

"Well, we've asked for that," said Johnny Bull. "We let that fat idiot bamboozle us into going out of bounds. We shouldn't have!"

"Not much use thinking about that now," said Nugent.

"It would have been of some use to think of it at the time! Didn't I tell you so?"

Four members of the Co. made no reply to that. Johnny Bull's common-sense had been disregarded at the time. It was really not much use "rubbing it in" now that it was too late. But tact was not included among Johnny's many good and solid qualities.

"I told you so," he went on, "and if you'd listened——"

"We didn't," said Bob Cherry, briefly.

"I know you didn't! But if you had——"

"If 'ifs' and 'ands' were pots and pans" remarked Nugent, "there'd be no work for tinkers. That's a proverb."

"If you had——!" repeated Johnny.

"Give us a rest, old chap."

"If you had——"

"My esteemed Johnny, if the if-fulness and the andfulness were the potfulness and the panfulness——"

"Well, I told you so," said Johnny, stolidly, "and if we have to go up to Quelch, we've got only ourselves to thank."

"Passed unanimously, and now give us a rest," said Bob Cherry. "By gum! Wouldn't I like to be just behind Bunter now, with my football boots on."

Vernon-Smith and Tom Redwing came out of No. 4 Study. They stopped, to look at the worried and disgruntled group in the passage.

"Anything up?" asked Smithy.

"Bunter hasn't come in yet," answered Harry Wharton.

The Bounder raised his eyebrows.

"Does that matter?" he inquired.

"Well, it does, as we lost him on the way back," answered Harry. "We shall have to tell Quelch where we lost him, if he doesn't turn up soon."

"You see, we let the fat cormorant hook on to our picnic up the river," said Johnny Bull, "and he was too jolly lazy to walk home. So he took the short cut through old Popper's woods, and we were asses enough not to leave him to it."

"Must have been asses," agreed Smithy.

"Well, I told these fellows so——"

"Is that nineteen or twenty?" asked Bob Cherry.

Johnny stared at him, blankly.

" Nineteen or twenty what ? " he asked.

" Nineteen or twenty times you've told us you told us so ? "

Grunt, from Johnny Bull.

" Well, I jolly well did tell you so——"

" That's twenty, at least," said Bob, " and that's the limit. If you tell us again that you told us so, we'll jolly well bang your head on the wall."

" Hard," said Nugent.

Another grunt from Johnny ! But he refrained from stating for the twenty-first time that he had told his friends so.

" Let's go down," said Harry, " may hear that the benighted bandersnatch has blown in."

The Famous Five went down to the Rag, where most of the Remove gathered after prep. But among the crowd of juniors, Billy Bunter did not appear.

As the minutes ticked on to bedtime, five members of the Remove grew more and more uneasy.

How any accident could have happened to Bunter in Popper Court Woods, they could not imagine. But if nothing had happened, where was he, and why did he not come in ? It was certain that, if any Greyfriars man did not turn up at bedtime, there would be a spot of commotion. The Famous Five would have to state what they knew. That meant admitting that they had gone out of bounds, with a " row " as the result.

It was not a pleasing prospect.

They were getting anxious about Bunter, wondering uneasily what on earth could be keeping him out of gates. At the same time they were yearning to kick him for causing so much worry and trouble. With these mingled feelings, they heard nine o'clock chime out from the clock-tower—and still there was no Bunter.

At a quarter past nine, Wingate of the Sixth looked into the Rag, and glanced over the juniors there. Evidently, inquiry on the subject of the missing Owl was beginning.

" Any fellow here know where Bunter of the Remove is ? " called out the prefect. " He hasn't come in."

There was no reply. Nobody knew where Bunter of the Remove was.

" Was any fellow here out of gates with him after class ? "

There was no help for it, and Harry Wharton replied :

" Yes : Bunter was up the river with us, Wingate."

" Didn't he come back with you ? "

" Um ! Only part of the way."

" You'd better go and tell Quelch. He wants to know."

" All right."

Five fellows, not in a happy mood, made their way to the Remove master's study. It was only ten minutes now to dormitory : and obviously their Form-master had to know what they could tell him on the subject.

They found Mr. Quelch frowning in his study. The vagaries of the troublesome Owl did not seem to have improved his temper. A pair of gimlet-eyes fixed sharply on the chums of the Remove as they presented themselves.

" Bunter is still absent, Wharton," said Mr. Quelch. " Do you know anything about it ? "

" He was out of gates with us, sir, but came only part of the way back with us," answered Harry. " He left us about half a mile from the school."

" Indeed ! Exactly where did you part company ? " asked Mr. Quelch.

Again there was no help for it !

" On the footpath in Popper Court Woods, sir."

Mr. Quelch's face, already frowning, became very grim.

" Wharton ! You are aware that Popper Court Woods are out of bounds for Greyfriars boys. You are Head Boy of my form : expected to set a good, not a bad, example to other boys. Yet you tell me——"

Harry Wharton crimsoned with discomfort.

" You have been out of bounds," exclaimed Mr. Quelch

" Yes, sir."

" I am surprised at you, Wharton ! I am very much

surprised, and very displeased. I should not have expected this of you," snapped Mr. Quelch.

Wharton made no answer to that. He could not explain to Quelch, that the obstinate fat Owl had taken the bit between his teeth, as it were, and that the others had followed where he led. Neither would it have been of any use : for obviously they should not have followed. In fact, Johnny Bull had told them so !

" Why did Bunter leave you ? " asked Mr. Quelch, in the same snappish tone.

" He fancied that a keeper was coming, and bolted into the wood, sir."

" Upon my word ! Then that must be the reason why he has not returned—he is doubtless lost in the wood," exclaimed Mr. Quelch, angrily. " This is very serious, Wharton ! You are very much to blame for having gone out of bounds, in company with a foolish and thoughtless boy like Bunter."

Wharton was silent.

" I shall have to see what can be done," snapped Mr. Quelch. " You may go now. Each of you will take three hundred lines. Leave my study."

In silence the hapless five left the study. They went down the passage with very expressive faces. A " jaw " for Wharton, and three hundred lines all round, was their reward for having followed Bunter's lead. At the moment, they had no sympathy to waste on a woeful fat Owl wandering in a wood. They were simply yearning to kick Bunter.

" The fat chump ! " breathed Bob Cherry.

" The dithering dummy ! " hissed Nugent. " We ought to have booted him, instead of following his lead."

" The oughtfulness is terrific."

" Well, I told you so, at the time," said Johnny Bull. " We've asked for this, and got it. I told you——"

" Did you say you told us so ? " asked Bob Cherry in a sulphurous voice.

" Yes, I did, and—yarooooh ! "

Four pairs of hands grasped Johnny Bull, as if four fellows had been suddenly moved by the same spring. After that interview with Quelch, patience seemed to have run rather short, in the Co.—and Johnny's reference to the undoubted fact that he had told them so, was the last straw. They grasped Johnny Bull, and banged his head on the passage wall. Crack!

"Yaroooh!" roared Johnny. "Look here—oh, crumbs—wow—you mad asses—leggo—wow——!"

Four fellows walked on, Johnny Bull followed, rubbing his head, in indignant wrath. However, he did not mention again that he had told them so!

CHAPTER V

LOST

BILLY BUNTER groaned.

Only by a dismal groan was Bunter able to express his feelings.

How long he had been parked in that oak tree Bunter did not know. It seemed rather like centuries to him. He had not the remotest idea of the time. Bunter had a watch—quite a massive affair : but it was useless to him for two good reasons : it did not " go " : and it was too dark to see the dial, even if it had been a going concern. Darkness lay like a pall of black velvet on the woods, and the hapless fat Owl could see nothing, except the greenish glimmer of eyes from the blackness below, of Tiger patiently watching.

He dared not descend with Tiger on the watch. He straddled a branch, his plump back leaning on the gnarled trunk of the oak, and waited. There was nothing for Bunter to do but to sit it out. He began to long for the keeper's return. Lines from Quelch, even " six " from his form-master's cane, would have been ever so much better than this. If that beastly keeper would only come back, and call off his beastly dog——!

It was a great relief when, at last, a sound of rustling in the wood announced that someone was coming. Then he heard the gruff voice of the keeper.

" Tiger ! "

A cheery bark replied.

Bunter blinked down. He could barely make out the burly form of the keeper in the deep gloom. The man was staring up.

" My eye ! You still there, you young limb ? " he exclaimed.

" Oh, crikey ! "

" Getting tired of that tree ? " asked the keeper, sarcastically. " Think you'd better come down ? "

Bunter, undoubtedly, thought that he had better come down. He was more than tired of the oak tree. But Tiger's bark was not reassuring.

" I say, keep that beastly dog off ! " he gasped. " I'll come down, if you'll keep that rotten dog off."

" O.K. ! Kennel, Tiger," said the keeper, and Bunter, with immense relief, heard the terrier scamper away through the wood.

The fat junior clambered down. It was really an easy climb down a thick gnarled trunk, but it was like Bunter to miss his hold, and roll down. He landed with a bump almost at the keeper's feet.

" Ow ! " howled Bunter. " Wow ! "

" Clumsy young idjit ! " said the keeper, doubtless by way of sympathy.

" Ow ! Beast ! Wow ! "

A powerful hand on a fat shoulder jerked Bunter to his feet.

" Now, then, come on," grunted the keeper. I've told the master there's a trespasser in the wood, and I got to take you to him. 'Op it."

" I say, what's the time ? " gasped Bunter.

" Turned half-past nine."

" Oh, crikey ! That's after dorm ! " groaned Bunter. " I—I say, I—I've got to get back to the school—I shall get into a fearful row——"

" You got to see Sir 'Ilton first," said the keeper, stolidly. " Come on with you, you trespassing young rascal."

Bunter had to come on, with that sinewy hand on his fat shoulder. He could not see a yard before his spectacles, but the keeper seemed able to thread his way with ease through the shadowy wood, and he led Bunter on without a pause, winding among the trees and thickets. But although the fat Owl could see nothing, he could guess easily enough that he was being led up to the house, where he was to face the lord and master of Popper Court. That prospect filled him with dread. It was not of much use to tell Sir Hilton Popper that his name was Smith or Jones, or that he belonged to Highcliffe: as Sir Hilton knew him by sight. But now that Tiger was off the scene, Bunter's hope of escape revived.

The keeper kept a grip on his shoulder, prepared for an attempt to dodge away in the dark. The fat Owl stumbled along by his side, till a distant gleam of lighted windows through the night showed that they were nearing Popper Court. Billy Bunter breathed hard through his fat little nose. If he could elude that grip on his podgy shoulder for even a moment, it would be all right. Once he was on the run, the keeper would never be able to find him in a thick wood as black as a hat.

Suddenly Bunter stumbled over, and fell. His fat shoulder slipped from the keeper's hand: but the man bent over him at once.

"Now, then, up with you, you clumsy young hass," he growled. And he grasped the fat shoulder again.

"Ow! wow! I've sprained my ankle," howled Bunter.

"Oh, rubbish!" growled the keeper. "Gerrup!"

"Ow! I—I can't get up!" yelled Bunter. "Wow! The pain's fearful. Ow! You'll have to carry me! Ow!"

"My eye! I can see myself doing it," snorted the keeper. "You look as if you weigh 'arf a ton. Look 'ere, gerrup with you."

"Oh, dear! I c-c-can't! My ankle's sprained," wailed Bunter. "Ow! It's like red-hot daggers—wow!"

"Rubbish!"

The keeper, grasping the fat shoulder hard, heaved. Bunter made no effort to rise, and his whole extensive weight was thrown on the keeper, who gasped as he heaved. Bunter, at last, was heaved to his feet, whereupon he immediately fell down again.

"Oh, corks!" gasped the keeper. "You weigh something, you do. Look 'ere, if your ankle's really 'urt——"

"Ow! ow! ow!" wailed Bunter.

"Blow my buttons!" said the keeper. He released his grasp of the fat junior at last, and stood looking down at him, puzzled what to do. "Bother you, you young rascal, giving a man all this trouble."

"Ow! ow! ow!"

"Oh, pack it up," growled the keeper. "I got to get you to the 'ouse somehow. Sir 'Ilton he says, bring him 'ere, he says, and I got to, and that's that. Look 'ere, you can lean on me and 'op it, see?"

"I—I—I c-c-can't!"

"I'm going to pull your ears if you don't," said the keeper.

"I—I mean, I—I'll try."

"You better," said the keeper.

Bunter was heaved up again. This time he stood on one leg, leaning heavily on the burly man, and holding to him.

"Now 'op it!" growled the keeper. "Come on! 'Old on to me and 'op it, blow you. 'Old on to my arm—like that—why—what—— Oh, corks!—you young villain you——" The keeper gave a roar of wrath, as he was suddenly relieved of Bunter's weight, and the fat junior shot away in the dark.

The sprained ankle, evidently, was a work of fiction! Bunter had only wanted to get loose from that sinewy grasp: and now he was loose from it. Seldom did Billy Bunter put on speed: but an arrow in its flight had nothing on the fat Owl, as he shot away into the wood.

For a moment, the exasperated keeper stood staring, as he realised that his leg had been pulled, and that, so far from being incapacitated, his prisoner was remarkably active! Then, with an angry snort, he plunged into the dark wood after Bunter.

Bunter ran hard.

He bumped into trees, he stumbled over roots, he tore through thickets, gasping for breath, heedless of scratches.

He could not see where he was going—neither could the keeper see him. It was only by sound that the man was able to follow. Bunter puffed and blew as he fled. His wind, always a little short, was failing him fast. But the crashing of the keeper in pursuit spurred him on. The man was after him—Bunter could hear him—and every moment he dreaded to be clutched from behind. With perspiration streaming down his fat face, his spectacles aslant on his fat little nose, Bunter charged desperately on, gurgling for breath, till suddenly, his feet catching in a sprawling root, he went over headlong. He rolled into a mass of hawthorns, spluttering. He would have scrambled up and carried on—but every ounce of breath was out of him now, and he could not. He lay in the hawthorns quite spent.

Had he been aware of it, it was the best thing he could have done. It was only by the sound of crackling bushes that the keeper was following him. As soon as Bunter lay still, that guiding sound was lost, and the keeper came to a halt. Bunter, as he lay gasping, heard him move again—but he moved in another direction, at a loss. Then the fat Owl heard his voice :

" You young rascal ! Where are you ? "

" Oh, crikey ! " breathed Bunter.

He realised that the keeper had lost the track. All he had to do was to remain still, without a sound. He remained still, hardly breathing, and listened.

For a good many minutes, he heard sounds from the keeper, as the man tramped to and fro, hunting for him in the dark. But the sounds died away at last. Such a search was hopeless, so long as the quarry kept quiet : and the man gave it up. Silence had never seemed so golden, to Bunter, as it did, when the last sound from the keeper died away in the dark wood.

The fat Owl sat up. But he did not stir further, till more than ten minutes of silence had elapsed, and he was assured that the coast, at last, was clear. Then he crawled out of the hawthorns.

Bunter was feeling considerably cheered. All he had to do now was to walk out of the wood, and trot on to Greyfriars. Certainly, a spot of trouble there awaited a fellow who rolled in after every other fellow had gone to bed. But Bunter had his excuses ready—he had lost his way in a wood—not Popper Court Wood—and Quelch could hardly come down heavily on a fellow who had had such an awful experience. He might even be sympathetic! Bunter hoped that that astute yarn would pull him through with Quelch. And he set out to walk out of the wood!

In the daylight, even Bunter could have done so with success. But he now made the interesting discovery that darkness made a tremendous difference. He tramped on in what he supposed to be the direction of Greyfriars, till he suddenly came in sight of distant lighted windows and realised that he was heading for Popper Court, the residence of Sir Hilton Popper. He blinked in dismay at those distant lights, and changed his direction, and the dark woods swallowed him up once more. Onward he dragged his weary fat limbs, winding among dark bushes and bewildering trees, but he did not reach Oak Lane, or the road, or anything else but shadowy trees and thickets.

And at length it dawned upon his fat brain that he could not find his way out of the wood in the dark! The yarn he had intended to spin Mr. Quelch was, in fact, true—Bunter was lost in a wood! He was wandering at haphazard in the dark, without the faintest idea where he was—the lane might be within a few yards, or it might be a mile off—he might be heading for Greyfriars, or he might be turning his plump back on the school—Bunter didn't know and couldn't tell!

The dismal Owl, tired in every fat limb, came to a dismal halt, and leaned on a tree, and groaned. Once more, he would have been glad to see even the keeper! But there was no sight or sound of the keeper. He was alone in the wood in the dark night: utterly lost! And he leaned on the tree and groaned. Then, too weary to make another effort, he slid down into a sitting position, and leaned his back on the trunk.

From somewhere in the far distance a chime came through the night. It was midnight.

"Oh, lor'!" mumbled Bunter. And his eyes closed behind his spectacles.

CHAPTER VI

BILLY BUNTER'S NIGHT OUT

"This way!"

"I saw him——"

"Follow me!"

"This way. This way!"

"There he goes!"

"This way!"

How long Billy Bunter's little round eyes had been shut behind his big round spectacles, he did not know. Loud sounds of crashing in the under-woods, and shouting voices, startled him out of the slumber into which he had fallen, and he sat bolt upright, blinking round him like a startled owl.

For a moment or two, he wondered where he was, and whether he had been dreaming, and was still in a dream.

Then he remembered that he was lost in the wood. But the dark, silent wood in which he had sunk down to slumber was no longer silent, and not so dark. Lights flashed before his dazzled eyes, and voices shouted, footsteps thudded, bushes crackled and crashed. Men, shouting to one another, were running to and fro: and among three or four breathless voices, Bunter, as he gathered his fat wits, recognized the sharp, strident tones of Sir Hilton Popper, which he had heard a good many times before.

He sat and blinked in amazement.

What was going on, he had not the faintest idea. He remembered that he had heard the chime of midnight before he closed his eyes; so it must be some time past midnight now. Such an outbreak of excitement, after midnight, in the dark and lonely wood, was enough to make the dizzy fat Owl wonder whether he was still dreaming.

But it was no dream!

Men with lanterns or flash-lamps were running about. In the light of a lantern, Bunter caught a sudden sight of Sir Hilton Popper—long, lean, with a leathery brown face, and sharp eyes. But he saw that the baronet of Popper Court was not dressed with his usual meticulous care. He was bare-headed : the neck of a pyjama jacket showed over the collar of a half-buttoned coat, and he had a boot on one foot, and a shoe on the other. Sir Hilton looked as if he had been suddenly roused from bed, and had thrown on the first garments that came to hand.

His mastiff face was red with excitement and anger. He was brandishing a big stick, as the light fell on him. Bunter blinked at him in terror.

Then the light passed, and Sir Hilton was lost in shadow again. But the fat Owl heard his voice, on its top note.

" Did you see him ? Hansom—Jenkins—Joyce—where is the rascal ? He has the stamp—I tell you, he has stolen the stamp—do not let him escape——"

" This way, sir ! " shouted a gruff voice, which Bunter recognized as that of the keeper whose acquaintance he had recently made.

" Jenkins ! Did you see him, Jenkins ? "

" Yes, sir ! This way."

More trampling of feet, rustling and crackling of bushes, and excited shouting. Bunter blinked and listened in quite a daze.

Evidently, they were searching for somebody. Bunter had dreaded, for a moment, that they might be in search of him. But he realised that it was not that. Somebody, according to Sir Hilton's words, had stolen a stamp—though why the baronet and his household should turn out in the middle of the night, in such a state of excitement, on account of a stamp, was quite a mystery to Bunter.

They had not come near enough to discern the fat junior sunk in grass and ferns close to the trunk of a shadowy tree. The chase passed quite close to him, and thundered on into the wood.

"Oh, crikey!" breathed Bunter.

Somebody, who had apparently stolen a stamp, was running, and Sir Hilton and his followers were in fierce pursuit of him: that much was clear to Bunter. And the fat junior picked himself up, to move away, and keep clear of them. They had not seen him: and the sound of the hunt was now at a little distance. Bunter turned his back on that sound, and groped away in the dark. Distant voices echoed through the wood, more faintly now to his fat ears. He groped hurriedly on.

The fat junior found himself in an open glade, where the branches were not so thick above, and a glimmer of starlight came through. But it was not light enough for him to see his way, even if he had known which way to go. He stood in the glade, blinking round him: when suddenly, the crashing of the hunt drew nearer again—crackling bushes, thudding footsteps, shouting voices: all sweeping through the darkness towards the hapless Owl.

No doubt the fugitive, whoever he was, had dodged his pursuers, and doubled back. But they were after him swiftly.

A shadow loomed up in the dusky glade. Bunter's startled blink fell on a dim figure—that is a running man, with a set desperate face, panting and panting for breath, running as if for his life, directly towards the fat junior.

Close behind the running man, came the roar of the hunt, filling the wood with din.

Bunter blinked at that desperate running figure in the dim starlight that filtered through branches overhead. But he had only a glimpse of it. For the next moment, the running man crashed fairly into him, and the fat Owl, with a gasping yell, went spinning, and rolled over. The running man, even more taken by surprise than Bunter by that sudden collision, sprawled headlong over him, winded to the wide.

"Oooogh!" spluttered Bunter. "Ow! Help! Yaroooh! Woooh! Help! Oh, crikey!"

"This way!" came a roar from Sir Hilton Popper.

"Quick: I see him—by gad! there are two of them—quick—seize him——"

The winded man, groaning for breath, struggled off Bunter. But he had no chance. Before he could gain his feet, the hunters were on the spot. Lanterns and flash-lamps concentrated on him: hands grasped him on all sides: and as he feebly resisted, his arms grasped by Jenkins and Joyce, Sir Hilton Popper brandished the big stick over his head.

"Ow! ow! wow!" Bunter sat up. "Ow! wow! Where's my specs? Mind you don't tread on my specs——!"

"Secure him!" roared Sir Hilton Popper, heedless for the moment of Bunter. "Hold him fast! Rascal! Attempt to resist and I will stun you!"

"We got him, sir," said Jenkins.

"Got him safe, sir," said Joyce.

The wretched man seemed safe enough, with a burly keeper grasping either arm, and two or three men gathering close round him. Sir Hilton's big stick was not needed, and he lowered it.

"Ow! Look out! Where's my specs?" howled Bunter.

Sir Hilton, assured that the hunted man was safe, bestowed an angry and astonished glance on the fat Owl.

"Who is this?" he rapped. "He looks like a schoolboy—— Boy! Stand up! Who are you? An accomplice of this burglar, hey?"

"Oh, crikey!" gasped Bunter.

All the party, even the prisoner, were staring at the fat Owl, as he groped in the grass for his spectacles, knocked off in the collision. Recognition came into Jenkins' face.

"That's the boy I told you of, Sir Hilton," he said. "The young trespasser."

"Oh! That young rascal!" exclaimed Sir Hilton. "Still in my woods—after my birds, I suppose. What? what? What are you groping there for, you young scoundrel? What?"

"Ow! My specs!" wailed Bunter. A glimmer of lantern-light caught the lenses of the spectacles in the grass, and Bunter spotted them, and grabbed them up. He jammed them on his fat little nose and blinked at Sir Hilton Popper. The long lean baronet frowned down on him.

"I've seen you before," he snapped. "I think I know you—you are a Greyfriars boy—your name is Grunt—or Hunt—or Shunt—what is your name?"

"Oh, crikey! Bunter, sir," groaned the fat Owl. "That beast ran into me and knocked me over—ow!"

The prisoner in the grasp of the keepers gave him a glare. He was a squat, low-browed man, with a most unpleasant face, and Bunter, as he blinked at him, edged a little further away. He did not like that man's looks at all.

"You silly young 'ound!" said the prisoner, in concentrated tones. "If I'd a 'and loose, I'd wring that fat neck of yourn. I'd 'ave got clear if you 'adn't been in the way! Blow yer!"

"Silence, you!" rapped Sir Hilton Popper. "Hold him, Jenkins, Joyce! He has the stamp—I know that he has the stamp—hold him while I search him for the stamp."

Why the lord of Popper Court was so deeply concerned about a stamp, was still a mystery to Bunter. But it was clear that he was very deeply concerned indeed, as he proceeded to search the prisoner. The man made no resistance, only giving Bunter evil looks: evidently attributing his capture to the fat junior who had been so unexpectedly in his line of flight.

There was a sudden exclamation from Sir Hilton Popper. It was almost a crow of relief and satisfaction. Something that he had taken from the prisoner was in his brown palm. It looked to Bunter like a postage-stamp, so far as he could see it. Whatever it was, it obviously afforded the lord of Popper Court the greatest and deepest satisfaction.

"This is it! Show the light here, Hansom! Yes, yes, this is it! Take that rascal away—he must be handed over to the poliee—I shall charge him, by gad! Grunter!"

He turned to the fat junior. " Grunter—did you say your name was Grunter——? "

" Bib-bob-Bunter, sir."

" Yes, yes, I mean Bunter. Bunter, you have been caught trespassing in my woods—you are a young scoundrel, Bunter. What are you doing here at this time of night ? After my birds, what—what ? Poaching young scoundrel ! What ? "

" Ow ! No ! " gasped Bunter. " I—I lost my way—I —I couldn't get out of the wood—oh, lor' ! "

" What ? What ? " From his height, nearly a couple of feet over Bunter's fat head, the lord of Popper Court stared down at him. " Lost your way ! Gad ! The boy is a fool—an idiot—a nincompoop ! "

" Oh, really, sir——"

" However, you have been partly the means of catching this rogue who burgled my house, Stunter. I shall overlook your rascality for that reason, Stunter. Did you say your name was Stunter ? "

" B-b-b-b-Bunter, sir."

" Oh ! Yes ! Follow me, Stunter—I mean, Grunter—that is, Bunter—follow me, and I shall send you back to Greyfriars. You are a young rascal, Gunter, but I shall pardon you, in the—the circumstances. Take care of that scoundrel, Jenkins—keep safe hold of him, Joyce—keep an eye on him, Hansom ! Punter, you young rascal, follow me."

Billy Bunter rolled after the baronet, as the party headed for Popper Court. His night out was over at last !

CHAPTER VII

BUNTER TELLS THE TALE

"HALLO, hallo, hallo!" murmured Bob Cherry, drowsily.

He opened his eyes, as the light flashed on in the Remove dormitory. Several other fellows awakened, at the sound of footsteps and voices. It was a couple of hours after midnight, and the Remove had been fast asleep, when the door opened, and Mr. Quelch came in with Billy Bunter.

"Lose no time, Bunter," said Mr. Quelch, in a voice rather like the filing of a saw. Quelch, plainly, was not in a good temper.

"Oh! Yes, sir," mumbled Bunter. "I—I say, sir, it—it's awfully late——"

"I am aware of that, Bunter. You need not speak."

"I—I mean, sir, m-m-may I stay in bed after rising-bell——"

"You may not, Bunter," answered Mr. Quelch, grimly.

A dozen fellows sat up in bed, staring. Bunter, evidently, had got home at last. Apparently Quelch had sat up for him: which accounted for the exceedingly grim expression on his speaking countenance. It was not a light matter for a hardworking form-master to sit up till two in the morning, waiting for a wandering Owl to roll in.

It was a relief to Harry Wharton and Co. to see the fat Owl, safe and sound. Evidently nothing had happened to him. They did not venture to speak while Mr. Quelch was present: and Bunter lost no time turning in: Quelch did not look as if he had much patience to waste on him.

In a few minutes, the light was switched off again, and the door closed on the Remove master. Then five or six voices were heard at once.

"Bunter, you fat ass——"

"You benighted owl——"

" Where have you been all this time ? "

" You potty porpoise——"

" You terrific fathead——"

" I say, you fellows, it's all right," said Bunter. " I can tell you I'm jolly sleepy. But it's all right. I say, did that keeper get you ? "

" It wasn't a keeper, fathead—only some chap taking his pimples for a walk," said Bob Cherry. " If you hadn't bolted, it would have been all right."

" Oh ! I thought it was a keeper ! I say, you fellows, I've had an awful time. But it turned out all right. I got lost in the wood after dark——"

" What the thump did you stay in the wood till dark for, you fathead ? "

" How could I help it, when I was up a tree, and a beastly keeper set his dog to watch me ? " demanded Bunter.

" Oh, my hat ! "

" After that he came back, and walked me off," went on Bunter. " Only I got away."

" Knocked him down as soon as looked at him ? " inquired Johnny Bull, sarcastically.

" Exactly," said Bunter.

" Wha-a-t ? "

" Fat lot I care for keepers," said Bunter disdainfully. " He had hold of my shoulder. I gave him a punch, and hooked it. He didn't let go because he thought I'd sprained my ankle, or anything. I just knocked him over, and went."

" Ha, ha, ha ! "

" You can cackle," said Bunter, warmly. " But I'll bet any of you fellows would have thought twice before knocking a keeper over——"

" And you'd have thought three times, or three hundred, you fat Ananias," said Bob Cherry.

" Oh, really, Cherry——"

" Well, I'm glad you've got home all right," said Bob. " But I've a jolly good mind to get up, and kick you all round the dorm."

" Beast ! "

" Didn't Quelch whop you ? " asked Vernon-Smith.

" No jolly fear ! " said Bunter. " Quelch has let me off ! You see, he practically had to, old Popper being a governor of the school, and putting in a word for me."

" Popper did ! " exclaimed a dozen fellows.

" Yes, rather ! He's a crusty old bean," said Bunter. " Still, there is such a thing as gratitude, you know, and after I'd caught the burglar for him——"

" After you'd whatted the whatter ? " howled Bob Cherry.

" The burglar——"

" What burglar, you howling ass ? "

" Oh ! I haven't told you that bit yet," said Bunter. " You see, there was a burglary at Popper Court—an awful ruffian broke into the place and pinched a stamp——"

" A stamp ? " gasped Bob.

" Yes—that was what old Popper said ! I thought it was an awful fuss to make over a stamp, but that was what he said. He was frightfully excited about it. From what I heard, they seem to have got after the burglar just as he was getting away with the stamp——"

" Penny one ? " asked Johnny Bull, with a snort.

" I don't know whether it was a penny stamp or a two-penny one, Bull. I know that old Popper was boiling over about it. He was awfully grateful when I caught the burglar, and he got it back."

" So you caught the burglar, did you ? " chuckled Vernon-Smith. His chuckle was echoed up and down the row of beds. The Remove fellows could not quite picture William George Bunter catching burglars !

" I jolly well did ! " declared Bunter, " and this is how it happened. I fell asleep under a tree——"

" That sounds true," remarked Peter Todd. " You'd fall asleep anywhere."

" Oh, really, Toddy——"

"And when you'd fallen asleep, you dreamed that you'd caught a burglar?" asked Skinner.

"I jolly well did caught him—I mean catched him—I mean——"

"Ha, ha, ha!"

"I was woken up by an awful row going on—old Popper, and three or four keepers and footmen, with lanterns and things, chasing after that burglar. He would have got away but for me. Seeing him coming, I leaped at him——"

"We can see you doing it!" remarked Skinner.

"Sort of!" chuckled the Bounder.

"Well, I jolly well did! Leaping at him like a—a tiger, I bore him to the earth, and shouted 'This way! I've got him!' Then they all came up and collared him! Mind, the burglar never fell over me in the dark, or anything like that! I sprang at him like a—a lion, and held him till they came up. Old Popper put his hand on my shoulder, and said 'Splendid! Plucky lad!' Those were his very words. I said 'Oh, it's nothing, old chap!' Just like that."

"Ha, ha, ha!"

"And old Popper said 'Come along with me, my dear fellow'. And they jolly well stood me some supper, too, and sent me home in the car," said Bunter. "And old Popper sent a note to Quelch, too. Quelch looked like biting me when I came in, but after reading old Popper's note he just said 'I will take you to your dormitory, Bunter'. So I'm all right."

"Is that the lot?" asked Bob Cherry.

"That's all, old chap."

"And now tell us what's happened."

"Eh? I've just told you what happened, haven't I?"

"I mean what really happened."

"Beast!"

"Something must have happened, if Bunter's let off," remarked Peter Todd. "Quelch was looking about as amiable as Rhadamanthus, when he brought him up. Can't you tell us what happened, Bunter?"

" I've told you ! " yelled Bunter. " If you don't believe me, Peter——"

" Ha, ha, ha ! "

" Well, it seems that the fat oyster is let off, anyway," growled Johnny Bull, " and we've got three hundred lines all round."

" Eh ! What have you got lines for, if you weren't copped ? " asked Bunter.

" We had to tell Quelch where we'd left you, you fat ass, when you didn't turn up for dorm," said Harry Wharton. " Quelch gave us three hundred lines each for going out of bounds in Popper Court Woods."

" He, he, he ! "

" Think that's funny, you fat chump ? " hooted Bob Cherry.

" He, he, he ! "

Apparently, Bunter did think it funny !

" He, he, he ! " cachinnated the fat Owl. " Fancy you fellows telling Quelch, and getting lines all round ! He, he, he ! You must have been a lot of fatheads ! He, he, he ! "

There was a creak of a bed.

" Well, I'm going to sleep. He, he, he ! I haven't got any lines ! He, he, he ! I say, is that some fellow getting up ? "

" Yes," came Johnny Bull's voice, " I'm getting up, Bunter."

" What are you getting up for ? "

" I'm going to swipe you with my pillow."

" Eh ? What ! Look here ! Keep off, you beast—wow ! Will you keep off ? " roared Bunter. " You swipe me again, and I'll jolly well—yarooooh ! "

Swipe ! swipe !

" Ow ! wow ! I say, you fellows—yarooop ! Will you stoppit ? " shrieked Bunter.

Swipe ! swipe ! swipe !

" Oh, crikey ! ow ! Gerraway ! Will you keep that pillow away, you beast ? Wow ! "

The pillow swiped, and swiped, and swiped again. Johnny Bull seemed to be putting his beef into it, and the fat Owl wriggled and roared, " Wow! Stoppit! Yaroooh! "

" There! " gasped Johnny. " Think that's funny, too? "

" Yaroooh! "

" Ha, ha, ha! "

Billy Bunter seemed no longer amused. Johnny Bull went back to bed, feeling better. Bunter, to judge by his remarks, was feeling worse.

CHAPTER VIII

THE SLEEPING BEAUTY

CECIL REGINALD TEMPLE, of the Fourth Form, stared.

Snore !

" My only summer hat ! " said Temple.

Snore !

" Fast asleep ! " said Fry, in wonder.

" Oh, rather," said Dabney.

Snore !

" The sleeping Beauty ! " remarked Temple.

" Ha, ha, ha ! "

Snore !

A snore was an unusual sound to be heard in morning break. It was no wonder that it drew the attention of Temple, Dabney, and Fry, as they came across the landing from the Fourth-form studies. They gazed at the plump figure of Billy Bunter, extended at ease on the settee on the study landing : his mouth open, his eyes shut behind his big spectacles : sleeping, and snoring.

In break, on a fine sunny morning, almost everybody was out of the House. Bunter had the study landing to himself, till Temple, Dabney and Co. came by.

Bunter, it was well known, eould do with lots of sleep. In that respect, Rip Van Winkle was a mere amateur compared with Bunter. Epimenides himself had nothing on him. The Seven Sleepers of Ephesus were merely also rans. Still, it was surprising for even Bunter to be fast asleep and snoring at ten-fifty on a bright and sunny morning.

Any Remove man, of course, would have known why Bunter had gone to sleep in break. They knew that the fat Owl had missed a lot of sleep the night before. But Temple, Dabney and Co. knew nothing of Bunter's wild adventures out of bounds, and they were mystified.

" He's going it ! " remarked Fry. " I've heard that that fat chap has nodded off in the form-room in the afternoon. But in morning break——"

" It's the jolly old limit," said Temple.

" Oh, rather," said Dabney.

Footsteps on the landing, voices and chuckles, did not awaken Billy Bunter. Unaware of the three Fourth-formers, he slept and snored on.

" Looks as if he won't wake till the bell goes for third school," remarked Cecil Reginald. " Perhaps not even then ! He's some sleeper ! "

" Might give him a shake," said Fry.

Temple shook his head.

" I'm goin' to give him somethin' else," he said. " A tip not to slack about goin' to sleep in the mornin'. Cut off to the study, Dab, and get me the tube of sky-blue from my colour-box."

Dabney stared.

" What on earth for ? " he asked.

" Bunter," answered Temple.

" Oh, my hat ! " said Dabney. And he chuckled, and cut back to the study in the Fourth-form passage.

He returned under a minute, with the tube of colour. Cecil Reginald Temple took it, and unscrewed the cap.

Fry and Dabney watched him, grinning. He squeezed out sky-blue water-colour from the tube, on Bunter's little fat nose. Any fellow but Bunter, doubtless, would have awakened, as the paint trickled on his nose : but the fat Owl of the Remove did not even stir.

Bunter's nose, generally, inclined to red in hue. But as Temple spread the paint over it, it looked blue—blue as the summer sky. The change in the fat Owl's appearance was quite startling. Fry and Dabney chuckled explosively, as they gazed at a fat Owl with a sky-blue nose.

" Oh, crumbs ! " murmured Fry.

" Oh, scissors ! " said Dabney.

" A thing of beauty is a joy for ever ! " said Temple.

THE CHANGE IN THE FAT OWL'S APPEARANCE
WAS QUITE STARTLING

"That's Keats—we've had it in class with Capper. Bunter isn't a thing of beauty, as a rule: but I'm going to make him a joy for ever."

"Ha, ha, ha!"

"Don't wake him," admonished Temple, "I'm not finished yet. There's a lot of colour in this tube, and Bunter's goin' to have it all."

"Oh, he won't wake," chuckled Fry. "Carry on, old man."

There seemed little danger of Bunter awakening. He did not stir under the decoration of his nose. Neither did he stir as Temple drew two large blue circles round his eyes, giving him an extraordinary appearance of wearing an extra pair of spectacles, twice as large as his own.

"Oh, crikey!" said Fry.

"Oh, jiminy!" said Dabney.

Spurred on, no doubt, by the appreciation of his artistic efforts by his two comrades, Cecil Reginald carried on with the good work. A sky-blue moustache was imprinted over Bunter's capacious mouth. Then both his ears were tinted sky-blue. The fat Owl's ears were not small: in fact, they provided quite an extensive ground for an artist to work upon, and the tube of colour was nearly empty by the time his ears matched his nose.

Happily unaware of the artist at work, Bunter slumbered on, snoring. Temple squeezed the last remnant of colour from the tube in a daub on his plump chin.

Then he stepped back, to admire his handiwork. Fry and Dabney were almost weeping with merriment by that time.

"Does he look a beauty?" asked Temple.

"Ha, ha, ha!"

"Think he'll make a spot of sensation when he goes down like that?"

"Ha, ha, ha!"

"He will have to wash," said Temple, thoughtfully. "They don't wash much in the Remove, and Bunter never, so I've heard. But he will have to wash before he goes into form—even Bunter! I don't know whether such a sudden and complete change will be good for him——"

"Ha, ha, ha!"

"Hallo, there goes the bell! Time we travelled!" drawled Temple, as the first clang was heard of the bell for third school. "Come on, dear boys. The sleeping beauty will be wakin' up."

Temple, Dabney and Co. went down the stairs, chuckling. Billy Bunter was left alone on the study landing once more, still sleeping and snoring. The grinning Fourth-formers supposed that he would awaken at the clang of the bell for school. But even the clang of the bell did not awaken Bunter. His snore continued, like a bass accompaniment to the bell!

Snore!

At a distance, downstairs, were hurrying feet, as the Greyfriars fellows went to their various Form-rooms. Harry Wharton and Co. and the rest of the Lower Fourth, gathered at the door of the Remove room, where Mr. Quelch let them in. But the gimlet-eye of the Remove master noted the absence of one member of his form. That member was still snoring on the settee on the study landing. The last clang of the bell died away, but the snore of the fat Owl went on, and on, and on! unending as the music of the spheres, though considerably less musical.

Indeed the fat Owl might have slept and snored on through third school, had not Trotter, the House page, chanced to cross the study landing on his lawful occasions. Trotter gave quite a convulsive jump at the sight of Bunter. His eyes bulged at the sleeping beauty.

"Oh, corks!" gasped Trotter.

He stood spell-bound for a long moment. Why Bunter had done this, Trotter could not guess—some sort of a lark, he supposed. So far as Trotter could see, Bunter had made himself up in that extraordinary manner, and then gone to sleep on the settee. It was quite amazing.

Trotter was good-natured, and Bunter was already ten minutes late for class. He gave the fat Owl a shake.

Snore !

Shake ! shake !

Snore !

" Oh, my eye ! " said Trotter. And he gave Bunter another shake, so energetic that it roused even the fat Owl from his slumbers.

Bunter's eyes opened drowsily behind his big spectacles. He blinked at Trotter, drowsily and inimically.

" Lemme alone ! Tain't rising-bell ! Beast ! " mumbled Bunter. Then he realised that he was not in bed in the Remove dormitory, and sat up. " Oh ! Oh, crumbs ! I say, has the bell gone ? "

" Ten minutes ago, Master Bunter," answered Trotter.

" Oh, crikey ! " Bunter bounded up from the settee. " I shall be late—and Quelch is pretty crusty with me already ! " Bunter rolled hurriedly towards the stairs.

" Hold on, sir," gasped Trotter. " You can't go into form like that, sir ! Hadn't you better get a wash first ? "

Bunter stared round at him, with an angry and indignant stare.

" What ? " he snapped.

Bunter was accustomed to little jokes in the Remove on the subject of washing. He did not want any little jokes on that subject from a House page !

" A—a—a wash, sir—hadn't you better wash your face——? "

" You cheeky fathead ! " hooted Bunter. " Mind your own business ! Of all the cheek——"

He wasted no more words on Trotter. Unaware of the unusual and extraordinary state of his fat visage, Bunter did not realise that Trotter was giving him good advice. It was sheer cheek, so far as Bunter could see. He gave Trotter a devastating glare through his big spectacles, and rolled away to the stairs : descended the same in great haste, and tore off to the Remove Form-room.

CHAPTER IX

BUNTER LOOKS BLUE

Mr. Quelch was frowning.

Quelch's brow was often severe. Now it was more severe than usual. The Remove master was not, in fact, at his bonniest that morning.

He had sat up to a late—a very late—hour, the previous night, on account of Bunter. A dutiful form-master like Henry Samuel Quelch could hardly go to bed, while a boy of his form was out of gates at night, wandering in parts unknown. He had been anxious about Bunter: and probably rather more angry than anxious. And when Bunter had, at long last, blown in, the note from Sir Hilton Popper that accompanied him made it necessary for Mr. Quelch's cane, which he had thoughtfully placed ready on his study table, to remain there unused!

Quelch could not keep such late hours without feeling the effects in the morning. And Quelch could not feel the effects in the morning, without passing on some of the same to his form.

Not that Quelch, a very just man, would have dreamed of dropping on any fellow because he was feeling tired, and peeved, and disgruntled. Quelch was always just. But when he was feeling like that, he was perhaps a little more just than usual! Little sins of omission or commission, which might have passed unnoticed in happier moments, drew Quelch's particular attention. Not for worlds would he have been unjust. But he was awfully just!

Lord Mauleverer had a hundred lines for yawning behind his hand. Vernon-Smith had two hundred for quite a small slip in con. Bob Cherry was almost scarified by the sharpest edge of Quelch's tongue for shuffling his feet. Skinner had an imposition for whispering to Snoop: and

Squiff had one for whispering to Tom Brown. In third school, the Remove were very much on their best behaviour. Nobody wanted to attract Quelch's gimlet-eye. And in third school, one member of the form was late—very late! Fellows who liked Bunter least felt sorry for him when he did at last show up, with Quelch in his present mood.

But Bunter did not seem in a hurry to show up. It would hardly have been safe to be a minute late, in the circumstances. Bunter was many minutes late. As the hand of the Form-room clock crawled round from eleven to eleven-fifteen, the frown on Mr. Quelch's brow grew deeper and deeper, grimmer and grimmer: and no fellow in the Remove would have been willing to be in Bunter's shoes for a term's pocket-money.

It was at eleven-fifteen that scuttling footsteps were heard in the corridor. Bunter was coming at last—a quarter of an hour late. At the sound of footsteps, Mr. Quelch picked up the cane from his desk. Apparently he was going to lose no time!

The Form-room door hurriedly opened. Every eye in the Remove turned on the fat figure that rolled breathlessly in.

Then there was a general gasp.

It was Bunter! There was no doubt that it was Bunter. Bunter would have been known anywhere if only by his circumference. But the fat face from which his spectacles gleamed was unrecognizable.

Fellows gazed at him like fellows in a dream.

Mr. Quelch's mouth was already open to address Bunter. But he did not address Bunter. He remained with his mouth open, staring, petrified, dumb.

Bunter rolled in.

Utterly unconscious of Cecil Reginald Temple's artistic work on his fat face, Bunter was naturally unaware of anything out of the common. He knew that he was late—very late. But that was all he knew. Why his entrance caused all the Remove to stare at him, transfixed, as if he had been the grisly spectre of a Bunter, he did not know.

He blinked anxiously at Mr. Quelch. The petrified gaze of his form-master surprised him. But the cane in Quelch's hand did not. He had a dire anticipation of establishing contact with the cane.

" I—I—I'm sorry I'm late, sir," stammered Bunter. " I—I—I never heard the bell, sir."

Mr. Quelch did not answer. He just gazed. All the Remove gazed, at a fat face decorated with a sky-blue nose, blue circles round the eyes, blue ears, and a blue spot on the chin. The ghost of Banquo did not startle Macbeth more than the blue-visaged Owl startled the Remove and the Remove master.

Bunter blinked at Quelch, puzzled.

" Kik-kik-kik-can I g-g-go to my place, sir ? " he stammered.

Mr. Quelch found his voice at last.

" Bunter ! " he gasped.

" Oh ! Yes, sir ! I—I never heard the bell, sir——"

" How dare you ? " shrieked Mr. Quelch. " Bunter, how dare you enter the form-room like this ? "

Bunter could only blink at him. He had to enter the form-room, to join up with the Remove. It was difficult to understand Quelch's question.

" Is he crackers ? " whispered Bob Cherry. " Is he off his onion ? "

" Is he ever on it ? " murmured Nugent.

" The crackerfulness must be terrific."

" Mad as a hatter," murmured Peter Todd.

" Potty ! " said Skinner.

" Is it a rag ? " asked the Bounder. " Is Bunter ragging Quelch ? Some nerve ! "

For once, Mr. Quelch was deaf to the murmur of voices in his form. All his attention was concentrated on the blue-faced Owl.

He did not suppose that Bunter had suddenly gone "crackers". Still less was he likely to guess that Bunter had gone to sleep in the morning, and that a playful fellow in another form had decorated him while he slumbered. To Mr. Quelch, this was a "rag"—an extraordinary rag: an unprecedented rag! Bunter was not only late for class: but he had turned up, perpetrating the most audacious rag that had ever been perpetrated in the Remove form-room. Quelch's amazement turned into towering wrath.

"Bunter! I repeat, how dare you? How dare you walk into this form-room in such a state?"

"Eh? I—Is anything the matter, sir?" stammered Bunter. The fat Owl was not quick on the uptake: but he realised that something was the matter, though he had no idea what it was. What Mr. Quelch meant by his "state" Bunter did not know. He could not see his own face!

"The matter?" gasped Mr. Quelch. "How dare you come into this form-room, Bunter, looking like that?"

"Like what, sir?" stuttered the amazed Owl.

"Like that!" shrieked Mr. Quelch. "Your face!"

"My fuf-fuf-face!"

"Are you in your senses, Bunter?"

"Eh? Oh! Yes!"

"Then why is your face like that?" thundered Mr. Quelch. "How dare you appear here, or in public at all, with such a face?"

Bunter blinked at him. Bunter's own opinion of his face was that it was unusually good-looking. No other fellow in the Remove shared that opinion: and indeed there were fellows who had told Bunter that his face would stop a clock. But Bunter certainly had never expected remarks from his form-master of that kind. Remove fellows might jest about his face, but it was amazing from the Remove master. Bunter's blink was indignant.

"What's the matter with my face?" he exclaimed.

"What is the matter with it?" repeated Mr. Quelch. "If you are in your senses, Bunter, you must know what is the matter with your face."

"I jolly well don't!" retorted Bunter. "My face is all right, I suppose. You let my face alone."

"Upon my word!" gasped Mr. Quelch. "Is this boy wandering in his mind? Bunter, are you not aware of your extraordinary face?"

Bunter crimsoned under blue paint. This was really too much! He forgot even his dread of his form-master's cane, in his indignation.

"You let my face alone," he hooted. "What about yours, if you come to that?"

"Wha-a-at?" gasped Mr. Quelch.

"My face is all right. Best-looking in the Remove, and chance it," exclaimed Bunter, indignantly. "I jolly well know that Dr. Locke wouldn't like you to make jokes about a fellow's face in form, sir!"

"Bless my soul! Bunter, your extraordinary face——"

"Tain't extraordinary!" yelled the indignant Owl. "Not so jolly ugly as yours, anyhow."

"Ha, ha, ha!" yelled the Remove.

"Bunter! How dare you——?"

"Well, you let my face alone," howled Bunter. "Making jokes about a fellow's face——"

"Ha, ha, ha!"

"Silence! Silence in the class! Bunter, if you have not taken leave of your senses, what does this mean? Why have you painted your face in this extraordinary manner?" roared Mr. Quelch.

Bunter jumped.

"Pip-pip-pip-painted!" he stuttered. "Who's pip-pip-painted his face? I don't know what you're talking about, sir."

"Ha, ha, ha!"

It dawned on the Remove, and the Remove-master, that Bunter was unaware of the remarkable state of his fat countenance. How he could be unaware of it was a mystery, but it seemed that he was!

"Bunter!" gasped Mr. Quelch. "Your face is painted——"

"'Tain't!" yelled Bunter.

"I repeat that your face is painted——"

"Tain't!"

"It is painted blue——"

"'Tain't!"

"Ha, ha, ha!" shrieked all the Remove, as they listened to that duet.

"Upon my word!" gasped Mr. Quelch. "The boy seems unaware of it, though how he can be unaware of it passes all comprehension. Bunter, are you not aware that your face is painted blue?"

"'Tain't!" bawled Bunter.

"Ha, ha, ha!"

Lord Mauleverer stepped from his place, taking his little pocket-mirror from his waistcoat-pocket. He did not speak: he held it up before Bunter.

Bunter blinked at him, and then blinked into the little mirror. What he saw there made him bound clear of the form-room floor.

"Oh! Oh, crikey! What—what's that?" spluttered Bunter. "That—that ain't my face! Why, it's all blue! Oh, jiminy."

"Ha, ha, ha!"

"I—I say, you fellows, who did this?" yelled Bunter. "Some beast has been painting my face——"

"Ha, ha, ha!"

"Bunter! Do you mean to say that your face was painted in this absurd manner without your knowledge?" exclaimed Mr. Quelch.

"Oh, crikey! Yes, sir! Oh, jiminy! Some beast must have done it while I was asleep—— I—I—I went to sleep in break, sir—I was sleepy after last night, and you wouldn't let me stay in after rising-bell—and some beast——"

" Ha, ha, ha ! "

" Silence ! " roared Mr. Quelch. " Such a jest upon this foolish boy is not a laughing matter."

" Isn't it ? " murmured Skinner.

" Ha, ha, ha ! "

" Silence ! The next boy who laughs will be detained for the half-holiday this afternoon ! " thundered Mr. Quelch.

Sudden gravity descended on the Remove.

" Bunter ! You will take three hundred lines for being late for class, and you will stay in this afternoon until you have written them. Now go and wash your face, you foolish and absurd boy."

" I—I——"

" Go ! " snapped Mr. Quelch.

Billy Bunter went. He was glad, at any rate, to escape Quelch's cane : but three hundred lines on a half-holiday, and an extra wash, were almost as bad. It was a dismal and disgruntled Owl that returned to the form-room, newly swept and garnished. The paint had been washed off, but Bunter was still looking blue !

CHAPTER X

A RUSH JOB

"CUT!" suggested Bob Cherry.

"Rot!" said Johnny Bull.

"Um!" said Frank Nugent.

"What do you think, Inky?" asked Harry Wharton.

Hurree Jamset Ram Singh shook his dusky head.

"The cutfulness is not the proper caper, my esteemed chum! The worthy and ludicrous Quelch would be infuriated."

"Let him!" said Bob.

"Rot!" repeated Johnny Bull.

Bob gave a disgruntled grunt.

Five fellows were faced with a problem. It was Wednesday, a half-holiday. The arrangements for that half-holiday had been made long since. Harry Wharton and Co. not being prophets, had been quite unable to foresee the consequences of letting the fat and fatuous Owl of the Remove join their picnic after class the previous day. The consequences had been three hundred lines each, all round. Those lines had to be handed in to Mr. Quelch before they sallied forth to carry out the plans already made for that half-holiday.

Quelch, perhaps, fancied that the leisure of a half-holiday gave those members of his form an excellent opportunity for getting their lines done! Certainly he was not likely to go easy, if they went out with the lines undone. He was not in the best of tempers with those members of his form—the escapade in Popper Court Woods had drawn upon them his grimmest disapproval. If Quelch did not receive those lines on time, he was likely to be, if not exactly infuriated as the nabob of Bhanipur expressed it, at least grim and unbending. Quelch, especially in his present mood, was not a "beak" to be trifled with.

On the other hand, an appointment was an appointment : and had to be kept. And the appointment was with certain members of the Fourth Form at Cliff House School—to wit, Marjorie Hazeldene and Clara Trevlyn. And Bob Cherry, for reasons which seemed good to himself, was very anxious not to miss seeing Marjorie. Hence his suggestion of " cutting ".

" It's all that fat idiot Bunter's fault," growled Bob. " We ought to have kicked him, instead of letting him roll along yesterday."

" Well, it was our fault we didn't, not Bunter's," Johnny Bull pointed out. Johnny was always ready to contribute solid common-sense : not always at the most propitious moment.

Snort, from Bob.

" Perhaps it was our fault too that the fat idiot insisted on coming back through Popper Court Woods," he yapped.

" It was our fault we followed his lead," answered Johnny, stolidly, " I told you so at the time, and——"

Johnny Bull did not finish the sentence. He jumped back out of reach. He was in danger of having his head banged on the wall again. Bob Cherry was giving him a most unchummy glare.

" Chuck it, Johnny," said Frank Nugent, laughing, " we've heard that one—oftener than we want to."

" Speech is silvery, my esteemed Johnny, but silence is the bird in the bush that makes Jack a dull boy, as the English proverb remarks," murmured Hurree Jamset Ram Singh. " A still tongue is an Englishman's castle, as another proverb remarkably observes."

Bob Cherry's frowning face melted into a grin, under the influence of those English proverbs.

" Well, look here, never mind whose fault it is, but we've just got to go," he said. " Marjorie and Clara will be walking back from Courtfield by the tow-path this afternoon, and we're to join them on the tow-path and trot on to Cliff House with them. Is that so or isn't it ? "

"It is," agreed Harry Wharton. "But——"

"Marjorie said they leave Courtfield at four——"

"Might be late," said Johnny Bull.

"Marjorie's never late," said Bob.

"Well, they're going to the milliner's," said Johnny. "You know what girls are when they get among hats."

"Rot!" said Bob. "They have to get back to Cliff House for tea, too, and they've asked us. Marjorie will be on time, and so will Clara, as she's with Marjorie. They'll be looking out for us, and we can't let them miss us. They'll expect to see us at Courtfield Bridge, as we arranged. Are we going to let them down?"

"No!" said Harry. "But——"

"Well, we can't get the lines done in time," said Bob. "That's that!"

Harry Wharton wrinkled his brows. Three hundred Latin lines was a large order. It was possible, of course, to put on speed. But it was a doubtful proposition. No member of the Famous Five, especially Bob, wished to fail to keep the tryst. On the other hand, Quelch had to be considered.

"Look here, we've got to do the lines," said the captain of the Remove, at last. "Quelch is shirty already, and we can't have another row with him. We shall have to rush them through."

"The rushfulness will have to be rather terrific," remarked Hurree Jamset Ram Singh, dubiously.

"And Quelch is quite capable of giving us the job over again, if he fancies that they're done too badly," grunted Johnny Bull. "Any job that's worth doing at all is worth doing well."

"Got anything better to suggest, fathead?"

"Well, we could ask Hazel to cut over to Cliff House on his bike, and tell his sister that we're kept in," suggested Johnny.

"Fathead!" said Bob Cherry.

"Look here——"

" Ass ! "

" If you've got nothing better to do than to call a fellow names——"

" Idiot ! "

" Pack it up, Johnny," grinned Nugent. " Bob isn't reasonable on that subject. You see, he doesn't want to miss Marjorie at Courtfield Bridge."

" I don't see that it matters a lot, so long as we let them know," answered Johnny Bull.

" You wouldn't," said Bob. " That's because you're a silly ass, and a fathead, and a born idiot, and——"

" Speech may be taken as read ! " interrupted Harry Wharton. " If we're going to do the lines, and get done in time to meet Marjorie and Clara, the sooner we get going the better."

" We can't get through in time," growled Bob.

" Let's try, anyway."

" Oh, all right."

" I say, you fellows." Billy Bunter rolled up to the worried and troubled group in the Remove passage. " I say——"

" Blow away, barrel," snorted Bob.

" Oh, really, Cherry ! I say, you fellows, you heard Quelch give me three hundred lines this morning," said Bunter. " It was all his fault that I was late for class, as he wouldn't let me stay in after rising-bell this morning——"

" Give us a rest ! "

" Beast ! I mean, look here, old chap ! Who's going to help me with my lines ? " asked Bunter. " Quelch wants them this afternoon. I can't do three hundred lines in one afternoon. I think you fellows ought to help, after all I've done for you. Suppose you do fifty each——"

" What ? " yelled Bob.

" Fifty," said Bunter, blinking at him. " If you fellows do fifty each, that's two hundred and fifty out of the three hundred, see ? I'll do the other fifty. I'm not lazy, I hope ! I'll do as much as you fellows. What about it ? "

The Famous Five did not answer in words. They were overwhelmed with lines of their own, owing to Bunter: and the idea of doing Bunter's lines in addition to their own did not seem to attract them in the very least. Instead of answering Bunter in words, they grasped the fat junior, and sat him down in the Remove passage, with a bump.

"Yaroooh!" roared Bunter. "Wharrer you up to? I was only asking you to do my lines, you beasts——"

"Get up!" roared Bob, "and we'll give you another."

"Beast!"

Bunter did not seem in a hurry to get up. Probably he did not want another. He sat and spluttered for breath: and the Famous Five dispersed to their various studies, to get on with their own lines—not Bunter's.

There was quick work in three Remove studies that afternoon. Seldom, if ever, had Virgil been transcribed at such a rate. But it was a long journey from "Arma virumque cano" to "finibus arceret": and it was four when, at last, the lines were done, and delivered in Quelch's study. And when Bob Cherry shot out of the old gateway of Greyfriars, his comrades had hard work to keep up with the strides of his long and sinewy legs.

CHAPTER XI

OUT OF BOUNDS

" THE short cut," said Bob Cherry.

" What ? "

" The short cut ! "

" You silly ass ! "

" Come on ! "

" Stop ! " exclaimed four fellows together.

Bob Cherry did not stop. He tramped on, and his friends hurried to keep up. He explained, over his shoulder, as he tramped with long strides.

" The short cut takes us out close by Courtfield Bridge. No other way of getting there in time."

" Why not walk up the tow-path from the boat-house ? " demanded Johnny Bull.

" It's past four already."

" Well, we shall meet them on the tow-path, sooner or later——"

" We fixed to meet them at Courtfield Bridge."

" If they don't see us there, they'll walk on."

" I know that."

" Well, then, what does it matter ? "

" Fathead ! "

Bob tramped on. His friends followed him, with worried looks. It was true that if the party walked up the tow-path from the school boat-house, they would not reach Courtfield Bridge, by the time Marjorie and Clara reached it from the other direction. The short cut through Popper Court Woods saved more than half the distance, for the Sark had a winding course, and the tow-path, of course, followed the bank of the river. That short cut solved the problem : so far as turning up on time at Courtfield Bridge was concerned.

Four members of the Co. considered it judicious to walk up the tow-path, sure of meeting the Cliff House girls somewhere on the way. Bob seemed to have no use for judiciousness. He was going to keep the appointment, and he was going to keep it on time. He had yielded to his comrades in the matter of the lines, though reluctantly. He was not going to yield now. He was going to be at Courtfield Bridge on time, if ten thousand Sir Hilton Poppers stood in the way, backed up by a legion of Quelches.

But the prospect of going out of bounds again in Popper Court Woods, after what had happened only the day before, was quite dismaying to Bob's chums. Having been called over the coals by their form-master for that very act on Tuesday, it was wildly reckless to repeat it on Wednesday.

"Look here, Bob——," urged Harry Wharton.

"Have a little sense!" urged Johnny Bull.

"After yesterday——!" said Nugent.

"Quelch will go right off at the deep end, if he hears of it," said Johnny. "As likely as not to send us up to the Head!"

"If we're spotted——!" said Harry.

"The spotfulness is a terrific probability——"

"Hold on, Bob," urged Nugent. "We're losing time, if we're going the other way——"

"And we jolly well are!" said Johnny Bull.

"Bob, old man——"

Bob Cherry certainly heard all those remarks from his friends. But he did not heed them. He turned a deaf ear—in fact, two deaf ears. Instead of heeding remonstrance and argument, he stepped aside from the lane, and made a jump at the fence bordering it. In another moment, his leg was over the top. On the other side of that fence, were the forbidden precincts of Popper Court.

"Stop, you ass!" hooted Johnny Bull.

"Come down, fathead!"

"Are you going to play the goat just as Bunter did yesterday, you duffer?"

" Haven't you any more sense than Bunter ? " demanded Johnny.

Bob glanced down at them.

" You fellows go the other way, if you like," he said. " I'm going this way. I'm going to be at Courtfield Bridge on time, as I said I would. See you later."

" Look here——"

" Stop ! "

Bob dropped on the inner side of the fence, and disappeared. His friends heard him pushing through bush and bracken. They exchanged glances. Bob had taken the bit between his teeth : and that was that.

" Well, are we going on ? " asked Nugent. " I suppose we're sticking to him."

" The stickfulness to the esteemed and idiotic Bob is the proper caper," said Hurree Jamset Ram Singh.

Harry Wharton nodded.

" Oh, come on," he said. " What about you, Johnny ? "

Snort, from Johnny Bull.

" Oh, let's ! " he said. " We let Bunter land us in a row yesterday—why not let Bob land us in another row to-day ? It's a silly-ass thing to do : but we are a lot of silly asses, aren't we ? "

And having delivered this opinion, Johnny clambered up the fence. A minute more, and all four were over it, and pushing through the underwoods after Bob, who was already well on his way towards the forbidden footpath that led to the bank of the Sark.

" Easy does it, Bob," called out Harry.

" Oh, come on, if you're coming," answered Bob, over his shoulder.

" If you crash along at that rate, you'll have every keeper at Popper Court on your neck ! " snorted Johnny Bull.

" Blow the keepers ! " answered Bob.

However, he slackened pace a little, and ceased to crash through bush and bramble. The wood, at that spot, was very thick, and care was required to progress, without announcing their presence to the keepers. Bob was quite determined to go by the forbidden footpath: but he realised that he did not exactly want another interview with an incensed Quelch. Caution was indicated: and Bob consented to be cautious.

The five juniors picked their way through the thick wood, and soon glimpsed the leafy footpath, which they had followed the day before, when they had encountered the trespassing gentleman with the pimples. But before stepping out into the open path, Harry Wharton stopped Bob by catching his arm, and came to a halt.

"Look before you leap, fathead," he said.

"Looks clear enough," grunted Bob.

"Make sure, ass."

"The lookfulness before the leapfulness is the sine qua non, my esteemed Bob," murmured Hurree Jamset Ram Singh. "It is no use locking the stable door after the cracked pitcher has gone to the well."

"Quiet!" whispered Nugent.

"Oh, what——?" began Bob.

"Quiet, you rhinoceros! I can hear somebody."

"Rot!"

"Listen, ass!"

Bob Cherry grunted, but he listened. Keeping back in the thick underwood, invisible from the footpath, the juniors all bent their ears to listen. And an unmistakable sound of footsteps reached their ears.

Someone, not yet in sight, was coming along the footpath.

"Oh, blow!" muttered Bob.

But he remained very still. To be caught at that point certainly was not the way to reach Courtfield Bridge on time. Jenkins, or Joyce, or Hansom, would not have been likely to allow the schoolboys to proceed on their way. Impatient, but cautious, Bob listened to the approaching footsteps, and waited for the unseen pedestrian to pass, and leave the way clear.

"Must be a keeper," muttered Nugent. "Quiet, for goodness' sake. Might be old Popper himself."

"Might only be that pimply chap we saw mooching here yesterday," grunted Bob.

"Think he takes his pimples for a walk in this wood regularly every day ?" inquired Johnny Bull, sarcastically.

"Br-r-r-r-r-r ! "

"Quiet ! " whispered Harry Wharton. "Look ! "

The juniors were still as mice as they caught the gleam of an eyeglass, in the sun-rays that filtered through the branches over the footpath. A long lean gentleman, with an eyeglass stuck in his eye, came into sight : and they were thankful that they were invisible. It was not a keeper : and it certainly was not the pimply trespasser : it was Sir Hilton Popper, the lord of Popper Court, himself !

"Oh, crumbs ! " murmured Bob. "Old Popper ! "

"The old-Popperfulness is terrific."

"Quiet ! "

Sir Hilton Popper came on, with his jerky strides. His brown old crusty face was clearly seen, and its expression was very far from amiable. Sir Hilton's temper was never very pleasant at the best of times : he was an autocratic old gentleman with a sharp temper and a sharp tongue. But it seemed unusually irascible at the moment, to judge by his look. His brows were knitted, his eyes glinted, and his lips were hard set. Whatever thoughts were passing through his mind, they seemed to be of a disturbing and irritating nature. But he did not glance towards the spot where the bushes screened the Greyfriars juniors. He had no suspicion that they were there.

As he was coming from the direction of the river, the juniors had only to wait quietly till he had passed, and then their way would be clear. They waited in breathless silence.

Sir Hilton came jerking on, till he was almost abreast of the spot where the thickets hid the Famous Five. Then, to their dismay, he halted.

For a moment, they had an impression that he had spotted them. But that was not the case. He did not glance towards their cover. He stopped on the other side of the footpath, where a fallen log lay under the branches of a spreading beech. And, to the utter dismay of the juniors, he sat down on that log, leaned his bony back against the trunk of the beech, and lighted a cigarette.

As he smoked the cigarette, the baronet sat facing the thicket that screened the Greyfriars juniors. They were not ten or twelve feet from him. A single movement must have drawn his attention. They did not venture to make a single movement. With deep feelings, they remained perfectly still, watching the baronet through the interstices of the thicket, and waiting for him to finish his smoke and go on his way.

And their feelings became deeper, when, having finished his cigarette, Sir Hilton Popper, instead of going on his way, lighted another!

CHAPTER XII

THE BLUE MAURITIUS

" WRETCHES ! "

Five fellows very nearly jumped.

That sudden exclamation, from Sir Hilton Popper, shot out suddenly like a bullet, startled them. It seemed certain that, staring directly towards their thicket, he must have spotted them, and that his remark was to their address.

But again it was only a false alarm. Sir Hilton was not addressing them : he was still happily unconscious of their presence. He was speaking to himself—referring to some persons unknown of whom he was thinking !

Bob Cherry winked at his comrades, who grinned. Sir Hilton little dreamed that his self-communings reached the ears of five schoolboys.

To whom he was alluding they had not the faintest idea. Probably any person who caused Sir Hilton the slightest spot of bother was, in his autocratic opinion, a wretch !

" Rats ! " said Sir Hilton.

Greyfriars fellows sometimes said " Rats " ! But Sir Hilton was evidently not using that expressive word in a slangy sense. The " rats " were apparently the same persons as the " wretches ".

The lord of Popper Court threw away the stump of his second cigarette, and the hidden juniors hoped that this meant that he was going on his way. But he did not rise from his seat. Instead of that, he took out a pocket-book from an inner pocket, and opened it.

From the pocket-book, he drew a folded printed paper. Five pairs of eyes being on him at such close range, the juniors could not help catching sight of the words " Income Tax ", in larger print than the rest.

They suppressed a chuckle.

This was the clue to Sir Hilton's ire.

It is improbable that any citizen was ever really pleased to receive a demand from his Inspector of Taxes for nearly half his income. If such a citizen existed, his name certainly, was not Popper! Sir Hilton was evidently displeased—and not only displeased, but extremely irritated, annoyed, and exasperated.

A gentleman whose estate was covered by mortgages almost as thickly as by oaks and beeches, and who was trying to keep up the appearances of thirty years ago, in an age of excessive taxation, could hardly be expected to smile amiably when he received official documents from Tax Inspectors. Certainly Sir Hilton Popper was not smiling. He was scowling almost like a demon in a pantomime.

Really, that Income Tax Demand Note might almost have curled up, and withered away, under the deadly glare Sir Hilton gave it.

" Spendthrifts! Wasters! " barked Sir Hilton.

In public, the lord of Popper Court certainly would never have dreamed of applying such opprobrious expressions to the great statesmen who handle the national finances. But Sir Hilton supposed that he was alone in the wood, and felt that he might let himself go a little, with no hearers but oaks and beeches.

" Pah! " snapped Sir Hilton.

He scanned the document with a malevolent eye, and laid it on his knee. Then he sat glaring, directly towards the juniors' thicket, luckily without his glare penetrating their cover. He had looked unamiable at the first view: but he was looking positively dangerous, since he had scanned that Income Tax Note. Only too clearly, Sir Hilton was in difficulties about raising the sum required of him by his Inspector of Taxes. Indeed he looked as if that official, had he been on the spot, would not have been quite safe from Sir Hilton's bony knuckles!

" How is a man to meet such demands? " asked Sir Hilton, apparently addressing that question to the green thicket where the juniors were still as mice. "Last year I had to sell a farm! The year before, to let my house to a bounder. This year I must sell the stamp."

The word "stamp" rang a bell, as it were, to the juniors. They remembered Billy Bunter's story of the burglar, and his extraordinary statement that that nocturnal marauder had stolen a "stamp" from Popper Court. Stamps, to the Remove fellows, were postage-stamps on letters, and they could not imagine the most enterprising burglar taking the trouble to burgle a postage-stamp. But they remembered now that there are stamps—and stamps!

If Sir Hilton Popper was thinking of selling a stamp, to pay his Income Tax, obviously it was not such a stamp as adhered to letters delivered at Greyfriars by Bloggs, the postman!

Rare stamps, worth only a few pence at the date of issue, might run into hundreds, sometimes thousands, of pounds, in value, according to the state of the philatelic market. Enthusiastic stamp-collectors, excited philatelists, had been known to give two or three thousand pounds for a rare stamp! Apparently it was such a stamp as this to which the lord of Popper Court was now referring.

"My stamp!" Sir Hilton's tone was now more mournful than angry. "My Blue Mauritius! The gem of my collection! There is no other resource! The Blue Mauritius will have to go."

He shook his head sadly.

Evidently the Blue Mauritius was dear to Sir Hilton's heart, and though it was going to be lost to sight, it was going to remain to memory dear!

Harry Wharton and Co. not being stamp-collectors, did not perhaps fully grasp what a blow this was to a keen philatelist. They knew little of philately and of the value of rare stamps. But the fact was that Sir Hilton, in younger days, had bought that Blue Mauritius stamp for a mere five hundred pounds, and it had been the apple of his eye ever since. It had been a great bargain at the time—he had been in luck. Now his luck was out—the Blue Mauritius had to go, to meet the ravenous demands of the tax-gatherers. Really, Sir Hilton was still in luck in one way, for the Blue Mauritius had increased in value during the passing years, and was now worth at least four times as much. But Sir Hilton did not look at it in that way. He was only feeling the wrench of parting with the gem of his stamp-collection—his beloved Blue Mauritius!

"It will have to go," said Sir Hilton, still apparently addressing his remarks to the juniors' thicket. "And to think——" He drew a deep breath. "To think that that burglar—that scoundrel—that crook—that iniquitous ruffian—nearly had it last night—that he got out of the house with it—that he might have escaped with it, had he not fallen over that stupid boy Punter in his flight! A two-thousand pound stamp. Good gad!"

Again the hidden juniors barely repressed a chuckle. This was the other side of Bunter's tale of burglar-catching!

"The wretch! The villain! The rascal!" Sir Hilton's opinion of burglars seemed even worse than his opinion of tax-gatherers! "The dastard! The knave! The—the—the——" Epithets seemed to fail Sir Hilton. "Luckily, he is now safe in the cells, and my stamp is safe! But—it must be sold!"

From a little socket in the pocket-book, Sir Hilton Popper drew a small object. The juniors could see that it was a postage-stamp. But they realised now that it was something very special and precious in the postage-stamp line. They were able to discern that it was blue in colour, and that it showed a profile of Queen Victoria. They also caught the words "TWO PENCE".

It was, in fact, a "Post Office" Blue Mauritius: worth the humble sum of twopence when issued a hundred years earlier in the British Colony of Mauritius: worth at the present day at least £2,000, its "scarcity" value.

Sir Hilton sat with the stamp between finger and thumb, gazing at it. Only a fervid philatelist could have fully understood and sympathised with his feelings as he gazed! Harry Wharton and Co. were not unsympathetic. But they did wish that Sir Hilton would pack it up and go.

"Oh!" breathed Nugent, suddenly.

"Quiet, old chap!" whispered Harry.

"Look!"

"Oh, gum!"

"Pimples!" breathed Bob Cherry.

The juniors stared blankly across the footpath, past the baronet sitting on the log under the beech tree. From behind that tree, a face had appeared. There had not been a sound—not the faintest rustle: the man moved as warily as a fox. Sir Hilton, unaware of him, did not stir. But all five of the Greyfriars juniors saw him, and recognised at once the man they had seen in the wood the previous day—pasty face, pimples, spotted necktie, bowler hat at a rakish angle, and all. And they saw that his narrow foxy eyes were fixed upon the precious stamp in Sir Hilton's brown fingers, with an intense gaze, his unpleasant face eager with greed.

Possibly the man had heard Sir Hilton's mutterings and mumblings. No doubt he knew the value of a Blue Mauritius, better than the schoolboys did. There was no mistaking the greed in his face.

The juniors stared across the footpath at him, hardly knowing what to do. They did not want to reveal their presence—very much indeed they did not—but they could scarcely have allowed the man to snatch at that precious stamp, without warning Sir Hilton. And he looked like it.

But at the point, the baronet rose from the log, apparently to resume his walk along the footpath.

He slipped the precious stamp back into the pocket-book, closed it, and, as he rose, slipped the elastic band round the pocket-book, to return it to the pocket from which he had taken it.

Then, with a suddenness that took even the watching juniors entirely by surprise, the foxy-faced man with the pimples acted. With a spring as swift as that of a panther, he was out of the wood into the footpath : and before the baronet even realised that he was there, he had snatched the pocket-book from Sir Hilton's hand : and, rushing on without a pause, shot across the footpath, and plunged into the thicket on the opposite side. It was all so sudden, and so swift, that Sir Hilton had hardly a glimpse of him.

Sir Hilton, so startled and taken off his guard that he did not seem even to understand what was happening, staggered against the beech. The thief, with the pocket-book in his hand, crashed through the thicket. Had that thicket been untenanted, as the man naturally supposed, certainly he would have escaped with his precious plunder.

But five Greyfriars juniors were in that thicket : and the thief, crashing through, crashed right into them. He gave a gasping yell of amazement and alarm as hands grabbed him on all sides, and he went heavily to the ground, Harry Wharton snatching the pocket-book from his hand as he crashed.

CHAPTER XIII

SAVED

"GOOD gad! What—who—how—what—— Gad!"

Sir Hilton Popper was spluttering wildly.

"What—what—who——!"

"Collar him!" shouted Bob Cherry, breathlessly. "We've got him!"

Sir Hilton, his old mastiff-face dizzy with astonishment, came striding across the footpath. The Popper intellect did not work quickly: but Sir Hilton realised that a thief had snatched his pocket-book and bolted into the wood with it, and in a startled, flabbergasted state, he was starting in pursuit. But the rustling, panting, scuffling, in the thicket bordering the path was quite a puzzle to him. He plunged on, and almost stumbled over a bunch of schoolboys clinging to a wriggling, struggling, panting man, who was fighting like a tiger to escape.

"What—what—what——!" stuttered Sir Hilton.

He stared dazedly.

He had hardly seen the man who had robbed him, so swiftly had the rascal appeared and disappeared. But he knew that this must be the man—and he knew Harry Wharton and Co. by sight. How they came there, with the panting thief struggling in their grasp, was a mystery to him.

"We've got him, sir," panted Bob.

"By gad! What—what——"

"The gotfulness is terrific."

"By gum! He's like an eel," gasped Johnny Bull. "Keep hold of him!"

"Good gad! That man has robbed me!" gasped Sir Hilton Popper. "What are you Greyfriars boys doing here? Good gad! Give me a hold of him—you may stand back—I will secure the scoundrel——"

"WE'VE GOT HIM, SIR," PANTED BOB

The baronet's grasp closed on the collar of the man's coat. He dragged him up, in a grasp that was much too strong for the slight, slim man to resist.

The juniors let go. Sir Hilton was more than able to deal with the sneak-thief, who was hardly more than half his size and weight : and the baronet evidently wanted to take matters into his own hands.

With a grip of iron on the little man's collar, the long lean gentleman held him rather like a big dog holding a rat. The prisoner panted and panted, and sagged in his grasp.

"By gad! My stamp—scoundrel—rascal—no doubt a confederate of that rascal last night—my stamp—my pocket-book—rascal—— Oh!" gasped Sir Hilton, "stop him! Good gad! Stop him!"

With eel-like agility, the little slim man suddenly wriggled out of his coat, and, leaving it in the astonished baronet's hands, darted away—so suddenly and swiftly, that the juniors had no chance of grabbing at him as he went.

In a split second, he vanished into the wood, running like a deer.

"Oh, my hat!" gasped Bob.

"That old ass——!" breathed Johnny Bull.

Sir Hilton staggered, with the empty coat in his hands. He stared at it, glared at it, almost gibbered at it : as if hardly able to understand, for a moment or two, that it no longer contained its former inhabitant!

"Good gad! The villain—my stamp—my pocket-book——"

"Here it is, sir!" exclaimed Harry Wharton.

"What? what?" Sir Hilton, about to rush into the wood after the fleeing sneak-thief, whom he would have had about as much chance of catching, as a tortoise would have had of catching a hare, turned back. "What——?"

"Here's your pocket-book, Sir Hilton."

The baronet blinked at it.

"My—my—my pip-pip-pocket-book," he stuttered.

"How—what—how—who—that is my pocket-book—how —how——"

"I grabbed it when the man ran into us, sir," explained Harry, with a smile. "It's all right, sir."

"Good gad!"

Sir Hilton almost snatched the pocket-book from the junior's hand. Taking no further heed of the fleeing man, already far away in the wood, or of the bunch of breathless schoolboys, he opened it, to make sure that the precious stamp was still safe within. His gasp of relief, as he saw the Blue Mauritius safe and sound, was like the air escaping from a punctured tyre.

Harry Wharton and Co., breathless, and more than a little untidy, after that sudden and unexpected struggle, grinned at one another. The thief had escaped, but they had saved Sir Hilton's pocket-book for him, containing the stamp which they could guess to be of considerable value, though its actual fantastic value they did not know. In the circumstances, Sir Hilton could hardly cut up rusty, they considered. For the moment, he had forgotten their existence.

However, having ascertained that the Blue Mauritius was still in his possession, Sir Hilton restored the pocket-book to his pocket, and became aware of the existence of the Greyfriars juniors again.

"Thank you, Warley," he said. "I think your name is Warley."

"Wharton, sir," said Harry, meekly.

"Oh! Yes! Wharton! I am much obliged to you, Wharton. You acted very promptly in getting the pocket-book away from that rascal—very promptly, very sensibly, very sensibly indeed. It contains an article of great value, Warley."

"Does it, sir?" murmured Harry, and the other fellows contrived not to smile. Sir Hilton was evidently unaware that they had heard his remarks on the subject of Income Tax and Blue Mauritius stamps!

"Yes, yes! Very great value indeed," said Sir Hilton. "By acting so promptly and sensibly, you have saved me from a very serious loss, Warley. Did you say your name was Warley or Warburton?"

"Wharton, sir."

"Oh! Yes! Wharton! Quite. But what are you doing here, in my woods?" added Sir Hilton. The Blue Mauritius being safe, the lean gentleman remembered that he was lord of Popper Court, fierce on trespassers. "You must be aware, Warburton, that these woods are not open to the public."

But the frown passed from Sir Hilton's mastiff face the next moment. If the juniors were trespassing, it had been a very fortunate circumstance for him: the gentleman with the pimples would certainly have got away with the Blue Mauritius otherwise. The frown gave place to a smile: or as near a smile as the baronet's crusty old face could get.

"Well, well, well, never mind that," he said, quite genially, "I am glad you were here—very glad, by Jove! Go away at once, and we will say nothing more about it. And I am very much obliged to you, Warfield."

"Thank you, sir," said Harry, rather wondering how many more variations of his name he would hear, if the conversation continued. "Come on, you men—— We'll get out at once, sir."

"We'll run all the way, sir," said Bob Cherry.

"Very good—very good—I excuse you, but go away at once," said Sir Hilton, with a wave of the hand. "I am very much obliged to you, Warrington, and your friends: but go away at once."

And Harry Wharton and Co. went away at once—that being the very thing they were most desirous of doing. They pushed on up the footpath towards the river, at a trot. Bob Cherry had said they would run all the way, for the excellent reason that only by keeping on the trot could they make up for lost time, after losing a quarter of an hour owing to Sir Hilton Popper turning up on the footpath.

They came out in a cheery if rather breathless bunch on the bank of the Sark, with Courtfield Bridge in view up the river. They kept on the trot until they reached the bridge.

" On time," said Bob, breathlessly.

At a little distance, coming from Courtfield, two graceful girlish figures could be seen approaching. Bob waved his cap to Marjorie and Clara. It had been a near thing: but the chums of the Remove were on the spot, waiting for the Cliff House girls when they came up.

CHAPTER XIV

HARD LINES

"Reddy, old fellow."

Tom Redwing smiled, and Herbert Vernon-Smith sniffed. Billy Bunter addressed Tom Redwing in the most cordial, indeed affectionate tones. It might have been supposed that he loved him like a brother.

Which, to anyone who knew Bunter, indicated that the fat Owl wanted something!

Smithy and his chum were on the way to the bike-shed, when Bunter happened. Redwing stopped, and Smithy snapped:

"Come on!"

"Oh, there's no hurry, Smithy," said Redwing, always good-natured. "What is it, Bunter?"

"Can't you guess what it is?" snapped the Bounder. "That fat ass has been mooching about for hours asking fellows to help him with his lines."

"Oh, really, Smithy——"

"Isn't it that?" snapped Smithy.

"I'm speaking to Redwing, Smithy! I know you're too jolly selfish to lend a fellow a hand," said Bunter, scornfully. "I say, Reddy, old chap, you heard Quelch say that I've got to hand in my lines before I go out——"

"You could have done them by this time," said Vernon-Smith. "Wharton's gang had the same lot, and they've done them and gone out. Come on, Reddy."

The fat Owl gave Smithy an inimical blink. No doubt he could have followed the industrious example of the Famous Five, had the spirit moved him so to do. But it hadn't!

It was one of Billy Bunter's happy ways to take more trouble to dodge a job of work, than would have been required to get it done. Not a single line of his three hundred had been written, so far.

He had asked fellows up and down the Remove to help him with those lines. But not a man in the Lower Fourth seemed disposed to use up a half-holiday doing lines for Bunter. With the selfishness to which he was sadly accustomed, they went about their own affairs, heartlessly regardless of a lazy fat Owl and his woes.

It would not have mattered so much, had it not been urgent and important for Billy Bunter to get out that afternoon. But it was both important and urgent. His sister Bessie, at Cliff House, had had a hamper, from home. So the urgency of the matter could hardly be exaggerated. Added to that, if it needed adding to, Peter Todd had gone out to tea, and there was likely to be short commons, if any commons at all, in No. 7 Study at tea-time. The matter was, indeed, so urgent, that Bunter had almost made up his fat mind to get those lines done without delay, by his own exertions. But not quite !

" You see, I've simply got to get across to Cliff House, Reddy," he said. " I've got to see my sister Bessie. She's had a—I—I mean, she ain't well, and I'm very anxious about her."

" Oh ! " said Redwing. His sympathies were easily touched.

" What's the matter with her ? " asked Vernon-Smith, whose sympathies were not touched easily, if at all. " Eating too much ? "

" Oh, really, Smithy ! If you had a sister, you'd understand a brother's feelings," said Bunter, reproachfully. " Poor Bessie ain't at all well, and I'm—I'm very anxious. I can't go out till those rotten lines are done——"

" Go and tell Quelch that your sister's ill at Cliff House, and he'll let you off," suggested the Bounder, sarcastically.

" Oh ! She—she ain't so ill as all that," said Bunter, hastily.

" I fancied not," jeered the Bounder.

"I say, Reddy, you'll lend me a hand, won't you?" asked Bunter. "You ain't selfish like Smithy. Do lend a chap a hand, old fellow."

Redwing hesitated. He was booked for a spin with his chum, and he certainly did not want to write lines. But he was all goodnature: which, in Billy Bunter's opinion, was synonymous with being "soft". If Redwing was "soft" enough to sit in a study writing lines, instead of going out on his bike, William George Bunter was the man to take full advantage of it.

"Gammon!" said the Bounder. "Come on, Reddy."

"Well," said Redwing, slowly. "If——"

"If rats!" snapped Smithy. "Is there a feed on at Cliff House, Bunter? I've heard that Wharton's gang are going over there this afternoon."

"They jolly well won't come in on Bessie's hamper," said Bunter warmly. "If they jolly well think they're coming in on it, they're jolly well mistaken——"

"Oh, my hat! Has Bessie had a hamper?"

"Oh! No! I—I mean—'tain't anything to do with a hamper—I ain't going over to see Bessie because she's had a hamper—nothing of the kind—I say, you fellows, don't walk off while a chap's talking to you—— Beast!" howled Bunter.

Smithy and Redwing did walk off, laughing: and Billy Bunter was left with his problem of lines still unsolved.

He blinked up at the clock-tower. It was half-past four. It was too late for Bunter to hope to get through three hundred lines, unaided, in time to get over to Cliff House for tea.

"Beast!" groaned Bunter. Sad to relate, he was referring to his form-master by that description.

He made a few steps towards the House, dismally making up his fat mind to get on with the lines. But he paused again.

There was a hamper at Cliff House. There was nothing for tea in No. 7 Study. And Bunter was in his accustomed state—stony! Not for the first time, he had been disappointed about a postal-order. He came to a desperate resolution. He was going to " cut ".

There would be a row if he went out with his lines undone. But that would come later. In the meantime, there was the hamper.

He turned his footsteps in the direction of the gates. He was going over to Cliff House to claim his " whack " in that hamper from home, chancing it with Mr. Quelch afterwards!

But alas for Bunter! Just as the fattest figure at Greyfriars School was rolling out of the gateway, there came a sharp voice:

" Bunter! "

" Oh, crikey! " gasped Bunter, spinning round like a fat humming-top, at the voice of his Form-master.

Mr. Quelch was standing at the door of the porter's lodge, speaking to Gosling. Bunter hadn't noticed him as he passed. But Quelch had noticed Bunter. It was like the fat Owl to " cut " under the very nose of his beak!

A pair of gimlet-eyes almost bored into the fat Owl.

" Bunter! "

" Oh! Yes, sir! " groaned Bunter.

" Have you done your lines? "

" Oh! Yes! No! I—I'm just going to, sir," gasped Bunter.

" You were going out, Bunter! "

" Oh! No! Yes! I—I mean no, sir! I—I wasn't gig-gig-going out, sir. I—I—I was just going to—to—to look at the scenery, sir——"

" Go into the House at once, Bunter, and write your lines. If you leave the school before you have handed them in to me, I shall cane you most severely, and double your imposition."

" Oh, lor'! "

Wearily Bunter turned back from the gates, and rolled away to the House. It really seemed as if the stars in their courses fought against Bunter, as against Sisera of old. In the most pessimistic mood ever, he rolled into the House, and into No. 7 Study in the Remove.

But his fat dismal face cleared a little, as he found Tom Dutton in the study. Dutton was deaf, and it was rather a labour of love to talk to him—which was doubtless the reason why Bunter had not yet asked his aid with those lines. Now it was a last chance. Dutton was adjusting trouser-clips, apparently with a view to cycling. Bunter gave him his most ingratiating grin.

" I say, going out ? " he asked.

Dutton glanced round at him.

" Well, what do you expect ? " he said. " A fellow who scoffs tuck like you must expect to be growing stout."

" I didn't say growing stout—I said going out," howled Bunter. " I say, will you lend me a hand with my impot ? "

" There's one on the table."

" Eh ? One what ? "

" Inkpot."

" Oh, crikey ! I never said inkpot, you fathead ! I've got three hundred lines to do for Quelch, and I've got to get over to Cliff House to see my sister."

" Better go to the matron, then."

" Eh ? "

" Mrs. Kebble will give you something for a blister, if you've got one. Where have you got it ? "

" Oh, crumbs ! I haven't got a blister ! " hooted Bunter. " I've got to go over and see my sister."

" Eh ? Did you say your sister ? "

" Yes, I did."

" Well, I'm sorry," said Dutton, staring, " but I can't help it if your sister's got a blister, Bunter."

" Oh, crikey ! I've got to go and see Bessie. She's had a hamper—I mean, she's ill, and I'm very anxious about the hamper—I mean about Bessie. If you'll do some of my lines for me, old chap——"

" It's downstairs."

" What's downstairs ? " shrieked Bunter.

" My cap."

" I wasn't talking about your cap," yelled Bunter. " Blow your cap ! Will you help me with my lines, so that I can get over to Cliff House and see my sister Hamper—I mean my Hamper Bessie—I mean, hold on, you deaf ass—I—I mean, old fellow—will you help me with my lines——"

" Eh ? Have you got lines ? "

" Yes, three hundred——"

" Well, if you blundered, you must expect lines, Bunter. You know what Quelch is like when a fellow blunders. You should be more careful."

" Will you do some for me ? " howled Bunter.

" I've got no time to do sums for you, Bunter—I'm going out on my bike. You said lines, not sums."

" Three hundred lines," raved Bunter. " Will you do half, so that I can cut over to Cliff House in time for tea—I mean, to see Bessie. You do half, and I'll do the rest——"

" Better do your lines before you rest," said Dutton. " Take my tip, Bunter, and get your lines done, and leave resting till afterwards."

And having given Bunter that sage advice, and having adjusted his trouser-clips, Tom Dutton left the study.

" Beast ! " hooted Bunter.

There was no help for a lazy fat Owl. If those lines were going to be written at all, it was evident that they had to be written by the fat hand of William George Bunter himself.

With a lugubrious fat face, he propped Virgil against the inkstand, and sat down to lines. And never had the deathless verse of P. Vergilius Maro been so utterly and thoroughly unappreciated by any fellow at any school.

CHAPTER XV

HOT CHASE

"THAT old ass!" said Herbert Vernon-Smith.

"Eh?"

"Old Popper!"

The long white road across Courtfield Common, with the town in the distance, stretched before the two cyclists, bordered by clumps of hawthorn. Ahead of them on the road—a long way ahead—the Bounder sighted a tall figure. Its back was to the cyclists—Sir Hilton Popper was apparently walking to Courtfield—but it was easy to recognise the lord of Popper Court, from a back view.

A mischievous gleam came into the Bounder's eyes, as he watched the tall, lean figure walking, or rather stalking, ahead. He gave Redwing a grinning glance.

"Rather a lark to make the old ass jump, Reddy," he said.

"Eh! What?" asked Tom Redwing, startled.

"Keep quiet till we're just behind him, and then bang on your bell like billy-O, and I'll do the same——"

"Smithy!"

"Make him jump, what?" grinned the Bounder.

"Don't be an ass, Smithy! Old Popper's a governor of the school——"

"I know that! I got a detention last week for landing on his dashed island in the Sark," said Vernon-Smith. "One good turn deserves another."

"Ten to one he will report you to the Head if you cheek him."

"My dear man," drawled the Bounder, "a cyclist's bound to ring his bell, to warn a pedestrian walking in the road in front of him. Don't you know the rules of the road?"

"There's bags of room to pass him. He will know it was cheek."

" I don't care if he does."

" Don't play the goat, Smithy. Look here——"

" Sermon may be taken as read," drawled Smithy. " No end of a lark to make the old ass jump ! It will be a tip to him not to stalk about with his nose in the air as if the whole county of Kent belonged to him. Are you on, Reddy ? "

" No ! I tell you——"

" Then watch me."

" Look here, Smithy——"

" Rats ! "

The Bounder put on speed, and shot ahead of his comrade. Redwing pedalled on at the same pace as before, watching him with an anxious look. He was not to be drawn into a disrespectful practical joke on the lord of Popper Court, and he was worried about the possible consequences for Smithy. Sir Hilton Popper was far too lofty and important a gentleman to be made to jump like a kangaroo with impunity.

But Smithy, as usual, was reckless of possible consequences. Sir Hilton had a way of making himself unpleasant, and Smithy did not see why he should not make himself unpleasant in his turn.

He put on a burst of speed, leaving Redwing behind, and then free-wheeled, his machine making scarcely a sound as it whizzed on. Sir Hilton Popper remained quite unconscious of the cyclist behind him.

He was likely to remain in that blissful state of ignorance, till the bell suddenly banged. Then he was only too likely to jump ! Smithy grinned with cheery anticipation.

But, as it happened, it was not Sir Hilton Popper who jumped. Smithy himself suddenly jumped, in his saddle, in surprise.

He was within twenty yards of the unsuspecting baronet, and his hand was ready on the bell. Another minute —but, in that minute, something quite unexpected happened.

Suddenly, from the clumps of hawthorns beside the road,

as Sir Hilton strode past, a figure shot out, and leaped right at the baronet.

The amazed Smithy glimpsed a pimply face and a spotted necktie. Harry Wharton and Co. would have known the man at a glance. But he was a stranger to Vernon-Smith's eyes.

In utter amazement, the Bounder stared, quite forgetful of his intended prank on the lord of Popper Court.

Sir Hilton was a big man, and the man with the pimples was small and slim. But the sudden and unexpected rush up-ended the tall baronet, and he went sprawling headlong over on his back, in the dust of the Courtfield road.

He crashed and spluttered.

Even as he crashed, the pimpled man was upon him, thrusting a thievish hand into a pocket—evidently aware of the pocket he wanted—and jerking therefrom a pocket-book.

"Oh, gad!" gasped the Bounder.

The pimply man had not looked towards him. He was too concentrated on the work in hand to heed cyclists on the road. The Bounder's astonished eyes saw all that passed, and Redwing, further back, saw it all as clearly. Both would willingly have intervened: but there was no time. The whole thing passed in a flash. The pimply man, leaping up from the sprawling, dizzy baronet, thrust the pocket-book into his own pocket, and sprang back into the hawthorns that bordered the road. He was gone in the twinkling of an eye, reappearing on the further side of the hawthorns, and running across the open common like a deer.

Hardly a couple of seconds later, Vernon-Smith jammed on his brakes, and jumped down, at the side of the spluttering lord of Popper Court. Sir Hilton sat up in the dust, his hat off, his eyeglass streaming at the end of its cord, his hand going to the pocket from which the pocket-book had been snatched.

"Oh! Oh, gad! Urrgh! I have been robbed—it was the same man—the man in the wood—he has robbed me—

my pocket-book—my stamp—the Blue Mauritius—good gad! Where is he?"

"Let me help you, sir." Smithy lent a helping hand, and the dizzy old gentleman tottered to his feet, gasping for breath.

"Where is he? My pocket-book——" Sir Hilton fairly shrieked. "The stamp! He has robbed me! Two thousand pounds—good gad—where is he?"

Redwing came whizzing up.

"After him, Smithy!" he shouted. And without waiting for a reply, Tom Redwing whirled his bike off the road, shot through the clumps of hawthorns, and disappeared behind them, on the track of the fleeing pickpocket.

"Coming!" yelled the Bounder, his eyes ablaze with excitement.

"Boy! Did you see—where is he—what——"

"He's cut across the common, sir—we're getting after him," called back the Bounder, as he jumped on his machine and tore after Redwing.

Sir Hilton was left standing in the road, gasping and spluttering. Sir Hilton, certainly, would never have had the remotest chance of recovering the purloined pocket-book. He did not even know in what direction the pick-pocket had fled. But the two schoolboys on bicycles had more than a chance. The Bounder drove hard at his pedals, and overtook Redwing.

Far in the distance, running like a deer, could be seen the little slim figure, vanishing across the common.

"Put it on, Reddy," panted the Bounder. "He's got the old bean's pocket-book—we're going to get it back."

"We'll jolly well try."

"We'll get him all right! Put it on."

The green expanse of Courtfield Common was rough and bumpy for cycles. The machines fairly rocked, as Redwing and Smithy drove at the pedals. But they did not heed the rough going. Rough as it was, a bicycle covered the ground faster than the swiftest runner could hope to cover it, and they gained on the running man at every whirl of the pedals.

They saw him look back, and a blaze of rage and alarm came into the narrow foxy eyes as he saw the two riders behind. One glance told him that they had witnessed the robbery, and were in pursuit. He tore on again.

But for the two Greyfriars juniors, it would have been easy money for the pimpled man. He would have disappeared into space with Sir Hilton Popper's pocket-book, and its precious contents, and Sir Hilton would have been extremely unlikely ever to see his foxy face or his pimples again. But with two sturdy fellows on bicycles behind him, it was a very different proposition. Either of them was a match for him, physically: but if he could have handled one of them, assuredly he could not have handled the two: and Slim Judson's only hope was in his legs. And muscle, in the long run, had no chance against machinery.

He tore on desperately, with the two cyclists rocking and bumping behind, but gaining fast. He disappeared from sight in a clump of trees, on the border of Oak Lane, and the Bounder gave a breathless chuckle.

"We've got him now, Reddy! He won't get far along that lane! We've got him, old man! Put it on."

"Looks like it," panted Redwing.

Even on the rough common, the cyclists had gained fast. In the open lane it was likely to be a very brief matter. They drove at their pedals, and whizzed on, nothing doubting now that they had their man, pocket-book and pimples and all!

CHAPTER XVI

ANY PORT IN A STORM

Cecil Reginald Temple, of the Greyfriars Fourth, had the surprise of his life that afternoon. Life is full of surprises, and the unexpected often happens : but what happened to Temple of the Fourth was so very surprising, and so very unexpected, that it left him in quite a dizzy state. Indeed, as Temple told Dabney and Fry in the study later, a fellow could hardly believe that such things happened.

Temple was out on his jigger that afternoon. He was looking his usual spotless and rather dandified self, and his gleaming bike reflected back the rays of the sun. At a leisurely pace—Cecil Reginald never hurried, even on a bike—he was progressing along Oak Lane, from the direction of the river, and towards the Courtfield road : the wide common on his left, the high fence of the Three Fishers on his right. In a cheery frame of mind, satisfied with himself and things generally, Cecil Reginald pedalled gently on, thinking about nothing in particular. And when a slim, slight, hatless man, panting for breath and red with haste, burst suddenly into the lane from a clump of trees on the edge of the common, Cecil Reginald gave him only a careless disapproving glance, not in the least interested in him.

But the slim man was interested in Cecil Reginald.

He bolted into the lane like a scared rabbit, stood staring up and down it for a moment, and spotted the Fourth-former of Greyfriars on the bicycle. It was then that the surprising and unexpected thing happened, which Temple told Dabney and Fry afterwards that a fellow could hardly believe. Temple, indeed, was so utterly taken by surprise, that he did not know what was happening until it had happened. He couldn't have foreseen such a happening. Temple of the Fourth was not, perhaps, very bright : but the brightest fellow at Greyfriars could hardly have guessed that an absolute stranger would suddenly rush at him, knock him off his bike, and grab the machine away. So wildly lawless an act had never come within Temple's experience before. It was, indeed, hard for a fellow to believe.

But it happened!

There was no doubt about that, for Cecil Reginald Temple found himself suddenly sprawling in dust, while a slim man with a pimply face was shooting away on his bike, going like the wind for the Courtfield road.

Temple sat up, with the earth and the sky spinning round him. The expression of bemused astonishment on his face was almost idiotic.

"Ooooogh!" was all Temple said. It was all that he could say. He sat and gazed after his disappearing bike like a fellow in a dream.

But in less than a minute, two cyclists came whizzing off the common into the leafy lane. Temple transferred his dizzy gaze from the disappearing bike, to Vernon-Smith and Redwing.

They braked, and stared round for the pimply man. The trees had hidden him, for a minute or two, from their sight. Now he seemed to have vanished.

Temple staggered up.

"You fellows——!" he gasped.

"Seen a man running?" shouted the Bounder.

"Oh, crumbs! Yes! He's got my bike——"

"What?" yelled Smithy.

"Look!" Temple pointed with a shaking finger. "He—he—he pitched me off, and pinched my bike! I say, lend me your jigger to get after him——"

"Come on, Reddy."

"I say," gasped Temple, as Smithy and Redwing whirled in pursuit again, "I say, he's got my bike—lend me a jigger——"

Temple's voice died away behind two Remove fellows

grinding at their pedals. The Bounder knitted his brows as they tore on.

"We had him, Reddy—fairly had him—and that blithering nincompoop had to let him pinch a jigger! But by gum, we'll get him yet."

"Put it on, old chap."

The bicycles fairly raced. It was good going in Oak Lane, quite a change from the rugged common, and the riders went all out. The man ahead was riding as if for his life, in the hope of shaking off pursuit. But neither Redwing nor the Bounder was likely to be shaken off. Redwing was determined, if he could, to run down the thief and recover the stolen pocket-book: while the Bounder was thrilling with the excitement of the chase, and would not have missed it for worlds. They were good men on a jigger: certainly equal to the pasty-faced pimpled man in that line, if not a little better. The pickpocket had a start: but he did not lengthen it, with all his efforts: and he had no chance whatever of getting out of sight.

"We'll get him!" said the Bounder, between his teeth. "A spot of luck for him to bag that booby's jigger—but we'll get him. Nobody about in this lane—but when we get out on the road——"

"Go it!" breathed Redwing.

They whizzed on.

At the corner, where Oak Lane joined the high road, the hunted man cast desperate glances to and fro. On his left the high road ran towards Courtfield—with Sir Hilton Popper somewhere along it. On his right, it ran towards the village of Friardale, passing the gates of Greyfriars School. The man was, for the moment, doubtful in which direction to turn.

But that was settled for him, by the sight of three schoolboy cyclists coming from the direction of Courtfield—Peter Todd, Tom Brown, and Squiff, of the Remove. Smithy and Redwing sighted them at the same moment, and the Bounder yelled, at the top of his voice:

" Stop thief ! "

The three juniors stared round.

" Stop him ! " roared Redwing.

" Stop thief ! "

Peter Todd waved his hand : Squiff and Tom Brown shouted back. But they had no chance of stopping the fugitive, for he turned in the other direction, and tore away towards Greyfriars.

Smithy and Redwing reached the corner, from Oak Lane, as Peter, Squiff, and Tom Brown reached it, on the high road.

" What's up ? " shouted Squiff.

" Pickpocket—he's got old Popper's pocket-book—and Temple's bike," shouted back the Bounder. " Come on."

Five cyclists careered on after the man with the pimples. Peter Todd and Co. were keen enough to join in the chase.

The hunted man cast a glance back over his shoulder. If he had had a thought of turning on his pursuers, he had to give it up now that there were five of them. He rode on at a frantic speed again.

" We've got him ! " chuckled Smithy. " Got him by the short hairs ! There'll be a dozen fellows to stop him when we get near the school."

A tall spire was in sight, over the trees. They were nearing Greyfriars. The school gates came in sight : wide open, on a half-holiday. A big senior was standing there, with his hands in his pockets, looking out. It was Coker, of the Fifth Form, and he stared at the chase as it came sweeping into sight—the pimply man, red and panting and thick with perspiration, going all out in his frantic endeavour to escape with his plunder : Smithy, Redwing, Peter Todd, Squiff, and Tom Brown, strung out behind him, all going like the wind. Coker stared in astonishment.

They were not near enough for shouting, but the Bounder released one hand from his handle-bar, pointed to the fugitive, and waved to Coker. The big Fifth-form man could have rushed out of the gateway in the fugitive's path.

But Coker of the Fifth was not quick on the uptake. He only stared, as the chase came rushing on.

"Idiot!" breathed the Bounder.

"Look!" yelled Squiff. "There's Wingate——"

"And Gwynne——"

"We've got him now."

Ahead of the hapless fugitive, coming up the road from Friardale, Wingate and Gwynne of the Sixth-Form appeared in sight. The captain of Greyfriars and his companion were walking back to the school from the village, with the sedate and stately pace that became Sixth-Form men and prefects. But they became suddenly alert at the sight of the chase rushing towards them.

"Stop thief!" yelled the Bounder.

"Stop him, Wingate!"

"Stop thief!"

The shouts reached the ears of the two Sixth-Form men: but even without that warning, they could see how the matter stood. They were rather quicker on the uptake than Coker of the Fifth.

"Stop him, Gwynne," said Wingate.

And they stood in the middle of the road, hardly a dozen yards from the gateway, from which Coker was staring, ready to grasp at the fugitive as he came whizzing by.

The pimpled man stared at them. Then he stared back over his shoulder, at five cyclists coming on. He was caught between the two parties, and his game was up. If he carried on, he was running into the grasp of the two big Sixth-Form men—if he stopped for a single minute, five eager pursuers would be all round him. For a moment he was nonplussed: and then, swinging round his machine, he shot in at the great wide-open gateway on his left. What that gateway was, and to what it gave admittance, Slim Judson did not know: probably he had never even heard of Greyfriars School. What it was to him, at the moment, was the only escape from clutching hands, whatever might be beyond it: it was a case of any port in a storm. His machine spun in at the gateway: and Coker of the Fifth, realising at long last what the matter was, grabbed at him, and missed, and Slim Judson careered onward into the Greyfriars quad—where a shout of astonishment greeted his unexpected appearance.

CHAPTER XVII

NO SALE

" FISHY, old man——"

" Yep ! "

" Come in, old fellow."

Fisher T. Fish grinned. He was aware of the value of " old fellow " from Billy Bunter. And he guessed, reckoned, and calculated that he was wise to why the fat Owl was addressing him so cordially.

Fishy was coming down the Remove passage, when Bunter's fat voice hailed him from the open doorway of No. 7 Study. He paused : but he did not " come in ". Fisher T. Fish was one of the few fellows in the Remove whom Bunter had not asked for help with his lines that afternoon. And if Fishy's turn was coming, he was prepared to reply with a brief and emphatic " Nope ! "

" I say, come in—I want to speak to you, old chap," urged Bunter.

At which Fishy's grin widened. Looking past Bunter, he could see a sheet of impot paper on the table. On that sheet seven lines of Latin were written. Billy Bunter had started at " arma virumquo cano " and arrived at " moenia Romae ". Then laziness had supervened. Of the three hundred lines that impended over the fat head of the Owl of the Remove, seven had been written, and two hundred and ninety-three remained yet to write. To that two hundred and ninety-three, Fisher T. Fish had no intention of contributing so much as a semi-colon.

" I guess I can year you from yere, old fat piecan," said Fisher T. Fish. " Cut it short ! There's somethin' going on in the quad, and I'm going down to see what's on. Make it snappy."

" You see, old fellow——"

"If it's them lines, forget it," said Fisher T. Fish, briefly. "I guess I ain't looking for work, Bunter. Not so's you'd notice it."

"'Tain't the lines," said Bunter. "The fact is, Fishy, I've been disappointed about a postal-order——"

"Aw! Carry me home to die!" said Fisher T. Fish. "If that's all you've got to spill, you fat clam——"

"I've got something I want to sell—something jolly valuable, Fishy. Come in, old chap."

"I guess I'll give it the once-over," said Fisher T. Fish, more cordially, and he stepped into No. 7 Study.

Fisher T. Fish, the business-man of the Remove, was always ready to do business. Fishy couldn't wait till he grew up before he exercised his gifts in that line. He guessed and reckoned that a cute guy who had been raised in New York could turn his dimes into dollars, even within the limited scope of school. At all times was Fishy prepared to buy any article for a quarter its value, and keep it in hand till he could dispose of it for twice as much as it was worth.

Sounds of excitement, shouting and calling voices, could be heard in the distance, from the quadrangle, and Fishy was curious to learn what was going on. But curiosity took second place when his business instincts were aroused. If Bunter had a cricket bat, or a camera, or bicycle-bell, or even a dictionary, to sell, Fishy was the man to give him next to nothing for it.

"Trot it out, big boy," said Fisher T. Fish.

"I hate parting with it, old chap," said Bunter, sadly, "but my postal-order hasn't come——"

"I guess I've heard that one."

"And that beast Quelch won't let me go out till my lines are done," groaned Bunter. "My sister at Cliff House has got a hamper, Fishy, and I can't go over just because that beast Quelch——"

"Make it snappy."

"And Toddy's gone out on his bike with Field and

Brown, and never bothered his head about a fellow in his own study," went on Bunter, too full of grievances to make it snappy. "Nothing for tea, Fishy, and I'm actually stony——"

"You keeping me here till the cows come home, while you chew the rag?" asked Fisher T. Fish.

"Oh, really, Fishy! I just hate selling my gold watch——"

"Your whatter?"

"My gold watch! It was a present from my Uncle Carter—my rich uncle, you know—and I believe he gave twenty guineas for it——"

"Then they did him out of twenty pounds fifteen shillings!" said Fisher T. Fish, derisively. "I've sure wondered more'n once why that watch of yourn hasn't rolled away, Bunter—rolled gold ought to roll——"

"Beast!"

"If that's the lot, I guess I'll absquatulate," remarked Fisher T. Fish, and he turned to the door. Fishy was prepared to do business, if business was to be done: but Bunter's gold watch did not seem to attract him.

That gold watch of Bunter's, in fact, was a little too well known in the Remove. If Bunter believed that it was made of gold, he was the only fellow in his form that did. So far as quantity went, that watch was all right—there was quite a lot of it. But the quality was not on a par with the quantity. If it had ever kept time, it must have been before Bunter came to Greyfriars School: nobody there had ever heard it tick. Once or twice Bunter had opened the case, and jerked a fat thumb into the works, in an attempt to get it going. But even that heroic method had never had any success. The watch, at the moment, indicated twelve o'clock. It had indicated twelve o'clock for whole terms. And the great probability was that it never would indicate anything else. It was, in fact, some terms since Bunter had taken the trouble to wind it. Something was wrong with the winder, among other things: it would turn and turn for ever and ever, without producing any effect on the watch.

Bunter held it out for Fishy's inspection, and Fishy condescended to give it a contemptuous glance.

" Just look at it, old chap," urged Bunter. " Even if it ain't solid gold, it looks just as if it was——"

" It sure looks as much like solid gold as a brass poker," said Fisher T. Fish, taking the watch, and turning it over in his bony fingers. " Has it ever kept time ? "

" Splendid time-keeper," assured Bunter. " It doesn't exactly go, but—but when it does go, it's a splendid time-keeper. And—and there's a lot of metal in it, Fishy."

" There sure is," agreed Fisher T. Fish, " it only wants to be just a leetle bit bigger, and a guy could use it to carry coals in."

" Look here, what will you give me for it ? " yapped Bunter. He would gladly have punched Fisher T. Fish's head for his remarks about that watch. But he had to restrain that natural desire, in the circumstances. " I'll take a pound."

Fisher T. Fish blinked at him.

" Say, whadyer know ! " he ejaculated. " Did you say a pound, Bunter ? "

" Yes, I'll take a pound, old chap——"

" I guess you'd have to look for a genuine bonehead to give you one," grinned Fisher T. Fish, " and then you'd have to catch him with his eyes shut."

Billy Bunter breathed hard.

In his dire circumstances, cut off from Bessie's hamper, disappointed about a postal-order, and with neither of his study-mates available to stand tea in the study, Bunter had made up his mind to part with that watch. He felt that it was hard to part with it. But parting with it was, apparently, going to be harder than he had anticipated !

" Well, look here, what will you give me for it ? " he demanded.

Fishy's reply was concise but clear.

" Nix ! " he said.

"Oh, really, Fishy——"

"I guess I wouldn't take it as a gift, old-timer." Fisher T. Fish dropped the watch on the table. "So-long."

"Look here, you cheeky beast——!" roared Bunter.

But Fisher T. Fish was gone. There was no business to be done in No. 7 Study, and Fishy was not wasting any more time there. He jerked away down the passage, interested once more in the uproar that was going on below.

"Beast!" hissed Bunter.

He blinked out of the study after the departing Fishy, and shook a fat fist after him. That valuable watch had been his last hope of raising the wind in time for tea. His last hope had departed with Fisher T. Fish. Bunter was strongly tempted to follow Fishy down the passage and punch his bony head. Indeed he would have done so, but for the probability of a return punch from a bony set of knuckles. So he contented himself with shaking his fist after Fishy, and glaring after him with a glare that almost cracked his spectacles.

But the next moment he burst into a fat chuckle.

Fisher T. Fish had reached the end of the passage, when a figure came suddenly bolting across the landing into the passage, crashing right into Fishy. There was a fearful howl from Fisher T. Fish as he went sprawling under the collision, and spread out on the old oak floor.

"Aw! Wake snakes! Great John James Brown, whadyer know! Whooop!"

"He, he, he!" cachinnated Bunter.

Fisher T. Fish sprawled on his back, and over him sprawled the figure that had crashed into him, and Billy Bunter, blinking from the doorway of No. 7 Study, chuckled loud and long.

CHAPTER XVIII

IN A HORNET'S NEST

"Stop thief!"

"Look out!"

"Stop him!"

"Collar him!"

"Bag him!"

It was a roar in the old quadrangle of Greyfriars. A hundred fellows were staring, shouting, calling. Seldom had the old quad seen such a spot of excitement.

"Oh, my eye!" gasped Slim Judson.

He glared round him like a trapped animal.

In sheer desperation, to escape immediate capture, he had turned in at that wide gateway, not knowing whither it led. But a few moments later he realised that he had got out of the frying-pan into the fire. In the Greyfriars quad he was in the middle of a hornet's nest.

The sight of a strange man, hatless, his face ablaze with exertion, careering into the quad on a bike, drew every eye at once. Fellows ran up from all sides—masters stared from study windows—even the Head looked out from his window in amazement. One stare round told Mr. Judson what he had done—plunged into a school: about the last spot he would have ventured into willingly. Mr. Judson longed for the open spaces—and he had landed in an extremely thickly-populated spot.

"Gum!" breathed Slim. "Strike me pink and blue! It's a blooming school—oh, strike me blue and crimson!"

Behind him, the pursuers came crowding in at the gateway: Wingate and Gwynne of the Sixth, Coker of the Fifth, Vernon-Smith, Redwing, Peter Todd, Squiff, and Tom Brown of the Remove. They were all shouting, pointing, or yelling.

SLIM JUDSON CAREERED ON, ON TEMPLE'S BIKE, WILDLY

" Stop thief ! "

" Collar him ! "

" Stop him ! "

Slim Judson careered on, on Temple's bike, wildly. Mr. Quelch stared from one study window, Mr. Hacker from another, Mr. Wiggins from a third : and from the big bay window of Common-Room, Mr. Prout, master of the Fifth, leaned out staring with popping eyes.

" Stop thief ! "

" Bag him ! "

Potter of the Fifth jumped in the way of the bike, and grabbed at the rider. Mr. Judson swerved to avoid him, and fairly ran into Greene of the Fifth.

Greene yelled and went over. The bike wobbled wildly, and curled up. Slim Judson landed on his feet, with the activity of a cat. He dodged Potter's clutching hand, and ran.

" After him ! "

" Collar him ! "

" Bag him ! "

No doubt Slim Judson still hoped to find some way out of the hornet's nest into which he had inadvertently run. Crowds of fellows were after him, round him, running to intercept him, and there really seemed no chance. But with a Blue Mauritius worth two thousand pounds in his pocket, Mr. Judson clung to the faintest wisp of hope. He ran and twisted and doubled like a hunted animal.

But there was no escape for him. He came to a panting halt under the big bay window of Common-Room, from which Mr. Prout leaned, and stared, and boomed.

" What is all this ? " boomed Prout. " What is all this unprecedented uproar ? Who is this man ? What is the meaning of this unparalleled disturbance ? What——"

Prout was suddenly interrupted.

Slim Judson stood, for a moment, panting, staring back at the swarm of fellows rushing him down. He had only a moment. Then, in sheer desperation, he leaped up on the low sill of the bay window, and plunged headlong in, knocking Mr. Prout aside as he did so.

"Oh!" gasped Prout, as he staggered. "What—what—— Oh!"

"Stop him!" came a roar from the quad.

"Stop thief!"

"Collar him, Prout!" yelled the Bounder.

Faces swarmed at the window. Slim Judson, plunging in, landed on hands and knees, but he bounced up like a ball. But as he bounced, a plump hand descended on his shoulder. Prout grasped him.

"Stop!" boomed Prout. "Who are you? How dare you—— Whooo-hooop!"

Mr. Prout had not expected to receive a vicious jab on the widest part of his circumference. In the exciting circumstances he might, perhaps, have expected something of the sort. But he hadn't! He staggered back from that jab, gasping for wind, his grasp slipping from Slim's shoulder.

"Ooooooooogh!" gurgled Mr. Prout.

Slim Judson cut across the room to the door.

"Urrrggh! Stop! Ruffian!" gurgled Prout. "Stop! I order you to—ooogh—stop——!"

Slim was not likely to stop! He fairly whizzed across Common-Room. Monsieur Charpentier jumped out of an armchair to intercept him. A swing of Slim's arm sent the little French gentleman toppling.

"Mon Dieu!" gasped Mossoo, as he toppled. "Ciel! Wow!" Monsieur Charpentier sat down, quite suddenly.

Slim tore open the door of Common-Room, and tore out. He found himself in a wide passage, with many doors on it. Some of those doors were open, and from one, Mr. Quelch was coming out, from another, Mr. Hacker.

"Bless my soul! Here is the man!" exclaimed Mr. Quelch.

"Stop him!" exclaimed Mr. Hacker.

Slim, panting, cast a wild glance around him. He had some vague hope of dropping out of a back window, and resuming his flight for parts unknown. But there was no chance of that.

Quelch strode at him, with a grim brow, followed by Hacker. Quelch was not a man to be jabbed like Prout, or toppled over like Monsieur Charpentier. Quelch could have handled Slim as easily as a terrier dealing with a rat. Slim did not wait to be handled. He darted frantically away. He found himself crossing a wide hall, from which a great staircase led to the regions above. There was a roar of voices. The Bounder and some other fellows were clambering in at Common-Room window : a whole horde rushed round to the door, and there was a roar as the breathless, panting fugitive was sighted within.

" Here he is ! "

" Collar him ! "

" Bag him ! "

Slim darted at the staircase. Again it was a case of any port in a storm ! He bounded up the stairs like a kangaroo, as a score of fellows rushed at him. He did those stairs in record time, and was well ahead of pursuit as he bounded on the study landing.

The interior of Greyfriars was, of course, quite unknown country to Slim Judson. His only hope was to escape from some window, before hands could be laid on him. He stared round him on the study landing, to get his bearings—and found himself staring at Fitzgerald of the Fifth, in the doorway of the games-study, at the corner of the Fifth-form passage.

" Howly mother av Moses ! " ejaculated Fitzgerald.

Slim did not wait for further remarks from Fitzgerald of the Fifth. He cut across the landing in another direction, and ran up the three steps to the Remove landing. From that landing a passage opened, and Slim bolted into it like a hunted rabbit into a burrow.

Crash !

Mr. Judson was much too pressed for time to take note whether anyone might be coming down the passage into which he bolted. Fisher T. Fish, though he knew that some unaccustomed uproar was going on below, naturally was not expecting a hunted man to shoot into the passage like a bolt from a cross-bow. Both of them were taken by surprise.

Fishy yelled and crashed, and over him crashed Mr. Judson. They mixed up in a yelling heap. And from the doorway of a study up the passage, a fat Owl blinked at them through his big spectacles, and cachinnated :

" He, he, he ! "

CHAPTER XIX

THE LAST CHANCE

" He, he, he—— Oh ! "

Billy Bunter suddenly ceased to chuckle.

Instead of chuckling, he jumped.

His little round eyes nearly popped through his big round spectacles, in his astonishment and alarm.

" Oh ! " gasped Bunter.

It had been fearfully amusing to see Fisher T. Fish knocked over, and sprawled over, by someone suddenly running into the passage. But as that someone bounded up, with a red furious face and blazing eyes, Bunter ceased to be amused. It was not someone belonging to Greyfriars, as he would naturally have supposed, who had crashed into Fisher T. Fish. It was a stranger to Bunter's eyes—a panting, furious, desperate-looking man, the mere sight of whom was terrifying to a fat Owl.

Slim Judson, almost winded by the shock, stood panting. He gave Fisher T. Fish an almost murderous glare—which caused Fisher T. Fish to squirm away from him and scramble up in frantic haste and bolt across the landing. Who he was, what he was, Fishy didn't know and couldn't guess : but his fierce and savage look was enough for Fishy.

Panting, the hunted man stared up the passage. He could not turn back—the roar of pursuit was behind him. His stare revealed only one person in the passage ahead of him—a fat junior, who was blinking at him in amazement and terror. The desperate look on Slim's face might have scared a stouter heart than Billy Bunter's.

Only for a second the man stood there, panting : then he came running up the passage. Bunter, certainly, could not have stopped him, if the thought of doing so had occurred to him.

But that thought did not occur to Bunter. What occurred to Bunter was to take to his heels—which he promptly did !

With a gasp of terror, the fat Owl flew up the passage, with a speed that would have done him credit on the cinder-path. He knew no more than Fisher T. Fish who or what the man was : but he knew that he was scared out of his fat wits as the man came running up the passage towards him : and his feet hardly touched the old oak planks as he fled.

Slim came speeding on behind him. His pattering footsteps gave the last touch to Bunter's terror. He was not in the least interested in Bunter : but to the fat Owl, it was pursuit. Few Greyfriars fellows would have deemed Bunter capable of the speed with which he flew up the Remove passage, and bolted up the box-room stair at the end.

Utterly unheeding him, Slim Judson hurtled on. But as he reached the open doorway of No. 7 Study, where the fat junior had been standing, he paused. For a fraction of a second he paused : then he darted into the study. Slim's peculiar way of life had taught him to take quick decisions. For the moment—though only for the moment—no eyes were on him—Bunter's back was to him, as the frightened fat Owl bolted, and the pursuers were not yet across the landing : and the idea of hiding, and watching for a chance to escape later, flashed into Slim's wary mind.

He shot into the study. Swiftly, but softly, he shut the door after him. Then he stood gulping in breath, in great gasps, while the perspiration streamed down his face.

Just within the door, standing close to the wall so that the door would hide him if it opened, he stood—and listened.

He had been only in time—barely in time. A roar of voices, a trampling of feet, sounded from the direction of the landing, and surged up the passage.

" This way," the Bounder was shouting.

" Where is he ? "

" He ran up this passage——"

" Come on ! "

Slim suppressed his panting breathing, as the uproar of shouting voices and innumerable footsteps surged up the Remove passage from the landing. If they looked into that study, he was cornered, like a rat in a trap.

But the rush went by the door of No. 7 Study, as it went by the doors of the other studies. For the moment, at least, it did not occur to the pursuers that the hunted man had sought cover in a Remove study. The chase thundered on up the passage to the further end.

A sharp voice came to Slim's ears : so near, that it made him catch his breath. Only the shut door was between him and Mr. Quelch !

" Vernon-Smith ! Redwing ! Todd ! Have you seen the man ? "

" He ran up this passage, sir——"

" I guess he bowled me over, sir—the piecan sure did bowl me over——"

" He's here somewhere——"

" He's got old Popper's—I mean Sir Hilton Popper's—pocket-book, sir—and he pinched Temple's bike to get away——"

" He must be found and secured ! The prefects will look for him ! All the juniors will remain in this passage, or go into their studies——"

" We can handle him all right, sir——"

" That will do, Vernon-Smith."

" But, sir——"

" Silence ! Wingate——" Mr. Quelch was interrupted, by a shout from up the passage.

" This way ! Somebody's in the box-room."

" Come on, you fellows——"

" I have told you to be silent, Vernon-Smith. Remain where you are. Wingate, Gwynne, Loder, please search the box-room for the man. I will come with you. All the juniors will remain here."

Every word came clearly to the breathless man listening inside the study door. Mr. Quelch stalked on up the passage, and ascended the box-room stair with Wingate, Gwynne, and Loder. The Remove master, and three hefty men of the Sixth, were certainly enough to deal with the fugitive, if they found him : but they left a noisy and discontented crowd of juniors in the passage.

"Cheek! He's our game, not Quelchy's." Herbert Vernon-Smith waited, judiciously, till his form-master was out of hearing, before he made that remark. "Like his dashed cheek——"

"They'll get him all right, Smithy."

"If he's dodged into the box-room——"

"Somebody's there——"

"They'll get him!"

Some of the speakers were quite near the door of No. 7 Study. Slim Judson gritted his teeth as he listened. For some reason, unknown to Mr. Judson, they supposed that he had dodged into a box-room, and for the moment, no one was thinking of looking into the studies. It was a respite : but likely to be only a brief one, for certainly they would not find him in any box-room : and a search of the other rooms was sure to follow.

On tiptoe, fearful of being heard by the buzzing crowd in the passage, Slim crossed to the window of No. 7, and looked out.

One look was enough for him. There was a drop of thirty feet outside the window : and, as if that was not enough, there were a dozen or more Greyfriars fellows in sight below. He backed quickly from the window.

There was no escape that way.

It was borne in upon the wretched thief's mind that there was no escape at all. For the moment he had a respite : but sooner or later—probably rather sooner than later—they would have him. He could not escape by the window, and to leave by the door was to walk into the hands of the hunters. With deep feelings, Slim had to realise that the game was up, and that he was booked to join his confederate in the cells at Courtfield Police-Station.

And in his pocket was Sir Hilton Popper's pocket-book, containing the Blue Mauritius, worth two thousand pounds : the biggest prize Slim had ever landed in all his career as a snapper-up of other people's property ! A tiny thing—a mere wisp of printed paper—but worth two thousand pounds to a collector—and when Slim was collared, as collared he must be, it would be found on him. His confederate had got away with it the previous night, only to be captured and lose it again : Slim, with what had seemed to him a great spot of luck, had got away with it in his turn, only to meet with exactly the same fate ! Slim could not help feeling that it was very rough luck.

But—— !

But Slim's cunning brain was working actively. They were going to get him—that was certain. Probably it was only a matter of minutes. But those minutes were his.

If he could hide the stamp somewhere——

They would find the pocket-book on him, but not the Blue Mauritius. So small an object could easily be hidden. And later, when he came out of the " stone jug ", he had a chance of recovering it.

It was a dubious hope. But it was all that remained to Mr. Judson. It was a chance, at least.

He grabbed the fat pocket-book from his pocket, and opened it. There were a good many papers in it, including the unwelcome missive Sir Hilton Popper had received from his Inspector of Taxes, and a wad of currency notes. Slim did not heed the papers, or even the notes. From a small socket, he extracted the blue-printed stamp, and returned the pocket-book to his pocket.

Outside the study, voices were buzzing. He did not heed them. He stared round him, in search of a hiding-place for the stamp. And a sudden hopeful gleam came into his eyes, as they fell upon a big watch lying on the table.

Some schoolboy—no doubt that fat fellow he had seen at the study door—had left that watch there. Slim snatched it up.

The value of Billy Bunter's big gold watch did not appeal to Mr. Judson. Even if he had been free to pick it up and depart with it, he would not have taken the trouble. It was of quite other things that he was thinking. He had found the hiding-place he wanted for the stolen stamp!

He snapped open the case at the back. There was plenty of space for so small an article as a stamp to be hidden within—more space than Mr. Judson needed.

In another moment, the case was snapped shut on a Post-Office Blue Mauritius Twopenny, worth two thousand pounds!

Slim replaced the watch on the table.

It was a wrench—a tough wrench—to part with the Blue Mauritius, even with a sporting chance of getting it back again later. But it was the only chance he had of getting his thievish fingers on it again. If they found it on him it was gone for good: now, at least, a chance remained.

Who would dream of looking for it in a schoolboy's watch? They would search for it, there was little doubt about that—search high and low. But the last place they would think of looking into would be a schoolboy's watch. And sooner or later, Mr. Judson would interview the owner of that watch, in some quiet spot outside the school! If it was that fat fellow he had seen at the door of the study he would know him again easily enough. If it was some other fellow, his task would be more difficult: but two thousand pounds was worth a spot of trouble. It was a chance, at least—but there was not the ghost of a chance, if they found the stamp on him.

Feeling slightly relieved in his mind, Mr. Judson listened to the buzz of voices outside the study. They would have him—they had as good as got him already—but they couldn't keep him for ever in the "jug". There was still an ultimate hope of getting away with the Blue Mauritius. Mr. Judson drew what comfort he could from that hope, as he waited for what was coming to him!

CHAPTER XX

ONLY BUNTER

" Oh, crikey ! " gasped Billy Bunter.

He flew up the Remove passage, and bounded up the box-room stair like a fat kangaroo. That awful-looking man, with his glinting eyes and desperate face, was behind him : and a bulldog on his trail could not have made the fat Owl put on more speed. He fairly whizzed. He shot into the box-room like an arrow from a bow, and slammed the door after him. He groped for the key, remembered that it had long been missing, grabbed the bolt, and jammed it home. Then, and not till then, did he totter towards one of the boxes, sit down on the same, and gasp and gasp and gasp for breath, quite winded by his wild flight from that unknown and awful man.

Footsteps on the stairs made him jump like a startled rabbit. His fat heart almost died within him, as the door-handle was turned from outside. Only the bolt kept the door from opening : and it certainly did not occur to Billy Bunter that it was Bolsover major, of the Remove, who was turning the door-handle. He had no doubt that it was that awful man : and he sat on the box, and quaked, his eyes and spectacles fixed apprehensively on the door.

Then there was a shout, followed by more shouting, a trampling of feet, and again the door-handle was turned. Bunter, with quaking heart, watched the door with popping eyes. It seemed that there were more than one of them—and the fat Owl's terrified imagination peopled the landing outside the box-room door with a swarm of desperate-looking men like the one he had seen in the Remove passage.

" Oh, crikey ! " groaned Bunter.

There was a heavy shove at the door outside, which made

it creak, and almost made Bunter's fat heart jump into his mouth.

Then came a voice, which to Bunter's utter amazement, was that of George Wingate, of the Sixth Form, captain of Greyfriars.

" The door's fastened inside, sir."

" Then the man must be here." This, to Bunter's further amazement, was the well-known rap of his form-master, Mr. Quelch. " The door must be forced."

" Oh, scissors ! " gasped Bunter.

Knock ! knock ! came sharply on the panels.

" Open this door at once ! " came Mr. Quelch's sharp voice. " We know you are here ! Open this door im mediately."

" Oh, crikey ! "

" Otherwise the door will be forced. I advise you to open it," snapped the Remove master. " Answer me."

" Oh, lor' ! "

Billy Bunter tottered off the box. That awful man, apparently, hadn't pursued him up to the box-room : it was Quelch, and Wingate, on the landing. The fat Owl tottered to the door.

Knock ! knock !

" Will you open this door immediately ! " snapped Mr. Quelch. " Answer me at once ! Do you hear ? "

" Oh, crikey ! " gasped Bunter.

He dragged back the bolt. The door flew open : and Wingate of the Sixth appeared in the doorway. The stalwart captain of Greyfriars had his fists clenched and his hands up, ready to tackle the hunted intruder, if the latter showed fight. He jumped almost clear of the floor at the sight of Billy Bunter.

" Oh ! What—how—where——" stuttered Wingate. " Bunter ! It—it—it's Bunter here, sir—only Bunter——"

" What ? " exclaimed Mr. Quelch.

He rustled in after Wingate. He gave the gasping fat Owl a stare, or rather a glare. and his sharp glance shot round the box-room. That room was fairly thickly populated by boxes and trunks : but it contained only one human inhabitant : William George Bunter of the Remove. There was no sign of the hunted man.

"Upon my word!" exclaimed Mr. Quelch. "Where——?"

"Not here, sir," said Gwynne of the Sixth, looking in.

"Only Bunter!" grinned Loder.

"Bunter! What are you doing here? Why was the door bolted?" thundered Mr. Quelch.

"I—I—I——"

"Where is the man? Was he here? Have you seen him?"

"Oh—yes—no—oh, crikey——"

"Explain yourself, you stupid boy," thundered Mr. Quelch. "Why are you here? What——"

"He—he—he——"

"What?"

"He—he—he was after me," stuttered Bunter. "An awful-looking man—oh, crikey—— I—I—I thought he was after me—oh, lor'——"

Mr. Quelch gave an angry snort.

"Pah! No one is here, Wingate, excepting that foolish boy. It must have been he whom Bolsover heard in the box-room, not the man we are seeking at all. This utterly stupid boy has caused us to waste time. The man must be found and secured—come at once. He may be in one of the attics."

Mr. Quelch whirled round and departed. Wingate, Gwynne, and Loder followed him. Evidently, the elusive intruder had to be sought for elsewhere. Several small rooms opened from the landing outside the box-room.

Billy Bunter rolled after them. Even the fat Owl realised that there was no danger, with his form-master and three hefty prefects on the spot. There was a shout from the Bounder, in the Remove passage. He was looking up the stair.

"Haven't you got him, Wingate?"

The Greyfriars captain did not answer: but it was evident that they had not "got" him. Mr. Quelch's brows were knitted. Minutes had been wasted, owing to Bunter's antics, and it seemed probable that the fugitive had been making use of them.

"Search the attics at once," rapped Mr. Quelch.

"Yes, sir."

Wingate, Gwynne, and Loder proceeded to search the attics. Mr. Quelch stood on the little landing, frowning. Billy Bunter edged past him, and rolled down the stair to the Remove passage.

"That fat ass!" exclaimed the Bounder, staring at him. "Was it you in the box-room, you piffling porpoise?"

"Oh, really, Smithy——"

"That blithering chump!" said Peter Todd. "But where's the pickpocket? Have you seen him, Bunter?"

"He—he—he was after me," gasped Bunter. "An awful-looking ruffian—he—he was after me—oh, crikey! I—I say, you fellows, who—who was it?"

"Only a pickpocket, fathead! He snooped old Popper's pocket-book, and he's got it on him. If you saw him, why didn't you collar him?"

"Oh, really, Toddy——"

"Up in the attics, most likely," said Vernon-Smith. "He can't get out—if he dodges the pre's, he will have to make a break this way. Look out."

"What-ho!" said Squiff, "we'll get him if he comes this way."

"Oh, crikey!" gasped Bunter.

He rolled hurriedly down the passage to his study.

Smithy, and most of the other fellows, were quite keen to collar the intruder, and rather hoped that he would dodge the prefects and give them a chance. Billy Bunter did not share that keenness in the very least. If there was the remotest chance of that desperate-looking man reappearing in the Remove passage, Bunter preferred to be safe in his study, with the door shut and locked!

He opened the door of No. 7 Study and rolled in.

A brassy glimmer on the table, from the sunlight at the window, caught his eyes and his spectacles. He remembered that big gold watch, which he had utterly forgotten in his terrified flight from the awful-looking man who had so suddenly appeared on the scene.

He rolled across to the table and picked up the watch. Fisher T. Fish had disdained it, and appraised its value at " nix ". But it was Bunter's gold watch : and he hooked it on the chain and restored it to his waistcoat pocket.

Then he turned to shut the door, and turn the key.

But he did not shut the door, neither did he turn the key. For as he turned, he became aware of another inhabitant of the study—a slight man with a pimply face and a spotted necktie, backing against the wall beside the doorway.

For a single instant, Slim Judson looked at Bunter, and Bunter looked at Slim Judson—his eyes popping through his spectacles. Then a yell of terror woke every echo of the Remove passage.

" Yaroooh ! Help ! He's here ! I say, you fellows ! Help ! help ! help ! Fire ! Murder ! Help ! Yarooooh ! Help ! "

CHAPTER XXI

CAPTURED

"WHAT the thump—— ?"

"What the jolly old dickens——"

"That's Bunter——"

"What—— !"

There were twenty or thirty fellows in the Remove passage, and they all jumped, and stared, and exclaimed, at the sound of a frantic yell from Bunter's study. That frantic yell rang and echoed, along the passage, from the landing at one end, to the box-room stair at the other. Bunter was putting on steam.

"Help! Help! Help! Help!" came Bunter's wild yell. "He's here—he's got me—— I say, you fellows—— Help!"

"Oh, gad! He is in a study—Bunter's study!" yelled the Bounder. "Come on, you men!"

Smithy led a rush to No. 7.

He hurled the door open, and rushed in. Peter Todd, Squiff, Tom Brown, Bolsover major, were at his heels. Fry and Dabney of the Fourth, Coker and Potter and Greene of the Fifth, came running up, and poured in after them. A score of fellows crammed round the doorway. If the fugitive was in that study, there was no escape for him.

And he was!

From Bunter's frantic yelling, it might have been supposed that the fat Owl was struggling for his life in the grip of a desperado. But it was not quite so bad as that. Bunter had backed as far as the window, to get as far as possible from the man in the spotted necktie, on whom his eyes and spectacles were fixed in terror. But the pimpled man had not made a motion towards him. Slim Judson knew that the game was up, and he was not in the least disposed to make a fight for it against overwhelming odds. He was leaning on the wall beside the door, with his hands in his pockets, scowling across the study at the yelling fat Owl, but making no movement towards him.

" Here he is ! " roared Smithy.

" That's the man ! "

" We've got him ! "

Slim Judson gave the crowding schoolboys a black look. Ten minutes ago, Slim had been making desperate efforts to escape : he had jabbed Prout, and toppled over Monsieur Charpentier : and certainly he would have put up any amount of jabbing and toppling now, had it been any present help in time of need. But as it could only have led to rough handling, with not the remotest chance of getting away, Slim scowled, but was otherwise quite lamb-like.

" 'Ere I am," he said, " that blinking winder's too 'igh from the ground to give a covey a chance ! 'Ere I am."

The Bounder paused. He was ready to rush and grasp, and so were the other fellows : but evidently it was not necessary. The cornered rascal was not thinking of resistance.

" We've got you, my man," he said.

" You 'ave ! " agreed Slim.

" And you've got old Popper's pocket-book," added Smithy.

Slim gave him a sharp look, and recognised him as one of the two schoolboys on bikes who had started the pursuit. His foxy eyes glinted at Smithy.

" You was quick off the mark, you was, young gentleman," he said. " If you hadn't been so 'andy, I wouldn't be 'ere now. I'd jest like to meet you in some quiet place on a dark evening, I would."

The Bounder laughed.

" I fancy I could handle you, if you did," he said.

" I say, you fellows, get hold of him," howled Billy Bunter, from the window. " I say, that's the man——"

" Coming quietly ? " asked Smithy.

"Quiet as a lamb," answered Mr. Judson. "Jest my luck to run into a blinking school! Who'd have thought it? Out of the blinking frying-pan into the blinking fire! It's 'ard luck on a covey!"

"Take his other arm, Reddy."

Vernon-Smith took one arm of the captured pickpocket, Redwing the other. They marched him out of the study—much to Billy Bunter's relief—into the passage, into the midst of a buzzing swarm of fellows of all forms.

Mr. Judson did not resist. He was, as he had said, as quiet as a lamb. The Bounder was grinning gleefully. Mr. Quelch was on the box-room landing—the three prefects were searching the attics. Quelch had taken the matter out of Smithy's hands: but it was Smithy who had made the capture, after all, while Quelch and the prefects were on a false scent.

"Somebody had better call Quelch," chuckled the Bounder. "He might be interested to hear that we've got the man."

"Ha, ha, ha!"

Peter Todd ran up the passage, and mounted the box-room stair. From the landing, Mr. Quelch turned a freezing eye on him.

"Todd! Go down at once."

"But, sir——"

"No juniors are required here," snapped Mr. Quelch. "I have told you to remain in the passage, Todd."

"Yes, sir! But——"

"Go back at once!"

"Oh! But—but I came to tell you, sir——!" gasped Peter.

"Another word, Todd, and——!"

"Oh, crumbs! We've got the man, sir!" shrieked Peter.

"Eh! What! What did you say, Todd?"

"We've got him, sir! He was hiding in a study——!"

"Oh!" ejaculated Mr. Quelch, "I—I—I see! Oh!

Quite! Wingate! Gwynne! Loder! Come this way! The man has been found."

Mr. Quelch hurried down the box-room stair. Wingate and Gwynne and Loder hurried after him. The loud voice of Coker of the Fifth was heard, as they descended into the Remove passage.

"You fags get away! Do you hear? I'll take charge of that pickpocket——"

"Mind your own business, Coker."

"If you want me to smack your head, young Vernon-Smith——"

"Barge that Fifth-Form ass out of the way, you men."

"Look here——!" roared Coker.

"That will do, Coker!" Mr. Quelch arrived on the scene. "Stand aside, Coker! Wingate—Gwynne—take charge of this man, and bring him downstairs. I will telephone for a constable immediately."

Vernon-Smith and Redwing handed the prisoner over to the two prefects. If Mr. Judson had been lamb-like before, he was doubly lamb-like now, with the two big Sixth-Form men gripping his arms.

Mr. Quelch rustled away. Wingate and Gwynne followed him, with the prisoner between them. Loder brought up the rear. Half an hour later Mr. Judson, in charge of a constable from Courtfield, was gone: leaving Greyfriars still in a buzz of excitement.

CHAPTER XXII

MISSING

" Hallo, hallo, hallo ! "

" Old Popper ! "

" Popping up again ! "

" The popfulness of the esteemed Popper is terrific."

" Looks jolly fierce ! "

Harry Wharton and Co., as yet unaware of the spot of excitement at the school during their absence, were walking back to Greyfriars from Cliff House, after tea with Marjorie and her friends. They had almost reached the school gates, when the Popper Court car whirled into sight, with Sir Hilton sitting in it as bolt upright as a ramrod, and with an expression on his face that was inadequately described as " fierce."

The Famous Five had often seen Sir Hilton Popper, and, almost as often, they had seen him looking grim, or grumpy, or fierce : and occasionally in a very bad temper. But they had never seen him looking quite like this before. His shaggy grey brows were knitted, and under them his eyes gleamed and glinted : his lips were set in a hard line : his whole look was that of a man in the worst temper ever. Probably others, as well as the Famous Five, glanced at him curiously as the car whirled past : but the lord of Popper Court was far too lofty a personage to care what the public might think of his black looks. Utterly regardless, and probably contemptuous, of all other inhabitants of the earth, Sir Hilton sat with knitted brows, glinting eyes, and set teeth, as the car whirled on—and the whole world, if it liked, was welcome to discern that something or other had come between the wind and his nobility !

" I wonder what's biting him now," remarked Bob. " He

looked almost good-tempered when we left him in the wood this afternoon."

"On somebody's track," said Johnny Bull, with a grunt. "Perhaps somebody else has been in his dashed woods—some other silly ass taking a short cut——"

"He's going to Greyfriars," said Harry Wharton, as the car slowed to turn in at the gates. "Somebody's booked for trouble."

"Can't be us!" said Frank Nugent. "The old bean was kind enough to forgive us, after we stopped that pick-pocket and he got his stamp back. Even old Popper wouldn't rake it up again."

"Not our esteemed selves this time," agreed Hurree Jamset Ram Singh. "But the esteemed and ridiculous Popper looks terrifically infuriated."

"Hallo, hallo, hallo. He wants us!" exclaimed Bob.

The car, about to turn in at the school gates, had stopped, as Sir Hilton sighted the five juniors in the road. He leaned from the window and waved an imperious hand, evidently as a sign for the schoolboys to come up. Apparently he desired to speak to them.

"Come on!" said Harry: and the Co. hastened their steps. What Sir Hilton wanted, they could not guess. Irritable and truculent old gentleman as he was, he could hardly be thinking of calling them to account, after all, for having taken that short cut through his woods that afternoon: after having magnanimously pardoned them, for services rendered. But it was clear that somebody, or something, had stirred his deepest ire.

They "capped" the baronet respectfully as they came up. He gave them a glare. But they were able to discern that that was merely because he was in a state of excitement and wrath. They were not the objects of his ire. Sir Hilton glared at them, simply because in his present frame of mind he could not have looked at anybody without glaring.

"Has the stamp been found?" barked Sir Hilton.

"The—the stamp," stammered Harry, astonished by the question. Unaware of the wild adventures of the Blue Mauritius since they had seen Sir Hilton in the wood that afternoon, the Famous Five were quite at a loss.

"Yes! The stamp! Do you not know what a stamp is?" Sir Hilton almost roared. "Are you a fool, boy?"

"Oh! I—I hope not," gasped Harry. "But—I don't understand——"

"The stamp that was in my pocket-book!" barked Sir Hilton. "The Blue Mauritius stamp! Has it been found? Its value is two thousand pounds! Has it been found?"

"I—I—I——" stammered Harry. "Has—has it been lost?"

"The boy is a fool! The stamp was not in the pocket-book when the man was searched at the police-station," hooted Sir Hilton. "Has it been found in the school? Cannot you understand, boy? The stamp is of great value—enormous value! It has not been found on him. From all accounts, he cannot possibly have got rid of it before he reached the school. Has it been found here?"

"I—I——" Wharton could only stutter. His comrades could only stare. No member of the Famous Five was able to make head or tail of this.

"Are you a blockhead?" exclaimed Sir Hilton. "I am asking you a plain question. Has the stamp been found? It is a matter of the greatest importance. Were you among the boys who seized him in the school?"

"Eh! What——?"

"Cannot you answer a simple question?" bawled Sir Hilton. "Good gad! What is my old school coming to, when a Greyfriars boy cannot answer a simple question? Has the stamp been found in the school?"

"We—we've been out all the afternoon——" gasped Harry. He realised that something must have happened at Greyfriars that afternoon, of which he as yet knew nothing. "We're just coming back from Cliff House——"

" What ? what ? Then you know nothing of the matter——"

" Nothing at all——"

" Then why did you not say so ? " hooted Sir Hilton. " Pah ! You are wasting my time with your stupidity ! Pah ! Drive on, James. Pah ! "

Sir Hilton sat back and the car turned in at the gates. Harry Wharton and Co. stared after it, and stared at one another.

" What on earth's been going on here this afternoon, while we've been at Cliff House ? " asked Bob.

" Goodness knows."

" Old Popper expects us to know, as well as goodness," remarked Johnny Bull, sarcastically. " Nobody's got anything to think of except his affairs. If he's lost his silly stamp again, the whole county of Kent ought to be sitting up and taking notice."

The Famous Five went in at the gates, extremely curious to know what had happened during their absence. They found a crowd of fellows in the quad, and a buzz of excited voices.

" I say, you fellows, you've missed it ! " squeaked Billy Bunter. " I say, they got him in my study——"

" Got who ? "

" Him ! " said Bunter. " He was hiding in my study, behind the door, you know, and I never saw him when I went in, and then I turned round and saw him, and——"

" And yelled for help ! " chuckled Peter Todd.

" Oh, really, Toddy——"

" He got my bike." This came from Temple of the Fourth. " Pitched me right off my bike in Oak Lane, and mizzled on it—the neck, you know—— ! I can tell you, I was jolly glad to find it here when I got back—my jigger, you know——"

" I say, you fellows, old Popper's here—I saw him in his car—— I say, he was looking awfully shirty about something——"

"But what's happened?" roared Bob Cherry.

"You fellows missed the circus," chuckled the Bounder. "We've been having no end of a time, haven't we, Reddy?"

"But what—— ?" exclaimed Harry Wharton.

"A man picked old Popper's pocket, on the Courtfield road, and cut across the common," said Redwing. "Smithy and I saw him, and got after him, on our bikes——"

"A fat pocket-book," said Smithy. "They must have found it on him at the police-station, when they searched him."

"We were after him," said Squiff, "and Wingate and Gwynne headed him off at the gates, and he dodged into the school——"

"Couldn't have known what he was dodging into," said Tom Brown, "all Greyfriars was after him in a minute."

"Nearly had him, when he bounced in at Common-Room window—knocked old Prout out of the way," chuckled the Bounder.

"Chased him all over the House——"

"He cut up to the studies——"

"Quelch and the pre's rooted after him in the attics——"

"And we got him, in a Remove study——"

"I say, you fellows, it was my study, and when I found him there, I just called out to the fellows——"

"Yelled like mad for help, you mean——"

"Oh, really, Smithy——"

The Famous Five pieced it together, from what a dozen or more fellows were telling them, all at once. It was startling news: but, from what Sir Hilton had said at the gates, they had a still more startling spot of news, of which the others were not yet aware.

"I wonder if it was the same man," said Bob, "might have kept an eye on old Popper, after getting away in the wood—— What was he like, Smithy?"

"Skinny little blighter, in a spotted tie——"

"Pimples?" asked Bob.

"Eh! Yes! All over his chivvy! Have you seen him?"

"I rather think we have," chuckled Bob. "He was after old Popper's pocket-book in the wood this afternoon, and nearly got it. So he had another shot at it, and got away with it——"

"They must have got it back, when they searched him at the station," said Vernon-Smith. "Old Popper's got it back all right."

"Something missing from it, though," said Bob.

"How the thump do you know?"

"I say, you fellows, you don't know anything about it! You've missed the whole show, and you don't know a thing——"

"My dear chap, we get the latest official news," said Bob, cheerily. "There was a stamp in that pocket-book——"

"A stamp?" repeated the Bounder, staring. "I expect there was something more valuable than a stamp."

"Not a common or garden stamp," chuckled Bob. "It was a Twopenny——"

"A twopenny stamp?"

"Just that!"

"And what the thump does a twopenny stamp matter, even if it's missing? Think old Popper's hard up for twopence?"

"There are twopennies and twopennies," explained Bob, "this one happened to be a Blue Mauritius Twopenny——"

"What about it?"

"Worth two thousand pounds——"

"Wha-a-at?"

"And it's missing from the pocket-book——"

"How do you know?" yelled a dozen fellows.

"Oh, we get the latest news," said Bob, cheerily, "official, I assure you. There's a two-thousand pound rare stamp missing from old Popper's pocket-book, and he's just hiked over to see whether it has been dropped about Greyfriars——"

" How do you know ? " yelled the Bounder.

Harry Wharton laughed.

" Easy ! " he said. " Old Popper told us, as we came in. That's why he's here."

" So if any fellow spots a blue twopenny stamp spotted about the school, it's worth picking up ! " said Bob.

" Oh, crikey ! " gasped Billy Bunter, his eyes popping behind his spectacles. " Did—did you say two thousand pounds ? Oh, crumbs."

" A Blue Mauritius——"

" Twopenny stamp——"

" Worth two thousand quid——"

" Dropped about the school——"

" Oh, my hat ! "

There was a buzz of excitement and astonishment. That item of news, supplied by the Famous Five, put the lid on, so to speak.

" I—I say, you fellows, he—he—he was in my study—we—we—we caught him there ! " gasped Billy Bunter. " I say, old Popper will have to come down with something if a fellow finds his stamp for him ! I say, he was in my study—he—he—he might have dropped it there——"

Billy Bunter left the crowd in the quad, and shot away to the House. If there was an article worth two thousand pounds lying about Bunter's study, Billy Bunter was going to be the man to find it—if he could !

But Billy Bunter was only the first in the field. As the news spread, there was a crowd, not to call it a cram, in No. 7 Study : and another crowd queueing up in the Remove passage eager to take a turn. With so many eager searchers, the precious stamp, if there, seemed certain to be discovered.

But it was not discovered !

CHAPTER XXIII

BUNTER ASKS FOR IT

"I SAY, you fellows—that old ass Popper——"

"Shut up, you ass!" hissed Bob Cherry.

"Oh, really, Cherry——"

"He might hear you, fathead."

"Oh!" ejaculated Billy Bunter, blinking round in alarm.

Bunter was pleased to regard the lord of Popper Court as an old ass: and, that being his opinion, he saw no reason why he should not express the same. But he certainly did not want Sir Hilton to hear him. Exactly what Sir Hilton would have done, had he heard the fat Owl describe him as an old ass, Bunter did not know: but he knew that it would be something painful.

It was morning break at Greyfriars, a couple of days later.

During those days, the excitement of Slim Judson's incursion into the school, and the loss of the precious stamp, had rather died out.

A hundred fellows, at least, had searched for the missing stamp. Policemen from Courtfield had searched for it. Inspector Grimes himself had gone over No. 7 Study, almost with a small comb. And the result had been precisely nil.

If that Blue Mauritius was really at Greyfriars, nobody had the faintest idea where to look for it. Most fellows doubted whether it was there at all.

Harry Wharton and Co. had their own affairs to think of, and had rather forgotten Sir Hilton's: till they were reminded by the sight of the lord of Popper Court in the Greyfriars quad.

He had been there when the fellows came out in break.

He was still there, unheeding the many curious glances that were cast towards him.

At the moment, he was rooting over the spot where Slim Judson had fallen from Temple's bike, after colliding with Greene of the Fifth. It was on the edge of a grass-plot: and the tall baronet was leaning over, stirring the grass with a stick—apparently in the remote hope of stirring up a Blue Mauritius stamp. A dozen times, at least, Sir Hilton had been seen about the school, poking and peering, in that delusive hope.

"Poor old Popper!" murmured Frank Nugent. "It's tough."

"I say, you fellows——"

"The toughfulness is terrific," remarked Hurree Jamset Ram Singh. "The esteemed Popper is a preposterous Tartar, but——"

"But we'd jolly well like to find his stamp for him!" said Bob.

"Yes, rather."

The Famous Five really were sympathetic. Tartar as Sir Hilton undoubtedly was, it was tough. They knew—though they had tactfully kept the knowledge to themselves—what Sir Hilton had been going to do with that stamp, owing to the mumblings and grumblings they had heard from him in the wood. It looked now as if his Inspector of Taxes was booked for a long wait!

He had nearly lost that precious stamp, on the occasion of Billy Bunter's night out. It had transpired, since Slim Judson had been in the hands of the police, that he was the burglar's confederate: his business being to spy out the lie of the land for his associate the cracksman. No doubt that was his occupation when Harry Wharton and Co. had come upon him lurking in Popper Court Woods. Had the precious stamp remained in its place in the library at Popper Court, it would probably have been safe from Mr. Judson, who was no cracksman.

But Sir Hilton had placed it in his pocket-book, for

conveyance to a philatelic dealer—the Famous Five knew why. That had given Mr. Judson a chance of trying his luck.

This time the stamp was gone. Mr. Judson had joined his confederate in the " stone jug " : but the precious Blue Mauritius was missing. The pocket-book had been recovered—without the stamp! Slim affected to know nothing of it—and certainly it was not in his possession.

" It's a giddy mystery," said Bob Cherry. " From what we hear, the man was on the run all the time, and never had a split second to open the pocket-book——"

" Until he was in the study," said Nugent.

" Yes : so if he took it out, it must have been there—and the study has been searched all over twenty times, and it ain't there."

" Old Popper seems to think that he may have dropped it when he pitched off the bike," said Johnny Bull, " but——"

" I don't see how he could have."

" I say, you fellows——" hooted Billy Bunter. " Do let a chap speak! I say, if a fellow found that stamp, old Popper——" The fat Owl blinked round again, to make sure that Sir Hilton was not within hearing. " I say, old Popper would have to stand him something—a fiver at least—but look here, it's no good a fellow looking for a thing that ain't there——"

" It must be about somewhere, if that rascal brought it here parked in the pocket-book," said Bob. " But where—— ? "

" The wherefulness is terrific."

" Well, look here," said Bunter, " that's the point. Was it in the pocket-book at all, or has that old ass made a mistake ? You know what an old donkey he is. Might have shoved it in his pocket, or something, and forgot where he put it."

" Fathead ! "

" Well, I've often forgotten where I put things," said Bunter.

Harry Wharton laughed.

"Very likely, fathead: but even you wouldn't forget where you put two thousand pounds, if you had it."

"That's all very well," said Bunter. "But if it was in the pocket-book, where is it now? Are you fellows sure you saw him put it back into the pocket-book, that day you saw him in the wood——?"

"Quite!" said Harry.

"He seems to have walked on to Courtfield, after we left him," said Bob. "I've heard that he was going to the station, for a train. The stamp was in the pocket-book all right."

"You fellows saw him take it out, and look at it, in the wood," said Bunter. "He might have done it again, and shoved it back into another pocket."

"Not likely."

"Well, if it's spotted about Greyfriars, it's jolly well worth looking for," said Bunter. "He would have to come down with a pretty decent tip, if a fellow found it. But a fellow doesn't want to take a lot of trouble for nothing."

Bunter, evidently, was in a state of doubt and perplexity. He was very keen to annex a handsome tip from Sir Hilton, for finding the stamp, if it was to be found. On the other hand, he had a very strong objection to exerting himself for nothing. He blinked at the Famous Five with owl-like seriousness.

"Might be in his waistcoat pocket all the time," he argued. "He's donkey enough——"

Bob Cherry chuckled.

"Better ask him," he said. "You can point out that he's donkey enough——"

"Ha, ha, ha!"

"Well, I expect he would get shirty, if a fellow put it like that," said Bunter, shaking his fat head, sagely.

"Go hon!" murmured Bob.

"But I'll bet you he's got it somewhere all the time," declared Bunter. "It couldn't have dropped out of the pocket-book, and if that pickpocket took it out in my study, it would be there now, and it jolly well ain't. Suppose he's got it in another pocket all the time——"

"I suppose it's possible——!" said Nugent.

"Not likely," said Bob.

"Jolly likely, I think," said Bunter, "and I'm jolly well going to put it to him. He couldn't make it less than a fiver if he finds the stamp——"

"Fathead!"

"Yah!"

Billy Bunter left the juniors, and rolled towards the tall baronet, who had now finished stirring the grass with his stick, and was moving away. He gave the fat junior a far from encouraging look as he rolled up. Bunter's solution of the mystery did not seem probable to Harry Wharton and Co., but the fat Owl had little doubt of it. He was going to put it to Sir Hilton Popper, anyway.

"Well?" rapped Sir Hilton, before the fat Owl could speak.

"I've been looking for your stamp, sir——!" began Bunter.

"Have you found it?"

"Nunno!"

"Then what do you want?" rapped Sir Hilton. It was only too clear that the lord of Popper Court was not in a good temper.

"Suppose—suppose it wasn't in the pocket-book at all, sir——"

"What?" barked Sir Hilton.

"I—I mean, suppose you put it in another pocket, sir, and—and forgot all about it——" stammered Bunter.

Sir Hilton Popper stared at him.

"Might be in your pocket all the time, sir," went on Bunter. "If—if you go through all your pockets, sir——"

"Good gad!" said Sir Hilton. "Do you think, you stupid boy, that I could have forgotten where I had placed an article of such value?"

"Well, old people do forget things, sir," Bunter pointed

out. "Lots of old people keep on forgetting things, sir——"

"What?"

"My grandfather——"

"What?"

"My grandfather was always forgetting where he put things, sir," explained Bunter. "Very old people do, sir——"

Billy Bunter got no further than that. For some reason, unknown to Bunter, Sir Hilton did not seem pleased by the suggestion that he had reached the age of forgetting things, like Bunter's grandfather. He did not speak: he reached out with his left hand, and grasped Bunter's collar. The stick, in his right hand, landed with a swipe on the tightest trousers at Greyfriars School.

Swipe!

"Yaroooooh!" roared Bunter. "Ow! wow! Oh, crumbs! Whooop!"

"Ha, ha, ha!" came from the Famous Five.

"Yow-ow-ow! Wow!" roared Bunter.

Sir Hilton put his stick under his arm, and stalked away. Billy Bunter was left wriggling, and the other fellows laughing. The lord of Popper Court was very anxious to find that Blue Mauritius, but evidently he had no use for suggestions from Billy Bunter.

CHAPTER XXIV

BUNTER ON THE WAR-PATH

" WILL you lend me—— ? "

" Sorry, old fat man——"

" Lend me——"

" Stony ! " said Bob Cherry, with a sad shake of the head.

" Oh, really, Cherry——"

" Try Smithy ! " suggested Bob. " Smithy's caked with oof—and he might lend you some—perhaps ! "

" The perhapsfulness is terrific," remarked Hurree Jamset Ram Singh, with a dusky grin.

Billy Bunter, in the doorway of No. 13 Study, blinked at the occupants of that study, with a devastating blink.

" You silly ass ! " he hooted, " think I've come here to borrow money ? "

" Eh ! Haven't you ? " exclaimed Bob, in surprise.

" No ! " roared Bunter.

" Well, wonders will never cease ! " said Bob. " I'd better put that down in my diary, as it's a thing that's never happened before. Friday—Bunter didn't want to borrow any money—— ! "

" You—you—you—— ! " gasped Bunter. " Look here, you silly, cackling ass, will you lend me your alarm-clock ? "

" My alarm-clock ? " repeated Bob, blankly.

There were four fellows in No. 13 Study : Bob, and the nabob, Mark Linley, and little Wun Lung. All four stared at Billy Bunter. All were surprised. Billy Bunter was a borrower of deadly skill, and there was hardly a fellow in the Remove from whom he did not extract little loans. How many half-crowns he owed to Lord Mauleverer he could not have counted, without going into high figures. How many " bobs " and " tanners " he owed to other fellows he could hardly have computed at all. He had even, on one historic occasion, borrowed a shilling from Fisher T. Fish: a really remarkable feat. At the word "lend" Bob had naturally supposed that it was a question of cash. The very last thing he would have expected Bunter to want to borrow was an alarm-clock.

The use of an alarm-clock was to wake a fellow up. Bunter hated being woke up. If there was one thing at Greyfriars that Billy Bunter loathed with a deeper loathing than lessons, it was the rising-bell in the morning. So his request for the loan of an alarm-clock was really astonishing.

"Yes, your alarm-clock, blow you," grunted the fat Owl. "Look here, will you lend it to me?"

"Do I hear aright?" ejaculated Bob. "Do mine ears deceive me? Do I sleep, do I dream, do I wonder and doubt—— Are things what they seem, or is visions about?"

"Ha, ha, ha!"

"You silly fathead!" hooted Bunter. "I want that alarm-clock——"

"But you can't eat an alarm-clock——!" argued Bob. "What on earth do you want it for? Can't you wait for rising-bell in the morning?"

"'Tain't for the morning," yapped Bunter. "I want to wake up at ten to-night."

Which reply caused No. 13 Study to gaze at him in intensified astonishment. Dormitory for the Remove was nine-thirty. At nine-thirty-five, as a rule, Billy Bunter's deep snore was heard, and it went on like an unending melody till the rising-bell clanged in the dewy morn. The very last thing Bunter had ever desired before, was to be awakened from balmy slumber.

Certainly, if he wanted to wake, after once his eyes had closed, an alarm-clock was needed. But why Billy Bunter wanted to wake up half an hour after bedtime, was a deep mystery—it was a new and astonishing departure from the usual manners and customs of the fat Owl.

"You want to wake up at ten to-night?" repeated Bob, almost dazedly. "You fat ass, if you're thinking of sneaking down to the pantry after lights out——"

"'Tain't that!" yelled Bunter. "I want to turn out at ten! They'll all be fast asleep in the Fourth-form dorm at ten."

"Oh, my hat! Is there anything to eat, in the Fourth-form dorm?"

"No!" howled Bunter, "'tain't that! It's that cheeky beast Temple! You know what he did when I was asleep on Wednesday morning on the landing——"

"Ha, ha, ha!"

"You can cackle," hooted Bunter. "If you think it's funny for a chap to have his face painted blue while he's asleep——"

"Ha, ha, ha!"

Apparently the fellows in No. 13 Study did think it funny!

"Well, Temple won't think it so jolly funny, at ten to-night," said Billy Bunter. "I never knew who it was the other day, but I've found out that it was Temple of the Fourth—those Fourth form smudges have been cackling over it, and I jolly well know it was Temple. I'd jolly well thrash him, only—only I couldn't, you know! But he's jolly well got it coming! If he thinks it funny to paint a fellow's face while he's asleep, perhaps he'll think it funny to get a pot of paint on his chivvy while he's asleep himself—he, he, he!"

"Oh!" gasped Bob.

Billy Bunter, apparently, was on the war-path. The remarkable appearance he had presented in the Remove form room, with his decorated fat countenance, had evoked merriment, in everyone but Bunter! Bunter, it seemed, was not amused. And having learned that it was Cecil Reginald Temple of the Fourth Form, who was the guilty man, Bunter had made up his fat mind to give Cecil Reginald "some of the same."

Cecil Reginald had caught him napping—and he was going to catch Cecil Reginald napping! Temple, certainly, was not likely to fall asleep anywhere in the daytime: but after lights out, it was easy. That was why the fat Owl had rolled along to No. 13 after prep to borrow the alarm-clock. Without some such aid, Temple of the Fourth would certainly have been quite safe from hostilities on Bunter's part, after lights out.

"Better give it a miss, Bunter," said Mark Linley, laughing. "If you wake Temple up with a pot of paint, something will happen to you soon afterwards."

"Didn't he jolly well paint my face?" demanded Bunter. "Making a fellow walk into the form-room painted blue——"

"Ha, ha, ha!"

"I shan't be there more than a minute," went on Bunter, "I'm not going to paint him as he did me—only just up end a pot of paint over his chivvy, see? I've borrowed a pot of paint from Gosling's shed—that's all right!—and I've borrowed Toddy's flash-lamp. Now all I want is your alarm-clock, Bob—you see, I might not wake up——"

"The might-notfulness is terrific," chuckled Hurree Jamset Ram Singh.

"Well," said Bob, laughing, "you can borrow the alarm-clock, old fat man: but I'd advise you to chuck it——"

"I'll watch it," said Bunter.

And he rolled away from No. 13 Study, with the alarm-clock under a fat arm, leaving the study chuckling.

When the Remove went up to their dormitory that night, there were three perceptible bulges on Billy Bunter's plump person. In one pocket was a pound pot of paint, requisitioned from Gosling's shed. In another, was Bob Cherry's alarm-clock. In a third, was Peter Todd's flash-lamp.

A good many Remove fellows, who were aware that the fat Owl was on the war-path, grinned as they noted those bulges. Luckily, Wingate of the Sixth, who saw lights out for the Remove, did not note them.

After the lights were out, and the prefect gone, Billy Bunter sat up in bed, and there was a sound of groping. Bunter was disinterring the alarm-clock from a pocket.

Crash ! smash !

" Oh ! " gasped Bunter.

" Hallo, hallo, hallo ! what's that ? " came from Bob Cherry's bed.

" Only that beastly clock ! I've dropped it—I think the glass is broken——"

" You fat chump ! "

" Beast ! "

There was more groping, as Bunter leaned out of bed, and fished for the fallen clock. His fat paw contacted it, and he picked it up.

" It's all right—it's still going," said Bunter. " It doesn't matter about the glass, as the clock's going——"

" You blithering owl——"

" Oh, really, Cherry ! I'll pay for a new glass, when my postal-order comes——"

" You burbling bloater ! "

" Well, it's going all right," said Bunter. " I've set the alarm for ten, and it's bound to wake me, close to my pillow. Now shut up and let a fellow go to sleep ! "

" You clumsy fat foozler——"

" Oh, really, Cherry, I think you might shut up, and let a fellow go to sleep, when a fellow's turning out at ten o'clock."

Bob Cherry did not immediately shut up. He seemed more concerned about the damage to the clock than Bunter was. He continued, for several minutes, to tell Bunter what he thought of him.

Only a deep snore from Bunter's bed answered. Lulled, perhaps, by the ticking of the clock close to his pillow, the fat Owl slid into happy slumber, and Bob's remarks passed him by like the idle wind which he regarded not.

Billy Bunter slept, and he snored : and if he dreamed, he did not dream that that bang on the dormitory floor had disarranged the alarm which he had carefully set for ten o'clock, and that it was now set for ten minutes to two! That was an interesting discovery that the fat Owl of the Remove had yet to make!

CHAPTER XXV

THE MAN IN THE DARK

Buzzzzzzzz !

" Urrrggh ! " grunted a sleeping fat Owl.

Buzzzz !

" Yaw—aw—aw—aw-aw ! "

Buzzz !

Billy Bunter was a sound sleeper. It was one of the things that Bunter could do really well. But even Bunter emerged from slumber as the alarm-clock buzzed and buzzed within a foot of his fat head.

He grunted, yawned, and sat up.

He groped for his spectacles, and perched them on his little fat nose, and blinked round him in the gloom like a drowsy owl.

Buzzzzzzz !

That alarm-clock had awakened Bunter. It had also awakened several other fellows, which was only to be expected. Three or four voices came from the shadows, addressing Bunter.

" Shut up that row ! "

" Is that that fat idiot Bunter ? Stop that row, you fat chump ! "

" Do you want me to heave a boot at you, Bunter ? "

" Can't you let a fellow sleep ? "

" I say, you fellows, it will stop in a minute," answered Bunter peevishly. He was not disposed to worry about fellows suddenly awakened from balmy slumber. He was already sufficiently worried by the prospect of turning out of bed—never a welcome prospect to Bunter.

Planning that just retaliation on Cecil Reginald Temple, earlier, had seemed quite a good idea to Bunter. Carrying it out did not seem too attractive, when the time came to turn out of a warm bed.

Bunter was strongly tempted to let the alarm run down, replace his fat head on the pillow, and go to sleep again, leaving Temple of the Fourth unpunished for his sins. Really, he could hardly be expected to bother about fellows who did not like being woke up in the middle of the night.

" Will you shut up that row ? " came a howl from Bolsover major.

" I tell you it will stop in a minute," snapped Bunter.

Whiz !

A boot sailed through the air, guided by Bunter's voice.

Bang !

" Yaroooh ! "

Bunter had not expected that. It took him quite by surprise when the boot banged on his ear, and tipped him over. He plunged wildly in the dark, tipped off the edge of the bed, and bumped on the floor, in a tangle of bed-clothes.

" Oh ! Beast ! Ow ! Who chucked that boot ? Wow ! "

" Do you want the other one ? " hissed Bolsover. " You'd better shut off that row, if you don't."

" Beast ! " howled Bunter.

Luckily, the alarm sputtered to an end. The raucous clatter ceased, and the silence was broken only by the spluttering of the fat Owl as he disentangled himself from sheets and blankets, and scrambled up.

Other fellows settled down to sleep. But Billy Bunter, being now out of bed, ceased to debate whether he should chuck it up and go to sleep again. Bolsover's boot had settled that point for him.

He groped for his trousers in the faint glimmer of star-light from the high windows, heaved his fat legs into them, and tucked in his pyjamas. Then he groped for slippers and put them on. That was sufficient attire for the trip from the Remove dormitory to the Fourth. Then he groped in pockets for the pot of paint and Peter Todd's flash-lamp.

The latter was required to pick out Temple's bed in the Fourth-form dormitory: the former, to decorate Cecil Reginald's countenance when found. With the paint pot crammed into his trousers pocket, and the flash-lamp in his hand, the fat Owl groped away to the dormitory door.

He blinked out cautiously into the passage. At ten o'clock, lights were out in the dormitories, but not downstairs. Masters had not yet gone to bed at ten: and probably many of the Sixth were still up. But not the faintest glimmer of light, not the faintest sound, reached the fat Owl as he blinked out. The deep silence and stillness of the House seemed to indicate a later hour than ten. However, Bunter knew that he had set the alarm for ten, so he had no doubts. He crept forth from the dormitory, without bothering to shut the door after him, and tiptoed away down the passage to the landing.

From that landing, several passages opened: one of them leading to the Fourth-form dormitory. Another led to the rooms of several of the masters. It was necessary for Bunter to be very cautious. He was surprised to see not a glimmer of light from the staircase. Usually a light burned on the stairs till the last bedroom door had closed. But there was not the faintest glimmer now: the staircase was a well of solid darkness. Only here and there a glimmer of starlight came ghostly from a high window.

On tiptoe, the fat Owl trod out on the landing. He could not venture to turn on the flash-lamp there, lest, at an unlucky moment, a "beak" might be coming up. He would have hated to meet the gimlet-eyes of his form-master just then.

But he did not need a light on such familiar ground. Cautiously, on tiptoe, he groped on the landing.

A chime came through the night, from the Greyfriars clock-tower: faint but clearly audible from the distance. It was followed by the striking of the hour. Boom!

The fat Owl started, stopped, and listened. He was sure that he had set the alarm for precisely ten, so it should now have been six or seven minutes past. But the clock was striking the hour: there was no mistake about that. He concluded that he must have set it a few minutes early. Boom! came a second time. As the fat Owl had no doubt that it was ten o'clock, he expected eight more strokes to follow.

But the rest was silence!

Billy Bunter stood quite still. It dawned upon his fat brain that something must have gone wrong with that alarm-clock. The deep darkness and dead silence of the House were explained now. It was not ten o'clock at night. It was two o'clock in the morning!

"Oh, crikey!" breathed the startled Owl.

In the deep silence that followed, he listened uneasily with both fat ears, and blinked round him in the gloom with uneasy eyes.

Two o'clock in the morning was a very different proposition from ten o'clock in the evening. Even Billy Bunter did not feel nervous about venturing out of his dormitory, when lights were on and masters up downstairs. But at an hour when all were sleeping, when nobody but himself was awake in the whole of the great building, it was quite different. A very unpleasant eerie feeling came over Bunter.

Instead of progressing towards the Fourth form dormitory, he stood where he was on the dark landing, hesitating. He was powerfully inclined to give up his expedition, and scuttle back to his dormitory. At such an hour, the darkness and silence were full of vague terrors—there might even be burglars. He remembered, quite unpleasantly, the recent burglary at Popper Court. Suppose——!

Creak!

It was only a faint creak from the staircase. But a roll of thunder could not have startled Bunter more.

He stood rooted, hardly breathing.

Creak!

All his vague terrors crystallized, at that faint sound. For he knew what it was—what it could only be!—the creak of ancient wood under a soft and stealthy footstep!

Someone—unseen in the dark—was on the stairs. The fat Owl's fat heart almost died within him.

It could not be a master coming up late to bed—nobody could have stayed up till two in the morning. Besides, a master would have turned on a light. It could not be some breaker of bounds, like Smithy of the Remove or Price of the Fifth, creeping cautiously home—at that hour! With a shudder of horror, Billy Bunter realised what it was—the stealthy footstep of some intruder from without! Terror rooted him to the floor.

A faint sound on the landing came to him. The unseen intruder had reached the landing, and was quite near him. A beam of light flashed in the darkness, and circled—the unseen man had turned on a flash lamp, to get his bearings.

The light moved round in a slow circle. A glimmer of it revealed the man who was holding it, to Bunter's terrified eyes. He glimpsed a slight figure, and a face with narrow foxy eyes—and pimples!

He could have fancied that he was dreaming.

For it was a face he had seen before—the face of a man who had been captured a few days ago in No. 7 Study: the face of the man who had been taken, in charge of a constable, to Courtfield Police-Station; the foxy, pimpled face of the man Bunter, and everyone else, supposed to be safe under lock and key.

Bunter could not stir. He could hardly breathe. Terror chained him. The glimpse of that rascally face was brief, but he knew the man—knew that Slim Judson was within six or seven feet of him. The slowly-circling light was approaching him, but he could not stir. It reached him——!

It flashed full on a fat, terrified face, with open mouth and starting eyes. There was a startled gasp from the man with the light.

"You!"

Evidently he knew Bunter again, as Bunter knew him.

The exclamation was followed by a swift movement towards the fat junior.

A wild yelp of terror escaped Billy Bunter, as he fled. His feet hardly touched the floor as he flew up the passage to the Remove dormitory. Whether the man followed him or not, he did not know. He careered frantically into the dormitory, yelling at the top of his voice.

"Help! I say, you fellows! Burglars! Yaroooh! Help! Keep him off! I say, you fellows! Oh, crikey! Help!"

CHAPTER XXVI

DOUBTING THOMASES

Mr. Quelch sat up in bed.

Something had awakened him—suddenly. It seemed to him that there was a sound of distant yelling, in the silence of the night. That seemed improbable, and he wondered for a moment whether he was dreaming. But as he listened, he realised that, improbable as it seemed, it was a fact. Indubitably, unmistakably, someone was yelling, in the middle of the night. He fancied that the uproar came from the direction of the Remove dormitory. An expression resembling that of the fabled Gorgon came over Mr. Quelch's face, as he stepped out of bed, and hurriedly grabbed up a dressing-gown.

He opened his door. Undoubtedly there was yelling: and a hubbub of excited voices: more clearly heard now that his door was open. With the Gorgonic expression intensifying on his face, the Remove master stepped out, and hurried across the dark landing. What hour it was, he did not know: but he knew that it was very late. If there was a disturbance in the Remove quarters at such an hour, Quelch was the man to deal with it promptly and drastically.

He flashed on the light, on the landing, and hurried up the passage to the Remove door. That door was wide open: and from within, came a perfect Babel of voices. Loudest of all were the dulcet tones of William George Bunter.

"Help! I say, you fellows, it's that man! I say, he's after me! Help!"

"What the thump——"

"Is that Bunter?"

"What's that fat idiot yelling about?"

"Put a sock in it, Bunter."

THERE WAS A SUDDEN BLAZE OF ILLUMINATION
IN THE REMOVE DORMITORY

" Shut up, you ass ! You'll have Quelch here."

" For goodness sake, shut up, Bunter. Do you want to wake the House ? "

" I say, you fellows, I saw him ! Oh, crikey ! Help ! I say, he's after me ! " yelled Bunter. " I can hear him coming up the passage——"

" Fathead ! "

" Chuck it ! "

" The fat chump's been frightened of the dark——"

" The frightfulness seems to be terrific."

" You'll have Quelch here, you howling lunatic——"

" Yaroooh ! He's coming ! Help ! " shrieked Bunter. Undoubtedly there were footsteps in the passage, and Bunter did not guess that they were Quelch's. " I say, you fellows, he's coming after me——"

There was a sudden blaze of illumination in the Remove dormitory, as Mr. Quelch, in the doorway, turned the switch.

Every eye turned on the doorway : and there was sudden silence, as the grimly frowning face of the Remove master was seen there. Only Bunter continued to yell.

" He's coming ! I say, you fellows, keep him off ! It's him——"

" Bunter ! " thundered Mr. Quelch.

" Ow ! Help ! Burglars ! Oh ! " Bunter blinked at his form-master. " Is—is—is that you, sir ? Oh, crikey ! I—I say, sir, look out—he—he may be just behind you——"

" Silence, you stupid boy ! How dare you make such a disturbance ? " Quelch fairly roared. " What are you doing out of bed, Bunter, at this hour ? Have you been out of your dormitory ? "

" Oh ! Yes ! No ! Yes ! " gasped Bunter.

Mr Quelch gave a grim glance at a crowd of fellows, sitting up in bed and staring. Nobody was out of bed excepting Bunter. Bunter, evidently, was the cause of the uproar : and that he was frightened almost out of his fat wits, was clear at a glance. He was fairly babbling with terror.

"You have been out of your dormitory, Bunter?"

"Oh! Yes! I—I saw him, sir——"

"You saw whom?" snapped Mr. Quelch.

"Him, sir!" gasped Bunter. "It was him, sir." In his excitement and terror, the fat Owl recklessly disregarded grammar. "Him, sir—it was him!"

"Who?" almost shrieked Mr. Quelch.

"That man, sir—oh, crikey! He was on the landing—he turned on a light—oh, jiminy! Then I saw him—that man, sir, the pickpocket—the man who pocked old Popper's picket—I mean the man who popped old Picket's pocker——"

"Will you tell me who or what you fancy you have seen, Bunter?" asked Mr. Quelch, in a grinding voice.

"I'm tut-tut-telling you, sir. It was that packpicket—I mean that pickpocket—the man who got old pipper's popper-book—I mean his pocket-book—the man who was copped in my study, sir——"

"Oh, my hat!" murmured Bob Cherry. All the Remove stared at Bunter. That the fat Owl had been badly frightened in the dark, everyone could see. But that he had encountered Mr. Judson within the walls of Greyfriars, no one was likely to believe. Mr. Quelch's gimlet-eyes almost bored into the fat junior.

"You utterly ridiculous boy," he exclaimed. "The man you speak of is under lock and key at the police-station——"

"But I did saw him, sir——"

"What?"

"I—I mean I did seed him, sir—I mean I sawed him—I mean——"

"Upon my word!" said Mr. Quelch. "You have been frightened by some shadow, you utterly stupid boy. How dare you leave your dormitory at this hour? Explain yourself! Why are you not in bed?"

"Because—because I—I got up, sir——"

There was a chuckle from some of the beds. It was stilled immediately by a glare from the Remove master. Only too plainly, Mr. Quelch did not consider this an occasion for chuckling.

"Bunter, you obtuse boy, if you do not explain at once why you left your dormitory——!" rumbled Mr. Quelch.

"I—I—I thought it was ten o'clock, sir," groaned Bunter, "the—the alarm-clock went wrong, sir! I—I was going—I—I mean I wasn't going—I—I—I wasn't going to the Fourth-form dorm to jape Temple, sir—I—I never thought of anything of the kind. I—I—I——"

"You were going to another dormitory, to play some foolish trick at this hour of the night!" exclaimed Mr. Quelch.

"I—I thought it was only ten, sir," groaned Bunter. "I—I wouldn't have got up if I'd known it was the middle of the might——"

"What?"

"I—I mean the middle of the night, sir. Then I heard it strike two, sir, and—and that man came up the stairs—him, sir——" The fat Owl shivered. "I—I thought he was after me—oh, lor'!"

"You incredibly stupid boy!" hooted Mr. Quelch. "The man Judson is in a cell at Courtfield—— You have been frightened in the dark. I shall punish you most severely for causing this disturbance, Bunter. You will come to my study after prayers in the morning, and I shall cane you."

"Oh, crikey!"

"Now go back to bed, and be quiet," said the Remove master, sternly. "There is no occasion for alarm, my boys," added Mr. Quelch. "There is nothing whatever the matter. Bunter, go back to bed at once."

"But I—I say, sir, ain't you going to telephone the police——?" gasped Bunter. "Suppose he's still in the House——?"

"Shut up, you fat ass," breathed Peter Todd.

"Oh, really, Toddy——"

"There's nobody, you fat chump," said Squiff.

"Oh, really, Field——"

"I have told you to go to bed, Bunter," said Mr. Quelch, in a voice resembling that of the Great Huge Bear. "If you utter another word, Bunter, I shall send for my cane, and chastise you on the spot."

Billy Bunter blinked at him. His terror of the pimply man lurking in the dark was great. But Quelch was a nearer danger! He did not utter another word. He plunged into bed.

Mr. Quelch breathed hard, and he breathed deep. His expression left no doubt that he was going to deal faithfully with the fat Owl, after prayers in the morning. He shut off the light, drew the door shut, and walked away: and Bunter's voice was not heard again till he was off the scene. Then it was heard.

"I say, you fellows——!"

"You blithering, burbling, benighted bandersnatch," said Bob Cherry. "Shut up and go to sleep, and let other fellows do the same."

"But that burglar—I tell you I saw him——"

"Fathead!" said Harry Wharton.

"It was that man——"

"Can it, ass," said Johnny Bull. "How could the man be here when he's in chokey?"

"I tell you I saw him——"

"Pack it up!" said Vernon-Smith.

"The packupfulness is the proper caper, my esteemed jawful Bunter," said Hurree Jamset Ram Singh. "Speech is silvery, but silence is the bird in the bush that makes Jack a dull boy, as the English proverb remarks."

"I—I say, Wharton, suppose—suppose he comes in here—I say hadn't you better shove a bed against the door, or something——?"

"You benighted ass, if there was a burglar, what would he want in a junior dormitory?" hooted the captain of the Remove.

" After Bunter's gold watch, perhaps ! " suggested Skinner.

" Ha, ha, ha ! "

" I tell you he was on the landing, and he turned on a light," hissed Bunter, " I saw him as plain as my own face."

" Well, that's plain enough, goodness knows," remarked Bob Cherry.

" The plainfulness is terrific."

" Ha, ha, ha ! "

" Blessed if I see anything to cackle at, with a burglar in the house——" howled Bunter. " Think I can go to sleep, with a burglar burgling about ? I shan't be able to close my eyes."

" You mayn't be able to close your eyes," said the Bounder. " But you'd better be able to close your mouth : for if you don't shut up, I'll get up and give you a spot of my bolster."

" Oh, really, Smithy——"

" Shut up, Bunter."

" But I say—— ! "

" Shut up ! " howled a dozen fellows. At a quarter past two in the morning, the Removites seemed to prefer slumber to Billy Bunter's conversation.

" Beasts ! " groaned Bunter.

But he shut up, at last. Evidently, nobody was going to heed his burglar story. And even Bunter realised that, after the alarm had been given, that nocturnal intruder was fairly certain to have taken himself off. The Remove settled down to sleep once more : and Bunter laid his fat head on his pillow, convinced that he would not be able to sleep a wink.

But that was an error on Bunter's part. In less than five minutes, a sound resembling the murmur of distant thunder was rumbling through the Remove dormitory. It was Billy Bunter's snore—and it went on non-stop till the rising-bell rang in the sunny morning.

CHAPTER XXVII

LUCK FOR BUNTER

Tap!

"Come in!" said Mr. Quelch, in his grimmest tone.

After prayers in the morning, Mr. Quelch had gone to his study. It was Bunter's duty, according to instructions, to follow him there, to take the painful consequences of causing a disturbance in the middle of the night.

Bunter, never a whale on duty, was not at all anxious to carry out that particular duty. There was delay, and Mr. Quelch's eyes were already glinting, when the tap came at his study door. The Remove master rapped out "Come in," nothing doubting that it was Bunter: and as he spoke, he grasped the cane that lay ready on his table, and rose to his feet. Cane in hand, with frowning brows, he stood ready for Bunter, as the door opened—and Inspector Grimes, of Courtfield, presented himself!

"Oh!" ejaculated Mr. Quelch, involuntarily.

He was taken quite by surprise.

He had expected Bunter. He had not expected Mr. Grimes, especially at such an early hour in the morning.

Mr. Grimes started a little, at the sight of the Remove master's attitude. He was about to say "Good morning!" Instead, he stared.

"Oh!" repeated Mr. Quelch. He had taken it for granted that it was Bunter, and he realised that he had taken too much for granted. The colour flushed into his cheeks, and he hurriedly dropped the cane on the table. It was quite disconcerting for a moment.

"Oh! G—g—good morning, Mr. Grimes! I—I was expecting—I mean—pray come in!" Quelch fairly stammered. "This is a very early hour—I—I was not expecting——" His colour deepened, as he detected a faint smile that flickered for a moment on the Courtfield inspector's stolid face. "Really, Mr. Grimes, at this very early hour——"

"Please excuse this very early call, sir," said Mr. Grimes. "I desired to see you as early as possible this morning——"

Mr. Quelch recovered himself.

"Pray sit down, Mr. Grimes. What is it?" His manner was as polite as he could make it. But he was disconcerted, and he had not yet had his breakfast.

However, Mr. Grimes did not appear to notice the edge on his voice. He sat solidly down.

"I am afraid, Mr. Quelch, that the recent occurrence here has caused a good deal of unusual disturbance," said Mr. Grimes, apologetically.

"It has, undoubtedly," said Mr. Quelch. "I may say that I had hoped to have heard the last of it."

Mr. Grimes coughed.

Greyfriars fellows had rather enjoyed the episode of Mr. Judson. They had rather liked a spot of excitement. But a school-master had no use for spots of excitement. School-masters preferred to keep on the even tenor of their way undisturbed. Mr. Quelch, no doubt, sympathised with Sir Hilton Popper, over the loss of his rare and precious Blue Mauritius. But he was chiefly desirous of hearing no more of Sir Hilton, no more of the Blue Mauritius, no more of the pickpocket, and no more of Inspector Grimes and the Courtfield policemen. More especially he did not want to hear anything more about any of them before breakfast.

"I am sorry, sir, that the matter is not quite at an end," said Mr. Grimes. "The loss to Sir Hilton Popper, sir, is of course very serious. I understand that the Blue Mauritius stamp, now missing, is worth upwards of two thousand pounds: and Sir Hilton has no doubt that it is to be found somewhere about the school——"

"Extremely improbable, in my opinion," said Mr. Quelch. "If your visit this morning means that further search is to be made, Mr. Grimes——"

"Not at all, sir," said Mr. Grimes, hastily.

"I am glad of it," said Mr. Quelch.

"I will speak frankly to you, sir," said Mr. Grimes, "more frankly than I care to do to Sir Hilton. I am not absolutely assured that the stamp was in the pocket-book at all, when it fell into the man Judson's hands. It was not found either in the pocket-book, or on the man, when he was searched: and from all the accounts I received, the man's flight was so hurried, so breathless, that he had no opportunity of removing it and concealing it—except during the few minutes he was out of observation in a schoolboy's study here. That study has been searched with meticulous care, and the stamp certainly is not there. Sir Hilton is positive on the point, but——" Mr. Grimes coughed again.

"Sir Hilton is occasionally somewhat forgetful, Mr. Grimes," said the Remove master, acidly. "Although he has known me for many years, he has addressed me as Mr. Welsh, and even Mr. Squelch: and a gentleman who cannot even recall a name——"

"Precisely so, sir," said Inspector Grimes, "Sir Hilton is quite positive about it, but I cannot feel equally positive myself."

"Nor I," said Mr. Quelch.

"But, sir, it happens that the matter may be put to a test, which may clear up doubt," continued the inspector. "If the man Judson did actually find an opportunity of concealing the stamp, while he was in the school, it can only have been in the hope of recovering it later, when he came out of prison——"

"No doubt! I presume that that will not be for six months, at least."

Once more the inspector coughed.

"I regret to tell you, sir, that it may be much sooner. In fact, the man escaped last night——"

"What?"

"I regret to say that he is now at liberty, sir," said Mr.

Grimes. " He escaped from his cell, and is now at large."

Mr. Quelch uttered a sound strongly resembling a snort. Then he gave a sudden start, as Bunter's strange story of the night before came back to his mind.

" Bless my soul ! You say that the man is at large ! " he exclaimed. " Bless my soul ! Then it is possible——"

" It is possible, sir, that he may lurk in the vicinity of this school, if in fact he did conceal the stamp here, to make some attempt to recover it," said Mr. Grimes. " That is why I am here so early, sir. Many of the boys of your form, Mr. Quelch, came into contact with the man, and would know him again at once if they saw him. You will appreciate how important it is for the police to be notified at once if he should be seen, anywhere near Greyfriars. If he knows nothing of the stamp, he is fairly certain to quit the neighbourhood, thinking only of his safety. But if he should be seen anywhere about the school, it will indicate beyond doubt that the stamp is indeed here, and that he hopes to lay hands on it. You see my point, sir ? "

" Bless my soul ! " repeated Mr. Quelch.

" If any boy who knows the man by sight should see him again—— ! " continued Mr. Grimes.

" It is possible that that stupid boy was stating the facts," said Mr. Quelch. " I had no idea, of course, that the man was at large, and when Bunter stated that he had seen him——"

Mr. Grimes gave quite a little jump.

" He has been seen ? " he exclaimed.

" A foolish boy, named Bunter, left his dormitory at a late hour last night, to play some insensate trick in another dormitory," said Mr. Quelch. " He was frightened in the dark—as I supposed—and caused a disturbance. He stated that he had seen the man Judson, on the dormitory landing—a statement which I attributed to terrified fancy—— But in view of what you now tell me—it is possible——"

" I must see the boy, sir," exclaimed Mr. Grimes. " I——"

Tap!

"That, I think, is the boy in question," said Mr. Quelch, as a tap came at the study door, and he rapped out "Come in!"

The door opened. A fat figure, a fat dolorous face, and a big pair of spectacles, were revealed. It was Bunter this time!

"Come in, Bunter," rapped Mr. Quelch.

Billy Bunter rolled reluctantly in. He blinked dismally at Mr. Quelch, then at the cane on the table, and then, in surprise, at Inspector Grimes.

"Bunter——!" said Mr. Quelch.

"Oh! Yes, sir," groaned Bunter. "I—I——"

"Mr. Grimes desires to ask you some questions. You will tell him exactly what happened last night when you were out of your dormitory."

"Oh! Yes, sir!" gasped Bunter. "I—I really did see that man, sir—he had a light, and he turned it on, and—and—I—I saw his face, sir—and—and—it was that pock-picket—I mean that pickpocket—who popped Sir Hilton's picket, sir——"

"Tell me exactly what occurred, Master Bunter," said Inspector Grimes, encouragingly.

"Oh, certainly, sir," gasped Bunter. And he proceeded to stutter out the tale of his thrilling adventure in the dark.

The Courtfield inspector listened attentively, putting in a sharp question now and then when the fat Owl wandered from the point. When Bunter came, at last, to an end, Mr. Grimes turned to the Remove master.

"There can be no doubt now, sir," he said. "The man was here, and he can have been here with only one object."

Mr. Quelch nodded.

"It would certainly appear so," he said. "If the man was here he can have had but one motive—to recover Sir Hilton's stamp——"

"Exactly! The information Master Bunter has been

able to give, clears up the doubt on the point, and is, indeed, extremely useful," said Mr. Grimes.

Mr. Grimes had a kindly heart. He had not failed to observe how the matter stood, and he was tactfully putting in a word for the unfortunate fat Owl. Mr. Quelch gave him a rather sharp look : and then gave Bunter a grim one. There was a moment's silence, and then he said :

" You may leave my study, Bunter."

" Oh ! Yes, sir ! " gasped Bunter. And he left it. A split second was sufficient to see Bunter out of the study ! It was a happy and relieved fat Owl that rolled away down the passage.

Mr. Grimes rose.

" The matter is now clear, sir," he said. " The man Judson was here, within a few hours of escaping from his cell : he lost no time. The Blue Mauritius stamp, sir, was his object, and it must now be taken as a fact that he succeeded in concealing it somewhere in the school. And his haste to make an attempt to recover it, Mr. Quelch, tells us something more—it indicates that he fears that it may be found—that its hiding-place may be discovered."

" It would seem so," said Mr. Quelch. " I conclude, sir, that measures will be taken to keep watch for the man, in case he should make another attempt to enter these premises——"

Mr. Grimes smiled faintly.

" You may be assured of that, sir ! We shall take all necessary measures, and I trust, sir, that the matter will soon be at an end."

" I sincerely hope so," said Mr. Quelch.

The inspector took his leave : considerably to Mr. Quelch's relief, as the breakfast-bell was ringing. As Mr. Grimes crossed to the gates, a fat voice reached his ears.

" I say, you fellows, it was all right, after all. Quelch looked as if he was going to bite, but he didn't whop me. Old Grimes was there, and I told him about it, and he jolly well believed me, if you fellows didn't! I can jolly well tell you that old Grimes isn't such a silly old ass as he looks!"

Which perhaps made Mr. Grimes, as he marched on, think that it was rather a pity that Mr. Quelch's cane had not, after all, come into action!

CHAPTER XXVIII

SQUIFF TAKES A HAND

SQUIFF of the Remove stared.

Squiff, at the moment, was perched on a high branch, in a massive old beech tree, that shaded the stile in Friardale Lane.

From the summit of that massive and ancient tree, there was a wide view over the surrounding country: the woods and fields and meadows of Kent on the one hand, the rolling sea on the other beyond the white cliffs: Greyfriars School, and Highcliffe, and the town of Courtfield, and many other objects of interest. It was said that the spire of Canterbury Cathedral could be seen from the top of that tree: and it was not uncommon for Greyfriars juniors to clamber into the high branches, for a bird's-eye view of the countryside. So there was Sampson Quincy Iffley Field of New South Wales, taking a rest on a branch, leaning back against the massive trunk, after a clamber to the top.

From that point of vantage, Squiff had a view of the footpath and the stile below, and of Friardale Lane winding away towards Greyfriars. And in the lane, he had also a view of a fat figure rolling along from the direction of the school towards the stile, with a big pair of spectacles flashing back the rays of the sun.

The view of Billy Bunter did not particularly interest Squiff. He considered whether to drop a handful of twigs on the fat Owl's head as he passed below, and make him jump. Otherwise, he was not interested in Bunter.

But a few moments later, he was interested.

Another figure came in sight, at a little distance behind Bunter. It was that of a short man, with a beaky nose, and very sharp little narrow eyes set very close on either side of it.

Squiff gave him a careless glance: and then fixed his eyes upon him, curiously.

There was nobody else to be seen in the leafy lane. Bunter, a little breathless as usual, with spots of perspiration on his fat brow, rolled on unconscious of the man behind him. That man's eyes were fixed on Bunter's podgy back, with such a furtive, stealthy expression, that the Australian junior, in the branches of the beech, could not help noticing it. He noticed, too, that when Bunter slowed down—as he frequently did—the man behind slowed down too. When Bunter accelerated again, the man behind accelerated again. And his narrow sharp eyes never left Bunter.

Squiff stared—and stared harder. It leaped to the eye that the man with the beaky nose was following Bunter—not merely walking in the same direction, as anyone might have been doing, but deliberately following him, keeping him in sight, and keeping always at the same distance behind him.

Which was remarkable, and drew Squiff's special attention. As he scanned the hard, narrow, beaky face, he remembered that he had seen the man before—hanging about the school gates. The beaky man had been there, when Squiff had come out, more than an hour ago. Squiff had noticed him in passing, and forgotten him again.

It seemed improbable that the man had been waiting there, till Bunter came out, with the intention of following the fat junior. Yet it looked like it.

Had it been Lord Mauleverer, or the Bounder, or Temple of the Fourth, or Monty Newland, or any such wealthy fellow, Squiff would have wondered whether the beaky man was a pickpocket, following a Greyfriars fellow to a lonely spot with the intention of relieving him of his cash. That was really what it looked like. But the most enterprising pickpocket could hardly have chosen Billy Bunter for a victim. Billy Bunter did not look wealthy. Remove fellows often heard of the wealth of Bunter Court, and of Bunter's rich relations. But they never saw any sign of it about Bunter. He was hardly worth the while of any professional snapper-up of unconsidered trifles. Yet undoubtedly it did look like it.

Bunter, equally unconscious of the Australian junior in the branches of the beech, and of the beaky man shadowing him, rolled on towards the stile. It was Saturday afternoon, a half-holiday at Greyfriars, and Bunter was rolling over to Cliff House to see his sister Bessie—perhaps with a faint hope that something might yet survive from Wednesday's hamper.

The fat Owl arrived at the stile, at length. He did not immediately clamber over it. He leaned on it to get his breath : always in short supply with William George Bunter.

Squiff, from above, watched the beaky man, curiously. The beaky man came to a halt, as Bunter stopped at the stile, still watching him. No doubt he could see that Bunter was about to take the footpath through the wood, which, if his purpose was robbery suited him admirably. It was obvious to the watching eyes from the beech that the man was waiting for Bunter to get over the stile.

Squiff's face set grimly.

A pickpocket or footpad who set out to pilfer from Billy Bunter was simply wasting his time. If Billy Bunter had any cash about him, it was not likely to amount to much. True, he had a watch and chain, and the beaky man couldn't know that the value thereof was what Fisher T. Fish described as " nix ". But he was not going to help himself even to Bunter's rolled-gold watch, if Squiff could stop him—and he had no doubt that he could. The sturdy Australian junior would not have hesitated for a moment to tackle him, and land a set of hefty knuckles on a beaky nose.

Bunter clambered over the stile at last, and dropped, with a grunt, on the inner side. At the same moment, the man in the lane got into motion. He shot forward, and reached the stile. Bunter was not six feet from it, when the beaky man leaped lightly over.

Squiff, watching him from the branch almost over his head, saw him shoot a wary glance up the footpath: obviously to make sure that nobody was in sight there. Then he ran at Bunter, and caught the fat Owl by a fat shoulder.

Billy Bunter spun round, with a startled squeak.

He blinked in surprise, and a little alarm, through his big spectacles, at the beaky face.

"I—I say—what—who—what—— ?" stuttered the fat Owl. "I say, you leggo! What do you want? What——?"

The beaky man did not trouble to speak. Grasping Bunter's fat shoulder with his left hand, he snatched at the watch with his right.

There was a brassy gleam, as Bunter's watch came out of his pocket, and a snap, as the chain parted.

Bunter gave a yell.

"Oh, crikey! You gimme my watch—why, you beast, you ain't going to pinch my watch—help—— Yaroooh!"

With a swing of his arm, the beaky man sent Bunter spinning. Bunter rolled in the grass and roared.

It was at that moment, that Squiff, on the branch above, went into action. He had been sitting astride of it. Now he swung with his hands, and dropped, fairly on the man below.

Crash!

A thunderbolt dropping from a clear sky could not have taken the beaky man more by surprise.

He was wary and watchful: his sharp eyes had ascertained that nobody was in sight—nobody on the footpath, nobody in the lane. He had been absolutely sure that no one was on the spot, or near at hand, excepting himself and Bunter. Squiff came like a bolt from the blue.

He landed on the beaky man's shoulders, fairly crumpling him up. One startled sputtering yell escaped the beaky man, as he crumpled. He pitched into the grass, Bunter's watch flying from his hand, and landing two or three yards away, his beaky face buried in grass roots. Squiff dropped on his knees on the sprawling back, pinning him down.

"Urrrrrrrgh!" came an anguished gurgle from the beaky man. "What—what—oh, crimes!—gurrrggh—ow! My back!—urrrggh!"

He wriggled like an eel under Squiff's sinewy knees, gasping, and twisting his head round to stare up at his unexpected assailant. Squiff gave him a cheery grin.

"Knocked you sideways, what?" he asked, pleasantly.

"Urrggh! Gerroff my back!"

The man struggled fiercely. But he could not dislodge the knee that pinned him down. Squiff had him down, and kept him there.

Billy Bunter sat up, spluttering. His eyes almost popped through his spectacles at the Australian junior.

"Oooogh!" gasped Bunter, "is—is—is that you, Squiff? I—I never saw you——"

"Neither did this johnny," chuckled Squiff.

"I—I say, he's got my watch!" gasped Bunter. He heaved himself to his feet. "I say, he's pinched my watch! My gold watch—— I say, Field, you make him gimme my watch——"

"There it is, fathead, where he dropped it. You can pick it up," said Squiff. He pointed to a brassy glimmer in the grass, and the fat Owl pounced on the watch. Fisher T. Fish might pronounce its value to be "nix," but Billy Bunter was very glad to recover his gold watch!—a poor thing, but his own, as it were.

"I say, that beast's broken the chain!" said Bunter. "Snatching a fellow's gold watch, you know—it's worth pounds and pounds, Field——"

"I don't think!" chuckled Squiff.

"Oh, really, Field——"

"Well, you've got your watch," said Squiff. He jammed a powerful knee a little more firmly into a wriggling back. "I'll look after this rat while you clear off, Bunter, but I can't kneel on him for ever. Hook it."

Bunter slipped the precious watch back into his pocket.

But he did not hook it. He eyed the wriggling pickpocket dubiously.

“ I—I say, suppose he gets after me again, in the wood ! ”

“ That's all right,” said Squiff, reassuringly. “ Show him that gold watch, Bunter—once he's seen it he won't want to get after it again ! ”

“ You silly ass ! ” roared Bunter.

“ Will you gerroff my back ? ” came in tones of fury from the beaky man, heaving under Squiff's pinning knee like the stormy ocean. “ I'll push your face through the back of your 'ead when I gerrup.”

“ I'll be there when you do it,” answered the Australian junior, cheerfully. “ You hooking it, Bunter, with that valuable gold watch of yours ? ”

“ I—I say, you—you won't let him get after me ? ”

“ Five minutes, start, old fat man ! Mizzle ! ”

Billy Bunter gave the wriggling man another dubious blink. Then he started. This time he did not proceed with his usual leisurely roll. Bunter was very anxious to get through the wood, and out of it, before Squiff's knee was withdrawn from the wriggling back under it. He started at a run, and in a few moments disappeared from view up the leafy path.

Squiff rocked, as the man under him made a tremendous effort. Evidently it was not the beaky man's view that Bunter's big gold watch was a thing of little value, for as the fat Owl disappeared up the path, he exerted every ounce of his strength to throw the Australian junior off—obviously with the intention of getting after Bunter, if he could. Squiff, strong and muscular as he was, had hard work to hold him down. But he did hold him down—grinding his knee into the small of his back till he howled with pain.

For a long minute, the man strove, fiercely and savagely : then, quite spent with his efforts, he collapsed in the grass, and lay panting and gasping, almost groaning for breath. After that, it was easy enough to hold him : and Squiff kept him pinned, till a good five minutes had elapsed. Then he removed his knee, and rose to his feet.

The beaky man staggered up, panting, his eyes smouldering at the Greyfriars junior. Squiff, standing between him and the way Bunter had gone, watched him coolly, quite ready for more trouble if the rascal wanted it. For a moment or two, it seemed that the man would spring at him: but a pair of very useful fists were ready if he did, and he seemed to think better of it. He gave the Australian junior a black scowl, and made a movement to pass on up the footpath.

Squiff stood like a rock in the way.

"No, you don't!" he said, coolly.

"I'm going through the wood——"

"You're mistaken—you're not! You're not going after Bunter," said Squiff. "Hop over that stile, and clear." He came a step nearer the beaky man. "Now, then, sharp's the word! Get going, before you get hurt."

The beaky man eyed him almost wolfishly. But no doubt he realised that the fat Owl was at a safe distance by that time, and that a scrap with the sturdy Australian junior would not serve any useful purpose. For a moment he hesitated, then he swung himself over the stile, and slouched away in the direction of Friardale. Squiff, with a cheery grin, sat on the stile, and watched him out of sight.

CHAPTER XXIX

A WILD NIGHT FOR SMITHY

HERBERT VERNON-SMITH caught his breath. His brows knitted darkly, and his eyes glinted under them. It was the sound of a dog's scampering feet under the old Cloister wall, that startled him, and brought that look of angry dismay to his face.

That sound would not have been alarming in the daytime. Gosling's mastiff might have run loose at any hour of the day, and the Bounder would have given it no heed. But it was a different matter when midnight had chimed from the old clock-tower. A Greyfriars fellow who was out of bounds at that hour of the night required to be very cautious about it, and to keep his proceedings exceedingly secret : the alternative being a painful interview with his head-master, and a morning train home.

After what had happened a few nights ago, wild horses would not have dragged Billy Bunter from the Remove dormitory after lights out. He was no longer planning nocturnal retaliation on Cecil Reginald Temple of the Fourth Form. Even a spread would not have tempted him forth. But the Bounder of Greyfriars was made of sterner stuff than the fat Owl. On Monday night, Smithy had an appointment with certain sporting friends at the Cross Keys : and the possibility of running into a shadowy form in dark passages or on dark staircases, did not make him think for a moment of washing it out.

Now that it was known that Slim Judson was at large, and had penetrated into the school in the dark hours, no one doubted that the Blue Mauritius was, after all, hidden somewhere in Greyfriars School, and that the pimpled man was after it. It was hardly to be doubted that he would make another attempt, unless the police succeeded in laying him by the heels in the meantime : and of that, there was as yet no news. But the hardy Bounder did not give that matter a single thought, when he crept silently from his dormitory, and slipped out of the House by way of the Remove box-room window. Smithy had the courage of his misdeeds : and he was not afraid of the dark, or of anything that might lurk in the dark.

Neither was he alarmed now, as far as any midnight intruder was concerned. What alarmed him was the danger of discovery by those set in authority over him. He had returned later than was his wont from his dingy excursion : tired, sleepy, not much comforted by having lost several pounds at banker to Mr. Joe Banks : and longing for bed and sleep. And, as he clambered on the cloister wall from the little shady lane outside, and was about to drop within, that sudden scampering in the shadows made him pause. Bunched on the wall, under the shadow of thick branches, he stared down into the gloom, gritting his teeth. He had to cut across a corner of the quad to get back to the House : and now he made the disagreeable discovery that there was, so to speak, a lion in the path !

He guessed at once why Gosling's dog was loose. It was a precaution against another surreptitious visit from Mr. Judson. After the last door had closed, and the last light was out, the mastiff had been loosed—for Slim Judson's behoof, if he came ! In the daytime, Biter would have taken no heed of Smithy, or any other Greyfriars man. But at midnight the matter was very different. A footstep would be enough to bring the mastiff careering up, waking the echoes with his barking. He might or might not sample the Bounder with his teeth : but he would indubitably draw attention to the fact that someone was there in the dark. And attention, out of bounds at midnight, was the very last thing Herbert Vernon-Smith wanted.

"The old fool !" breathed Smithy. He was referring to Sir Hilton Popper, whose missing Blue Mauritius was the cause of the trouble.

He could have wished, at that moment, that he had not taken up the chase of Mr. Judson on Courtfield Common. If the pickpocket had got away with the Blue Mauritius, Smithy would not have been in his present scrape. But it was rather too late to think of that !

He listened intently.

The scampering died away in the distance. Biter had not spotted him, so far, and had scampered off.

If he had gone to a safe distance, Smithy could make the venture. He had to make it, sooner or later : he could not stay where he was. He could have kicked himself for having left his dormitory at all. But again, it was too late to think of that.

A sound came to his ears, as he listened, and he gave a start. It was a sound, not from within, but from without—a stealthy step in the little lane outside the wall. Someone was there, in the dark.

Smithy's heart beat unpleasantly. He stared from the dark shadow of the branches over him, and discerned a stout figure, looming dimly in the night, a few yards from him. Another figure loomed still more dimly. A faint voice came to the Bounder's ears in the stillness.

" Did you hear something, Rance ? "

" I think I did, sergeant."

Smithy hardly breathed. He realised that he might have guessed that a watch was kept on the school, after Mr. Judson's visit : but he had not given it a thought. There were two policemen in the lane outside the cloister : and he might have walked into them ! Certainly, they were on the watch for a pimpled pickpocket, not for a Greyfriars fellow out of bounds : but if they found him—— It seemed to Smithy, for a moment, that he could already see his head-master's stern face, and hear Dr. Locke pronounce the words " Vernon-Smith, you are expelled ! " He scarcely dared draw a breath, as he stared into the shadows at the two dim forms.

One of them moved closer to the wall, staring up.

Obviously, they had heard some faint sound from the Bounder as he climbed, and were suspicious. If they turned on a light——

He dared hesitate no longer. He dropped within the wall, hardly a moment before a beam of light flashed out. He had been barely in time. He had to take the chance of the mastiff now. Swiftly, but lightly, he ran in the shadows, only hoping that he would reach the House before Biter heard or scented him. Smithy had had more than one escape in his career as a " bad hat " : and this looked like being the narrowest of all—if he did escape !

Scamper ! Bark ! Bark ! It was Biter again, at a little distance, but only too evidently aware that someone was about. Then, to his astonishment, the Bounder heard a sound of rapidly running feet. Someone else was out in the quad—running ! It flashed into his mind who it must be ! But he had no time to think, for a moment later someone unseen crashed fairly into him, and sent him spinning.

" Oh," gasped the Bounder, as he spun.

He went over helplessly, sprawling on the ground. He heard a startled gasp from the unseen man who had crashed into him, and who was reeling from the shock.

" Oh ! Strike me pink and blue ! Ow ! "

But in a second, the man was running again. Biter was careering on his track, and he had no time to lose.

The Bounder sat up, dizzily.

Running footsteps died away in the dark. If it was Judson, he was gone. But scampering feet, and two eyes that looked like green fire in the gloom, were terribly near : and Vernon-Smith bounded up, and ran.

Bark ! bark ! bark !

The dog was behind him. Biter had been chasing an intruder, and, as the Bounder ran, doubtless Biter took him for that intruder. The unseen man had vanished, and Herbert Vernon-Smith now had Biter's particular attention.

M

And, remembering what Biter's teeth were like, the Bounder ran as he had never ran on the cinder-path, his feet hardly touching the ground. From somewhere he heard a calling voice, and then another, without heeding them. The Bounder raced on, and reached the outhouse below the box-room window. There a rain-pipe was the means of ascent to the leads under the window by which he had left, and by which he had planned to return. That rain-pipe required rather careful negotiation by a climber. But Smithy had no time for care. The mastiff's jaws were snapping below him, as he made a desperate spring, caught the pipe, and dragged himself up.

Bark ! bark ! bark !

Biter had missed him only by inches. He was jumping, prancing, barking, making the night ring with his deep voice. There were footsteps, and flashing lights, in the distance. Breathless, panting, the Bounder clung to the rain-pipe : but he dared not pause. Up he went, wildly clambering, in terror every moment lest a light from below should flash upon him and reveal him. Almost winded by his frantic efforts, he dragged himself on the leads, and sprawled there panting for breath.

" 'Ere, Biter ! Good dorg ! " It was Gosling's voice. " Wot I says is this 'ere, Mr. Rance, Biter was after somebody——"

The Bounder crawled along the leads to the box-room window. He was thankful that it was a dark night. Otherwise, he must have been seen, as he pushed up the sash he had left unfastened, and plunged in at the window. Breathless, panting, his forehead wet with perspiration, he closed the window and fastened the catch, and sank down on a box to recover his wind.

He was almost giddy with his narrow escape. But he had escaped : and in less than a minute, he was stealing on tiptoe down the box-room stair, and creeping past the Remove studies. Another minute, and he was tiptoeing up the dormitory staircase, hardly able to believe in his good luck when he reached the door of the Remove dormitory.

All were sleeping there. The Bounder crept quietly into bed: but it was long before he could sleep—after the wildest night out that he had ever had.

CHAPTER XXX

BUNTER IS WANTED

"HALLO, hallo, hallo! Grimey again!"

Bob Cherry made that remark, in break on Tuesday morning. And the Famous Five glanced at a solid, stolid figure that came in at the school gates. They smiled a little as they glanced.

Inspector Grimes, of Courtfield, had become quite a familiar figure at the school, of late. And here he was again: on the track, the chums of the Remove had no doubt, of that elusive Blue Mauritius stamp. He had had no luck, so far: but evidently the plump inspector was a sticker!

That the Blue Mauritius was somewhere about Greyfriars, few now doubted. But spotting it was quite another matter. It looked rather like making a search for a needle in a haystack. Even Sir Hilton Popper, who, as the Famous Five knew, had been relying on the sale of that Blue Mauritius to satisfy the demands of his Inspector of Taxes, had ceased to wander about the school, poking into odd corners. So small an object, in so extensive a place, really needed a lot of looking for: and the lord of Popper Court had apparently given up the faint hope of discovering it.

"Grimey is a sticker," remarked Johnny Bull, as the inspector from Courtfield walked across to the House. "He's sticking to it."

"The stickfulness is terrific," grinned Hurree Jamset Ram Singh. "But the findfulness of the absurd stamp is a boot on the other leg."

"Pimples knows where it is, I suppose," said Bob, "but they've let Pimples slip through their fingers. His coming here the other night shows that the jolly old stamp is spotted about Greyfriars somewhere. It seems that that fat ass Bunter did really run into him on the dormitory landing——"

"That's queer, too," said Harry Wharton, thoughtfully. "What the dickens was the man doing up in the dormitories? He was cornered in the Remove studies, and never went up the upper staircase at all: so he can't have hidden the stamp up there."

"Hardly," said Nugent. "I daresay he would pick up anything that came handy, while he was on the spot: but there's nothing up in the dormitories——"

"Except Bunter's gold watch!" grinned Bob.

"Ha, ha, ha!"

"I say, you fellows." Billy Bunter rolled up. "I say, old Grimey's here again—he's just gone in to Quelch. I wonder if he wants to see me."

"Well, if he wants to see you, old chap, there's one thing you'd better do at once," said Bob.

"Eh? What's that?"

"Wash!" said Bob. "He won't be able to see you otherwise."

"You silly ass!" yelled Bunter. "I say, I think very likely Grimey wants me. He said the other day that I had been very useful——"

"Well, you couldn't expect him to say that you were very ornamental——"

"Yah! I shouldn't wonder if he wants to see me," declared Bunter. "I'd be jolly glad to help, you know. Old Grimey isn't very bright, and a fellow with brains might be jolly useful, if he could only see it. It was me who spotted that pimply beast the other night, when you fellows were snoring in bed——"

"Better not let Quelch hear you put it like that," chuckled Bob.

"Eh! Why shouldn't I?" demanded Bunter.

"Quelch might expect you to say 'It was I who spotted the pimply beast'," explained Bob.

Bunter blinked at him.

"Well, I like that!" he exclaimed, indignantly. "It wasn't you, Cherry—it was me."

"Ha, ha, ha!" yelled the Famous Five.

"Blessed if I see anything to cackle at. It was me," hooted Bunter. "Cherry wasn't out of bed at all—it was me——"

"Ha, ha, ha!"

"Making out that it was him!" Bunter was almost breathless with indignation. "It was me all the time——."

"You blithering burbler," roared Bob. "Quelch wouldn't let you say 'It was me——'"

"I didn't say it was you! I said it was me."

"Ha, ha, ha!"

"No wonder Quelch is going a bit grey!" gasped Bob. "Teaching Bunter grammar is enough to turn a beak's hair white in a single night."

"What's the matter with my grammar, I'd like to know? We ain't talking about grammar. We're talking about that pimply beast that I spotted the other night. You never spotted him, Bob Cherry—you jolly well know it was me——"

"Ha, ha, ha!"

"Why not make it I?" chuckled Nugent.

"But it wasn't you——"

"Oh, my hat!"

"Are you going to make out that it was you, Nugent, as well as Bob making out that it was him?" hooted Bunter. "Why every man in the Remove knows that it was me. Me all the time."

"Ha, ha, ha!"

"You can cackle," snorted Bunter, "but it was me, as you jolly well know! And if Grimey wants to see any chap here, it won't be one of you fellows, but me, so you can put that in your pipe and smoke it."

At which the Famous Five chuckled again. It did not seem probable to them that the Courtfield inspector wanted to see Bunter, or had any use for his brain work. But a surprise was coming. It came in the shape of Trotter, the House page, who emerged from the House, glanced round, and then came across to the group of juniors.

"Master Bunter——!" said Trotter. "If you please, sir, Inspector Grimes would like to see you, in Mr. Quelch's study, sir."

Billy Bunter grinned. He grinned so widely that his fat grin extended almost from ear to ear. He gave the Famous Five a vaunting blink.

"He, he, he! I say, you fellows, what do you think now? What? He, he, he! Who is it Grimey wants to see? He, he, he!"

And Bunter, greatly bucked, rolled off to the House, in high feather: leaving five astonished juniors staring.

But Trotter's mission was not yet finished. He went further afield, to apprise Peter Todd that he also was required. Then he looked for Tom Dutton, to give him the same information. From which it appeared that Inspector Grimes desired to see all the inhabitants of No. 7 Study in the Remove. Dutton had to be told three times, crescendo, before he heard aright: then he told Trotter that there was no need to shout, and followed Peter Todd into the House.

Billy Bunter, at the door of Mr. Quelch's study, blinked round, surprised and not pleased, to see his study-mates coming up the passage.

"I say, you fellows, wharrer you want?" he asked. "Think Grimey wants to see you?"

"Sort of," assented Peter.

"Well, that's rot!" said Bunter. "He wants to see me! No need for you fellows to barge in. You'd better clear off, Toddy, and you too, Dutton."

"Eh?"

"Clear! You're not wanted to see Grimes."

"They have one in Common-Room, I believe," answered Dutton, staring. "What do you want *The Times* for, Bunter?"

"Oh, crikey! I didn't say Times—Grimes!" hooted Bunter.

"Rot!" said Dutton. "You don't get much about crimes in *The Times*. One of the cheaper papers, if you want to read about crimes."

"Not crimes—Grimes!" shrieked Bunter. "You're not wanted to see Grimes."

"Talk sense, Bunter! You don't see chimes—you hear them! Besides, you weren't talking about chimes at all——"

Peter Todd, grinning, tapped at the study door, and opened it. Bunter had to give it up, and the three inhabitants of No. 7 in the Remove entered Mr. Quelch's study together.

CHAPTER XXXI

DRAWN BLANK

INSPECTOR GRIMES was standing by the window, in Mr. Quelch's study, solid and stolid. He was looking out into the quadrangle : but his ruddy face turned towards the three juniors as they entered, and he gave them a genial nod. His eyes, very keen under his plump brows, scanned them. Mr. Quelch, who was seated at the study table, rose.

" Here are the boys, Mr. Grimes," he said. " Todd! Dutton! Bunter! Inspector Grimes wishes to speak to you. You will tell him anything you can."

" Yes, sir," said Peter and Bunter.

Tom Dutton looked puzzled.

" Did you say can, sir ? " he asked.

" Certainly," rapped Mr. Quelch.

" What can, sir ? Do you mean a water-can ? "

" Bless my soul! Inspector Grimes, I should explain that this boy, Dutton, is somewhat deaf, and liable to mistake what is said to him." And with that, Mr. Quelch quitted the study, without explaining to Dutton whether he had meant a water-can or not.

Mr. Grimes smiled faintly. There was a slight edge on Mr. Quelch's voice, which indicated a little edge on his temper. Possibly Mr. Grimes guessed that the Remove master was fed up with the affair of Sir Hilton Popper's missing stamp, and considered that enough of his valuable time had been wasted on it. However, Mr. Grimes had his official duty to do, even if it irked Mr. Quelch, and he proceeded stolidly with the business in hand.

" You three boys belong to the study, Number Seven, in which the pickpocket Judson was captured last week ? " asked Mr. Grimes.

" Yes, sir," said Peter.

" I was there, Mr. Grimes," said Billy Bunter. " Toddy and Dutton were out—they don't know anything about it——"

" I think you were one of the boys on bicycles who joined in the chase of the pickpocket, Master Todd," said Mr. Grimes, apparently not hearing Bunter.

" Yes—I was with Field and Brown, and we joined up with Smithy and Redwing, sir. We were after him when he dodged in at the gates."

" I found him in the study——! " recommenced Bunter. " If there's anything you want to know about that, Mr. Grimes——"

" From the various accounts I have received," said Mr. Grimes, still deaf to Bunter, " the man was hotly chased, and hardly out of sight for a moment until he hid in that study. It appears to be certain, as doubtless you know, that he removed a valuable rare stamp from Sir Hilton Popper's pocket-book while it was in his possession."

" We know all about the Blue Marumptious, sir——! " said Bunter.

" Now, listen to me carefully," said Mr. Grimes. Bunter wondered whether the inspector had become as deaf as Tom Dutton. He did not seem to hear the fat Owl at all. " It appears that the man removed the stamp from the pocket-book, and concealed it : apparently in the hope of finding an opportunity of recovering it later. From all appearance, he can have concealed it only in the study in which he was out of sight for a few minutes."

" Oh, it ain't there, Mr. Grimes," said Bunter. " I've looked."

" The study has been searched with such thoroughness, that we are satisfied that it is no longer there," went on Mr. Grimes, " that is why I desire to question you boys, as belonging to the study."

" I've looked everywhere——" Bunter re-started.

" On Friday night," resumed the inspector, still ruthlessly

regardless of Bunter, " the man is known to have entered this building, at a late hour——"

" I saw him, sir ! It was me ! If Nugent or Bob Cherry make out that it was them, it's all gammon. It was me all the time."

" On that occasion, the man was seen on an upper landing, a flight of stairs above the Remove studies," said Mr. Grimes, stolidly. " He could easily have entered the study undetected, but he had some reason for going up to the dormitory floor instead. This would seem to indicate that he had some cause to think that the hidden stamp, though undiscovered, might have been transferred from the study to a dormitory."

Peter Todd gave a quick nod, as he saw the inspector's point. Billy Bunter blinked at him, through his big spectacles, wondering what on earth the old ass was driving at. Tom Dutton gave no sign. He had not heard a word, so far.

" You see what I mean, Master Todd," went on the inspector. " The stamp may have been hidden in something, such as the pocket of a blazer hanging on the door, or some other garment that may have been left about the study, and that may have been removed by the owner before the search was made for the stamp."

" I get you, sir," assented Peter.

" Oh ! " said Bunter. The fat Owl understood now what the " old ass " was driving at. Indeed, it was clear that something of the kind must have occurred if the Blue Mauritius had been hidden in No. 7 at all, since it was no longer there. " Oh ! I see ! I wonder you didn't think of that before, Mr. Grimes."

Inspector Grimes breathed rather hard for a moment. But he did not yield to his natural impulse to box Bunter's fat ears.

" Now, I want you boys to make an effort to recall that afternoon," he went on. " You seem a very intelligent boy, Master Todd : and I have no doubt you will remember whether you removed anything from that study—any article whatsoever—after the man Judson had been there, and before the study was searched for the stamp."

Peter Todd wrinkled his brow. But he had to shake his head.

"Nothing at all, sir," he said. "I've an old blazer hanging up in the study, but it's still there. Nothing at all."

"Not even a book you may have borrowed from another boy?" suggested Mr. Grimes. "A book, or a box of instruments—or anything? The stamp may have been in it."

"Nothing at all, sir," said Peter. "Bunter may have—— He's always leaving things lying about——"

"Oh, really, Toddy——"

"Now, Master Bunter." Mr. Grimes took cognizance of the fat Owl's existence, at last. "Can you remember whether you removed anything from your study, after the man Judson had been there?"

"Oh, yes, sir," answered Bunter, cheerfully.

"What was it?"

"My lines, sir."

"Your lines?" repeated Mr. Grimes.

"I had lines for my form-master," explained Bunter. "Quelch wouldn't let me go out till they were done, and so I couldn't go over and see my sister Bessie at Cliff House—she had a hamper——"

"Keep to the point, Master Bunter."

"That's the point, sir—I had to stick in the study and do my lines, and I did them after that man Judson was there, and took them down to Quelch, but it was too late then to go over to Cliff House, and——"

Mr. Grimes breathed hard again.

"The stamp can hardly have been concealed in your lines, Master Bunter, if you did them after the man was gone," he said. "Did you take anything else from the study before the search was made? A jacket—a blazer—a cap—a book—even a handkerchief——?"

"Oh, no, sir, only my lines. Quelch said——"

"That will do, Master Bunter." Inspector Grimes turned to Tom Dutton: his last hope. "Now, Master Dutton——"

"Did you speak to me, sir?" asked Tom.

"Oh! Yes!" Inspector Grimes remembered what Mr. Quelch had told him, and put on steam a little. "Do you remember removing anything from your study last Wednesday afternoon——?"

"I don't think so, sir. It was quite a fine afternoon. I was out on my bike, and never noticed that it was muddy, at all."

"Oh!" gasped Mr. Grimes, "I was speaking of your study."

"Yes, sir, I heard you. It wasn't, that I know of. Did you notice whether it was muddy, Toddy? You were out on your bike, too."

"Oh, my hat!" murmured Toddy.

"He, he, he!" from Bunter.

"Do you remember last Wednesday afternoon?" bawled Mr. Grimes.

"Oh, yes, sir! That was the day that pickpocket dodged into the school—they found him in my study."

"Somewhere in that study, he is known to have concealed a stamp."

"I shouldn't wonder, sir. All the fellows said he was a pickpocket, but he may have been a tramp too."

"I said stamp!" roared Inspector Grimes.

"Eh?" Tom Dutton looked bewildered. "Did you say stamp?"

"Yes: stamp!"

"I don't think Mr. Quelch would like me to stamp in his study. What do you want me to stamp for?"

"Upon my word!" gasped Mr. Grimes. He put on full steam, and roared, "A stamp—a rare stamp—was concealed in your study."

"Oh, yes, I've heard about that, sir! There's no need to shout at a fellow—I'm not deaf——"

"The stamp may have been hidden in some article, removed from the study before the search was made by the police. Did you remove any such article ?" bawled Mr. Grimes.

"Oh ! No !"

"Such a thing as a book, or a cap, or a blazer—— ?"

"I don't use an ink-eraser. If I did, I shouldn't take it out of the study—I should want it there !"

"Or a book—— ?"

"Did you say cook ?"

"No ! Book !"

"Oh, hook ! Yes, there's a hook on the door—Toddy keeps his old blazer hanging on it. That's the only hook I know of in my study."

"I—I think that will do," gasped Inspector Grimes. "You may go, my boys. If you should learn, Master Todd, that any article was removed from your study, at the material time, you will inform your form-master, who will communicate with me."

"Certainly, sir," said Peter.

The three juniors left Inspector Grimes with a knitted thoughtful brow. He had no doubt that Mr. Judson had concealed that precious stamp in No. 7 Study in the Remove : and he deduced that it must have been concealed in some article removed from the study before the police came. From the circumstance that Mr. Judson, on the occasion of his later visit, had been up among the dormitories, he deduced further that the article was probably something that would not be left permanently in a study, but might be carried up to a dormitory. He had hoped for confirmation of that theory from the occupants of No. 7 Study—and he had drawn completely blank !

He might have been enlightened, had Billy Bunter remembered that his gold watch had been left lying on the study table during Mr. Judson's brief sojourn there. But that trifling circumstance had not lingered in Bunter's memory. It was a puzzled, perplexed, and somewhat irritated police-inspector who watched the three juniors leave the study—little dreaming that one of them was carrying away with him the precious Blue Mauritius of which he was in search !

CHAPTER XXXII

BUNTER IN LUCK

"HARRY, old chap—— ! "

" How much ? " asked Harry Wharton, resignedly. Billy Bunter blinked at him.

" Eh ? Wharrer you mean—how much ? " he demanded. " Think I was going to ask you to lend me some tin ? "

" Oh ! Weren't you ? " asked Wharton, in surprise.

" No ! " roared Bunter.

" Then why did you call me Harry old chap ? "

" Oh, really, Wharton ! It's Wednesday, you know——"

" I had an idea that it was, as it was Tuesday yesterday," assented Wharton. " Did you work that out in your head ? "

" I mean, it's a half this afternoon, you silly ass," howled Bunter, " and Bessie's got tickets for the circus at Courtfield. I've got to meet her in Courtfield at a quarter to three."

" Then you'd better be a little more careful than usual with your con in third school," advised the captain of the Remove. " If you get put into Extra——"

" Never mind that," said Bunter, peevishly. " I shall want to know the time, you know. Bessie won't wait for me if I'm late, I know that. My watch has stopped——"

" Why not wind it up ? "

" I keep on winding it, and it doesn't make any difference," explained Bunter, " the beastly winder goes round and round and round, but the watch doesn't go ! It's a jolly good watch, you know——"

" Must be," agreed Wharton. " Sounds good ! "

" I believe my Uncle Carter gave twenty guineas for it——"

" They must have seen him coming ! "

" Or twenty-five," snapped Bunter. " It's a jolly expensive watch, thirty-five carat gold——"

" Oh, my hat ! "

" Or forty," said Bunter, " but—it doesn't keep time, at —at present. I'm going to have it repaired when I get a postal-order I'm expecting. But—it isn't going now. Will you lend me your watch for to-day ? "

" Oh ! "

" Only for to-day, you know," said Bunter. " I've just got to keep time this afternoon, or Bessie will hike off without me. You know what girls are ! I know it's only a paltry cheap watch you've got, old chap——"

" Eh ? "

" Nothing to look at, compared with my splendid gold watch. But it does keep time, doesn't it, and that's what I want. I don't mind it being a cheap old turnip, really. Lend it to me, will you ? "

" You put it so nicely," said Harry. " Can't you borrow somebody else's watch, you fat ass ? "

" Well, I asked Smithy—I'd rather wear his watch than yours, of course—but he only laughed. I asked Mauly, too, but he walked away before I'd finished speaking. That's why I'm asking you, old chap. You can wear mine for to-day, if you like," added Bunter, temptingly, " you needn't mention that it's mine, either—you can let the fellows see you swanking with a magnificent gold watch, for once."

Harry Wharton laughed. If he had been disposed to " swank " with a gold watch, Billy Bunter's big brassy specimen was not the one he would have selected for the purpose.

" Blessed if I see anything to cackle at," said Bunter, irritably. " Look here, the bell will be going for third school in a minute. Will you lend me your watch for to-day ? "

" Oh ! Yes, if you like," said Harry. " Mind, if you lose it, or break the glass, or anything else, I'll burst you afterwards. Here it is ! "

The captain of the Remove detached the watch, and Billy Bunter—with a disparaging blink—slipped it into his waistcoat pocket. Certainly, it was not an expensive watch: not at all the watch Bunter would have chosen, had Smithy and Lord Mauleverer been more amenable. Still, it had the modest merit of keeping time.

"Not much of a thing, is it?" said Bunter. "Not the sort of watch a fellow would care to wear, really! Still, nobody will see it, in my pocket," added Bunter, apparently drawing comfort from that circumstance.

"You fat ass——!"

"Oh, really, Wharton! You needn't call a fellow names, because he's got a splendid gold watch, and you've only got this tin thing, or whatever it is. Look here, if you wear my watch, mind you take jolly good care of it—it's not cheap tin like yours, you know——"

"Thanks: I wouldn't be found dead with it," answered the captain of the Remove, politely, and he walked away.

"Beast!" yapped Bunter, no doubt by way of expressing thanks for the loan of the watch. And he rolled up to his study, to deposit in the table-drawer his own imposing gold watch, which, magnificent as it was, in Bunter's estimation at least, was useless for the purpose of keeping an appointment on time.

That worry off his fat mind, another took its place, when the bell rang for third school. Bunter could not help feeling a little uneasy about his "con". True, in a numerous form like the Remove, a fellow could always hope to escape being called upon to translate. That hope was always with Bunter, springing eternal in his podgy breast. Under its influence, he had spent "prep" the previous evening in the armchair in No. 7 Study, while Toddy and Dutton were working at the table, "chancing" it with Quelch once more.

Now, he rather wished that he hadn't chanced it. Quelch might not call on him to construe: but, again, he might!

He was beast enough, as Bunter knew only too well. And if the fat Owl handed out " howlers ", it was quite on the cards that Quelch might give him Extra School. Which would wholly, completely, and totally " dish " the circus at Courtfield that afternoon.

There was a wrinkle of unusual thought in Bunter's fat brow, when Mr. Quelch let the Remove into their form-room for third school. Prepared Latin was tough going, for Bunter: unprepared Latin was an insoluble problem. He could only hope that Quelch would pass him over.

Quite unaware of that worry on the fat mind of the fattest member of his form, Mr. Quelch did not even glance at the Owl of the Remove. Wharton, Nugent, Johnny Bull, Bob Cherry, were called on in turn: Mark Linley, Hazeldene, Squiff, Tom Brown, Wibley, Ogilvy, Russell, Fisher T. Fish, Micky Desmond, and Peter Todd. And then——!

" Bunter! "

" Oh, crikey! "

" What? What did you say, Bunter? " exclaimed Mr. Quelch.

" Oh! Nothing, sir! I—I never said ' Oh, crikey ', sir! I—I didn't speak——"

" You will go on, Bunter."

Billy Bunter could have groaned. He blinked at his book. He did not even know the place.

" Lucus in urbe——" whispered Peter Todd, over a fat shoulder.

" Lucus in urbe fuit media——! " mumbled Bunter.

" Construe! " snapped Mr. Quelch.

There was nothing for it but to make a shot at it! Billy Bunter was about to make a shot, which would have missed the mark by a very wide margin, when a tap came at the form-room door.

Tap!

Never had Bunter been so glad of an interruption. It was a respite, at least. The form-room door opened, and Trotter appeared.

Mr. Quelch gave him a sharp, not to say an irritable, glance.

"What is it, Trotter?" he rapped, before the page could speak.

"If you please, sir, a servant from Popper Court, with a message for Master Bunter from Sir 'Ilton, sir."

Mr. Quelch compressed his lips. He did not like interruptions in lesson time. Sir Hilton Popper, if he had a message to send to a member of Mr. Quelch's form, should obviously have chosen a more appropriate moment. However, Sir Hilton was a member of the governing Board of Greyfriars School, and not to be disregarded.

"Very well!" snapped Mr. Quelch. Trotter departed. "Bunter!"

"Oh! Yes, sir!" gasped Bunter, his little round eyes dancing behind his big round spectacles.

What message Sir Hilton Popper could have sent him, Bunter could not guess. An invitation to tea up at the Court, perhaps, in acknowledgment of his usefulness on the occasion of his night out in Popper Court Woods. True, the last time Sir Hilton had seen him, he had whopped him with his stick, which perhaps made an invitation to tea at Popper Court improbable. But whatever the message was, it called Bunter away from the form-room, just in time to escape "con".

It was sheer luck for Bunter, for he had been about to construe that passage, "There was a light in the city", which certainly would not have satisfied Mr. Quelch, and might have put him in danger of Extra. Now it did not matter a boiled bean to Bunter whether there was a light or a grove, or indeed anything else, in the city. Bunter was in luck!

"Where is the man waiting, Trotter?"

"In the visitors' room, sir."

"You may go to the visitors' room, Bunter, to receive the message from Sir Hilton Popper.

"Yes, sir," trilled Bunter.

And he rolled joyously out of the Remove form-room, leaving less lucky fellows to carry on with "con". With a cheery fat face he rolled into the visitors' room.

CHAPTER XXXIII

THE WATCH THAT WENT

THE man standing by the window in the visitors' room was quietly dressed, with a clean-shaven face, and his manner was deferential as he turned towards the fat Owl of the Remove. He looked a respectable man-servant, and Gosling had had no doubt when he let him in, neither had Trotter doubted for a moment that he was other than he stated. Neither did a doubt cross Billy Bunter's fat mind, as he blinked at him through his big spectacles. There were at least six or seven men-servants at Popper Court, and this, so far as Bunter knew, was one of them. Not for a moment, did William George Bunter dream that he was about to have the surprise of his fat life.

The window, which looked on the quadrangle, was wide open. Nobody was to be seen in the quad : only Gosling, in the distance, standing by the door of his lodge, stolidly contemplating the pigeons. The man had been looking from the open window, with very keen eyes in a smooth sleek face. But he turned at once as Bunter rolled in.

" Master Bunter, sir ? " he asked, deferentially.

" Yes ! " Bunter gave him a patronising blink. " Trotter says you've got a message for me from Sir Hilton Popper ? "

" Precisely, sir ! You are the young gentleman in whose study a pickpocket was caught on Wednesday last week sir ? "

" That's me," agreed Bunter. He was quite interested. Apparently the message from Sir Hilton had reference to the affair of Slim Judson and the missing Blue Mauritius.

" Then this note is for you, sir," said the sleek man.

He came deferentially towards Bunter, taking an envelope from his pocket. Bunter held out a fat grubby paw for it.

THE WATCH WHISKED OUT OF BUNTER'S WAISTCOAT-POCKET IN HIS HAND

What happened next seemed to Billy Bunter like a fantastic vision from some extraordinary nightmare.

The sleek man, as he drew nearer, did not place a note in the fat hand. Instead of doing that, he made a sudden snatch, and the watch whisked out of Bunter's waistcoat-pocket in his hand.

With the watch in his right hand, he gave Bunter a violent shove, with his left, sending the fat junior sprawling on his plump back on the floor.

There was a heavy bump as Bunter landed. Utterly amazed and dazed, the fat junior sprawled on his back, gasping.

The sleek man did not waste even a glance on him. Leaving Bunter sprawling, he thrust the watch into his pocket, and ran to the window. Bunter's dizzy blink glimpsed him jumping out into the quad.

Almost in the twinkling of an eye, he was gone.

" Urrrrrggh ! " gurgled Bunter.

He sat up dazedly.

So utterly unexpected and extraordinary was that sudden happening, that he could hardly believe that it really had happened ! His fat brain was in a whirl. A man-servant from Popper Court, with a message from Sir Hilton, pinching a fellow's watch and knocking him over ! It was amazing—astounding—stupefying !

The fat Owl staggered to his feet, spluttering for breath. He stared from the window through his big spectacles. The sleek man, running, was almost at the gates : Gosling staring at him, no doubt wondering why so respectable-looking a man-servant was putting on such undignified speed.

" Stop him ! " yelled Bunter. He waved excited fat hands from the window. " Gosling ! Stop him ! Stop thief ! He's got my watch ! Stop him ! "

Gosling, at the distance, did not even hear. He stared blankly at the running man, who was past him in another moment, and whizzing out into the road. He vanished from Gosling's eyes and Bunter's spectacles.

" Oh, crikey ! " gasped Bunter.

The man was gone ! He was gone with the watch he had so suddenly and unexpectedly snatched from Bunter—the watch Harry Wharton had lent the fat Owl just before third school. Billy Bunter was not destined to keep his appointment with Sister Bessie with the aid of that watch ! That watch had vanished into parts unknown with the sleek man who had snatched it.

" Oh, crumbs ! " gasped Bunter.

He stood blinking, almost dithering. The amazing occurrence made his fat head feel as if it was turning round. He tottered out of the room at last, and made his way breathlessly back to the Form-room.

Monty Newland was on " con " when Bunter rolled gasping in. He was interrupted.

" I—I—I say, sir——! " spluttered Bunter, in wild excitement. All eyes turned on his fat excited face.

" You need not speak, Bunter," rapped Mr. Quelch.

" But, sir—I—I—he—he—I——"

" You may go to your place, Bunter."

" But—but I've had my picker pocked," gasped Bunter. " I mean, my pocker packed—I mean my pocket picked——"

" WHAT ! "

Even Quelch forgot construe, at that startling statement. His gimlet-eyes fixed on the wildly-flustered fat Owl.

" What did you say, Bunter ? " he rumbled.

" That man, sir—that man from Popper Court—he—he—he—he pinched my watch, sir, and—and knocked me over, and—and—and bolted with it ! " stuttered Bunter. " He—he—he's gone, sir, and—and he's got the watch—— He jumped out of the window, and bi—bub—bob—bolted, sir——"

There was a general jump, in the Remove. Even Lord Mauleverer came out of his placid accustomed calm, and jumped. Every man in the form stared at the fat Owl. Quelch's eyes almost pierced him like gimlets.

" Bunter ! What do you mean ? Explain yourself at

once. It is impossible that anything of the kind can have occurred. What do you mean ? "

" It—it did, sir—he's got the watch—Wharton's watch—Wharton lent it to me because mine doesn't go, and he's got it——"

" Impossible ! "

" He did, sir—he snatched the watch, and biffed me, and wumped out of the jindow——"

" What ? "

" I mean, jumped out of the window——"

" Bunter, collect yourself, and tell me at once what has occurred, if indeed anything has ! " snapped Mr. Quelch.

Bunter babbled it out, breathlessly. The Remove listened in sheer amazement. Quelch listened, quite as astonished as his form. It was hard to believe that such an occurrence, utterly unprecedented in the history of Greyfriars School, really had occurred. But, evidently, it had !

" Upon my word ! Extraordinary ! The man cannot have come from Popper Court—that is impossible—a pretext to obtain admission—but—but—— Extraordinary! Most extraordinary ! I shall notify the police at once—Wharton, I shall leave you in charge of the Form for a few minutes."

" Yes, sir ! "

Quelch, convinced at last that the almost impossible happening had happened, hurried from the Form-room, to get on the telephone to Courtfield police-station. There was an excited buzz in the Form-room, as the door closed after him. Billy Bunter, seldom the cynosure of all eyes, " had the house ". Every fellow wanted to hear every possible particular.

" I say, you fellows, he can't have been a man-servant from Popper Court, after all, just as Quelch said—that was just an excuse to butt in—— I say, Wharton, wasn't it jolly lucky I had your watch on, and not my splendid gold watch—— ? "

" Ha, ha, ha ! "

" Frightfully lucky, you fat idiot," said Harry Wharton.

" I told you I'd burst you if you lost my watch——"

" Well, I couldn't help that man pinching it, could I ? Who'd have thought it, you know ? Man coming here making out that he had a message from old Popper, and pinching a fellow's watch and bolting——"

" Blessed if I half believe it," said Skinner.

" Oh, really, Skinner——"

" Well, it seems to have happened," said Bob Cherry, " but I'm blessed if I can make it out. Can anybody ? "

Nobody could ! How the man even knew Bunter's name was a mystery. Nobody was likely to guess that a man with a beaky nose, who had snatched Bunter's watch at the stile in Friardale Lane on Saturday afternoon, and had heard Squiff address the fat junior by name, had passed the information on to a friend in the same line of business ! The whole episode was astonishing and almost incredible. But—it had happened !

Mr. Quelch came back to a buzzing, excited form. But one grim glance from the gimlet-eyes stopped the buzz and subdued the excitement : and, after that thrilling interlude, P. Vergilius Maro resumed the even tenor of his way in the Remove.

CHAPTER XXXIV

BEASTLY FOR BESSIE

"MARJORIE!"

"Yes, Bessie."

"Can I borrow your mac?"

"Oh! Yes, if you like."

"Clara!"

"Well?"

"Can I borrow your brolly?"

"No!"

"Cat!"

Those remarks were exchanged at the doorway of No. 4 Study, in the Fourth Form at Cliff House School.

Bessie Bunter, whose ample proportions and big spectacles gave her a remarkable resemblance to her brother William George, blinked into the study through the said spectacles, at Marjorie Hazeldene and Clara Trevlyn. To her two requests, Marjorie had replied in the affirmative, Clara in the negative. Marjorie always found it difficult to say "No!"—Clara, evidently, found it less difficult.

"You can see that it looks like rain, Clara," said Bessie, reproachfully. "Perhaps you'd like me to be caught in the rain without a brolly."

"Why can't you take your own brolly?" demanded Clara.

"Because it's broken in three places, and split up, and the handle's come off," snapped Bessie. "That's why I want you to lend me yours."

"Then I'll lend it to you, when I want it broken in three places, split up, and with the handle off," said Clara. "Not till then!"

"Cat!"

"I've heard that one!" Clara pointed out.

" Look here, I've got to walk as far as the Courtfield road, to get the bus," said Bessie. " If it comes on to rain I shall be drenched, without a brolly. And you can see it's going to rain. There's a few drops already. I simply must go—I've got tickets for the circus. Billy's meeting me in Courtfield to go with me, at a quarter to three. Will you lend me that brolly or not ? "

" Not ! "

" Cat ! " said Miss Bunter, for the third time. " Keep your old umbrella ! I shouldn't care to be seen with your shabby old brolly, anyway. I can borrow Barbara's. She said she wouldn't lend it to me, but she's gone out with Mabel, and she hasn't taken it. Where's that mac, Marjorie ? "

Miss Elizabeth Bunter rolled away, provided with a mac, though minus an umbrella. In the lobby downstairs, she selected Barbara Redfern's umbrella, which Babs so luckily had not taken with her when she went out with Mabel Lynn. But Bessie's luck was out !

" Bessie ! "

" Oh ! " Bessie Bunter blinked round at the voice of her Form-mistress. It was just like Bellew to have an eye on her at the most inopportune moment. " Yes, Miss Bellew."

" Is that your own umbrella you are taking from the stand, Bessie ? " asked Miss Bellew.

" Oh ! Yes ! I mean, no," stammered Bessie.

" Put it back at once."

The word " Cat " trembled on Bessie Bunter's lips. But she did not utter it. Miss Bellew could be characterised as a cat only when she was safely out of hearing. With deep feelings, Bessie Bunter replaced Barbara's umbrella, and extracted her own.

But an umbrella broken in three places, split up one side, and without a handle, did not seem very useful if it rained. Having blinked at it, Bessie put it back, and sallied forth umbrella-less, trusting to Marjorie's mac.

It was extremely irritating, for the weather to turn rainy, on a half-holiday, when she had to cover the distance to Courtfield. More than a few drops were falling, as Bessie rolled down Pegg Lane : and the drops increased in number as she proceeded. They spattered on a fat face, and dimmed a pair of big spectacles.

The rain was coming down quite hard, by the time she reached the stile that gave access to the footpath through the wood. At the stile, Miss Bunter paused, undecided whether to carry on. It would be all right when she reached the bus-stop on the high-road, but that was at a considerable distance. One of the winding footpaths in Friardale Wood led to it : but the falling rain and dripping branches did not look inviting.

On the other hand, Miss Bunter had tickets for the circus, and they were available only for that afternoon. Billy, too, would be waiting for her at the corner of the Market Place in Courtfield. Billy, it was true, could wait !—Miss Bunter was not deeply concerned about Billy. But she did not want to waste the circus tickets. So, clambering over the stile, she pushed on.

Ten minutes later, in the middle of a drenching, dripping wood, she rather wished that she had turned back, after all.

It was a regular downpour, now. Clara's or Barbara's umbrella would not have been of much use, with the rain coming down in a flood, and the wind blowing among the trees. Hoping that it was not likely to last long, Bessie parked herself under a tree, to wait for it to stop.

But, as if specially to annoy Bessie, it did not stop. It came down harder. It poured. Wet and dripping branches were little protection. Bessie realised that she had to make for shelter, and, leaving the tree, she headed for the old wood-cutter's hut. It was merely an open shed, where old Joyce, the wood-cutter, piled logs : but it was a shelter from the rain, and Bessie was very glad to reach it.

The hut had three walls and a slanting roof. The interior was more than half full of piled logs, and was dusky and shadowy. Certainly it was not such a spot as Bessie would have chosen for shelter : but it was the only shelter available for a mile or more : and she plunged into it, glad to get out of the rain.

But the rain and the wind followed her in : and the fat junior of Cliff House threaded her way through the stacked logs, to the furthest extremity of the hut, and sat down on a dry log there, between the rear wall and the piles of fuel.

There neither the wind nor the rain reached her : and the fact that Marjorie's natty mac was becoming considerably smudged and stained by contact with the logs, did not worry Miss Bunter. She was thinking of her own discomfort, of being late for the circus, and of that beastly rain which seemed as if it would never stop, and had no leisure to bother about other people's macs.

Pat-pat-pat-patter came the rain on the roof. It pattered, and splashed, and almost banged, on the corrugated iron, and ran down in floods, drenching the earth in front of the open hut, and forming in pools.

For a good half-hour it went on, Miss Bunter's feelings growing deeper and deeper as she listened to it.

But at last, at long last, it slackened.

The pat-pat-patter grew lighter : the water no longer ran in floods from the roof. Bessie began to think of venturing forth again. She was still thinking of it, when a footstep splashed in a puddle in front of the hut, and a surly voice reached her ears :

" Cor ! What weather ! Strike me pink ! "

" It's leaving orf, now we got 'ere," said another voice. " It would ! "

Bessie Bunter gave a little jump. Then she sat very still ! Tramps ! was the terrifying thought that flashed into her fat mind. Tramps—in the middle of a lonely wood ! Bessie hardly breathed.

She could hear two men pushing into the hut. Had the rain still been falling heavily, possibly they would have followed Bessie's example, and pushed on to the rear of the hut, and indubitably found her there. But the rain was almost over now, and they remained near the entrance. A smell of tobacco penetrated to her. They had lighted cigarettes.

"You wet, Slim?"

"Ain't I just!"

"Shiny don't seem to be coming yet. 'Arf-past two was the time, and it's past that now. Think he's got it?"

"I shouldn't wonder! He's got nerve, Shiny has, jest the man for it. After all, it's easy. That fat cove don't know a thing about it. It's still where I put it—we should 'ave 'eard if it had been found. It ain't been found—so it's still there."

"Cor! That fat covey's watch is worth something!"

"You was a fool to lose it Saturday, Beaky, after getting your 'ands on it. You couldn't show up after being seen, no more than I could, and we had to let Shiny in on it. That makes three for the divvy."

"There's enough to go round, Slim."

"Yes—if he's got it!" Slim gave a grunt. "If he ain't, I shall 'ave to try it on again at the school: but I tell you, Beaky, it ain't easy, with that blinking dorg loose. He'd have had me, Monday night, only there was some other covey about in the dark, and the dorg got after him instead. Cor! I can tell you, the sooner I get away from 'ere, the better I shall feel—too many coveys about these parts know a bloke's face. If he's got it——!"

Slim interrupted himself, to strike a match and light another cigarette. Every word came clearly to the plump schoolgirl behind the stacks of logs. Bessie hardly dared to breathe. They had, evidently, no suspicion that anyone was there: she had only to keep silent. That "Beaky" and "Slim" were discussing some robbery, she could not fail to be aware: they were not merely tramps: they were thieves. If they found her there——! Silence was not one of Miss Elizabeth Bunter's gifts: but she was as silent as a mouse with the cat at hand.

" 'Ere he is, Slim ! " came a sudden exclamation.

Bessie heard a sound of tramping feet in puddles. A third man had joined the two lounging in the entrance of the wood-cutter's hut : a man, if Bessie could have seen him, with a sleek smooth face, and the look of a respectable man-servant.

" Got it ? "

" I got it all right, Slim ! But——"

" But what ? "

" There's nothing in it ! I opened it and looked ! It's the fat covey's watch all right—he was wearing it, and I got it—but there's nothing in it—nothing but the works—— Look ! "

" Strike me pink and blue ! That ain't the watch ! " Slim's voice was almost a yell. " 'Tain't anything like it ! "

" That's the watch he had on."

" You fool you, it ain't the watch ! Not the one that I see him put on ! Nor anything like it," howled Slim.

" I tell you it's the one he had on, and I snatched it, and——"

" Strike me blue and crimson ! Cor ! First Beaky lets a schoolboy scare him off it, and then you goes and pinches the wrong watch ! Cor ! " Slim's voice thrilled with anger and indignation. " Fat lot of use you are to a covey, you two ! I lets you in on a big thing, and this 'ere is 'ow you 'andle it ! Strike me pink ! "

" Sold ! " said Beaky, dismally.

" I tell you this was the watch he had on——" persisted Shiny.

" Then he must have changed it ! Look at this—H.W. engraved on the back. Think a covey named Bunter would 'ave H.W. on his watch ? He must have borrered it— 'tain't his watch ! Cor ! If this 'ere ain't enough to make a man chuck up the 'ole game and turn honest ! It is that ! " Slim almost wailed.

" The game ain't up yet, Slim," said Beaky, comfortingly. " We got to get 'old of the right watch——"

"We 'ave that!" said Slim. "We got to get after that fat covey Bunter and get that watch off 'im, and we got to do it quick, afore he 'appens to open it! Cor!"

There was a shuffling of feet in wet grass and puddles. The three rascals who had met at the solitary wood-cutter's hut were going—much to Bessie Bunter's relief.

The last words she had heard had made Bessie almost forget her terrors, in her astonishment. She did not need telling who the "fat covey" named Bunter was! These three rascals—Slim, Beaky, and Shiny—were after Brother Billy's watch—why, was a mystery that a more powerful brain than Bessie's might have failed to fathom. She knew that watch: and that its actual value was precisely as appraised by Fisher T. Fish, "nix". Yet these three lurkers of the under-world wanted that watch, and wanted it bad—had evidently made attempts to possess themselves of it, and were planning to make further attempts! It was just amazing to Bessie!

Footsteps died away in the wood. But it was long minutes after the last footstep had died away, that Bessie Bunter ventured to peer out of the wood-cutter's hut through her big spectacles, and finally venture forth, and resume her way to Courtfield.

CHAPTER XXXV

IT HAPPENS AGAIN

" FRANKY, old fellow——"

Frank Nugent grinned.

" No ! " he answered, without waiting for Bunter to continue.

" Beast ! I say, Bull——"

" No ! " said Johnny Bull.

" Yah ! Inky, old chap——"

" The answer is in the esteemed negative," grinned Hurree Jamset Ram Singh.

" I say, Bob——"

" Bow-wow ! " said Bob Cherry.

Harry Wharton laughed. Billy Bunter did not address him, alone among the members of the famous Co. He was, at the moment, of no use to Bunter. Bunter had already had his watch !

They were in the Rag, looking out at a quad shining with rain. Bunter, really, should have started for Courtfield before this : but he was not likely to start in a heavy downpour of rain. Bessie had had to start earlier, as Cliff House was twice the distance from Courtfield. The fat Owl waited in the Rag for it to stop. Now, at last, it was stopping, and Bunter was prepared to get a move on. But, owing to the strange and startling occurrence in the visitors' room, that morning, the fat Owl was still in want of a watch.

Watches were made to go : and Harry Wharton's had gone ! No other member of the Co. seemed disposed to trust his time-keeper in Bunter's fat hands. The fat Owl blinked at them reproachfully : but, like Pharaoh of old, they hardened their hearts.

" I say, Smithy——"

" Rats ! " said Smithy.

" Toddy, old chap——"

" Watches ain't safe with you, old fat man," said Peter, shaking his head. " You'd have lost your own watch the other day, but for Squiff—now you've lost Wharton's. I'd rather you didn't lose mine."

" Well, there ain't likely to be another pickpocket about," argued Bunter. " I wouldn't mind wearing that old tin turnip of yours, Peter, if you'd lend it to me. I simply must know the time this afternoon—I'll bet Bessie wouldn't wait a minute for me, and she's got the tickets. If I had the tickets, it would be all right, and it wouldn't matter if I missed her, you know—but she's got them. I say, dear old Bob——"

" I'll tell you what," said Bob, " I'll lend you——"

" Your watch ? "

" No : my alarm-clock ! It keeps jolly good time, and you can have a new glass put in, while you're in Courtfield."

" You silly fathead ! " roared Bunter.

" Ha, ha, ha ! "

Billy Bunter certainly wanted to make sure of the time that afternoon. But he did not seem to like the idea of carrying an alarm-clock in lieu of a watch ! He gave Bob Cherry a devastating blink through his big spectacles.

" Well, I've got to get off," yapped Bunter. " If I miss Bessie, and don't get to the circus, it will be your fault. Blessed if I ever came across such a selfish lot ! Selfishness all round, as usual ! It's enough to make a fellow grow selfish himself, mixing with you lot ! Yah ! "

The fat Owl turned to roll doorward. Peter Todd glanced after him, hesitated, gave an expressive grunt, and called out :

" Here you are, fathead ! "

" Oh ! " Bunter revolved on his axis, blinked at the watch Peter was holding out to him, and grabbed it. He gave it a disparaging blink—even more disparaging than the one he had given Harry Wharton's that morning.

Undoubtedly it was not an expensive watch. Wharton's at least was silver, with a monogram on the back. Peter's was a Waterbury of uncertain age. It kept time: and Fisher T. Fish would probably have valued it at considerably more than "nix". But compared with Bunter's own splendid gold watch, it was, in the fat Owl's opinion, as moonlight unto sunlight, as water unto wine. He gave a sniff as he put it into his waistcoat pocket, thereby expressing his opinion of the watch, and his grateful appreciation of the loan.

"Mind you don't lose it," said Peter.

"Blessed if I see that it would matter much, if I did," said Bunter, agreeably. "If I lose it, Toddy, I'll buy you another just like it—I can afford half-a-crown! He, he, he!"

With that gracious and grateful remark, Billy Bunter rolled out of the Rag, with Peter's Waterbury in his pocket. Peter's glance followed him, as he went, with quite an expressive expression!

"Nice chap, Bunter," remarked Bob Cherry. "How they must love him at home, and what a pity they don't keep him there! Well, the rain's stopped, my beloved 'earers, and we can get out and breathe."

Sunshine followed the rain: and the crowd of juniors in the Rag were glad to stream out into the quad. Billy Bunter was rolling cheerfully down to the gates.

He did not observe a man loitering on the other side of the road, as he rolled out. Had he observed him, he would not have recognised him as the sleek man who had called at the school that morning: for Shiny now had an artificial moustache gummed to his upper lip, and a cap pulled low over his forehead, which gave him quite a different look.

Bunter, quite uninterested in a man loitering by the roadside, rolled out unregarding.

But if Bunter was not interested in the loiterer, the loiterer undoubtedly was interested in Bunter. His eyes snapped at the sight of the fat junior coming out at the school gates.

Shiny, indeed, could hardly believe in his good luck! He had been there hardly ten minutes, since leaving his associates in Friardale Wood. He was hanging about the school on the mere chance of the " fat covey " coming out that afternoon. And here was the fat covey! Shiny had got the wrong watch once! He was going to get the right one this time!

Then, as if to exasperate Shiny, the fat covey stopped, took a watch from his pocket and blinked at it, and then, rolled in at the gateway again! Shiny breathed hard and he breathed deep, and his eyes fairly glittered at the back of Billy Bunter's fat head.

Oblivious of Shiny, Bunter rolled in again, and blinked round him through his big spectacles. He spotted the Famous Five and rolled up to them.

" I say, you fellows——"

" Hallo, hallo, hallo! Lost Toddy's watch already, and want to borrow another?" inquired Bob Cherry.

" Oh, really, Cherry! I say, I shall be late if I walk it," explained Bunter. " I'm late already, really, but I expect Bessie's late too, as it was raining. Who's going to lend me a tanner for the bus?"

" The who-fulness is terrific."

" I say, if I don't go by bus, it's no good going at all, and——"

" Dash it all, it's worth a tanner not to see Bunter again this afternoon," said Johnny Bull.

" Beast! I—I mean, if you've got a tanner you don't want, old fellow——"

" I haven't! I've got one I do want—here it is."

A fat paw closed on the sixpence, and once more Billy Bunter revolved, and rolled. He disappeared out of gates, leaving the Famous Five discussing what they were going to do with the remainder of the afternoon. Bob Cherry's suggestion was a ramble on the cliffs: at which Nugent winked at three other members of the Co., and there was a smile. The way to the cliffs lay past the gates of Cliff House School!

But the discussion was suddenly interrupted. Having seen Billy Bunter roll out at the gates, Harry Wharton and Co. supposed that they had seen the last of him for the afternoon: agreeing unanimously that it was well worth a "tanner". But that was quite an error. Hardly two or three minutes had elapsed since Billy Bunter had rolled out of view, when he came into view again—bolting in at the gates at top speed, his little round eyes almost bulging through his big round spectacles, and yelling at the top of his voice.

"Hallo, hallo, hallo!" ejaculated Bob, staring. "What——"

"That fat ass——!"

"What the dickens——?"

"I say, you fellows," Bunter yelled frantically. "I say, I've been robbed—my picket's been popped—Woddy's totch—I mean Toddy's watch—oh, crikey—I say, he's got it—he snatched it—oh, crumbs——!"

"Who's got it?" yelled Bob Cherry.

"That man—a man—he rushed at me in the road, and snatched it—I say, you fellows, he snatched it and pushed me over, just like that beast this morning—I say, he's wot the gotch—I mean he's got the watch——" Billy Bunter babbled, breathlessly and incoherently. "I say, he's got it—he patched it and snushed me over—I mean he snatched it and pushed me over—I went down bump—oh, crikey——"

"Come on!" exclaimed Harry Wharton.

He ran for the gates, with his comrades at his heels. A dozen other fellows had heard Bunter's startling announcement, and they rushed after the Famous Five—among them Peter Todd, anxious for his Waterbury. They came out of the gates into the road in a breathless crowd.

But there was no "man" to be seen.

Shiny, with a snatched watch in his pocket, was already

heading for the open spaces, and he was well out of sight. The Greyfriars fellows stared up and down the road, round and about, in vain. There was no pickpocket in view—not the ghost of one.

"Gone!" said Bob Cherry.

"The gonefulness is terrific."

"And he's got my watch!" gasped Peter. "Why, that fat villain hadn't had it more than ten minutes—and it's gone! My watch——"

"This beats the band," said Vernon-Smith. "Why is somebody after Bunter's watch specially? This is the third go——"

"Goodness knows!"

"I say, you fellows." Bunter rolled out. "I say, have you got him?"

"No, ass—he's gone."

"With my watch!" roared Peter. "You fat ass——!"

"Oh, really, Toddy! I can't help pockpickers packing pickets, can I—I mean pickpockets picking pockers—I mean pockets! And it wasn't worth much, was it, old chap? You haven't lost much, you know——"

"You fat, frabjous, footling fathead——"

"Well, I think you might be a bit sympathetic, Toddy, when a fellow's been pushed over, and had his picket packed—I mean his pocket picked. But I say, you fellows," Bunter remembered the circus, "I've got to get off—I say, who's going to lend me a watch?"

"What?"

"A watch——!"

"Oh, my hat!" gasped Bob Cherry. "Who's going to lend Bunter another watch to be pinched? Don't all speak at once!"

"Ha, ha, ha!"

"Well, I think one of you fellows might lend a chap a watch, when he's got an appointment to keep. That cheap one of yours will do, Bob, if it keeps time."

"That cheap one of mine is staying in my pocket, old fat

man," chuckled Bob Cherry. "You'll have to manage with that splendid gold watch of yours, Bunter."

"Well, it doesn't keep time, you know. I've wound it up dozens of times, but it won't go! Will one of you fellows lend me a watch?"

"Ha, ha, ha!"

"Blessed if I see anything to cackle at! A fellow must wear a watch," snapped Bunter. "If you won't lend me your watch, Bob——"

"No 'if' about it."

"Well, will you cut up to my study and get mine? It's in the table-drawer?" snapped Bunter. "I may as well put it on."

"And you may as well fetch it," grinned Bob.

"Beast!"

"You'd better let Quelch know what's happened," said Harry Wharton.

"I've no time. You can tell Quelch if you like. Cut up to my study first, and get my gold watch for me——"

"Fathead!"

"Beast!"

Nobody, it appeared, was going to lend Bunter another watch. Nobody was even going to cut up to his study and fetch his gold watch for him. It seemed hardly worth while to cut up to the study himself, for a watch that wouldn't go. So the fat Owl rolled away for the bus, watch-less: and at least safe from pickpockets. And by good luck he found Miss Elizabeth Bunter in the Market Place: so the loss of Peter Todd's watch really didn't matter after all!

AND while Brother Billy and Sister Bessie were rolling into the circus at Courtfield, three men—one with pimples, one with a beaky nose, and one with a sleek smooth face—in a secluded spot in Friardale Wood, were gazing, with an expressive gaze, at a Waterbury watch—the second wrong watch that had fallen into their hands!

CHAPTER XXXVI

GREAT EXPECTATIONS

" I SAY, you fellows."

" Oh, blow away, Bunter ! "

" Oh, really, Wharton——"

" Shut the door after you ! "

" Oh, really, Nugent——"

" Buzz off, bluebottle ! "

" Oh, really, Cherry——"

It was quite a party in No. 1 Study in the Remove. The Famous Five were all there, and Smithy, and Tom Redwing, and Peter Todd, and Squiff. No. 1 Study was fairly roomy, but nine fellows filled it almost to capacity : and nobody present seemed to think that there was room for a tenth—especially one who was double-width ! Billy Bunter, as he blinked into that study through his big spectacles, could not, by the widest stretch of his fat imagination, have fancied that he was persona grata there.

But he did not blow away. Neither did he buzz off. He shut the door, as requested : but he remained on the inner side thereof.

" I say, you fellows," squeaked Bunter.

" Hook it ! "

" I've got something to tell you——"

" Go and tell somebody else."

" I've just got back from the circus——"

" Queer they let you get away ! "

" Beast ! I say, Bessie told me something—— I say, I wish you'd let a fellow speak ! " howled Bunter. " It's about my watch——"

" Bother your watch ! "

" And bother you ! "

" Blow away ! "

Billy Bunter's fat face was excited. Apparently, he was full of news. He had come there to surprise and startle the Remove fellows. But not a fellow in No. 1 Study was interested. Nobody wanted to know. They seemed interested only in seeing Bunter's podgy back!

But that view was denied them. Bunter's podgy back remained in the door, and his fat face and spectacles remained on view.

"I say, you fellows——"

"Oh, my hat!" exclaimed Bob Cherry. "Is that fat bluebottle still there? Won't somebody swat it?"

"Beast!" roared Bunter. "I tell you——"

"Travel!"

"You'd better go down and see Quelch, Bunter," said Harry Wharton. "He wants to see you——"

"Blow Quelch!"

"I've reported to him about Toddy's watch going——"

"Blow Toddy's watch!"

"Grimey is coming over about it——"

"Blow Grimey!"

"He won't go till he's fed," said Squiff. "Give him a bun and roll him out."

"Oh, really, Field——"

"Will you blow away if we give you a bun, Bunter?"

"Beast! I haven't had tea," said Bunter, "it was too late for the scrum in hall when I got back from the circus. You've got a spread here. I think you might ask a fellow to join up, after all I've done for you. That looks a decent cake. I say, you fellows, I'm going to ask you all to a topping spread to-morrow. I'm expecting——"

"If you say 'postal-order', I'll buzz this loaf at you!" said Johnny Bull.

"I'm expecting a lot of money to-morrow. I'm going to sell my gold watch," said Bunter, impressively.

"Ha, ha, ha!"

"You can cackle——!"

"Thanks: we will! Ha, ha, ha!"

"Well, you jolly well wouldn't cackle, if you knew!" snorted Bunter. "Fishy wouldn't give me anything for that gold watch when I asked him last Wednesday. I'm jolly glad now that he wouldn't! Of course I always knew that it was jolly valuable—forty-four carat gold, and all that. But now that I know that a gang of crooks are after it——"

"A which?"

"A whatter?"

Bunter seemed to have interested the tea-party in No. I Study at last. They all gazed at him as he made that startling statement.

"A gang of crooks," said Bunter. "Bessie heard them, and she told me at the circus. She said they must be off their chumps to want my watch—I mean, she said I'd better take jolly good care of it, as it was so valuable—— You see, she got into old Joyce's wood-shed out of the rain, and they met there and she heard them—there were three of them, she said—she didn't see them but she heard them—talking about my watch—three crooks, or gangsters, or something—they're after my fifty-six carat gold watch——" Bunter gasped for breath.

"Oh, my hat!"

"Did Bessie go to sleep in old Joyce's wood-shed?" asked Squiff.

"Eh? No."

"Did she dream all that awake?"

"You silly ass!" howled Bunter. "She didn't dream it at all! I can tell you she was jolly scared! Only she was behind the logs, you know, and they never saw her. Three of them—and one was that man with the pimples, because she heard the others call one of them Slim, and you know that pimply beast was called Slim Judson, it came out after he was run in—— So it must be the same man, the one I found on the landing that night, you know, and she said the others were called Beaky and Shiny, and I expect one of them was that beast with a beaky nose who tried to pinch my watch on Saturday, when Squiff jumped on him, and the other's the beast who came here this morning, I expect, making out that he had a pessage from old Mopper—I mean a message from old Popper—and he hadn't all the time, and——" Again Bunter paused for breath.

Harry Wharton and Co. gazed at him.

Now that Billy Bunter was able to get his story out, it was coming out with a rush. And they were interested at last, and considerably astonished.

" They're after my watch ! " said Bunter, " and it must be awfully valuable for a gang of crooks to get after it, see ? I mean to say, they've got hold of Wharton's watch, and Toddy's watch, but it's my watch they want—my splendid gold watch, you know. Well, they wouldn't take all that trouble for nothing, would they ? They jolly well know how valuable that watch is, see ? "

" My only blue bonnet ! " said Bob Cherry. " Is it possible that somebody's seen that watch of Bunter's, and fancied it was gold——"

" Oh, really, Cherry, I know jolly well that it's sixty-two carat——"

" Rot ! " said Johnny Bull. " A blind mole with its eyes shut could see that it wasn't, Bob. It's not worth anything at all."

" I tell you, they're after it ! " hooted Bunter. " Bessie heard them say they'd got to get after Bunter—that's me—and get that watch off him. One of them said they'd got the wrong watch, with H.W. engraved on it——"

" Mine ! " said Harry Wharton.

" And now they've got Toddy's, too," said Bunter. " But you can see now that they were after my watch all the time. They didn't want your cheap one, Wharton, or your old turnip, Toddy—they wanted my valuable gold watch. And now I know it's so jolly valuable, I'm jolly well going to take it down to old Lazarus in Courtfield to-morrow and sell it, see ? I may get fifty pounds for it ! Or—or a hundred——! "

" Ha, ha, ha ! "

" Well, if you get a hundred quid for it, you can square that tanner," remarked Johnny Bull.

" I say, you fellows, don't you think it shows that my gold watch is jolly valuable after all ? " asked Bunter. Perhaps a spot of doubt lingered in his fat mind. " I mean to say, why should three packpickets—I mean pickpockets—get after my watch, unless they knew it was awfully valuable ? "

" Beats me ! " said Bob Cherry.

" The beatfulness is terrific."

" Blessed if I make it out," said Harry Wharton, wrinkling his brows. " It really does look as if somebody's after Bunter's watch specially. Squiff stopped a man grabbing it last Saturday. Then that blighter barged into the school this morning, and snatched my watch—he must have supposed that it was Bunter's, as he was wearing it—and then this afternoon, Toddy's watch—he must have supposed that that was Bunter's, too, as he had it on——"

" But what the jolly old thump could anybody want Bunter's watch for ? " asked the Bounder. " I suppose he's not short of tuppence to buy one like it, if he wants one."

" Oh, really, Smithy ! My seventy-two carat gold watch——"

" Beats me hollow," said Tom Redwing. " We all supposed that that man Slim Judson was hanging about after old Popper's precious Blue Mauritius stamp—now it looks as if he wants Bunter's watch—but why——"

" The whyfulness is preposterous ! " said Hurree Jamset Ram Singh, with a shake of his dusky head.

" Well, I fancy it's like this," said Bunter. " He was after old Popper's stamp at first, but that's lost, and he's chucked it up : and now he wants to get hold of my watch instead."

" And go home loaded with loot, after all ! " remarked the Bounder, sarcastically.

" Ha, ha, ha ! "

" Well, if the watch ain't jolly valuable, what do you think they're after it for ? " hooted Bunter. " Think a crunch of books—I mean a bunch of crooks—would waste their time getting after a watch unless it was worth lots and lots."

" But it isn't ! " said Nugent.

" It jolly well is ! Why, old Grimey is after that man Slim, and it's jolly dangerous for him to hang on in this neighbourhood, with the bobbies after him, and he's doing it just to get after my gold watch ! I say, you fellows, I want you to come with me to-morrow when I go to Courtfield to sell that watch—half a dozen of you, see—they might get after it again—in fact I'm pretty sure they would—I ain't going out alone with that watch, I can tell you—— And you can see me safe home with the money, see ? "

" The whole threepenny bit you'll get for it ? " asked Squiff.

" Ha, ha, ha ! "

" It's all rot," said Peter Todd. " I can't make it out, but we jolly well know that that man Judson is after old Popper's stamp——"

" He's after my watch ! Bessie heard him say so, quite plain. That's why he's still hanging about. He was jolly well after it the other night, when I saw him on the landing —I see that now ! " declared Bunter. " A fellow takes his watch up to bed, and he was going to root through the dorms till he found me—and my watch ! Ain't that plain enough ? "

Bob Cherry whistled.

" By gum ! It does look like it ! " he said.

" It does—it do ! " said Squiff. " He couldn't have been after old Popper's Blue Mauritius up in the dormitories, if he hid it in a study."

" Hardly," agreed Harry Wharton.

" Grimey thinks so," said Peter Todd. " That's why he was asking us questions yesterday in Quelch's study. He thinks the man hid it in something that might have been taken up to a dormitory afterwards—such as a blazer, or anything——"

"That's possible," said Harry. "Old Grimey's got his head screwed on the right way. That might easily have happened——"

"He was after my watch——!" yelled Bunter.

"Rot!" said Johnny Bull.

"The rotfulness is terrific."

All the fellows in No. 1 Study shook their heads. Undoubtedly, it looked as if Slim Judson and Co. were after Bunter's watch. All that had happened to Bunter looked like it, and it was confirmed by what Bessie had overheard in the wood-cutter's hut in Friardale Wood. Judging by the look of the thing, Slim Judson had forgotten all about Sir Hilton Popper's precious Blue Mauritius, and was concentrated on Bunter's watch, and had called in the aid of two rascals of his own kidney to help him in obtaining possession thereof. But as Billy Bunter's famous gold watch was only worth the sum named by Fisher T. Fish, "nix", how could it be so?

The fat Owl blinked at them in angry indignation.

"I say, you fellows, you'll jolly well see to-morrow, when I take that watch to old Lazarus in Courtfield," he yapped. "It's as plain as anything that it's awfully valuable, with those three pickpockets after it. That man Slim jolly well knows what it's worth."

"You fat ass, he's never even seen it." said Bob.

"He jolly well has," retorted Bunter. "I'll bet he saw it on the table in my study the day he was here."

"Well, if he saw it, he knows it's worth about threepence——"

"Twopence!" said Johnny Bull.

"Catch me giving twopence for it," said the Bounder.

"Oh, suffering cats and crocodiles!" exclaimed Peter Todd. He jumped up from the table, his face ablaze with excitement. "Bunter, you fat foozler——"

" Oh, really, Toddy——"

" You frumptious chump——"

" Look here——"

" Mean to say that that watch was on the study table when that man Judson was in the study last Wednesday ? " shrieked Peter.

" Yes, it jolly well was ! You see, I'd shown it to Fishy, and he wouldn't buy it, and he chucked it on the table, and then that man came racing up the passage, and I cut off to the box-room and forgot it——"

" Oh, holy smoke ! " gasped Peter. " Then it was in the study with him——"

" Eh ? Yes ! "

" And you put it on afterwards ? " yelled Peter.

" Yes, when I got back to the study, before I saw him there ! So he jolly well saw it, and of course he knew at once how valuable it was, and that's why he's been after it ever since——"

" Where is it now ? " shrieked Peter.

" Eh ? I left it in the table-drawer in my study when I went out——"

Peter did not wait for more. He rushed to the door, and darted out into the passage. Billy Bunter blinked after him, in astonishment.

" I say, wharrer marrer ? What—oh, crikey ! I say, you fellows, where are you all going ? " yelled Bunter.

His eyes popped behind his spectacles, as the whole crowd of juniors in No. 1 Study rushed after Peter Todd.

Bunter was left alone in the study.

" I say, you fellows," he yelled.

But answer there came none ! Why Harry Wharton and Co. had all rushed out of the study in that extraordinary way, Billy Bunter had no idea. But, as it happened, nothing could have suited Bunter better. He was left alone—with the spread on the study table ! He dropped into one of the vacant chairs, and the next moment the most capacious jaws at Greyfriars School were working to capacity ! Where they had gone, and what they were up to, Bunter didn't know—and he couldn't have cared less. Wherever they were, he only hoped that they would stay there long enough to give him time to deal faithfully with the good things on the table. And he lost no time!

CHAPTER XXXVII

AT LAST

Harry Wharton and Co. fairly hurtled into No. 7 Study. Peter Todd was first man in: but the Famous Five were at his heels, and Smithy, and Redwing, and Squiff, close behind.

Every face was wildly excited.

Billy Bunter had come up to No. 1 Study, with the intention of startling the inhabitants thereof. But he had startled them more than he could have dreamed. Quite unintentionally and unexpectedly, he had given the whole party an electric shock.

For the same idea had leaped into all minds. The Blue Mauritius had been hidden in No. 7 Study. Inspector Grimes surmised that it must have been put into some article later removed from the study—such as a blazer, or a cap, or even a handkerchief—anything that might have been left about a study and taken away afterwards. And now the fat and fatuous Owl of the Remove had revealed, quite casually, and with no idea whatever that it was a matter of any importance, that his big gold watch had been in the study at the time, lying on the table while Slim Judson was there, and that he had put it on again.

Mr. Grimes had not thought of so unlikely an article as a watch, but of more likely things like a blazer, or a cap, or a book. But the watch had been there—Judson must have seen it—must have known that the room would be searched for the Blue Mauritius—that it would be safe only in an article likely to be taken from the study. Nothing could have suited him better than a watch which, as it happened, had been left on the table, but which obviously the owner must intend to put in his watch-pocket again.

Judson had hidden that stamp in something—and it was

not a cap, or a blazer, or a book, or a handkerchief—was it in that watch ?

Was that why the pickpockets were, so inexplicably, so desperately, in quest of a watch which, on its intrinsic merits, was worth precisely " nix " ?

It had not, of course, occurred to Bunter. But it occurred to all the other fellows in No. 1 Study: and they poured helter-skelter into No. 7. Peter, first in the field, grabbed the table-drawer, and pulled it open—so energetically that it came out, scattering its contents over the study carpet.

Papers, a gum-bottle, an indiarubber, several pens and pencils, and other such articles, rained on the floor—and among them, a heavy object thudded down—— Billy Bunter's big gold watch.

" Hallo, hallo, hallo ! There it is——"

" That's Bunter's ticker——"

Peter whipped it up.

Eight eager fellows gathered round him, treading recklessly on papers and pens and pencils. The excitement was quite at fever heat. Did that glimmering old brassy turnip of Bunter's contain a rare stamp worth two thousand pounds ? Certainly there was room for it inside—lots of room. Skinner, indeed, had said that Bunter's watch was big enough to take in a lodger. But was it there ?

" Quick, Toddy——"

" Get it open——"

" Let's look——"

" We are on the esteemed tender hooks, Toddy——"

" Buck up ! "

Peter Todd snapped open the case. The works—such as they were—of Bunter's big watch were revealed. But not wholly. A fragment of paper was there. It glimmered blue.

" Great pip ! " gasped Peter.

" Oh, gad ! " said the Bounder.

" My only hat ! "

" The stamp—— ! "

"The jolly old Blue Mauritius——!"

"Eureka!"

"The Eurekafulness is terrific!"

They had more than half expected it. But it was a thrill to see it. And there was no mistake about it. It was a postage-stamp: once upon a time worth the humble sum of twopence: worth, at the present moment, at least two thousand pounds, and probably more.

The Famous Five had had a glimpse of that stamp before, in Sir Hilton Popper's hand in Popper Court Woods. The other fellows saw it for the first time. But they all knew what it was. They gazed at it.

That celebrated stamp, of which only a dozen are known to be in existence, showed a left profile of Queen Victoria, the word "Post Office" on the left-hand side, "Mauritius" on the right, "Postage" across the top, and "Two Pence" along the bottom of the stamp, with a rather crude ornament in each corner. It was printed in a deep blue. It looked, to non-philatelic eyes, worth nothing at all; but the eyes of any philatelist would have lighted up at a glimpse of it. It was one of the dreams of a stamp-collector's life! In the philatelic world, it was worth the huge sum of two thousand pounds, that being its rarity value. And there it was—sticking in Billy Bunter's gold watch, where the cornered pickpocket had hidden it a week ago!

"So that's it!" said Bob Cherry.

"That's it!" said Peter.

"Two thousand quid!" said the Bounder, with a whistle. "Worth no more than the watch we've found it in, really, if it wasn't for collectors——"

"Good news for old Popper!" said Tom Redwing.

"The goodfulness of the news is terrific," said Hurree Jamset Ram Singh. "The smile of benevolent equanimity will replace the preposterous frownfulness on the absurd countenance of the esteemed Popper."

"Better take it down to Quelch at once," said Harry Wharton. "The sooner it's in safe hands the better."

" Come on," said Peter. " We'll all go, as we all found it. Quelch will be jolly glad—I fancy he's fed up to the back teeth with Popper and his stamp."

" March ! " said Bob Cherry.

Nine fellows crowded out of No. 7 Study, and marched down the passage : Peter in the lead, carrying Bunter's gold watch, the other fellows in procession behind him.

A fat junior, busy at the table in No. 1 Study, gave a jump of alarm, at the sound of many footsteps coming down the passage. But to Billy Bunter's relief, they passed the door of No. 1, and tramped onward to the landing. Apparently the tea-party had forgotten the spread, and forgotten Bunter. Bunter, only too glad to be forgotten, continued to deal with the spread : while Harry Wharton and Co. marched across the landing to the stairs.

Coker of the Fifth, at the corner of the Fifth-form passage, stared at them.

" What's that game ? " he called out.

" Oh, we've found old Popper's stamp for him," answered Bob Cherry, carelessly. " There's been such a fuss about it, you know, we thought we'd take it in hand."

And the procession marched on down the stairs, leaving Horace Coker staring.

At the foot of the staircase, they came on Wingate and Gwynne of the Sixth. The two prefects turned a severely inquiring gaze on the mob of hilarious juniors.

" What do you fags fancy you are up to ? " asked Wingate.

" Snuff ! " answered Peter.

" What ? "

" There's been such a spot of bother about old Popper's stamp that we thought we'd find it for him—— ! " explained Peter.

" You've found it ! " exclaimed Wingate and Gwynne together.

" Sort of ! We're taking it to Quelch."

" How on earth did you find it ? " exclaimed the Greyfriars captain.

" Oh, we just looked in the place where that man Judson hid it, you know. Elementary, my dear Watson ! " said Bob Cherry.

" Ha, ha, ha ! "

The procession marched on, to Masters' Studies. Harry Wharton tapped at his Form-master's door.

" Come in ! "

There was a snap in the voice within. It did not sound as if Mr. Quelch was in his bonniest temper. However, Wharton opened the door, and Peter marched in with the watch, and the rest followed him in. Then they became aware that Mr. Quelch was not alone in the study. Inspector Grimes of Courtfield was with him.

The inspector glanced at the crowd of juniors, and raised his eyebrows slightly. Mr. Quelch fixed his gimlet-eyes upon them, with a grim and portentious frown. Indeed he seemed, at the moment, to be trying to reproduce the frightful, fearful, frantic frown of the Lord High Executioner, as he stared, or rather glared, at this unexpected and numerous invasion of his study.

Quelch was not, in fact, in a good temper. Mr. Grimes was there again—and while he had a proper esteem for that efficient officer of the law, he was quite tired of seeing him at Greyfriars. Now, added to the troublesome affair of the missing stamp, was the puzzling and irritating affair of the pickpockets who seemed to be making the fattest member of his Form the object of their very special attention. It was all very annoying to Mr. Quelch : and while he contrived to be polite to Mr. Grimes, he seemed to have no politeness whatever left over for the swarm of juniors crowding into his study.

" What does this mean ? " he rapped. " Why have you all come here ? Wharton—— ! "

" If you please, sir——"

" I am engaged at the moment ! What do you mean by crowding into my study in this manner ? Eight—nine of you—upon my word ! Go away at once."

"But, sir——"

"Take a hundred lines, Wharton——"

"Oh! Yes, sir! But——"

"You see, sir——!" gasped Peter.

"Take a hundred lines, Todd!"

"But, sir——!" exclaimed Squiff.

"Take a hundred lines, Field."

"Esteemed sahib——!"

"Take a hundred lines, Hurree Singh."

Mr. Quelch rose to his feet. He pointed to the door.

"Go! All of you! At once! Not a word more! The next boy who speaks will be caned! Leave my study instantly."

Nine fellows became dumb, on the spot. Quelch's hand was already reaching for the cane on his table. Really, it looked as if the heroes of the Remove, having marched Sir Hilton Popper's precious stamp into their Form-master's study, would have to march it out again!

But Peter, without speaking, laid the Blue Mauritius on the table, almost under Mr. Quelch's nose.

The Remove master stared at it.

He was no philatelist. On other subjects his knowledge was wide and extensive: but he had yet to learn the value of a scrap of paper a hundred years old. Having stared at that scrap of paper, he gave Peter a grim look.

"What is this? What do you mean by bringing a used postage-stamp to me? Are you in your senses, Todd?"

Inspector Grimes jumped. He jumped as if he had touched an electric wire. He fairly bounded. Portly as he was, with plenty of weight to lift, Mr. Grimes was on his feet in a fraction of a split second, bending over Quelch's table, and staring at the stamp. Then he clutched it up.

"The boys have found it!" he gasped.

"What——?"

"This is Sir Hilton Popper's lost stamp, sir," said Mr. Grimes. "The Blue Mauritius, worth two thousand pounds, and these boys appear to have found it——"

"Oh!" gasped Mr. Quelch.

He understood.

The thunder cleared from his brow. No doubt he was glad that the lord of Popper Court would now recover his lost property. Probably he was gladder that the troublesome affair was now at an end. Peter had not exaggerated in stating that Quelch was fed up to the back teeth with old Popper and his stamp!

"Bless my soul!" said Mr. Quelch, quite genially. "That—that is Sir Hilton's stamp—— I—I—I see—— I quite understand! You have found the missing stamp——"

"Yes, sir."

"Oh! Hem! Um! You—you need not do the lines, my boys, of—of course! I—I did not understand, for the moment! I am very glad that the stamp is found! Please tell Inspector Grimes and me where you found it."

Which the juniors were only too pleased to do. Inspector Grimes' eyes opened wide, and Mr. Quelch's wider, as the tale of the discovery of the stamp was told.

"In Bunter's watch!" said Mr. Quelch, with a deep breath. "Upon my word! That stupid boy——"

"That utterly stupid boy——!" said Mr. Grimes.

"However, all is well that ends well," said Mr. Quelch, with a smile. "I am much obliged to you, my boys. Inspector Grimes is much obliged to you. And I am sure that Sir Hilton Popper will feel much obliged to you. You may leave my study."

And Harry Wharton and Co. left the study, taking Bunter's watch with them, and leaving the precious Blue Mauritius in the official hands of Mr. Grimes. In a cheery crowd they tramped up the stairs, to carry on with the spread in No. 1 Study, and tell Bunter the thrilling news: and, in view of the great occasion, to welcome the fat Owl to a "whack" in the spread!

But they need not have bothered to think of Bunter in

connection with the spread. Bunter had done all the thinking that was necessary in that matter.

"Hallo, hallo, hallo!"

"Bunter——"

"We've found it——"

"In your preposterous watch——"

"And we——"

"Here! What? Where's Bunter?" exclaimed Harry Wharton.

"And where's the spread?" roared Johnny Bull.

Bunter was gone! The spread was gone! It was easy to guess where the spread was. It was inside Bunter! It was no use looking for the spread. And it was not much use looking for Bunter. Like the hunter of the Snark who suddenly beheld the Boojum, he had silently vanished away! —and with him had vanished the spread, to the last plum and the last crumb.

CHAPTER XXXVIII

BILLY BUNTER'S REWARD

" FAIR play's a jewel ! " said Billy Bunter.

" Eh ? "

" What ? "

" I say fair play's a jewel. Ain't it ? " demanded Bunter.

He blinked at Harry Wharton and Co. in the Greyfriars quad. The Famous Five had come out of the House, and were glancing, in passing, at a car on the drive. They knew the car from Popper Court. The lord of that demesne, apparently, was at the school.

Billy Bunter was blinking at the car, through his big spectacles. But he turned his little round eyes, and his big round spectacles, on the chums of the Remove as they came out : and, rather to their surprise, propounded the indubitable proposition that fair play was a jewel.

" What do you mean, you fat ass ? " inquired Johnny Bull.

" If anything ! " remarked Nugent.

" I mean what I say—fair play's a jewel ! " said Bunter. " Old Popper's with Quelch now. He's come about that stamp being found, of course."

" What about that ? " asked Bob.

It seemed probable that Sir Hilton, now in possession once more of his Blue Mauritius, and in the happy state of being able, at long last, to meet the demands of his Inspector of Taxes, had called at Greyfriars, to acknowledge, with a few gracious words to Mr. Quelch, the service rendered by boys of his Form. But why Bunter was interested was rather a puzzle.

" Well," said the fat Owl, " he's got his stamp back, hasn't he ? It wasn't my watch those pickpockets were after, as it turns out, but that stamp ! I thought I was going to get a lot for that watch——"

"Ha, ha, ha!"

"I mean to say, anybody would have thought it was worth a lot, with three pickpockets after it——"

"They won't be after it any more, old fat man," chuckled Bob. "Now it's known that the stamp is found, they wouldn't take it as a gift. I expect they've mizzled before this—but if they haven't, you could walk that watch right under their noses, and it would be as safe as houses."

"Well, it's a jolly good watch," said Bunter. "Eighty-six carat gold, and all that. It would keep jolly good time, too, only it won't go. But I ain't going to sell it, now. After all, a fellow likes to wear a gold watch! But I was saying that fair play's a jewel! Ain't it?"

"Passed nem. con.," assented Bob.

"Old Popper's got his stamp, worth two thousand pounds, so they say. Well, fair play's a jewel——"

"We've had that!"

"And he's jolly well bound to stump up something for getting his stamp back," said Bunter. "That's fair, ain't it?"

"Rot!" said Johnny Bull.

"Oh, really, Bull——"

"The rotfulness is terrific."

"Oh, really, Inky——"

"Bosh!" said Nugent.

"Oh, really, Nugent——"

"Piffle!" said Bob.

"Oh, really, Cherry——"

"You fat chump!" said Harry Wharton. "Do you think we're going to stick the old bean for spotting his stamp?"

"Eh! I wasn't speaking of you——"

"If you mean Toddy——"

"I don't mean Toddy! I mean me," yapped Bunter.

"You!" exclaimed all the Famous Five, together.

"Me!" said Bunter. "Wasn't it in my watch? Wasn't it to me that those crangsters and gooks—I mean gangsters